Saga of the
Light Striper

SAGA OF THE LIGHT STRIPER
THE REFRAMING OF A NEW WORLD

RICK STUEMPFLE

iUniverse

SAGA OF THE LIGHT STRIPER
THE REFRAMING OF A NEW WORLD

Copyright © 2023 Rick Stuempfle.

All rights reserved. No part of this book may be used or reproduced by any means, graphic, electronic, or mechanical, including photocopying, recording, taping or by any information storage retrieval system without the written permission of the author except in the case of brief quotations embodied in critical articles and reviews.

iUniverse books may be ordered through booksellers or by contacting:

iUniverse
1663 Liberty Drive
Bloomington, IN 47403
www.iuniverse.com
844-349-9409

Because of the dynamic nature of the Internet, any web addresses or links contained in this book may have changed since publication and may no longer be valid. The views expressed in this work are solely those of the author and do not necessarily reflect the views of the publisher, and the publisher hereby disclaims any responsibility for them.

Any people depicted in stock imagery provided by Getty Images are models, and such images are being used for illustrative purposes only.
Certain stock imagery © Getty Images.

ISBN: 978-1-6632-5215-9 (sc)
ISBN: 978-1-6632-5216-6 (e)

Library of Congress Control Number: 2023907068

Print information available on the last page.

iUniverse rev. date: 09/20/2023

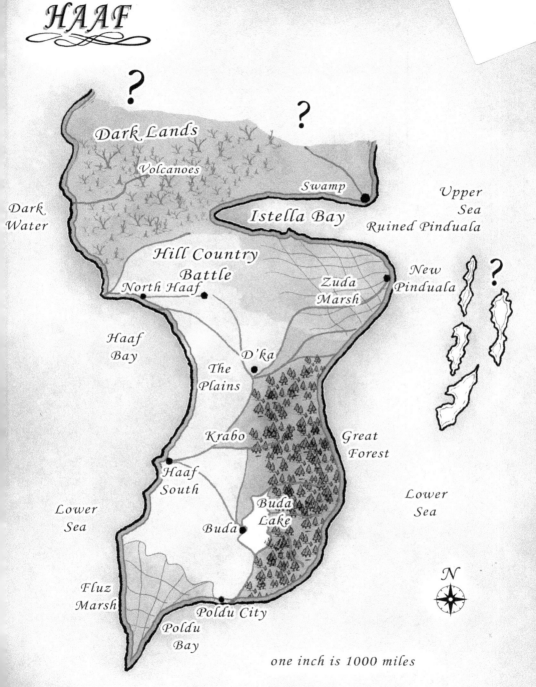

Volume 1

Chapter 1

When is enough…enough…what evidence pushes us over the top? How do we make changes and not rip apart the present?

The King anxiously paced the stonewalled room of his personal quarters above the High Council Hall. The news received from his highest in command, Commander Chaplain Vosnob had changed: the Kyykki seemed to have disappeared, almost in a single dawn. After two generations of intermittent hostilities across the Haafian entrenchments and fortifications, the unexplained change sounded alarm: from one end of Haaf to another.

Though the King was the king, he recognized, from past experience, that his powers remained severely truncated. Thus, the Haafian Light Stripers discovered themselves still involved in the lingering debris of the ages past War, and also with the clerics of the Church and the self-righteous, self-serving merchant class.

The common serfs, those who formed the vast majority of the Light Striper as well as society-at-large, sought only to control the meagerness allotted them, which, at present lay in jeopardy. Much of what transpired at the so-called 'higher levels' of society was totally inappropriate for them. Little Love was lost between the serfs and the arrogant lazy royalty of Haaf.

Now that the 'damned one', god of the Kyykki, having somehow instantly maneuvered his troops to parts unknown, the nervous High Council quickly voted to elevate the hero of The War, a much older Vosnob, to full Commander of the Light Striper. Without difficulty, they easily assumed, Haafian society would return to normalcy within a couple of full double moon cycles.

Vosnob, a deeply devout and practical fellow, properly acknowledged but refused to appreciate his new 'gift'. Nor did the ageing hero, a label he found personally offensive, assume half of what the High Council earnestly desired. Their fickle assumptions, which they believed automatically, delivered them from any personal responsibility, Vosnob ignored. Such moneyed persons lived by the power of their personal pocketbooks. For Haafian royalty, faith was but a word in their lives, nothing more. Vosnob did not forget this hard-lesson from The War.

"Shut your mouth, if you know what's good for you." Sarg whispered.

"Why?" Luuft replied, a bit more than half indignant.

This evening, their first off-duty evening within a full double moon cycle, their first time for relaxation since being on the front trenches, their first time to get a shower, their first time for a hot meal—and after only five minutes of leave, Sarg has the guts to tell him to shut up.

"I've been shut up for six dawns, Sarg……..And the last thing I'm going to do is shut up!"

"Don't bet on it Stripers!" The stern voice directly behind them was terrifyingly recognizable.

Luuft immediately froze. Sarg come to attention. Both of them could have killed each other. The Revered Vosnob, Chaplain Captain of the Light Striper, Commander General of the Army, Military Advisor and Life Member of the High Council of Haaf had spoken.

Somehow, Vosnob had ridden his Striper right up behind them. Until that last moment, even Sarg didn't notice. Now it looked like their leave had simply evaporated into nothingness.

"Stripers!"

"Yes Sir!" It was a unison voice.

"At ease men!"

"Yes, Sir!"

"You don't have to shout, I'm not deaf."

"Yes sir."

Vosnob slowly brought his Striper around. Except for his voice and reputation, the angular Haafian could have any officer. He even dressed exactly the same way: mid blue double breasted tunic with cuffed sleeves tucked into baggy yellow breeches which in turn were tucked into black knee boots. All seams were decorated with gold trim. From red leather shoulder strap hung his famous broadaxe; the very same one he used to destroy the demon Beizel. About his waist hung his rank denoting sash; yellow and silver stripes. As usual, he was bareheaded, allowing his slivered hair to outline his creased olive-skinned face as a halo might have.

He remained one of the few Haafian Officers the Light Striper would follow into hell and back. An officer who, like most all officers, began at the bottom as a common serf and rose strictly by merit. This hero of the War, this man who brought about the required changes after the War, this man who still camped with troops on the field, now had two of his Light Striper troopers in a cold sweat.

Vosnob dismounted. Vaad stayed right beside him, almost as if to protect him. Such could be true, for this was the same Striper that carried Vosnob during the War. He was still a magnificent beast; a little over seven feet at the shoulder, charcoal black mane, beautiful silver and black stripes and his well-honed six-foot antlers still retained a bit of fuzz. Not that Vaad looked that different from the other Stripers in the squadron, but he had a certain dignity and attitude that definitely set him apart. Just ask the grooms who had their feet flattened while the Striper gleefully snorted.

Sarg and Luuft remained at attention. Vosnob stood but two paces away.

"Enough, I didn't come here to inspect the troops. I need some help."

The two men looked at each other and then back to Vosnob.

"Does that surprise you? Have you all ready forgotten your training in the Holiness code?" He said in a somewhat teasing manner.

"No, I don't think so, sir." Said Luuft truthfully.

"I can tell that you haven't." Vosnob replied, staring Luuft eyeball-to-eyeball.

"You've spoken the truth. And we are bound to do those at all times, aren't we?"

"Yes", said Luuft, rather shakily. "But what has that to do with helping you?"

"Does any person know everything?"

"Some think that they do. But no." Luuft paused on his answer, quite unsure of what his Commander expected.

"Then the matter is settled. I told you the truth. I need your help. And, as is only rightful, I will expect the both of you to help. I am correct?"

"Yes Sir." They both said, quite soberly, to an unknown future.

"Good! Let's begin." With that Vosnob reached out, squeezing Sarg with a huge hug. Sarg returned the hug. Luuft about fell over. "Sarg, you've been out of my sight for too long. It's good to see you again."

"You too, Vosnob. Looks like you've put on a few pounds?"

"Not really. It's just that I've been forced to wear this so-called armor under my tunic. Can't hardly move the right way. Maybe it will disappear."

"Be careful my friend, I don't want to come to your funeral."

"I be careful. Look who's talking. The man who has been a spy for so long that some only remember his reputation and a strange one it is at that. For a dozen moon cycles at a time you've disappeared into the southern Dark Lands for us. Thanks to you, we know things have changed. The Kyykki have some kind of Captains now. That's still extremely hard to believe. They seem to have some type of guttural language……And spears. We even have a bit of a map. Don't we, Sarg." Vosnob laughed.

Luuft's head spun as if he were to lose his mind. He thought after three years as a Striper he understood quite a bit. All this was highly irregular. Maybe he was dreaming. "I didn't know…….." Luuft stammered.

"Was there a reason for you to know? The very fact that you didn't know proves my point. Sarg is good at what he does. And now more reconnaissance work is required."

"I think I'll miss you, Sarg." Luuft announced, quite out of turn.

"Not so fast, my son. No one goes alone."

Sarg roared with laughter. "Ah, so maybe I get to teach you a few things. Of course, maybe you get killed."

"That's not…..funny." Luuft choked on his emotions, more than on his embarrassment.

Vosnob continued smiling while he spoke. "No, it really isn't funny. Dead Light Stripers, unlike a few unnamed merchants, usually aren't very helpful. Sarg, you will keep this man alive." His smile instantly disappeared. "To business, Luuft, your village is on the edge of the south swamp, down by the Fluz Marsh."

"Yes, the family lived just outside of Poldu. My Father is a tracker for all the 'richies' and royalty who venture down from Krabo. Sometimes they pay pretty well, especially if you make them look good. Actually, if they didn't see me shoot, they thought they really got the deradh. They really did. Its still is difficult to believe their presumptions and dishonesty." Luuft found himself a bit overwhelmed, a condition leading to his overworked explanation.

"Their dishonesty?" Chuckled Vosnob. "But I like how you understand the game. It will be most useful."

Luuft felt his face burning-again. Vosnob caught him with his own words.

"Back to business. Something seems to be going on in Zuda Marsh. It's not like our friends to be out of the Dark Lands. Its not territory that we've ever known them to use before. And it's not a place where neither Haafians, nor Yidans usually travel. However, it's dense enough and so enormous that the 'damned one' could conceal his entire Kyykki army there. Or at least, the majority of it….The two of you are going on a little journey. I want a report from you within four double moon cycles….You'll be leaving tonight."

"Sir? How is that possible?" Luuft struggled with his sense of duty. "We're due to report back in two days. It'll look like I've deserted."

"I must apologize for the little lad, Sir. He's not been in but three years. There's a lot of the more practical things he's got to get under his belt....I suppose we do this the old way?"

"I'm really impressed, Sarg. I had thought those blows which split your helmet might have damaged your memory. Which, if I'm not mistaken, never has been your strong point?"

"Only for those confounded social events. Somehow they fall when there are just better places to be."

"And when you get back, you'll go to work on that. That's an order, from me in behalf of good living." Vosnob enjoyed watching Sarg squirm.

"Staff Master, front and center!" Vosnob shot a friendly glace at Sarg. "Yes, the old way. It works."

A torch suddenly appeared in the near distance. As the light came closer they all heard the voice of the grizzled Staff Master. "It's close to the middle of the night! You vagrants better know what you're doing, if you know what's good for you! I've had troopers sent away for less, you know! Why... I was in the middle of....."

"A good dream, I surmize." Finished Vosnob.

The flashy-eyed grey bearded man stopped cold. His long hooded robe did not hide his shaking however. "My lord, I didn't....." "Yes...Yes... Yes Sir." He shook nervously: he'd do anything to relieve himself of this embarrassment.

"Do you know these men?"

He squinted a bit: the sleep still with him. "Yes My Lord. This be Sarg. He's the platoon leader. And this be Luuft. A good trooper, little wet behind the ears though, Yes, My Lord, I know these two." He began to regain his composure.

"They're your men? And you are responsible for their actions? Then you know how they should be dressed?"

"Of course, My Lord. That's my job. Been doin' it for nigh three thousand moon cycles."

"Is that why your men smell and look like the Kyykki? Is that whey they are up at all hours of the night? Maybe they require some retraining exercises?....What do you think?"

Actually, the first statement was true, after a full double moon cycle at the front line their uniform needed some strong washings. So too for their bodies. Front lines have a proclivity for dirt and filth, especially as the lines are simply jumping-off points for further exploration into the Dark Lands of the torrid north.

The Staff Master immediately lost all of his regained composure. "No no, My Lord. This has never happened before." He was begging now. "You can check my reports, please check my reports."

Vosnsob looked away from the petrified man. "All right then. I must believe you, its part of the Holiness Code. However, I'm still looking at two smelly, dirty troopers. They're your men, what say you?'

After an excruciatingly long pause, he replied. "I believe," The Staff Master said carefully picking his words, "I believe that some retraining may be in order for the two of them. I believe that would do just fine. I can't allow them to set a bad example for the rest of the squadron."

"That does sound reasonable. However, your squadron is at the barricades. We are to expect an attack most any time. Can we afford these two men?"

The Staff Master determined to proceed most cautiously. "My Lord, I humbly confess that this is most difficult. Mounted archers are most valuable ….and…and…yet, if they are here to contaminate the squadron…. well, I just don't have an answer, My Lord."

"Then, with your permission, of course, might I suggest a suitable answer?"

"Retraining usually takes eight or more moon cycles. What if we simply send them off for four cycles? That should set the example for the men and get these two acting and smelling like real Light Stripers again. What do you say?"

"Agreed!" He couldn't wait to get this mess cleaned up. "Then you will send them off immediately. I expect them to be in reserve camp before dawn. "Any problems?"

"No, My Lord."

"Good!" Vosnob mounted Vaad, his charger and left as quickly as he arrived.

"Get your bags and go." The Staff Master dictated. He turned and headed for his tent. "Don't have too much fun." He mumbled.

Luuft kicked Sarg in the foot. "He's in on this too, isn't he?"

"You can bet your pointy ears and olive-colored skin he is, maybe."

Vosnob later turned in for a few hours of sleep. Sending out Sarg and Luuft was the last item on his list for this dawn. The first, a special envoy to the High Council meeting at Krabo: that Aide-de-Camp galloped out prior to dawn. Now he could only wait until the messenger returned or the 'strangely absent' Kyykki attacked. Wisdom of experience said to him, 'Rest now, only the Holy One, blessed is His Name, knows what is coming.'

Etan watched Krabo rise triumphantly in the far distance. Even at thirty miles out the new capital city impressed everyone. It was huge walled fortress, being ten miles from point to point as plotted on a six pointed star pattern. The six gates and their eighty foot towers stood at the end of each point. The gates were thirty feet wide and were so constructed that the Iron Gate plus the three iron fences under the tower and the draw bridge closed simultaneously. Most of the outside walls were thirty feet thick. Through its subbasements, it had connections to each of the six towers. The source for the granite was the Eastern Mountains, the densest rock known.

The serfs lived on the inside, along with the merchants as were the selling houses and bazaars, but the serf's fields were outside between the star points. Grazing extended outward for several miles.

The entire city stood has reminder and a defiance of the past: D'Ka would never happen again. Krabo's construction took ten hundred moon cycles...ten hundred moon cycles of fear and desperation.

Etan remembered the exception within the fortress: the home Church. This simple two storey wood building stood just inside the main gate. It was the clergy's witness to the people that fear is not overcome by granite but through faith. Faith dwells in truth and that alone sets people free. Krabo was the city built on fear. Etan realized this paradox was obvious to most residents.

He arrived on time. The twenty mile check points on the main roads and their garrisons provided for that. It took minimal time to remount. He covered nine hundred miles in a single moon cycle. Now he had the chance to rest and wash up before the High Council Meeting. Considering the awesome political power of the merchants, he needed the rest....even more than he needed it from the long hard ride.

Vosnob's primary aide-de-camp was well known in the city. Not that his silver trimmed forest green uniform hid him, or that his singular way of speaking inculcated the Holiness Code without actually quoting it. Rather, his scribal abilities more than once unveiled the fraud of the merchants. One lost his head, many more stuffed the jail cells. Etan knew he faced more of them this evening. He promptly forgot those thoughts as he entered the North Gate. Krabo was his home and there was time to visit family.

A note from Etan had been forwarded to the King. Etan requested permission to speak on behalf of the Commander of the Light Striper, Chaplain Captain Vosnob. It was a needful thing to do, however, no one dared to challenge the right of Vosnob to speak. Etan left without waiting for a reply. It caught up to him on the steps of the Church. A side glance from the messenger assured him of the expected answer. As he walked to the altar, he jammed the message into his weathered boot.

"Etan! Welcome! It's been a long time...Ah....I can see this is a serious visit, isn't it?"

"Jabbi, you certainly know that's the only way I get here anymore." He shot back. "……………..But enough…… How are you?"

"Not as well as I'd like to be. There's a certain buzz in the city I can't put my finger on. It should make me happy, instead it gnaws at me…. I can't find the truth in the matter."

"Have the termites eaten at the walls again?" Etan smiled though he sensed the Priest was deep into something.

Jabbi kept in touch with the happenings among the common people. That came from spending time in the bazaars and homes, a habit acquired before the Kyykki invasion came. His credibility remained untouchable. After the War, that same credibility gave him the power to assist in reconstructing the new government. Now he served as First Advisor to the King, a job that demanded much from a 'supposedly' old man.

"Perhaps, I need to apologize for my remark, but you get too serious, Jabbi. It's not good for this heaviness to weigh on you. Time to share the truth. Two will carry the burden easier than one."

"Obviously, it is never by coincidence that you are here. There are no accidents are there? The Holy One, Blessed be His Name, watches us closely. Why do I tend to forget that?" Jabbi reached back to his old habit of self-depreciation. "You are correct, my friend……Time to share……. Some Priests are too cozy with the Merchants…Come, there is much to share."

The men walked to the altar and prayed. How simple the altar Etan thought, too bad nothing else followed suite.

The altar, a simple bench constructed of oiled wood. Over the middle lay a plain white cloth upon which sat the symbols of the faith: an unadorned silver chalice and a well worn copy of the Holiness Code. With "The Truth frees us all." Jabbi abruptly ended the prayers.

They spent the afternoon in Jabbi's small cluttered office, pleasant room with scroll and book stuffed shelves flanking the window. An oak desk was slammed into the wall and two leather covered chairs finished off the room. Etan sat, long legs stretched out as Jabbi rambled on. Across the courtyard rose the mighty High Council Hall.

Jabbi explained that he'd never known the merchants to like him. He had little time for their incessant talk and rapacious greed and even less patience with their inherent dishonesty. But lately, this standard situation changed, not much, but enough to cause worry. Some had invited him to dinner, others had a few suggestions as to how to spread the Faith. This didn't fit. What reason lay behind this change? He didn't believe the Kyykki challenge had much influence here, except that, with the Kyykki hovering just beyond the barricades, the merchants harvested money hand-over-fist. Did they now have too much money? Something uniquely off-balance existed here. Jabbi found it most disturbing.

Etan's family shared some of the same anxiety. But they rejoiced in it: the merchants were finally finding the Faith. Jabbi was not so sure, nor was Etan.

"Jabbi, my friend, there isn't that much I know about this new situation…..But I share your concern. The merchant's change of attitude is strange, to say the least, especially as their real god is called gold…..Perhaps tonight's meeting will yield more information. …Let's meet afterwards. My answer from Vosnob won't arrive tonight."

"Are you sure?"

"I'm sure we'll have plenty of time to talk…..See you at council."

The High Council chamber held, supposedly, three hundred fifty people. They sat between sixty foot high pillars specifically designed to intimidate. People were not always the final authority here. Jabbi's original design ideas had proved themselves well: the cathedral-like atmosphere settled people to an almost civil level. The Church Guards stood ready to escort the unruly, irregardless of class, to the street. It was clearly a case of Church tyranny, but without some semblance of order, this Kingdom might fall as quickly as its predecessor.

That said, a meeting of the High Council usually proved the Haafians uncilvized. Meetings were notorious for their blatant disregard of politeness, the personal right s of others and anything that resembled the Holiness Code. Haafian culture took this paradox in stride. A regulated outlet from the rigidity of the Holiness Code was essential. Past history proved that a 'tight lid' on society produced mindless lip service to the Holiness Code. Trust and respectability disappeared. Secrets and scheming became a way of life.

The High Council meetings were designed to be a partial curative for this. Two hundred persons had permanent seats. However, anyone could speak to the gathering. The speaker was free from recrimination and revenge as long as he or she dealt with what he or she perceived to be the truth of the matter-at-hand. The permanent members acted as jury. Being that the merchants and lesser nobles held the permanent seats, the type of cases heard remained somewhat limited. The Church commented on all proceedings.

The Church Guard, composed of Knights, had change of enforcing all judgments. Being, therefore, independent of the nobles and merchants, they were also isolated from them, and often received the brunt of popular animosity. It may have been that way irregardless, as the Church Guard was recruited from the serfs. Paradoxily, the serfs had little power, yet when organized, the reverse was true. Even in the High Council hall, the serfs had gained a bit of power.

But with the merchants growing closer to the Church, Etan became anxious, as was Jabbi. They knew how the 'unwritten' system worked. Holiness had little to do with the outcome in too many cases. The Church was not above being 'bought'. Nor did the serfs forget merchants getting rich over land deals in the War Zone. That territory where the Kyykki died was unholy and thus removed from the serfs only to be sold, secretly, at low prices to merchants. The Church collection overflowed with donations. A riot ensued when this news leaked out. Many merchants lost their heads as did some of the Church hierarchy. But the serfs still lost their land:

their ability to be productive. The northwest sector of the country now belonged to merchants.

This concern headed Etan's list. Vosnob wanted new troops to secure this area. All things considered, he'd wish for an easier assignment. He knew that the Northern Army commanded by Vosnob stood ready to defend the land. But, he and many others, doubted the land would ever return to its rightful owners.

The army ran on fairness and merit, thus often opposing merchants and the Church. Here a male serf might rise to be a commander. Here practicality ruled, not tradition or birthright. Here honor still carried much weight. But if the Kyykki attacked as they did during the War, there were not enough troops on the front lines to stop them. Etan came seeking more troops. This would require an almost unanimous consent. The sell would be difficult. After all, news from the front held that all was quiet. He shuffled his feet on the cobblestone leading to the High Council Hall.

Somehow he managed to rearrange his frame of mind before entering. Jabbi met him on the steps. Etan saw Jabbi motion to the Captain of the Church Knights.

"Yes, Sir."

"Just keep it looking formal, Captain. I need to know the mood inside."

"It's rather calm today. Probably because the King is to show."

"What's the King doing here?" Even when Etan came for funding to maintain the extended front line, the King refused to show.

"Do you want rumor or truth? There's a little of both." The Captain smiled.

"Let's start with the rumors. They have more power in the common mind. ..Besides, its rumor you'll be fighting, eh Etan?"

"Just what I need….Another wise guy."

"Then you forgot what you told me a few hours ago? Then you certainly are in trouble……………….Glad I'm here to help you out."

"All right!....." Etan turned to the Captain. "About those rumors?"

"It seems the King has had a change of heart. He's beginning to act like a King. He's requested and received first-hand reports from the front. The treasury is up-to-date. The King imposed heavy new taxes on the nobles. They are ready to revolt, except they won't have time...All those of age are being enlisted in the training squadron."

"Unbelievable."

"I agree, Jabbi....Which training squadron?....I don't need those idiots in my way."

"Rumor says, 'Krabo'."

"So the good King wants to fight. I never thought he had the stomach for it."

"Nor I." Murmured Etan. "I've heard stories of his swordsmanship, horror stories."

The tubas blared, not once, as usual, but three times. The King had arrived and had taken the floor. It was his royal prerogative, even if he was elected to his post. Jabbi told the Captain to meet them in the chapel after the meeting. He requested a special watch for a merchant named Kracik. Quite a dirty fellow, but there was not enough evidence to implicate him.

The Captain bowed. "See you both later. Don't be too surprised if you hear more strange things."

The pair took the steps two at a time and moved into the main hallway. The Captain deftly cut his way through the crowd to his seat at the head of the Church Guard. The tubas blasted three more rounds. This time, with the aid of the flat sides of their swords against a few bottoms, the room quieted. Merchants seated themselves on the right and the nobles on the left. The Priests sat at a platform at the end of the hall, towering over all. The King and his court sat directly below them, yet still above the merchants and nobles. Serfs and others scrambled for whatever seats and standing room remained.

Etan and Jabbi sat with the merchants. Etan was still impressed by the ideas Jabbi incorporated into the Hall. His singular ideal held true: If Haaf were to survive, then a stable government was required. All about him, Etan saw the stability, from seating arrangements to the speaking area. The Priests, sitting above all, aptly demonstrated the Holiness Code.

The crier's thunderous voice woke Etan from his mental wanderings. "All rise! ALL RISE! ALL RISE FOR THE KING!!!!"

As if one, the entire group stood in silence. The King entered from the side. A hushed whisper ran through the crowd: the King walked in— unescorted—dressed in full battle armor. Not like that of the Light Striper, but of the ancestors: full plate armor from head to foot. He carried a golden visored helmet in his right hand. His ill-fitting broad sword dragged on the marble floor, making a racket. He walked to his seat and dropped his helmet there. After bowing to the Priests, he walked to the center of the speaker's floor,

"Even Vosnob wouldn't have expected this." Etan thought.

The King slowly looked about the Hall, studying each facial expression. He was not the wised or most experienced King, nor had he ever been construed as the most sincere. Now, as clumsy as he was, this is the most regal and imposing as he'd ever been. The entire assembly just stood, stunned, confused. Was this the King they elected? This new image, just a cover? In loud silence the people waited.

"You have my permission to sit." The King roughly commanded. He sounded like a line officer, not a King, not the stodgy politician merchant they elected. Not the sneak who tried to run the show behind the High Council's back. Not one person sat.

"I said....'SIT'........'SIT DOWN!'........NOW!"

As one, the hushed body sat.

"You haven't heard me speak like that before. ..You should have. I apologize for the miserable way I have behaved as your king. Its time for me to separate myself from the Church...the merchants...and, especially, the nobility... I do so for the sake of out Haafian future."

Everyone remained stunned, except for the leaders of all three groups. Their bright red faces expressed both betrayal and anger.

He motioned to the Church Guards. They carried forth the Altar table. It was another simple trestle table of dark oiled wood. On it were the symbols of the faith: a small wooden chalice with a white star painted on it and the Book of the Holiness Code.

"I formally protest to the entire body. This King has gone too far! Now he assumes the duties of the Church." The old High Priest trembled with righteousness as he spoke from his vantage point on the platform above the gathered participants.

"You may sit down my friend. I plan no usurpation of your Holy office ......However, you are wrong. The fact is, I haven't gone far enough....yet." He paused for a moment and studied the crowd. "My friends, my people, relax. I have a story to tell you. A story that is still rather strange for me and a story that is the reason that I stand before you today, ready to lead you against the Kyykki....But that is getting ahead of the story."

"Many of you believe that I was out hunting these last five double moons. I did intend that. However, even though I was not exactly a religious man, I felt pulled to the Snow Mountains. The closer I got to the old monastery, the more I felt the call was from the Holy One, Blessed Be His Name."

There was a gasp from most who were gathered, a religious King in Haaf was highly irregular. Some of the Priests had tears in their eyes. But the merchants and the nobles immediately became suspicious. A newly religious King sounded ominous: they might end up losers.

"I spent my time in guided prayer, thanks to the Brothers there. The longer I stayed the more I struggled with my dreams. Dreams are powerful. Yes, dreams can be sent by the Evil One. That's why I needed the help of the Brothers. The first dream is one that I wish I could forget. It spoke in clearest terms of the punishment waiting for me if I continued to do nothing in the face of the oncoming evil from the North. I knew I needed to change, but I had not the courage to do so…..I enjoyed the life of idleness, of making deals with you merchants and with you nobles…..I tell you most truly, those meaningless days are herby terminated….It is high time for all of you to get to work, honest work that brings glory to the Holy One."

Some of the merchants prepared to leave. The Church Knights blocked the exits. The Church Knights were bigger and most willing to engage in a fight. The King had another idea.

"Time in the lower prison for rudeness is appropriate, you unfaithful merchants! ….Take them away! And their property shall be sold and used for the Holy War."

There was an outbreak of approval. Even some merchants were clapping and every one stood. The priests silently nodded their blessings. A bit of disciplining now-and-then assured reverence and order.

"Come to order! There is only so much room in the prison." The King laughed. "Sit down and I will tell you of my great dream and its meaning. As it transformed me, so too will it transform all of you." He waited for every one to sit before continuing.

"My dream…..my dream was not one I did not ask for, nor even after receiving it, was I convinced that I was the one it was intended for. No, do not think I accuse the Holy One of being wrong. Much the opposite, why should one such as I be chosen? Again, I am ahead of the story.… In my dream, the black evil forces from the Dark Lands attacked our forces with numbers and hatred unknown…beyond all imagination…They and their monsters trampled and killed and devoured everything that they touched. Our forces, though faithful, were not enough save the country.….. The second scene was that of idleness and unfaithfulness, of politics and business as usual. As if there was no war! Then the hordes broke in and devoured these people. I woke from my dream. I was terrified! There was no hope for us I screamed!...My screaming brought the brothers to my room. They listened to my dream. With tears in their eyes they agreed with me. A nation divided and idle, a nation without a vision….can defeat no one…can not defend itself!"

It was almost too quiet. The stark reality of another war struck home with the usually indifferent. No one could guess what the King might say next, especially if you happened to listen to the rumors floating about the city. The King walked around the altar several times before speaking again, needing time to control his emotions.

"I found myself without hope for the dream was about our land. A land where a few faithful defend those of us who live without a care and live without sacrificing as does the Light Striper. I know why Vosnob is more the leader than I will ever be. He follows the precepts of the Holiness Code; we only pay it lip service. As the dream showed, this stupidity will cost us everything.…..We cannot and we will not go on this way!" The King raised his voice measurably.

"These are the changes that go into effect this day." With that the King pulled a large paper from his sleeve. He looked it over and then rolled it up. "Before I tell you about your new way of life, you need to know the rest of the story.…I was terrified about the dream. It was true. There seemed to be no future for us…Then one of the Brothers suggested that the dream might not be over. Dreams, he noted, if they originated from the Holy One, usually did not have but two parts, but three. Three, you understand, is the Holy number.…..It was a bit of a solace, enough to try to sleep again.…The third part of the dream came. This was different vision.…In it, a huge white eagle flew above the land. The eagle appeared from nowhere. It circled above the cities and the crop lands. Everyone who saw it, followed after it. The eagle lead the people to the Battle and far beyond.…There the eagle dropped down on the black hordes of Kyykki. Nothing could stop the eagle as he plowed through the enemy ranks.… nothing…not clubs nor spears…nor numbers beyond counting.…..Then as if by a divine signal, those who followed the white eagle went over the wall and pushed the Kyykki back into their black belching holes.....As quickly and as unexpectedly as he had come the eagle disappeared." The King was visible shaken. He bent at the waist as if carrying a heavy burden. "The brothers also helped me with this dream. They considered it divine. It is the answer to our situation! It is a sign of victory given by the Holy One, Blessed Be His Name!"

"You have to be stupid to not see what's coming." Etan whispered to Jabbi.

Jabbi gave him an elbow in the ribs in reply.

"We are no longer without hope!" The King thundered. "The identity of the great white eagle is known!............... I'm the great white eagle."

A rush of unbelievable disbelief rattled through the visibly shaken crowd. No way could this be possible. No way could this man even use a sword. NO.

The King anticipated this reaction. "You aren't convinced, are you? I can't say that I blame you. As I began, I apologize for being an irresponsible King...Let me explain. First, as was confirmed by the brothers, the dream is divine. Second, remember that the Holy One works in mysterious ways. He will call to serve Him whomever He so desires. And as the Holy One called, so too will He protect...I am no warrior, but the Holy One has called. I will go...Which brings me to the third point, how do I know that I am the white eagle? Why not the famous Vosnob? Or something or someone unknown to us at present? .....Because, since as long as there has been history, the herald for our family has been the white eagle. I am the chosen one." The true humility in the King's voice was missed only by those headed to prison.

"We have little time to lose. With the backing of the Church and with the powers I have as King, this is what will be done." The King unrolled his paper and began to read, "Due to the crisis in our land, I, your King, make the following declaration, which shall remain in effect until after Haaf is once again free of the evil which seeks to destroy her. First, all merchants will be triple taxed. This money shall come from their treasuries. No additional taxes will be placed upon the serfs. This money shall support the new squadrons requested for the Light Stripers."

The few merchants who dared to groan or whine were immediately hauled away.

"There will be no more of this unfaithfulness!" The King became deadly serious. "Second, all nobles, at their personal expense will join me at the front before the end of this cycle. You will follow me into battle. Such is the high calling for nobility. Those not reporting for duty will be considered traitors and shall be killed on sight."

The King eyeballed each of the nobles. They drew back in fearful response. "You do understand, don't you, my Lords?"

Their response was mixed. "Long live the King!" Was heard from the minority. For a few, their need to prove themselves had been answered. Most were stunned and confused. Death seemed to stare at them for the first time. The cowards kept quiet. Maybe they could somehow break a leg.

The merchants chimed in, "Long live the King!" Even the staid Churchmen chanted, "Long lives the King!"

The King motioned for silence. "There is a third item....All Churchmen, upon ordination, shall serve for five years as teachers and preachers. They shall serve in every town, every village, and every hamlet where more than fifty people live." The King faced the Church hierarchy. Even though he was looking up to them, they exhibited much anxiety. "You were called by the Holy One to serve ALL his people. Now you will do it! I, your King, called by the Holy One, blessed be His Name, have spoken!"

The paper was laid on the Altar. The King took up his helmet. He looked about. "What are you waiting for? We all have work to do! Until it is done, this High Council is dismissed. That is all." The King started to leave. No one else did. "Guards, gently remove these people." He murmured.

Chapter 2

Sarg depended on intuition concerning what Vosnob actually wanted him to do. This 'format of freedom' had become pretty standardized throughout the double moon cycles. As the Commander usually sent him on a dangerous mission only to be given green troops to work with, Sarg demanded this freedom to accomplish the given mission. Still, Vosnob's consistency in this particular matter of green troopers hit a raw nerve with Sarg. But this time Vosnob improved upon his standard procedure; Luuft was assigned to him.

Ten cycles. That's how long Sarg had known Luuft. Most of the troops Vosnob assigned were collected along the way, at predesignated places. That way, if they never returned, fewer questions were asked. There wasn't much that Sarg could about the situation. Maybe it was best that way. After all, he wasn't exactly regular army. Dreams of the old farm and his family were never far from him, even though they were long gone. His family never made it to D'Ka when the Kyykki hordes overran the countryside. He was at South Haaf when the attack came. Even though it was usual for him to be at South Haaf during the harvest, he never forgave himself for not being at home. Later, the merchant thief Kracik bought his master's land and half of the rest of the valley for almost nothing. Sarg had no family and no place to return. For that vile transaction the Church was rightly blamed. Sarg still held a grudge. Inside was a bitterness that refused to budge. Suddenly, a huge dark shadow, one emanating from nowhere, tore Sarg from his personal thoughts.

"Scatter!" Yelled Sarg.

The entire group and the pack Striper charged for the trees that overhung the side of the road. The dark shadow passed. No one was hurt. Nothing happened. Sarg studied the sky to see where or what the shadow was. The bright noon day blinded him.

"Never saw anything that big before! What was it?" Luuft didn't care for surprizes.

"Try big, fast, deliberate." Such was Yauk's analysis.

"Real smart! Why do I need a wise guy?"

"Probably because you can't figure it out for yourself!" Yauk shot back. Luuft pulled his broadaxe.

"Knock it off, both of you! I've got more to worry about than a few hot heads. Put that away! Yauk, keep your mouth shut!"

Luuft hovered at the edge. It was the forth day in the saddle, the forth day of hard riding without a break, eating and riding, sleeping and riding. He got off one Striper only to get another one. Sarg said they were supposed to get a break at Pinduala. That was only a sunrise and a half away.

Sarg mentally deliberated about these two green troopers; big and big mouthed Yauk and the skinny, poorly uniformed, [clothes were at least big enough for Yauk to wear] I-refuse-to-talk-to anyone Breel. The kid was always trailing behind, a bit like a lost puppy.

"I've had it with Yauk!" Luuft said to no one particular.

"What's the problem? You asked a question and you got a rather well-thought out answer. The dark shadow was big. But it was also deliberate. It was not some accident. We spies are being spied on." Vauk thoroughly enjoyed himself. "Anything that could make a two hundred foot shadow and then be gone, as if it never really was, certainly had the power to kill us. The point is, it didn't. It's probably been watching us for quite a while."

"So why then did it give itself away, smart guy?"

"Easy, it realized it had nothing to fear from us. And, before you get more stupid, no, the thing did not originate with any of the damned Beizel's descendants. You know they aren't able to work in the bright day light. They require clouds or a rain storm."

Luuft mumbled something about a well placed funeral. Then he turned his Striper and moved out in front of the group. Breel galloped up to ride with Luuft, his baggy uniform flopping in the breeze.

"Ha! There's our shadow!" Yauk gestured towards Breel. He remained rather proud of his remarks, in spite of the fact that no one actually listened.

"You know, Yauk, the time is coming when I'm not going to be able to stop him." Sarg was serious. "So, even if you are one of those university types from Buda, keep your mouth shut!"

"I'll try, however, someone must be clear headed about this shadow mystery." A hint of arrogance tinted his voice.

"Then you let me think about it. And that's an order!"

"Yes Sir!" Snapped Yauk. He still wasn't thrilled about this spying business. He intended a law practice. His personal endeavor aimed at cleaning up the unholy mess created by the Church after the War. The Holiness Code demanded righteousness. The Church, he believed, carried the responsibility for the current land injustice. Delineating out how the land was condemned and then restored was a mystery. But if the names could be found, then he would really be spying. He searched for a paper trail, not the wilderness trail.

The four troopers had been following the equipment road. This trail, running directly behind the massive bulwarks, was designated the logistical resupply route for the troops on the front line. Because of the duration of the Trooper's stay, it became more of a bazaar road, with shops and peddlers doing an excellent business. Nor did one have to look too far to see the brothels and the ale houses. These were also flourishing. The troopers took this in stride, all except for Breel, that is. In fact, everyone knew when they were getting near one of those places just by the way Breel's complacency disappeared. Instead, for some unknown reason, he transformed into a monstrous ogre ready to smash and burn the brothels and ale houses to the ground.

Sarg called an inspection halt at the last blockhouse. While the three waited outside, pretending to be the serfs they were dressed like, Sarg went inside and presented Vosnob's personal credentials to the Staff Master. The shaken man called for an immediate inspection of the troops.

They failed miserably. No complete duty roster, no one on top of the sentry post, a few 'original' uniforms and not enough supplies for even one short siege. However, the most serious offence was the half-empty arsenal; the spears and arrows being scattered over the practice yard. This atrocity was futilely explained as ordinary target practice. Sarg wrote up an ugly report and sent it by special carrier directly to Vosnob. Then he demoted the Staff Master to Trooper. The post went on ten day alert, until Vosnob said otherwise.

After 'assembly' sounded, Sarg addressed the so-called troopers. "It is most obvious, and most deploringly so, that this outpost has forgotten not only its duty to the nation but also the Holiness Code. You are the first defenders when the Kyykki come, especially should they be wise enough to believe they might outflank us. They would eat you alive in less than ten minutes. You are not prepared!....You are not ready!....You are not the Light Striper! You and your games.....You and your stupidity.....You and your lack of commitment....If I ever hear just one more thing, anything, that tells me you have neglected your duties, I'll personally shoot each and every one of you.. ....Do I make myself perfectly clear!"

"YES SIR." No unison reply here. And not quite a serious enough reply for Sarg. An extremely elemental and long-remembered lesson was required.

"Luuft, you and Vauk take these troopers out for a run. However, they aren't fit to be called Light Striper, so they'll run without the Stripers. About ten miles might help them get serious, what do you think?"

"An excellent idea!"....Troopers! At the right! Fast walk!" Two hundred troopers moved out more quickly than ever before. This time they were encouraged by a whip. They'd return by midnight, at least a few of them would.

As they trotted by, the gaily decorated tent city emptied out her whores. Others came to see the excitement. They were having quite a party about it all.

"Breel, its time we cleaned up the rest of this camp. There's just too much filth here. Tell me, how many brothels do you see?" Sarg asked with an intriguing smile.

"Three and four ale houses." His voice quavered like that of one too young to join the Light Striper.

Sarg had a slight personal problem with that, a fighting man should sound like a fighting man. Still, efficiency, commitment and skill counted more to him. "Then you'll need just seven arrows to get rid of them."

Without a single word, Breel pulled his bow off his shoulder, lit an arrow and sent it off to the farthest brothel. Within a few moments the tent blazed. The remaining unsocial institutions began burning in less than a minute. Breel actually reveled in this responsibility. The tent city became flame city.

"Fire is the way to purify things." Breel remarked flatly. "So says the Holiness Code."

For whatever value it had, this was the first time Sarg recalled him grinning.

"Might you be one of the Holy One's messengers?" Sarg commented, but deep inside, he wasn't too sure if he was half serious or not.

Breel replied with a mysterious smile, then turned to watch the entire tent city burn. A moment later, the dark shadow passed over them again. Sarg traced it for but a few seconds; again, it flew into the sun and vanished.

The reddish dawn produced four rested troopers. A surrealistic landscape now surrounded them: burnt offerings from the tent city left the ground charred and smoldering, the block house, being constructed of white granite, loomed high as the victor. The now totally exhausted albeit serious troopers responded as one man, one uniformity and to one duty. An evening of remedial training was all that was required. By mid-day Sarg was ready to move on.

"Do you really think the Kyykki would attack from the swamp?"

"No, Luuft, I don't think so. Its out of their usual territory. They've always come directly from their volcano ridden land. Like they wanted the heat and the dryness, not heat and water."

"But," countered Vauk, "Isn't our mission to see if that hypothesis holds any truth? After all, its only a short move to the north and they can come pouring out onto the plain. It would be a great flanking move....."

"You seem to believe that we have no intelligence reports from this area. That may be rash on your part. And that rashness will cost you. You're too presumptuous for your own good." Sarg said.

"Aha, then I know why I'm here! Vosnob told me my education was incomplete until I got some dirt on me. He said I had good potential, but it was worthless...not tested. Well, At least I got the best teacher in the Light Striper."

"I'll try to take that as a complement." Sarg's grin belied the tone of his voice.

As they rode towards Pinduala, they noticed a real change in the air; it reeked of dead and decaying matter, especially when the breeze came from the north. Breel took it the hardest; he puked every few minutes. The ground also changed: it became soft underfoot and from the dead trees bordering the road, it appeared that the swamp was moving southward. No swamp insects chirping, no animals. Not even a sound from the great water, which they could now see in the distance.

The first items were disturbing, the latter was simply a matter of knowing that when the two moons were on opposite sides of the land, which was regular enough to predict, tides did not exist.

The ride remained a quiet one, until the stone village came into view. The Light Striper squadron living there actually had few Stripers compared to its 'navy'. This was the home port for the 'hidden' navy that only a few knew existed. Even the King remained ignorant of it. The navy based itself a hundred miles off the coast, on the islands. They kept the three hundred or so ships afloat by fishing and trading. Sarg shared this unknown information with his fledglings. He enjoyed seeing their dumfounded faces as much as he enjoyed being a few steps ahead of them. As more and more revelations became known, the Troopers began to realize their limited knowledge of the current situation.

Just as the Pinduala guards caught sight of the four, Luuft challenged everyone to a race to the gate. Breel, even though keeping up the tail end, as usual, answered by kicking his spurs into the Striper. With his ill-fitting uniform flapping in the wind, Breel imitated a dancing scarecrow.

"Damn! You Cheat!" yelled Luuft as Breel passed him. It took him the entire race to catch up. Breel won.

"So!" Luuft jammed the words in Breel's face. "So what do you want for a prize? Clothes to fit or a body to put them on?"

Breel answered in his most polite tone. "I had no idea that you would be so generous. Allow me a few days to think through your most generous offer. I should not want to be so cheap as to offend you."

Luuft glowed redder than the noon day sun. But as the other two stood by to witness the exchange, he felt caught. Honor would hold him to his stupidity, and it would probably cost him dearly.

It took a few moments minutes to get through the gate. Security was stepped up since Sarg was last here, then anything and anyone could just walk through. The city was prepared for a long siege. All walls had been reinforced from the inside. The multiple arrow shooting machines were well-placed for massive volleys. The catapults sat 'at ready', disguised as ordinary hay wagons. Such mobility for siege machines was relatively new, but the advantages of such equipment were obvious. The old straw huts were replaced by stone ones. The guise used belonged to some noble ideal about helping the poorest. In reality, a major fire hazard disappeared.

The barracks of the Light Striper lay on the east side of the city, just to the north of the docks. This too, was now built of stone, rising to four stories, allowing it to become the tallest building in town. Even the new stone chapel didn't compare in height.

Each Trooper deliberately, per Sarg's orders, took a different path through town. They would compare notes during supper at the barracks. Sarg tied his Striper and headed for the ale house. He knew drunks had very open mouths that seldom connected to their brains. Breel headed for the bazaar. He had the excuse of finding an expensive gift, but a check on the imports and exports would also tell who was in town. Luuft decided just to walk the back alleys. Not safe, but these street types had good common sense. Besides, Luuft felt at home with city people. Vauk meandered towards the chapel. He had questions that demanded the truth. He might find some clues there.

Breel missed supper. The rest feasted on roast beef with greens and melons on the side. The ale was warm but the local juice somehow wasn't. Because most of the patrols left for the night, the large room was empty. The heavy wood tables blended in with the white washed floor. One corner, the barrels of arrows, had cushioned seats. There the three withdrew to compare notes. Sarg cared only to listen.

Vauk commenced. "The priests are jumpy and nervous. They talk of something unholy invading the city. It might be invisible, like a spirit, but that's conjecture. The whole effect is that trust has left, suspicion is creeping in. If it's any more contagious, even the Light Striper might become affected."

"Ghosts and spirits walking about the city? And just how do we stop these, provided, of course, that they exist?" Luuft mocked.

"Do holiness and evil mix? Use your brain." Vauk refused to take the tempting bait Luuft laid out.

"So what do you propose? The Church will consecrate the entire city? Ha, You'd put the blessed merchants out of business. That's the real evil here....not some spirits."

"Keep your mouth shut." Sarg cautioned Luuft. "Now, just what did you hear?"

"Well, street people tend to see things more down to earth. There's a major problem. But it has nothing to do with this evil spirit stuff. At the docks, a few strangers have been seen. Tall and they wear hoods, stay in the shadows. Usually in groups of three or four. No one knows if it's one group or a few. They don't buy nothing, don't say nothing, except to themselves. Since they arrived, sometime during the last two cycles, bodies, dried out like a mummies, have shown up at the dumping ground. Trouble is, they used to be dock workers......Your evil spirits conjecture mummifying spells, Lawyer man? Well, do they?"

"Obviously, the evil is real." Sarg thought out loud. "It uses its victims to achieve a goal: stir up the city, rip its cohesiveness away. But why Pinduala? What would the damned evil one want with this place? The answer to th......"

The door opened and then slammed. A bloodied Breel just stood there, his tunic and pants shredded, as if by small razors. His color, ashen. His slimy broadaxe hung from his left arm. It was bloodier than the sack he carried. The sack produced a gut wrenching smell. It came from the green stuff oozing from the sack. Breel wobbled and then shook it off.

"Explain this!" He let go of the bag. Two greyish skeletal heads rolled out. Green ooze bubbled from their severed necks. "The third one got away, but not all of her." A long fingered hand dropped from the sack. Breel stared, glazey-eyed, at the heads, then stumbled and collapsed. He hit the wooden floor like a boulder.

"All rise for the King!" The page bellowed. The superb acoustics of the Council Hall reverberated with his voice. The whole assembled Council rose even as he spoke. It was now three full cycles since the King dismissed them all. The atmosphere became thick and tense, if not entirely foreboding. The King placed demands before the group. They were now to give accounting.

The King entered the hall, this time dressed as a serf, sandals and all. He paused before the Church leaders prior to speaking.

"WE, and I mean WE, are being called to account for our deeds and misdeeds. Not ONE of us, not even those standing behind me, is free from the offence of irresponsibility. When we execute responsibility, we bathe ourselves in Holiness. This is the ONLY route to the nation's salvation. Nothing less will suffice, unless we care to perish." His voice was not stentorian as at the last High Council session. Now he portrayed himself as deep with wisdom and earnest with the Faith, a combination that proved formidable, especially to the merchants.

"I have accomplished the tasks that were needful. I choose to declare this because I deem it essential to set the example." He paused. "I begin with our terminal gathering as the 'old' High Council. I laid a judgment and a conditional responsibility upon each of your vocational strengths, spiritual leadership, economic leadership and nobility or rather---as it now stands accomplished---military leadership." He paused again. "My accounting was, and remains, to define your mission and to organize the nation to confront the evil of the Kyykki. Yet, the merchants persist in the most recalcitrant activity. They gloat in deferring to others to discharge their profession. This conspiracy is ended. Six of this group died yesterday. They did not withstand the rope about their necks."

A Loud silence rose from the gathered. This half-educated minor noble, whom they help select to be King, had both defied and broken from their powerful grasp. He did it with impunity. Even before the War, no King had ever challenged their authority. While the merchants squirmed in their seats, the 'new' military silently wrung their hands in merriment. At last, a King of their own kind! Indeed, the glorious old days of the ancient history were returning.

"I admit, I play the tyrant. But you shall also play. You must feel the burden of judgment; you must bear that serious responsibility also..... This is the case. Today, with two of the guard, I went to buy Stripers, the best reddish-blacks, for the new military." The King eyed those gathered with a stare that brought them shivers.

"We were all dressed as serfs. We had a procurement document from the King, with his signature and seal. Fifty heavy mounts, at least three years old, were required. We paid for them in advance, at a fair price agreed to by both parties. Delivery for the fifty mounts was for noon today. The mounts which arrived stand outside this building. They are good mounts, except there are but forty, not fifty. My men and I returned to the merchant demanding a satisfactory explanation. As the King was in most demanding tyrannical mood, so we explained to the merchant, we were intent having all the answers......The merchant instantly became outraged! We were accusing an innocent man of fraud! Then he produced the bill of sale. It read, forty mounts, not fifty. It was the bill I signed, however. I have witnesses to that. ...The document was altered, the smudge marks are still visible."

A guard paraded the altered document before the assembly. The alteration job was not skillfully done. Anger rose from each side. Such injustice, such defiant corruption was intolerable. So murmured those present.

"Beyond this," continued the King, "Is the buyer's copy of the transaction. I have that with me."

Another of the guard presented this second document to the Council. The only difference between the two was the number of Stripers ordered.

"The other cases I judged were just as profoundly perverse. In each, an attempt to impoverish the Nation for personal gain was clearly manifest. It is robbery! It is treasonous! It shall not go unpunished!" The King quieted himself. "Now all of you must decide. Do you believe a crime against the nation has happened?

There was a pause, such opinion was never called for in the past. In fact, more than a few took pride in such underhanded dealings. Now they were forced to judge one of their own. From the side of the nobility rose the first voice. "The king has made the case, let justice prevail! Hang the merchant!"

Within the next moment, the cry, "Hang the merchant!" created an ear splitting din. Most of the merchants joined in. Though their smiles were suppressed, the clergy tacitly approved.

The King raised his arms: the Council quieted. "We are agreed on the first question. We move to the second. What's the sentence?"

Again, the Council roared, "Hang him! Hang him!"

"One moment, my fellow Council members." After a strange eerie moment, the Council obeyed. The dark somber voice from the merchants section belonged to Kracik, the rich merchant from the north. "Thank you, dear colleagues.... My King, I beg audience to address the Council." The voice begged only in words, its dark tone threatened.

"Permission granted."

"I ask all of you to search your hearts, for a man's life obviously hangs, ...pardon my impoverished vocabulary...upon our verdict. Yet in all fairness to the accused, not only has he been denied the ethical procedures of defending himself, but also, we do not even know who this person is? Has he a name? Who is it that we sentence? For all I know, and I do not intend to ridicule the King, this person could be a Kyykki!" His voice tinged with rage. His red, sweat streaked face clearly indicated that his disciplined words were ready to detonate, allowing his true self to be broadcast.

Laughing and snickering slowly invaded the Council room. Definitely, Kracik's support remained minuscule. The King won a round. Yet he knew the battle was far from over. Kracik's questions required respectable answers....prompt answers.

Again, the King raised his arms. Murmuring prevailed more than quiet. The King waited. He then brought his head up. The guards flew into action; the flat of a sword on a few dozen openmouthed heads regained the silence.

"You speak with great eloquence. I confess that you construct a few valid points. However, to infer...to insinuate...that the King is so deficient as not to recognize a Kyykki, goes too far. That insult should not stand without redress....However, during this crisis, I choose to ignore your blatant lack of propriety. As for your questioning the man's identity, what difference does it make? Are we to restrain justice through favoritism? As far as I know, the Holiness Code makes no exceptions for a man's power or prestige. Justice is only justice when it remains blind." He turned to the clergy who were sitting above him, "Tell me, is this the way it is?"

A nod of their heads proclaimed the King correct.

"Your last question dealt with the accused defending himself. What does the man have to defend? His honor? His dignity? His patriotism?"

The Council broke out with muffled laughter, aimed at the defiantly enraged Kracik.

The King immediately called for sentencing. Before the Council responded, three guards slammed the accused into the center of the hall. He stumbled and fell. A hood covered his face. The Council had an instantaneous reply, "Hang him! Hang him!"

The pandemonium became overwhelming. And the presence of the accused only heightened the outpouring of support for the King's new way. Kracik took one step back, only to discover guard at each elbow. A sickeningly sweet smile appeared on his usually taciturn face. The stomachs of many quivered when they saw it

"Get up!" the King commanded the accused.

The guards yanked the accused to his feet. His hands remained tied. His dress seemed familiar; a long yellow with gold trimmed robe, maroon colored riding boots that matched his wide belt.

"See the traitor!"

A guard ripped off the hood. The Council froze. Kracik went white. The man was Ruje, Kracik's youngest son.

"Justice is blind. Justice is true. Justice will be done." Intoned the King to the frozen Council. He heavy-heartedly looked to Kracik. "I would have defended my son also." Words were somber. "I remind all of you that you made the judgment. You are responsible and you, like myself, will carry the burden of your actions. As you have spoken, so let it be...... Ruje, tomorrow at noon, you shall hang. You have condemned yourself by your own greed and selfishness......Take him to the dungeon."

Shock upon shock impacted on the Council as they began to consider the gravity of their actions. The King successfully thrust them into reality and actively living the Holiness Code. Some would never forgive him for that. Many, thinking business over, rose to leave, only to find the Church guards blocking the doors.

"In all fairness," Began the King, "All three parties must give account. We've dealt with but one. Please be seated."

The 'old' nobility, now renamed 'military', were next. Required to arrive at Krabo for military preparation, some had gone the other way. Again, such actions proved one traitorous, defaulting on the nation and the Holiness Code

"There can be no sympathy for those who willfully deny their country. Nobility are subject to regulation as much as the serfs are. No! More so! The Holy One, Blessed be His Name, gave the greater responsibility to those born into superior station. They will set the proper and righteous example."

Some merchants could appreciate the King's balancing act. He, potentially, had the power to proportionate the score. This hope they now hungered for: an impartial and objective king.

"The guards are rounding up the dishonorable nobles. Some, I believe five, were executed. A few others repented thoroughly, relinquishing their title, all land holdings, and all assets of any type. After five years in prison, they are free to transform themselves into serfs."

Nobility, especially the uppity families residing in the southern part of Haaf, despised equality. The 'new' military gave them both disciplined employment for the first time in their lives, and experiential education concerning sweat, dirt and blood. This amused the merchants, who, if nothing else, understood the concept of strenuous labor.

"Those who were righteously executed had their titles, properties and inheritances confiscated and placed in the King's trust. Following the coming War, such titles, properties and the like shall be granted, by royal decree, to those deemed worthy by their achievements during the War. Birthright is denied anyone. Honor and dignity will be earned through personal achievement, following the example of the esteemed Light Striper."

The merchants relished the King's polemic. Some equality could be realized in the future. Nobility just might enhance one's stature in society. This, instead of providing bait for ridicule, is what those sitting opposite the merchants were now compelled to prove to the nation; that nobility concerned itself with these new principles as the merchants cared for theirs.

"Finally, the Church and its clergy: your's is the highest of callings. But, you have blemished yourselves! By keeping, by hoarding, the teachings of the Holiness Code. They have never reached the serfs! You pitiless scoundrels! You allow His people to live in ignorance! You damnable hypocrites! You preach condemnation to those you never tried to help! Your days of fine food and relaxation are terminated forever!"

While some had thought to take on the Church before, now, in front of the nation's leaders, the King willing and earnestly brought them to task. Everyone gasped: the old ways evaporated right in front of them. Was anything constant or sacred anymore? What happened to tradition? Few would remain foolish enough to challenge this King's actions. But, as the old system now crumbled, little latitude was left for others to out-maneuver the King.

Now the Churchmen were panic stricken, it clearly showed on their strained, sweating faces. By adhering to the Holiness Code, they felt protected and confident. The code denounced them: the clergy were called by the Hole One to be servants, not to be the served.

"The monasteries are now schools for the most talented serfs. The clergy who once inhabited those too staid and too cozy establishments are now being dispersed through out the nation. Each and every hamlet will now include a chapel and school. The tax money the Church receives shall pay for each and every clergy who is rightfully following THE calling. Nor shall the Church proclaim herself impoverished and thus levy unjustifiable taxes. The Church will use her finances to promote the Holiness Code to everyone in the nation." The King paused, looked over the audience. Indeed, every one was inordinately attentive. "Let me establish evidence of the Church's error. Those of you who have actually seen or read the Holiness Code we 'supposedly' abide by, stand up!"

Approximately two hundred fifty had gathered in the hall. Less than twenty stood.

"I have justified my point. This must come to an end. Holiness cannot defeat evil when no one knows what Holiness is....Members of the clergy, I bid you no malice, but your transgressions need corrected." The King faced the disturbed and apprehensive clergy as he spoke. He awaited a reply.

All remained silent for a few minutes. "My king," solemnly spoke the usually remote High Priest, "You have indeed spoken the truth. We confess to the Holy One, Blessed be His Name, that we are neglectful of our calling. Our repentance will be manifested in our actions throughout the country." His words were honest, and as he held power over the clergy, some credibility was restored. "Might I have permission to impose a question upon the King?" The High Priest asked with a shaken demeanor.

"You may."

"I, and the rest gathered here, perceive you a transformed man. We have spoke of it at some great length. It is frightening to many, even myself...."

"You had a question?"

"Sorry, my King.....There is so much to think about. ...My question: was it not through the pilgrimage you took to the Brothers that you were reformed and that you actually studied the Holiness Book?"

"Yes, and yes. That was two questions, but consider yourself forgiven."

The King said. "The nation needs to know the power of the Word. It is essential for our well being. True, I am no longer who I was, but I take no credit for the conversion. It is a gift from the Holy One, Blessed be His Name. My responsibility is to do what I have been called to: free the nation from evil, from both inside and outside........."

The King never finished. For, as if a gesture of unified support for the King, the clergy soundlessly rose and joined hands. The High Priest retrieved the chalice, brought it down the staircase to the King. The King was transfixed as he mentally acknowledged the symbolism of this action: the King was being accepted as one with the clergy. Kneeling before the High Priest, the King received the chalice, possessing it for but the moment when the priest's hands encompassed the top of his head and blessed him. To conclude the ceremony and fulfill the liturgy, the King stood and embraced the High Priest. The holiness, mixed with some confusion, both reflecting themselves in the King's face, communicated both honesty and truthfulness.

The 'new knights' clumsily rose to ungainly presented swords, saluting their King and Commander. "Long live the King!" Rolled off the pillared walls and into the city.

Merchants usually refused such formal ceremonies, but after a brief debate, stood and bowed to the King. Even Kracik rose and bowed; a man encompassed by guards has few choices.

The King began to summarize. "I am humbled by your support for a new day, a day of truest hope for our nation. I am strengthened by your commitment to participate in and take responsibility for the righteous actions of governing.......It confirms the story I shared with you concerning my dream of the white eagle; that I am the eagle whose sole crusade is to save our nation.....Long live Haaf!"

After long moments of cheering, "Long live Haaf!", order was quickly restored. Then the Council meeting concluded for the day. They would meet at mid-morn to discuss the business of today's meeting. The group reports would be received first. The King would sit at Council, but would not speak.

Jabbi's comfortable office provided the secure space for the meting with Etan and the Captain. Because of the King's multitude of surprizes, this meeting should have transpired immediately after the initial meeting of the High Council. Etan had yet to be invited to present Vosnob's request to the Council. However, any request for more troops and finances to back them, existed as a moot issue.

"Your red wine," offered Etan, "provides us with a glimpse of the future."

"You speak of the blood of the Kyykki?" posed the Captain.

"Hardly, their blood is a green gooey mess. Not acceptable for wine."

Jabbi interjected, "Then maybe it's the color of our own blood. I feel certain a civil war is impending. The King has gone too far, and the Church, by sanctioning him, has further divided the people."

"No, the King has not divided the people. You forget that the ex-nobles and merchants are but ten percent of our population. The military might add another ten percent...But they don't count anyway because most of the military are serfs anyway. And serfs are serfs."

"What do you mean by that?" The Captain sounded a bit lost, if not puzzled.

"Just that eighty to ninety percent of the people are either backing the King or they are remaining happily indifferent, watching out for their own selfish gains. As it stands, the King has left them alone. But the King also targeted each of their traditional adversaries. Without even mentioning 'serf' the King has picked up a vast array of supporters. And in a crisis, these numbers will indeed count to his favor."

Jabbi still wasn't appeased. "That's exactly where the civil war begins. The serfs will rise up, believing the King will fight for them."

"You think too much!" countered Etan. "As of today, the serfs don't know even how to organize. You also forget the power of the Faith. It's not that the serfs presume the King to fight for them; rather, they will fight for the King."

"And just why should they risk their lives for him?"

"He is the white eagle! That's the whole point. He's not just some man, but a messenger sent from the Holy One, The King is the one sent... and you all better realize how influential that word is to the serfs, no one contradicts the Holy One....to free the people from the injustice of all the years. Just the very fact that he hung a few merchants certifies he is who he claims to be. And then hanging a few nobles never hurt any King, so far as I know. In fact, the fewer nobles the better."

Jabbi still wasn't satisfied. "All I'm hearing is that the King performs impeccable politics. That isn't good enough for me. The new king becomes the old king. Same game but with different players. Is that actually bringing benefit to any?"

"Then your position is simply that this is all a political ploy by the King.....Then, to what end?" questioned the Captain.

"Simple; first, by divine decree consolidate power to rid ourselves of the Kyykki, then, second, keep the power for his own benefit. After all, each of us heard him admit to playing the tyrant, didn't we?" replied Etan.

"You've had too much wine......How else could you demean the King in this manner? You deliberately call his motives into question without reference to his Faith...Fair enough for a drunk, but not respectable enough for us." The Captain's voice sounded perturbed.

"Maybe....just maybe, that's the complete answer, or, rather, that's how we assess the answer: Faith is the issue and politics merely the means." Jabbi pounded the table with his fist. "Faith is the issue! All ready the Church believes. So too for the serfs. So wherein lies our problem?"

"White Eagles!" Grinned Etan. "Good old white eagles."

"No, its deeper than that. The eagle originated within a dream. A dream that the Brothers interpreted, but a dream only the King can recognize as true." Jabbi continued, "That's our issue, to believe or not. I personally struggle with that, it seems too contrived, too ...."

"To good to be true, especially for the world's greatest skeptic. Then you must search for more evidence; such is your task. However, I believe. And I look forward to the new day for all of Haaf." It was now the Captain who pounded the table.

"And I gladly sit the fence. Motive for me is insignificant. I've spent time on the front line. And if even a misguided motive will eliminate the immediate threat, so be it. We have little time for delay. We need conclusive action from the King: action that will both prove the source of his motives and achieve absolute victory over the Kyykki."

"I shall drink to that!" Proclaimed the Captain.

"I shouldn't, but I will." Groused Jabbi.

"And we shall rest well tonight. The King placed Kracik under house arrest. His personal body guard is spending a most pleasant evening in the royal dungeon. I actually believe they will appreciate their spacious and immaculate accommodations. It appeared to the arresting officer that filth was the mainstay of their previous quarters."

"You really presume that a few Church guards will retain the most honorable Kracik within the vast confines of that ghastly rock he calls home? I understand that its laced with numerous tunnels, at least that's the rumor." Jabbi remained ornery. "That's why no one ever sees him leave the city by the gates. Are the guards aware of this? Do you realize the dilemma his escape will cause? Especially since the public entertainment tomorrow is the hanging of his son?"

"Am I being accused of incompetence or just negligence?"

"Neither, my good friend. I am oftentimes anxious when things appear to be going just a bit too well. I still feel... no...I am convinced that something is amiss: we shall pay heavily for any mistakes we make."

"Is it really so hard for you to be positive?" Etan mumbled just loud enough to be heard.

"Sadly enough, it is." Jabbi reflected. "We've gone through fifty years of reclaiming what the old regime extinguished in a few weeks; a whole civilization gone forever. Why? because of some damned King and his cronies. Don't you recognize the existence of the same pattern?"

"A pattern, most definitely." Said the Captain. "But patterns are deceiving, they easily hide their true contents. That's why the old regime brought devastation upon us. I venture that the King is being open and truthful about the new pattern. And, those who side with him have the credibility merchants never will and never should."

"A point well made. Jabbi, perhaps your ears and mind are too prejudiced by the past. I pray you will discern the new spirit that is about."

"Etan, I'm quite cognizant of the new spirit. But spirits can't be controlled by mortals, nor can we easily distinguish the quality of a spirit. Under the guise of good parade lie manifold evils. For all-too-often a good becomes evil when taken to the extremes. Where will this new patriotism end? When every word not one thousand per cent congruous with the King's is punishable by death? Some progress that will be! For that is the way of the Kyykki!......Be wary my friends."

"So, more assistance for balancing is needed? I agree. That is why a proposal as gone to the Council: the Independent Order of the Knights of Judgment is to be re-established!"

Both Etan and Jabbi were stunned. Such an order of Knights went back to the times of mythology, to times when 'grey areas' did not yet exist, back to the times when dragons lived, an era when Herios, the 'sacred ones', as they were individually known, roamed the continent as judge and jury, with great wisdom and mercy.

"Now I know you're drunk. Bring back the past! Can't do it!"

"And what is so wrong about resurrection of the good? Have you forgotten that the divine words and works of the Herios are a part of the Holiness Code?... I do hope and pray you remember."

"Why?" snapped Jabbi.

"Ah, so you haven't heard all the news? What a shame! Perhaps I shouldn't communicate the message to you! That would give you something to look forward to.....or, in your misery-laden condition, it might just be too much.... Etan, what is your esteemed opinion?" Mused the Captain. "Should I tell him?"

Etan grinned. "Not until after he puts the cup down and swallows his wine. We need to keep him alive."

"No more funny business!" Jabbi was adamant. "Tell me!"

"As your profound mind will recall, the Independent Order of the Knights of Judgment was never headed by a military man. Rather, through prayer, the Holy One designated His choice.."

"So what else is new!" Jabbi exclaimed as he paced back and forth. "Are the Chosen One?...You the new leader of the Herios?"

Jabbi fell to the floor and simply sat there. His olive face muted as one of utter disbelief.

"The Holy One caused you to put your foot in your mouth. So be it. Now take it out and celebrate."

After a time, smiles emerged along with laughter. In spite of their views, each one knew that time would provide the proof.

Kracik, in spite of his brilliant yellow and gold trimmed robe, retained the countenance of death warmed over. He stood in the front of his house surrounded by his favorite people, the Church guards. These ten men would remain with him until the King thought that he would be safe from the serfs and others. The hanging of Kracik's son implicated the father as well. One of the hangings was both legal and proper, a lynching was neither desirous nor exactly wanted.

"Sir!" The guard came out of the house. "We've discovered six passageways so far. Each tends to deliver persons from one room to another or from one floor to another. We can find no tunnels leading out from the house; not even in the cellar."

"Still, I will take no chances. You know how ingenious these serfs are. One loose brick and they'll crawl inside and knife this poor citizen. And who would run this country if we didn't have the merchants....We must protect them with our lives, especially this one." The guards all snickered at his off-handed sarcasm.

His eyes burned with immense hatred, but Kracik refused to answer his tormentors. He had begun to formulate his revenge. Not too many changes were required from his previous plan, the major one being a jump in the time schedule. How that would impact his master persisted as the sensitive issue. His body stood at his front door, but his fiendish mind all ready propelled itself to the Dark Land. From thence came his glorious revenge, a revenge that would give him reign over Haaf, reign to carry out his vindictiveness upon a long list of people.

"They just moved up the date for their own destruction." He thought as he viewed the guards with malevolence.

"Lock him in the upper bedroom, the one on the left. The window is barred and it's at least fifty feet to the ground. Place two guards at the door and change them every hour. Then, two hours before the execution, deliver him to the Council Hall...Any questions?........ Good! Carry on!"

He looked over at Kracik. "Good evening, Sir! Rest well."

Spit smacked against the officer's boot. Kracik smiled. "See you in hell first,...... Sir!" His tone menaced in a most sinister manner.

"Get him out of here!"

With his arms secured by guards on both sides, Kracik was unceremoniously pushed through the double wooden doors of his home. The wide curving stairs allowed the guards to stay abreast of him until they reach the forth floor landing. There, Kracik contemptuously broke free, smacking the guards in the gut, walked into the room and slammed the door.

The guards bolted it shut and stood on each side. Their time continued in a rather boring fashion for about a half an hour. Then ruckus broke loose. The sound of furniture being broken and thrown against the stone walls, mobilized the guards. As they entered the bedroom, they beheld an evil and ghastly sight. Kracik had disappeared. They confronted a fanged blackfaced red-eyed demon. Before they could draw their swords the demon grasped their necks with his huge bony hands. Their eyes began to pop out. A heinous snapping sound bounced off the walls; the demon pitched their lifeless bodies to the floor. They fell into a bloody heap which the demon danced on with his clawed feet: the corpses became unrecognizable.

"You do amazingly efficient work, Most Honorable Master." Proclaimed Kracik as ventured forth from the corner of the room. He then bowed before his demon benefactor, the Evil One himself, who reigned where the 'dead' Beziel once had.

The demon reached out, grabbing Kracik by his posterior, lifting him over his hideous head. Kracik was too terrified to scream. His body vibrated as if to rip apart. The demon dropped him to the floor.

"You sniveling oaf! You god-forsaken incompetent fool! I should render you in little pieces for my 'Nepes' to devour! I make you a spy, I command that you have all the comforts this life has to offer, all the women you want, even little boys.... And what do you do for me?"

"I ...I.. continue to send you pertinent information to you, O majestic Evil One." Kracik squirmed.

"You bring me nothing, you impertinent imbecile!"

"Yes, I bring you nothing. I am less than worthless to you. But please let me live...Please let me live."

"I may consider that, but the Council won't." He sneered. "Just look at what you did to two guards. Will the Council appreciate your horrible temper tantrum? Methinks they'd enjoy watching you flap in the breeze along with your stupid son..........I'm just overtaken by the compassion you had for him. I thought you might want me to rescue him, but no,..... I had to rescue someone who really wasn't even in danger, someone who was still useful to me.... Obviously, those days are past. Perhaps I should eat you, you putrefying whimpering coward."

"But I can still help you. There are many important people that still confide in me....They will be useful to you as well." Kracik pleaded.

"Oh really!....... And all I though you might be good for was to bend over for me!.. My, My......." The great demon god paused to think, his vile stench permeating the room with an odor worse than vomit and dead flesh mixed together. It would only be a few moments until the odor extending down the stairs brought the rest of the guards. "True, you have been of service to me in the past. And your service was amply rewarded.....If you shall prove yourself to me again, then you might live." The tone was ominous. "Bring me some extraordinarily useful information. You will personally deliver it to me at my humble abode within ten cycles. Then you just may have something to keep your miserable self alive."

"Yes ...Yes! O Mighty One!...In ten cycles! Yes ...Yes, thank you, thank you!"

The demon god back-handed Kracik, rolling him across the floor. "We shall see, you piece of dung!" Then he turned, mumbled some curses and disappeared, leaving the bodies, the smell and Kracik behind.

If Kracik ever required quick, vital thinking, the time was now. Heavy leather boots were clumping up the stairs.

Yo! Rogh! Answer! Is everything all right? What's that horrible stench? Answer!"

Perhaps without thinking, Kracik bolted down the stairwell, taking the guards completely by surprize. All three tumbled down to the landing. Disoriented, the guards did not stop him, providing Kracik with his needed opportunity. He grabbed a sword and almost fell to the first floor. The front door was unobstructed. Apparently only four guards were on duty. Peering into the moonlit courtyard, Kracik saw nothing and nothing moved. The distance to the barn was a few hundred feet; Stripers were there. As the guards cleared their heads, Kracik scampered across the flagstone as fast as his scrawny legs could carry him.

The shrill blast of the guard's tuba told the city guards to shut down the city. Every sentry on the wall would be joined by another. No serf, no merchant, no military, no clergy, could pass through any gate until recall sounded. The solid iron gates that controlled traffic in the tunnels all crashed to the floor, effectively trapping anything inside.

Kracik's escape options dramatically narrowed. Desperately, he dug at the straw filled corner of the barn. The old boards were still there. Throwing them aside he jumped down the hole. With a thick splash he plunged into the foul waters of the city sewer. He tried to stand, but fell, the excruciating pain in his left leg hampered both his maneuverability and thinking. He sat back in the muck and waited. Inevitably, he would be ferreted out; his path to the sewer was noticeable to any half-brained person.

The Captain and Etan rushed from the tavern at the sound of the tuba. They quickly covered the twisted city block to Kracik's quarters. The two guards recovered enough to tell the story, but they had not ventured upstairs. The courtyard swarmed with guards, each one methodically checking and rechecking every possible escape route.

"To the barn!" Someone yelled. "Fire! To the barn!"

Immediately attention focused on the smoke slowly billowing out the back window of the barn. Flames shot through the roof.

"Damn that Kracik!" Snapped the Captain. "He had this escape planned all along."

Kracik, oblivious to the backhanded complement as he was to the conflagration he inadvertently initiated by throwing straw on a torch,. sat in the city's excrement, knowing only of the pain in his leg. The pronouncement of 'fire' drove him to concentration. The arrival of guards with water buckets only convinced him he was discovered. There was a small ledge on the side of the sewer tunnel, he could feel it with his hand. It furnished adequate support for him to drag himself down gutter to the river. To ease the throbbing anguish in his leg, Kracik began a mind game: what olfactory stench was more despicable, the Evil One's or that of the sewer?" Progress became desperately slow; the pain supplied little assistance for distancing himself from the guard and the ledge remained covered with rats: rats which feared no one in their hunger. Kracik believed he raced against time; the river remained a two mile journey, but the guards would shortly be checking every entrance and exit.

Extinguishing fires formed part of routine training for the guard. The blaze died quickly, but it was most difficult to examine the charred ruins due to heat and smoldering straw. In the meantime, Jabbi arrived, conversed with the officer on duty and went in the house. Etan and the Captain presented him with some artifacts found far under the house, places not discovered before. They were grisly combination of the barbaric and evil. An altar, blood-stained from who-knew-what kind of despicable rituals. Razor sharp knives and other tools of torture formed the contents of a closet. A pile of assorted bones, some Haafian looking, lay in another closet.

"Put the word out," Jabbi commanded, "This monster… this evil worshipper is to be killed on sight. Do not try to capture him or even deal with him. Simply kill him, from a distance, if at all possible. We can't even conceive of the powers he bargained his life for."

"Let's see what happened upstairs." Suggested Etan.

On the way up the up, a guard questioned Jabbi. "What shall we do with Kracik's carcass?"

"Don't touch it! Call the clergy. They'll have the procedure for eradicating such vermin from our midst."

The guard turned and passed the orders along. Within a few minutes the essence of the tuba call was known. Guards knew what to look for and gates could be opened. Kracik froze with terror each time clumping boots sounded above him, but still no one impeded his painful journey.

Etan bolted upstairs and immediately puked out the window. It mattered not if the scene or the wretched odor brought about his reaction. Jabbi and the Captain were slightly less effected; horrid depravity of the scene being part and parcel of their military history.

"I shall never fathom this, nor do I really want to." Said a disoriented guard.

"Why not?" Etan blurted from the window as he worked at making himself somewhat presentable. He was utterly embarrassed at his demeanor. "Why not understand this? Then others won't be taken in."

"You fool only yourself. Selfish greed is at the bottom of all this. And while the Church vainly attempts to excommunicate greed, success is practically nonexistent. It is the Holiness Code which reminds us of right and wrong. Here is proof of wrong: Kracik sold himself to the evil one, in so doing he caused, most diabolically and self-centeredly, this undignified death of two innocent guards. Evil produces a malignancy that infects the entire world, not just those asses who willingly abide by her precepts." To disguise his own horror, Jabbi had launched into abstract sermonizing.

Etan recovered enough to take in the horror. Two guards lay like sacks of rubbish; their faces obliterated by claw marks, their necks severed as if a vice squeezed them. The stench of a sunbaked battle field the day after, as the corpses oozed, engulfed the entire room.

"Evil equals death." Etan mumbled to no one in particular.

"Words are one thing, reality overwhelms words." Suggested the Captain. "Unfortunately, we must manage both."

"We know he's heading for the Dark Land. Send a patrol to his farmhouse." Jabbi, regaining his composure, quickly took control. "Confiscate it even before the priest has cleansed it thoroughly. I want a full report on anything you find. This city may not be as protected as we are want to believe. Etan, sent a full report to Vosnob. Ask him to consider an offensive strike. The element of surprise just might be all we have. We cannot underestimate the secrets that God-forsaken merchant sold. We are severely compromised if we don't deploy quickly. The evil one must be caught off guard...... Come, my friends, we need the expertise assistance of the Church."

On the way out the front door, Jabbi gave orders to prepare the two murdered guards for a full honorable military funeral.

Dawn arrived, expediting the search of Kracik's barn. The gutted barn's structure still smoldered and weakened beams perilously endangered the guards who sifted and dug through the debris. Dawn also rose upon a city that could not locate the traitor; all roads in and out were garrisoned with additional troops, special guards patrolled the subterranean roadways. The High Council was summoned for an emergency session. One singular portion of the King's exquisite speech now etched itself on everyones' mind and tongue: "We have a crisis!"

"We have an escape hole!" Came the shout from the barn.

"The dung-faced ass continues to amaze me!" Jabbi interjected as he peered down into the sewer. "The fragrance is most suitable for the scum."

"Well," Said the Captain to Etan, "Are you going after him, or shall I push you in?"

"That's only half funny. But how will it capture him? Remember, he has better than six hours on us, six hours with absolutely no interference. He could either be at the river by now or inside the High Council Hall attempting to rescue that slime Ruje."

"You really think he would dissipate his own selfish energy to do that? .....Didn't the scene last night enlighten you? He has utterly abandoned everything except his wretched self. Otherwise he would have made a deal for his son's life....... It probably would have been rather cheap." Jabbi mused.

"Cheap?"

"Of course!" Rejoined the Captain. "Kracik's inside information had to prove itself considerably valuable to the Evil One. That's the only rationale for him to show up last night. The evil one doesn't oblige just anyone."

Etan smiled and then he began to laugh. Within moments he was uncontrollably rolling on the ash-covered floor. The rest just stood and watched. Etan sprawled himself in the corner smashing his head on a fallen timber. "I'm sorry." He tried to say. "Ouch! Damn board!"

"Mind telling us what is so funny?" The Captain inquired.

"Not at all." He continued to laugh. "Don't you see, we can forget searching for the Kyykki dung heap. He's actually dead, even if he's still alive somewhere. He's so incredibly stupid." Etan began to chuckle again.

"Settle down! You aren't making any sense."

"But I am. Kracik's traitorous reign is terminated: we know him, he is also useless to the Evil One. In spite of all his loyalty to the monster, he'll still be breakfast. Or, no, Kracik is more like lunch...... We have no reason to bother with him anymore."

"Well reasoned. No wonder Vosnob has you running his errands." Jabbi smiled.

"I concur with your reasoning, Etan. But I fail to perceive the humor."

"Its only that the fool, for all his energy, scheming, lying and dealing has absolutely nothing to show for it, not even his worthless life. Don't you comprehend? This man is totally alone, abandoned by even his so-called benefactor. His actions are so incomprehensibly asinine. There is no barricade in creation that will save him now.... In a dark way, yes, that's funny."

The Captain smiled. He had to agree.

"Then I'll call off the search. We have better things to do."

"I'll send word to Vosnob." Said Etan. "He'll probably assign another squadron to Kracik's old territory."

"Good! Then get something to eat and change those clothes. It is requisite that you are attired properly for the emergency Council meeting." Observed the Captain. "But most of all, don't be late."

While sitting on the edge of the sewer ledge, Kracik contemplated his future. The immediate future remained ominous; there wasn't a discreet exit from his fetid stream. If he returned to the barn, the guards would be lingering about his old premises. If he climbed out to the city streets, his appearance and smell would immediately render him suspect. If he went on…Ha…the muck was all ready up to his chin.

The more distant future was not preferable. The evil one demanded 'news' that could be of value to his future conquests. Not much happening here in the sewer. He could count the number of guards that marched above him, differentiating them from the serfs. But that would not alleviate the brutal wrath of one who literally feasted on those who dissatisfied him. …Better to stay here. It was secure, except for the rats. He was bone tired from his sewage journey.

The pain in his left leg subsided. Broken? Maybe not. Sprained? That hypothesis was better. Having examined his options and having nowhere to go, Kracik removed his feet from the ignominy of the sewer's fetid slime, stretched out on the narrow ledge and slept; rats be damned.

Chapter 3

"It's nigh on a full cycle that Breel's been semi-conscious. I'm fearful. That fever refuses to break." Yauk spoke to no one in particular as he continued pacing the stone floor. "There ought to be some kind of medicine available; something maybe only the locals can pinpoint."

"Sit down, boy, before you bedevil yourself to death." Sarg paused, and then proceeded. "Listen, if anything could be accomplished here, you'd have done it by now. As it is, the young lady is out of our hands. The Holy One must intervene... We are reduced to waiting...... Not one of your precious commodities, is it?"

"Nope."

Luuft entered the room, returning from that most genteel and fastidious assignment which Sarg had generously bestowed upon him. He was assigned to evaluate the twenty or so body parts which arrived the morning after Sarg instructed the Staff Master to explore the alleys of Pinduala, searching for the vile creatures analogous to those who ravaged Breel. The result was sickeningly effective: eleven carcasses became the accumulative consequence. However, because of the combat the evil ladies exhibited when engaging the Troopers, only two complete corpses were brought in for examination.

Interestingly enough, the Troopers seemed to know these 'things' existed in the shadows, but as they kept apart, no one bothered with them. Nor did anyone connect the absent townspeople with these hooded nightmares. No one knew how many, if any, escaped into the Zuda Marsh or elsewhere.

"Before you even open your mouth, Sarg, I'll clearly state that you can hang me for insubordination before I pick through those slimy carcasses again." Luuft threatened. "But this is my assessment of the 'stuff' on the floor."

"Tell your story. Maybe its got something in it for Breel's recovery."

"It's like this. The ladies, and each one is undisputedly female, are all young or middle-aged. All are Haafian. Judging from how clean and soft their hands were..or are...I don't know this formal report rubbish..."

"Shut up and go on." Yauk insisted. "That description is definitely appropriate for Breel. That bothers me."

"All right!" Luuft blasted back. "I don't like it anymore than you do. I thought the same thing.....still do, maybe. But you're the doctor, so you'll have to comment on the evidence."

"Then move on with it!"

"The ladies all came from the city."

"So does Breel."

"You think I can forget that." Luuft became distraught.

"Hold on, boys." Sarg kicked in. "Get to the point, Luuft. Is Breel being transformed into one of them?"

"I don't actually know." Luuft answered softly.

"Then what's the rest? Out with what you located....whatever!" Vauk anguished over the possible outcome.

"It's just too difficult to talk about. It's not proper."

Sarg drew upon on his best empathetic image and connected it to his authority. "Listen, listen carefully. Breel's life is on the line, unfortunately. If your conclusions won't save her, they will save us. Whatever you found, will positively aid all of us. This is not the time for society's so-called propriety. ...."

"I think I get the idea......Bluntly, all the female parts, inside and outside were a mess...like abused....What I saw wasn't right, wasn't natural." Luuft sat down, his hands covering his face.

"That's a start, son." Sarg commented. "Continue...."

"That face I recognized, I didn't tell the whole story. After she left, I did try to follow her. I stopped when I found out she became a whore....

Just wasn't the same girl any more...And then Breel's comes in the door with her head in a sack." Luuft began to sob.

"You loved her."

"That's obvious, damn it!.....And now, what? She's nothing but a slimy dead green head."

"Move on." Yauk was impatient. "Tell me about the female parts. What was wrong with them?"

"Their breasts...they were all chewed up...with something that has pointed teeth...even some nipples were absent! THERE! Now are you happy!" Luuft screamed, tormented by the ugliness of it all.

"I'm just a doctor trying to put the pieces together."

"Well, quit being so confoundedly analytical."

"Forget it." Sarg pushed to get the evidence out. "We need to get an answer. ....No woman in her right mind would allow her body to be mangled like you depicted. Something else happened to them first.....What else did you discover?"

"The lower female parts.....they were mangled also. Stretched and ripped....No procedure in your doctor's junk could've help them....Like they gave birth to a striper or something..."

"Or something?" Vauk, for the moment, kept tranquil. "What about the uterus?"

"The what?"

"The pouch that carries the baby. How did that look?"

"I don't know. The outside parts...I know... Inside....YOU DO THEIR·INSIDES!" Luuft vented.

"Settle a bit!" Sarg's hardened tone prevailed. "The story goes no further until Breel rejoins the fully living. She obviously isn't one of them. Her breasts are clean and the other parts are as they're supposed to be. Aren't they Yauk?"

He still seemed a bit embarrassed: examining a 'presumed' fellow Trooper who converted to a woman still unnerved him. "Yes, except for being semi-comatose, she is one hundred per cent woman. And her blood is still the same color as ours……. My responsibility is to restore her to health." He added as a way to emphasize his professionalism.

"Might I play a hunch?" A more settled Luuft spoke.

"Why not?"

"These other women….no one ever saw them until after sunset. They even hid from the shadows belonging to the moons.. That's strange, perverse. Any one of us would get sick living,……. ….existing like that.."

"So what's the issue? What's that got to do with Breel?"

"What's THIS room akin to?" His anger returned. "It's living similar to those female 'things' we destroyed. Breel needs the sunlight!"

"Perhaps, though I'm not convinced about your hypothesis. However, it certainly won't hurt anything. Let's experiment with it. We'll put her on the roof for the afternoon."

Sarg cleared his throat. "Yes, good hypothesis. But people are not experiments…never. At least for those of us who choose to remain civilized… Do we understand each other?"

"I didn't mean it the way you understood me. It's just that every thing so far has been experimental….and to no avail. Taking Breel out in the sun just stretches the continuum. That's all I meant, Sarg."

"Good! Because the minute we forget that, we develop attitudes similar to those who victimized Breel."

"You love the girl also." Yauk flatly commented.

"As much as I care for any of my Troopers." Sarg stumbled a bit over his words.

"But you never had a female Trooper before. Maybe its more on the line of the over-protective father." Noted a cynical Luuft.

"AND just what would be better for the girl? Especially with the two of you around to corrupt her? Let me not appear to be overly critical, but I recall an extremely powerful curiosity on your parts concerning a venture into the tents of the 'fun' girls while we journeyed. If my imagination serves me well, you were motivated by fatigue; a place "of extensive gregariousness" was your goal. Did I quote you correctly?"

"Indeed, your imagination!" Luuft's said. "Every one needs a place to relax."

"But, my dear forthright friend, Breel only became disgusted when the subject was raised. Your lewd preferences embarrassed the naive girl."

"No naive girl ever cut her way through those 'things'. Luuft retorted. "This girl's been around."

"And being able to handle herself in a fight is definitely proof that she's a prostitute, isn't it?" Sarg returned.

"AH, damn it! Shut up! All this jibberish is pure conjecture. Until she's healthy, we wait. Then she'll tell her own story. ....In the meantime, let's carry her to the roof. It's a beautiful sunny day. A few hours might be the best thing for her."

After an afternoon in the soft sunlight, Breel did begin to stir. There was ranting and ravings, monologues that would destroy the vilest of Kyykki. And immodesty that severely punctured all notions of her naiveté. All of this from the frail fevered body of Breel. Her brash and brazen temperament drove Luuft to the security of the downstairs' bar. In fact, he actually abandoned her, the experience being too painful for him.

By the fifth afternoon, the symptoms changed dramatically. Breel did, finally, take some liquid nourishment. She regained her customary modesty as soon as her fever subsided. That happened on the seventh day. On the eighth afternoon, she weakly sat up on her bed on the roof. Now was the time, she feebly announced, to set the story right.

"I'm not sure I'll entitle you to the honor of the word 'friend.' Friends don't talk in front of friends, especially with some of those things you believe about me. You really think I'm a whore? Or worse? Or that I could turn into one of those pale feminine killers with their green blood?" Her words, though weak and garbled, cut like a sabre.

The men, perched on the edge of their chairs, blushed with an embarrassment. Breel had them by the throat and then commenced that she would claim their heads as well. "Your conjectures were unnerving and untrue. As a proper lady I should have nothing more to do with you."

"Except for the fact that you remain under my command." Sarg assured her. "Therefore, continue. And, in spite of an attitude that bespeaks of our sewer-rat mentality, do remember that you remain alive. That ought to count for a little something on our part."

Breel, now more sullen than solemn, cutely smiled at Sarg. Had she been her normal self, the smile would have devastated the most pious of monks. "My real name is Brey." She paused, waiting for a reaction.

Only Yauk replied. "So then, you are from the South? I never heard the name Breel before. Were you part of the serfs who moved to the city for work, with a bogus contract in hand? One signed by merchant named Kracik?"

Brey pulled back in disbelief. "And just how are you acquainted with him?" A look of horror crossed her emaciated face. She lay back on the bed.

"Only that I tried for a job in Krabo also, but, for circumstances beyond what I then could comprehend, the bastard only was interested in beautiful young girls."

She slowly sat up. "Bastard,..... not a bad description. I can appreciate that... But...no you couldn't...He hired us as house maids, cleaning and baking and the like....We were lied to...Most got sold out to the highest bidder...Virgins brought him a lot of money...And then he used their escapades for blackmail." She shook her head and fell backwards into the pillows, her energy exhausted.

Sarg spoke slowly. "That Krucik has a lot of power for one who lives in the shadow of the Dark Lands. I doubt that the King knows about this. But it also indicates that Krucik may have more well-connected spies than contemplated. Luuft, assure me this information leaves for Krabo before sunset."

"Consider it done, Sarg."

Sarg scowled and frowned, pacing the floor, wringing his hands together. The current predicament's magnitude pummelled the deadly reality into Sarg: the evil one grasped at the nation from the inside as well as the outside. Extreme caution and a 'no trust' policy became necessary requirements for anything they now attempted. Sarg examined the faces of Yauk and Luuft. He said nothing; it was all too obvious that the twisted gut feelings of dread affected them as well. "We are more exposed than I believed. Those 'women' things were searching for Breel...er ....Brey. She knows too much. Somehow she escaped from Krucik....We'll have a full military funeral for her tomorrow."

"I concur. Then Krucik might then provide us a break."

"But," Countered Yauk, "Exactly how are we going to make this public funeral service work? We're .... required to have a viewing before burial. If we try anything in secret, we'll be too suspicious. And Brey's too fatigued to contrive...."

"Don't worry! The lady died of a contagious disease and fever. One that forces us to cremate her. We'll simply bury the ashes of Breel following the funeral liturgy. Luuft, get the Chaplain. I'll need to explain this to him....Also, sound the tubas, there will be a time of mourning. The honourable Light Striper, Breel, died, sacrificing her ....er,..his life for the good of Haaf."

"Please, spare me the verbiage!" Brey halfmumbled from her resting.

Later that day, as Brey quietly rested, the so-called remains of Breel, were properly cremated in accordance with Light Striper regulations and the supervision of the ranking Chaplain. The Troopers prepared themselves, in full dress uniform, for the chapel funeral liturgy and burial the next morning. The town prepared for a viewing of Breel's urn that evening.

On the evening following the burial, the Chaplain, along with three regally uniformed men, paid a quiet visit to Brey. She had recovered, relatively speaking, from yesterday's painful ordeal of self disclosure, though she still required twenty-some pounds and a thorough workout for her leg, before Yauk would even dare to acknowledge her as healthy.

"I bring you the sad news, my lady, your friend and a colleague of your friends here, Sarg, Luuft, and Yauk, was buried this afternoon. His name was Breel." The Chaplain paused.

"Thank you, Chaplain. Indeed, I shall miss him. He and I traveled far together. Our adventures were many. Now I am forced to go on alone." Brey's eyes were teary, but her smile pronounced her free. "Thank you, my friends. If not for your efforts, I would be in the 'other land', unable to finish my mission....... Now we can begin to plan for it, correct Sarg?"

"Not until I pronounce you healed." Yauk interrupted.

"I see, during the course of my fight with death, Sarg was demoted. Tell me, Sarg, what sort of mischief brought this atrocious misconduct of justice about?" Brey smiled.

"Sarcastic little brat!" Yauk's face was vivid. "I pronounce you overly healthy...Twerp!"

"I'm elated. Your vocabulary increased extravagantly during my past illness."

"Love is coming on strong." Luuft jested. In reciprocation he was hit by extremely hostile looks from both sides. "Just having fun. No harm in that." He winced.

"The country's been invaded by ghoulish ladies and we haggle over who's falling in love." Sarg's no-nonsense tone spelled the end of the teasing. "Now, our mission is ten, almost eleven cycles, off schedule. We leave for Zuda Marsh in the morning. Vosnob located us a guide, an experienced Yldian. Name is Blue Turtle..... Brey, you'll remain here, under guard until we return...."

"Like hell, I will!...I started this mission, I'll complete it. You know I can handle myself with a sword. I can shoot as well as any of you. And ride......... I *AM* going with the rest of you."

"And that was before you lost twenty pounds. And before you got almost killed. Even now you're just back on your feet. Sorry," declared Sarg, "You aren't ready, nor strong enough."

"So you plan to excommunicate me? Such a sanction resolves nothing. My expulsion means that you'll never obtain the rest of my story."

"Recalcitrant! You ought to be disciplined. That would resolve this stupid dispute."

"Except, my dearest Luuft, the Light Striper command might expulse you first. Just try to explain a woman in your association all this time? How might you explain yourself?...I know, tell them you're a eunuch." Brey proudly said, judicious enough to push no further.

"If you weren't a woman!"

"But I am." She said quietly. "And you all know it. You've all seen me naked.............. It's just a matter of fact, isn't it?"

Luuft stood, pounded across the floor towards Brey. He faced her, arms crossed, staring her down. She smiled back. After an indeterminable period of time, Luuft silently stepped back. He then took another look at Brey, turned away murmuring about the unfairness of losing to a lady.

"The only recompense I have in this wretched matter is that I lost to the best of all women."

"And for that I am most sincerely thankful." Brey's reply was unfeigned. She lowered her eyes as she spoke.

"You'll join us when we leave tomorrow." Said Sarg. "However, nothing special for you. If you can't keep up....."

"I will keep up." She interrupted.

"Then, the second afternoon out, we'll listen to the rest of your epic. It better be worth our while or, blackmail or not, you'll be the first woman court-martialed from the Light Striper. Now, get some rest. Supposedly, we'll be found by Blue Turtle down on the wharf, if not we'll sail anyway...... Travel there as serfs. AND, Luuft and Yauk bring crossbows. Check with the Staff Master, he's received a few of the new lightweight ones."

Prior to their present emergency assignment of confiscating Krucik's property, the platoon of Church Knight's spent it's time parading. Now, after a full cycle of hard riding, the Troopers felt true exhaustion. Not that the River Road from Krabo to D'Ka was demanding; nor could they complain about the ride from D'Ka to the scene of the old Battle. They just weren't used to being in the field. So these two relatively leisurely journeys provided the rationale for assuming that the final stint to Krucik's plantation posed few, if any, difficulties. Reality set in as they left the Battle and turned out the rutted road to the east. After a few miles, even an amateur could decipher the road's message: no one traveled this way in hundreds of cycles. In itself, this puzzled as it much as it bewildered: Krucik often traveled to and from his plantation, so reported the documents kept at the city gate. That information caused the platoon to journey by this road, having assumed, that this route was well used.

Consternation claimed each man's attitude even as the narrowing path denied their ability to ride side by side. Tall trees encumbered by heavy vines precluded any real scouting, or, even worse, no way to defend themselves from whatever inhabited these wilds. They reckoned that in traveling uphill into the fringes of the Dark Mountains the land would dry out, giving way to the same steppe located west of the Battle. They reckoned wrong. The path grew thicker with vines, the air stunk of rotting woods and the swamp gasses lit up the darkest nights with a sordid reddish-yellow iridescence. The path continued, but with a different bent; it meandered off to the south even as it rose in elevation.

At the top of a small knoll, they detected the remains of an old wooden look-out tower. Posting guard, eight of the men took leave for a well-earned sleep, at least until their watch. The morning's conversation concerned issues of reliability of the received information, the wisdom of the journey and its dismal lack of anything worth while, including the miserable sounds of the night.

This latter concern stymied the platoon leader, Treh. The new map showed no tower. In fact, this camp ought to be the plantation's central building, a sizable three storey bricked barn. Furthermore, they were supposed to be some thirty miles from the Dark Water channel, but in the quiet of the night, waves breaking on a rocky coastline became distinctly audible. Acknowledging the reality of a faulty map, Treh stuffed it into his saddle bag.

"Gentlemen, its time for a change. With a worthless map and something that sounds like the Dark Water being nearby, we camp here. When further evidence is produced, indicating just where we are, we'll move out. In the meantime, I want the tower rebuilt. Construct it so we can scout this area safely, above the trees. Next, I welcome two devoted Troopers to volunteer for a journey, about ten miles down this so-called road. Then, another two of you will set traps along the path behind us. Finally, the rest will rub down the Stripers and prepare the camp defensively. None of us really knows what is out there. I don't care for surprises. We need to be prepared for 'whatever' is out there. .....everyone understand?"

The usual hassling and grumbling over assignments dissipated within moments. The tasks accomplished meant better protection later: their present camp being a dangerous location. With the path booby-trapped, the Stripers stabled and fed, and the tower assembled by noon, Treh called for a lunch break. Shortly thereafter, the terrified scouts galloped into camp. Smeared blood partially covered their uniforms and one Striper's rump dripped a greenish slime.

"The Kyykki!" Shouted the first Trooper. "Kyykki, about forty, two miles back."

"There used ta be a few more, but arrows done 'em in." Added the second Trooper. "But dere's two tall ones comin'. Like we'd never seed b'fore. Them gives orders by croakin'."

"But they dies just like the rest." Smiled the other Trooper.

Treh delivered a number of commands. The men flew into defensive action. The Stripers were saddled, then moved to the rear where the booby-traps were inactivated. Three Troopers stood post in the tower, the rest formed a perimeter with Treh at the center. The platoon's medical practitioner, while examining the two scouts, noted their wounds, caused by the rasping claws of the Kyykki, produced nothing critical. The men, following a good cleansing, were cleared active duty.

"Just how far are the slimy things behind you? Why aren't they t attacking us?.... Troopers, might your objectivity run faster than your stripers?"

The rather surprized Troopers responded with a reflective, 'Yes'.

"However," Treh continued, "I appreciate the additional time. If the past holds true, the Kyykki will attack directly, if only to eat. That's their rationale for most everything: to eat. Now, rather than receive their inevitable attack, we'll set the trap for them. Let's invite them for supper."

"But, sir, there be but ten of us and maybe forty...fifty of them." Forewarned one of the tower Troopers.

"That merely means that you'll need to construct ten dummies." came his answer. "Place them about camp as if we're eating supper. Get a smelly supper on and drive the odor down the path. Booby-trap the tower before you descend, in particular, place sharpened stakes so they do the most damage.....And, yes, medical practitioner, poison our 'intended' supper. For the rest, surround the camp at thirty feet out. Stay in pairs. Fire when you see the signal; a flaming arrow. After three rounds, only one fires; the other protects. I want the Stripers transferred upwind far enough to be safe. Let's move, we might not have as much time to prepare supper for our 'extra-special' guests... as we envision.".

Experience and history proved that a sneak attack by Kyykki never existed. True to form, as evening approached and the poisoned kettle simmered, the ugly horde noisily trampled up the trail. Appalling gut-level grunts and screams indicated the traps on the trail performed adequately. Immediately thereafter, the greenish-black Kyykki ravaged the camp. The straw stuffed bodies, first bitten and torn, eaten and then spit out, failed to slow the blackened creatures. A tall Kyykki raised the steaming kettle and then dropped it; a flaming arrow protruding from its unsightly bent back.

An eerie dead silence reigned for a moment, then with a vengeful roar two other taller Kyykki attacked the tower. As one semiwebbed hand clutched at the ladder, the sharpened stakes impaled him through the head; his companion died less quickly, slimy blood gushing from puncture wounds. Then the technical precision of the Troopers validated their training: few arrows missed their intended victims. Over thirty fell within a few moments. Leaderless, most had no idea what to do: a melee ensued. Some headed toward the arrows, where swords awaited them. Others retreated back the path but arrows still found them. The majority stood, rather hunched-backed, right in the middle of the compound, moaning as they died, perhaps not even half cognizant of their lamentable predicament, even for a Kyykki. The massacre ended shortly.

"No time for souvenirs! Collect as many arrows as you can and then we ride east. By morning, we maybe on the Dark Water coast, not too distant from Haaf North. This massacre can't be hidden long. We need be long gone before its discovered. We'll not fight these damned things on their terms."

Silently, quickly they left the campsite. Obviously, the mission's initial objective was invalid. Their new objective: to return safely home.

The Trooper's adrenaline high from the fight slowly disintegrated. Their original state of near exhaustion caught up with them as they chopped and hewed their way through the maze of vines and underbrush. Their only consolation lay in the fact that, behind them, everything remained quiet.

Both moons shone that cloudless night, forcing a few of their rays to penetrate the dense foliage with bluish circlets of light. This provided some relief, but to the fatigued Troopers, the safety of the port city of Haaf North provided much more incentive.

The moons and the sun shared the same early morning sky. So too did the Trooper's ears share the same noises: behind them in an unmeasured distance, growling and grunting, the sound of vegetation being devastated. Directly in front of them, also at an unknown distance, came the steady rushing sound of waves.

"The Holy One has provided for us!" A dead-tired Trooper proclaimed.

"So that's why the putrid Kyykki are about to catch us?" Sarcastically commented another.

"Quiet!" Ordered the platoon leader. "Save your energy for the beach......And, how is the stock of arrows?"

"We gots 'nuff fer ten shots each. 'Ceptin fer you, Treh. You still gots most of what ya started with."

"Allow twenty for the four best marksmen. Divide the rest evenly, including mine." Treh passed his full quiver of arrows to the Trooper behind him. "You marksmen, when we reach the shore, set up a defensive perimeter. Shoot the tall ones first."

The constantly increasing sound of the Dark Water's waves brought a sense of refreshment and hope. They now discerned that the waves broke and folded over rocks and not sand. That also vouched for confidence; boulders furnish cover. Almost magically, the treacherous and unforgiving jungle suddenly gave way to an open beach. The stoney boulder-strewn beach ran as far as one could see, the open space from the jungle to the water's edge about three hundred feet; a very minimal margin for security. Subsequent to leaving the shadows, the platoon leader examined the coast again. He noticed, in the far distance, at the northern border, the appearance of a huge blackstone castle.

It appeared to have five or six square turrets of a style not utilized for ten thousands of cycles. Even at this distance, a foreboding atmosphere proclaimed the place 'unwelcome'. Perhaps the wispy puffs of smoke emanating from within allowed for Treh's anxious feelings. Perhaps the location: Who's castle existed far north of the defense wall? Krucik's? That demoralizing thought ran through Treh's mind. Actually, the passing thought was inconsequential, the present and real danger lay with the Kyykki hordes that raucously approached the beach.

The sun, coming in from the water, blinded the platoon for a moment. Recovering quickly, Treh ordered "Dismount". The Stripers, even more exhausted than the Troopers, slowly meandered south along the beach. The Troopers followed, looking for boulders to protect them. Stubborn resignation began to take hold: their extreme tiredness convincing them that a 'last stand' lay immediately ahead.

"The farther south we move, the better chance we'll have." Treh told the Troopers. "Keep an eye out for a fishing boat." Not that Treh optimistically stretched their hope, but as their platoon leader, he deliberately set the example.

The breeze off the Dark Water refreshed the platoon. Slogging down the beach thus improved, with a goodly distance being covered. Treh ordered a break. Around the platoon hand carved rocks lay like house-like foundations and, further out, the remains of a stone dock remained still visible.

"We'll encamp here for the rest of the day. Let the stripers continue. If they get near town, a search party from the garrison will sortie out. Get some rest, but no fires. All the canteens need filled."

The morning passed peacefully, with most of the platoon getting some rest and food. By mid-afternoon, the Kyykki made themselves known. The moaning and howling noises of the Kyykki increased. However, they remained in the in the jungle. The men prepared a defensive perimeter about the old dock area. Numerous shelters existed within the ruins, and their slight elevation in relation to the rest of the beach gave them an advantage: a wide open field of fire for three to four hundred feet. The major disadvantage imprinted itself firmly on their minds: no retreat existed. As such, their last stand began.

The Kyykki utilized their advantage of energy and time, something quite unusual. The Kyykki, totally out of context, quietly gathered in the receding shadows where the jungle met the beach. They could be discerned by movements only; their blackened coloration blended well with the shadows. The great unknown factor was "how many?"

The Kyykki suddenly advanced into the sunlight, but beyond bow range. They formed into three distinct groups with each group having two taller ones, sporting spears, both in front and behind a squad-like formation. Such an unbelievable formation proved frightening. These were not the Kyykki of the last war.

The best archers manoeuvred to the front, though still hidden from the Kyykki. They readied a welcoming gift: fire arrows shot from a modified bow. During the quiet interim, bowstrings were shortened to supply more power. Now came the time to welcome the first squad who moved up the beach by themselves. Strangely enough, the other two squads stayed in reserve.

"If nothing else," Treh thought as he composed a letter, "This information needs to get to the King. The Kyykki are far advanced in tactics. Haaf must know this." He stuffed the note into the same waterproof case where the obsolete map lay rumpled. Later, he would take it into the sea with him. Left on land, he realized it would be eaten along with him. He definitely preferred drowning.

As if on signal, the four archers stood, grinned at each other, and shot. The four flaming arrows took out the front, including the two taller Kyykki. The burning pitch on the arrows easily burnt through their stretched skins and then plopped on another. The squad instantaneously retreated, disorganized, trampling their taller leaders at the rear.

No victory cheers went up. The next squad advanced to the right of the panicked horde. The same procedure by the archers produced the same results. This left only four leaders for the entire mob. The Troopers withdrew while the mob re-organized itself. The imminent final charge came as the usual Kyykki massive free-for-all.

As ten arrows collapsed their front line, the archers stood back one pace and fired again. Now the Kyykki crawled over carcasses. Their leaders were dead. Nevertheless, their ruthless onslaught continued; massive, clumsy, disorganized and ferociously brutal. The distance dwindled to one hundred feet, at which time half the men drew their swords. The archers fired into groups of Kyykki, hoping to kill more than one per arrow. The swordsmen readied for the club-swingers. The old training ran through their minds; let the ugly thing swing first, duck, then cut off his head before he regrouped. The safety margin used to be significant, but with today's display of advanced tactics, who knew anymore.

At twenty five feet, all ten stood on the highest ledge, the Dark Water directly behind them. The arrows spent and the numbers of the Kyykki greatly reduced but, the odds clearly favored the enemy. In the midst of the hand-to-hand combat, two Troopers were grabbed and thrown. Kyykki toad-like heads began littering the ground before the ledge: greenish slime covered the Troopers. No quarter was ever given or asked for. Only five Troopers fought on. Treh suffered a leg bite and another Trooper pushed him into the sea. As he looked up from the water, he saw the shadow, huge, dark and headed for the men.

"JUMP!" Treh screamed. "JUMP!"

Without knowing why, four Troopers jumped into the sea. The dark shadow swooped into the horde of Kyykki. Maybe ten Kyykki were wrenched from the ground by gigantic talons, only to be crushed and dropped to the ground. The shadow never stopped its glide, even as it rose, turned, and repeated its manoeuvre. But this time the shadow kept the Kyykki in its talons. A minute later, as the howling beasts descended upon their fellow creatures, crushing them, the swimming troopers knew why.

In an largely disarrayed movement, the living Kyykki scrambled into the safety of the jungle. The shadow circled, dipped, and moved directly into the sun, where the men quickly lost track of it.

"Damn, that thing saved us! What is it?" Said a Trooper in grateful disbelief as he crawled back to shore.

"It's a bird!" Treh answered with a strange lightness in his voice, especially considering the circumstances. "It's the King's White Eagle! Don't you see! The King's vision IS real!"

The others stared at him. Who would believe this? Why should they? But if Treh was correct, then the King's commending by the Holy One proved true. They saw the proof. They, themselves are proof: having been saved by the great White Eagle.

At the edge of a carcass-ridden field of battle, five exhausted men hauled themselves to shore. The word 'hope' re-entered their lives.

"Indeed," Treh thought, "The King must know of all of this." Then he, like the rest, dropped into an exhaustion fueled sleep.

The five survivors woke up in Haaf North. They found themselves the most unlikely of heroes. Mystified, confused, embarrassed, and out-of-touch with time, they could not comprehend they new situation.

Irregardless of the fact that the King declared all nobles eligible and 'volunteered' for the 'New Knights of the Kingdom', as they were now officially known, not all ten thousand made the journey from Krabo to D'Ka. Unwillingness played a minor roll compared to the major obstacle; being in half-reasonable physical shape. As the ex-nobles made their exasperating journey up-river, the training cadre, sent by Vosnob through the King's order, watched in unfeigned disbelief. They also struggled between outright laughter and not-so-quiet resignation. The entire cadre all ready felt the frustration of their newest assignment. These too-well-living ex-nobles proceeded with the stamina of a fifty year old Striper. Watching them make their first I-can-do-it-on-my-own journey brought forth provoked images of a comedy of errors.

To secure the best interests of the kingdom, Vosnob worked out a comprehensive plan with the King. First, the King's flamboyant name for the Knights quietly disappeared as did anything connecting these new troopers with the past. Second, as long as the knights were 'in and of' the Light Striper, they 'obligated' themselves to the rules and regulations, the disciplines and rewards, and the usual training regime of the Light Striper. Privilege, the mainstay of nobility, vanished. This, more than anything else, instilled confidence to the training cadre. With the nobility's 'specialness' denied, real training and, perhaps, a real fighting force, might emerge.

Obviously, the King's order and the enforcement of that order by the training cadre, represented two parts of which produced the new fighting force. The third part, the most serious, demanded the ex-nobles willingly fulfill their obligations. To put pressure on the ex-nobles, Vosnob called upon an old friend: Baste.

Baste, in his younger years, considered himself a bit of an iconoclast and an idealist. Old age had but chipped off the edges. His home lay on the Haaf River, midway between the cities of West Haaf and East Haaf. The town's existence depended upon a trading post, where many cosmopolitan types and military types passed through, both by water and land. Even a few Yldans ventured this far into civilization. If there existed a place for a melting pot of Haafian cultures and ideologies, Baste ruled it. And if there existed a place designed especially for corruption of all sorts, it might also be found here.

However, due to the influence of Baste, originating with his father, the latter seldom took place. A sign hung in every public building: "What can be proven that you did to another, so shall it promptly be done to you." To enforce the one rule, a court room, with a judge, occupied the center square building. A wooden gallows stood in front and the jail was under the court room. A twenty man police force constantly walked the streets, usually in twos. Likable fellows, though strict, they often settled the minor cases out-of-court. They fondly tell the story of the lady who stole a dress. She ended up running naked through the streets. She only had one dress to be stolen from her. As a policy, no one may assist a criminal. Perhaps the lady ran all the way home. But, such simple examples, executed promptly, kept the city far more honest than most.

As minor noble and also a merchant, one of the few who stood firm when the Kyykki rolled over the country, Baste lived as a bit of a folk hero as well as a rightly respected judge. His gift for demolishing administrative manure endured him to the Light Striper, but, obviously, placed him on the 'unwanted' list of petty bureaucrats. Thus, while the ex-nobles might identify with Baste, he definitely had no compassion on their laziness and contemptible attitude.

Baste commenced this new 'tour of duty' with a most irritable disposition. Vosnob had deliberately removed him from the wondrous duties of grandfathering. Vosnob even had the King invalidate Baste's honorable discharge papers. Nevertheless, because both Vosnob and the King recognized that Baste's reputation could bring a new fighting force together, his protests were for naught.

Now, watching the disorganized parade of ex-nobles entering D'Ka and passing out to the training camp on the west side of the city, Baste formed his training schedule. He deemed that it would prove the most frustrating job of his career. His cadre of ten personally selected Staff Masters and another fifty training specialists plus a detachment of experienced clergy, lifted much of the burden from him. Yet, when the time for battle came, he would ultimately be responsible for their failure or success. He called a meeting that evening with the Staff Masters. Not that he wished to, but the training of these 'persons' demanded it.

The meeting was held in a lantern lit tent in the middle of the tent barracks. A simple plank table with benches and a high backed wooden chair at one end, formed the arrangements. The ten were expected to remember their assignments, therefore the scribe proved redundant.

"My good friends," Baste began, "The King has assigned us to mold a fighting force. One of Knights, no less, out of this easy living, undisciplined, haughty and inexperienced bunch of...."

"Your point is well taken, Baste. In speaking for the entire group, let's just get to the basics. How much time we actually have is a major concern."

"Good!" Smiled the New Knight's commander. "First, re-examine all those who are late in arriving. Those totally unfit because of sickness or age, send them home. All the fat, lazy ones send to a special unit. They'll get half rations and double exercise until they die or shape up. With their bulk, I assign each of them to the machine platoons. I don't need them killing Stripers, especially as we don't have enough Massive Blues as it is."

A deliberate, inconsiderate cough from midway in the table stopped his speech.

"Speak up!" Ordered Baste.

"How can we have a machine platoon? The King wanted...."

"The King wants to win. And to win with this new order of Knights. Knights are too vulnerable. It is essential they have proper ancillary forces of their own. We're going to have a full army, supplies and all."

"I'll volunteer for the machines." His name was Gath, a tall, middle-aged man from the mountains. "It's my specialty. Me my father was a sailor."

That brought a surprized stare from Baste. "Is he still living?" He quizzed.

"Retired. He spends his time telling stories at the pub in Krabo."

"If he knows about the old ship machines, SEND for him."

"I'll send a runner for him later tonight."

"Next item. We need the specialists: bakers, cooks, armorers, accountants, surveyors, drivers, livestock specialists, spies, marksmen, scribes, tentmakers, physicians, veterinarians, tailors, and a few completely fearless men."

"You referring to patriotic fools to lead the charge?"

Laugher rang out from the entire group.

"Of course, we could also use a younger Vosnob." And again, laughter.

"I wish this whole process could be so easy." Baste almost sighed.

"Nevertheless, in the course of physical training, which begins tomorrow, watch for these types. I want three platoons of each included in the squadrons along with other specialists you deem indispensable."

"But what about those who are incompetent? Nobility seems to inherit that trait, …………..or maybe they just hoard it." Laughter again presented itself, but clearly as a disguise for the tension.

"We shall need all the laborers, drivers and engineer workers you can find." The reply came from Gath who had begun to size up his responsibility. "As I see our situation, there will be about six squadrons. Probably each of them will require an unusually large machine platoon, maybe two, to off-set the inexperience of the Knights proper."

"Well put, my friend." Commented Baste. "But you haven't gone far enough. From what I've seen, the best we'll produce is four knight's platoons per squadron. We'll try to mount half of the rest. They'll be trained as 'lights'."

"So far we've commissioned nine of the twenty platoons. Excuse me, nine plus one half of the remainder. That leaves us with six platoons unaccounted for…… I don't plan on splitting these 'nobles' up any more than is essential." Advised one of the seasoned Staff Masters.

"Have no worries. The other six platoons will be infantry." Baste stared down the table, watching disbelief flood most faces. "Yes, infantry. It will be advantageous to bring them back, especially as a new taller breed of Kyykki is reported. They use spears, ten foot ones."

"No way! No infantry!" Shouted an older man. "This is a disgrace of great magnitude! I won't hear any more of this, even from you, Baste."

Baste's fist exploded on the table. "I suspected your integrity had long ago abandoned you. You operate from a brain that refuses to catch up to today's reality. These are NOT the Kyykki of the War, no more than we are the Light Striper of fifty-five double moon cycles ago….I find your attempts to reproduce the past misdirected if not somewhat arrogant."

The old Staff Master stood, sword drawn over his head. With one quick smooth motion, Baste clutched the nearest goblet and, with a flip of his wrist, launched it down the table. The old man fell on his rear when the goblet, wine and all, clobbered him in the chest. A hearty round of applause and cheers went up from the rest as the old man climbed into his seat.

"That," Baste reflected to all present, "Is the Light Striper infantry conquering the over-estimated New Knights." He sat down and slowly examined their faces. "I have made myself clear?"

All heads nodded in agreement.

"Then to business. Because the Kyykki have a new trooper, taller and able to effectively use spears, we change tactics. The infantry will be formed and used. Ayhn, this is your responsibility. Take half of the best 'nobles' to form your core group. This unit will be as respected as any other, including the specialists and the machiners."

"While appreciating your offer," Said Ayhn, "I have no experience with infantry. I've been cavalry all my career."

"Yes, and a most excellent one at that. We're all familiar with your awards and exploits. Now, think of the infantry, standard archers to the rear, the front ranks, standing shoulder to shoulder, piercing swords at their sides, each carrying a twelve foot lance. Imagine them at a fast walk, ploughing through ranks of Kyykki, the blades of the lances......."

"Yes," Interrupted Ayhn. "I get the picture. A moving wall of lances, with well co-ordinated maneuvers, ought to destroy the Kyykki ranks."

"Its refreshing to see that not everyone's brain atrophied during the past double-moon cycles." He paused. "I'll give you nine cycles to prepare these 'whatever' for a demonstration. There will be no parades until they earn one. ....Furthermore, each of you has a Chaplain assigned to your headquarters. I expect this man to be trained as the rest, to live like the rest. And, he will have full authority over all moral issues. The first one being that all women are headed home today. And they shall stay home..... Now, good night."

Overwhelmed, completely and totally overwhelmed: that's how the King showed himself to those in the city. Not that it really mattered, as most of Krabo felt the same way. Their supposedly unimpregnable fortress city, had fallen prey to a flying, fire breathing beast. A people and a King who arrogantly thought themselves safe from the Kyykki and other evils, now lived with that fallacy.

The painful truth of the matter showed that the Kyykki and their damned leader could do as they pleased. Proof lay in the courtyard across from the High Council Hall. What should be done? The King posed that question first. In reply, the remaining High Council members, far less than half, gathered soon after the dead beast polluted the city. Paradoxically, the day glowed with a positive sunny warm mid-morning.

The nervous High Council found their King even more nervous. He couldn't even sit, but paced the floor, murmuring. The time to engage the new reality that the fire beast demanded as well as the news from Vosnob, from Treh, from Jabbi and even from the Church hierarchy, presently demoralized, began. Rumors spread that the clerics erudite theology had crumbled, leaving no foundations for the Haafians to understand yesterday's massacre.

The time for ceremonies in the High Council room vanished. Serfs jammed themselves into every nook and cranny, anxiously awaiting a word of hope or a least an explanation for what happened. The Captain began the meeting by introducing the first report.

Jabbi rose and walked to the center of the hall. "There is some good news to report to you this morning: we found the body of the traitor Krucik. His water logged carcass washed up on the river bank some three miles south of the city. The only explanations are that he either got through the city and then somehow fell into the river or that he never left the city. It seems that we neglected to thoroughly inspect the sewer system. In either case, the traitorous bastard is dead." Without waiting for any response from the people, he sat down.

The King continued pacing as Etan delivered a message from Vosnob. Every eye in the Council Hall fixed on him. "I have two reports to share with you. I'll try to keep them succinct. The Kyykki have returned. They continue to send raiding parties to the wall. Their losses are in the thousands. There is a new Kyykki: taller and smarter. It uses a spear. The second message comes from a scouting party. The enemy has a new type of spy: lazy Troopers at the front lines. They are under court martial at this time. Reserve troopers are HQ'd at the outpost."

The council members just sat, devoid, it seemed of any feelings except those of despair and self-pity. The serfs murmured among themselves.

"So what!" Sputtered a robe-bedecked merchant. "Beasts from the air......... breathing fire, bigger and better Kyykki, ex-nobles called to fight......ha, I watched them 'try' to ride out. Our wives could defend us much better."

"You oafish moron!" Howled the King, wagging an agitated finger at the man.

"Tell me you feel any differently. Or will you hide behind your 'great White Eagle' piety?" The agitated merchant responded. "What do you REALLY have to offer us? A treaty with the Kyykki?" The merchant stood and walked towards the King, who had all ready drawn his sword.

Before either uttered another word, or executed a deed, the Captain stood between them. "This is exactly what the damned evil one intended, isn't it?" His powerful voice resonated throughout the hall. "We shall indeed be easy prey for him if we are terrified by one dead flying beast and a new type of evil warrior........ So what?....... Are the rules abrogated? Should we just pack up and leave?...Sit down, merchant!"

Without comment, the King replaced his sword in its scabbard. Then he too, sat down.

"Next report!" Jabbi broadcast.

Etan drug an old man with a white beard to the center of the floor. "I present to you the beast slayer. A heroic man, who using his experience, knowledge and common sense, launched the fatal arrow into the beast's green slimey guts. His name is Wygga, the sailor....Also do I commend to you the soldier who lead the attack on the beast, decapitating his wing. Come from the shadow, my friend." A handsome but gawky man crossed the floor. "This is Vaal, a man flying beasts will respect from this time forward......My King!" Etan turned to the monarch.

"Ah, er, er, yes. Thank you Jabbi, er, Etan....." The King returned to the center of the room, bearing two heavy cloth bags. "As a way to show our appreciation for your unselfishness in saving our city from certain destruction, I present you with this token." Then he unceremoniously dumped the bags into the hands of Wygga and Vaal. Walking the floor like an old man, the King resumed his seat, leaving two embarrassed and puzzled men standing in the middle of the floor. They, in turn, shuffled off to their seats, not realizing they carried a small fortune in gemstones.

"What's next?" Sighed the dispirited King.

"A report from the Church Hierarchy." Said Jabbi.

This time the Church Hierarchy, sitting with the merchants, instead of their usual section, simply stood for their report.

"I speak this morning for the Church and for the Holy One, Blessed be His Name."

In proper silent reverence, everyone stood until the Churchman bid them sit.

"First, this unholy and damnable beast which descended upon the city, bringing naught but evil, is...........is called a dragon..........." His voice was barely audible. "A dragon...a damnable creature from....." His voice trailed off.

The word 'dragon' brought rapt attention from everyone. With one word the council transformed its despair into a focused, albeit terrified energy. No eye nor ear strayed from the Churchman. "I believe that your minds are easily read: you question the dragon, anything but a dragon. I am correct?"

In the now crowded Council Hall, all heads moved to affirm the Churchman's deduction. Not that any them wanted to, but the truth is the truth, like it or not.

"From the description found in the Sacred books, the beast can only be a dragon. It is reptilian in nature, elemental because of its use of fire, semi-divine through its ability to fly, yet of nature as well for it can be destroyed, never to return to life again. Furthermore, and this is the crucial point of our struggle as the Church, something commonly known by all of you, such dragons no longer exist. The Holy One, Blessed be His Name, personally eradicated them all when they endeavored, through their own powers, including that of speech, to induce all peoples to worship them.......... Your crisis is understandable; ours is unfathomable and overwhelming..... Outside this building lies the skeleton of a beast that cannot be. They were all annihilated tens of thousands of cycles ago by the Holy One himself. None ever existed within this age of ours. They are the evil manifestations of the past age."

The gathered crowd missed no word, nor any implication, nor any nuance of the Churchman's talk. They whispered among themselves. But not so much about the dragon, but about the fact that the Church itself had openly admitted to a crisis of the Faith. This hit them harder than the dragon's existence. The once secure anchor that grounded the people swayed: the stenchridden proof decomposing in the courtyard, its victims buried outside the city and those who destroyed the dragon were not the Holy One but ordinary Troopers.

"Obviously, we are in a crisis: if the Sacred word is erroneous at this juncture, then can we trust it at all? Or, can we begin to envision another rationale for the dragon's existence, one that does not call the Sacred word into question. Or, we can, as some have idiotically suggested, pretend there is no dead dragon on our doorstep. ......OUR FAITH PERMITS NO SUCH LIES!"

The boldness and velocity of the Churchman's delivery stunned the audience. It took integrity to deal with this ominous reality, yet, in spite of the obstacles, the Church refused to take the easy out. It would plumb the depths of the crisis. To those listening, here existed indisputable hope; the truth would be found. The people would live by the truth, for in truth is righteousness, and their hope.

"Now, the vastness of the problem, our crisis of Faith, to be exact, will take time to solve. And your prayers as well. All the resources of the Church will be utilized and the people will be kept informed of any....and I mean any....developments. Beginning this day, we call all the faithful to prayer each day. The words you heard here this day will leave tonight by courier for all the parishes in Haaf."

The crowd slowly filed out-- nervously hopeful, but inwardly anxious, desperate. How fragile Faith is: one dead dragon questions its ultimate authority. How resilient and strong Faith is: its followers, its practitioners, claim the inherent power of its Truth to establish a new answer. Or, maybe something altogether different. The new path which lay ahead would be traveled solely in Faith. The possibility of living with a paradox existed.

The King, however, retained his languidity, seldom bothering to touch the same reality of his people. The Church Knights gently escorted him to his quarters. The summoned physicians gathered. After some lengthy and arduous discussions with the Captain, decisions were reached. The King, until his malaise ended, must decentralize his power. A cabinet composed of Etan, Jabbi and the Captain would advise the King. Vaal's quick promotion placed him in the Captain's old role. A council of three Church Theologians would meet with the King and his advisor's every fifth day. The Haafian Kingdom needed to continue as before, even a dead dragon didn't negate the Kyykki.

"Well, what do you think?" Yganak questioned Running Cloud as he laid out the taller Kyykki on the table.

"The thing smells as bad as the others."

"Wonderful! The first time we get one of these 'things' up close and you worry about smell."

"If I don't warn you about it now, you'll be unprepared when the rest attack. Then how will you measure it?"

"So....open the windows and jam the doors."

"This second-in-command stuff has made you pretty bossy, even obnoxious...I guess I expected it."

"And just what is meant by that remark?"

"You've forgotten the ancient Yldian wisdom. I ascertained as much the other day. You really need to come to the village for a few cycles."

"Just get to the point...before this 'thing' rises and walks away!" Yganak 's limits were sorely tested.

"Allow a Haafian to rise above his ego, and his ego mandates the world."

"I never heard such jibberish before."

"Quite true." Commented Running Cloud while wiping off his weapons. "Quite true. I just concocted it."

Yganak almost threw the dead Kyykki at Running Cloud. Instead, Running Cloud began reciting his findings concern the dead 'thing'. "Its almost two foot taller than the other Kyykki, making it eight and one half foot tall. Almost as tall as a mounted Light Striper?"

"About a two foot difference, to our benefit."

"Could be reason for concern, especially with spears. We both witnessed what happened out on the hill."

"I'm well aware." Yganak said tersely. "What else?"

"Quite a number of things, actually. Examine the length of the torso. It retains the frog-like inverted triangular back. Means weak legs when standing, weak back for throwing anything, but plenty strong for hopping at great speeds.....Then, the longer, stronger arms. Hardly frog-like at all, except for the webbed hand and no thumb. Again, no danger from accurate spear chucking. But here's the significant alteration: the 'thing' has a neck."

"So what?"

"Do any of the short ones have a neck?"

"No."

"See the advantage of the neck?" Running Cloud twisted the carcass's head back and forth and up and down. "Understand this significance? Both greater mobility and intelligence." Running Cloud answered his own question.

"Intelligence?" Yganak sneered.

"Think! These things can now grab their prey simply by turning its head and not its whole body. Just like a long-necked bird fishing in the shallows. Or, a snapping turtle. Or, too much like us." A bit of dread crept into his voice. "Now look at this face.... Eyes that face forward, not off to the sides, like reptiles..... This thing has much better vision than his smaller colleagues. And, the cranium is much larger. See the bulge behind the ear holes?"

"So, its not just a bigger old style Kyykki?"

"No, unfortunately, we're looking at a whole new species........ another vile.....nauseating.... creature.....A most dangerous species.......... Almost half-person, or.... headed in that direction." Running Cloud paused.

Yganak offered another 'real' problem. "Just what, or how did this happen?"

"When you know you'll share it all with me." Said Vosnob. He made his way into the room.. "I wasn't sure about the smell coming from here. I thought it was just the two of you!" His grin was short lived. "You stupid morons...."

"Does he always speak in redundant tones?" Quipped Yganak.

"Damn it! You two imbeciles could be dead."

"Needless-to-say, we aren't." Said Yganak. "But now that you finally got here, maybe we can put some pieces together."

Vosnob flustered. As competent as these two proved time and time again, their reckless unorthodoxy still bothered him. He also cursed their unserious manner, if only because it kept them one step ahead of him. "Obviously, then you know about the brief I received from Sarg yesterday?"

"Does it add anything of substance to explain this 'thing'?"

"I'm not sure. Is that 'thing' male or female? How much 'person' might it be? What about its ability to reason independently? And..."

"Stop right there, Vosnob." Running Cloud more than encouraged. "As you might be able to see, the body is not dissected. Being of a reptilian nature, the sex organs are internal. So, give me a moment." He drew a heavy line about where the navel might have been. "Stand back, I've not skinned one of these afore. But I'll tell you one thing; this skin is much different, it fits uncommonly well. Nick this skin and they'll bleed, but don't expect them to explode anymore." Knife now in hand, Running Cloud now meticulously carved the carcass across the line. "My word!" He exclaimed.

The greenish blood dripping onto the stone floor had bright red streaks mingled through it. The blood's consistency was much thicker and the sliminess, absent.

"Damn! My hypothesis is true! This is some sort of half-half beast. It wrenches my guts out. This is utterly abominable. Its blasphemous.... That's what it is."

"Then you better not want to see the rest." Running Cloud stated soberly. "It doesn't get easier, biologically, or, in your case, theologically. Quite frankly, we need a Shaman for this unnerving debacle."

Yganak walked over to the stretched-out carcass, peered into the deep incision Running Cloud made and then hurriedly went to the nearest window and puked.

"Well, I did warn you. Those innards aren't a pretty sight. However, this thing isn't female. No pouches for eggs or, maybe, 'little things'."

"If that wasn't so ludicrous, I'd personally have you hauled in for blasphemy." Yganak muttered from the window. He continued to restore his dignity, though, with one's head out the window, it became rather enigmatic. "So, 'it' is a male? Are there any reproductive organs present?"

"I really wouldn't know. Why don't you come over and show me what they look like." Running Cloud grinned.

"No thank you. But, with all of your trapping and skinning experience, can't you tell?" Yganak queried. "This worries me. If they reproduce quickly, substantial alterations to our military plans and procedures are clearly in order."

"And since when did I die and leave you to panic over a dead 'thing'?" Vosnob inquired. "You don't even have the whole story."

"AH, good. I arrive in time for the theology debate." Remarked the too-stout Chaplain as he burst into the stone room. Their barriers were, obviously, too frail against the chaplain's bulk He apprehended the best seat in the room. "Now, just exactly how are you defining this matter?"

"I thought you were the Shaman, not some damned proctor." Yganak challenged.

"Oh, I'm forced to do both. There are a phenomenal number of theologically illiterate officers in the military, you know." The man was jovial, almost elated, as if an official summons empowered him. He'd give and take as the others did.

"Where did you find this beast of a man.......again?" Running Cloud questioned Vosnob. "He's enough to ......"

"Handle whatever you can ...?" Smiled the rotund Chaplain.

"I almost thought I'd enjoy your obnoxious company again, Oros. Alas, once more I'm proved wrong." Running Cloud said.

"Most inappropriate. That is the nomenclature you bring to my mind....Anyway, ...And, the first one of you to crack another stupid grin will also be the first man to fly out that window." With a stubby finger he pointed to the window overlooking the carnage. "Rather a gruesome place to land, I would think."

With dimly surpressed grins, Running Cloud and Yganak made their way to other chairs. Vosnob initiated his usual pacing, ignoring the banter.

"This is where we begin." Commented Vosnob as he unrolled the dispatch from Sarg. "This is the core of his writing. Its concerns the brutal beating of a Trooper by some emaciated, pale skinned women with sharpened teeth. According to the report, these 'women' were Haafian, Haafian prostitutes. Most of them lured into this profession by one Krucik, now dead. This is evidence from a person who miraculously escaped his wiles."

The other three listened intently. Vosnob only covered details once. He would then move into the major principles involved and their ramifications. Exactly why Oros stumbled into the group was as a mystery. So implied the commander-in-chief.

"Now, a physician in the group, one Vauk, dissected one of these creatures. Listen carefully to his findings. I quote from Sarg: 'these women creatures were bitten and badly chewed up about their nipples. Evidence shows them also to have given multiple births, though from the sustained damage to their external sex organs, these births had to be so large as to permanently damage the women......I surmize that whenever these women lost their usefulness at birthing they were put to use as spies. How many there are is unknown as is the range of their influence...'"

Vosnob paused, glancing about the room. Was the message getting through? He decided to continue reading. "We have scoured the city [Pinduala] to remove any remaining spies. I suggest the same be done throughout the nation. They are only out at night, usually in groups of three or four, wearing long raggedy hooded robes. Any wounds incurred from them require immediate professional care. The fevers run dangerously high....Also, their blood is no longer pure red." He crumpled the paper and tossed it on the floor. "As you can see, the evil one has not been sleeping since the Battle. No, by using our own women he creates a new race of Kyykki. DAMN HIM!"

A dismal profound silence pervaded the group.

"We build a wall, the damned evil one builds a new people." Murmured Yganak. "It is not conceivable! Oros! Tell me this is pure conjecture! A ridiculous hypothesis!"

"Then you want to hear lies." Oros immediately replied. "Unfortunately, I cannot obey. The fact is, the hypothesis is not a hypothesis. It is the truth."

"Then has the Spirit abandoned us?" Running Cloud asked, his bronzed face broadcasting anxiety.

"No, my friend." Comforted Oros. "The Spirit has naught to fear from the machinations of the evil one."

"Then why has this happened?"

"Why did it happen the first time?"

"Because we..."

"WE!" Repeated Oros. "You know the answer. The irresponsibility of 'we' almost cost us the nation last time around. This must be avoided at all costs."

"And just how are we to defend Haaf from such evilness?" Demanded Yganak. "Can we also create another people?"

Oros crossed his arms on his barrel chest and gently leaned back in his chair. "A comment made a few moments ago......concerning the lack of information, not having the entire story?"

From the far side of the room, Vosnob spoke. "And that is why I called you down from the mountains."

"Well spoken............ I certainly didn't volunteer."

"Then share your story with us. Only when the pieces are known can we proceed."

"The King needed to be convinced that 'evil' is happening. And that some of our own people were intimately involved." Oros glanced about the room, seeing only bewildered expressions on two faces. "Don't be so astonished! The King is nothing special when it comes to discerning the events of the world. We practically had to kidnap him and carry him to the mountains."

"So the Yldians were right on target."

"Yes, we knew that they knew, but with so little importance placed on the King by your people, we had to move quickly."

"But you did call for the High Shaman. And, if I correctly understood, he had a significant positive impact upon the King."

"You hear extremely well...... The King's visions were directed, in part, by the council of the Shaman. The King can be stubborn. If he didn't know about the 'evil' then he didn't have to deal with it. ....Sounds much like a merchant, if I may venture my own opinion in this matter."

"Move on with the story." Said Vosnob.

"There isn't much more. The King required a transformation or else we were doomed to repeat the past ruination of Haaf. We made certain that it happened. And that it happened in time."

Yganak spoke. "Why do you continue to use 'we'?"

"Because I was there. The brother monk the King mentioned?...... Oh, one more thing. Since the last war, our order has been sending spies into the Dark Lands. Often, no one returned. This, in itself told us that the damned evil one continued. Stagnation is only the way he wants us to view him. Actually, he's rather progressive, in an evil way, naturally."

"Naturally." Yganak blew sarcastic. "So which side are you on?"

"The faith teaches us to be realistic and truthful, even if it hurts and even if it causes us to sound sacrilegious."

"But you haven't delineated the source of the evil? How does the Holy One allow this evil mixing of the soulless ones and people?"

"I wonder," Oros suggested, "I wonder if you take the faith seriously? Does not the Holy One encourage us to make decisions? Are we not created in his image, an image that is living and therefore, changing? But unlike the trees, who have no choice in their changing?"

Yganak winced. "So, WE are responsible?"

"Ah, you learn fast. That is precisely the point. We were, by the wisdom of the Holy One, given the ability to decide. We are also held responsible for how we use this freedom."

The door to the stone room burst open again. A runner, totally out-of-breath stood there, gasping. With a motion from Vosnob he crossed the floor and presented Vosnob with a diplomatic stamped-and-waxed document.

"Sir, this is from your Aide-de-Camp, Etan. I am to await your immediate reply before leaving."

"At ease, son." Vosnob took the report. "Now, get some food and rest downstairs. I'll call for you when the reply is in order."

"Sir, thankyousir!" Gasped the Trooper. He quickly left the room, leaving the peculiar report in the Commander's hand.

"Highly irregular, isn't it?" Vosnob asked no one in particular. "This is the first message waxed-and-stamped. Etan is not so formal. Obviously, something is amiss." Vosnob tore the report open even as he spoke. Then he began to read. "The dragon, so identified by the Church, is dead in the courtyard outside of Council Hall. Half of the Council are also dead, as is Krucik's son. The King is safe. However, the Court Physicians have put him on 'inactive' status until he is back in control. Evil reality has overtaken his senses at this time. A council of three is appointed to carry out his duties: the Captain, Jabbi and myself. The Church is working towards a theological explanation for this, especially for the people, who presently feel a spiritual vacuum. "When an evil beast can terrorize the city at will, then who are we to fight against it? And where is the Holy One?" Just a common comment from a baker. I will continue to keep you informed. Please send reply in code advising your intended actions and how we can coordinate with you. ETAN."

Vosnob paced the floor. Oros prayed, shaking all the while. Yganak appeared pale. Not one ever expected a dragon. The Holy One dealt with them; they remained as part of the extinct age.

Running Cloud made the only comment. "Why are we so plagued by a DEAD dragon? Gather your wits about you! The dragon was killed by us. That should put everything into perspective."

"You are quite right." Said Vosnob. "When evil believes its losing it fights harder and uglier. Is that not correct, Oros?"

"Indeed! But a dragon! It's been tens of thousands of double moon cycles since those two hundred foot beasts roamed about. Well before our age began. The evil one must be desperate to use such a trump card so early."

"Perhaps. But you assume that the damned one creates dragons? That presumption contradicts the reports coming from your 'spies'. Now, which is correct?"

"I have a great fear of dragons. Mention them and I shake. I've never seen one, but now one lies dead in Krabo."

"Will you please focus on the question."

"Yes, ah, yes." Stammered Oros. "Truthfully, I don't believe a dead dragon can do much damage. His appearance did the damage. Demoralization is the label I'd give it. But the equation remains stable: nothing has really changed."

"You don't sound sane." Said Yganak.

"Then listen carefully. Did not the master of the dragon expect the dragon to return, mission fulfilled?"

"Of course!"

"But it never happened. The dragon died in the city. Somehow, even though caught completely off-guard, someone, probably the Church guards or the Light Striper contingent, killed it. That says alot for how fast and efficient our forces are....... True, half the High Council was also killed. But, the ex-nobles all ready left the city. So it fell upon the merchants to suffer for their country...... I relish some small justice in that."

"Vosnob, this man is cynical beyond all reason." Running Cloud advised. "I think he shall remain with us."

"So be it!"

"AMEN!" Added Yganak.

"Then, Oros, your responsibility lies in front of you. Advise the Church heads: rebuild the Haafian morale from a spiritual perspective.... To you Yganak, make sure every squadron knows how to watch for and exterminate dragons. Find out what weapons were used. You know the rest, but don't forget the New Knights at D'Ka....And you, Running Cloud, I really can't command you at all."

"Hardly, I outrank you. But, might I suggest that two clan groups join you. Dragons and other Kyykki need to eat. Well prepared poisoned food might help even the odds."

"Accepted, thank you....Runners will leave in the morning. Your letters will travel with them. I'll finish mine this afternoon. I seems that Etan can't ferret out all the spies...At least not until this letter reaches him.....I'll see you all for supper? By that time the carcasses shall be disposed and the air will be clean."

"Right! See you for supper?" And Yganak bolted out the door.

Running Cloud and Oros already left.

Chapter 4

"Albasla'. Are you sure that's the rightful name for the skiff?" Vauk asked. He walked up and down the gangways all morning searching for the vessel the Staff Master engaged for the next stage of their journey.

"As if you'd even recognize a skiff. You probably think it has oars and is seven hundred feet long." Brey teased him, but with just the right touch of malice.

"A skiff has one lateen sail and one stern sail, miss smart.."

"That's quite enough, you two." Sarg suddenly appeared behind them. "Anymore of this and we're all liable to believe you actually care for each other. Another week of this and we'll all think you're married." Sarg was only halfjoking, his instincts told him something was going on, but he refused to comment any further.

The other two pretended not to notice each other's blushing face. They neared the northern end of the wharves at Pinduala. Still dressed as serfs, they booked for the unregistered islands in the Upper Sea. The trip's design included both negating any spies as well as obtaining information from the 'unknown' Light Striper navy who inhabited the string of islands.

In spite of her considerable verbiage to the contrary, Brey remained weak and underweight. Sarg simply utilized this to provide an excuse to ferry his sickly daughter and his lazy son out to the islands. Sarg did not have to lie to the port authorities about Brey's condition.

Luuft boarded another skiff the pervious night. He left in full field uniform, being listed as a replacement trooper for a platoon that fell into rotation. In his provisions Luuft transported the weapons for the group. Now, at sea, he wished the bag contained something more useful, especially as he spent the majority of the voyage with his head hung over the rail.

"Not every Light Striper Trooper be cut out for sea duty." is what a kindly ensign told him. The words made no impact on his sour stomach.

Earlier, on the dock, the Staff Master promised the four of them a reunion long before they headed into the Zuda Marsh. That, and a polite smile, were all they received. Sarg requested a guide for the Zuda, one Blue-Turtle, a Yldan,. He received no acknowledgement. The Staff Master left for the wharf without a hint of an answer.

"There she is!" Vauk pronounced with unusual zeal.

"You'd think he'd just entered the most holy Church in the Kingdom." Commented Sarg. Vauk had simply read the name off the ship's stern.

Brey gave him a cute smile. Sarg still had difficulty seeing her in the peasant skirt and blouse. Not that it didn't become her; it did. Too well, perhaps, judging from the rather lewd remarks of sailors and the deckhands. Sarg worried about Brey getting well....if they whistled at her now........

The trio paused on the causeway. The 'Albasla' moored to their right. But a ship three hundred feet long with a beam of almost thirty and three masts was totally unexpected. She rode considerably high in the water, especially for being loaded. Passenger cabins were located both fore and aft of the masts, a bit unusual. A load of huge rough cut timber; squared poles about one hundred feet long, were lashed to the gunwales. This freighter ran first class. Sarg wished he could have thanked the Staff Master for the gift.

"You be the Sarg party of three?" Yelled an ensign from the bow.

"Yes, we are." Responded Sarg.

"Come aboard! Yer cabin's waiting. We cast off in ten moments. The gang plank's slippery, ye bees careful." He turned and went back to whatever he was about.

On board, a sailor showed them to a cabin in the stern, just aft of the third mast and one deck below. Utilitarian and clean adequately described the room. Four doubled-over cots lined the walls, the lower ones functioning as benches. A folding table occupied most of the rear wall, excluding the large shuttered window. Vauk conjectured their cabin measured ten feet by ten feet. Flanking their cabin, were quarters for the junior officers.

After unbolting the shutter to open the window, Sarg recognized this freighter possessed more armament than any freighter he knew. The window lead to a five foot wide passageway designed as a magazine, with disguised loopholes for crossbows built into the outer wall. A solid knock on the door moved Sarg to slam the shutters before anyone else knew what was there.

"Might I enter." The voice conveyed an undecipherable accent. "I am Ellom, Captain of the freighter Albasla."

"Please." Brey said, almost coyly.

The Captain, Ellom, decked out in Light Striper uniform, except with the long mid-blue tunic shortened to waist length and the usual yellow trousers were off-white, presumably due to the salt water, entered and bowed. His build showed nothing out-of-theordinary. But Brey giggled at his bare feet.

"Aye, ye bees a landlubber. But them fancy shoes o' yours will get ye swept off the deck too quick. And you be too purdy fer fish food."

Brey blushed and kept her eyes on the floor. A muffled guffaw rose from Vauk.

"I see ye found out this no be a freighter, Sarg. I 'spected one with yer reputation not to waste much time." Ellom looked directly at Sarg. "Unfortunately, the rules be that I can't show ye much more, 'cept what ye see from the decks. Not personal, mind ye, but secrets be secrets."

"We certainly understand, Captain." Sarg spoke for all. "But can you say when we might disembark?"

"We be slippin' the ropes now. Jist leavin'. Ye Light Striperrs be impatient." He grinned. "Best I can say ...be three dawns, then ye all can walk again....Supper be at seven on the deck...If ye be in need, pull yon rope." He pointed to the window where a large knotted rope extended down from a hole in the ceiling. "Please excuse me, we be heading out." He quickbowed to the three, pivoted and headed up the stairs to the bridge.

"Welcome to the Navy of the Light Striper, my friends." Announced Sarg to some perplexed children of his. "And you didn't know how widespread my exploits were known, did you?"

"Well, no." Vauk dryly replied. "But then, this is all a secret, isn't it?"

Brey actually laughed, but speedily caught herself. Drawn by curiosity, she re-opened the shutters. "So this is a ship-of-battle?"

"Try battleship, Brey." Groaned Sarg. "I don't want you sounding too illiterate while on board."

"I didn't realize how over-protective you could be." Brey said smiling as she swung her skirt about. "I wonder what weaponry lies on and above deck?" And before anyone responded, she bound up the stairs, tripped on the top one and smashed her face on the deck. She looked out at a set of bare feet.

"Ma'am, ye be better off if ye used the railing." Said the seaman as he helped her up. "Ye be all right. That's a bad limp ye have. Ye sit here, while I gets the ship's doctor."

"That won't be necessary." Said Vauk, who stood over her. "I'm her doctor. I thank you for your most courteous concern for her welfare."

Without a word, the seaman continued on his way.

"Now, you silly damsel, I just hope you didn't re-open the wound on your leg. Another set of stitches ....."

"Let it go." Cautioned Sarg. "Remember, we're just some landlubbers journeying to the islands."

"But can you still walk?"

"Your damn right. I CAN WALK!" Brey pulled herself up by a rope and hobbled twenty feet to the rail. "See!" She painfully sneered.

Pinduala swiftly disappeared into the foggy morning as the three huge faded red triangular sails literally glided the ship across the waves. The three walked arm and arm, Brey in the middle.

They casually meandered about the ship's decks including a tour of the bridge area. In private, their conversation focused upon the partially visible armament. Some never existed inland and some weaponry, provided weaponry is what it actually is, remained undecipherable to them. Maybe time would provide the answers. After all, Captain Ellom stated 'three dawns', but a secret mission means all proper rules are suspended.

The mid-afternoon sun's direct rays gave Sarg the perfect rationale for sending Brey to their cabin, her vehement protests notwithstanding. Then the two proceeded on a more adventurous tour of the ship. That ended abruptly, but politely, as an ensign blocked their entrance way to below deck.

"But we are passengers!" Sarg protested.

"And passengers stay above decks. That be the rule." The ensign replied with all due respect. "The only exception allowable be if you were a merchant checking the validity of the invoice."

"I apologized for my Father." Said Vauk. "He is too used to having his own way, especially about HIS castle."

Sarg's face did not deny the lie: he appeared belligerent. The ensign accepted this as his justification. He then showed the men to the upper decks.

"You might want to see how we catch supper." The sailor suggested.

"Thank you." Came Sarg's terse acknowledgement. He kept some other, more choice words ready for Vauk, just as soon as the right opportunity appeared.

The contraption far up the bow caught their attention. Familiar and yet unfamiliar is how the 'thing' puzzled their minds. They approached the contraption's crew to further investigate. Indeed, a crossbow. However, its cramped size and the fact that four sailors, using a winch to draw it proved totally incongruent. A conventional machine that would take four men, would also be mounted in a wagon and weigh over three hundred stone. This machine could be easily held by one man, though it was post mounted.

Its bolt was fully six foot long, including a two foot barbed head. The barbs were explicitly designed to prevent the bolt from being torn loose from the intended target. At the other end of the bolt hung a steel ring through which passed a flexible, sturdy braided rope. This rope, which laid coiled at the base of the crossbow, then ran to a stanchion where it tied off.

"Wha' cha know 'bout this yer girl?" Said the proud man who appeared to be the crew chief. "Most landlubber types 'ner seed one 'o dees. Probly think ye can't make sumtin like this.....Hey, I be right?" He looked Sarg right in the face.

Sarg moaned something, but then remembered his disguise. "You are right, my good fellow. I don't know much about this 'girl' of yours. How does she work?"

"Effens ye got 'bout ten moments, yer goin' learn." The proud sailor answered. Without waiting for a comment, he stripped to the waist, exposing a short heavy muscled frame decorated with too many scars. With an old rag, he slopped some fish oil on the groove where the bolt would ready itself. Then he checked the bolt and the rope. "Load me girl up, maties. It be time fer supper."

Two men loaded the bolt while the third checked the mounting and raised the sight on the crossbow. He then readied a second bolt. Their target was sighted off the starboard bow. The alert came from the crowsnest on the foremast. Out on the ocean, some one thousand feet off, jumped a school of high finned sharks. The ship turned towards them, soon cutting the distance in half.

Yauk and Sarg stood, intently watching, fascinated by the teamwork as well as by the concept: catching fish with a crossbow. A sailor gently removed them to a position farther down the gunwale, safely out-of-the-way. 'Cause landlubbers might get hurt', he apologetically explained.

"HOLD STEADY!" Called the bowman. And the ship slowed in the water.

"STAND CLEAR!" And the crew stepped back.

TWAAAAANG! The bolt sped across the wave tops to its prey. The rope played out behind it. It took but a second to hear a 'thud' as the bolt impacted the shark. For a moment, the shark jumped in agony, then splashed to the ocean, dead.

"HAUL AWAY!"

A winch wound in the rope attached to the dead shark. While that progressed, a second shot achieved the same goal. Supper would be excellent and bountiful. The high-finned sharks, when hoisted to the deck, ran twenty five feet long. They could bite a man in two, and they certainly could swallow a man, but they tasted excellent.

Supper consisted of the thickest shark meat stew they had ever eaten. Served hot from the kettles which had been hauled to the poop deck from below, it became the best meal of the dawn. Judging from their size and condition, Sarg surmized the kettles also held burning pitch or oil. Everything on this 'freighter' did double-duty. The oily taste of Brey's tea caused her stomach distress, which was eleviated when Vauk shared his wine with her. Captain Ellom politely insisted that no young lady should drink anything but tea.

Being the sole passengers, they were obliged by the Captain to join with him on the bridge after supper. From that vantage point, they experienced a ship sighting off the port side. The Captain cautioned them that if she turned out a pirate ship, they would spend considerable time in their cabin. 'Valuable passengers must be kept safe.' is how the Captain worded it.

The other ship continued to increase in size, and rather quickly too, for the Captain changed the Albasla's course to rendezvous with the unknown vessel. Within a brief period of time, the other vessel became recognizeable as a sister ship of the Albasla. That observation, combined with the fact that no 'call to arms' sounded, determined that no pirate ship existed.

"Furl Sails!" Came the order from mid deck.

A hundred sailors climbed the rigging and slid out on the yard arms and spars. Six huge faded red sails disappeared, leaving the ship bare, skeleton-like.

"Ready the spars! Fore and Aft!" Sounded the next command.

The masts and other sundry parts of the sailing ship ingeniously transformed into a loading dock, the masts doubling as the cranes. Most of the crew attended to this massive transformation.

At this juncture, the three passengers recognized the ship as the real cover-up, the ultimate disguise. They also discovered that over three hundred troopers of the Light Striper called this 'home'.

Sarg could only guess at how many such freighters patrolled the waters of the Upper Sea and the southern coast of Haaf. And, not even a handful of land-lubbers were cognizant of this 'gift.' Certainly, the Holy One exercises His will in mysterious ways. Sarg's beatific thoughts were dismantled as the Captain's rough commands flew by.

"READY THE DOCKING!" He hollered in his still undecipherable accent.

The squared hundred foot logs formerly lashed to the gunwales now swung cross deck to rest perpendicular to the ship. The sister ship ran parallel to the Albalsa, at an estimated distance of four hundred feet. Then she too, furled her sails. As the distance narrowed to a hundred feet, the lundlubber trio watched in silent fascination as the other ship also prepared to 'ready the docking.' Never before had they seen anything so precise and so well executed. Now the ships paralleled each other at twenty feet, barely drifting in the swells.

"DOCK NOW!" Bellowed Captain Ellom.

The huge logs floated above the gunwales for a second, then slowly and deliberately reached out to the other vessel, guided the mast cranes. On the other ship, crews armed with pikes and ropes received the logs, lowering them to both gunwales. The heavy spars were then manhandled into final position: resting and then tied to both gunwales with the previously chopped notches in the spars fitting perfectly. In short, two ships became one; one huge double-hulled twin-masted 'freighter'.

As a final step the sailors ran planking over the spars and the twenty foot expanse of sea. This deck provided the space for just about anything one could imagine. That evening, its usefulness served for the swapping of crew and materials and, much later, a rather raucous sailor's party. A more civilized and genteel get-to-gether, set in the Captain's quarters began at the first moon-rise. All ensigns and other officers would to be there in full dress uniform. The passengers, especially one pretty lady, would also be expected to attend, properly attired for the occasion. So said the note found in their cabin.

"Well," Sarg drawled. "How about we show up in full uniform? That's what's expected. Maybe we'll be able to throw them a surprize or two. After tonight's spectacle, I believe we owe them a few."

"But then, should Brey be exposed? She's all ready been assailed by too many sailor's looks." Vauk voiced his concern.

"Am I to believe that you may be jealous, good doctor?" Brey was a bit more than coy, especially with her flashing eyes. Something in her question went beyond teasing. Vauk quickly put the thought and its implications in the farthest corner of his mind.

"I really didn't mean to disrupt your train of thought." Brey finished. She obviously knew how to reach him.

Sarg's cool, "Enough of this!" bought him two angry stares. "Let's get moving. The first moon will soon be out in full and as the Captain's quarters is directly overhead, we have no excuse for being late, not even fashionably late."

Without much forethought Sarg began to strip. A giggle from Brey caused him much embarrassment, which he covered with something about the need to have a blanket divide the room; a separation of officers and enlisted men. Then, realizing the implications his remarks created for Brey and Vauk, he almost blew a gasket.

"Forget what I said. Vauk, hang up the blanket! And then get over here with me."

Brey responded with a rather cute titter.

"Careful, or you'll be up on charges for insubordination." Sarg threw back at her.

"Why Sir, I could never think of such a thing?" The lady made herself convincingly innocent.

The blanket up, they changed. Sarg demanded a formal inspection before they left the cabin. Vauk wore his ten year ribbon and his doctor's insignia.

"Take that off, you ARE NOT a doctor!"

"But I am." Vauk soberly replied.

"But you told us otherwise."

"Unfortunately, I lied."

"YOU WHAT!"

"I had no intention of hurting anyone, but to keep ourselves a bit more disguised, I lied. Too many people find doctors easy targets." Vauk said.

Brey pretended to be hurt. And Sarg missed none of it.

"Picking doctors as easy targets. Interesting. I thought people only chased you for your money." Now Sarg entered the sport, though not with Brey's approval.

It came as a shock, but, somewhere, at sometime, Brey had altered her uniform. With a few tucks and darts, it demonstrated her definitely feminine attributes, even if the doctor complained about her being underweight. Apparently, the doctor had a few things to learn.

Sarg simply adjusted her first year ribbon and cursed under his breath. "What am I doing with a woman in my outfit?"

They headed up the staircase to Captain Ellom's quarters. They arrived last, to the stares of many surprized Light Stripers. Seated about the room, in full Light Striper regalia of blue and yellow were the ensigns, the petty officers and both Captains. In the corner stood Luuft, smiling at the amazement on the officer's countenances and at how beautiful Brey looked. For their part, rendezvousing with Luuft furnished a most unexpected surprize. The old Staff Master kept his word.

Sarg broke the ice by formally introducing Brey, a first year veteran of the ever progressive and deliberately misleading, to the enemy of course, Light Striper. This obliged no arguments. How could it? The entire Light Striper 'navy' lived as one hundred percent deception and disguise. So Sarg reasoned with himself before he entered the Captain's quarters. A hearty round of applause confirmed his reasoning and the following toast, presented by Captain Ellom himself, put everyone at ease.

With other guests introduced, the usual one-upsmanship story telling time ensued. With Brey's presence, even though tacitly accepted as true Light Striper, the stories remained 'slightly' more refined than usual. That is, until Brey, in a most offhanded way spoke of the pale skinned females who attempted to devour her. Her tale of the sword play and heads and arms flying through the night air spewing greenish slime, clearly startled all but three persons present. Sarg silently committed himself to stuffing a rag in her mouth if she began the story of burning down the prostitutes' tent city.

Luuft finally hailed Vauk and informed him of his voyage. Luuft would remain with Sarg on the Albasla as the other ship, which had plates for various names, had scheduled to break away at sunrise. Luuft shared his impressions about the discipline and the coordination of this 'sea going' Light Striper. He occupied his time on the other ship with the armoire, a young man whose inventiveness produced both the new crossbow as well as the bolt used for fishing. Their discussion centered on using the new crossbow on land, as an offensive weapon. Luuft picked up enough information to design an experimental version when they returned to Haaf. At which item, Vauk only smiled.

Finally, the two gleefully watched Sarg defend Brey from all and any advances. The vast majority were innocent to all but Sarg, the dutiful Father. The one real threat, an overly ambitious ensign from the other ship, more than a little drunk, somehow tripped over Brey's foot and fell out the Captain's door. He never returned.

"Gentlemen.... and lady." Announced the Captain. "I thank you all for a most delightful evening." He specifically winked at Brey. "But now, its time to move on. So I bide all of you, including the ambitious, but absent ensign, Good Night."

Everyone left feeling quite well and laughing. And tripped over a semi-conscious ensign heaped at the bottom of the steps.

The war tubas split the air with their 'call-to-arms' long before the Captain's promised sun-up arrived. Men clamored up the rigging to assume their crossbow positions in the crowsnest. Archers appeared everywhere along the exterior gunwales. But most of the action happened on the open deck areas where huge catapult machines set up for action. The foremost one was mounted on a rotating platform permitting it to fire in any direction. The other could be moved manually, but was readied to fire off the port bow. All this could be seen from the door of the guest cabin. The foursome reported directly to Captain Ellom.

"I appreciate this. But you have no experience in this type of fighting, especially as it involves pirates. Haafian and Yldan types. Have you fought against your own kind before? Its not the same as fighting against the 'soulless' ones, you know."

"But we are Light Striper." Luuft interjected.

"Aye, That's true." the Captain thought for a moment. "We won't close with the pirates until sun up. Take that long to run them down..... So, Luuft..."

"Yes Sir!"

"You and the rest head to the other ship. Stay with that armoire friend of your's. You might as well learn something you can take with you...And his ideas aren't as unique as you might think, most came from his father."

"Let's move!" Said Sarg. "Thank you, Captain!"

The passage to the other ship had its mishaps: the bridging deck remained constantly slippery with the spray off the bows. Vauk almost fell overboard and Brey lost her footing trying to disembark at the far end. The armorer readily caught her; but then was totally embarrassed to discover Brey wasn't another trooper. Brey's distress likewise proved embarrassing: grabbing a woman about the chest just didn't sit right, even with an unending stream of authentic apologies.

"PIRATE SHIP OFF STARBOARD BOW!" Came from high on the mast. som

"Time to load up!" Quipped the armorer, his mood altered by the lookout's alarm. "There's two bows on the bow. I'll handle one, Luuft. The other is yours....There's your crew." He pointed to the other three.

"But they know less than I." Luuft begged.

"No matter, usually we only get two of the four bows running. Now we got three.....maybe...Anyway, them pirates won't expect three...And surprize is a magnificent weapon, right?"

"Yes indeed, my boy, yes indeed. Let's have at it!" The smell of battle excited Sarg.

And with the pitch melting and the oil bubbling, the weaponry and the armor smells, as well as the determined attitude of those around him, everyone felt a sudden rush of energy.

"Just do EXACTLY as I do!" Turned out to be the only command given by the armorer.

They arrived at their position in the bow just as the figure heads proved themselves false. They dropped to the water line exposing cast iron rams. Another component of the light Striper 'navy' now became obvious to the landlubbers; these two ships fought as one. As they looked up, even the sails brought this message home; big triangular sails stretched out between the masts of the two hulls. The military strategy went undisguised, even to a landlubber: ram the pirate ship. The high-finned sharks would finish off anything left.

"SHIP AT TWO THOUSAND! .... READY ALL WEAPONS!"

Brey and the others failed to notice how fast they had gained on the pirate ship. In fact, as they now finally took a hard look at it, quite a shock awaited them. The pirate vessel resembled a dark fairy-story boat: a dragon head in the bow with a huge tower behind it, cluttered with crossbows. Iron plates hung from the gunwales. A catapult in the stern opened fire; large stones splashed in front of the Albasla. The Pirate's greyish sails spread to fullest capacity in order to outrun the Light Striper.

"FIRE TO DE-RIG ONLY!"

"Explain that!" Growled a perplexed Vauk.

"Just watch over there." Responded Luuft.

The armorer swung his crossbow around, taking aim at the huge main sail on the second mast.

"Change heads!" He yelled. In a few breaths another bolt lay in the groove. Its head measured a full five feet in diameter, each of the six blades made from razors.

He returned to sight in his weapon, then fired. The bolt arched upward, then curved into the upper right corner of the sail. What the bolt failed to do in demolishing the sail, the wind provided; making small tears large ones that refused to harness the wind.

The bolt from the other ship finished off the sail. Luuft's crew hadn't loaded yet. Before they did, two more bolts left for the pirate ship, but with little success.

Meanwhile, the pirate catapult scored a direct hit on the bridge and then one the poop deck, putting the rotating catapult out-of-order. Albasla's catapults returned fire, to no avail; the pirate ship being too narrow.

"FIRE WHEN TARGETS PRESENT THEMSELVES!"

"Damn strange command. I guess they don't waste ammunition."

"Not exactly." Retorted Luuft. "Each man knows how far his weapon reaches. The closer we get, the denser gets the air...."

THuuud! A bolt struck the gunwale in front of them.

"Time to send them a return gift!" The crossbow crew made ready, utilizing a bolt with a with a heavy iron head. "Made to blow a hole in the side of the ship. Let's see if she works." The armorer aimed and shot.

The distance between the two ships rapidly dwindled to less than five hundred feet. Luuft aimed at the gunwale surrounding the catapult. He missed, the shot ripping through the wood underneath. The other two crossbows affixed lines to the stern of the pirate ship, as if they were shooting sharks. Bolts rained down from the crowsnest, keeping most of the pirates in hiding. A ball of fiery pitch hung above the pirate ship for a moment and then, slowly descended on their single catapult. The next moments confirmed a new feeling, a new sound, this being the first time in battle the three heard cries of pain and agony; sounds of dieing among the enemy. Its effect slowed the enthusiasm of the 'new' crew, just as the Captain prophesied.

"PREPARE TO RAM!"

Four platoons of heavily shielded Light Striper moved to the bows. The armorer's crew and Luuft's crew moved to the stern. Not all dodged the bolts and arrows all the way to safety. Luuft received a bolt through his foot and the armorer's first crewmate died with an arrow in his neck.

The Albasla turned enough to ram the pirate ship at a thirty degree angle instead of smashing through the stern. The port side delivered the first blow. The slamming jarring motion knocked many off their feet. The pirate ship heaved sideways into the other ram. It crunched through the heavy timber at the waterline a few moments later. With the pirate ship caught broadside by the rams, the assault platoons plunged onto the pirate deck.

From the stern, one could only judge the battle by the horrid noises. Smoke obscured all vision beyond twenty feet. The now emptied deck provided for a margin of safety for the wounded who were carried back to the doctor, which now included the hobbling Vauk. The wounds were barbaric: hacks and holes, burns and arrows, mangled limbs....and everywhere, blood. Vauk couldn't verify who he treated.

The war tubas sounded 'recall.' Troopers slowly backed off the pirate ship as the crossbows strove to set her afire. All wounded and most of the dead returned to the ship. The pirates had to fend for themselves. The boarding bridges raised, throwing a few pirates into the sea and a few more onto deck. No quarter was asked, none given. The men in the crowsnest fired again, even though sighting targets through the smoke and the movement of the ships prevented much accuracy.

"PRE-PARE TO DIS-EN-GAGE!"

Sails flew by Vauk and Brey. They dropped to the deck as the booms reversed so the command could be obeyed. Then, as the sails grabbed the wind, the booms raised and a wrenching twisting sound commenced as the Albasla backed off the rammed pirate ship. A loud splintering noise declared the rams free. Most bolts and arrows ceased; the worst of the battle over.

Luuft gathered his friends for the purpose of examining the course of the battle and the damage. Brey called this barbaric, though she headed fore with the others. Luuft grabbed a piece of timber for a crutch. The pirate's bolt hadn't done any real damage. They moved along the gunwale watching the water, which soon filled with bodies, most without uniforms. The pirate ship listed badly, if the Albalsa didn't back up any faster, she'd soon be entangled in the pirate ship's rigging. Some Light Striper, with the standard broadaxe, stood at-the-ready for this possibility. What was peculiar and unique, to the four, simply went as standard operating procedure for the crew.

Once at the bow, the seriousness of the onslaught engulfed them. Parts of bodies, of broken helmets, of bashed-in shields, of broken wood and bent mental, littered the area. The two crossbows disappeared, maybe into the sea. An arrow went whizzing overhead. The corpses were collected for proper burial, at least for the Light Striper. Dead pirates ended in the sea.

Brey looked over to the sinking pirate ship. She witnessed desperate actions: men trying to help other men, men still shooting arrows, men finding something to cling to as the ship went under, men creeping out on the masts and yardarms to find haven on the Albalsa, only to be shot off by those in the crowsnest. This ugliness, this wretched horror, this living vision of hell, fire and all, firmly etched itself in Brey's mind. She would demand an explanation of this....this abhorrence....And not just from Captain Ellom, but also from the ship's chaplain. She started to turn away from the entire scene, to curl up in the cabin, to sleep.

"Brey! Brey! Look to the ship's rail!" Cried Vauk. "You know those 'things', don't you?"

Brey stumbled and turned. She looked and went white with rage and horror. The deck hatch now opened, 'things' dressed in greyish robes with gaunt faces streamed up from the hold. Any pirates in their way were hideously butchered by their teeth and nails. A few, recognizing their plight, stood at the rail, begging for help. Perhaps a hundred hooded figures soon filled the deck. An ensign called for a boat to rescue them.

"Ensign!" Roared Sarg. "Do you have permission to board that ship?"

"Those women will die, Sir."

"Those are NOT women. They are beasts from Hell, sent by the damned evil one himself."

"You don't know that!..... Get ready to shove off!"

Sarg drew his broadaxe. "Come with me or you're dead!"

The ensign paused, cursed, but went with Sarg.

"Watch that so-called woman on the stern platform. Do you see her?"

"Yes."

"Good. Tell me, what is this 'woman' doing?"

"Why, she's bending over, to help......MY....Damn...."

"Having a problem, ensign?

"She's eating .....eating ....the pirate."

"Yes! Now still want to rescue these cannibals?"

"NO.......nosir, sir, thank you, sir."

"Just trying to educate you junior officers." Said Sarg as he put his broadaxe away.

Brey burst open with rage. First she cursed, then cried. Finally she picked up a crossbow, shooting as many 'things' as possible. The ensign, declaring the women to be unholy cannibals, ordered his platoon to shoot them. Their greenish blood immediately identified the 'pale ladies'. Within moments, none were living.

Brey kept shooting long after the pirate ship's hulk sunk. Vauk stood beside her, waiting for her rage to dissipate, to empty itself out of her, forever. As the double moons rose, out of bolts and energy, she began to sob. Vauk put his arm around her and they slowly made their way through the debris and destruction to their cabin on the other ship. For Brey, this ending dawn spoke of two battles; each won in its own peculiar way.

While still recovering at Haaf North, Treh called for a scribe to record the events surrounding the platoon's exploits into the Dark Land. The scribe appeared confused by this, indicating that he thought their commissioning, by the King, sent them to find Krucik's home and guard it.

"That is correct." Said Treh. "But that isn't what transpired. There is simply too much here that defies my reasoning. Too much evidence that indicates we're all part of 'something else' that includes both the Holy One, Blessed be His Name, and the damned. Nor do I believe that we have much time to prepare."

"So you disobeyed the King." The scribe returned.

Quickly realizing the scribe existed in a domain foreign to his, Treh changed topics and tactics. "I want three copies of this report. I will read and seal two of them before they are dispatched; the third is my copy. They will be ready by.." Treh paused as he thought the timing. "By the first moon tonight. Have riders ready to leave before the second moon."

"I will do all except the last. That is beyond the scope of my scribal responsibilities." The young man announced coolly.

"If you don't do it, you'll find yourself unemployable. Scribes without fingers ......Get the message, you fat oaf."

Treh's threat put the scribe to diligent work. The report Treh dictated covered one long scroll. And though the scribe missed no words, his attitude acknowledged him as disbelieving or else as altogether overwhelmed by the content. No matter, he completed the scrolls on time, the copies verified by the post Staff Master and sent off prior to the second moon's arrival.

The two copies first went to D'Ka. From there, the King's copy headed down to Krabo; the copy for Vosnob headed towards the Wall, no one knowing exactly which outpost or tower might be visited by Vosnob. Within two cycles, Treh received confirmation that both reports were safely delivered. That confirmation, however, totally ignored the horrendous problems it caused at both destinations.

As per the new policy, the King's copy first went to the committee of three; Jabbi, the Captain and Etan. They were stunned. The organization of the Kyykki combined with the episode of the dragon indicated their foe had anticipated the Haafian response. Thus pointing to the dreadful fact that the spies had done their work well. Treacherous and greedy Haafians were permanently written into the equation; an equation that sought to undermine Haaf's future.

The item concerning the four hundred foot White Eagle: the committee would have liked to censure the report. But the truth is the truth, as testified to by the five survivors. This bird created such a stir in the imagination. Was it sent by the Holy One? Such happenings, 'miracles' were recorded. The interpretation became problematic as well; the huge eagle was not the King, not controlled by the King, nor did the King even know such eagles existed. Perhaps no one actually did. And then, for what end did this knowledge apply? Would the eagle ever appear again? Were there more of these birds? How and where do they dwell?

Before advising the King, the three wisely summoned the Council of the Church Elders, an independent body of the erudite sages, at least in public's mind, to discuss the matter. They could gather within the cycle. The Council of the Elders needed to travel from the north end of Lake

Buda. Until such time, the three explained that they studied a 'rather technical' report that required interpretation for the King's understanding.

Calling upon the Council of the Elders is a particularly serious matter. These persons represented the core of orthodoxy, the most learned of the Faith. Supposedly, they detached themselves from politics and economics, having been called by the Holy One to a life of study and meditation. From time to time, they issued pronouncements for the populace, most of which were never read; the topics being too esoteric. At other times, everyone listened, for the Elders answered a request by the King, or the High Council or, in a small number of cases, an ordinary serf. Whether the information was utilized or not mattered little: in either case, their directive became the bottom line: nothing existed beyond their final utterance. For tens of hundreds of cycles this standard practice continued.

Long before the two cycles turned, a lone raggedy man entered the city and silently proceeded to the High Council Hall. In one arm, he held a strange staff: it hooked at the upper end. Over his shoulder hung a leather bag, very worn. His grey hair parted in the middle, and then braided down over his ears, a style seen only in some old parchments, but an ageless style for the Yldans. However his aged face disguised whether he was a Haafian or an Yldan. An unusual nuance surrounded him, causing people to open doors for him, and no one bothered to ask for his identification. Now he stood before the door to the room where the Council of Three ate. With a gesture from his crooked staff, the guard moved from the door and the door opened. He casually strolled in taking off his leather bag, he turned and faced the three, who stood at their table, speechless.

"Let's get to work, friends. I have some information for you." His voice even understated his looks. Here, the Head of the Council of Elders, probably the only 'known' Elder behaving like a serf. The three bowed from the waist in respect, and then obeyed the Elder by sitting down.

"Might I trouble you for some tea?" His tone was soft, yet it obligated one to obey.

Etan poured another cup and slid it across the table.

"Thank you. Its been a long walk." He took a sip and returned to the matter at hand. "If we understand correctly, credible information is needed concerning a huge white eagle, theology of the evil one, and some items concerning the King."

"That is correct." Jabbi said.

"First, the Eagle is a special bird, but not a sacred one. Long ago there were thousands of them. They lived in this land, until driven out by our civilization and our wanton destruction of their environment. Stealing their eggs is recorded in our history....... Most stupid...... Where they went is somewhat of a rough conjecture: try north of the Dark Lands." He paused for another sip of tea.

"North of the Dark Lands?" The Captain puzzled.

"Should you believe that the Holy One only created Haaf with its two races and the Dark Lands? If the truth be known, we haven't begun to explore this gift of ours. Yet we blindly and stupidly insist that we are all there is. Be not so presumptuous, my friends."

Three men flushed with embarrassment, not just about the Elder's admonition, but also concerning the implications for the future. The idea that another whole civilization or whatever, lay far beyond the boundaries of the world they presently knew, unsettled them. Moreover, the immense power of the Holy One racked their thinking.

"Now, as for the evil one. Remember your lessons. He is not created, like you and I. Therefore he is immortal. However, he cannot act with assistance from others. No more than you and I can act or live independently. His goal is to rule. But he can only be strong when his followers are strong and when his followers have what he desires most, souls."

Etan and the Captain drew back, aghast. Such horrid thoughts hadn't entered their minds.

"Then the evil one needs people to carry out his work?"

"What do the events of the immediate past tell you?"

"Well put." Jabbi commented. "Most of us just refuse to admit the fact that we can be bought, bribed or otherwise coerced into being unfaithful. Not one of us is invulnerable."

"Thank for the cheerful message." Retorted Etan.

"As for the King. Why has he been set up as a 'special gift' from the Holy One? And to the exclusion of most everyone else? There is no modicum of fairness here and certainly no justice. Beyond that, if what you've done isn't corrected, will not even the serfs find they have no personal stake in the future?... So, its all up to the King, isn't it? ....Now is the optimal time to retrieve the King from his cloud prison." Graciousness filled the Elder's pointed words.

The three easily discerned the Elder spoke from the heart and from love for all the people. He finished his tea and rose to leave. He threw his leather bag over his shoulder and reached for his crooked staff. "I have answered your questions?"

"Indeed. That and more. There is much here for us to disseminate." Etan replied.

"Then I have ended my work here. Thanks for the tea, my friends. Now I must meet my grandson." He patted his leather bag. "We're going fishing."

The incredulous three smiled at each other as the Elder rambled down the hallway and out the door. "Going fishing!?" They all thought. Here indeed was an extremely special man: an Elder.

The dispatch to Vosnob had some difficulty reaching him, not that he broke contact with his forces, but that he remained constantly on the move, making additional decisions appertaining to new defensive measures for the 'Wall'. The runner found him and Yganak located some fifteen miles west of Battle.

Running Cloud had departed for the mountains. This a matter now involved his people more fully. His people and their skills were essential for victory. That much Oros made extremely clear.

Vosnob accepted the dispatch and read it while he and Yganak rode to the next outpost. His face grew dark, foreboding.

"The report is that bad?"

"Perhaps. The Church Guard platoon sent by the King, to locate Krucik's home, was ambushed, then saved by a huge white eagle that not only plucked the Kyykki from the ground, but dropped them from the sky to kill more Kyykki."

"This is serious?"

"There's no reason to doubt the authenticity. This Treh even knows about the taller Kyykki and writes about their battle formations: attack in three parallel formations acting in coordination with each other."

"Impossible. Such mentality means that the soulless ones might be 'getting' souls................ I don't know if that's a question or the truth...... Either way its dangerous."

The seriousness of the letter caused them to slow down the entire column. Conversing about weighty issues is difficult at a canter. Now, reining the stripers to a walk, they continued.

"I believe we shall soon see scaling ladders and maybe towers from the Kyykki." Suggested Yganak.

"But we aren't prepared for them, are we?"

"No.....Nothing save hand-to-hand combat. We'll never have the numbers for that. We'll check to see what the armory can provide......I don't care for this escalation. Fighting soulless ones is one thing, but now its beginning to resemble the feudal ages."

"I'm not sure I understand you, my friend."

"Its just that in the feudal ages, we fought each other. Real people killing real people. In our hearts, we aren't prepared for that type of war, none of us."

"Give the Evil One credit, Yganak, he seldom runs out of obstacles for us......Maybe we still have time........ We're not killing frogs anymore. We're killing the worshippers of the Evil One......That motivation, which is the truth, ..."

A galloping messenger riding a sweating striper caught up to the column. The Staff Master brought the carefully sealed document to Vosnob. The document's authors were the Council of Three.

"I hate to get this much mail, keeps interfering with the work." Vosnob snapped as he torn it open. He read the contents silently to himself, then, without comment, passed it to Yganak to read.

"Don't just keep your mouth shut. Tell, what do you think?"

"Basically, the Elders confirm our discussion. The eagle is for real. So too is the plan of the Evil One to escalate. And, the King needs to be glued somewhere, if only for the people's benefit."

"Pretty much my thoughts as well. I want to explore this eagle matter further. This 'Treh', I'm sending him to find the bird or birds. He'll have a ship and an augmented platoon. Tell him to head west and then north."

"Why west? There's nothing out there but water."

"Maybe, maybe not. You read the report."

Before long, another dispatcher, armed with the request for an assignment from Vosnob to Treh, galloped off for Haaf North.

Vosnob told Yganak, "It's time for the final battle."

Yganak deliberately choose not to answer.

Three dawns later, the rising sun up brought high seas. It also found a rested foursome headed east in a tiny single sailed raft, one patched together from wreckage of the pirate ship. Their lateen sail only filled to half in the weakening breeze, causing the raft to shudder each time the waves careened over the bow, keeping each of them thoroughly soaked. Their vision of the Albalsa and its safety rapidly diminished. Now these landlubbers became victims not only of the sea, but also of any of the high finned sharks, of any change in weather conditions, or, of any pirates sailing between them and the distant shore. A few gifts brought them encouragement; Captain Ellom's directions and a map of the coast line, provisions for a week and three casks of fresh water. Luuft brought the weapons he secreted in his cabin upon his initial embarking at Pinduala.

The bench seat that held the stern together occupied the less-frail but not-yet-fully-recovered Brey: exhausted enough to sleep even knowing that three not-so-experienced men were handling the raftt.

"Ellom really didn't give you a time frame for making land, did he?" Vauk asked Sarg.

"With this tub, he didn't dare to. Its not exactly like riding a Striper. But I suspect that we aren't more than one or two sun sets away."

"You mean we're stuck here for the night?" Luuft broke in, worried. "And how do we manoeuvre in twilight?"

"The same as any dummy would do on land." The now awake Brey blurted. "Follow the stars." She still reclined on the bench, her head resting upon a bag of supplies.

"So you're the new morale officer!"

"Why not? You certainly didn't put in for it!"

"All right!" Sarg expressed himself commanding tones. "This verbal battle is ended. Its going to be sufficiently difficult for all of us as it is, even more."

"Are you intimating that a woman will cause more problems than she cures?"

"Possibly. I don't want to sound harsh, but women are not part of the Light Striper. And you're a wounded one at that."

"At that? Am I just a burden?....No, I bother your consciences. I force you to think of women in new, different ways, just by being here....That,.. I believe,...is something quite positive."

"Perhaps it is, but give us a ten thousand cycles to think about it."

"No way!" Cried Brey, as she kicked Vauk in the rear.

"AYE!" He bellowed and went overboard.

Sarg reached out with a pole and redepositted him in the boat.

"Do anything close to that again Brey, and we'll all know you love the soggy doctor. And.....afore you open your mouth, if you even attempt a stunt like that again, you'll be carrying the biggest pack once we reach land. I hope I've made myself clear."

"Yes, sir." She mumbled, yet still very pleased with herself.

"I'm not about to lose a good trooper because of some silly lover's thing." Sarg finished his sermonette.

"But these charges you make have no factual basis." Protested Vauk.

"Since when did love or does love need concern itself with something as stupid and insipid as facts." He replied.

The midday heat increased to the point where no one remained awake. The four slumped and rested, dangerously oblivious to anything that might happen. The shadow passed over them, several times, totally unwitnessed. Its slow careful sweeps over the boat presented an image of a caretaker. And, until the first moon rose, the shadow sojourned with them. Shortly before the rising the shadow dove, plucking up a high finned shark that became too inquisitive about the raft. Much later, as Luuft roused himself, the shadow quietly glided to the north and disappeared.

"LAND!....LAND!" Yelled Luuft waking up everyone with his good news.

Sarg jumped to his feet. "What land?"

"Look at those gleaming lights dead ahead."

"That means a village. Could be trouble. Pirate village....Trim the sail and head us to the north."

Vauk, now alert, wrenched the tiller from its old position and forced it to turn the raft almost ninety degrees. "That should do the job. But I don't understand the lights. We're supposed to be too far north."

"Naturally. Just like twin-hulled ships don't exist. And just like the Light Striper is totally ignorant of anything that can float. We better be careful about everything." Commented Luuft. Then he began to re-check the weapons he brought. "I wanted to save this for later. However, your appreciation might be greater if I show you now."

"Wonderful, strange lights of an unknown village, Brey still sawing wood, an uncharted seacoast and you want to play games. May your trinket be worthy." Vauk, the cynic, dryly proffered.

The insult provoked Luuft to heave his bag into the corner of the boat. Then, miscalculating the reach of the boom, Luuft let it swing perpendicular to the boat to maintain the boat's new heading. This action resulted in Luuft whacking himself in the back of the head, knocking himself unconscious.

"Well," Sighed the pragmatic Sarg. "We now have a hospital ship. One doctor and one crew and some stupid surprize in Luuft's bag."

A small craft running parallel to rather significant waves is almost tantamount to suicide, that's how any sailor will explain it. Landlubbers who don't know this precious information pay an incredibly high price for it. No sooner did the raft swing its bow north than the first wave tumbled over the low gunwale, almost swamping it. Brey tumbled from her perch on the stern seat into the foam and supplies. The following wave proceeded to half-capsize them, only by Sarg and Vauk throwing themselves against the port side of the boat, did it right itself.

Sarg took immediate action: he jammed the tiller back to its old position. Vauk grabbed the boom and mustled it back to its former position. Its line broke, forcing him to hold it. Then came another wave. This one came over the corner of the stern. The craft now lay even lower in the water, but as its direction regained the original course, the waves no longer threatened to capsize the craft.

"Turn Luuft over before he drowns!" Vauk yelled to Sarg.

The task proceeded quickly; both Luuft and Brey were tied to the mast with their drooping heads well above the water level. Sarg tossed a piece of rope to Vauk. The boom made secure, Vauk joined Sarg in bailing. Brey appeared somewhat alert, but fear showed in her eyes. She said nothing, even when he saw Luuft tied up next to her. When the water receded to ankle depth, the men allowed themselves a break.

"Brey, you strong enough to be untied?"

"Only if you can promise NO more 'sink the boat' games, Sarg."

"I don't believe I'm able to do that. I'm only half the sailor you are."

"Set her free, Sarg." Vauk interrupted.

Brey turned her head and sneered at him.

"I'm serious, Brey. When we hit shore, you'll need all the strength possible."

Brey realized he wasn't being the wise guy, but actually was being considerate. Nevertheless, she furnished him with another immoderate sneer.

Luuft's incomprehensible groaning and curses were the tell-tale signs he'd soon return to his normal self. That left three to keep the boat moving west AND only west. Bailing continued. The water level dropped rapidly, until it barely covered one's foot. At this point, they rested.

But rest, however much needed, however much desired, allocated itself to the future. Within what seemed barely a few breathes, the boat struck something with such force as to dislodge two hull planks. Water thrust itself in so swiftly that the boat literally sunk around them. Then it acquiesced faster than it began. The boat leveled itself as if resting on the bottom with the warm water being about knee deep. Waves now splashed in over the stern and then went running out the bow. Even though only a few waves were of the serious variety, those few methodically demolished their boat.

"Untie Luuft afore he drinks too much of this salt water."

Brey untied him while Vauk undertook the job of getting him to his feet. Luuft's sense of balance hadn't returned. Sarg helped to steady him as Brey gathered and then tethered all the equipment to the mast. Then she came and huddled with the others. In the darkness, hope receded as did the waves.

I'm not sure we can do anything until dawn." Sarg said. A sense of dreariness stuck in his voice. "I don't know how far shore is or even what we're stuck on, or how stable it is."

"I'm always fascinated by your optimism." Vauk, pummelled by a wave, spit out the words.

"And I suppose YOU have more pleasing options for all of us!" Brey half-sneered and half-cried. She reached the end of her strength, a mental strength which kept her injured body moving.

"No, I don't. ....Well, if you haven't all ready, pray to the Holy One, blessed be His Name. Pray for our survival."

Brey stared at this man with amazement. Faith meshed itself into her life, but she never once thought it valid for Vauk. Waiting for dawn, the four stood about the wave battered mast, silently praying as they observed their boat disappear, board by board.

Dawn's haziness brought enough problems without being further modified by the mist. Vision persisted in being extremely poor. The one comfort they thanked the Holy One for concerned the temperature: it remained remarkably warm all night.

As the dawn became fuller, the troopers examined their perilous situation. Except for the planks they stood on and the mast, the boat no longer existed. Most of their supplies remained intact, but waterlogged, rendering some of the boxed food inedible.

"Which way is the shore?" Asked Vauk.

"That way." Sarg pointed westward.

"Then let's get moving. We aren't helping ourselves by standing here."

"But how deep is the water?" Brey asked fearfully. "I can't swim."

"It doesn't matter." Sarg added. "We'll take it step by step. Those of us who swim will help the others. Each of us will carry some of the supplies."

Luuft had regained most of his sensibilities. He grabbed the weapons bag and the last keg of water. He also took the initial step out of the defunct boat. The rest watched, not knowing what to expect. Nothing happened. The water remained less than knee deep, even after Luuft paced off ten feet.

"Let's move." Sarg said. "We'll follow Luuft, single file. Brey, you're in the middle. I want five steps between each of us." He paused to pick up the rope. "Luuft, tie this over your shoulder and pass it to me."

Soon a single file of shriveled-skinned troopers slowly made their way west, utilizing the sun to stay on course. The melting haze immensely increased their vision. Fewer waves now caught them off-guard. The scene that slowly appeared before them indicated a plain of shallow water extending westward into a denser haze. They heard waves breaking, demonstrating a near-by shore. The implications of this impacted everyone simultaneously: they ran. Which, as they later realized, became a good two mile trek. As they finally plodded onto the sand beach, they noticed the remains of their boat scattered about.

"Strange, very strange." Mumbled Sarg.

"This whole mission is strange."

"No, you idiot! Look about! Did these piles of timber all come from one boat? Seems this area of the Upper Sea might be a 'shipwreck beach'."

Luuft glanced around and nodded his head in agreement. "We certainly aren't the first visitors here."

They stumbled their way towards a group of unrecognizable trees, but trees that would, nevertheless, provide a welcome shelter from the relentless sun. There they inventoried what supplies remained. The water kegs stayed intact; the breads spoiled. The weapons needed cleaned, and the crossbows' strings required drying before they were useable. The paper and pens, securely wrapped in waterproof skins, remained undamaged.

Luuft cut some branches off a shrub and pushed them into the sand. Then he removed his shirt and hung it there. On two other poles he turned his boots over. Vauk followed.

"It feels good to dry off." He claimed.

"Well mind your manners, there's a lady present."

"I guess she wants to sit about in wet clothes, from what I can see. Still has her boots on."

"She'll dry off her way."

"Thank you, Sarg." Said Brey while she emptied out her boots and placed them on some poles.

"Until we get an idea of our location. We'll stay put.... Brey, you and Vauk take the first watch. Get us up at high mid-noon. Guard the water..... And everyone get a drink."

The assignments worked well, especially as the first watch lasted less than a fraction of the dawn, allowing Brey some time to recuperate. By the next dawn, Brey had dried off and rested. Luuft shot a wild pig with his new 'toy'; a regular size crossbow that had the same style head and rope as did the one on the bow of the Albasla, only in miniature. During their first cooked meal in two sunsets, they planned to leave the beach for some higher ridges they observed. The distance appeared a relatively easy march except for the fact that this 'jungle' had no paths, no roads. It offered them masses of vines, creatures unfamiliar to them, and a genuine uncertainty about the evening.

From the angle of the sun, Sarg hypothesized that they might be above the Dark Lands. Should this be true, not only did they travel in totally unexplored territory, but also in a land that never showed up on the maps. But, from Sarg's position, this way of infiltrating the Dark Lands not even the Kyykki could suspect.

At the bleak cloud-streaked dawn, Sarg passed out the weapons to everyone, the rest of the items were divided up and packed. Luuft, acting as point man, carried the least. Brey got to carry the ham.

As they were entering the jungle, Vauk cried out. "Look! The shadow! The shadow is here!"

Before anyone else responded, the shadow darted into the sun, making itself all but invisible to the other three.

"Its there………. Probably never left us really……. Just wish I knew whether it was friend or foe." Remarked Sarg.

The second moon lit the top of the knoll when the exhausted quartet finally rested. Their five mile journey, as estimated by Sarg, existed in reality as a living nightmare. It began with Luuft hacking a tunnel through the intensely dense underbrush and sticky vines. Difficult as this was, it was also the easier piece of the trek. The underbrush, after some three hundred feet, gave way to branchless trees which soared hundreds of feet into the air, and once there, lavishly spread an umbrella canopy. Sunlight could not penetrate the lushness of the canopy, nor did the canopy submit itself to allow moisture out. The resultant environment, one appreciated only by the thousands and thousands of unknown insects, quickly drained their strength. The grey semi-darkness combined with mucky bare surfaces of this high humidity 'place', did little to help morale. Unnerving sounds constantly invaded their ears, but only shadows were observed; shadows which did not stir. Aromas of putrefying vegetation and who-knows-what-else assaulted their sensibilities.

Thus, over the course of travel, the tension, the pressure and the inhospitable environment thoroughly devitalized each of them. The small clearing on the knoll offered the first glimpse of the sky since mid-dawn and the first breathable air as well. Luuft passed the water keg to everyone, leaving it empty. Brey shared the rest of the roasted ham.

Believing no one about, nor could be, Sarg allowed everyone time to sleep. They would try to remove the garbage smell and the muck they carried up from the jungle in the morning. Luuft suggested they might find game up here to eat as well.

They all woke to the smell of burning wood, of clean smelling clothes and something like boiling stew. White rounded clouds dotted the clear blue sky. The image evoked a perfect unreality.

"About time you all be up. See the sun? Its at mid-dawn and we got a few miles left to hike. This be unsafe here, but better than your stompin' in the jungle."

They stared at the bronze-red Yldan who sat by the fire, calmly stirring the stew. He appeared quite young. His trousers, though worn, were Light Striper issue. Soft leather moccasins completed his attire.

"Come on, up! My name be Blue Turtle. And," He said pointing to each one. "You are Sarg, and Breel, and the docter Vauk. Welcome to the Zuda Marsh. You just traveled through the worst part of it that anyone ever choosed."

Without knowing exactly why, they obeyed this Blue Turtle. Breakfast, actually lunch, filled the empty stomachs and tasted well. Brey, who quickly yet softly corrected Blue Turtle concerning her real name, found a secure spot over the edge of the knoll to wash up and change. The four found their boots in ruins; neither the salt water nor the wretchedness of Zuda Marsh exhibited a compassion for leather. As they checked over their crossbows and washed up Blue Turtle quietly burned their filthy clothes.

"Not to disturb you, friend. But how are we going to get along without our clothes?" Sarg questioned.

"Vosnob set up everything for you. All that you want is available at the outpost." He tossed each of them a sack filled with new clothing. He said quietly. "Please remember, you all be dead."

"How?" demanded Vauk.

"Seems you got on a ship called de Albasla."

"SO!"

"She be a pirate ship. You all got on the wrong ship and its no secret to anyone what pirates do to loyalists."

"Wonderful!" Luuft tried to smile. "Not only are we lost, but dead."

"Actually, neither of the two be true." Blue Turtle spoke with a straight face. "This be north of the Dark Lands. From the village we see the Dark Smoke Mountains."

"Village? You said outpost." Luuft questioned.

"You don't trust much. Village ...Outpost... who cares."

Blue Turtle's understatement gave rise to the first laugher in a while. Luuft refused to comment further.

Meanwhile, Blue Turtle picked up the kettle and his short bow and headed down the knoll at a trot. The others grabbed what equipment remained and pursued the Yldan. They caught up to him as he entered the village, some three miles south.

Gargantuan pine trees camouflaged the small village. Behind a briarwood barricade twelve long houses spread themselves in a semi-circle. Platforms high in the trees reminded the party of the crowsnest on the Albasla: they performed the analogous function, with the exception that signals in the Yldan village were those of birds. As Blue Turtle promised, the view was extraordinary....and ominous. The Dark Lands' sky, belching smoke and all, not more than ten miles away, as the birds flew.

Perhaps fifty Yldans inhabited the village, approximately half women. However, no children lived in the village. Sarg's military experience told him this village stood as but one of many 'villages' set up to watch over the Dark Lands. He also recognized the 'village' as temporary. Respect for the Yldans' dedication occupied Sarg's thoughts.

"You don't stand in the doorway, move in. We be friendly, especially because of Vosnob."

As they entered the defensive compound, the Yldans surrounded them, gawking at their strange appearance. These Haafians, with their brownish skins, slanted eyes and brown and blonde hair were a genuine novel entity. They did share language, or rather a close proximity thereof.

"Its been a very long time since we've seen many Haafs, you probably noticed that all ready.......We have two long homes set up for you. When you return from your bath, we'll eat. Tomorrow I'll lead you to 'the edge'. From there you'll begin your mission. I'll send word to Vosnob for you. Any questions?" Asked Blue Turtle.

"Yes. But first, We appreciate your most generous hospitality. And thank you for going out-of-your-way for us." Sarg began.

"The Holy One, does not He expect as much from us?" Blue Turtle interrupted.

Sarg continued, nodding his head in acknowledgement of Blue Turtle's testimonial to the Faith. "I'm not acquainted with 'the edge'. What exactly is this 'edge' that prevents you from continuing with us?"

"You will need to wait until tomorrow." He turned and headed for another of the long houses.

The houses assigned to the troopers were pointed out. Brey found herself lead away by a few women to a smaller long home towards the rear of the compound. The baths, intensely hot and steaming, also gave off the aromatic smell of healing spices.

Another set of new uniforms awaited them as did new weapons, each appropriately modified by the Yldans. Wide-brimmed leather hats and soft moccasins replaced their hoods and boots, respectively. The uniform material being twice as thick and strong as normal issue, provided them with the knowledge that over 'the edge' the terrain became much rougher. Their tunics, modified to waist length with a leather belt, also gave rise to the need for freedom of movement. An extra uniform was included with their other supplies.

The extravagant supper supplemented by dancing, brought a kinder ending to the dawn than the previous dawns. The Yldan story dance depicted the perils of living. But it also functioned as a dance of hope, for the Holy One, depicted in the form of a bird flew everywhere to aid His people. When the eagle's shadow fell on the good, they smiled and rejoiced. Conversely, when the eagle's shadow overtook the evil and the unrepentant, they immediately perished. The impact of this orthodox symbolism imbedded itself on the four. Birds began to take on new meanings for them.

The next morning found them traversing a narrow path leading from the village to 'the edge'. Blue Turtle instructed them concerning the two essential items for survival over 'the edge': water and weapons. The Troopers believed they carried more than enough of each. Their revised instructions now altered their destination; their departure for home sent them down a river which ran 'supposedly' between the volcanoes. Such were the final words of Blue Turtle before he tossed the ropes over the side of 'the edge'.

Luuft cautiously approached this 'edge' and peered over. "Its a few hundred feet down!" He exclaimed.

"Three hundred until you reach the rapids at the bottom." Blue Turtle said flatly. "You'll discover a series of nitches along the cliff wall. They're fifty feet apart. That's a rough estimate, of course."

"Thanks for the warning." Luuft dryly commented.

Blue Turtle paid no attention to the remark. He simply reacted by handing Luuft the first pair of heavy leather gloves. "Lower the supplies separately, but keep your swords." Blue Turtle advised Sarg. "May the Holy One watch over you." He silently disappeared into the forest.

The four resumed their original mission, full of misgivings and anticipation of what mysteries lay before them. While descending the treacherous ledges of the great cliff, Vauk observed their uniforms' coloration to be identical to that of the cliff. Even the rope had been made an off-yellow color. He appreciated this extra margin of safety.

"Do you enjoy the smell?" Asked Brey.

"You mean the fact that this place resembles an unkempt latrine?" Quipped Luuft.

"Exactly."

"Have you ever worked with a soft yellow mineral named sulfur?" Sarg's way of terminating conversations often worked. "Listen, we're defenseless here on the cliff. We're not carrying these weapons for nothing. The quicker we're down, the better off we'll be. Let's keep moving."

The final ledge placed them squarely in the middle of a stream that probably eroded most of the cliff. Its undrinkable noxious water provided a reason for thankfulness. They fully understood the value of their water kegs, heavy or not.

From a hillock nearby, Luuft surveyed the terrain. "Its empty." He told the others. "No trees, no vegetation at all to speak of. There's no evidence that any other source of water will materialize. The closer we get to the volcanoes, the darker everything becomes. Ash and soot, I presume. I did see some yellow marshes. They bubble."

"Then we're avoiding that area." Brey firmly announced.

"I thought Sarg was the leader." Vauk said off-handedly.

A typical Brey sneer answered.

The stultified area incorporated an element of soullessness: no nurturing influences existed, only a painful deadness. The air kept passively still, empty of energy, even the stream they followed seemed directionless. In the distance rose huge hollow and blackened tubes, some dripped red-molten slag from their pinnacles, others like never-ceasing chimneys poured soot and smoke into an indifferent sky. However, most waited, lifeless or apathetic, a community of the dead, an appropriate loathsome monument to the damned evil one.

"Now that we've arrived, Sarg, what exactly are we to ascertain about this blasphemous world?"

"We're here for two reasons: to map out the landscape and the environment and, secondly, to get a fix on the real strength of the Kyykki."

"But," Retorted Vauk. "Others have done that all ready."

"Not true. There is no corrected or useful map of this area at present. And the spies that you refer to, never got as far inside the Dark Land as we presently are. Even the Yldans never went further than their outpost."

"Wonderful."

"Shut up, Luuft." Brey challenged him with a hardness unnoticed before now. "Let's get the job done."

Being wary of ambushes or what traps, let alone any bizarre type creatures, might exist in this vast wasteland, they judiciously kept to the hilltops and sheltered ridges to even out the equation. Brey and Sarg had crossbows at the ready; the other two kept a firm grasp on their swords.

Their trail meandered through the terrain in a southernly direction. Every mile Sarg paused to make some notes on his chart. Presently, they emerged from a long path-like channel that terminated on a ridge. Both, rather perplexingly, provided concrete verifications of being constructed, not natural, edifices. The ridge, from the bottom where the group stood, ran north and south, forming itself into an arc. The arc itself then stood before the first supposedly 'dead' volcano. The unreal scenario did not fit the pattern of anything heretofore seen.

"I have a strange feeling about this place. Its evil and threatening." Said Vauk.

"Maybe we're what's threatening to it." Suggested Luuft.

"Quiet." Demanded Sarg. "Everyone sit until I map this out."

"Why not get a better view from the ridge top?"

"Because, Brey, I fear there's something on the other side deliberately waiting for us."

"That's an unfair tactic, using fear."

"My administrative principles inform me to keep notes and make maps in safe places. I don't believe the other side of the ridge is synonymous with congeniality."

"But you have no evidence ...."

"I have my guts and my instincts, ...experience.... And you don't think of this channel and ridge as 'unnatural'?"

Brey thoughtfully kept her mouth shut. Her usual sneer never surfaced. Her appreciation for Sarg's wisdom grew.

When Sarg finished his cartography, he signaled for Luuft to climb the ridge; Vauk would trail him by fifteen feet. The ridge sloped easily for the first two hundred feet. But its open barrenness, being slippery as well, gave them men an uneasiness. The soft-packed yellow dirt easily came loose underfoot. The next thirty feet achieved an angle of some sixty degrees. The men crawled up the slope, which had become mucky. Luuft reached the top, where he found a wide level track. Then he dropped over the other side to investigate. Then he just as hurriedly ricocheted down the slope, passing Vauk. He refused to stop until he slid into Sarg.

"A giant yellow lake and there's 'things' in it." He puffed out in his excitement.

"How big?" Sarg calmly removed the cover from his mapping supplies.

"About eight or nine mile miles wide. Reaches all the way to the volcano."

Sarg made deliberate notations on his map. "How deep?"

"No idea. But deep enough for something to make Haafian size waves. And then there's clouds of darkness in the lake, like schools of black fish. It smells like a latrine, one made of sulfur, of course." He smiled impishly at Brey.

"Is there a beach on the other side?" Sarg asked, not removing his eyes from the map.

"About ten to twenty feet wide. Hard to tell because of the waves."

"Or because you only took a few breaths to explore the area?"

Luuft didn't respond. But Brey provided the equalizing 'I-goteven' sneer. Sarg packed up and lead the three up the ridge. Vauk received them at the summit.

"Its not fish, Sarg. Looks more frog eggs or tadpoles. But if that water is even half as bad as it smells, I can't explain their survival. That whole yellow lake is nothing but a cesspool with waves."

"I can smell that much for myself. I don't like it at all. Smells like a horde of Kyykki." Sarg examined the lake, finding Luuft's rapid observations to be quite accurate. "I owe you an apology, Luuft. Your reconnaissance is amazingly accurate."

"Thanks."

"Now, though I have dreadful premonitions about this place. We need to get some water samples for our report. Vauk, get the jar from the pack. You're going over and down to the beach."

Shortly, Vauk found himself on the softest beach in the world. The yellow muck claimed him all the way to his knees. He quickly retied the rope under his shoulders for safety. The wall behind him being too steep and too soft to climb, the rope became his only salvation. The unhealthiness of the putrid water needed no verification: it even had a tendency to curdle. The lake's very existence resisted various explanations, even the most primitive ones. Yet those 'things' in its malignant waters 'lived'. However, as those black 'things' refused to swim near shore, to capture them meant wading into the thick rancid liquid. He glanced upwards to see Sarg motioning him into the lake; a most unreasonable duty, he thought, but one he could not refuse.

One mucky step after another he moved into the yellow waves. As reticent as he was about entering the water, he now found one small benefit; the weight of the water packed the yellow dirt. He stood waist deep watching for a swarm of 'black things' to move closer to him. They suddenly did, with a horrid unbridled vengeance. They set upon Vauk to devour him. He felt their little razor sharp teeth rip and slash his trousers. He jammed his jar into the midst of the swarm and screamed at the top of his lungs.

"GET ME UP!......I'M BEING EATEN ALIVE!"

The first yank on the rope pulled him down into the water. He watched the ugly little beasties bit at his nose. They squashed in his hand like mealie bugs. The next pull dumped him on the shore, but the 'pests' refused to quit. They were no longer just scraping the skin. He began turning blood-red from their bites. The next pull bounced him up the soft cliff, where Sarg ripped his tattered clothes off him. Sarg and Brey squished another twenty of the 'pests' that latched onto his legs.

"Damn, this isn't natural at all. Its too corrupt." Muttered Sarg as he grabbed a wet cloth from Brey.

"Welcome to the Kyykki breeding ground. I believe they thought I might be their legitimate food." Vauk spit out disgustedly and then paused before his next enunciation. "The motive behind the creation of this 'lake' is rather obvious: it produces millions of the soulless ones. It also demonstrates betrayers in our midst. The evil one didn't construct this by himself."

The others just stared at Vauk. His assessment allowed no comforting assurances, but a vivid recognition of the powerful darkness that has the capability to snatch anyone. The existence of the 'lake' established that anguishing truth.

Vauk took the cloth and began to wipe himself down. "Get me that antiseptic. This quagmire can only produce an infection."

Brey produced the bottle of oily pine-smelling ointment. It was a particularly potent medicine, used for Kyykki wounds from the battlefields, where every bite brought great agony, fever and pain. After cleansing his body, he donned the uniform Luuft tossed to him. Brey finally and politely turned her back, preferring to act as guard.

"Well, there's your damn sample, Sarg.... You better find it profitable, because I'm telling you that I'm not going back again..... Too risky. Those 'things' will virtually eat you alive."

Sarg put his finger in the jar and withdrew it with a yelp. A 'thing' firmly imbedded itself on his finger. Luuft squashed it, but not before he also observed that the 'thing' resembled a miniature Kyykki, about a half-finger long. This did little to assuage the expression of contempt which covered his face.

"Welcome to the reproductive center of the kingdom of the evil one." Luuft said to no one in particular. "And we're here to challenge its authority." He murmured.

"If you want to preach, you'll have to enlist at the seminary."

"If that's what it takes to leave here, Vauk, I'd do it immediately."

"Wonderful!" Sarg half muttered, still shaking his bloody finger. "I have my volunteer to combat wickedness."

Luuft, surprized, wondered what Sarg planned. His wait ended just after Sarg swabbed some ointment on his finger. "Luuft, take this jar of vermin to the Yldan village. Find out what poisons they can offer us to exterminate the population of this lake. Then, send word to Vosnob about our findings so far and a copy of the maps as well."

"Are you sure we need kill these 'things', Sarg." Asked Brey. "It seems such a move would destroy our cover. We four can't fight the entire Kyykki...."

"Good point. Except that there is no guard for this place. It could easily be a full double moon cycle before they realize their new recruits are dead. Furthermore, by sacred covenant you know we are to engage evil and destroy it. There are no exceptions."

"Brey is right Sarg." Vauk added. "Before we destroy this lake's fetid contents, we better position ourselves miles away. In spite of being here during the 'daylight' and witnessing no protection for the lake, no one leaves their future army to fend for itself."

"But this is not, I repeat, not, regular army. The evil one has no sense of compassion. If those 'things' of his devour each other, then they are trained killers before they know what we even look like. He doesn't need all those countless billions..." Sarg paused to consider another ghastly proposition. "... And we haven't the foggiest conception of how many of these lakes exist."

"Its argument to argument, but you have the authority." Brey deliberately sidestepped the unwanted idea.

"Thank you, Brey...... Pick up the jar Luuft. We'll wait here for you. Be careful."

"And I thought you never cared about me." Luuft smirked as he picked up the jar and his 'special' crossbow.

"You really need that?"

"You expect me to crawl up the cliff?" And he left at a trot.

The others moved back to the channel and pitched their yellowish colored tent. Until Luuft returned Sarg worked on completing his maps,. Vauk collected data concerning the lake environment, and Brey, because of lowest seniority, got to maintain their camp.

Luuft sighted the base of the cliff when he heard shouting, screams and the honking of 'something'. If its dimensions equaled its volume, the 'honker' instantaneously became a creature he would do well not to challenge, so he told himself.

Sticking to the meagre cover offered by the eroded sides of the putrid stream, Luuft cautiously maneuvered himself to where the four-some touched bottom earlier. Then he glimpsed up the cliff.... almost dropping his crossbow. The awesome sight alienated him.

The monstrous honking creature figured large enough to secure its behemothic front feet on the bottom landing, fifty feet up. Its rear legs sunk into the stream, while its massive tail shifted back and forth, producing a cloud of bitter tasting yellow dust. His second look, after washing the dust from his eyes, showed the monster one hundred feet long, dark red in color, covered with yellow splotches and possessing a whip-like forked tongue. This tongue retrieved at least one Yldan, judging from the red blood running out the monster's mouth.

Luuft felt himself immediately engulfed with rage. It mattered little to him that the beast's smooth skin all ready held arrows or that the Yldans on the other landings engaged the beast with whatever weapons they found; namely rocks. He cocked the crossbow to maximum tension, tied the end of the rope to a large stone column, and crept up underneath the monster. Without a word, he aimed and shot. Then deftly jumped off to the side to reload.

The bolt caught the monster in the soft part under its chin. By sheer force it broke through the beast's skull, breaking the bone between it's eyes. Enraged, it stood solely on it's hind legs. The rope went taut, forcing the beast off balance. It staggered, then fell with the loudest obscene honk yet. It's enormous body dammed the stream and sent a final cloud of filthy yellow dust into the air. From a safe distance, Luuft sent another bolt into the writhing monster. This bolt entered its eye, demolishing the brain. The beast went limp.

Only at this point did the Yldans realize what transpired. A yell went up from those on the cliff and those on top. Luuft smiled and waved. A party lead by Blue Turtle quickly descended to meet him.

"How many of these 'things' do you have around here?" He asked.

"We really aren't sure. They patrol about the perimeter at irregular intervals."

"What happened? I thought you never came down here."

"Not usually. We had an order for sulfur to fill. We came with a guard, but this monster kept quiet. He killed three guards."

"Can you usually kill these 'things'?"

Blue Turtle turned away, angry. "Where are your priorities?.... You care so little for my people?.............. Three men killed...You say nothing."

Luuft paused for a most awkward time. "I apologize. Three good men lost to the beast....Three men who will not be able to destroy these 'little' monsters." Luuft handed his jar of Kyykki to blue Turtle. "We found a lake full of these horrendous things."

Blue Turtle, turned and bowed stiffly, a tacit acknowledgement of Luuft's apology. Then he peered inside the jar; a look of disgusting wonder filled his face. "So the damned things reproduce as if they are frogs. Frogs with teeth."

"Indeed, and there are billions of them, all floating and living in a cesspool. A very unnatural cesspool, at that."

"And the pool ..er...lake is guarded by monsters like this? We've never ventured inside as far as you have. Our poisons rely on time to work. And our bows don't have enough force to split open skulls." Said Blue Turtle.

"Neither, do ours. This crossbow is a new model, used on some ships.

Requires a long time to cock, but she'll punch through five inches of planking... Here, you keep this one." Luuft tossed him the weapon.

"Thanks."

"I returned for your assistance. Those jarred Kyykki ....."

"We have a problem."

"Why? All I require is some of your pink root. Can I persuade you to dump a few gallons into the lake?"

"That's the issue: our vermifuge is extremely potent, however deliberately poisoning the all ready polluted doesn't produce many casualties. By definition a poison is a substance foreign to the receiving party, such that the receiving party has a minimal defense mechanism. Therefore, the poison is fatal, provided it is a true poison for the appropriate organism."

"Thanks for the intellectual background. But I just need something synonymous with 'death to the Kyykki'. But you're informing me that nothing is available. That's not what I wanted to hear."

"You go too far.."

"Well, you have thirty or so of the bastards in your hand. Let's try those formulas on them. It shouldn't take too long for the best one to surface."

The Yldans erected a table near the top of the cliff. The entire community gathered and the chemists put their formulas on trial. Most had no perceivable effect, being that the immature Kyykki were stultified before the tests began. The addition of more poison into their putrid environment simply accelerated a normal principle of their lives. After all, the fetid lake never received any sanitation, just more filth.

That hypothesis caused Blue Turtle's brother to bring a simple chemical called 'bleach' to the table. His contribution brought about a hearty round of laughter.

"Why laugh at my contribution, friends." He said with a pronounced smile. "Your's have not faired well.... The principle behind a poison is that the receiver has nothing in its person by which to defend itself. Am I correct?"

Every head nodded.

"Good... Continue to follow....These abominations to the Spirit have a reticence to all poisons thus far. Why? Because they are nothing more than living poison themselves. A culture based on degradation...not just morally, as we all are accustomed to, but also physically. Think, until now, the breeding of these wretched soulless ones remained hidden. Today, using the Light Striper, the Spirit provides us with the solution....It is not obvious? The poison for the Kyykki is not more poison, but the opposite...... Purification,...Bleach!"

He smiled and then dropped one spoonful of dry bleach into a large jar. Within a breath, the Kyykki writhed in agony, then collapsed, dead. Now, a generous round of applause and cheers greeted the chemist.

"How much bleach is on hand? Blue Turtle queried.

"Only dry............twenty gallons."

"Then we go with twenty gallons. Before the second moon, the Kyykki of the lake will return permanently, to the deadness from which they emerged."

"Just one question, my friend." Luuft shouted across the table. "Just how do you propose to get the bleach into the lake? Do you have any engines?"

"I thought, this being a joint effort, that you would provide for us." Smiled Blue Turtle.

"Give me some time. We'll carry the parts with us. I'll need thirty five men."

At the rising of the first moon the Yldans gathered at the stream bed, deployed to follow Luuft to the rancid lake. They began by climbing over the monster's corpse. In spite of the ill-boding darkness, the argument for safety precluded any torches being lit. The expedition to the lake went as scheduled. While surprised by the problematic episode of the dead monster, the others concerned themselves more with Luuft's return and the poison. The promise of a clean lake enthralled Brey, who also associated the bleach with purification. She held such an ideal as her public, uncontested conviction.

Luuft estimated the range of the makeshift throwing machine to be two-tenths mile, at best. Sarg called an informal council to suggest that they concentrate the bleach within a small area of the lake. With his idea accepted, the machine set and readied, Sarg waited for the loading. If this proved effective, the Yldans would continue to 'clean up' the cesspool lake on their own.

Within a matter of several breaths, the machine initiated lobbing two gallon skins of bleach over the ridge. Blue Turtle acted as spotter. Each lob, re-adjusted by twenty feet, presented an arc pattern which, when pushed shoreward by the waves, formed an area of 'clean death' for the Kyykki caught within. To ascertain the results of their bombardment, some Yldans jumped the ridge and dragged part of the shoreline with a fishing net. Of the thousands of infantile Kyykki harvested in their net, none were viable.

In anticipation for another round of 'bleaching the lake', they pushed the machine into a carefully concealed cave excavated on the back side of the channel. A quiet celebration ensued, meaning lots of smiles, time for supper and some rest for Luuft. With the argument for bleach decisively conclusive, Sarg scribbled another note to Vosnob. "Be sure to add bleach and other antiseptics to our arsenal of machine bombs."

Baste's realignment of the New Knight's training regime proved a wise one, to a point. The numbers of those ex-nobles talented enough to form mounted squadrons resulted in numbers far less than expected. Of the original six squadrons authorized to receive such training, qualified recruits survived to form only four. Even so, Baste consistently refused to lower standards, which endeared him even more to Vosnob and the serfs, but produced obvious friction within the ranks of the ex-nobles.

To Baste too many ex-nobles refused to seriously incorporate their limitations into their 'self-perfect' image. That mirror of truth being normally excluded from their life-style. Thus, the number of traumatic training casualties and accidents ran twice the normal. The result finally produced a New Knight formation the strength of three squadrons, not the anticipated six.

The other training, Baste's demand for specialists, out-produced itself: the literacy rate among the New Knights ran both high and quite competent. Logistical concerns also promised a good future: the parallels between managing a large estate and that of a squadron or a platoon were sufficiently numerous that a crossover from one to the other became mainly a process of changing nomenclature.

The machine platoons received a mixed review: the effort involved to build the machines remained beneath the 'dignity' of some. Gath sponsored a few public and mandatory attendance 'whippings' that decisively put an end to such 'dignity'. Sweat became a cherished word in their vocabulary, especially because Gath also rewarded the productive troopers: the best got to fire the first shots. Others found reward by promotion to crew chief: the one who calculated the angle of fire and tension strength for each shot.

The sore spot became the one so identified at the first meeting called by Baste, that of the infantry. Even with public whippings there persisted an inborn rebellious spirit. "Nobles were created to ride!"

Ayhn did not consider this a ludicrous statement. This newly created group had no allusions about who they were and were not. Ayhn, pushed to the limit, responded with a hanging for one who refused to repent of his mutiny. Actually he did respond, but spitting in the well-respected squadron's chaplain's face only confirmed his intransigence. The man's followers rapidly dissipated, but more positive actions remained essential to the formation of a solid fighting force. Ayhn asked for an audience with Baste to discuss an idea that might substantially improve morale and quality of the infantry. It began by renaming them 'Phalanxers'. Ayhn's reply arrived in the form of an invitation to a 'long table' meeting.

Baste sat at the head of the candle-lit table. The scribes posted at the corners of the tent readied themselves, but, as usual they did not write anything. Gath found himself across the table from Ayhn. A rotund Chaplain, obviously of some influence, presented a new face at the table. Baste gave him the seat to the right.

Baste stood and everyone quieted. "Before we hear the reports of progress and 'other things'," His face rather stern, "Grant me the privilege of introducing Vosnob's favorite Chaplain, the mountain man, Oros." Then Baste half-innocently smiled at Oros, knowing the character all-too-well.

The chair slid back as Oros rose to shake hands with Baste. A devilish smile flashed from the mountain man's face as Baste, struggling to keep his composure, straightened out his fingers.

"I thank you all for this opportunity to speak to you. I bring blessings from Vosnob, to be sure, but I also bring you grim tidings from events of the Dark Lands. When I met with my fellow chaplains this morning, I found myself immensely disappointed. The abounding attitude in this 'training camp' is fun, in spite of the disciplinary actions taken." His intense mood disturbed some of those sitting at the table: their eyes studied the floor, attempting to avoid Oros.

"War!" Oros shouted, grabbing everyone's attention. Then he lowered his booming voice. "War is very near. And YOU aren't ready for it!" He angrily exploded. Such broadcasting inspired a few feeble chuckles; intimidating, but of little substance. Noting one cute smirk, Oros promptly yanked the man out of his seat by his collar and dropped him.

"My friends, when I desire smiles for being funny, I'll notify you." He turned to the squadron leader who remained on the floor. "Should I kick you?...Get up, you fool! Bring that sack to the table."

The man looked at the size of the sack and then looked sack to Oros, his eyes begging for a reprieve. "I carried the sack this far," Said Oros, "You'll carry it to the table, unless you'd like to serve as my lackey for the next...."

The man tugged at the large sack even as Oros spoke. Then he puked, causing even the scribes to snicker. However, the fetid odor from the now opened bag, began to reach all. A few more puked. The veterans nervously awaited the repulsing contents. Oros claimed the victory as the man unceremoniously dumped the bag's contents on the table. With the exception of Baste and Oros, the other members present hastily backed away from the table. The head, an arm and a leg from the taller Kyykki now horribly decorated the table. Traveling in the sack from the outpost at the Wall neither helped their appearance nor their rotten odor.

"Recognize your enemy." Oros said flatly. "Not pretty, but bigger than the old model. Notice the larger head and the beginning of a neck. This creature thinks. He chooses. He's ten times more dangerous than his fathers. He also uses a new weapon, a ten to twelve foot spear. He's accurate with the damned thing, but, as of yet, he cannot throw it. He has no thumb.....Why are you looking at me? Examine the parts for yourselves!" His mood precluded any further quibbling; everyone surrounded the table, examining the parts.

Baste and Oros gathered to seats away from the table.

"I want the camp to see these parts." Baste told Oros. "Then I'm breaking camp. It's time to put some fear into the men. A skirmish or two will accomplish that. These 'nobles' are just too damned uppity for their own good."

"You have my blessing." Oros responded. "Except I need to share one more item."

"And that is?"

"The blood from the Kyykki is no longer slimy green; red is mixed with it."

Baste's face went white. "I trust this is a joke. Please?"

"No, its the truth and you understand the implications as well as I do."

"They are no longer soulless, then." He whispered.

"I can't be certain on that point, but I am sure on the other point. These creatures are becoming too much like us. Those parts are proof that the evil one has been very energetic since the Battle. He's done more than dispose of his former master. And, we must assume he's been able to buy off some of our own people."

"Does the name Krucik mean anything to you?"

"Not really, should it?"

"He sold out years ago. He's dead now."

"Dragons? Indeed, we've heard the story. I tell you truly, their reappearance will make the last war seem insignificant."

"Perhaps. But the dragon was easily killed."

"But the stakes have been raised immeasurably. The evil one is coming at us with all he has."

"And that is exactly why I'm taking this army to the front. Vosnob suggested we take the battle to them, before he has all his forces ready. I chose to ignore that suggestion until now. You all ready knew that, of course."

"Of course."

"Tell Vosnob your object lesson achieved its goal. We'll begin to break camp in a few dawns."

"I'll let you tell him. I'm assigned to meet with the Council of Three in Krabo." Then he lowered his voice to less than a whisper. "We need to get the King back on board."

Baste nodded, sadly. His heart told him the King might not return to duty. But the people required a leader, especially one who was called by the Holy One.

"You are prepared for more dragons?" Oros asked as he walked out the tent, almost unnoticed by those crowding about the table.

"Yes, Gath received aid from the guard at the city. His equipment is ready to go. The machine crews believe the stuff is for running lines over obstacles."

"Better let them know the entire truth. A dragon is frighteningly paralyzing. But you know that."

"Only as much as I know someone who is a bit like his father, except he doesn't have quite the weight to throw around."

"So you know about Gath. I swore to him I would keep any relationship out of this."

"Vosnob told me, years ago when we were inspecting some troopers.... Don't stare at me, I tend to believe in merit selection as well as you do."

"Yes, you do. But this information is not to extend to any others."

"You worry way too much. I'm surprised it hasn't depleted the extra weight you carry." Baste smiled.

"I'm not aware of any 'extra' at all."

"You never really enjoy facing a mirror, do you?" Baste said flatly.

But Oros faded into the night instead of answering.

The following dawn brought a whole new dimension to Baste's mission: the New Knights headed to battle, to war. "May the Holy One, Blessed be His Name, guide and strengthen us." Baste prayed throughout the restless night.

Midday found Oros walking briskly along the river road to Krabo. In his mind he realized that Vosnob's message to the High Council, via Yganak, had all ready determined its course. That type of efficiency pleased him. It also reminded him that the Council of Three was ably running the country, at least for the present. But knowing the army of the Light Striper trained to destroy dragons, that, he savored the most. The dragons formed the Evil One's final weapon, a last resort. With their obliteration, the Evil One stood quite defenseless before the righteous. Then, the Evil One's demise would prove the lies: he might protect himself and live forever, but he would exist in a powerless vacuum. Oros paused, quizzing himself on his anxiousness about the basics of the Faith.

Oros also wondered if that message of hope is preached and taught by the clergy sent out into the country side. The message is powerful, if wisely and truthfully presented. The clergy should know that the Evil One is nothing in and of himself. His power, his real strength, derives from what he can convince others to do for him, or, more substantially, what he is able to convincingly project upon the community. Terror-stricken people and a fear-driven populace are counted as his 'ancient' and inferred victories. But truth combined with grace de-emphasized such tactics: Divine truth, when applied by the people, provided for their continued salvation. Moreover, it provided the Holy One's counterpart to the Evil One's lies about salvation, life and power.

Prior to giving battle to the dragons and other abominable creatures Oros's itinerant preachers must communicate this Holy truth to all the people. Within a few dawns, Oros would personally oversee this Holy mission. It must be adequately promoted.

Krabo shrank from the same bright optimistic city Oros left a while back, not even the great square had been totally refurbished. Atop all towers, even those of personal residences, chapels and businesses, stood new crossbows, waiting the arrival of the next dragons. And, except for a few merchants conferencing with the clergy and a double guard at the doors, he found the huge High Council Hall devoid of any real agenda. The atmosphere boded shadowy, empty. Here, Oros found premise for his conjecture concerning the demise of the King.

The Captain met Oros in a chamber room upstairs for lunch. The other two, Etan and Jabbi, conferenced with the King's physicians in another part of the suite.

"Overwhelmed enough not to be able to put the pieces back into place." Is how the Captain described the King to Oros. "I believe, unfortunately, that his ability to lead, without considerable assistance, is unalterably impaired. We're examining all options that are available to us, including possible replacement."

"Rather extreme, isn't it?"

"Not when you consider the fact that the ex-nobles consider 'A King' as the only proper one to lead them against the Kyykki."

"That's true enough, but for the wrong reason. The King is as poor a trooper as the other nobles." Oros went on to explicate the difficulties at the training camp outside D'Ka as well as the order for the New Knights to bring battle to the Kyykki.

"Fascinating, they're actually headed into combat without the King. I never would have thought that they would obey the Light Striper regulars."

"Their training has emphasized personal readiness, not blindly following the King. There's been enough disciplining to swiftly mature the 'lazy boys'. And, as most failed stripermanship, they'd be too embarrassed for the King to come to lead them."

"Most interesting. Perhaps this will buy us the time we need to reach a better solution for the country....But if most aren't mounted...."

"Infantry, Captain, infantry. Heavy fifteen foot lances in four or five ranks, backed by crossbowmen and archers. Six platoons per squadron. By the time they're engaged in battle, the mounted Light Striper ought to be but two platoons, in spite of what Baste believes."

"A countermove to the taller, 'thinking' Kyykki?"

"I believe it is...."

"And just what should a good churchman believe?" Jested Etan as he and Jabbi entered the room.

"Welcome an old wandering preacher with an insult will you." Oros shot back, a bit of a smile on his round face.

"Insults do tend to get your attention, I've noticed." Said Jabbi flatly as he took a chair at the table. "Anyway, I'm glad you are here."

"When you get serious this early in the dawn, trouble is brewing."

Etan attempted to comfortably lean himself into a corner, but his face, drawn and worn, gave him away. "I have neither the endurance nor the temperament for this advisory position." His voice conveyed the solemnity of one in confession"

"Are you convinced of that truth? Or am I listening to a loss of patience and sympathy due to overlong hours? Either way the emotions get tromped on." Oros' listened with his heart to their hearts.

"I know the King's role must be radically altered. More than three responsibilities completely overwhelms him." Etan's usual optimism gave way to a realistic appraisal of the King, a change made possible by the trust level of the group. "He can't continue, unless he is specifically assigned a few duties. And if he's busy doing that he can't ruin the other programs and administrations that he feels he must meddle with."

"He's not quite the King-of-all-trades, isn't that the real problem?" Oros posed the option. "But then, can any one really fulfill what we all demand of a King?"

"I doubt it." The Captain replied. "But what do you recommend, my dear Chaplain?"

"I balk when you get formal." Oros raised his heavy grey eye brows. "Send the King to the front. The New Knights, at present, are headed by the river road to the front. Baste is taking the battle to the Kyykki."

Jabbi and Etan were taken back by Oros' announcement, even though they should have expected something startling.

"But what if the King is killed? Jabbi protested.

"Haaf has need of a martyr."

"Damn, you are a cynical one, Oros."

"Well, is it not the truth? To keep the King here is to invite internal troubles. To send him forth on his divinely appointed mission is most appropriate. Is that not what you've told me?"

"It is." Answered the Captain. "It's high time our White Eagle got himself back to work. If none of you objects, he'll leave with his guard early in the morning."

The group nodded their heads in assent. Etan took a seat across the table from Oros.

"There are more agenda items?" Queried Oros. "I have some fishing to do, and I'm late all ready."

"With your father and son." The Captain's statement sounded like a set-up.

"Good, then you've seen my father. I often worry about him. Quite old, a little fuzzy about directions sometimes."

"Should we have guessed he was your father?" Etan asked.

"Hardly, he probably didn't tell you his name, and by his very imposing yet unassuming countenance, none of you even bothered to ask....Don't get rattled, it happens all the time." He shifted back into his chair and took up a cup to play with. "Now I believe that we all have more to do than talk about my father." The fact that others presented Oros with different fathers never really bothered him, probably because he wasn't too sure either.

"Yes, we can all play with our cups." Jabbi sarcastically intoned.

It became readily apparent to Oros that the group of three was beyond exhaustion. They had taken up residence in rooms adjacent to the King's. Being zealously dutiful, they ignored their own needs. Therefore, they had been slowly reduced by the King's abject moodiness. From one moment to the next he became anxious, then jealous, then depressed. His forgetfulness chanced to ruin the kingdom; he could neither remember what he had signed nor the substance of that which he signed. The only grace in the entire matter consisted in the knowledge that the King refused to initiate anything. This Council of Three, existing as his harried neighbors, endured all of this for quite some time. Therefore, when Oros announced taking matters of consequence into his own hands; sending the King to the front, Oros met no resistance.

"Do what must be done." The Captain stated without much emotion. "The future of Haaf lies upon the image of the King." Depression tainted this added note.

"Put not your faith in mere mortals, my friend." The robust cleric challenged him.

"You know exactly what I mean, Oros." The Captain growled.

"Yes, but now I want all of you to pay attention. As soon as I get through, you'll all be able to rest."

As a reply, though not necessarily a positive one, three chairs re-adjusted.

"Good. Consider the following. For a scum like Krucik's son, the evil one lets loose with a dragon. It's analogous to sending the entire Light Striper to save a drowning cow. The overkill borders on ludicrousness. The question is, why? Why not keep the dragons to mow down whole squadrons of unprepared Light Striper? Why waste such a prime weapon on a scum like Ruje?"

"We've spent too many hours on this all ready. Our conclusion is that the evil one, being imperfect, can miscalculate as well as any of us. Obviously, the dragon was meant to succeed in both the rescue, indicating a type of omnipotence on the evil one's part, and, perhaps as more important, to demoralize the people. After all, if the Evil One's beast can raid the capital city at will...? ....But it failed, producing the opposite effect in the people...."

"With the exception of their King." The unhappy Captain added to Jabbi's analysis.

"But what if the damned one really had no stake in this rescue at all. He merely tested us. Getting us to prepare for an invasion from the sky. And we forget to watch for an attack from other directions?"

"Just what are you implying? That there exist monsters underground?" Etan wasn't too sure of his own words.

"That's just my point. Is it not a standard military tactic to throw the enemy into a state of off-balance, either by false security or misdirection?"

The Captain concurred. "You better know that it is."

"Then, is it being used against us? And we're not doing anything about it?"

"I refuse to believe that the evil one has tunnelling creatures ready to come up at us from below."

"And when you were younger did you not criticize those who challenged your notion over the non-existence of dragons? I seem to remember....."

"You remember all too well." Etan embarrassingly replied.

"Then my point is well-taken?"

"Rest assured."

"Then I'll move on. You received, sometime back, a note forwarded through Vosnob, originated by Sarg concerning the existence, and then demise of some rather bizarre palish women."

"Yes, and we followed through with our orders. We located two large groups of the 'ladies'. One headed from Buda Lake to the northwest."

"Towards Krucik's palace?"

"We believe so. None of them survived. Their carcasses were burnt." The Captain acknowledged.

"And the other group?"

"Headed east, up the side road to Pinduala. Literally thousands of them, plodding along. Some officers got the feeling the very sunlight could destroy them. Maybe as many got away as were exterminated. No one really knows."

"You all realize these were in league with the Evil One. We have grizzly evidence they served as more than spies. We conjecture these creatures somehow served as 'mothers' for the 'taller' Kyykki. How is that for a sneak attack?"

"He turns our own people against us." Etan's face burned.

"Exactly. Now those 'ladies' weren't exactly tunnelling creatures, but, in essence they undermined our whole society. And we still have no idea as to how long they've been at large."

"So we've got to cover the skies and also the land, even disbelieve our own people?" Jabbi harshly questioned.

"Yes. But don't stop there." The burly chaplain instructed. "The waterways, both the seas and the rivers, are they guarded?"

"Never really thought about it before." Said the Captain. "But it makes sense. If the damned one has flying things, why not swimming things?"

"That's pretty much the thrust of my argument. While the troops are all gathered to the north...."

"We get invaded from the east by swimming creatures." Added Etan. "Can things get any better?"

"Yes, they will. In preparing for any eventuality, we must cover all possible means the damned one will use to topple the Kingdom. Therefore every person is needed....It functions thusly: All serfs now are required to report any strange things they detect. The local chaplains will act as the clearinghouses concerning which are real and which are a vivid product of a serf's imagination."

Jabbi wasn't too happy with the idea. "You ask too much from the people. They are not suited for such strenuous thinking. Fighting, yes. But responsibility for the nation's safety, Oros, you've gone too far."

"Really? Then do want to do the job by yourself? The more we involve our people in the war, the better chance we have of winning and the lesser chance of losing them to the evil one's treacherous promises."

"He's got you Jabbi. And what harm is it if all our people get involved? Then the Captain answered himself. "They receive an ownership."

"Then is it settled?"

Jabbi held out a bit longer; his protests designed to keep face. The end result, however, was that Oros' original edict, signed by the King, went to all cities, villages and hamlets of Haaf.

The edict itself was brief: To the proud citizens of Haaf, being a responsible people and a people faithful to the Holy One, Blessed be His Name, are hereby commanded by their King to fulfill these solemn and essential duties in the war against the Evil One.

1) All sightings of unnatural or unusual things will be immediately reported to the local chaplain for prompt investigation.
2) You are to know that the Kingdom depends upon your labors to defeat the evil that surrounds us. Every job done well, every eye and ear kept open, every promise kept, provides for a safer, more secure Haaf.

I am most certain that you will endeavor to fulfill your calling in this war as I am certain of mine.

The King's signature and seal had been affixed. Copies left before the next dawn. Oros slept well that night. The Kingdom had begun to wake up to the reality of the Evil One.

While a parade, brass band, well-wishers and all, gave the King a rousing send- off to accomplish his divinely ordained mission against the Kyykki, Oros finished breakfast. Later he met with the Council of Three, now unburdened from their exhausting duties as the King's unofficial babysitters.

"I trust you gave your fond farewells to the King." Oros smiled.

"And may the farewell be a long one...... I pray he doesn't get homesick." Jabbi's mood allowed more sarcasm than cynicism.

The Captain wandered in, re-reading the report from Treh. He paused and handed it to Oros. "I don't think this is something you've read yet. It did much to confirm my faith."

A broad pudgy hand received the document. After a few moments he began to shake, almost off his padded chair. He put the paper down and then started to speak. "A·A·A·A·A·White EEEEEAGLE!" is all his emotional state allowed him.

"Calm down, Oros." Etan demanded. "Calm down."

"I'm trying......A A A White eeagle."

Jabbi silently reached over the table and poured a cup of cold water on the man. The radical change in environments speedily brought Oros about.

"Damn it!" He sputtered. "I find your UN-practical jokes intolerable."

"So you all ready took a bath..... But that isn't the concern. We are fearful that your shaking might damage the building."

"Damn it!" He cried as he toweled off his face. "I am speaking of this trumped up report.....I almost believed it."

"You better believe it, Oros, we sent Treh out to find Krucik's palace, or whatever 'he' called home. Treh's report is authentic. He's one of the best Church Guards. He's presently recovering at the garrison in North Haaf. About half his platoon killed by extremely well organized Kyykki. The platoon's only salvation was this White Eagle who used Kyykki as one would drop stones on ants."

"I only start to shake when I read about dragons.

"Did you hear anything I said?" The Captain inflected his words with great earnestness.

"Yes...... But I struggle with white eagles. And I'm supposed to believe the size of this bird? Better than twice the size of a dragon?"

"We had a problem with that figure also." Confided the Captain. "However, each survivor gave the same approximation: a wing span of some four hundred feet. The tail is short and rounded, but the back of the head seemed to have a large boney protuberance, as if its beak needed a lever."

Etan supplied the additional details. "Yet from whence and to whence the white eagle flew continues unknown. Treh felt it deliberately flew into the sun."

"It's for real then." Oros' doubting slowly dissipated. "Even the Holiness Code is very cautious about such creatures. Only at the beginning of time when land was minimal did they exist in great numbers. The Holy One used them to watch over his people, before He caused the Church to be."

"Allow me a stupid question." Said Etan.

"Allowed."

"When the Elder visited us, he also spoke of the white eagle. He said they existed with the earliest Haafians. Actually, he claimed we drove them away. And then they headed north, to the far side of the Dark Lands. Why are your details different?"

"An Elder..."·Oros shook his balding head, noticeably disturbed. "I strongly suggest you take his word above mine."

"Why?" Asked three voices simultaneously.

"Simply because my studies deal strictly with the Holiness Codes. The Elders spend their time with the rest of the sacred books. Some history, some rules, some stories...like parables, I've never seen them."

"Then, the birds do exist? And, most likely, they're on our side?"

"I would wholeheartedly agree with that." Oros' shaking rapidly diminished.

"Another question then: what is the relationship between the dragons and the white eagles? What does the Holiness Code proclaim?"

"From the little I understand in this matter, the Holy One did not create the dragons." Oros paused.

"Go on." Urged Etan. "Finish the story."

"Unfortunately, that is all I know. Rumors and hearsay must be discredited. Traditions tend to obscure the facts in favor of projecting one's slanted point of view."

"So the origin of dragons is unknown as is any encounters they might have with the huge white eagles." Jabbi attempted to interpolate the few facts.

"No, the Code states that dragons showed themselves to the world only after the Evil One set himself up as a rival to the Holy One. As he is, in essence as well as in substance, inferior, so too, it follows, is anything he might try to create. Not create, as out of naught, as does the Holy One. Perhaps 'form' or 'mold' is the better terminology. And whatever life force they have must derive from the evil one himself. He cannot create life……"

Jabbi commenced pacing the hardwood floor. His face contorted as he wrestled with Oros' information. Finally he spoke. "If I understand you, Oros, the Evil One can only take life away. He cannot take it and remold it into something else…."

"Correct, so far. With one exception, one we've seen all ready. Those who willingly give or sell themselves into his service, he can remold, rework anyway he so desires."

"Those women could become dragons, then?" Jabbi ventured.

"That is a real possibility. But I refuse to be the authority on such matters where my ignorance intrudes."

"How enthralling." Quipped the Captain sarcastically.

"But what of the soulless ones?"

"To animate them, he must first divest himself of part of his own life force. For them to grow stronger, he grows weaker. But he appears stronger because of the vast numbers of Kyykki and the fact that they protect him."

"Then what happens when the Kyykki are slaughtered?" Asked the Captain. "Does their life force return to him or has he lost that part of him forever?"

"I have no idea. Of such deeper things, again I confess my ignorance."

"Who might have such knowledge? Your father?"

"I can't even tell you that. I suggest to you however, that such information, because of its depth will be confined to the category of 'mystery'. If we had the answer to the strengthening of evil, we'd have won the battle tens of thousands of cycles ago."

"So," Said the Captain, with some stoicism in his voice, "We have no option than to go after him."

Oros leaned back and took in the high decorated ceiling. "That's the path that's been set before us." His philosophically oriented musing irritated the others. Then he spun about in his chair to finish. "But then, it seems that the Holy One has provided allies...... We must find them!"

"A search for the White Eagles?"

"I believe that's the jist of the matter at hand. To neglect a gift from the Holy One is a rather stupid maneuver on our part; one that could easily cost us....."

"The entire Kingdom." Jabbi concluded. "We aren't stupid. But 'we' are busy administrating the Kingdom. You, on the other hand, seem relatively free. Therefore, by the powers invested in me by the High Council and the blessing of these other two, I proclaim you "Official White Eagle Searcher of Haaf"."

Oros almost began to shake again, especially when both Etan and the Captain applauded Jabbi's proposal. His rotund physique quivered and he held his stomach, then he tumbled back into his favorite chair. He sat there in a daze, as if transported off to an unknown dimension. Questions to him went unanswered, even water to the face produced nothing. The three then sat and observed.

As the sun set, Oros returned from where ever part of him had been. "Thank you for waiting. You never realized what you commanded...I realize that now.....And I completely forgive you."

The three were half-dozing, but revived quickly enough to catch most of Oros' utterance. They paused, waiting for more, but Oros remained silent, a wry mystical smile on his round face.

"I guess I need to explain?"

"That would certainly shed light on your and our forgiveness." Countered Etan.

"You've assigned me to a Quest. Do you actually realize what you've set up for me?.......... A Quest!"

"I find it most appropriate, especially for a chaplain." The Captain slowly iterated with intentional emphasis.

"You are all serious about my going on a Quest, aren't you?" Oros deliberately studied each of their faces. "Maybe I should wait until your details of my Quest are in before the forgiveness part becomes effective."

"But you have no recourse to such. And, I might remind you, we've all ready been forgiven."

Unfortunately, Oros knew Jabbi's assessment as correct. "I guess I'll not be fishing for a while." He sighed as if his entire world had come apart. "Then I shall begin. However, its MY quest, so I'll direct it to suit me."

"We thought you'd hold to that line. Though the debate ended with two for and one against you taking control."

"And just when did this 'debate' transpire?" Oros demanded of Etan.

"You did spend a half dawn in some unknown territory...... Or perhaps you don't recollect your own change in disposition at all." Etan matter-of-factly replied.

"I am fully aware of the dimension I fled to." Oros announced defensively. "But, due to the nature and substance of my encounter, I am not a liberty to share any of it with you."

"So ...you are now selfish as well as fat." Jabbi laughed. He ducked as the iron goblet went flying by his head.

By early next morning, Oros, with monetary and material benefits provided by a most willing--at least from a safe distance--Council of Three, began his 'most secret' Quest with a highly befitting breakfast; one of ten separate courses. He then met with the others to outline his tentative plan. He would travel without fanfare or without an entourage; a squad of plain clothed Light Striper would accompany him as students. An extra person, an expert in being a bodyguard, would join them as well.

His name was Rux, a towering scarecrow of a man with bushy hair and ferret-like eyes. And a scurrilous reputation which would effectively disguise Oros.

The North Haaf destination, selected as the place to meet Treh at the garrison there, should prove an easy journey. Once there, Treh and the remainder of his platoon would join the Quest. New plans would be drawn up at that particular time. These would be the last reports sent back until the Quest reached its conclusion.

Due to the Spiritual nature of the Quest, as well as its essential secrecy, the Captain personally recruited the squad from his own guard. A securely protected report documenting all these events would be hand delivered to Vosnob by Etan. Jabbi readied himself to leave within a few dawns to find Oros' father and glean what information he might before Oros left from Haaf North. This allowed the Captain to play 'king' for many, many cycles, much to his chagrin and the group's laughter.

They shook hands, possibly for the last time, no one really knew what the future might deliver. Quietly, Oros descended the stairs into the Great Hall of the High Council where he met Rux. The odd looking pair mounted their Stripers outside. The selected squad arrived to meet them at the North Gate of Krabo.

Their journey to Haaf North should have proven the easiest part of the Quest. Instead, Oros chose to head due north, hoping to secure some information from Baste before continuing. Without further consultation, he also dismissed the hand-picked squad: they were to meet him in Haaf North, with this 'Treh' and a ship outfitted according to his specifications. He handed the squad leader a worn leather bag containing the necessary information and sent them along to North Haaf.

"Just me and you." Rux commented after a while.

"Who else is really needed?" Oros curtly replied.

"Aren't we touchy..... Sounds like you need some more room." And he fell in behind Oros.

"Get up here." Oros sounded a bit aggravated. "This Striper is sweating too much. I think he's sick."

"Just working too hard, Oros." Rux claimed. "Pardon my manners, but the Stripers just aren't built to carry someone like you."

Oros face slowly burned red. "Another lousy 'fat' joke."

"No." Rux replied without emotion. "Just the truth. When we arrived at the New Knight's encampment I'll secure a suitable mount for you."

Oros remained indignant, but he also recognized the truth of the matter.

Chapter 5

In spite of the legends, Sarg never camped in the Dark Lands, at least until the past few dawns. This uncharted territory remained a mystery of horror and intrigue to Haafians. Treading inside the damned one's domain just wasn't done: it almost smacked of territorial heresy. The Dark Land existed as a wretched wasteland threatening to devour all who dared travel through her. The present night, barely discernible from the overcast dawn, now brought as many horrors to life as did the monstrous creature back at the cliff. The Dark Land resembled hell. And like hell, it tormented the spirit as well as the body.

A double posting of the Yldan guard did little to quell the anxiety brought about by the croaking, gurgling, yelping noises which, when combined with the tedious breeze bringing the unearthliness of the lake's stench into camp, made for universal uneasiness. This 'hell' was of no one's particular liking. Yet this very 'hell' they invaded, by Vosnob's commission, to explore and, whenever possible, exterminate is what presently constituted home.

One other significant noise caught their ears; that of a constant continual slow beating. In their huddled deliberations they reached no conclusion, except for the fact that it might possibly be wings. However, any creature whose flapping resembled what they heard withstood being discerned. For some, this added another fear, yet for many others, it was fatefully accepted as simply part of their assigned mission. Whatever terrors and assorted evil things inhabited the Dark Land, now faced extinction. Knowledge of this 'hell', as the Yldans and Sarg sought to utilize it, meant the end of the its evilness.

Sarg labored over his maps throughout the night. He discovered the lake's luminescence allowed him to work from the edge of the ridge. In spite of Brey's vehement protests, Sarg refused any safety precautions. The

Yldans, whose night vision exceeded that of the Haafians, kept an alert about him.

Neither of the moons shown that night; the dense dirty clouds being thick enough to defeat their yellowish rays. Dawn brought a different scenario: the sun penetrated the dismal cloud cover, causing it to dissipate, and bringing temperatures well above that which they had endured in the jungle. The renewing of vision also permitted a truer sense of reality and a dismissal of many fears.

Dawn also delivered the signal to commence plans established during the night. The Yldans constructed rafts deliberately built to disintegrate once they floated partially across the lake. This made more sense than tossing bleach via a make-shift catapult. Sarg continued mapping the area. But Vauk and Luuft he charged to reconnoiter the lake as far south as the supposedly 'dead' volcano. Sarg had seen evidence--piles of the luminescent material drifting across the cesspool waters. But what was it? Breel against her formidable vocal will, acted as scribe for Sarg. Precluding any major mishaps, Sarg's directions for the scouting expedition were designed to bring everyone together as night fell. The rafts, laden with containers of dehydrated bleach, then would sail.

The Yldans' journey back to the cliff went without incident. However, the carcass of the gigantic beast, as it began to decompose, drew enormous black flies. As Yldans found out, enormous 'biting' black flies. A dusting of bleach exterminated the flies as well as helped the odor and sanitary problems with the carcass. The eight available casks of bleach went forward. Word spread throughout the other villages to send more.

The return trip, unfortunately, revealed the identity of the slow flapping sound: two dragons. As the Yldans rounded a low hill approximately half way to the lake, the first two men disappeared in a ball of flame. The dragons hovered above.

"Run!"

"Hide!" Commanded Blue Turtle as he quickly assessed their situation.

A second ball of fire landed where most of the party, in greatest haste, had departed. This dragon landed not one hundred feet from the group. The other kept watch from on high, making slow clumsy circles.

"Use the crossbows! Aim for any soft spots!" Blue Turtle ordered. He moved to the center of the trail, aimed at the right eye of the beast, and fired. Deftly, the beast knocked the shaft out of the air with its right clawed paw, as if to mock the Yldan warrior. Then the beast advanced upon the group, moving slowly, deliberately. Its huge three foot eyes hungrily surveyed the surviving Yldans.

Other bolts flew through the air. Each, in turn merely bounced off the hardened scales that covered most of its immense body. The beast paid little heed to such trivial annoyances; his red eyes fastening themselves upon the casks of bleach. As the Yldans continued spread out and fire more bolts against the beast, he simply lumbered down the trail until he was within twenty feet of the casks. Then his long neck stretched out permitting him to sniff the casks, which had been coated with grease to prevent leakage. He sniffed twice, then viciously bit into the first cask, lifted his head to swallow it and gave out the ugliest, ghastliest noise any Yldan ever heard. Yellowish blood spurted from his mouth and his head began to sway. His eyes went blank. He rose up his enormous bulk as if to fly, but fell, sprawling across the trail. He shook from head to tail and then died. Even as copious amounts of bleached out entrails ran from his mouth, bolts flew, hitting the beast's eyes.

"Watch...." Cried Blue Turtle, but too late. The second dragon, from a secure perch in mid air, vaporized some Yldans who moved from cover.

Blue Turtle turned and fired at the now diving beast. The broad head of the bolt caught the dragon on the wing, ripping a long slash. The beast quickly pulled up, roaring and belching smoke. With what appeared to be great effort, the beast clumsily, lopsidedly flapped in the direction of the volcano.

"Quick!" Yelled Blue Turtle. "To the lake. Before this beast brings his friends."

The remaining seven casks were rapidly drug along the path to the camp area. Time to savor their victory over the dragon was indefinitely postponed. As the blackness of the surviving dragon blended into the blackness of the volcano, the Yldan party entered the camp.

A few terse sentences from Blue Turtle told the waiting Sarg the essentials. The party had also watched the wounded dragon. Brey alone identified the creature as such. Now, the commodity of time suddenly vanished. The dragon's capability to pass on news of the intruders would bring trouble.

"To the lake!" Sarg commanded. "Before the other dragons come to assail us." Inside his head, he never imagined half of what they had been through so far. "And just how much of this information would reach to Vosnob?" He wondered silently.

In the hazy yellowish-grey of mid afternoon, the bleach laden rafts pushed out into the lake. As expected, the rafts with their deadly contents were viciously attacked as soon as they hit the yellowish water. An ugly hideous battle ensued; one pitting the smaller against the larger embryonic-like Kyykki. The victory of the larger sent the rafts bobbing out to deeper water. There the scouting party witnessed a half-grown Kyykki leap from the lake's depths, swamping the raft by landing on it. Immediate death rewarded him well as the thousands who crowded about the raft. The bleach attacked the Kyykki as transgressors of the highest magnitude; it swept over the lake with a righteous vengeance close to what one might expect from the Holy One.

Blue Turtle turned to the people and spoke. "We have seen the evil can be defeated, but also note that the bleach will soon deplete itself as the lake's filthy waters dilute it. We have more work to do. But we shall rejoice later, for the time is coming when the Holy One himself will dispel this filth from his creation with the breath of His mouth."

The stunned party witnessed Blue Turtle's prophesy. Sarg found it difficult to comprehend. "I am not familiar with your statement. Where is it found in the Holiness Code?" Sarg questioned.

"It is not written on paper which cannot last, but upon the hearts of our people who pass it along. As the Holy One once provided us with a 'good' world, which has been contaminated by the damned one and by us, so the Holy One will return to re-new his creation. This is the prophesy."

"And it provides for problems. That which is of the oral tradition contains the uncertainty of the mind. That which is written avoids the contamination of the mind. Second, even in the midst of this present peril, your words allow for laziness. Just sit back and wait for the Holy One to do it all."

"You mock me!" Blue Turtle retorted, enraged. "You kill the Spirit in order to promote the written, which is dead. In no way do we Yldans stand idle! Look about you!"

"And the evil one delights in this talk." Brey loudly injected. "Even as we destroy his domain, we cripple our efforts with these ridiculous theological diatribes. Why can't both stand as equals....the Spirit and the Written?" She offered.

"Never!" Replied Sarg and Blue Turtle simultaneously. However, they did return to the work at hand.

A secure base for the Yldans to continue cleansing the lake came first. Then time for Sarg and Brey to meet up with Luuft and Vauk. The theological controversy which separated the Haafians and the Yldans since the beginning would most definitely resume later.

Luuft and Etan explored a deep ravine, one that ran from the eastern end of the lake and circled down behind the volcano. Then the flapping noise caught their attention. From a covered rocky ledge, they watched the staggering beast fight his way to the volcano's major opening, a jagged hole some three hundred by two hundred feet resembling a single eye high on the volcano's slope. The Troopers' gaze transfixed on the dragon as much by their abhorrence of the beast as fascinated by its power.

Intently they stared as it approached the jagged opening. Its huge eyes full of agony, it's involuntarily flight erratic, a yellowish substance draining from a ragged wing, the gigantic beast made a determined glide for the opening. A crashing noise followed by a hair-raising roar filled the ledge where the men hid. The beast undershot the landing, smashing into the almost vertical wall of the volcano. Now, try as it might, the sheer forces of gravity pulled the beast down to certain doom in the lake fall below. With most pitiful roars and desperate clawing from its four taloned feet, the creature slowly slid into the fetid black water. Both Luuft and Yauk realized the beast knew its fate: it would be eaten alive, the hunter became the feast. Blackish water churned and boiled, the dragon fought back, slicing and crunching numerous half-grown Kyykki. But the odds denied him any hope of victory. As his wings were chewed into clumpy masses, his head shot from the cesspool lake for the last time. The churning and foaming from the fortuitous banquet lasted into the night.

A silently moving figure, now peering from the fissure's rim into the lake, caught the men's attention. Its height, medium, and it looked a soft ebony color, but its eyes bulged huge enough for three ordinary men. Its pointed ears appeared sliced off close to the skull, and not too skilfully at that. It's beak-like mouth, protruding below a bobbed nose, exposed more than a few fanged and broken teeth as it cursed the fallen dragon.

"Most damned beast!" It raged. "Suffer for thine own stupidity. Suffer double, for thou saw not fit to share thine information with thy master. May thou suffer a long time in thy lake tomb, O thou damned dragon. And where is thy mate? When she returns, she too will feed mine little 'Nepes'." The creature then placed what should have been arms on the volcano's ledge, but its arms were blackened tendrils, ending in most repulsive clamps.

The men shuddered in contempt and horror. Luuft wrote in the dust with his finger. "Is this the evil...."

Yauk quickly erased it and shook his head 'no'. And then, after a pause, wrote, "I don't think so."

Luuft looked away and scribbled, "Wonderful".

An incomprehensible cursing continued, then paused. The 'demon' gazed across the lake and screamed. "My babies, my 'Nepes' are dying! I can hear their screams! They beckon me to preserve their lives!" The monster pounded on the rim, sending stones down the slope into the putrid waters. His screaming went unabated.

Luuft sensed anguish in the demon's tone. But he knew not whether it derived from the demon's actual concern for his 'babies' or from his apparent lack of power to save them. One thing became certain to him at that moment; the 'thing' they watched could not be the Evil One. Haafians believed that the damned one was without emotion.

Finally, the 'demon' turned his back to the rim, exposing an excoriated back, one that oozed a slime which dripped into the waistband of his bronze colored trousers. Yauk's stomach went queasy, some-thing most rare for this physician. Then commands were heard, followed by various smokings, as if different fires began flaring. Shortly thereafter, in a column of twos, ten dragons left the volcano's fissure, heading for the far end of the lake. As the last pair flew off, the 'demon' showed himself at the opening again.

This time he spoke softly, but with intense anger. "Go my naggas! Go! Defend the lake from the intruders who seek to kill my babies.....my precious nepes. Go! Destroy!" His voice now reached its peak as he waved his blackened tendrils as if he too had wings. "GO! DESTROY!" Turning, he disappeared into the vast depths of the volcano's interior.

Luuft and Vauk watched in horrified agony as the dragons winged their way towards the camp. Their options bordered on despair. Warning their fellow Troopers at the camp-- -simply impossible. Furthermore, without weaponry so as to divert a portion of the attack, they felt helpless. Finally, with the impending attack, reporting to Sarg became foolhardy. Thus, divine intervention notwithstanding, they decided to explore the volcano, collecting information to supplement their present report. This continuation of their mission presented itself as the only viable alternative, even though meant deserting their friends.

The base of the volcano had no guards. It didn't need any as no entrance ways existed along the north side, so they quickly discovered. Subsequently, they headed towards the eastern slope. There, where the cesspool-like lake lapped the volcano, they saw a series of Haafian sized openings, all located approximately ten feet above the waterline, each with a large ledge attached to it. Nothing provided evidence for the purpose of these strangely fashioned openings. As they crawled nearer, they froze. Indiscernible utterings came from inside. Then, to their utter horror, at each of the openings stood a few of the 'pale women', exactly the type who attacked Brey and like those whom the high finned sharks ate. These 'women' lead some taller Kyykki by the hand to the ledge and, following a vicious kiss, pushed them into the lake. Instantly, the blackish water foamed, turning more greenish as the parade of victims continued. The men quit counting after a hundred victims were sacrificed to the 'demon's babies', his nepes. The scene buffeted their sensibilities, assailing their sense of ethics.

"Why," Whispered Luuft, "Would they deliberately destroy their best fighters?"

"Watch." Vauk whispered back. "Each of those 'things' has a defect."

Quite true. A few fingers here, an arm there, many had slight limps, but the more significant disfigurements belonged to the face: missing ears, some eyes. Most were simply more grotesque than any Kyykki previously seen.

"So, the damned one is trying to create his own people." Vauk said flatly.

"But that's blasphemous. It can't be done."

"Then you explain this in other terms."

"I don't...I can't."

"He's simply ferreting out the defectives in order to improve the race of Kyykki. He does it with singular compassion; a kiss of death."

"Such novelty you bring to a situation."

Vauk shrugged his shoulders. "Maybe we can even the score. Let's follow them inside."

"Now?"

"Of course, then we can be the next meal."

Luuft winced at his own stupidity and shut up.

"We'll wait until dark."

Luuft just nodded and began checking his weapons.

The Yldan guards quickly noticed the fast approaching column of dragons. They also observed the ravenous appetites of the flying beasts. Three glided down to the lake's surface for a mouthful of young Kyykki. As Sarg scribbled afterwards, "Their divine mistake; refusing to comply with orders, proved fatal." The three feasted from whitened patches on the lake; patches whitened from by the bleach. All three dragons subsequently dropped from the sky, screeching and blowing slime from their mouths. Panic-stricken they floundered in the yellowish lake, fatally assailed by their intended meal. The white-capped seething waters witnessed their complete destruction.

No Troopers remained at the camp. They jogged towards the volcano, missing the dragons' demise. Sarg and Blue Turtle, when alerted to the impending danger, jointly decided to attack the volcano. Waiting for the dragons or retreating bordered upon pure stupidity, so the small band moved forward. That, they figured, was not exactly what the dragons expected. The attack upon their eyrie would come unexpected, giving the small band of Yldans and Light Striper a significant advantage over the enemy. Uncertain about what assistance the advance party of Luuft and Vauk might provide, Sarg began to formulate alternative plans. He appreciated the assistance received from the evening's darkness.

Only the flapping of the dragons detracted from their attack on the volcano; everyone kept concealed until they slowly flapped by. The dragons seldom surveyed the ground, preferring to study the cliffs. With the dragons now headed towards razing the cliff-side with their fire, the company traveled at a dead run along the edge of the lake's ridge. They carried three small containers of bleach, and each trooper controlled his own weapons. Blue Turtle personally commanded the rear guard, which kept two newer style crossbows at the ready. Sarg took the point while Brey struggled alongside in his shadow.

As darkness slowly surrounded them, the forest above the cliff, now frightfully blazing from the dragon's raid, reflected light off the lake to the volcano's side, making for grotesquely flashing silhouettes. Sarg rested the company where Luuft and Vauk left some supplies. Believing both Troopers would return to collect their supplies, Sarg decided to set up camp. Because the volcano's debris made for a defensible camp, no one complained about the cramped space.

Sarg privately consulted with Blue Turtle. "What action would you prefer? Wait until the dragons to return? Or, do we infiltrate the volcano before they return?"

"Perhaps no action. We saw only three dragons drop. We can't do battle with seven. especially since we have no conception of what lies inside or 'if' we can get inside. I think you are too far ahead for such 'action'." Blue Turtle struggled to be polite in spite of his true feelings concerning Sarg's recklessness.

Sarg didn't overlook this change in attitude. "I owe you an apology. It's not that we have a squadron with us, is it?."

"No, it isn't."

"Then we wait until we hear from Luuft and Vauk."

Blue Turtle smiled rather wistfully. "I concur."

The bleak darkness of the night arrived and yet the dragons hadn't returned to their nest. Sarg struggled with this development, concluding that it, like most of life, had potential for both blessing and curse.

Then Vauk And Luuft stumbled in, their eyes bright with shock and amazement, their countenances bracketing a look of riveting insanity. They stank of the fetid water.

"There's a whole damn city in that volcano!" Vauk blurted out.

"Its got rooms and storages, breeding tanks and..."

"And its full of the 'pale women'." Vauk interrupted Luuft. "Also, there's some type of ceremony beginning, dancing and drums...Not sure what else."

Shortly thereafter Sarg silenced the two, ending their unceasing barrage of horrid details. Then Sarg sat the two down and sent for Blue Turtle. Brey showed up as well.

Blue Turtle carefully weighted his words. "Can we get inside to destroy them?"

"Yes." Luuft replied. "However, the slope to the entrance is directly over the lake. One slip and you're a 'nepes' supper."

"Nepes?" Asked Brey.

"That's what the 'demon' calls his 'babies'; those things who live in the cesspool."

"What 'demon'?" Demanded an alarmed Blue Turtle. The two then proceeded to report more of their findings of the day. The two leaders closely examined all the evidence, asking and re-asking questions. After Blue Turtle satisfied himself with their reporting, Sarg shared with them the effects of the bleach and the end of three dragons.

"Four, you mean." Corrected Luuft. "The sick beastie smashed into the volcano wall and slid into the lake." He announced with mock sympathy.

"Is there another way out?" Sarg questioned as he constructed their plan of attack.

"Possibly. We found a carved staircase heading down. It's at the rear of the volcano." Vauk articulated. "We didn't have time to explore further." He cautioned.

"But the staircase appears to lead out?" A stressed Blue Turtle wanted precision.

"I can only vouch for what I heard. From the stairs I heard rushing water." Vauk declared.

"And what about this ceremony? Can we get there?"

"The entrance I spoke of, Sarg, leads to a shallow ridge some forty feet above the floor." Answered Vauk.

Sarg's facial expression clearly indicated he wanted to attack, in spite of the fact that their exit might not actually exist.

Blue Turtle masked his intentions by asking a question. "What about the return of the dragons?"

The 'naggas'? I don't have any idea. We both saw them leave."

What's this 'naggas'? Are we learning 'demon' language?" Brey enunciated sharp enough to cut the air. "And how do we kill them?"

"The same way we always do." Sarg said with equal force, putting Brey back in her place.

"Not good enough!" She continued. "There are too many."

"Then you have something exceedingly superior." Sarg imposed with sarcasm.

"Yes, as a matter of fact, I do!" She challenged. She passed around an arrow, its head covered with a thick a bleach paste. "Now, won't something this despicable weapon be to our advantage. Even a touch of bleach to their skin incapacitates them.... Is this not correct?"

"And I thought you were above such." Smiled Vauk.

"I still am." Brey deafeningly announced, though with a quick blush.

Sarg ignored the small talk, but stalled the attack until everyone filled their quivers with the bleach-paste bolts and arrows. Even though his knowledge of the volcano's interior depended upon Luuft and Vauk's thorough observations, Sarg felt unsatisfactory and restless about his fragmentary knowledge. Nevertheless, he determined to attack.

The cliff-climbing Yldans easily scaled the volcano's steep exterior. Once inside, the powdery dust of countless double moon cycles often lay knee-deep, slowing the expedition's attack. The narrow ridge ran exactly as Luuft and Vauk described it; some forty feet off the floor. The breathtaking albeit nauseating view could scarcely be communicated. The distance to the far side measured well over a thousand feet; in looking up, the volcano closed it yawning mouth to less than two hundred feet. The floor, what could be examined due to the proliferation of dancing and bouncing Kyykki, was relatively flat and filthy. The sources of light came from the far west end of the room: the first originated from a band of swiftly flowing lava that semi-encircled a stage area, the other light came from an altar fire built on the stage. This light stood in front of a huge polished surface which, in reflecting light into the room, also partially blinded those who faced it.

A number of dried carcasses littered the stage floor, enough of a repulsive sight to gap most civilized persons. Green-yellow slime covered the floor surrounding two stout poles which flanked the altar. Riveted to the poles were two sets of shackles; one high, the other low. To the left of the altar, in a half shadow Sarg espied a narrow stairs. Presumably they went up into the dragon's eyrie, perhaps not.

Blue Turtle, noticing that their ledge bridged the lava river, silently led the men forward. The incessant methodical drumming covered any noise they created. The Kyykki appeared too intoxicated to even pay attention to debris falling from the ledge. Their advance to the stage area immediately stopped as the 'demon', now flanked by two semi-nude women, descended from the stairs.

This same creature was the one Luuft and Vauk observed. Now the creature's power manifested itself, bringing an awesome fear to the Yldans. For them, this 'thing' unmistakably was the Evil One. And they invaded the heart of his territory. Even Blue Turtle felt a twinge of panic as he stared at this huge-eyed, shiny black, tendrilled armed 'thing'. His disfigured face caused many of Yldans greatest discomfort, for mutilation marked one with a sign of disobedience and of deliberate failure.

Through sign language, Blue Turtle ordered his men to wait and to rest their weapons. He needed no loose arrows to ruin the surprize attack.

Then, a demanded hush, almost deafening in contrast, brought focus to the procession at the stage area. Flanked by the women, the 'demon' began a speech. Blue Turtle and Luuft crawled into crossbow range and waited.

The 'demon' spoke, loudly and yet with a hollowness that rang of things dead and hopeless. "My children, hear the words of thy father, thy creator." He paused his raspy voice to cough. "I bring thee presents, presents for the ablest of mine children." He pointed to the women who flanked him. "They belong to any of thee, my children....Any who can jump over to thy father."

A great ear splitting howl erupted from the gathered Kyykki. The women gasped in horror as they suddenly realized the 'demon's' intent. But it was too late; a crew of the 'pale women' emerged from the stairs and chained the Haafian women to the posts. Then reaching out with his tendrils, the 'demon' ripped off the skirts the women wore, leaving them naked and screaming.

With a haughty revengeful laugh, the 'demon' turned towards his children. "They are thine, my children, after I am finished with them." He turned again towards the women. This time, using the clamps at the end of his tendrils, he ripped a breast off each one. One he devoured immediately, as his children howled. The other he tossed across the lava chasm. Two Kyykki roasted in the lava in their innate greed to retrieve 'their father's' gift.

The Yldans in the ridge froze at the revolting horror. Brey reached for her bow, only to discover it in Vauk's grasp. He shook his head 'no'.

Never in the world's history had anything so abhorrent to their senses been witnessed. The two women hung from their shackles, semi-conscious from shock.

"May the Holy One bring them death." Whispered Luuft.

"Let it come quickly." Added an anguished Blue Turtle.

Further down the ridge, Vauk forced his hand over Brey's mouth: her sobbing reminded him of the Albasla incident. Luuft, kneeling in from of them, remained frozen, trance-like, as if this 'stage' scene battered down his last resistance to putting the missing pieces of the 'pale women' into perspective. In his mind, he did some massive reshuffling; these 'pale women', he realized, were volunteers, not victims. Perhaps, a bribe of some grandiose proportions bought them for the damned one's service. Whatever doubts he entertained prior to the stage episode, disappeared forever, replaced with a vile repugnance. He reached for his crossbow. Sarg's arm restrained him.

"Wait a little longer." Sarg said quietly. "Our time is soon to come. This 'demon' deserves his name, but not his life."

Vauk withdrew his hand.

The 'demon' once more raised his tendrils, signaling the 'loud' quieting of the massed Kyykki. "Now, my children, I, thy father, have finished with these women....Those who might have them as well, I now invite to cross over to me." He stood back from the edge of the stage, surrounded by the 'pale women'. He smiled lustfully as they attended to every part of him.

Within a moment, several Kyykki ventured a jump. Most belly flop into the lava stream, writhing with great anguish and even greater stench as they died. Their horrifying screams echoed throughout the cavern. The 'demon' and his 'pale ladies' raucously laughed at this abhorrent sport. One taller Kyykki shoved and jostled his way to the front. He properly saluted his 'father' with a deep bow. The 'demon' ingratiatingly smiled in return, giving permission to the taller Kyykki to jump without hindrance. The taller Kyykki savagely cleared out a circle of space for himself, sending a few lesser Kyykki bouncing across the floor. His excitement aptly demonstrated itself by his focused intensity. A running leap placed him precariously on the lip of the stage. Then, as if to assist him, the 'pale one' who stood by the 'demon' offered her hand. As the Kyykki reached out, she kicked him in the face. He fell backwards into the lava, gurgling curses through his greenish slimed face. Even before the rest of the Kyykki could chaotically cheer the sport, 'father' added to it. He smashed the 'pale one' in the back with his clamps, spinning her into the lava. Her tormented cries reached no ears, such was the gleefulness of the crowd.

During the depraved distractions, Blue Turtle relocated the Yldans across the lava stream and behind the stage area. Sarg now brought up the rear guard. As the 'demon' stood to watch, with pleasure, his wench die in the lava, Blue Turtle lowered his arm, the signal to fire. Instantly, thirty five arrows flew into the crowd, creating no more chaos then all ready existed. Only with the second round, when the first began to fall, did some concern arise. But most paid little attention, presumably 'father' simply played another cruel game. Those on the stage saw nothing. The arrows' targets fell in the darkness.

After six rounds, the crossbows targeted their selected victims. They let loose on the 'demon'. A broadhead bolt completely severed his leg. His 'pale ones' thought it hilarious, until they too discerned the pain of the bolts. Then, in a knee-jerk panic, a few tried to escape up the stairs, but found their way blocked by four Yldans who slid down ropes from the ledge. Sabres finished them off, their bodies pushed into the lava stream.

Slowly, the Kyykki finally realized 'something' extraordinary was happening. They rushed the front seeking support from 'father'. There they saw him laying on the stage, bleeding a mixture of slime and red blood. He desperately grasped at anything which could support him. He crushed two of his 'beloved' 'pale ladies'. He crawled to his foot, using it for a crutch. The next bolt, sent with love from Vauk, removed his head from his neck.

"Love these broadheads!" Vauk shouted.

"So do I!" Brey replied in a loud grimly determined voice. Then she shot the last 'pale one' in the shoulder. She stumbled and dropped off the stage; the lava claimed her. "Those who sell themselves to darkness deserve their judgement." Her voice resonated like steel.

"Move quickly! Into the corridor! Now!" Yelled Blue Turtle.

Another crisis developed unexpectedly; the Kyykki carcasses piling up over the lava stream caused it to overflow its banks. The spreading lava now threatened the entire company, because the entrance to the staircase escape ran below the floor level. The dangerous situation granted insufficient time to safely get everyone into the tunnel. Without a word, Sarg and Vauk drew their swords and waded into the massed and disorganized Kyykki, cutting a slimy path for the others to follow. The Yldans behind them used their sabres to keep the path open while Luuft lead the rest into the corridor and down the stairs.

"Back up slowly to the tunnel!" Ordered Sarg. "Use their bodies to block the way."

It remained as easy to obey as for the order to be given: the Kyykki still hadn't fathomed their predicament. Their inferior attributes and lack of experience precluded their recognizing an attack, especially one upon their castle, their home. Carcasses piled up as fast as one could hack them down. The tunnel became impassable, at least for the time being.

"Let the others get safely down to the water." Sarg instructed. "We'll follow after this tunnel is blocked. However, Kyykki carcasses aren't the best for stopping anything."

The Yldans approved of his sarcasm by nods of the head.

In examining the staircase corridor, Sarg noticed several wooden doors set into the wall. "We'll use those to block the tunnel. Be careful when you open them...."

The Yldans stared, bewildered.

"Remember...... our friends, the dragons? Be careful!"

The first door fell off its hinge without undue effort. The room behind it smelled moldy. The second room found twenty 'pale ladies', all ready to attack. A Yldan received a severe wound in the arm and face. The 'pale ladies' found a strange mercy in the Yldan's sabres: they died quickly, no torment of a long painful dying.

"A third door will finish the job." A Yldan commented.

"Yes." Said Sarg. "But no more casualties. Be extremely careful." He grabbed a torch from its wall sconce and handed it to the Yldan. "When I kick the door open, toss the torch across the room. Don't move until I do."

The heavy iron-banded door fell forward into the room, creating a cloud of dust.

"When the atmosphere clears, we'll enter."

"Gentlemen," Called a graciously feminine voice from the rear of the room. "You have my permission to enter, provided you come in peace."

Sarg, startled, backed up. "Careful! This might be a trap."

The same voice replied. "You have a loathing for your superior's behavior that is quite unhealthy, my good man."

"And just who might it be that I am loathing?" Sarg said rather irritably.

"Are you not then of the shepherd class?"

Some of the rear guard, including Vauk, gathered about the doorway, both intrigued and mystified by this unreasoningly bizarre conversation. Sarg signaled for the torch to be tossed in.

"You are such incompetents. The torch has a proper place on the wall. Are you not familiar with sconces?" The voice now gently scolded Sarg.

"Yes, my good lady, I am familiar with wall sconces. However, exactly what is a 'shepherd'?"

Giggles from at least two other voices echoed off the hard stone walls of the chamber. They reminded Sarg of the polite giggles, the ones where hands covered the mouth, the ones he recollected from the royal parties his wife forced him to attend.

"I understand that royalty has bid me entrance. I obey and bring my second with me." Sarg announced most dignifiedly. His mind raced ahead, trying to put these confusing pieces together. If these women were 'pale' he would personally kill them.

"Ladies, it appears that we are rescued."

Sarg, with Vauk three steps behind, strode into the room as if he owned it. When he saw the ladies in the shadows, he quickly lifted his slimy sword.

"Put that 'thing' away!" Commanded the oldest of the three beautiful pale blue ladies. She spoke and Sarg and Vauk heard, but her mouth and the words formed a distended variance. "We can not harm you."

Sarg, unsure, refused to obey. Bows at the doorway targeted the three ladies.

"How can we be sure? Your appearance is that of many whom we've recently killed, ...before they would have killed us, of course."

"I too am familiar with those degenerate 'creatures'. In spite of some devious color tampering, they are not us nor are we them........ We are Tath royalty."

The voice of Brey called from outside the chamber. "We discovered flatboats! They're waiting, move it! Even the dumbest Kyykki won't stop till we're eaten....or worse." Brey's anxiety pushed her to repeat herself many times. The longer she spoke the more unsettled her voice sounded.

Then sounds of wood being hacked and torn reminded everyone that extreme danger lurked up the hallway. Sarg commanded the Yldans to use the third fallen door to reinforce the barricade. Before they moved, the slender pale blue lady moved across the floor as if traipsing upon air, such grace filled her movements. The others followed her at a slight distance. Vauk and Sarg stumbled out of their way.

"Allow me," She softly spoke while she moved through the doorway, "To negotiate with these uncivilized black frogs."

"But.." Protested Vauk.

"They shall obey me." The firm demeanor of the slender lady certified that her words had tremendous power. From across the black stone floor, Sarg noticed that her height and that of her two female companions was approximately a foot shorter than himself.

Without orders, the entire rear guard instinctively formed about the lady and her two companions. The trio gazed into the wooden barricade. The older lady spoke, but again, her words did not match what they heard. The dissonance between what they heard and what transpired, appeared magical, mystical and unnerving.

"Listen, O hungry ones. I have the gift of food for you. A gift from your 'father'." Silence rang from the barricade. The lady continued. "Your food lies in the lake. Go and eat! Nepes are your food! I, Queen Sjura, servant of your 'father', command you to eat. Everyone one of you shall eat. Now go! Tell the others! I command you."

Sarg and the others heard muted shuffling sound. Then a plethora of undecipherable remarks echoed in the cavernous ceremonial room as the lady's message spread through out the gathered Kyykki.

"They will bother us no more. Shall we adjourn to the flatboats? I believe that's what some young lady called them." Again, her mouth and her words fought each other. Nevertheless, the entire rear guard followed the trio down the darkened corridor to the awaiting Troopers and the flatboats.

The long corridor gave semblance to having been designed by a drunk snake. Unkempt as the cavern, debris made their passage dangerous. Descending towards the sound of running water was the sole redeemable factor of the corridor. Brey's voice kept beckoning them. But her message bouncing off the dark rough stones walls kept anyone from recognizing the true distance to the landing she spoke about.

Abruptly, the corridor thrust itself to the left, opening upon a large docking area, more than adequate for the four flatboats tethered there, The area was well lit, compared to the rest of the volcano. Supplies of ordinary food stuffs lined the dry walls, as if they had recently been delivered.

Casks of water occupied a corner. It wasn't the scene expected, but then, neither did anyone expect royal personages, nor a true opportunity to safely depart the Dark Lands. Many prayers of thankfulness reverberated off the tunnel's arching walls.

"Why might all of you be staring, instead of bowing?" The leader of the strange trio of ladies asked without malice or belittlement. She appeared slightly bewildered; what should have been, wasn't.

Brey moved quickly on an uptake. "We are unaccustomed to such formalities, my Lady, but be assured that we greet you with all due and proper respect." With that she politely bowed from the waist and motioned for the rest to follow suite.

I thank you................"

"Brey, my Lady." Blue Turtle offered.

"I thank you..."

"Blue Turtle, my Lady."

"Brey and Blue Turtle, I thank you." Said the Queen, sounding a bit exasperated. "My subjects call me Queen Sjura...Queen Sjura of Tath." Her retainers politely giggled again, to which the Queen replied with a quick curt stare. They both immediately retreated into an elegant, if completely artificial, propriety.

Blue Turtle's hand never left his sword hilt, and in the back-ground he heard the familiar sounds which reminded him that the three would become porcupines if they detected one small irrational motion. In spite of every thing these Ladies appeared to be, blue skinned women retained an abhorrent reputation. Strained politeness existed in the midst of the impending crisis. No other words sounded as each group sized up and peremptorily judged the other.

Sarg broke through the barrier. "I introduce to you three blue ladies who, in ways I admittedly do not comprehend, but do wish to." Sarg spoke, casting a glance at Queen Sjura. "By speaking to the Kyykki, she sent them into the lake for food rather than allow them to assault us at the upper end of the corridor."

"Then the Kyykki, by word of this 'Queen' have committed suicide? Is that what you ask me to believe?" Luuft's voice ranged between a sneer and disbelief.

"It is what we bear witness to." Answered one of the Yldans. "In truth it happened, but for why and for what reason, I cannot answer...Indeed, part of my heart warns me of the possibility of a deeper motive for their action. Though good or bad, that I cannot tell you either."

"What is your name, most honest Sir?" Asked the Queen.

"Deep Owl."

"Then, Deep Owl, what might I do to allay your fears? Where would you suggest I begin?"

After a moment, the sensitive Yldan replied. "Your mouth, my Lady.......... Why is it we see your mouth move, but the words we hear do not match the words you use? This places you in the realm of that which we strongly disapprove: magic."

The Queen's face turned white and the retainers grabbed her as she began to fall. Someone shoved a wooden crate, useful as a chair, under her.

When she recovered, she proudly stood. "Magic is too dangerous for mortals. I am mortal. I do not use magic, such is for our God alone, should he desire.... That is one issue we shall need to discuss. As for my voice, that is easily explainable." The Queen raised her left hand. There, on her second finger, she exhibited a heavy-banded gold ring into which set an oval stone, bright orange in color.

"Watch the ring." She said, explaining. As she spoke, the ring glowed brighter with a pulsing. "I do not speak a language anyone, my retainers excepted, would comprehend. Nor do you speak a language that I, on my own, could understand. The reason we are communicating is due to the power of the ring. It has the power, or gift, if you prefer, to translate all languages."

"Then I declare what you use, the ring, as magic." Declared an alarmed Deep Owl. "Are you striving to deceive us? That would be particularly unwise. Your lives are still held in judgement."

"Then will you judge without all essential information?"

He dropped his head. "That is wrong. ..Please, ..Continue your story."

"I shall, Deep Owl...This ring, one of seven identical rings, came to our people as a gift from our God. Each ring has the same power: to promote communication between the created peoples that they might be 'one people' again as they were at the beginning of time. One ring was destroyed in a foolish war among our people ten centuries ago. Now each tribe has a ring, which is the property of the royal house. I received my ring from my mother the moment she died. My daughter shall receive her's the same way. As long as I live, the ring cannot be taken. That's what the 'demon' waited for." Such warm atmosphere created by the Queen's theology and honesty rested fears and suspicions. Thousands of questions, however, yet remained and would for some while. Another culture, an unknown people, collided with that of the Haafians and Yldans. Putting the newly emerged pieces together would require efforts that, at this juncture, time did not permit.

"I believe that a check on the situation in the ceremonial room will prove that Queen Sjura, regardless of our countless unanswered questions, is a true ally against the Kyykki. If what we heard is true, the room should be rather empty and the small Kyykki in the lake, well-fed." Sarg delivered his words with a sense of relief as well as a challenge to all present.

Luuft took five Yldans with him to inspect the ceremonial room and to check on the situation with the lava. Blue Turtle instructed supper be prepared and provisions made for a night's stay, including triple guards. A small party, under the direction of Deep Owl, scouted the stream's course by following along the walkway that bordered it.

Brey insisted on staying with the three females. In spite of their presently abhorrent color, she found great comfort in their company.

The next morning, morning according to the ditates of Sarg, not necessarily those of the environment, brightened into a truer reality when the torches relit the corridor. It also brought forth much information which Sarg and Brey collected from Queen Sjura, and Tiello and Jelkio, her two retainers. These two were the same age as Brey, but of much different disposition.

Sarg reserved the morning for writing his report to Vosnob. The time would be utilized by the troops for readying transportation down the stream. The evening's patrol, led by Luuft, discovered Queen's Sjura's words true: the majority of Kyykki committed suicide. The few remaining were ferreted out by Yldan patrols being guided through the maze of passageways by Tiello and Jelkio. These incursions succeeded even though communications depended entirely on hand signals. These patrols 'bleached' pools set up for breeding Kyykki and demolished all equipment found. A blood smeared altar to the evil one now existed only as a pile of rocky debris. Even the dragon's filth-laden lair, in the far upper reaches of the volcano, they cautiously explored. The dragon's continued absence provided much anxiousness for the troops, but Queen Sjura seemed strangely unconcerned.

Sarg's report to Vosnob:

We camped inside the bowels of the volcano this past night. As we attacked and defeated innumerable Kyykki of all sizes as well as a few dragons, rest becomes us all. As noted in my previous report, we have much success using bleach against the Kyykki. It will also eliminate dragons, should they ingest the bleach. Casualties, to date, have been borne by the Yldans. Most were vaporized by a dragon, one was wounded by the 'pale women' [who infested this volcano as servants of a high priest of the evil one]. Both are dead.

Furthermore, we found ourselves the unwitting rescuers of a New People, Taths. These Taths are basically a nomadic peoples. There are but six tribes for the whole country, which I believe is located north of the Dark

Land. The Dark Land merely divide us, the Dark Land no longer exist as the most north a person can travel.

These Taths do not speak a language we understand. Their God [whom Queen Sjura claims has no name, for that would allow people to have some power over God] provided the Queen with a ring that functions as a translator for all languages of peoples as well as some non-peoples. Queen Sjura actually spoke, using the ring, to the Kyykki in such manner that they committed suicide in the lake, which resides to the east of the volcano.

There is too much here to write about, but I suggest a 'royal party' be sent along the coast north of the Dark Land to make contact with these Taths.

The following is essential in making contact with the Taths. They are a bright light blue color with rounded eyes, oval ears, and a formal polite disposition. They are about a foot shorter than us and are petite in build, even the men [though we have not seen any]. They are intelligent, but confusing. For them, for example, distance is measured solely by time, and descriptions are given from a 'bird's eye view', as if these Taths could fly. Watch out for an animal the size of a Massive Blue, if not larger. They are known as sheep and provide for most beautiful garments called woolen, its even warm when wet.

Finally, the Taths are ruled by women and the priests are also women. They have a city which the Queen says is north and inland from a great swamp. I reckon this to be our Zuda Marsh. Much is still being processed about the Taths. As I figure it out, it will be reported. May this report find you in good health.

"Damn it!" Sarg complained.

"What's the problem, Sarg?" Asked Brey.

"There's no way this report can be sent. I'll just have to take it with me."

"Not a bad idea. By then you'll be able to compose a coherent one."

Brey smirked. "You've completed your duty. The law is fulfilled. Now take a break before we leave here." Brey ordered.

The far end of the docking area became the scene of considerable unmilitary maneuvering: it seems both Tiello and Jelkio drew the attention of just about every trooper. Language easily crossed barriers with two pretty and young ladies involved. From their giggles, both Tiello and Jelkio acked as true flirts. A fact not wasted on Brey, who knew exactly what Vauk thought, and showed her displeasure by throwing a rock at him.

Vauk turned and saw the jealousy on Brey's reddened face. "I'm obviously missing something here." He literally said the words with a demand for an instant answer. "Well?"

"Why are you over there?" Pointing to the flirtatious two.

"Why not? They are most charming. And we have the chance to learn a new language and about a new people."

"And look into those big round eyes. And drool when you stare at those non-existent bodices they wear."

Vauk's face grew hot as he blushed. "Well," He stammered, "Those long gowns are more attractive than a military uniform."

Brey smacked his face before she even realized what she did, so instinctive... They caught each other off-guard. They stood, glaring at each other. Then glares transformed into sheepish grins and then laughter.

Vauk spoke first. "You've made a claim I didn't know any thing about. It's quite an unfair tactic, you know....even a painful one." He said while gently rubbing his cheek.

"I know." Brey replied. "I'm sorry." She said almost too softly for anyone to hear. She turned and walked away, her face covered with tears.

Vauk followed her to the end of the docking area, near the corridor entrance. Without a word, he placed his hand on her shoulder, pulled her around and kissed her. "It's more fun being part of the secret when I know I'm in it." He said, wiping her tears away.

Deep Owl's report to Blue Turtle included strategies for negotiating the subterranean stream. The four boats would follow close on each other, except for those places where another stream joined in. As these were possible locations for an ambush, one boat at a time would clear. Evidence that torches were previously used caused some alarm. To be secure along the lower waterways the flatboats would travel with four oarsmen and one trooper at the tiller. The rest kept armed and at the ready.

"What about a stopping point?" Asked Sarg.

"As far as we could tell," Responded Deep Owl. "This tunnel is endless. Without torches, we travel in darkness."

Sarg coughed at the ridiculousness of the latter statement and mumbled. "The latter is obvious. But no end to this tunnel? That is difficult to believe."

"No end as far as we could discern." Deep Owl responded sharply. "I have no idea where this goes. Maybe we should try to return the way we came?"

"With all the dragons just waiting for us to show ourselves." Sarg annoyance showed.

"My good friends, what has started must finish." Queen Sjura interjected from her seat a few steps away. "My rescue needs completion. When I arrive back in Tath, your responsibilities shall be both terminated and rewarded." She spoke with the polished air of nobility and of an astute diplomat.

"To the boats!" Called Sarg giving Deep Owl and the Queen a look which acknowledged more than words could ever cover.

"At least the stream is straighter than the corridor." Brey commented to Vauk after they'd spent two meals on the boats. "According to Deep Owl's signals we're well beyond the explored distance."

"That's exactly my worry, this territory is unexplored and yet we keep on going."

"Are you really that concerned for my safety?" Brey suggested with a strange and somewhat devious smile.

"Yes...and no." He answered while scanning the black corridor walls. "I need to keep the mission concerns separate from personal concerns. It's not easy."

"That's true." Brey wistfully acknowledged. "But some day..." She never finished the sentence. Vauk instinctively pushed her aside as he felt something move. A breath later a crude spear splintered on the board where she sat.

"Ahead faster! Attackers!" Vauk yelled from the first boat.

Ahead stood a ghastly repugnant vision, shadows from their torches created more than a nightmare. The 'demon' which Sarg deftly beheaded, now challenged the troopers from a walkway not less than an easy stone's throw. He stood on the concave side of the bend in the tunnel, surrounded by an easy dozen of his most advanced 'children'. With one tendril, he used a crutch and with the other he held his still functioning head.

This time, thanks to the Queen Sjura's ring, the Kyykki's words were translated for all to hear. "Kill them funny skins. Kill. Eat."

"Funny skin am I!" Deep Owl bellowed as he let the first arrow loose. A Kyykki splashed into the water, followed by the rest.

"Attack by water!" Vauk barked. He drew his broad-axe. "Get the oars in!"

The last command come too late: a Yldan oarsman flew from his seat into the stream with a horrifying groan followed by a crunching, snapping sound. The second flatboat, guided by Sarg, attacked those remaining on the ledge. Sarg sent his sword flying into the bodiless head, splitting it open from skull top to jawbone. Then as their flatboat smashed into the ledge, Sarg and five others brought suffering to those who did not jump. Six were quickly sabered. The 'demon', now without a functioning head to provide directions, stood motionless as Sarg hewed his blackened frame into small pieces. Then used a flour keg to smash the head into yellowish-green pulp.

The last two boats veered away from the encounter, and docked a little ways downstream, where they picked on selected targets and rescued their own wounded. The tunnel now stank of Kyykki, as their arms and heads floated by.

"Damn it!" Cursed Blue Turtle. "Four men lost and another four wounded." He sized up their situation "We cannot afford another ambush."

"There won't be another one." Sarg called from the walkway. "The 'demon' is gone for good...Unless this slimy pulp can put itself back together."

"Burn the pulp! I don't enjoy his damnable surprizes!" Blue Turtle returned. With that he tossed a torch to Sarg.

The slime moaned as Sarg burnt it. Sarg shuddered. He continued burning until all rendered to dust. "I must trust your judgement more often."

"No thanks! I simply hate this bastard"

"Doesn't everyone!" Brey cynically enjoined.

Tiello and Jelkio, without aid of a common language, ably tended to the wounded.

The two Yldans bodies, two of four they were able to find, Blue Turtle wrapped and placed in the last boat. This boat carried supplies and was manned by Deep Owl and four others. Blue Turtle expected a proper burial for his men.

The following two dawns saw the usual monotony of the tunnel once again controlling the company. Their sense of time quickly deteriorated. Meals became the standard way of expressing any progress. After seven meals as well as a lengthy stop to tend the wounded and rest, the water's speed increased rather dramatically. The sound of waves breaking over rocks echoed through the tunnel.

The first boat hit a rock and violently swung about, smashing into the second boat. Three men went overboard, finding the water only waist-deep. The third boat veered around the collision only to run aground some hundred feet ahead.

"Light!... Daylight!".... Someone hollered from the third boat.

"Send out a scouting party." Sarg directed from the second boat.

Luuft lead the party along the broken boulder-strewn walkway; half of the group he positioned in the stream. The sizable breakers became too large as to prevent easy passage. Off on the right, however, another tunnel began, or so it appeared.

"We'll explore the sunlight first." Luuft said.

Their discovery led them to be thankful for both rocks and low water. A plummeting three hundred foot waterfall splashing into a wide luxuriant valley below was their awe inspiring discovery. The stream simply rounded a bend and dropped---well below the base of the volcano.

What a wondrous difference! The air once again lived: clean, bright and fresh. In the valley below, greenery, a magnificent forest, flourished. White clouds skittered across an actual blue sky. In front of them, though maybe twenty miles away, shot up another ugly blackened volcano and still another one on the left. These looked as dead as the present one, yet as similar. 'Dragon holes' existed near their peaks. The valley inspired them; beautiful and pure and alive: a concrete paradox of their present environment.

"I don't understand what this is all about. A curious vision of paradise in the middle of hell?" Luuft waxed philosophical as the feeling of release bubbled up within.

"Does it matter?" Retorted a practical Yldan, still caught up in the dismal atmosphere of the Dark Land. "We are here just scout. ...... Besides, this is not the direction we travel, in spite of the view.......... But the area is large enough to provide for a quiet camp....with FRESH AIR." The swiftly changed environment finally effected him.

"Certainly. I'm sure the dragons would be most appreciative." Luuft annoyingly responded, mostly to defend himself against the fellow's overwrought sense of practicality.

"And what says there are anymore?"

"I do, those six are still somewhere. And who knows how many live across the valley." Luuft's spirit wasn't up for an unending argument. His enthusiasm, fueled by the spectacular view of the valley, slightly retreated. "Let's explore the other tunnel."

The other tunnel provided easy access to the flatboats, even when fully loaded. But the rushing water compounded the dangers of the route. Its one redeeming virtue was that its path continued straight. Very faintly, at bottom, a pale light flickered.

"I believe that's the end of the tunnel." Luuft hypothesized.

"Could be. That would make it lower than the waterfall. But we'd probably be in a valley further to the south." His comments were interrupted by a voice from the other side of the tunnel.

"Here's a rope. No,.. a whole system..... for moving cargo up the stream....It's in well-kept condition."

"Now we know how the supplies got in. Time for us to get out!" Luuft's energy level received a boost from the news. Luuft reported back to Sarg who quietly and earnestly conversed with Queen Sjura.

"My rescue is becoming most difficult." She spoke with an inflection of dismay, one whose genuineness cut through the disconcerting incongruity between her words and her mouth.

"But your rescue is an accident. We had no idea you were here. We are on a scouting mission for the Light Striper."

"Yes, you've tortured me with that animal. I can't believe such a beast exists. But, more importantly, there are no accidents. Our God knew we needed rescued. Our God summoned you to provide."

"We don't know your God."

"Maybe you should. Our God cares for all creation."

"I'll concur with the latter statement." Sarg said brusquely.

"Did not God create all?"

"Yes."

"Does God appreciate and enjoy the diversity God created?"

"I believe so." Answered a wary Sarg. Theological discussions made him nervous, usually because they dealt with issues that had little practical substance.

"Then why did you accuse us of being 'ugly blue flesh eating' monsters when you first rescued us?" She flatly demanded.

"I've gone over this before...."

An over-anxious Luuft broke in. "Sarg, and Queen Sjura, I welcome the opportunity to report daylight, daylight from a tunnel leading to a waterfall. There lies a beautiful valley at its base. But we remain surrounded by these ugly volcanoes." Luuft quickly learned the Queen appreciated a more formal style of speaking. She listened better at those times.

Queen Sjura's rounded brown eyes went wide open at Luuft's description. She began to hyperventilate. "Where is this view?" She curtly demanded as she placed her slippered feet in the stream. Tiello splashed after her as she ran downstream.

"This way!" Luuft called after them. Within moments he caught up with the two and escorted them through the boulder strewn stream.

Sarg and others, made curious by the commotion, also headed for the waterfall.

Once there, the Queen allowed herself to be swept up in deep emotions; both sobbing and laughing simultaneously. Tiello guided her to a rock where she could sit. Jelkio stood by her side until she partially regained her composure.

"We are forbidden to walk down there anymore. This is the Holy Valley our priests have spoken of. This is where God created the Taths, where they lived before their apostasy. Gaze and wonder, my children. This was our home. Now it is home to dragons."

Tiello's eyes asked more questions than her mouth could utter. "How..... do you know this is the place?" She stammered in Tath.

"We are surrounded by the four old smoking mountains. Through the middle of the valley runs a single stream. That gap," Queen Sjura pointed to the north, "is where we left, ashamed."

"This is where the Tath ancestors demanded God's name?" Tiello asked tearfully.

"Yes, sadly enough, it is..... Here we demanded to control our God by having a name for God in our possession..... Here our God caused us to leave until that time when we might simply live by trusting God."

Sarg found himself caught up in her heavyhearted story. Such a wondrously peculiar God he thought and such a people. To live simply by faith, that's a goal he believed everyone should strive for.

"To this day no one has attempted to enter the valley. Dragons guard the valley."

"Your God created 'dragons'?" The gross inconsistency dumbfounded Sarg. Then he ventured a reasonable explanation. "Then you must have two Gods?"

"No. There is but one." The Queen wasn't entirely shocked at Sarg's suggestion. "The dragons came after we left. How or why, we do not know." Answered a saddened and wistful Queen Sjura. "We had once conjectured that the dragons existed to keep us out. That argument isn't plausible: if true, then our God would never see our faith in action. Thus we could never return."

"I believe I understand most of what you say." Said Sarg. "Your God moved you to test your Faith........... But your God has not deserted you? Is that correct?"

"It is." Tiello replied softly. "That's how we knew you came to rescue us."

Sarg looked down into the pristine valley and kicked a rock over the edge. "Such faith." He murmured over and over again.

Luuft, however, pursued a different course. "Is it safe then for us to be here? Will the wrath of your God descend upon us?.................. What about the dragons?"

The Queen graciously deferred to Luuft's anxiety and the anxiety of most of those standing about by answering each question. "It is only the valley which is forbidden. Here we have not disobeyed anything our God required. Second, I believe we were supposed to see the valley. It is part of our journey in faith. This view is a most vivid reminder of what we left and where we might return. ....I don't know about the other dragons. But the ones who flew out to conquer you, are now destroyed."

Obviously, the latter claim, a profusely bold statement, brought about numerous questions. The Queen only asked for patience. The answer would manifest itself in God's time. Though somewhat annoyed and overly curious, most were willing to bide their time. Then, until long past sundown and the rising of the double moons, the Queen and her devoted attendants stared into the undefiled valley, their ancient, forbidden homeland.

Sarg and Blue Turtle provided a secure encampment at the mouth of the tunnel. A restful quiet night, one without dragons, tunnels, Kyykki and any other unkindly surprizes is what they prayed for.

Delicately bright invigorating morning sun is what the troopers and their royal company received. It performed a miracle in restoring vitality to the overwrought troopers. The fresh air also woke up their senses, such that a full half-day became occupied with bathing, shaving, washing clothes and other sundry things that separate peoples from the rest of creation. Sarg had a special tent erected and hot water prepared for the all the ladies. But he wasn't sure who he protected from whom. Tiello and the blonde Jelkio enjoyed the men's attention a bit too much for his liking. Sarg, believing Vauk needed relief from a glowing Brey, sent him and Deep Owl to explore the subterranean supply tunnel.

"Find out far we can travel without being seen. I assume you can do that much."

"Actually, we can't Sarg." Vauk shot back. "We've never done this before. But, maybe you have a special ring that can make us invisible and we'll have absolutely no problems at all." Sarcasm rolled with his words.

"I'll keep the lover in line." Deep Owl assured Sarg. The most inauthentic compassion plastered all of his naturally reddened face.

"More friends such as the two of you, I don't need." Vauk shouted over his shoulder as he turned the bend and headed down the tunnel.

Deep Owl caught up with him quickly, but his smirking grin persisted. As they examined the intricate workings of the towing mechanism one fact loomed all-to-true; the machine's construction proved it constructed by Haafians. This fact forced the two to reshape their thinking; their next skirmish could be fought against their own kind. Part of their stomachs sickened.

"Its certainly not an unreasonable supposition." Vauk said. "In fact, this just might provide the missing pieces for us."

"Missing pieces?"

"Where the 'pale ladies' come from and what happened to those who were banished?"

"Yes, of course." But Deep Owl realized that Vauk wasn't focusing well. "Get your mind on the mission." Deep Owl's voice threatened.

Vauk turned to embed his fist in Deep Owl's face, when unexpectedly, the tension in the machinery's ropes disappeared and the cogs began to rotate. The dim light at the end of the tunnel faded.

"Supplies are coming." Hoarsely whispered Deep Owl.

"And I thought the tunnel collapsed." Retorted Vauk. "We'll continue with the other item later." He said without a grin.

"Sorry, but Tiello and I will be traversing a little known path later on." Deep Owl announced flatly.

"Damn!"

"Ah, your vocabulary increases." Deep Owl continued to tease as they quickly ascended to the top of the tunnel.

Sarg's wanted to capture the crew and the supplies as quietly as possible. A net stretched across the tunnel's ceiling, situated where the flatboat crew would be most vulnerable, at the bend in the tunnel. The deeper water there naturally demanded a modification in their transport technique. This demanded a pause in flatboat's journey, the perfect place for an ambush.

"Use this after the net falls." Blue Turtle handed a Yldan a grey ball of leaves filled with sleeping powder. "It takes a half day to wear off, but one breath will instantly send someone to dreamland."

The flatboat's mile tow up the fast-moving stream took most of the afternoon. By then, everyone knew that only one boat would be arriving. It had a crew of four on board and three following on the walkway. These latter had the responsibility of keeping the cogs running properly. Their off-key singing exemplified their secureness in this underworld.

There was no fight, no resistance, in fact no activity at all from the seven man crew. Their unbelievable sense of security left them one hundred percent vulnerable. The net fell and the ball collided with the boat crew. Their eyes went white. They just rolled out of the boat into the stream. The Yldans rescued them from a watery death. The three on the walkway succumbed to a leaf laced with the same potion Blue Turtle provided for the flatboat crew.

Sarg immediately had the seven Haafians trussed up until later. The sight of such dregs sickened him. He noticed the ill-boding countenance of Brey's face. Sarg wisely provided her with a responsibility far from the prisoners, for their own safety.

The flatboat went under quarantine; its cargo to be inventoried immediately. Sarg assigned Brey to this duty. Somehow she felt relieved. Her findings produced awe, consternation and rage. The boat's manifest listed several well-known and respected merchants and two nobles as contributors or dealers. The supplies on board included rather ordinary items, such as food stuffs and flour and salted meat. These Brey turned over to Tiello and Jelkio. Their next meal was designated as a feast, the first in many cycles.

She found some small items that provoked her. They especially disturbed Sarg. Maps were found inside a hollowed-out book. These incredibly accurate maps included the underground tunnels and supply routes under the city of Krabo. The second map delineated the major strong points along the wall with some scratches showing, once again, the subterranean supply routes. Sarg wistfully noted that most scratches were inaccurate. The third map went into immediate usage. It consisted of the route from Haaf North, through the mountains and then down to the coast where an "X" marked a place as 'Krucik's'. The merchant was no stranger.

Working the map backwards might furnish their escape route. Ideas of revenge, a righteous revenge, flooded Sarg's mind once again; a portion of that territory once belonged to him.

The ladies pulled a richly gold-and-silver inlaid mahogany trunk from inside a heavy wooden box, along with several smaller trunks, just as ornate as the large trunk. The large trunk and the smaller ones, Brey had carried to the ledge, where she might inspect their contents without danger from the water. Unfortunately, she opened one of the smaller boxes first.

"You probably would look most alluring in such outfit." Vauk said to Brey, a big excited grin on his face. Perhaps he expected Brey to be embarrassed about the extremely scanty, albeit, lacy feminine undergarments she pulled from the trunk. Instead, she held them up for everyone to see.

"I believe these to be about the right size." She said almost disinterestedly, as she held the top up to the front of her uniform. "A whole lot prettier too. Don't you think so, Vauk?"

He turned six shades of red as Brey's demonstration focused not on her teasing behavior, but on Vauk's awkwardness. He didn't answer, so Brey took the endeavor to another level. "Would you like me to model it for you?" She asked with a definite leer that left the Troopers roaring with laughter. Even the Queen enjoyed the show, from an appropriate distance, of course.

"Well, are you going to answer or do I have to teach you everything?"

"Where is your propriety?" Vauk said as boldly as possible under the circumstances.

"And where might your's be?" She quickly responded. "All you care to do is hold hands?" A wall of laughter poured over Vauk. He had no escape.

By now, Queen Sjura had a picture of the future. Quickly she summoned Jelkio and Tiello to capture Brey and her trunks of feminine clothing. Another comment from Brey wasn't needed. With big grins to the Troopers, and a special one from Tiello to Deep Owl, the girls swooped down on Brey and carried off the trunks. With their now famous giggles, they bounced along to their tent. Brey, now rankled, hastened after them, much to Vauk's relief.

"Vauk." The Queen called.

"Yes, my Lady?" He puzzled.

"With all due circumspection, I suggest you learn something about the way women communicate their feelings."

"I find myself at a loss, my Lady. What is it that I have done?"

"Perhaps its what you haven't done." Said the Queen, looking away from Vauk. Without another word, nor a answer from Vauk, the Queen gracefully walked to the tent where the trio of young ladies were beginning to hassle over the expensive dainty and alluring clothing.

Sarg, upon seeing the 'delightful' disturbance, called for the rest of the flatboat to be unloaded. Three casks of ale and one of wine were among the easily identifiable merchandise. A straw filled wooden box containing fragile glass-like bowls and mixing sticks proved mysterious and puzzling. But Vauk recognized these items as standard for the mixing of medicinal components.

"All I can tell you is that these are far too large for anything a doctor would be interested in. Maybe an alchemist or a wizard or a sorcerer...a magician.... might use something like these." Vauk estimated.

"Then we have our answer." Said Blue Turtle. "Would not the evil one be considered a sorcerer? Especially since he's into breeding his 'children.'" His voice became sickening as he thought some more. "Remember the rooms Deep Owl described for us."

"You mean when his patrol ransacked the empty volcano?" Asked Luuft.

"Exactly." Blue Turtle said. "There were rooms full of strange equipment and trenches dug into some floors. And one room stank of decayed flesh...."

"How about the evil rites of that 'thing' Sarg turned into pulp. Remember the altar Deep Owl 'delicately' delineated for our educational benefit." Luuft added with a sense of disgust.

"But it was for your benefit." Deep Owl proclaimed as if his dignity had been undermined.

"Certainly, it was!" Sarg announced. "But its time to find out the real answers. Bring one of the prisoners here. A little persuasive interrogation will clear the air."

"Let's wait until after the feast." Suggested Queen Sjura. "We all could use some food." Sarg shook his angular head in agreement; he found it most indelicate to defy her. However, he easily convinced himself of his hunger.

The tribunal met at dusk, after supper. Those appointed to hold the interrogation included Deep Owl, Brey, Blue Turtle, Luuft and Sarg. Queen Sjura, by her own special order, asked to participate. Sarg asked her to sit by his right side and to keep the ring in view. The group convened in a semi-circle with torches behind them and a small fire in the middle. This stark setting in the dank corridor proved rather intimidating.

The first of the prisoners arrived, arrogant and wet from the water used to bring him back from his dreams. "I am a freeman. I have nothing to say to you. I protest ...."

"You have no power here." Brey said softly. "Your life is on the line. We are the Light Striper."

The man's face showed he understood; he hid his arrogance. "I know de Light 'iper." He muttered. "Them killed me village."

"Only if you were a Kyykki." Sarg said bluntly. "Anymore lies and your head will float down stream without the rest of you." Then Sarg raised Queen Sjura's hand to show the filthy prisoner her ring. "Notice, my friend, that the ring's orange glow. That proclaims that the truth has been spoken. Should it ever change color, consider yourself a dead man."

The slob stood taller, a gleam of arrogance returned. "What do I know which it werks?" He challenged.

"Enough of this arrogance." Blue Turtle said without much emphasis. "He is a traitor, take him away."

The Yldans who restrained him, removed him from the tribunal's circle, returning him to the temporary prison. There, in front of the other prisoners, they summarily executed the traitor. The other six suddenly had a wealth of information to provide the tribunal. When the last of the serfs, as they actually turned out to be, finished his garbled testimony, the tribunal rested, exhausted.

"I suggest we wait until dawn to summarize." Brey recommended.

The tribunal dispersed without another word. Some to eat, some to sleep. And Queen Sjura to check up on her blonde attendant. Vauk, waiting on the pathway to Brey's tent, found himself just wasting time, at this particular moment she had a full schedule. She did, however, accept the red flower he plucked from a bush growing to the side of the falls.

When breakfast finished, Sarg recalled the tribunal to session, though, today, the meeting began in the warm sunshine.

"I'm glad we only have another section of tunnels before we're done with them." Luuft began.

"Except," Cautioned Deep Owl. "There are two sets of 'real' guards and these fellows think. They're Haafians."

"You don't need to remind me." Sarg cut in. "We need to, first of all, appraise what we were told last evening."

Queen Sjura offered the first analysis. "I found the last six men truthful to the point of pain. In spite of their depravity, they still appreciate living. And, as they explained, their 'demon's prurient interests lie in vile sexual pleasures. ....I'll not repeat the base details, which caused me nauseousness last evening." She paused to wipe her eyes. "That's the primary reason for either buying or kidnapping young ladies." She paused again, weeping. "There are times when this ring is nothing more than a curse."

"I'll vouch for that part." Brey said under her breath, but loud enough for everyone to hear.

"But the ladies performed a more abhorrent role: the 'demon' used their inner female parts to create his 'children'. I could have strangled the one who told us that." Deep Owl murmured as the Queen sobbed and Brey's face showed the tension she felt.

"Some things I'd ...."

"Want to forget about? Hide under a rug? Ignore as the truth? Do not for get who you are, Deep Owl." Blue Turtle sermonized.

"I'm not." He replied defensively. "But the evil dark things mark the soul of those who simply hear about them. They rob innocence and induce an orientation antithetical to our culture."

"Get off this purity kick." Sarg barked. "We're called to deal with what is, not the world we envision. The point is, peoples are bought, most people have a price. The ladies sold out for a pleasurable life. These serfs sold out to another master, one who lied. Now they're all either dead or captured."

"I have a reshaping to do with my own thoughts about our culture. All the traitors! The backstabbers!" Luuft sighed. "This power of the evil one pervades the nation. How will we achieve victory when...."

"Why should you not have expected this?" The Queen asked.

"I find myself looking for simple answers. There aren't any. Its one thing to say that, quite another to understand what it means. I don't....I hate realizing that I'm not much different from those others. I have the same feelings. I could be bought." Luuft stared at the ground in front of him.

"Yes..." the Queen acknowledged. "However, by recognizing the truth inside you. You also maintain a tremendous resource for the choosing you must do. You are facing the truth. That is proper for the faithful in Tath. We spend years getting to know ourselves."

"Are you positive your God doesn't have a name?"

"Yes, Sarg. I am. Our Gods may have some similar ideas, but our God would never allow God's word to become encoded on paper and thus become dead and stagnant."

Blue Turtle smiled at that. "I favor that your God is likened unto the spirit side of our God, the Holy One, Blessed be His Name."

"No. As we discussed earlier, our God allows for no such rampant subjectivity. Our God sends us prophets when there is something God wants us to know. We live from one prophet to the next."

With tempers slowly wore wearing thin, Sarg ended the debates. "Theology and the study of comparative religion is all well and good. But," Announced Sarg in his most authoritative tone. "We have just another dawn before this flatboat crew is due at the bottom. Its time we put the pieces together."

"An ambush is the best way to go. Fill the boat up with the troopers and head down. Surprize is still our best weapon." Luuft voiced his a plan.

"But that still leaves us with ten in the boat and twenty on the docks. And maybe another twenty serfs above ground. Account for them? Its tempting to believe we'll get them all, but not especially true." Blue Turtle commented.

The boat goes down slow, so it doesn't break up. Except for a rear guard and a party for the Taths, the entire company will stay behind the boat. A trio dressed appropriately as serfs will amble down the walkway. Those in the boats will have bows, the rest will charge; half to the docks and the balance up the stairwell to the surface. Deep Owl will lead the archers. Luuft will command the rest. I'll take the docks. Blue Turtle, you take watch over the Queen..."

"I severely object to such mandated rules, my dear Sarg." The Queen said coolly. "We ARE capable of taking care of ourselves. Our health after two years in this volcano is proof."

"Though I do not understand 'years', at this moment it is of little significance.... And, you may object, my dear Queen. But as you are part of this company, you are subject to its rules. If you weren't royalty, however, I could put you in the boat.... Can you shoot well?" Sarg had a broad but serious smile.

The Queen flustered for a moment. "I believe your motive proper, Sarg. I shall do as you say."

"Thank you, my Lady."

"And who has the rear guard?" Queried Brey.

"You do. Thanks for volunteering." Said Sarg matter-of-factly. "We'll be leaving at early morning. The one-eyed serf said they eat lunch upon arrival."

"What about lunch now?"

The afternoon witnessed the Yldans testing their shooting skills, though out of respect for the Queen, no arrows were shot into the valley. The constant guard watched only blue skies with soft clouds and non-existent dragons. But the guard did behold a wondrous sight; Queen Sjura, Jelkio, Tiello and Brey arrived for supper dressed in the finest of gowns, having procured them from the largest trunk.

The four literally swept into camp, causing many pleasing smiles and a bit of 'deliberate' confusion as all the troopers turned their heads to stare. Queen Sjura wore a full length gown of grey-blue velvet trimmed with the finest white lace at the hem and the edge of the bell sleeves. For the first time, she wore a crown, a rather modest one consisting of a medium wide gold band fronted with four precious stones that formed a diamond. Her three ladies-in-waiting wore matching ankle length gowns of deep pink. These were also trimmed in fine white lace at the hem and about the neckline. The shoulderless gowns came with lacy shawls that teased the best from their femininity.

Queen Sjura waited until all the camp had gathered before she spoke. "Sarg, my good friend, is it not time for supper? The four of us are awaiting our feast."

Sarg stared, a bit stunned, at first not recognizing Brey, the 'temporary' lady-in-waiting. The beauty of the Queen also caught him off guard. More than just her queenly grandeur that rattled his mind; her manners, the way she carried herself all brought back memories of his late wife. He shook his head as if to rid himself of the new reality: after all, Queen Sjura is royalty. She is a Tath and he a Haafian. No, this stupidity must cease at once, he demanded of himself in a low undertone.

"Sarg," The Queen gently repeated, "We are awaiting supper."

Her remarked caused him to half stumble from his daydream into the real world. "You were saying, my Lady?"

"Only for the third time, Sarg."

The ladies giggled, except for Brey, who wasn't too secure in her new role. But all noticed Sarg wasn't quite himself either. Obviously, he needed some relaxation also; such a concept materialized because of the Queen's presumption: a party might prove the corrective for Sarg.

"Its time for the supper to begin." Announced Queen Sjura not waiting on Sarg to catch up. Then she turned and smiled at Sarg. "I have chosen you as my escort." She said to everyone as she stared Sarg in the face. "Yes, the Queen will have her rescuer as her royal escort." She reached out and took his tensed arm before he could protest. "Ladies," Ordered the Queen, "You shall not be seated without an escort. It is only proper."

A near riot ensued as Jelkio tried to choose from too many of the overanxious Yldans.

"Your flirting has come back upon you, dear Jelkio." Called a voice from the crowd.

"Who is this one who called out?" Demanded the Queen, a wry smile upon her face."

"I am." Answered a stockish Yldan archer with a resonant voice. He stepped out in front of the Queen. His long brown hair was parted in the middle and braided down over his ears. A single white feather hanging from a leather necklace showed him to be warrior of some renown. As usual for the Yldans, he wore only baggy trousers. "Queen Sjura, my name is One Fox." He said politely, but without bowing.

The Queen looked him over. "Jelkio, One Fox is your escort for the evening. His example of honesty may be to your benefit."

One Fox flushed for a moment and then found Jelkio on his arm. The troopers saluted him with a roaring cheer and a few whistles. Jelkio spent an uncomfortable evening adjusting to a different type of man. Brey had little trouble dragging along Vauk as her escort, though Vauk's embarrassment troubled her and began a lecture that would last until after the two moons passed over. Tiello quietly moved next to Deep Owl, they spoke much but bothered little with words.

A few rounds of ale and a feast for the troopers guaranteed a night of strange tales, fascinating dances and music. At Sarg's request, none of the usual jokes. Dawn would bring the designated raid, but the evening brought back the return of life at its best. Talk and friends, wine and food, and the always tempting promise that tomorrow, because of now, would provide the 'stuff' that makes for beautiful endings.

"A well planned raid!...... Damn!........Damn!" Sarg swore. He stood alone at the squalid town's only gate; his face blackened, his uniform wet and tattered his skin swollen and bleeding.

Ashes continued to pour down upon the few survivors as did scalding water from the newly erupting volcano. They only had time to sprint up the stairs into the mud hut village. The singular fact that the village appeared empty set the troopers preparing for an ambush along its crooked narrow and garbage strewn lanes. But nothing came of it, except that the slower they proceeded, the greater their casualties.

"Head over that ridge!" Sarg yelled with both rage and grief.

Over fifteen Yldans died at the bottom of the tunnel. The moment the raiding party arrived at the docking area, from the center of the pool an infernal mixture of flame and lava erupted up into the open air above the pool, taking parts of the flatboat with it. The swirling, boiling water, throwing waves over twenty feet into the air, swept away most. The cavern's docks then disintegrated as molten lava flooded over top of them.

Their agonizing cries for help still rang in Sarg's mind. His ability to control the situation didn't exist. And, in spite of his mental block against 'magic and sorcery', Sarg found this disaster beyond any coincidence. All along, he now realized, deliberately planned obstacles had thwarted their efforts to finish the mission. The cost, especially in innocent lives, tormented him.

"Keep going! ..Head for that patch of trees! Watch out for an ambush!" Sarg's efforts focused on getting the survivors away from the volcano's suffocating ash and droplets of molten rock.

As of yet, Luuft and Deep Owl remained unaccounted for as did Jelkio. The Queen, Vauk and Brey created a pathway to the safety of the thicket Sarg pointed out.

"Damn!" Sarg continued to swear. "First the dragons, no first the jungle, and then... the other beast.. And the demon...twice the demon.... and now, an empty dock, a deserted town...and a volcano that explodes at the precise moment we arrive...." Sarg seething incessantly mumbled to himself as he aided the survivors leaving the town's gate. A few were severely burnt and wouldn't last the night. Friends carried wounded friends. Two men, with but one leg each, drug each other through the gates. One died as he reached it. Sarg picked up the other one and carried him to the thicket. His torment became unbearable as he realized that no others survived.

"DAMN!" He roared.

Sarg continued to swear as he covered the distance to the thicket at a dead run. He laid the man beside the others Vauk doctored. The Queen prepared bandages from whatever supplies she found. The water casks were lost, but a spring bubbled from the center of the thicket, that proved a blessing of sorts. The walking wounded and others, now commanded by Blue Turtle, began building a defensive wall about the wounded.

"I doubt it'll stop anything!" Blue Turtle barked at Sarg.

"Let it be!"

"But we are defenseless at present."

"Can you keep a volcano from attacking?" He retorted with unusual cynicism. "Can we still do anything?" He questioned himself, though he said the words loudly.

"Are we dead?" The Queen's voice bit deeply into Sarg's sense of self-remorse.

Sarg shook his head, making no verbal reply. He quickly surveyed the makeshift camp ....or, rather, the field hospital. Six Yldans suffered from severe wounds, mainly burns. Even the Queen had a few scald marks on her legs and arms.

Then the attack came, crudely and loudly. The attackers numbered fifty, according to Brey. Haafian serfs attacked, armed with short swords and round shields. Their full tilt charge came from behind a low rise off to the right of the thicket, about two hundred feet away.

"Perfect range for arrows!" Blue Turtle intoned with a sense of vengeance. Each arrow bought a serf a cruel death, but only four arrows survived. He drew his sabre and waited.

The remaining crossbow took out the two lead men, ripping through the metal shields into their chests. As the hand to hand combat began, the renegade Haafians collided with the Trooper's line with only half their original number.

Three furious troopers wielding broadaxes sliced through shield and man alike; each cross cut as deadly as the forward one. Sabres danced faster than the untrained attackers imagined. They fell quickly and none broke through. Tiello and the Queen, both brandishing kitchen knives, had taken their places at the field hospital.

"Duck!" Roared Blue Turtle to Tiello as a wounded Haafian plunged himself through the front line in a desperate effort to break it. The man jumped up in front of Tiello, savagely swinging his sword down upon her head. She stood there frozen, the kitchen knife pointing out from both her hands. Blue Turtle caught the man in mid air with a kick. Off-balance, he planted himself firmly on Tiello's knife, his own sword nicking her in the upper right arm. He looked at her, blank-faced and died.

The Haafian serfs, what few still lived, began a disorganized retreat. Their formation had no discipline, providing easy targets for the vengeful Light Striper. Sarg cut the last one down just a few feet from the rise that sheltered the attackers. "Hard to stop a broadaxe with a bare hand, isn't it? You stupid fool!" Sarg cursed the dying man while he retrieved his thrown broadaxe from the Haafian's bloody chest. He stood on the rise, exhausted and yet mindful of the friends he lost. Vengeance did not become him; once he proudly stood behind that. Now vengeance found its place in his life. But the uninvited quandary bothered him.

After he checked out the rise, Sarg called out "All clear, there are no more." He dropped over the rise and came back with a sack of Haafian supplies. "Send some men over to get the rest....And collect the arrows."

That evening the two moons did not show, the ugliness of the dark clouds from the still frothing volcano blotting them out. It made the night more foul for the troopers, especially the wounded. Tiello shook from her shock and horror all night, even when Blue Turtle tried to console her. Such savagery tore holes through her. The Queen, with aid from a few Yldans, did her best to provide a meal.

Off, at the corner of the camp stood Sarg, silently wrestling with his faith. "Magic does not exist. But now else to explain the carnage about us? Is it mere accident that we are prevented from our mission? True, this is not our land. This is evil land. But does that preclude the Holy One from having power here? Are we suffering because His power is limited to Haaf?" Then he cried out, feeling a deep in inward pain when he realized the extent of his machinations. He crossed the boundary into heresy and he knew it. Yet, ideas of 'magic' refused to be silenced. A gentle hand touched his shoulders. He turned to see the Queen.

"Take this." She gently said, handing him a metal cup filled with a hot tea. "You must rest, you know. However, if I might be so bold, I believe you are much like my late husband. He never rested until the answers matched the questions."

"You are kind, my Queen" He took the tea and drank it all.... "How long have you been listening?" His embarrassment showed in his voice.

"Long enough to know you must talk to me."

"But," He began to protest.

"But I'm the Queen, correct!" She emphasized each word. "Now, by your standards, the Queen is only to be served."

"Well, yes." He said slowly, feeling that trouble showed on the horizon.

"Then you shall serve me by sharing those heresies with me...." She paused, as if a bit frightened about her own feelings and needs. "Besides, I do miss having conversation with someone on my level."

She reached out her hand to Sarg. Without really meaning to take it, he did so with almost an inner sense of relief. A log lay nearby, furnishing an excellent spot for a long talk.

"I need to tell you that God has power, even in this ungodly environment. My proof is you and the rest. We prayed, for four hundred and some days for deliverance. From our position, as prisoners of the demon, deliverance might have been given as death." She hesitated as the grief and ugliness from her captivity began to cause her to stutter and then cry.

"I thank you for your affirmation to your God." Sarg almost whispered.

He put his arm about the Queen's shoulder. For the longest time, no one spoke.

"I'm glad we were able to assist you in escaping. But for us, it was unintentional. We had no idea who or what existed in this evil domain."

"You had no need to be intentional; God guided you." The Queen's eyes still watered. "And, I believe, from your perspective, our God should have no such power over those who don't know God."

"Yes." But the answer presented the feeling of deep thoughts under the surface.

"Share with me?" The question was genuine.

"I hate to even think about it, milady. but at this juncture, I'm not sure where the Holy One is. We have only one God, as your people do. But it seems His power might have some limits, where your God can reach into hell and pull you out...." Sarg's pained voice gave evidence to this jumbled mixture of new and old thoughts, some he recognized as heresy."

"How do you know your Holy One is powerless here? Where is your evidence? If your Holy One's power is limited and yet He is your protector, then tell me, how is it that you remain alive?"

"My Lady....." Sarg took a deep breath. "I have no answer, except that I know the damned one is atrociously devious. Perhaps it is 'it' which causes my great doubting. And this 'its' territory."

"Then your God and the evil one are equals, each sharing a portion of the land to the exclusion of the other?"

"Forbid such a thought!" Sarg became overly nervous. "Then we are without hope, if evil and good are but equals." His journey into melancholy became heavier.

"Then might I offer an alternative?" The Queen's voice trembled slightly as she dared pursue another route. She knew full well that her alternative might destroy a faith that provided both meaning and nourishment for Sarg.

"My Lady," Sarg dispiritedly said. "My heart is torn. These are questions I've never pondered before. I've never known of their existence before. Once, I believed we were forbidden to even question. Now I am forced to....If I am to be at peace.....If I am to know the truth.... Please, share with me." Only after his wife's death, almost four hundred double cycles ago, had Sarg felt such a desperate emptiness.

"Forbid my boldness, my friend." Her voice sustained a quavering: she harbored no desire to hurt Sarg, but she knew her very words could. Such responsibility she received at birth, being part and parcel of her royal office, nevertheless now she wished she might be a simple commoner whom Sarg would willingly argue with.....

"Think of it this way." She slowly began. "Might there not be Gods of areas of land, Gods of nations, yet one Almighty God who is supreme beyond all the others?" Her voice filled with intrepidation as she uttered her final words.

Sarg sat motionless, frozen to the log. He felt as if his head and heart burst into a million fragments; ones that were irretrievable. Certainly, he discovered a logic in the Queen's suggestion, but it far surpassed his true comprehension. More than one God? Lesser Gods? How many? And why? The Holy One, a sub-servient God? An ordinary geographical God? A God circumscribed by water on three sides and the Dark Lands on the north?.. Sadly, he had nothing by which to defend his old position. Nothing he could think of. His only hope now lay in the Holiness Code and those who priests who interpreted it.

"This is much too heavy a suggestion for me to bear, My Lady." Sarg spoke as controllably as he could. "I don't have enough time to fully explore what you have suggested. Such questions actually belong to the territory of the clergy."

"You are angry with me?" She hesitantly asked.

"I really don't think so. It's not you. I recognize you are trying to help me. I appreciate that." His voice lost some weakness. "But in unlocking such a new dimension in my mind, several other items then also need re-explained or redefined."

"What might they be?"

"Magic, for one....Magic exists." Even though the Queen visibly recoiled from his words, Sarg continued. "Magic is forbidden to mortals. You said that yourself, my Lady. But, if there are Gods in competition for certain parcels of land, then magic is their way of manipulating us to do their will?"

"It cannot be so!" Queen Sjura exclaimed, drawing back. Now her world, once as rock-stable as Sarg's began to crack. "Such capriciousness, especially of God, is intolerable. What foundation shall be provided for our stability?" Alarmed would be a gross under-statement for the Queen.

"Don't be afraid, my Queen. Perhaps, as I continue to dwell on this mystery, it actually was supposed to be...this conversation, that is. You see, we each had a God, a God trapped inside the only boundaries we understood. But, can a God be a God if we people define what and what not God can do? A God who is God only because He has people to define Him?..........Can you understand my ramblings, my Lady?"

"I.. I'm not sure. But freedom belongs to God. We have no right nor way to remove it..... But we do, don't we? In our minds and within our cultures.....Perhaps,.... you are right. Maybe God is working to bring about a greater appreciation of God. One that transcends our current misconceptions."

"There is too much here for mortals. We should not be so bold as to question things of which we are ignorant. This 'God' business belongs to the clergy." Sarg tried to extricate himself from the controversy once again.

"Then what are you doing in this evil land?" Queen Sjura readily caught him.

Sarg blushed slightly. "Perhaps I am here to rescue a Queen?"

Prior to their meager breakfast, Sarg and Vauk left the thicket planning to investigate the filthy mud-and-stone village. Vauk wanted to see if their journey might be continued downstream. Sarg went to look for evidence of magic. If he had been using a wrong set of rules...well, he just wanted more substantiation.

The slimy buildings, all equally coated with greyish dust along with a modicum of lava pellets, lost their roofs to fire. The place was deserted, no one about, no one alive, that is. They buried the Yldan who died at the gate in a shallow grave. They approached the stone staircase leading to the docking area, now covered with a thick coating of lava. A sturdy rap from Vauk's broadaxe, however, cracked it open. Once the hole was large enough, Vauk silently crawled in, followed by Sarg.

Beyond belief, beyond shock, they found the dock busy, as if nothing had ever happened. The men stared at each other in utter disbelief. A flatboat just arrived and serfs were about their usual duties. Any and all damage caused by yesterday's volcanic eruption simply didn't exist anymore, except for a larger hole in the volcano's roof. Even the stones on the dock were visible and appeared worn, as if nothing ever happened. Some giddy young females in long transparent gowns were aboard the incoming flatboat. Sarg inwardly groaned with disgust and with pity.

But signs of any more Yldans, dead, alive or captured didn't exist. Jelkio, Deep Owl and Luuft remained in the same categories. While the two expected this to be the situation, neither had prepared himself for the heartache it brought.

They left as quietly as the arrived, not desiring to be chased back to camp by the renegade Haafians. They returned to camp by mid-morning. Neither of them actually believed they pitched camp over three miles from the village.

On approaching the camp's perimeter, Queen Sjura came running towards them, violently waving her arms. Brey ran two steps behind her, fully armed. The Queen suddenly stopped when the men stood only ten feet away. She pointed to her orange stone ring;. It pulsed like never before. Then she pointed to the thicket and finally put her finger to her mouth, signaling 'quiet, no one speaks.' Brey handed Sarg a written note as the Queen stuffed her hand, ring and all, into the a heavy cape she usually wore.

After reading the note, Sarg's anguished contorted face showed he understood the new situation. He passed the note to Vauk who stupidly began to read it out loud.

"O' my love, its nice to be with you again!" Exclaimed Brey as she kissed him and then whispered into his pointed ear, "Shut up! Read! To yourself"

He did so, immediately. "Tree talks. Will attack directly."

Vauk's face went pale, showing both disbelief as well as shock. He automatically turned his head towards Sarg, awaiting a command.

First, Sarg motioned for the ring to be exposed to the tree's hearing, then he spoke. "Yes, its good to see all of you as well. But, we are tired. Let's return to camp for some food and.......and........everyone should receive some time off. What'd you think, Vauk?"

Caught off-guard, Vauk stammered until Brey kicked him in the right leg. "Aa aa Yes, Commander. A rest is needed. ....An excellent idea. The troopers would enjoy an afternoon nap." A quirky smile from Brey told him he finally caught on. He gave her a snarl in return.

"Come, Vauk," Brey coaxed. "Your pride needs mending." Her eyes showed her to be extremely serious in spite of her tone. "Time to get back to camp."

Sarg grabbed the note from Vauk. Then he stooped down and wrote in the ground: Have Queen set up for meal. Move wounded and supplies over rise. NOW." Vauk and Brey walked ahead into camp, Sarg gently escorted the Queen to the camp's hospital. During their slow walk, Sarg used hand signs to explain he planned to evacuate camp as quickly as possible, while allowing the tree to believe the opposite. Queen Sjura indicated not only that she understood but that she also heard the tree bragging about how quickly it enveloped people with their branches. Sarg winced at the 'welcome' information.

"Quickly, Troops!" Sarg called out. "Before I can grant you an afternoon of rest, we'll have inspection. Full inspection. Forget nothing." His tone and gaze let the troopers know something wasn't right. They hobbled quickly into inspection formation, even though nothing approaching a uniform existed.

The tree instantly reacted, its food was leaving. As the men moved into formation, great branches moved and dropped down to encircle them. The leaves dripped with a sticky sappy substance, powerful enough to rip off clothing as well as flesh.

A Trooper screamed out as he was lifted into the higher branches and then, dashed upon the ground, some twenty feet below. Some troopers attacked the tree; finding it not impervious to their sabres, but its branches retained numerical superiority.

Queen Sjura spoke. "The tree is laughing at us. Considering us surrounded, it desires to play with us. Kill us one-by-one."

"Not true!" A defiant Sarg screamed and gestured with his broadaxe. "Today, you shall die!" He cried out. Then he placed his broadaxe on the ground. He placed his hands together in front of him, aiming both index fingers at the huge tree occupying the center of the thicket. "In the name of the Holy One," Sarg intoned half-way between a curse and a prayer. "You shall die!....Now!"

A deep rumbling came from the heavens even as a blue halo surrounded Sarg. From his pointed fingers shot a solid bolt of blue lightning. As Sarg fell back from the recoil, the bolt struck the tree shoulder high on its massive trunk. The tree shrieked in a way that forced everyone to cover their ears. The massive high pitched vibration lasted a few breaths, then suddenly terminated. As the Queen and the other survivors watched in reverent awed silence, the huge tree slowly split from crown to root. Its branches limply uncurled, freeing six Yldans. The leaves yellowed, browned and then turned to greyish ash. Before their eyes, the rest of the once arrogant tree also turned to ash. Before Sarg recovered, only a blackened hole remained where the evilness once reigned.

The Queen, suddenly remembering that Sarg lay upon the ground, turned and bent over. She held him in her arms and kissed his forehead. He recovered with a start, frightening the Queen.

"What happened?" Sarg demanded. He shook his head, complaining of dizziness and headache.

"Maybe you can handle it." Suggested the Queen. "But it did throw you on the ground. And its safe to say, the whole thing came from your God, the Holy One."

"Is everyone safe? The tree?" Sarg became nervously excited.

"Yes, thanks to the power of your God." The Queen restated with awe and reverence.

"Then the Holy One answered?"

"Let me show you." Offered Vauk as he helped a groggy Sarg to his still shaking feet.

In the fifty feet to where the tree once defiantly stood, a thin scorch line continued to smolder on the earth. A ten foot crater existed at the end of the scorch line. Sarg peered into the hole, awe struck and humbled.

"I humbly thank you, O Holy One." He prayed as he fell to his knees.

The other Haafians did the same. The Yldans simply bowed their heads while the Queen and Tiello wept. Sarg continued in a daze. What happened was unbelievable. His God answered his cry for help. His God watched over him personally. His God had no limits.

Much later, as they prepared to head south, around the squalid village and its volcano, Sarg explained the scene back at the docks. It was so incredulous that almost every detail had to be verified by Vauk. Then as the journey commenced, Sarg walked next to Queen Sjura. Vauk and Brey acted as the rear guard, though more for the opportunity to share their common loss than to protect the Troopers.

None dared speak of what happened, it seemed too Holy, too sacred, to profane with common talk. And who was Sarg?

"My Lady," Said Sarg after they walked for some time. "I wish to thank you for last evening. I confess you severely pained my heart, but the question did find an answer."

"Yes, Sarg, it certainly did." The Queen responded in a manner that invited Sarg to continue. She took his hand as they walked, a very bold move for a queen, especially a Tath queen.

"I refuse to believe in magic. Magic had nothing to do with what transpired at the thicket.... Miracle is the proper name for the God event..... The scene at the dock demonstrated the power of the damned one, working, of course, in his own domain."

"Are you certain you understand where you're headed with this?"

"I believe so. I had to know for myself about the Holy One. He appeared to me in my dream last evening, simply saying, "Trust Me"."

"And that's exactly what you did." Queen Sjura interjected.

Sarg walked quietly for a while. "My Lady, the Holy One has power, power in a territory I erroneously thought He had no control over....I am ashamed of myself...I have failed in my Faith, my God, the Holy One........ Yet the Holy One, when I too boldly asked for His assistance, did forthrightly answer me."

"Does questioning still alarm you so? Did not your Holy One's reply serve to answer your questioning?.....If He had been angered by your so-called insolence, why was the tree destroyed instead of you? ...How might you answer that, My Lord?" She squeezed his hand tightly and presently him with a warm smile.

Sarg blushed. "My Lady, even this hand holding is unbecoming. I am a serf, you are royalty." Sarg's nervousness resonated in each syllable he uttered. His mind jumbled and tossed; two extremely separated items he simultaneously needed to settle. "My Lady, this is way too much for me. Your friendship is a wonderful reward of itself...... I seek nothing from you.

What you desire goes beyond the bounds of our cultures and of common propriety."

"I think not." The Queen strongly challenged. "You are the one who is beyond me or any other royalty..... You are a Prophet!"

"A Prophet?" Sarg flinched, here, he recognized, came another dreadful change.

"A Prophet, one who acts on behalf of God, your God for the benefit of His people. Is that not what you did, and was it not based solely on faith?"

"Yes, my Lady......... Except there are no prophets in Haaf. The Holy One acts through His word for our benefit."

"The Holiness Code. The Code which Blue Turtle instructs me does not allow the Holy One His rightfully due freedom. Blue Turtle tells me of the Holy One's spirit which sends dreams and messages to whomever He so chooses...... Yet you both claim to have the same God."

"Yes, my Lady." Sarg's nervousness expanded as he ascertained the trail of the Queen's logic.

"I've spoken with Blue Turtle. He believes you have been given the gift of the Spirit. That you will be able to use it whenever needed. He does not deny that the term 'prophet' applies to you. In fact, he claims that each generation has such a person as you. Even one Vusnoobe, he claims, has none of the power you demonstrated." She sprung the trap, Sarg found himself caught.

"My Lady," Said Sarg. "I must think on all of this."

"Nonsense." She flatly replied. "You know all ready that you cannot refuse the Holy One. If He called you to be a Prophet, you are a Prophet....... All the Yldans believe that. They stand in awe of you and rightly so."

She paused and then turned to the Troopers behind her, Troopers who had been listening all along. She spoke loudly. "Hail, the Prophet of the Holy One." Then she knelt before the unamused and embarrassed Sarg in humble respect.

"Hail, Prophet of the Holy One." Blue Turtle said as he also knelt, humble and earnest.

Then followed the other Yldans. "Hail, Prophet of the Holy One." And they too knelt along with Brey and Vauk.

Sarg slowly shook his head in disbelief. He had only wanted to be a Light Striper Trooper. Instead, his skill promoted him to the right hand of Commander Vosnob, then to secret missions, now he became a Prophet..... And Queen Sjura loved him, perhaps? He wasn't sure what the future held, but like most commonsense Haafians, he knew he must accept the present. A Prophet, even a disinclined one, so be it.

Knee high brambles, briars and a continuous grey sky set a dismal atmosphere for the next four dawns as the wounded and tired Troopers proceeded hacking their way southward. A lack of anything resembling a trail and an irregular stony terrain significantly added to the problems of transporting three wounded Yldans. Small springs appeared at irregular intervals, providing adequate water supplies, but depleted food stuffs plagued their healthiness. Finally, after skirting around four huge volcanoes and two more of the 'breeding lakes', the sky intermittently gave way to a brighter yellowish hue and a sweltering dry breeze. Shade was nonexistent from the beginning, but now, with the change in weather, it contributed to the death of a wounded Yldan. At the so-called evening of the forth dawn, as the dry wind blew a darker grey over them, the scouting party reported a narrow valley heading off in a southwest direction. So far, the heavy, disconsolate four dawns, allowed Sarg to ponder his new responsibility. The quietness helped the others to adjust to it as well. That which is Holy is also found to be both risky and somewhat fearful, and definitely, unnatural. Every evening, about their circles, for fear of the dragons and other demonic beings, they shared their stories. So too for the fifth night. The stories centered about their immense losses, over half of the initial party. The conversation dwelt upon the unfairness of their experiences, especially the fact that funerals weren't possible, and, until now, no one really had time even to mourn for the dead or for themselves. How would the Holy One react to their neglectfulness? Once the issue broke into the open, all eyes turned to Sarg for the answer.

Sarg began with a disclaimer. "I am not a learned clergy, nor have I spent great amounts of time studying the Holiness Code. I have only recently been made a Prophet. I had no desire to be one. And I remain unsure of the responsibilities of a Prophet... ....But, you have asked for an answer. ...I too mourn, for my friends, for those who perished before I actually knew them, for those who simply left my life.t....And my life feels empty."

The Troopers heavyheartedly nodded their heads in full agreement. Their out-in-the-open feelings pushed Sarg to go on.

"I'm not sure how to place the events of our mission into perspective." Sarg went on, rather pensively. "The Holy One loves us all. He desires that we use our abilities to the fullest, if the cause be good and proper. Righteous, yes, that's the Prophet's vocabulary,......I guess."

His last remark elicited a slight snicker from the group. He felt a bit more at ease; maybe he could be a Prophet without fitting into his preconceived Prophet's mold.

"Anyway.......That's my rationale for our mission: we came to explore this evil land that those who follow us might defeat these evil things we all know about....It will also mean the end of their vile and abominable practices. ...We are all part of that plan....But, fighting evil...." He paused in an effort to clear things in his own mind. "Fighting evil is costly, to our friends, to ourselves, to our minds and hearts. Fighting evil changes us and others. We have become as one, though we are of three races. .... Others, the Haafians who suffered when they attacked us, give into evil. For them it is costly also." Sarg simply summarized some basic truths. He had nothing new to offer. Such a dangerous undertaking, he desperately wished not to begin. "I find one very important difference, an essential difference here: the Holy One loves us and will not use us to serve a selfish notion."

Snickering flared up at Sarg's gaff. He regained his composure without speaking: a Prophet's silence, he quickly learned, carried great weight.

"I hope to finish momentarily. The evil one uses his people for his own insulting purposes. He cares nothing for their faithfulness, only that they perform according to his wishes. Should they fail, he kills them. There is no love, only fear."

The Troopers continued to stare at Sarg. He felt the pressure to continue. But then, he realized he had forgotten the original reason for his speech: the disappointment of the Holy One for not having the funerals. A moment later the thought returned to him. "The Holy One loves us, he does not condemn us for what is not possible. We have done our best in mourning for our friends. They are not forgotten; we remember their lives. If we are still fearful about the Holy One's judgement, then we have yet to fully appreciate His love…There is no more that I have to offer you."

Sarg stood up and slowly wandered away from the Troopers, who sat quietly distilling the Prophet's words. The words were special, and somehow, in spite of Sarg's avowed awkwardness, they reached into the depths of the Troopers. Sarg experienced a strange tiredness, one that went beyond his heart to his soul. He also felt a separation from the others. Is a Prophet to be alone? Is he now so different? As if an answer, the small hand of Queen Sjura gently grasped his. When they returned to the campsite, everyone except the posted guard, was sleeping.

"Perhaps, we'll have something to eat after we get to the valley."

"Wishful thinking, Brey?" Vauk tried to make her smile, but Brey, like the rest, suffered from severe exhaustion.

The dry heat had continued unabated, even during the dark grey night. Yellowish skies proved no kinder than the light grey ones, except that everyone believed the gradual modification meant that safety, that is, the border of Haaf drew nearer. Even the narrow valley, with its contrasting green vegetation and a blue ribbon of water running its length, promised respite from the dreary wasteland they trudged through.

Getting to the valley proved the immediate challenge. The trek amounted to another three miles. To the Trooper's dismay, the wasteland ended abruptly at the valley's edge; a sheer black basalt cliff dropping some fifty feet to its overgrown floor.

Without warning ten dragons, flying in a line, instead of their usual languid cluster, approached swiftly from the north. Their blackened ugly forms silhouetted upon the yellowish sky, their long necks straining to ensure that they screened every foot of the acrid territory. The Troopers, outlined against the green valley below, were soon spotted. The single line of dragons maneuvered into three parallel lines as they clumsily circled for their kill.

"Spread out! Aim for their eyes! Queen Sjura, here, please!

Tiello, Brey, get the wounded away from the edge and see what you can find for ropes." Sarg bellowed the orders as he stood forward, his back to the valley, his broadaxe in hand to greet the dragons.

They uneasily landed in crooked line a hundred feet away. A horrendous looking demon, much like the one twice-killed in the tunnels, swung down from the first dragon. "I bring a message from my master." He croaked in a deadening monotone.

"Why should I care about your master's wishes?" Sarg shot back with a sneer.

"It might save your lives. Are they not valuable? And, are you not outnumbered?" He croaked out the words and spit on the yellowish-grey ground. It steamed when it hit, leaving a hole in the dried turf.

Sarg waited until Queen Sjura stood beside him before he replied. "It sounds as if your slimy master has sent a piece of garbage to lie for him. Nonetheless, what filth do you offer?"

"A deal!" He croaked louder than before. Anger quickly built inside of him; it lept from his blood red eyes. He spat again. "You stole the Queen and her two retainers from my master. He demands the return of his most valuable property."

"How much might they be worth?" Sarg answered, sounding intrigued. Queen Sjura stomped on his foot in reaction

"My all powerful master decrees you shall keep your miserable lives." The croaking, because of the demon's anger, became muddled.

"So, you speak then for the Holy One? By what authority? Where are your credentials?" Sarg goaded the demon on.

"My master IS the all powerful one." He slipped back to a more reasonable croaking monotone.

"Your master is a filthy slime eating pig!"

"You should watch your language, my master may rescind his kind offer...... Now, what do you answer?" The demon took a step or two in each direction trying to control his seething anger. He spit enough that a circle of steaming vapor surrounded him. "How do you answer?........ My master demands a quick reply."

"Then why did the idiot send a fool like you? Your ignorance is greater than your ugliness! Even ...."

"You have gone too far Haafian."

"I suppose I have. I've been from one end to the other of this cesspool. Quite frankly, it still smells better than you. How about moving downwind?....Do you know which direction that is? Allow me to point it out for you." Before the demon could react, Sarg pointed his broadaxe over the cliff. As he turned back around, a crack of thunder sounded.

"Tell me the offer again?" Sarg said with a wisp of a smile.

"You know the offer my great master made: Give me the three women and the rest of you live." He then headed towards Sarg, his fists waving angrily in the air. I'll rip you apart...."

"Wrong idea!" Sarg announced flatly. He raised his broadaxe over his head to defend himself. "All evil creatures gathered here, die!....NOW!.... Know the power of the Holy ONE!" Sarg roared. A blue blade of fire shot from his broadaxe blade. Whatever the blue blade touched immediately sliced in two. Sarg spun in a semi circle, ten dragons fell in twenty retching pieces, stumpy legs without back, wings or head. Then Sarg stared down the demon. "Still want to deal!"

The demon looked about, then charged, full of hatred and rage. Sarg methodically raised his weapon and brought it low, then, before the demon fell apart, the blue blade ripped him from side to side. Four smoldering pieces bounced on the hardened ground. They steamed as did the dragon carcasses.

"Burn the damn idiot." Sarg called to Vauk. "I don't want to kill 'it' again."

"My Lord," Queen Sjura's voice grieved distressfully. "Why did you bring me here to witness this?"

"I really didn't plan it this way." Sarg said, a little embarrassed. "I didn't know just what would happen. I didn't know if I would understand the demon without you being here."

"But you had an idea." Queen Sjura plunged to the heart of the matter. "I hope... a good one, my Lord. These battles and gore are getting too stressful for those of us of royal blood." Her tone, though only half serious and a bit out-of-character, still demanded a satisfying return.

He put his head down and kicked the dirt. "My Lady, I had two things in mind. First, if we were to lose to the garbage out there," He pointed over his shoulder to the steaming carcasses, "I wanted to be with you."

"You faithless..."

"I know, how selfish of me, my Lady" Sarg replied with dubious sincerity. "But should I apologize? What is the royal protocol that I must accustom myself to?"

Queen Sjura paused for moment, the strange wondrous implications of Sarg's word's ringing though her mind. Then she looked up at Sarg with a bright shine in her eyes. "That is the strangest marriage proposal I've ever gotten....I accept!"

Sarg staggered and then fell. His strength gone, as before. Or did he reel from Queen Sjura's remark? When he woke, the answer still evaded him. But Queen Sjura refused to leave his side.

Later that day, after Brey found ledges for the Troopers to descend into the valley, Queen Sjura, not one for loose ends, posed a question to Sarg. "What, my Lord, was the second reason you wanted me near you when the dragons arrived?"

Sarg glanced up at her smiling face as he went over the edge and flatly remarked, "I wanted to know if dragons had a language."

"You just wait!" She yelled.

If a paradise existed under grey-yellow sky, the valley would aptly suffice. The humidity recovered to a bearable level, the water ran free and pure, and the trees presented themselves to the troopers as givers of tasty fruits of oranges, limes, nuts and cherries. A Yldan shot a large deer. The extravagant supper, compared to the paltry staples of the last few days, could only be superceded by the Queen's announcement concerning Sarg's proposal. It was. And shocked silenced reigned into the evening.

Because of the relative safety of the valley and its caves, Sarg proposed to camp here until the Troopers caught up on much needed rest. Within a few days, the two wounded were promoted to walking wounded. As best they could, the troopers re-outfitted themselves. Not only was bathing mandated, but also clothes washing and mending. The Yldans began cask and arrow making and also repaired their sabres and others weapons. Sarg and the Light Stripers resharpened their broadaxes, thankful that they had stuffed them in their packs.

Sarg sat apart, trying to write a few reports before he forgot some 'essential' items. His dilapidated leather pouch survived along with its contents: it never left his person. Queen Sjura, along with Tiello and Brey, concocted others plans.

Sarg still buckled at being a Prophet, though he began to understand it probably had very little to do with theology. For that he remained most grateful to the Holy One. He pondered the new power: if he could destroy evil, could he not heal the faithful? He wasn't willing to use others to receive an answer. He thanked the Holy One for Queen Sjura, now simply 'Sjura', who spent many long evenings listening to him.

And, "Yes, dragons do have a language." Sjura called to him after he dropped her off at the women's cave. She deliberately took her time to answer.

"I should've thought so!" He growled to himself while walking to his cave.

Chapter 6

The King's extravagant parade at D'Ka resembled a carnival more than anything else. It was supposed to be a full military inspection. Wives and children had arrived the day before, all bringing excessive entourages. Space on the training field disappeared, forcing the formal inspection to be transferred from the camp to a farmer's field west of camp. This sat none-too-well with Vosnob nor with Baste, but the King's decree demanding the presence of the New Knight's families could not be ignored. Baste, however, had deliberately sent the message to the families as late as possible.

By mid-day, the New Knights awaited inspection by their King and by their Commanding Officers. The hot weather combined with a lack of any breeze, quickly took its toll on the green Troopers, most notably, among the Knights Proper, as they had commissioned themselves.

"Shiny armor is about worthless." Vosnob mumbled loud enough for the King to hear. Vaad, his huge striper, whinnied his support for the remark. Baste simply ignored the remark.

"I'm well aware of your opinions, Vosnob." Came the King's terse reply. He had donned the finest plate armor ever crafted, etched and then filled with gold in the most intricate of designs. Even his Striper, instead of the usual cloak, wore armor, the frontispiece being that of a large eagle outlined in silver. The King took Vosnob's comment personally.

In another moment, the three men would turn from the flank to front the men. The field bristled with banners hung from the lances of the mounted troops. Their shields bounced the sun's rays into the crowd, partially blinding them.

The infantry, mainly because of Ayhn's exertions and strict discipline, received their rightful place of honor: front line, flanked by the Knights Proper. Their new phalanx and its aggressive flexibility completely defeated the Knights Proper in every training encounter. They were uniformed similar to the regular Light Striper Troopers except for the use of cuirass and greaves. Their tunics remained mid-blue but the baggy trousers had been replaced by white tight-fitting hose.

Gath, his expertise combined with that of his father, the dragon killer Wygga, in the construction of and deployment of war machines, placed his entire squadrons across the rear of the formation. Except for the fact that the Troopers wore moccasins, they were uniformed exactly as their unknown counterparts who sailed the Upper Sea. This included the sloppy wide brim hats. For today, Baste integrated his 'specialized' troops with the infantry. The old veteran wasn't about to deploy all his secrets to a crowd containing at least a 'few' spies.

The traditional tuba fanfare brought the troops to attention, even those suffering from the heat at least froze as they were. The second fanfare, this one with trumpets added to the tubas, acknowledged the presence of the King of Haaf. At that point, the King, followed by a subdued Vosnob and Baste, turned the corner and cantered to the middle of the front line.

In salute to the King, all helmets and hats were doffed until the King gave permission for them to be returned. But the King never gave the signal. While the armored Knights Proper found relief in the mistake, the infantry and machiners did not. The King just sat in front of the troops, lost in some weird daydream, a strange mystical wispy smile on his face.

"My King." Baste whispered to the Haafian monarch as he and Vosnob moved forward to flank the King. "Begin the inspection."

The King acted as if deaf. He just stared, head on, into the troops gathered before him. Ayhn, standing at attention directly in front of the King, signaled to Vosnob with his eyes that the King was frozen, paralyzed. Vosnob gestured to Baste to pick up the King's reins. Once accomplished, Vosnob took command of the inspection.

"Troops!" Barked Vosnob with an authority that brought hope to the veterans on the training staff and fear to the green troops. "A-TEN-SHUN!"

The infantry snapped as if one man, but the New Knights sloppily effected the identical move. The machiners moved in two groups into position, the footmen preceding those mounted on the Massive Blues and those on the machines themselves.

"Commanders!" Vosnob continued. "To the Fore!"

The commanders of the three units present rode forward; Gath and his father, Wygga, from the machiners, and Ayhn from the infantry. Presumably, the King represented the New Knights. Baste quickly maneuvered to take the King's place, tossing the reins back to Vosnob. The four commanders faced Vosnob who stationed himself to the right of the still uncomprehending, semiconscious King.

"Gentlemen," Vosnob quietly spoke only to the four. "You see our predicament."

All four simply nodded, their stiff formal dispositions quite square-faced and military.

"The inspection will go forward as planned. I'll meet with you after supper in my tent." He said quietly then paused, looked about, resuming his Chaplain Commander's stance. "DIS-MISSED!"

For the next hour Vosnob, with the King reined in tight, the trio deliberately rode along the ranks. Vosnob stopped often to make verbal commendations as well as judgements. Enough to keep most of the Troopers' minds off the King's rigidity and silence.

Yganak and Etan anxiously watched the crowds. When they recognized the King refusing to function, they also began to inventory the gathered families to observe their re-action. The King's physicians, standing far to the left of Yganak, tried to break through the guards to reach the King. Locked lances properly dissuaded them.

As Vosnob and Baste, still holding the King's reins, returned to the front, their inspection now complete, the tubas signaled. "At Ease". With fear and trembling, as well as jolt of reality, the Troopers, including the overbearing New Knights executed the finest drill movement of the day.

However, Vosnob brought the New Knights' overt pomposity to naught; their dismal showing at inspection would prove costly.

"Troops!" Commanded Vosnob. "This day I have seen what Haafians are able to do IF they choose to put their will to it. I am impressed with the quality and the patience of your superior officers. They have endured much from your arrogance. Most of it, is abated. Which is the only reason you have passed the inspection. However, I have no sympathy for the New Knights. Your behavior, your whole demeanor bespeaks of undue disdain for the military...You will have to prove yourselves upon the field of battle. You have proven nothing to me today."

Vosnob had cleared his remarks with Baste beforehand. Too much political maneuvering and too much money passed around within the New Knights. In spite of the King's orders, essentially Vosnob's orders, a few Line and Training officers were quietly bought. Time refused to permit altering the New Knights composition, but pressure could be brought to bear upon their lamentable performance, especially as produced by their incompetency at inspection. Vosnob aimed to embarrass them before their fellow Troopers and families.

"Therefore," Vosnob continued in his authoritative tone. "All Troopers, excepting the New Knights, will join me for supper. You will bring your wives and families with you. ...The New Knights will assume double guard duty until further notice." Vosnob signaled for the tubas to sound "Attention".

After his blasting lecture, Vosnob turned command of the troops over to Ayhn, who dismissed the troops. Complete chaos ruled the farmer's field. The sole exception being the half of the New Knights who understood the impact of Vosnob's criticism. They slumped on their saddles, not even bothering to visit their families.

"That's a good way to gain a few more powerful enemies, my friend." Baste remarked over the din.

"I didn't have any choice. I'm not stupid enough to believe their motivation is pure. These are not serfs. They are not proven in battle." Vosnob's seriousness alarmed even Baste.

"Then what shall we do?"

"Exactly what the King came for."

"We're taking these troops to the front?"

"No."

"No?"

"Exactly!....You are taking the troops to the front...actually, you'll be leading them into battle."

"I beginning to think the other side paid you well." Baste's cynicism had just a touch of lightness to it.

"Actually, they promised me something before the Battle. But, they've never delivered." A crusty smile shot across his face.

"And what might they have promised you?" Baste now rode next to Vosnob, still keeping the paralyzed monarch close to him.

"Something about being the next King."

Baste's belly laugh caused the paralyzed King to slide from his mount. Fortunately the King's physicians stood nearby to catch him. Using the ensuing chaos for cover, they bundled the King off to a Line Officer's tent. There they conducted a full examination of the King. As Vosnob had so graciously given the troops the 'leave' for the evening, the physicians had until dawn to revive or transform the King. Vosnob thought little about these men, but he could not figure out why.

By the rising of the second moon, all the officers Vosnob expected to gather at his tent arrived, joined by Yganak and Etan. A representative from the King's physicians also sat at the table. A rotund figure dressed in a hooded robe sat half hidden in the corner, drinking. Baste claimed one end of the long plank table, Vosnob took the other. Across from Yganak sat Gath. Wygga declined a seat at the table, preferring to join the hooded figure in drinking. Ayhn seated himself directly across from Etan. The physician squeezed himself in between Gath and Ayhn.

"What a strange gathering." Baste announced rather dryly. "Its time to begin." He motioned for the physician to report.

The thin bearded Haafian stumbled to his feet. "Is there a particular reason why I should report first?" He said with a nasal voice twinging with slight animosity.

"Yes." Vosnob answered without bothering to look up. "Just do what you're told."

The man's disposition caused him to unleash a number of curses upon Vosnob. A flying tankard smacked him in the back of the head.

"Ye bees r'spectful." Came Wygga's peculiarly accented voice. "Dis man bees yer commander."

"But I'm not in the Light Striper." The physician sullenly protested, his pride hurt. He kept his real anger in check. He turned to face his half-hidden assailant.

"Yer sho is." Wygga replied knowingly. "Iffen the King be Light Striper and you'd b'long ta the King, then you'd 'ficially beed Light Striper."

"You crazy old drunk!" The physician screamed.

"Pro'bly, but I'se be right and you'd be Light Striper."

The physician immediately bolted for the tent's door, muttering about the 'damnable' people he had to associate with. Two guards politely returned him to the table, his feet twitching in the air. He settled himself once they jammed him tightly into the chair.

"Wygga is a respected veteran." Vosnob flatly explained. "He is also correct. You are Light Striper as long as the King is on active service. That means if I hear anymore insubordination from you, I'll have you flogged before the troops at dawn." Vosnob rose and stared down the man. "You understand?" The commander's voice threatened.

Color washed itself from the man's face. "Yes." He whimpered and lowered his face to the table.

"Now." Vosnob began again. "Let us hear the report on the King."

There was an uneasy pause before the physician started. "The three of us are at a loss. The King's symptoms are those of one who is susceptible to seizures. However, we find no evidence of this illness within his family."

"Why are you at a loss?" Baste demanded. "The King has seizures. Your responsibility is to prevent them in the future. I presume you have the proper medicine?"

"Therein lies the issue. Seizures are of two types: the wild and the frozen. Obviously, the King suffers from the frozen. We have a potion to bring him about, but none exists to prevent the seizure. In fact...quite truthfully.." The thin man nervously continued, "We cannot predict when or if he'll suffer another seizure."

"So you're incompetent!" Shouted Baste.

The physician shuddered with fear; his weakly voice trembled. "No, but our knowledge has limits."

"Can you even tell us what produces the seizures?" Baste roughly asked.

"No." Whimpered the physician. "Perhaps its stress. Perhaps its some food. Perhaps his mind..."

"Bunch of illiterate fools." Mumbled Baste. "Your skills are as severely retarded as you are..... I believe it derives from an old tradition of the King's physicians coming from a payment system. Whoever can buy his way to the King becomes his physician. Competence is not a qualification. Is that not true, you incompetent oaf?" Baste's words shoved the thin man into his seat even further.

"Yes." Came another whimper.

"Etan, as one of the council of three, is there any reason why such stupidity should continue to be inflicted upon the King?" Vosnob saw a smile on Baste's face as he spoke to Etan.

"None. Traditions are not written, they are easily augmented."

"Then," Said Baste as he again stared down the physician. "You and your companions have a new occupation....Guards!" The two men who 'sat' the physician entered the tent. "See that the doctor and his two friends find some stable work. They'll need to be occupied there until we engage the Kyykki."

"Yes, Commander Baste." The older guard replied. They hoisted the physician from his chair and left.

"Next order of business?" Vosnob called.

"The King's future, or better, the limits of the people's faith in him to lead." Etan said.

"Go on."

"Yganak and I watched the crowds today. Most were ignorant of the King's debility. That's to our benefit."

"And the troops were too frightened to look up at the King." Added Ayhn.

"But the New Knights saw him at an eye-to-eye level. They saw the blankness of his face. I think that maybe part of the problem." Gath interposed. "I'm glad they'll be too busy to spread their observations."

"Perhaps." Replied Vosnob, a bit leery. "Perhaps, we need to isolate the New Knights? What do you think, Baste?"

"I don't believe it would hurt any. We'll just pull their squadrons into one unit. They can spend some time becoming totally self-sufficient."

Vosnob nodded his approval. "Good. ...And now the King will be attended to by our regular staff physicians. I am aware of their training and competence."

"I see no reason to alter our plans." Baste announced. "We'll proceed to the front after worship tomorrow morning. You are prepared, Oros?"

The fat Holy Man struggled to rise from his chair. "I am ready for that. But then I shall continue on my Quest."

All eyes turned to meet his.

"No one has entered a Quest in a couple of hundred double cycles." A surprised Yganak shot out.

"All the better to begin one now." Oros replied with a touch of finesse. "And, before we go any further with this. This Quest is a secret." He smiled as if to dare anyone to push him on the issue. "Also, my appointed bodyguard is tired of wasting time. We'll leave after lunch."

"I'se knowed you'd stay ta eat." Wygga spat out with a good deal of self satisfaction. The entire group enjoyed the old sailor's 'wisdom', to the chagrin of Oros, who promptly dumped himself back into his chair.

"Is there any other business?" Vosnob's tone meant that the meeting soon ended.

"Yes, one item." Said Yganak. "What exactly are those 'ships' with the three shooting platforms on them?"

Gath began to laugh to be joined by Ayhn and then most of the others. "Better ask the old man in the corner." Gath laughed as he spoke.

"I'se 'posed ta have all da answers?" The old man enjoyed the attention. "Them bees dragon killers. Got's ten of 'em. Some good first mates ta use 'em, too."

"Dragon killers? First Mates?.....You planning on joining the navy?." Then Yganak stopped suddenly, his voice had a bit of awe. "You're the Wygga who killed the one at Krabo."

"That bees me."

"And you just put the crossbows on 'ships' with wheels?"

"Yep. 'ceptin' we also put the ropes on."

"May I inquire as to why ropes are required to kill a dragon?"

"Natur'ly, my son...Ya sees, when ya hit the dragon with da shaft, da head flies open, rippin' out his guts. But da beastie kin still fly 'way. Soes, iffen ye puts a rope on the shaft, the beastie will rip out 'is innards afore he kin fly ta safety. Careful," He chuckled, "Ye mighten git hit by dragon innards droppin' from the sky. ....'en dragon guts smell rite poorlie."

"We'd not be takin' any wounded then?" Sounded a delighted Yganak trying very hard to imitate Wygga.

Wygga almost fell off his chair laughing. The rest of the group enjoyed the old sailor's cynical humor as Yganak did, causing Vosnob to end the evening's meeting. They'd casually meet after worship, as the troops moved out for the front.

Oros' preaching set the tone for the march to the front line. Today began a new day for Haaf, a day in which the forces of the evil one, which, most unfortunately, included some Haafians, would soon spend their allotted time in hell. The message focussed upon the key theological rationale for the impending battle: it is and would continue to be, a Holy War. Haaf, their country, and their families would only remain free of the damned one if they were willing to earnestly fight. By ending the sermon with a call to allegiance to the Holy One, Blessed be His Name, Oros deftly gathered the various mind sets: fight against evil, serve the Holy One willingly and remain faithful to family and country.

Following the final hymn, Oros sent each force to the front with its own benediction. It required more time and energy, but with the King both present and seemingly well, Oros saw the addition as indispensable. Even so, at the officer's tent, he sat first at table.

In the near corner of the tent stood Vosnob, the head staff physician and a tall Yldian, a bit on the older side of life. Their conversation appeared hushed, tense and well-guarded to Oros. Without a trace of humility, he burst in upon the trio, using his piled up plate as a wedge. "Is the one called to the higher issues of the campaign to be ignored?"

"I had prayed as much." Said a straight faced Running Cloud.

"Didn't work, did it?"

"We were in the process of evaluating that 'sermon' of yours." Running Cloud lied. "Want to hear our verdict?" He challenged.

"I'm not sure." Oros lied back.

"But we are, so shut up." Vosnob dryly responded. He put a mock pout on his face, but Oros did obey.

The staff physician re-commenced speaking, refusing to acknowledge Oros' immense presence. "We are still determining which type of poison got mixed in with the King's wine. Most of what he brought from Krabo is contaminated. And, each poisonous bottle has a small 'c' carved into the cork top."

"But it is definite," Vosnob clarified. "The King's been poisoned for some thirty or more double moon cycles."

"Then, what becomes of him now?" Asked Running Cloud.

"We'll need time to ascertain the correct poison. Only then can we begin the antidote, if any. And only then will we know if this is as sick as he becomes."

"Or if he will slowly die." Added Oros.

"Yes," The staff physician soberly agreed. "That is a possibility we all need to consider, especially as you head to the front."

"How long will your search for the poison take?"

"I brought a shaman along to speed up the process." Running Cloud answered Vosnob. "Unfortunately, I believe there maybe a Yldian connection. Haafian poisons are too crude to induce the effects suffered by the King."

"Exactly my thoughts." Iterated the staff physician.

When they realized the long term effect of the poisoning, a silence enveloped the four; each one having an individual picture of the chaos mitigated throughout the nation, and the Light Striper in particular, by an incoherent King. A king brought low by the evil machinations of the evil one.

"The damned bastard goes deep to thwart our Holy purposes." A piqued Oros mumbled as he broke the deadliness.

"Let's get moving... Oros," Vosnob stared down at the fat man. "You are not part of this meeting. In fact you and Rux left some time ago for Haaf North. Treh is waiting for you." He turned to the staff physician. "Find out all you can. Keep me abreast of all significant findings. And I don't care to hear about the petty squabbles you have with the shaman concerning methodology. You understand?" His firm tone added even more gravity to the physician's chores.

"I truly understand... But," He hesitated.

"Go on."

"The King's physician's should have known about this. I suspect them...."

"I have too. Allow me to watch them. If we scrutinize them well enough we might discover their connections to the Yldians."

"I'll see you all at the front." Running Cloud said as he turned and walked out the tent door. He stopped and called back. "I have five hundred in front of the first wall. They're headed to Battle. I'm sure you'll let us in."

"Only if you promise to refrain from your drumming." Vosnob half-teased. But Running Cloud vanished.

"Vaad is waiting, Sir!" Called a guard from the tent door.

"Thank you." Vosnob returned. "See you two later on." He walked out and swung into the saddle. His double platoon awaited him. They headed east, to inspect the outpost Sarg's report denounced. He also had a few connections to renew at Pinduala's barracks.

A military campaign of such grand magnitude had not existed since the Battle times. Nor had anyone seen such a convoy move as this one. The supply wagons, all two hundred of them, each pulled by three teams of Massive Blues, formed the center of the convoy. As the terrain was relatively flat and grassy, the wagons traveled wide: four abreast. Flanking them were the infantry, fully armed and with full field kits. Then came the War Wagons, single file, pulled by two teams of the Massive Blues. The crews rode the animals, while the crew chief and the loaders rode the wagons. Wygga's Ships, by Gath's order, traveled randomly throughout the caravan, their lightness allowed for three Massive Blues to pull them. The driver rode the first Blue while the crew of six studied the sky constantly, each of the three crossbows at the ready. Finally, the New Knights formed the outside wall. With ribboned pennants cluttering the sky, they slowly walked their Massive Blues at the same pace as the rest of the convoy. With their burnished armor mirroring the bright sunlight back to the fields, even the blind could not mistake them, so reported the scouts who ranged far ahead. Every officer, regardless of rank, rode a Striper, making them the least visible members of the convoy.

Baste allowed five days for the northeast journey, knowing full well it would severely tax the troops and their mounts. The route took the New Knights through grasslands that changed to high prairies that slowly rose into the Dark Mountains. In this far distant semi-desert area only one outpost existed. The 'Wall' was fragmented, leaving large portions of territory unfortified, though patrolled. Maneuvering in this barren and quiet sector provided the means for Baste to ascertain the best plan of attack once they reached the staging area. In a few dawns he'd know which troops to count on and which would cost them a battle.

In spite of the extra demands Vosnob placed upon the New Knights, an attitude change developed amongst them, as did the number of painfully beaten Knights. Baste smiled wistfully as they came each evening to report the injustices foisted upon their pre-eminent persons. He took no action, fostering the concept of policing their own ranks. Each complaint, however, was written down by one of the Chaplains and the complainant spent the rest of the evening with the Chaplain. This procedure quickly diminished the number of complainers.

On the third day, a scout riding a sweat soaked Striper, abruptly reined in before Baste. "Commander?"

"Speak."

"We've located the Yldian volunteers. Five miles due north."

"Yes?" Baste puzzled. "We've known that."

"They've come under heavy attack from the taller Kyykki. About three thousand or so."

"How are they holding up?" Baste's knitted eyebrows.

"They've formed a circle. When I left, they were still holding."

"And where are the rest of your scouts?"

"Picking off the Kyykki from the back."

"Get a fresh Striper, alert the next outpost…"

"All ready done, Commander."

"Then signal the Yldians the New Knights are coming."

"Yes, Sir." The scout vanished into the convoy and then left immediately on a fresh Striper.

Immediately Baste's aides received an array of orders for urgent delivery. Half the War Wagons and all the New Knights would head north to the battle. The rest would follow at the current pace, but on full alert.

The entire column swiftly changed directions. The New Knights moved out in double column of ten with the War Wagons in the middle. Baste personally lead them. After cantering for four miles through the grasslands, the terrain turned to a semidesert quality; dust, stones and shrubs. The column slowed to a walk as Baste conferred with the scouts as well as with the other line officers.

"It appears that our Yldian friends are doing quite well." Baste smiled. "They have a new weapon, a most interesting weapon: ordinary bleach! It effectively kills the Kyykki."

The line officers, being an experienced and pragmatic group, accepted this new development with far less emotion then Baste.

"Now, the outpost garrison is also under attack. One of those asinine frontal attacks….. That gives us the opportunity to safely test the New Knights. We'll deliver a regular frontal attack at the gallop. Make sure the troopers veer around the Yldians. No chasing after any survivors, the War Wagons can do that…… Keep them tight after the fifth rank, Gath!"

"Yes."

The New Knights Changed formation. At a half mile from Yldan's circle, they were in charging ranks.

Baste issued more orders. "Pull two War wagons on the far flanks and one in the middle. On their third volley, commence the charge…….. Gath!"

"Ready Sir!"

"What I need is assurance that your father is back with the main column."

"Can't give that, Sir."

"OH?" Posed Baste, as if he didn't all ready know the answer. "Where is the old man?"

"He brought one of his dragon ships along. He figured the men could use some real target practice...with moving targets."

"Damn sailor." Baste muttered, knowing, in spite of the fact that he had personally requested Wygga's assistance, he would never control the independent old fool. "Gath, tell your father he gets only six shots. But I want more than six bodies."

"Giving the stubborn old man a challenge?"

"Now, would I do such a thing?" He put his spurs to the Striper's flanks.

Gath placed his father's 'ship' next to the War Wagon in the middle of the front rank. Actually, Wygga's ship moved far out front before the New Knights arrived. When Gath pulled up, the old man and his crew grinned from ear to ear.

"Ye misseded da round, Gath." He spoke with undiluted pleasure.

"I'se figurred that we kill a group at a time. Jist watch!" He turned to the crew chief. "Fire jist like da last one, matey!"

The crew chief sprung the latch which prevented the four foot head from spreading before hitting the target. Then he rechecked the rope, making sure he secured it to the bolt but nothing else.

"Ye careful 'bout da elevashun!"

"Yes Sir!" Then he carefully aimed and fired. The bolt flew in a deadly arch with the rope trailing behind it.

A wretched howl, full of grief and fury, exploded from a mass of Kyykki. They became the victims of the two thousand foot shot which easily ripped through their dense ranks and then entangled them in the rope.

"Now, son, I figgure dis be what we kin do at dis range. Got's ta be closer."

"Looks just fine to me. You stay put." Ordered Gath. "All of you stay put."

"But I'se need ta test out 'nother idee."

"You will stay put!"

The old man stammered a while. "Look ye. Iffen dis werks, we save lots 'o troopers. See, wees take two ropes and tue de fer end ta gether. When wees shoot, de rope circles 'round 'em. Mow dem damned devils right over."

"You will stay put until Baste arrives." Then Gath turned his Striper and headed for the other War Wagons. At two thousand feet, Wygga's ship stood flanked by the first rank of the New Knights. Then the charge of the four thousand began; their brisk walk turned to a canter then to a full gallop with but two hundred feet to go. Their lines became erratic, but their countenances delightfully grim. Inexperience be damned.

The manic Kyykki paused, shocked as they first heard and then saw the heavy metalled knights bearing down on them. At fifty feet the lances dropped, leveled at the Kyykki. The Kyykki instantly moved into a rough defensive formation: spears pointed upwards, the butt to the ground, but their timing proved miserably late. The huge Massive Blues plowed through them as if they didn't exist. The broadhead lances cut through the unarmored Kyykki bodies so well that few broke. What numbers of Kyykki the first rank of Knights missed, the second and third ranks finished. The final two ranks mopped up survivors.

All the excitement gave Wygga time to move his 'ship' into the center of the Yldians circle, where he commanded his rambunctious crew to practice on the Kyykki deserters. Though rather unconventional, Wygga allowed the Yldian's leader to fire a round. At one thousand feet, he barely missed.

"Not bad 'tall fer a Yldian. 'specially dis bees yer first shot." Wygga had a friendly grin on his face.

Running Cloud smiled, satisfied with his uncritical evaluation, but more due to the battle's ending. The Yldians, surprized by the impact of the charging Knights, became even more elated by well-substantiated success of each bleach soaked arrow. One nick on the Kyykki's blackened skin quickly killed.

A low-lying cloud of dust suddenly appeared behind the rise to the north, some three thousand feet distant. Wygga spotted it from his raised perch in the 'ship'. As he turned, another, larger cloud of dust emerged from the east.

"Ambush!" Wygga yelled, pointing to the two dust clouds descending upon the knights and the Yldians. "Load and tie them ropes ta gether." He commanded the crew.

The tuba sounded to reform ranks. Baste modified the call to place the fourth and fifth ranks of the Massive Blues in the front ranks. The War Wagons rapidly formed a defensive circle with the Yldians. Baste personally held the first and second ranks back, forming them in two columns, and then sending them back, as if a slow retreat. Once back, they would regroup to attack on the flanks.

Running Cloud handed Wygga a heavy sack. "Tie this to your bolts. I guarantee you a better average. Be careful, the stuff is razor sharp!" Then he left to assume command of the defenses. The heavy sack contained Running Cloud's flattened razor sharp wire, neatly coiled in twenty foot sections. Wygga studied it for a moment and then, with a broad grin commanded the crew. "Tie it on. Yer goin make a messy out der."

As Running Cloud sized up the situation, they were suckered into a well-prepared ambush. This strategic advancement on the part of the Kyykki caught the New Knights and their Yldan allies off-guard. Even with the arrival of the New Knights and the War Wagons, the odds remained bleak; an estimated ten thousand Kyykki ungainly hopped and loped towards them. The ground reverberated with their unnerving stomping.

At one thousand feet Wygga's 'tied' bolts launched at low level. The rope broke before inflicting any significant damage. Running Cloud commanded the firings from the War Wagons. He spaced the volleys to keep a constant deadly rain upon the Kyykki at six hundred feet. The Yldians positioned themselves to individualize their targets. The defensive plan produced a massacre, building a wall of blackened carcasses. Even so, a few Kyykki safely negotiated the arrow barrage.

At seven hundred feet, the 'ship' focused her three crossbows north and fired five volleys. The flattened razor sharp wire hummed as it sliced though the air, bouncing in wide uncontrolled circles and arcs behind the broadhead bolts. When the razor wire hit the first mass of Kyykki, nothing but slimy bits and pieces of the enemy remained as the uncontrollable wire outperformed its intended duty. Once grounded, the wire continued its deadly duty, maiming every Kyykki it touched. Their advance floundered for some time. Then it began again when enough carcasses buried the razor wire.

"Fire agin, maties!" Yelled Wygga. "Wees gots ta slow 'em down."

Three more bolts spun off into the charging Kyykki followed by three razor tails. At five hundred feet the impact stunned and stopped the charge, leaving a massive slime covered carnage in its wake. The War Wagons kept the air filled with bleach covered arrows. Round after round arced into the tightly packed ranks of Kyykki. Now, at four hundred feet, the Kyykki crawled over their dead to maintain their assault.

At three hundred feet, the tuba sounded 'charge'. Slowly, ranks four and five of the New Knights picked up momentum. Fifty feet from the Kyykki lances dropped. The New Knights slammed through the Kyykki at full gallop. Sheer numbers snapped lances and slowed the charge; the

Massive Blues bogged down as they encountered belly high piles of dead and dying Kyykki. Frozen and immobilized, the Knights drew their broadswords to fend off those who crawled over the piles of their own dead.

However, the more numerous twelve foot Kyykki spears produced a distinctive advantage over the four foot broadswords: the hardpressed knights started tumbling from their mounts as the hideous blackened Kyykki overran them.

A whining, strangely crunching noise emerged from the south. Slowly, at first, the Kyykki's attack drifted northward. Then, their speed increased. The stalled Knights were being attacked only on the left. The piles of Kyykki increased in front of them as barrages of sky-darkening arrows struck them from the south. Then the arrows suddenly stopped, leaving a void for the Knights to hear the wretched and pitiful sounds of their wounded.

From the southeast came the deep sound of 'charge' blown by the tuba. Ranks one and two cantered around the back end of the repositioned War Wagons, pivoting at their southern corner. After lowering their stained lances, they cut into the rear of the Kyykki forces on a broad front, moving northwest. This pincer move enveloped most of the Kyykki and pushed the rest towards their northern force.

Gath's War Wagon, now pulled by a double set of Massive Blues, forcibly plowed its way through this morass, heading north, passing directly in front of the immobilized fourth and fifth ranks, its crossbows maintained their constant fire. Other war wagons followed, firing in high arcs that effectively encouraged the Kyykki to propel themselves north even faster.

The Kyykki assault from the north stalled, ten feet from the Yldian defensive circle. Wygga's supplies of the razor wire expended themselves, but his bolts continued their devastating toll. At point blank range, with broadheads out full, they easily obliterated a six foot swath of Kyykki. The five War Waggons not re-positioned also fired at point blank range, creating an unclimbable wall of Kyykki some fifteen feet high. As their stall now transformed into a leaderless stop, the third rank of knights smashed the Kyykki on their flank, pushing them east into the survivors heading north. As the two groups collided, the Knights reined in at a safe distance, watching as the War Wagons discharged their arrows into the remaining thousands of Kyykki.

The rest of the column advanced far enough to deal with a few stragglers. The lance-pole infantry, at a quick march, began to position themselves to the fore of the Knights, providing them with a much needed reprieve. The Chaplains and Staff Physicians immediately went to work as did the Quartermaster's Staff. The rest of Wygga's dragon ships set up for full defensive action along the enlarged outside perimeter.

A dread calmness that began spreading over the battlefield stopped when a menacing darkness mysteriously moved in like a misty fog. Its finger-like projections swirled down from high, where a single blackened cloud quickly expanded to immense proportions. The tired mounts grew restless and agitated; the Troopers, nervous. What was bright day, now was dusk. Everything appeared as greying shadows, as if the differences between the living and the dead faded into a bizarre nothingness.

As quickly as the darkness descended, it raised enough to show the New Knights their future. To the north, and east, and west, silently stood the greatest horde of Kyykki ever assembled. They stood at least a mile deep, a mile deep of tightly-packed blackened spear-armed Kyykki. Three thin skeletal demons, each dressed in a blood red robe, floated forward to the Haafian front line. Ayhn's infantry, in deep phalanxed formation skittishly held their ground. Their inexperience produced great concern for Baste.

"Stand your ground. First rank, kneel! Ground your lances! Archers, at the ready." Ayhn walked along the line, bolstering the men's confidence. "Quartermaster staff! Get double tubs of arrows!"

The demons stopped fifty feet from the front line. Their hollow sunken eyes scanned the line, probing for the fears they would later use to their advantage.

Baste rode up behind Ayhn. "What do they want?"

"They have yet to speak." Ayhn replied. "My father told me about these things. If you chop them up enough, they can be killed."

The nervous infantry snickered.

"You're almost as funny as Running Cloud."

"I take all the compliments I can get."

"So you finally got your first one?"

Baste didn't have time to enjoy his insult: the middle demon moved in front of the other two and raised his hands, signaling he desired to speak. Baste signaled back and slowly rode through the line towards the demon. He stopped at a distance of thirty feet, refusing to move closer. The smell of meaningless death pervaded the atmosphere.

"Speak demon!"

"As you command, my Lord." The demon's voice boomed as hollow as his eyes and just as empty. The combination, dreadful.

"I shall never be your Lord."

"As you wish." The tone ominously rang throughout the battlefield.

"I have better things to do." Baste called to the demon as he began backing his Striper.

"I shall speak quickly." Intoned the demon. "I bring you an offer from my Master."

"Why should I care?" Baste baited the demon.

"He promises to all who will follow him, riches beyond riches." The demon called out in a voice that no trooper missed. "My master seeks those who are wise and talented to bring peace to our broken land." Though powerful, his words lacked conviction.

"And if you follow after the Holy One, Blessed be His Name, you shall keep your worthless life."

A murmur of approval rippled through the infantry's ranks.

"If you walk to me now, the promises are your's."

"Keep them for yourself, demon. We know your Master. He's a notorious slovenly liar."

The infantry's approval rang louder this time. Some even laughed, though more from anxiety than anything else. The demon's eyes began to burn with unhidden hatred. Nonetheless, he stood silent, waiting for any troopers to step towards him. No one stirred.

"Your time is over, Haafians!" The enraged demon thundered. "Prepare to die!" He turned and walked back to the others as Baste rode into his own lines.

"Wygga!" Baste quietly called.

"Yessir!" He returned with a whisper.

"You want them?"

"Yessir!" Wygga's eyes covered his whole face with a wicked glee.

"You got to get all three." Baste sternly ordered.

"Jist watch!"

Before he turned his head, three bolts, broadheads full open, discharged from Wygga's ship. Each plunged into its intended demon target, catching two in the chest and the head demon in the back, exploding them into six grizzly pieces. A roar went up from the troops. And peculiar darkness partially returned.

"Wygga!" Baste bellowed over the cheering troops.

"Yessir!" His voice excited as a child.

"You shot the damned demon in the back." His voice had a sense of false remorse.

"Thank ye, Sir." Wygga replied with the greatest false modesty.

In the long agonizing silence which followed, the lines reformed and the wounded received proper attention. Quartermasters and their staffs redistributed supplies allowing for the machines to work at full capacity as well as provide a well-designed program for withdrawal. Runners spread away to the outposts, requesting reinforcements. Booby traps and poisons covered the heaps of dead Kyykki. Even a few strands of razor wire were recovered. The deliberate logistical business commanded by Baste and Running Cloud kept the anxiousness of waiting from demoralizing the inexperienced troops.

From a hastily erected thirty foot tower, Running Cloud surveyed the assembled Kyykki. Their strength lay to the north and the east. Their western contingent amounted to less than half the others. Unless they radically changed their straightforward tactics, the Kyykki had to descend into a ravine on the north before reaching the troops. On the east, the rolling hills provided only distance as an obstacle in their attack. The New Knights withdrawal route lay due south, down an undulating slope presenting few obstacles for either side.

"But it's not a retreat." Baste constantly emphasized to some of the newly appointed Line Officers. "We'll simply be attacking from another direction."

Running Cloud, Gath and Ayhn, gathered for a pre-battle conference. Exasperation, because of Baste's tenuous nomenclature, bothered them. Their sobering tone concerned the future; if this became a "last stand" then everyone would make sure the Kyykki paid dearly. While they had faith in their tactics, the astronomical numbers of visible Kyykki, quickly diminished their personal faith.

"Quitters." Mumbled Running Cloud. "You act as if are all alone. Where has your Faith gone?"

"Faith is still here. I'm just being realistic." Gath mumbled back, slightly embarrassed.

"Faith works to produce hope." Running Cloud continued his sermonizing. "And we have more work to do before the damned soulless slime attack."

"And just what needs to be done?" Baste's rough tone of voice declared he had been listening.

"We can safely enlarge our perimeter." Running Cloud said calmly. "To the top of the ravine on the north."

"Go on. How do we hold it?"

"By using the supply wagons for plows. As the Kyykki stumble up the slope, we'll roll the wagons down on them. Coated with some poisons, of course."

"Of course." Groused Baste. "I'm just glad you and your people are on our side."

"It's only because you pay better." Running Cloud said blandly.

Grins appeared on almost everyone's face.

Gath spoke. "Besides plowing, I'd like to turn a few wagons into shooting towers. No matter which way them come, height will be to our advantage."

"Get to those things." Baste snapped. "I'm not sure what 'their' hold-up is."

The attack came, without the usual doumy-doumy drumming and dancing, just as an almost indecipherable dusk arrived. The Kyykki forces to the north and east advanced in regular columns, confounding most veterans. Their slowly plodding pace deliberately saved energy for the suicidal-type charge. The dim light prevented all but a few details to become exposed, the most significant being that the taller Kyykki commanded the others. Their bright yellow-green eyes, drifting up and down as they loped forward, sabotaged the Kyykkis' efforts to blend into the haziness of the dusk, permitting Gath's men to call range with excellent accuracy.

The dragon ships opened fire at fifteen hundred feet. All the horrendous implements attached to the bolts turned the first hordes of the eastern columns into slimy blackened piles. Twice more the Kyykki attacked the same way, to be defeated the same way. The result produced another wall of Kyykki carcasses fifteen hundred feet out. This prevented the New Knights from charging and protected the Kyykki who next advanced.

"They have an effective way of limiting what we can do." Ayhn cynically commented.

"Most things are easily done if there is no concern the troops." Baste's tone reflected his strong sense of ethics. The damned one achieved results with the mass suicide, the concept sickened Baste.

The Kyykki demonstrated the same tactic when their northern attack commenced. The poisoned wagons, covered with bleach paste, with the addition of a few War Wagon volleys, halted the attack at the point where the deep ravine transformed into a sickening shallow gully. Again, such a tactic prevented the New Knights from attacking.

A third attack followed immediately from the west. All the Kyykki comprized the taller type and carried spears. Scurrying towards the fortifications, they broke from column formation into line as they approached within one thousand feet.

Suspecting a ruse, Baste allowed a minimum of archers to decimate them. He then commanded the infantry to quick-march, in full formation, to the Kyykki's wall on the east.

With a nauseating howl, the Kyykki threw themselves over their self-made barricade. Arrows sent the first rolling down upon their comrades. Those who safely made it to the top, summarily skewered by the lances of the Phalanxers. But the sheer masses of suicidal Kyykki gradually forced the infantry back.

Promptly as the pitch black night of a no moons night forced itself upon the battlefield, the Kyykki disappeared. The troopers found themselves confined to a space less than five hundred feet on the east. The paradoxical blessing existed in that the lost territory was unusable to either side, being stacked six to eight deep with dead Kyykki and almost five hundred feet wide.

The next attack, at dawn, commenced with ten dragons flying in from the north and Kyykki from the west. During the darkness of early morning, the Kyykki abandoned the east, shifting the entire force to the north and west. Wygga waited, ready; if his experienced teams could collapse an entire Kyykki column, they could take down the dragons.

"Yuse gotta shoot 'em under de wings." He reminded them in his usual upbeat voice. "Make 'em fall on der owns."

The first bolt flew out as the dragons approached two thousand feet. It ripped through a wing and then wiped out a few Kyykki before digging itself into the turf. The wounded dragon haltingly reversed its course and glided to a landing far behind the Kyykki lines. The next dragon ship sent an entire volley into a dragon, bringing him down almost instantly. His ripped steaming carcass slammed into the ravine, smashing hundreds of Kyykki and rendering a hundred foot of frontline impassable.

Two more dragons were forcibly retched from the sky before a fifth closed in to demonstrate their vile ferocity. Diving from the greyish heavens, the beast swooped low over the observation tower, breathing fire. It yanked the tower from the ground only to drop it on the mounted Knights. Casualties ran high, most crushed and burnt.

The onslaught of the northern most Kyykki commenced simultaneously with the dragons' appearance. In columns that refused to quit, they clumsily traipsed over and through their own dead, into volleys of arrows and lance fences which refused to give ground easily. But, as happened on the east, the north became a barrier to both friend and foe alike. The piles of Kyykki being well over ten feet high in places.

"The evil bastard's strategy is working." Baste thundered. "He's going to close off the west next."

"Only if we can keep this rate of firing up." Gath replied. "Its been a half day of fighting. The energy level dwindles."

"I believe its time we thought seriously about leaving." Baste gave the prearranged signal to begin loading up. To surprize the Kyykki, all preparation was accomplished silently. The Knights would provide the initial diversion by striking out to the west. Once through the Kyykki lines, they were to head south to join the column.

"How many dragons left?"

"About four, Baste." Gath yelled from his wagon. "They're very wary about getting too close."

"Might they follow us?"

"I don't think so, or they'd come after us before now."

The light grey of mid-day suddenly dropped into densest black. The stench of rotting flesh invaded the atmosphere, causing everyone to think 'death'. The rancid bleak darkness swiftly took shape, rearing itself up into the heavens like a spire and then reaching out with a haziness that solidified into two clawed hands. The hands extended, vaporous arms forming behind them. The spire transformed into a ghastly fang-filled maw above which two yellow eyes glared down upon the troops. Hatred filled the narrowing eyes as a gnarled serpentine nose shot out from between them. An immense transfixing power emanated from the focusing of his clawed hands with his vision, causing each trooper and each Kyykki to physically freeze. Thinking remained, so too did the sense of hearing; eyes could move and watch, but nothing else. Then, as the last of the airborne arrows collided with its target with a dull thudding noise, an unimaginable silence reigned supreme over the battlefield. It was cold, lifeless, and evil, able to defeat most powers except that of gravity. Its horrid maw opened, but the hollow sounding words it uttered were appraised only by the mind.

"Listen you wretched creatures who serve the bastard Holy One! Listen well to me, your Savior or your Destroyer. I return to claim my land and my people. Haaf and beyond are rightfully mine. I will have them back!"

The roaring that filled each man's head would have driven him to suicide. Their immobilization prevented the action: they could not even scream at their mental anguish. The evilness of the creature overpowered the sensibilities of the men, causing many to ask for death.

"I read your stupid, insipid thoughts, wallowing in self pity, crying to a bastard god who refuses to hear you. Where is your asinine god?" He haughtily bellowed deep inside their minds.

Then the damned evil one suddenly became quiet, transforming himself into something almost likeable. Gleefully he smiled down from his cloud level perch. "But I listen well to my followers. If you desire death, I shall grant your desire."

Suddenly the men's minds thought otherwise. The will to live clouded out other thoughts except for a horrid fascination about this Dark Lord, or, as others recognized him from the Holiness Code, the damned Evil One.

"I am the omnipotent God. I am the one the other gods bow to, in fear and trembling. Now I grant you that special privilege. As I, in my great beneficence, allow others to live, including your so-called Holy One, so I shall allow you to live. Such is my beneficence to those who willing obey me. All the rest, which are but garbage, shall perish. I will slaughter and torture those who refuse me. None shall live who does not fear me and tremble when he knows I am present."

The thick heavy darkness changed, becoming even more oppressive. Each Trooper's heart felt enveloped by the evil one's clawed hands. With each threatening word the damned one uttered, the tightening strengthened. The torturous grip steadied when it reached the apex between life and death for each trooper. Then the evil one spoke in a soft condescending tone, clearly recognizing himself as the absolute ruler of life and death.

"Shall I destroy all of you, like so much filthy vermin? I can you know." His cockiness most gratuitous. "I·AM·THE·OMNIPOTENT ONE! ..But, I, in my great beneficence, will give you life. I only demand that you curse your old impotent god who cannot assist you. Your damned god who refuses to answer." He suddenly spoke softly with a sympathetic leer. "Then I demand that you pay homage and allegiance to only ME!" He roared so loud as to cause blood to drain from the troopers' ears. Then, for an undetermined period of time, his voice became silent and still. "YOU!" He suddenly screamed. "You are in my hands. I choose life for you or I choose death for you." The grip about the men's hearts tightened slightly. "I, in my great beneficence, decided to choose life for you."

The stifling grip about their hearts immediately vanished; the Troopers breathed. "See and feel my absolute power!" He gloated. "Now, those of you who desire to keep the life I gave you, come to me. I·COMMAND·YOU, COME·TO·ME."

A vehement blinding wind careened downwards from the evil one's maw, creating a smooth passage way through the Kyykki carcasses piled up on the east. The trail, violently smashed into each man's mind, lead from their temporary fortifications through the Dark Lands to a singular reddish-black volcano surrounded by a cold, dark lake.

"Follow the trail, if you desire to live. I will protect you from all others. My grip is maintained about the hearts of the others. Those lovers of the false impotent god will not destroy you. ....You who wisely choose to follow me: announce it to me! Curse your bastard old god! Then I will free you, to follow me."

Shortly after his demonical voice stopped ringing in their minds, the Troopers discovered both their voices and their necks free to move. The eerie silence remained for but a terse moment.

"Damned be the Holy One." Yelled a thick set New Knight. Before the words finished, he tumbled off his Massive Blue, staggering towards the path into the Dark Land. He walked stiffly; his will immediately sapped by the damned one and yet mesmerized by his promises. His mount, however, continued in the frozen position, as did all those remaining faithful to the Holy One.

Slowly, the number and volume of curses increased. A minority of men from the infantry, the New Knights, the machiners and the specialized squadrons began ambling out of the barricade. Their paralyzed gait, the shuffle of persons robbed of their dignity, of their very immortal souls, proved agonizing to the remaining faithful. Single file they moved towards the east, leaving their entire lives behind them. In voluntarily cursing the Holy One, they forever forfeited their family, friends and faith. A life of freedom, albeit, one with the usual responsibilities, died, destroyed and then swapped for a living death which wrapped itself in lies.

A depression, a righteous anger, filled the hearts of those who stood frozen, totally unable to detour their foolish comrades-in-arms. They sadly gazed, tears running down their faces, as the cold, stone faced troopers passed by....... one-by-one.

As each 'former' New Knight, machiner or infantry Trooper reached the entrance of the formidable wall of Kyykki carcasses, surrendered his weapons and armor to the dead Haafians: those who sacrificed their lives to stop the wretched soulless ones. Without protection or food, the faithless troopers then continued. As the last of some five hundred fifty passed through the morass, the ferocious wind that opened the passageway now returned to eradicate every trace of it. And the sky retained its sickly dead grey color. The 'dead' oppressive atmosphere returned.

Just slightly at first, the ground began to tremble, and a strong blue streak rent the deathly grey overcast sky. Without a sound each trooper found himself freed from the malevolent grip of the evil one. No trooper was exhausted. Those wounded had limbs restored, gashes healed without scars. Those on the verge of death, sat up, then stood. Within the encampment, all were healed and reinvigorated.

Before anyone moved, or rejoiced, the earth trembled again, this time more forcefully, causing a chasm to develop between the barricaded troops and the Dark Lands on the north and east. The Dark Land receded from view. What once stretched upwards from the battlefield into the Dark Lands, now disappeared from view as the earth continued to tremble and moan.

"Be at peace, my people!" Came a clear authoritative voice from the ever-widening blue streak in the sky. The voice was sincere and kindly, banishing every shred of fear and torment fostered by the evil one. "Be at peace! You are safe!"

No reason in all creation could prevent the troopers from recognizing the voice. Something deeply instinctive, deep into the soul, instructed them as to the character of the 'new' voice. Some fell to their knees in adoration, others froze in reverent awe, still others became entirely confused and panicked. The Chaplains tearfully gazed into the bluing sky, giving thanks for their immanent salvation.

"Stay within your barricades." The voice commanded.

Troopers grabbed their weapons and rushed to take the proper places in line. The full robust lines denied that any Troopers deserted, as if such filthy traitors never lived. Baste summoned for the war tubas to sound. Troopers clicked to attention, then to 'at ease', anxiously awaiting the next event.

The brightest blue cloudless sky effortlessly blasted its way through the Dark Lands, dispelling all greyness and revealing a land devoid of life. The measure also brought forth an angry, familiar voice.

"Who dares disturb my victory!" The Evil One's unabated arrogance broke forth. His wispy, black-cloud image instantaneously reared up into the sky, to fall back just as quickly, severely stricken by the brightest blue sky.

"I do." Replied the authoritative voice of the Holy One. The voice retained all calmness and security, reimplanting hope within the Troopers.

The Evil One pulled himself up into the sky again, full of rage and animosity. He endeavored to blanket the entire sky with his deadly greyness, but found himself surrounded by a blue sky that kept his expansion to a well-defined minimum. He roared and cursed at his confinement. "Damn you!"

"I have often warned you about the force of such language. To all present, to all who hear you, you are the damned one."

His roar turned to shriek that caused the earth to jump. But the roar hardly bore the power of omnipotence. "I confined you to your own land. Get out of here."

"But you are the one with no land. After all, I am the Creator, not you." The Holy One's calmness further incensed the Evil One.

"What is it that you brag about?" The sneer filled with hatred. "Where were you when over a thousand of your so-called faithful cursed you and joined me?" His statement attempted to undercut the Holy One with ridicule.

"Just once may you speak the truth. The actual count is five hundred fifty three." The ghastly face of the sky imprisoned Evil One drew back into hideous contortions. "Now, you have far acceded your limitations. This slaughter before me is proof....How do you plead?" The forceful intentionality of the Holy One demanded an answer.

"I have done nothing that is out-of-line." He lied without any hint of remorse or guilt. "I am the perfect one. You answer to me, you damned...."

"Yes!" The voice a bit weary. "I've heard all of your lies before. Furthermore, your power is only that which I allow you to have. ....I have decided to remove some of it. I will have the people know you as you really are; a sniveling, cowardly liar."

"You can't touch me." The evil one's enormous struggles to break through his blue sky confinement availed not. His anger boiled over into unbridled rage. "I hate you, FATHER! And I hate the rest!"

"We've known that for thousands upon thousands upon thousands of cycles. Your irresponsibility has shown us what you are. Unfortunately, you tried, once again to destroy my creation, my people. For that you shall be punished."

A tortuous scream rang throughout the Dark Lands, lasting until the first of the moons rose. The blue sky continued into the night. The troopers witnessing this divine drama still remained at their posts, transfixed and utterly fascinated by the discussion and totally overwhelmed by the theology exploding upon them.

"Rest and eat, my children." Came the concerned voice of the Holy One, falling gently from the heavens. "Nothing will happen until I alone make that choice. Furthermore, do not grieve for those who are missing. They chose in freedom just as you did."

As a they prepared and then ate a hot supper, a bright brassy concerto, provided by the Holy One, filled the air, obliterating the howling whimpering sounds produced by the damned one. Baste, as best he could under the circumstances, placed the men on regular guard duty and set about putting the camp into order.

Towards dawn, the Holy One spoke. "Stand forth."

"I'll be damned before I obey you!"

"We've covered this territory before." With that the Holy One spread the damned one across the sky in a film so thin as almost to dissipate him. "Watch!" He roughly commanded.

Again the ground began to shift. This time the Kyykki army, still frozen in position, vanished down a newly opened chasm into complete oblivion. The traitors from the New Knights suffered the exact same fate. The chasm then transformed into a five hundred foot cliff. A sheer drop of black polished granite now effectively separated the Dark Lands from Haaf for a fifteen mile stretch. Dark robust rain clouds then dropped their contents into the newly created valley, ruining its toxicity.

The eyes of the Evil One bulged with horror as he watched his so-called 'territory' transform. His maw foamed at the fate of his now defunct army. But he was quite powerless to hamper anything the Holy One proclaimed.

"Listen well. This is your punishment".

"You have punished me enough all ready." He bellowed with a stubborn defiance.

"No. I haven't punished you at all. The destruction of your army and of the new recruits is an example of true justice. Your punishment is another issue altogether." The Holy One's calm composure easily displaced the damned one's animosity.

"I am the Omnipotent!" Challenged the evil one.

"And that is the last time you will utter a deceiving word." The Holy One countered. "That is your punishment."

A huge dripping sneer slowly materialized, discontinuing his previous arrogance. A hollow evil laughter emanated from his gaping maw. "You have....n...this power over me!" A sudden sense of futility struck the evil one. "You da...m....." With all his ferocious might he fought against the Holy One's prescribed punishment. "You Blessed One, my Father." He blurted out, totally embarrassed and profoundly incensed. "You can't take away my power."

"But I all ready have." The Holy One politely acknowledged. "From this time forth, you shall communicate the truth and only the truth when you speak. You will, naturally, think your lies. But no longer will you share them with anyone or anything. That is your eternal punishment."

"What if then I choose to become silent?"

"That is simply your choice. The blessings from that would be reaped by all of us." He spoke matter-of-factly, no malice nor cynicism implied. "Now, off with you!"

With his blue sky prison released, the evil one abruptly departed for the hinterlands of his wretched domain. The deadly greyish sky returned to conceal the Dark Land, though the blue sky forcefully remained in place over the granite cliff and the newly forming lake below.

"My children," The Holy One spoke to his people. "Remain alert, he is clever, nor is he defeated, nor is he without those who sympathize with him. The war is yet to come." Before the Head Chaplain could humbly petition him, the Holy One vanished, leaving dual rainbows as a testimonial.

Bewilderment mixed with awe overwhelmed the camp. Noon arrived before Baste re-established any semblance of order. Not that the Troopers refused their orders, but that the remarks of the Holy One quite effectively challenged the Holiness Code, the mainstay of their lives and the basis of community life in Haaf. Even the leaders, Baste included, remained unnerved by the Holy One's words. The easiest solution lay in discrediting the 'voice' and its all-too-well demonstrated power. Not even the most secular trooper however, backed that stupidity.

At mid-afternoon, Baste assembled the squadron commanders as well as all the Chaplains in his tent, which he had removed to a field one mile from camp. The agenda had but a single item: provide truthful and adequate answers for what had transpired. Once they reached that goal, no matter what the time, the entire camp would be summoned to a hearing.

The six Chaplains sat at the far end of the table, opposite from Baste. Gath and Ayhn arrived a bit later than expected.

"How nice of you to drop by." Baste delivered with a forceful sarcastic tone.

The two grabbed seats without commenting.

"You offer no explanation?"

"There's just a few too many fights over theology." Replied Ayhn. "And after all that's happened, its a little difficult to imprison the men."

Baste grimaced and made a couple of peculiar noises in his throat. "Obviously, without the aid of the Holy One, this meeting would concern the letters sent out to the families of the Troopers who died. Now, because of the Holy One's words and actions, our whole theology, our Holiness Code is in disarray. Chaplains, I beg you," Baste earnestly pleaded. "Give us something useful, something practical."

A tall bony Chaplain, sitting towards the corner, rose to speak. "I can only offer a humble summary that we've been able to truthfully answer." His voice surprized everyone; it was strong, bold and clear. "We believe these issues are the most important: that the Holy One might have a son, the evil one. Yet the Holy One never made such a claim, but the damned one did after he was forced to speak the truth. Therefore, the Holy One is not the only god. Next, the Holy One alluded to 'others' who might ally themselves with the evil one. We do not unanimously believe the Holy One meant other 'gods'. However, neither can we be sure. A flood of disbelief combined with anger rolled through the tent. The whole concept of many gods, in, at least, partial competition with each other was outright heresy. And now this heresy came with the approval of the Chaplains.

"Before my colleagues and I are condemned, allow us the benefit of our entire summary." The powerful voice had a bit of an edge. "True, you believe this a heresy. I, rather, we, are convinced it isn't. Actually, the crux of the whole matter is not the Holy One, but each of us."

"You are accusing us of being heretics?" Ayhn gasped, unwilling to consider the validity of such an outrageous statement. "We stand firm in orthodoxy. We have the Holiness Code. What we are witnesses to is not in the Holiness Code."

"Exactly our premise." Said the thin white-robed Chaplain. "Our assumptions have fuelled this critical situation."

"What assumptions?" Baste quietly asked, inferring for the Chaplain to continue.

"With all due respect towards our Yldian brother, Running Cloud, and his wisdom." He motioned towards the solid reddish skinned Yldian. "Ask him if he finds our situation problematic."

"Well, Running Cloud, do you not find any of this just a bit overwhelming?"

"I do. Indeed, I do." He replied most thoughtfully. "This is the first time I've heard the Holy One speak....This is also the first time I've witnessed Him at His holy work: providing for us. Those things have deeply impressed me, and strengthened my faith, but they do not overwhelm me."

"Might I call upon you to tell us why this is true for you?" The Chaplain carefully positioned himself for a break-through.

"You may....... It's a matter of assumptions." Running Cloud began. "Haafians have always assumed that if the Holiness Code doesn't specifically articulate an issue, then it is considered null and void, a total non-issue."

"That's outrageous! I demand an apology for your abuse of the Holiness Code!" One of the squadron leaders burst out.

"I agree with him!" Added another. "All that is necessary is contained, in its totality, in the Holiness Code."

A loud commotion ensued, forcing Baste to call for guards to settle everyone. "We are not here to destroy each other! We shall have order!" His huge fist thudded down on the table. "Are we clear on this matter?" He threateningly demanded.

The ruckus abated quickly.

"Chaplain, clear the air for us! Why is it that Running Cloud's testimony is so important to your case?"

The thin man stretched out a knobby finger, pointed directly at the man who first objected. "You are the reason why there is so much confusion. You have assumed the Holy One is stuck within the pages of the Holiness Code. You have assumed that the Holy One could not be greater than His word. Therefore, you have assumed that the Holy One is finite, as we all are. You are the true heretic!" He waved his bony finger at everyone in the tent. "All of us who would place any limitations upon the Holy One, better beg for His mercy."

An angry hush, full of prayer and other murmurings, as well as a few penitent tears settled upon the gathering. Their convictions, when mirrored, proved false. By actually granting omnipotence to solely the written word, the Divine author of the book had become substantially forgotten. Tears fell from many faces as the truth settled in.

"Bless the Holy One, my friends." The Chaplain persuaded those gathered. "Bless the Holy One, for He has shown us, without malice nor punishment, the error of our assumptuous ways."

This area of agreement brought them together. But in agreeing, room opened for a major shift in theology. This presented problems, many becoming iconoclastic, in spite of the resent evidence to the contrary. The Holiness Code never once mentioned a 'son'.

"This is why I prevailed upon Running Cloud. We are all aware of their theological construct that we Haafians have disdained for thousands of cycles. That is, the Holy One works beyond his own word by use of his Spirit. Spirit is a word we Haafians refuse to place in our vocabulary. Spirit is a concept of the Holy One that is beyond our control. We Haafians enjoy controlling too much to allow the Holy One that space. Yet, should the Holy One be truly confined to the pages of a book, then His freedom to be the Omnipotent Holy One we witnessed this past dawn is fully denied. Nothing of what transpired is found in the Holiness Code. And if the Holy One did not provide for our salvation, who did?" The Chaplain ardently pounded out every syllable of his final sentence. He paused and then spoke in but a whisper. "My friends, is it not wondrously beneficial that the Holy One is much more than a book?"

Mystified, those gathered sat pensively, as if balancing upon a sword blade. Great freedom lay on the one side and the comfortableness of tradition lay on the other.

"It can not be expected that any of you dissociate yourselves from our Haafian traditions. As your Chaplain, I urge you to acknowledge the events of yesterday and its implications as a blessed addition to your faith. We have learned, with His great mercy, that we should never impose any limitations upon the Holy One."

"Then you destroy our ship, leaving us drown."

"Only if you so choose." The Chaplain shot back to the original troubled leader. "There is another way to choose."

"And what might that foul choice be?" He reproachfully questioned. "I am to convert to the damned one?" He snickered.

"If you so choose." The Chaplain replied shortly. "There is plenty of room in his devastated ranks for all varieties of fools."

The man drew his sword, only to find that Ayhn's blade prickled his sweaty throat.

"Sit down, my good man." He gently invited the squadron leader.

Promptly, the fellow obeyed.

"I strongly suggest the rest of you open your minds to the Holy One's truth: as the Holy One lives so too does our faith. To live is to embrace the revealed Truth. And the Truth is what sets us free....We all witnessed that during the battle. We observed our omnipotent God in action against the damned one. We witnessed the effortless victory of the Holy One. And nothing of what we witnessed is written down……. To live is to change, to mature. That which refuses to grow, especially our Faith, is dead………. The Holy One deliberately placed this specific crisis upon us…….. Shall we choose life or death?"

"I respect the soundness of your argument." Baste slowly responded as his wrung his hands in a lost desperation. "But where does that leave us? What is our guide?"

"The Holiness Code remains valid, Commander, if that's what you were referring to. We continue to use it as before. However, the essence of our Faith is not a book, but a relationship with the Holy One. Therein lies the modification we need seriously consider."

"But the Holy One is so distant, so Holy and majestic." Baste hesitantly protested.

"You were present at the battle, Commander?" The Chaplain's said sternly.

"Yes."

"Did you witness a distant, too-Holy-for-us-God?….. A God who divinely extricated us from certain defeat?"

"No."

"Did this God who saved us, proceed according to any written code, or did He operate upon His own unimpeded initiative?"

"He acted on his own…….maybe he responded to our prayers." Baste recognized his struggle was shared by many at the table. "The old ways die very hard, don't they, Chaplain?"

"Indeed." He answered sympathetically. "Our traditions have the power to enslave us much worse than the Evil One could."

"But what about the notion of other gods? The damned one being the Holy One's son, for instance?" Gath spoke, prompted by Running Cloud. "Stretching one's Faith beyond the confines of a book, especially when confronted with irrefutable evidence, is not too difficult. But now we find ourselves surrounded by many powerful gods.......?" He trailed off, overtaken by his own mixed and jumbled thoughts.

"Obviously, the Holiness Code mentions no other gods. However, none of us can rightfully deny the damned one's words, declared truthful because of his divinely given punishment... We confirm that the evil one is a god....of sorts. We knew of his immense power. We allow for the fact the he probably was quite close to the Holy One at one time. Just how close the relationship is has not been revealed to any of us."

There was little discussion about that matter; obviously what the Holy One publicly confirmed, however indirectly, obliterated Haafian society's stories and assumptions. That piece of solid evidence came as a welcome relief. And if the changes in theological focus proved unbalancing to many, the truth of the damned one's real influence and power returned the equilibrium. Only the Chaplains remained unaffected by the radicalness of the dramatic developments, making their influence throughout the leadership significantly stronger.

Small discussions around the table now replaced the Chaplain's summarizing. The fanatically stubborn old purists rapidly lost their influencing power. The key to the whole matter rested in the explicit demonstration of the Holy One's protection of His people, something none might forget. Baste quietly left the meeting to attend to his Troopers.

As he meandered through the campsite, how bizarre he thought. There are no wounded and dead. Thanks to the Holy One, casualties were non-existent. Then, concerning the leadership and conduct of the New Knights, their loyalty and their combat skills had been severely tested. They passed their test successfully, and with the identical agony every Trooper before them experienced. The King, still recovering in the field hospital at D'Ka, would be proud of his New Knights.

Evening approached with first moon's rising. Conversations became subdued and personal as each man seriously restructured and then restructured his thoughts about his Faith. Most shifted towards a similar conclusion, though the routes traveled to get there were as varied as the men present. The Holy One, Blessed be His Name, cared for His people. He deliberately acted to protect them from evil.

"Chaplain." Gath called out across the tent. His word drew the attention of all those gathered. All eyes focused on the thin white robed man who sat with his back to the table.

He turned on his chair. "Yes?"

"Chaplain..." Gath hesitated. "We...some of us...I...have come to the conclusion that we're...I'm... now forced to live without direct answers."

"You want me to bless your conclusion?" Posited the Chaplain.

"Yes." Gath answered humbly. "Or else provide us with the corrective."

"Perhaps the word you seek is 'ambiguity'." Offered the Chaplain. "'Ambiguity' refers to living each day without knowing all the answers. 'Ambiguity' causes much stress and anxiety. 'Ambiguity' forces us to live as Haafians and Yldians ought to: by Faith and not totally by knowledge."

"Then it is permissible to live in ignorance?" Gath responded incredulously.

"No, we are bound to make the most of what we are given. Just look at your father, for example." The thin bony man began creating wispy smoke-like caricatures of the leaders by gesturing with his bony fingers. Most laughed outright, including Gath. "Have I made my point?"

"But..."

"No 'buts', my son. It's this straight forward: we learn to live knowing that come whatever, the Holy One is for us. And none is more powerful than the Holy One, Blessed be His Name......And Amen. .....I'm tired."

So ended the meeting.

A summary to both the King and Vosnob, rapidly sped across the flatlands. A third copy, more theologically detailed, destined for the Church Council and the Elders, left the following morning.

Baste, unlike Running Cloud and the Chaplains, wrestled with sleep all night. A new day dawned, a new day undreamed never before. A new creation, or is it a new civilization, involving many peoples and gods about commence war? So pronounced the Holy One. And, again and unfortunately, Baste landed right in the middle of it all. He whimsically thought of the old days, when he took his grandsons fishing......That would wait...No one knew how long....But the next time Vosnob showed up, if he dared, a terse, blunt day-long 'dressing down' speech awaited him.

Oros made little effort to disguise his animosity towards Rux. The thin, gangly bodyguard provided the enormous priest with the appropriate mount: a Massive Blue. While Rux protested that he merely went about his 'bodyguard' business, the thinnest hint of a smile did not go unnoticed by Oros.

"Are you sure I may not need two of these animals?" Oros sarcastically intoned.

"Perhaps," Rux said flatly. "But then it would decidedly more economical to purchase a wagon for you."

"Disgusting!"

"I thought so too." Rux shot an impish glance at Oros.

The Massive Blue stood a good foot taller than Rux's Striper. It boasted twice the girth, causing the corpulent priest to ride with his feet protruding at a most undignified angle, and the stirrups to dangle and swing empty as the two rode along the village road. Their destination lay far to the west, at Haaf North, where some 'bird watcher' named Treh awaited them.

This, the eleventh dawn of their journey; eleven dawns of nothing. The serfs along the route ignored them, until after the Massive Blue went by, then laughter exploded. The other problem occurred when the serfs were forced to give way. They more than adequately replied by curses of the vilest type. Had either man been in uniform, the tension producing curses would have remained inside their stupid skulls. This wasn't the proper way to initiate the Quest.

"We'll stop in the village ahead for the night." Oros suggested to Rux.

"Do you promise to behave yourself?"

Oros's face grew livid. "For the last time, Rux, I'm telling you that bed was a deliberate trap. By caving in upon me, the Evil One sought to incapacitate me or even kill me. He doesn't want me on this Quest."

Rux replied rather blandly. "Yes, Almighty Oros, you have so told me. Yet it may be a long while before I will believe such a horror story. I am well aware that such a significant personage as yourself must be the very individual on whom the damned one would spare no chicanery to abort this Quest."

"Your sarcasm is not amusing."

"Then shall I tell you a joke?"

Oros choose to ignore the remark and rode on in sullied quietude. Revenge would happen, but only after much prior orchestration. Oros easily found his verbal sparing partner in Rux. Actually, Rux's unique sophistication made him more than an equal, but Oros refused to deal with that particular truism. Nor did Oros willingly grant that the Council of Three, Jabbi in particular, bestowed upon him the best bodyguard possible.

"Ha!" Oros smiled to himself. "When the oaf turns sideways he disappears. Just what I deserved, an invisible bodyguard."

This village differed little from most others: its main crossroads and square were of paved cobblestone. At the center of town stood the market, the Church, and the Inn. The whitewashed buildings implied a sense of values and dignity, and, just maybe, adequate food. Rux quietly noticed that behind the facade lived the actual town; dirty little twisting alleys, rough shacks and a few too many filthy children running loose.

As they pulled in front of the inn, Oros, slipped from his Massive

Blue, landing in a leap on the ground. Rux patiently waited as the priest stumbled to his feet and dusted himself off.

"How polite of you to offer your able assistance." Oros snapped.

"Why, how generous of you to notice." Rux responded with the lightest touch of sarcasm.

"Your time is coming." Oros angrily threw back at him.

"I suppose it is." He nonchalantly replied.

"I'm going in to get supper. Take the animals to the stable."

"Only if you promise to save me some food."

"I've had about enough of the 'fat' remarks...Anymore and I'll have you replaced."

"That's extremely doubtful." He answered dryly. "Cause if I turn sideways they can't find me to replace me." He smiled broadly.

Oros snorted an exasperated wheeze and trundled into the inn. The interior grossly belied the exterior. Low beamed and smokey, with the only light deriving from the table candles' flickering; the deep shadows created an unwholesome atmosphere. The pitted wooden floor was littered with broken mugs and rotting food. The oilskins which patched the windows effectively prevented the sunlight from entering and the fouled air from leaving. Two groups of local men, each quite inebriated, took possession of the middle of the filthy room. Oros quietly ambled to a table in the near corner to the door.

"Whatcha' be wantin'?" Called a rough female voice from across the room.

"Just some stew for supper. Enough for two." He said mildly.

"I'll betcha you eats fer two." She said with disgust in her voice. As she approached the table, her well built figure attracted a few invitations from the drunks. "Sorry boys, but I don't come free."

Maybe you don't c..." Oros heard a snap and a yelp as the waitress yanked the chair out from under the poor sap and then smashed it over his bald head....."At all." He finished.

266

She then kicked him in the head, leaving him to bleed on the floor.

"Now mister," She said to Oros as if nothing out-of-the-ordinary happened. "Fore ya eat, I wants ta see some money."

Oros dug his chubby fingers into his bag, pulling out four copper pieces. "That should buy supper plus two mugs of ale."

She grabbed the money, scraped it and casually slipped it into her low cut blouse. "Ya, this be 'nuff."

She turned, deliberately kicking the drunk in the head again. His friends at the crusty table howled with delight. With a rough and teasing curtsy, the waitress proudly accepted their approval.

Two burly stinking men from the other table came to Oros's table. They brusquely sat down, uninvited, one on each side of him. He felt a sharp point focussing in on his ribs. "We're 'bout ta have a short talk." The man said with a miserable accent. "I talks, yoos lis-den."

Oros nodded his head nervously. "I listen." He repeated.

"Good." Said the other man. His accent slightly worse than his sewage smell. "Then I won't bees pokin'so hard." He pressed the blade into Oros's ribs once again. "Will I?"

"No. I shall listen to whatever you two gentlemen have to say."

"There's a person who wants you just to forget about the Quest."

Oros wide-eyed fanatical gaze took the men by surprize. Then he flipped the table and made for the door. Both men seized him before he got to the doorway.

"He be right. He said we'd have ta kill him." Snarled the man with the knife.

"Too bad we couldn't buy him off.....Maybe not, 'cause we gat to keep the money for us." They drug the stricken Oros out the door and around the corner. No one paid any attention to the commotion.

"I'd let the fat man alone, friend." The voice, clear and strong, came from Rux. He stood in the middle of the alley, seemingly unarmed.

The smelly man with the knife stepped behind Oros, putting the blade point in Oros's mouth. The other man just snickered.

"Better go your own way, stranger, if ya know what's be good for you." The second scoundrel haughtily purred.

"This be the best help you can find anymore, Hanmer?" Rux cynically questioned the man behind Oros.

"Yea, I guess it is. Quality ain't what it used ta be." He shot a glance at his assistant. "But what ye be doin', Rux?"

"Not too bad. Money's pretty good, especially for one like him."

"Ye ain't changed too much. How much is he worth to you?" Hanmer drawled.

"Nothing anymore. I've been paid." Rux admitted matter-of-factly.

"Then you certainly won't mind if we take him." Said the other man.

"Yes, I would." Rux unexpectedly jerked his left arm, spinning a dagger into the burly man's chest. With a stupid look on his face, he turned towards Hanmer and died.

"Not fair!" Hanmer exclaimed.

"I don't play fair!" Rux said as he spit on the ground. "Now, I'll give you to three to let the fat man go."

Hanmer grabbed Oros even tighter. "When you count three, he's dead." Hanmer retorted. "You can't reach me behind this here fat boy."

"Maybe we got a stand off?"

"Only if you really want the fat man to continue living."

"I believe I do." Rux commented. He then placed his two hands together and rubbed them, looking quite nervous. Immediately, Hanmer fell to the ground, a crossbow dart protruding slightly above his right ear.

"Thanks for not moving Oros, you made the job much easier."

The rotund priest quivered. "Just how did you shoot him?" The priest was completely baffled by the ninety degree shot. "How do you shoot from a direction different from the one you're in?"

"Do I ask, do I pry into your gifts?"

"Not as of yet."

Rux retrieved his dagger from the dead man, wiping it off on the dead man's grease stained tunic. Then he placed his hands together again. A bolt struck the dead man in the same hole used by the dagger. "Now the locals will all be roaming the countryside for a man with a crossbow. ...We can eat in peace. ...You didn't forget to order did you?" Rux placed his hands together.

"Stop that." Oros yelled. "You tend to make me a little unsettled."

"Think you might be more unsettled if your throat had a whole in it." Rux replied with a vicious delight in seeing Oros squirm.

"Your time is coming." Oros predicted. "Your time is coming."

The thick stew tasted far better than the environment dictated. Oros and Rux sat with their backs to the wall, half on guard, half inquisitive as they watched the search for the crossbowman begin. No one cared much about Hanmer, but the other fellow hailed as some sort of local hero, one who enjoyed stalking the Kyykki. One local fellow even boasted a necklace made from Kyykki teeth, a present from the dead man.

As strangers in the village, Rux and Oros expected to be questioned. For some undeclared reason, no one paid them much attention. Rux surmized that the difficulty concealing a crossbow on one's person kept the villagers from wasting time with the strangers. He also knew that their mounts and the goods on the pack Striper would be thoroughly searched, if not altogether stolen.

As a witness to their innocence and ignorance of the two murders, Oros and Rux spent the night in the rat and bug infested room above the dining room, along with twelve others. Neither man actually slept, Oros from contemplation of Rux's most unorthodox gift and its benefits, Rux from suspicion: Hanmer seldom worked alone. But something else worried him more, Hanmer's right forearm showed a new tattoo, one of a flying dragon. Once on the road, he fully intended to engage Oros in a conversation about these items.

Breakfast consisted of the same stew and the mugs of ale. The rough talking waitress showed a wispy mystical smile on her face.

"Had a good night, I see?" Rux absently queried.

"Bout the best in a few hundred nights." She answered without a hint of embarrassment. That was left for Oros.

"Must you." Oros jabbed the thin man in the ribs with his fork.

"Why not? What else she have? You offer her something better?" Rux responded sharply. "Damn Churchmen!" He muttered. "They criticize but never fix."

"Unfortunately, I tend to agree with you." Oros said. "We are the best hypocrites in Haaf." Guilt hung on his words.

"I just might get to like you, Oros." Rux grinned.

Their journey from the village commenced with empty saddlebags, just as Rux predicted. However, the two Stripers and the Massive Blue had been well cared for and adequately fed. Once out-of-town, they turned towards the north, following a forest track. This gave them some protection from the brisk early autumn winds as well as the opportunity to converse.

"What do tattoos signify to you, Oros?"

"Strange question." He paused for a moment. "Why do you ask?"

"You did see the flying dragon one on the right forearm of Hanmer, didn't you?"

"It thrilled me about as much as the real ones do."

"What do you make of it? After all, it's a relatively new one."

"I can't be sure, but there may be a secret organization involved. One that knew who I was and where I'm going...Tell me, did you know I was on a Quest?"

"No, as far as I was concerned, you were headed to Haaf North. Once there, some Light Striper officer named Treh was to ship out with us."

"Not bad. But there are some errors. Treh belongs to the Church Knights, and he's 'just' been promoted to officer." Oros said. "Then exists a more significant problem; one that I really don't want to consider: a spy well-planted in the higher echelons of the Church."

"Yes sir. You people really are the foremost hypocrites."

"This isn't funny, Rux!" Oros's markedly strained tone punctuated the air.

"True, but you're not going to correct the situation here."

Supper consisted of roasted pheasant, one that Rux shot shortly before they camped for the night. The misty glen, about three hundred feet off the trail, abounded in dense shrubs and had a small artesian well bubbling up, forming a pond deep enough for fish and room enough to take a much needed bath. The abundant moss provided for a most conformable bed, no rats and no bedbugs, just a few ever-present spiders. Both men slept well.

As the blazing morning sun cut through the mist, Rux and Oros, refreshed, cantered along the forested trail.

"By lunch we'll pass by a large farm. We'll restock there." Rux commented.

"Think they'll serve us a cooked meal?" Oros smiled.

"Only if you dress proper. People act differently when you Churchmen parade about in your fancy gowns."

"You really have to rub it in, don't you."

"Don't take it personally. It's just an interpretation from an outsider. A person just ought to practice what they demand from others, nothing less nothing more. I've seen very few Churchmen practice that."

"What about the King shoving the clergy into every village to teach?" Oros countered.

"Simply proves my point. The King ended their uppityness, not the Church Hierarchy. The people will enjoy having the priests about. For once their 'betters' are confined to the same life as most of them." Rux spoke, but he focussed his energy on the clearing ahead. His stomach's turnings warned him of danger; instinctively he put his two hands together as he passed the pack Striper's tether to Oros. Oros smiled politely, acknowledging a problem ahead.

With a yowling growl, six ruffians with swords attacked Rux as he entered the clearing. He neatly dispatched them within moments, a bolt through each head.

"Not overly intelligent." Rux remarked. "They actually attacked frontally, as a group. I hardly had to aim." He swung off his Striper to examine the dead. Oros clambered off his Massive Blue to join him.

"Not just another coincidence, is it?" Oros thought out loud.

"I wish! Look here." He held up the forearms of two of the attackers, each identified himself with the flying dragon tattoo. "Any of these faces look familiar?"

"Not after you've put those holes in them." He sarcastically replied.

"I can remove the bolts." Rux said, almost innocently.

"Forget I said anything." Oros announced caustically.

"If you so direct." Rux continued to examine the fallen men. All were Haafian, middle-aged. Most showed significant degrees of recent sunburn, as if they usually spent most of their time inside. Their hands showed none of the calluses and muscles that are peculiar to those devoted to manual labor. "These idiots are the poorest, rawest recruits I've ever seen."

"Makes your responsibilities easier."

"And you proclaim me...."

"No matter, this tells us we better find another way to Haaf North. I'd like to get there alive."

"I didn't think you worried about such things!"

"Shut up and ride!"

And so they did, as Rux proceeded to carve a path through the forest. They meandered all day in a westerly direction, every now and then encountering another path or farm road.

"Might you explain just how that crossbow of yours works?"

"Oros, I'm devastated!" Rux mocked. "I thought you Churchmen knew all about 'gifts'."

"I know exactly where it originated." The fat priest shot back. "Tell me how it works."

"Its all a simple matter of analyzing angles. I know from whence I shoot, to what I ricochet off and thence to the intended target."

"So that's how you seem to shoot around corners?"

"Didn't I just say that." Only his ridiculous smile kept Oros from flattening him with the back of his pudgy hand.

"Then what occurs if your target moves?" Oros deliberately taunted him as he stared him directly in the eyes.

"You know, old boy, if you could ride a normal Striper, I'd have to look down at you." He smirked and quickly deflected the on-coming hand. "Nice try! You need more speed and an improved manner of surprize."

What if your target moves?" Oros cynically challenged.

"Aren't we getting touchy." Rux released Oros' hand. "No target can move that fast."

"And just how fast are 'we' moving?"

"About the same speed as you need to catch your ugly fat reflection in the mirror." Rux yelled over his shoulder as he kicked his spurs into the Striper.

"Damn you!" Oros bellowed. He trotted on, vainly attempting to catch the more agile Rux.

Late in the afternoon, he caught up to Rux at the edge of the forest. Beyond the large ripening wheatfield rose an immense brownstone castle. No moat, but the twin walls provided clues as to the strength of the castle. Some untended cows meandered through the pasture on the north, but nothing else. Emanating from the chimney of the castle's rounded keep poured dark smoke tinged with red.

"Krucik's place, isn't it?" Rux asked Oros as he rode up behind him. "Stay in the shadows. I'd rather we not be seen."

"But I don't see anyone, even on the walls."

"That's what really concerns me. The old man is dead and his son got squeezed by the dragon. His wife's been dead for nigh a thousand dawns. So who's got the castle fire going?"

Before Oros replied a curdling scream tore through the tranquil atmosphere, causing the cows to run and the mounts to bolt. The atmosphere converted to evil and cold. The texture of the castle's smoke changed to darker black with a green tinge.

"Any ideas as to what it is?"

"My guts inform me I don't want to know." Rux said rather pained.

"Can you get us inside?" Oros commanded.

"Why not just go around it? My responsibility is to get you to Haaf North in one piece. The skinny old man told me to keep you from becoming a hero or, worse yet, a martyr."

"What skinny old man?" Oros curiously posed.

"You forgot what your father looks like?"

"Damn you!"

"You used that phrase twice now. Shouldn't I hear your confession? Rux goaded Oros.

Oros flushed, turning somewhat bluish in the face. He quickly regained his composure. "If, and only if, it actually was my father then you'll be able to identify him by name." He spoke quite confidently.

"Fat chance!" Rux coughed. "Stupid, insipid trick....I wouldn't tell you that, even if I knew it."

"You have thus gained some semblance of...."

"Credibility? Why, thank you so much.....Now, if we remain within the confines of the forest, we'll safely circumnavigate the castle."

"Forget it. We're going to pay these castle types a Holy visit, a secret visit."

"I don't like what you say."

"You don't have to like it. Now get my long tube out of the saddlebags. We're going to exterminate some of the damned one's faithful followers."

"You enjoy this, don't you?"

"I am a Church Guard." Oros answered bluntly.

Until the first moon rose, they studied the castle through the long tube. The few guards posted obviously did not take their responsibility seriously, as most finished off one bottle after another, oblivious to the environment. The well-worn path leading to the south side of the castle ended at the rusted gate, one long unused. Shadows of people in long robes glided silently along the top of the keep, as if expecting someone or something.

"So, how do we get in?"

"Easy, every castle has a chapel. Under the altar is a passageway to the outside."

"Every castle has an escape route?" Rux asked incredulously.

"You actually expect me to answer that."

Rux refused to continue the discussion. Instead he chose to prepare their cold supper. Following supper, the two cautiously walked the three mounts around to the east castle wall. No one hailed them, nor did they see anyone. Oros motioned for a halt towards the corner of the east wall. Rux tethered the mounts and removed Oros' sword from the saddlebag.

"Dig here." Oros whispered as he pointed to what appeared a piece of rocky debris.

"Are you sure about this?" Rux wondered out loud. "How do you know about this place? You've been here before?"

"Shut up and dig."

A few spade fulls of dirt disclosed a rounded iron plate, now indifferently rusted. The rust discolored the stone blocks which held the three foot plate.

"Don't just stand there gawking. Move the plate."

The unyielding iron simply ripped Rux's hands. An iron bar, used as a wedge, poked a hole in the center of the plate. Stagnant, repellant air blasted up through the hole, knocking both men over and destroying the majority of the rusted plate.

Rux picked up a few pieces. "You didn't tell me about boobytraps." He whispered angrily.

"It wasn't supposed to be."

"Your 'supposed to' is going to kill us both."

"And you aren't ready to die? Is that your problem?"

"Shut up!"

Beneath the rusted remains of the plate, lay a tightly twisted staircase which continued issuing fetid smelling air, enough to nauseate both men. What little light from the second moon dared to penetrate the dank staircase reveled dirt and dust covered steps, the skeletal remains of a few small animals and plenty of crawling insects.

"Just your sort of place, isn't it, Oros?" Rux obnoxiously vented as he held out an unlit torch to him. "You go first."

Rux almost died trying to quiet himself from Oros' grand entrance into the tunnel: Oros missed the first step and then bounced step by step to the bottom, emitting a groan with each bump. A cloud of aged and stench-filled dust erupted from the tunnel as the well-rounded priest collapsed at the bottom of the shaft. Silence ruled for a moment, then Oros sputteringly called for his torch. Rux dropped it down the stairs and waited for light before descending.

The small slippery steps descended over twenty feet, terminating in an oval shaped room which could effectively contain a half platoon. An extremely narrow stone archway designated where the tunnel now headed. Oros had all ready jammed himself into it, and, with a measured amount of unpleasant shoving from Rux, found himself in the tunnel proper, where the dimensions measurably enlarged. However, being well over six foot tall, Rux discovered the tunnel's four and a half foot height placed a grand imposition upon his dignity.

The tunnel continued to run downward, then leveled off. His hand felt wet and sticky, but Rux had only touched the staircase. Upon grasping the torch, he observed the color of the wetness: red.

He grossly contorted his face as the depraved implications of the blood horribly pounded their way into his senses. "The scream?" He hoarsely called to a visibly shaken Oros.

Oros' face went beyond pale, his countenance frozen. He slowly nodded his balding head in agreement. He placed his hands over his face blocking out the truth. Finally, when he lifted his face, righteous anger shot from it, catching Rux off-guard.

"Let's go!" He whispered tersely. "The evil upstairs shall be avenged."

Grabbing the torch from Rux's hand, the fat priest scrambled up the staircase like a rat. Rux followed a few steps behind. Soon they both peeped out the four holes installed in the altar ages ago, when it served Haafians with hope. They surveyed a ghastly environment where nothing sacred lived and where a debauched sacrilegious cult celebrated. A few drunken guards leaned against the front pews, another one, farther back, seemed intimately involved in pursuing vile pleasures with a gagged, but still-shrieking female. The rest of the vast darkened chapel reeked of rottenness and other decay. A puddle of blood remained on the floor, next to the altar, but no body. The stained glass windows had been planked shut against the purifying sunlight. Smelly oil burning braziers hanging from the heavy beamed ceiling cast long dismal shadows across this once Holy space.

"Makes you really want to hurt someone, doesn't it?" Muttered Rux.

"Exactly." His face stern and determined. "And the best way to cleanse something is to burn it down!"

"I am beginning to like you, after all." Rux said after he shot both guards. They fell noiselessly into heaps on the dirty wooden floor. "Where do we find the rest?" He asked with a smile.

"They'll be above us, on top of the keep."

"Then we'll just have to 'keep' them up there until they're well cooked." Rux declared. "But what about the rest?"

"Let's go hunt them down." And with that terse remark, he swung open the door on the back side of the altar. "That moronic heretic in the pew belongs to me."

"As you wish. But 'keep' it quiet."

The guard in the pew had too much trouble with his breeches to notice Oros behind him.

"Good Sir." Oros whispered loudly.

The startled man lurched around to confront Oros. He was well met by a swift stroke of Oros' sword which dumped his guts into his half-dropped breeches. The man's eyes blazed with incredulous horror.

"Good Sir." Oros calmly repeated. "I do believe you've dropped something.

The severely shocked guard sheepishly looked down at his guts, then fainted. Oros ungagged the girl; her appearance being vaguely familiar, somehow bothered him.

"Look here." Called Rux. "All these idiots have the tattoo." He then spotted the girl and smiled. "Will we be having stew again tonight?" He asked in a most polite manner.

"Only iffen me 'onor is restored." She replied testily.

"Honor is one thing. Revenge is quite another." Rux continued. "I believe its the latter you really want."

"You means I wants 'dem all killed." Her voice softened, but the accent still plagued Oros' hearing.

"Then we have a deal." Rux put out his hand and the two shook. "Stay here until we return....As for your friend, he isn't dead. I'll leave the honor to you."

"You really ir a gentleman." She said. Then, suddenly realizing her current state of undress, hurriedly continued. "And a gentleman don't look neither." She said abruptly, but without embarrassment. "Turn around!"

The two quietly left the chapel to explore the rest of the darkened castle. Oros lead the way to the kitchen, which they found empty. So too for the pantry.

"I do believe everyone is on the keep. I suggest that they gather here only for their ceremonies."

"Then how did they get in, Oros?"

"Through the gate that connects with Krucik's private mansion. Follow me."

"Why not, nothing else going on." He murmured.

They exited the kitchen into a small garden and then into the yard beside Krucik's mansion. Four careless guards leaned on the gate there. Once around another corner of the mansion, a glance through the dirty stained window demonstrated that the once elegant mansion had become a filthy barracks.

"How many?" Oros asked.

"Enough to make for an interesting challenge. But first we'll rid ourselves of those guards."

"And as soon as they drop over, out comes all the idiots from the barracks." Oros disapproved.

"Not if the bolts fasten the guards to the wall."

"You can actually do such a wondrous thing." Oros embellished his sarcasm.

"As easily as you can spill someone's guts. And you didn't even ask his name....... What will the wench think of your manners."

"Shut up."

Rux wasted no time 'bolting' the unsuspecting guards to the wall. After blocking all other entrances out of the mansion, Rux walked calmly through the front door. Halfway up the stairs to the second floor he folded his hands together and began shooting. Most never realized they were dead. Oros joined him as they began to explore the second floor. The formal dining room littered with maps and charts provided a curious sight.

"What you do make of them?"

"They are maps of most of our cities in the south." Oros said angrily. "This is definite proof that some Haafians are traitors......... Monstrous!"

At his outburst, three officers smashed through the side door. Two raised their swords, the other a crossbow. Oros crouched as the first officer swung. The sword overshot its mark and Oros punched his head into the man's stomach, tossing him over his shoulder and out the window. Rux easily dispatched the second officer. The third fired before he died. His bolt struck Oros in the calf.

"Damn it!" He yelled as he wrenched the bolt from his calf. Rux tossed him a rag to bind the wound.

"There's a few more coming." He warned. "Can you walk?"

"Just give me a crutch."

Six more military types burst through the same door. They charged Rux without pause. All terminated their charge within a sword's stroke of Rux. Oros hobbled about the tables, gathering up maps and charts, stuffing them into a large linen sack.

"Turn the candles over." Rux called to Oros.

The dusty, paper cluttered room caught fire easily. Rux moved from room to room, finding the place deserted, while Oros hobbled down the stairs. Without pausing to check for other sentries, they made for the kitchen, Rux half-carrying Oros. At the kitchen Oros explained the intricacies of the twin staircases that ran to the top of the keep. Rux would block them while Oros and the girl, provided she hadn't escaped on her own, collected adequate combustibles to fire the entire keep.

Oros found the girl standing over her dead captor. In spite of her apparent hardness, tears dropped from her eyes.

"He begged me to kill him." She spoke without turning towards Oros. "His eyes were filled with pity."

"So you left him just to burn later on?" Oros queried. "You're a hard woman. No mercy!"

"Damn you!" She screeched at Oros. "And just what mercy did he have on me? You sound like one of those idiot priests!" She snapped at him so close that he thought his nose bled.

Oros restrained himself from pursuing her argument, fearing bodily harm if he offered another explanation. "Listen," He asked her. "Can you help me gather wood and oil to burn this place down?"

"Where's the skinny guy?" She hotly demanded.

"Upstairs. He's blocking the staircases so we don't have any survivors." He said weakly.

"You're wounded.... How?" As she calmed down the phony accent slowly returned.

"Soldiers in the mansion." He said flatly and then he saw the fear on her face. "Don't worry. They're dead....Rux killed them."

Rux tramped back with a broad smile cluttering his narrow face. The other two completely ignored him, being busy up-ending the pews and piling them under the oil filled braziers.

"They're drunk and calling on Beziel, or something like that, to accept their sacrifice." Rux commented.

"Those damn bastards!" The girl yelled. "Ela was my friend. ..... They just cut her heart out......And then showed it to her....She was still alive...." She burst into tears and grabbed Oros with a strength that almost suffocated him. Oros gently placed his thick arms about her...."Thanks."

Oros, arms still about the girl, glanced at Rux. "Can you shoot the braziers."

"Can you disembowel a heathen with one stroke?"

"The bastard deserved what he got!" The girl defended Oros.

"Sorry." He gingerly replied. Rux then grimaced as he noted the blood running Oros' wounded calf. "You really are more effective without the accent." He bowed to her. "My lady, Nadre."

Nadre froze with fear, squeezing Oros all the tighter. "Stay away from me.....you.....you."

"Rux is the name." He quietly announced. "Oros, whom you've just about suffocated, is my client."

Realizing she injured Oros, she suddenly set him free. Oros rapidly sank to the ground, gasping for air.

"I'm not here to return you. You are free………. and I don't really know you are here."

A strange bizarre look came across her face. "But, you know me?" She said quietly and yet bewildered.

"I work for Baste." He answered, trying to sound innocent. "I'm the one who discovered you stealing at the market." He took a long breath. "Baste is now at the wall, fighting the Kyykki. He has no time, nor do I, to concern ourselves with a few stolen potatoes…………………. I hope you believe that."

Oros pulled himself up to almost standing. "Enough." He weakly called out. "We'll finish this morality debate later. ...My dear Nadre, consider yourself safe. You have my word for it as a priest."

Nadre shrank back in real embarrassment. "I'm soory....sorry." She roughly stammered, trying not to look at Oros. "I didn't ....I really didn't... Know."

"Ah!" Grunted Rux. "Don't worry about those words. The fat man is tough….. Believe me, he's heard much worse....And lived."

Nadre managed a quick smirk while Oros glared his vehement disapproval. She then tidied herself up a much as possible. "How is your leg doing?" She tried to change the subject.

"Shoot down the braziers and let's get out of here." Oros barked.

"Yes, my wonderful master." He laughed, pushing his hands together, tumbling, one-by-one, the oil filled braziers from the ceiling the wooden pews piled below. Ten small conflagrations rapidly gathered strength, creating a most appropriate inferno of judgement for those above.

From the sheltered canopy provided by bordering trees, the trio silently watched the keep burn and then collapse. For a while the dry wooden pews fuelled the hundred foot flames which jealously enveloped the entire structure, restructuring the night sky. They carefully scrutinized the gate, not one person emerged from the mansion.

"Have you all seen enough?" Oros sourly articulated.

"You're just hungry." Rux returned as he threw the pack striper's tether to Nadre. "You're free to go."

"And just where might I go?" She asked bluntly. "No, I'll stay with the two of you.... Besides, its not proper nor safe to leave in the middle of the night." Her accent disappeared altogether.

"You really think that's wise?" Oros posed as a corrective.

"If wisdom was ever one of my stronger suites, I'd be elsewhere." She corrected Oros. "Actually, I prefer safety. And I find it here." She smiled smugly. "Besides, you need a nurse and you both need a meal."

"Well, I be thinkun youd doo right gudd, missy." Rux innocently spat out, trying to mimic her old accent.

"Shut up!" Oros replied. Then he muttered something concerning the disadvantages of his leg wound. "Now you're forced to retrieve some wood for the fire."

"And you, priest." Nadre stared Oros in the face, backing him down with her compelling tone. "Are going to have a most pretty lady at your service." She presented him with sweet seductive glance that caused him more agony than any confession.

The pouring rain rudely woke the exhausted trio. The sky turned grey with blustery cold thunderclouds. In the near distance the keep smoldered and steamed, however, it now stood less than twenty feet tall. The strong brownstone walls of the mansion formed a blackened perimeter about a massive jumble of broken and charred beams, beams that once kept the heavy tiled roof in place.

Rux erected a rough canvas shelter to protect Oros, whose wounded leg swelled to twice its usual dimension. With an unusually large hairpin, Nadre lanced Oros' calf, allowing a copious amount of yellow puss to drain. That extraordinary piece of nursing relieved his pain but not his consternation.

As the drizzly evening approached, Rux decided to wait until noon the next day before continuing their sojourn to Haaf North. Nadre remained close to Oros, and though she acquitted herself well, appeared to be apprehensive.

"The demons never quit eating at your soul, do they?" Rux tried to draw her out.

She pretended to be deaf, though tears welled up in her large brown eyes and rolled down staining her bodice. She pensively glanced at Rux, her eyes effectively communicating.

"My demons still bother me now and then." He modestly confessed to her. "Took quite a while for me to believe I might be worth something..... besides dead." He paused, watching for Nadre's reaction.

As an immediate reaction wasn't forthcoming, Rux recommenced his story. "Quite frankly, I forgot about you...and the stealing, until after I returned to the inn for supper. I've usually put things in a priority order. Capturing you, Nadre, a simple thief, and please, take no offence, wasn't paramount for me. As it's been over a hundred cycles, the case against you is terminated....... Quite frankly, Nadre, you are free."

"But free for what?" She angrily cried out through her tears. "I escaped to that stupid town, where no one knew me and no one really cared. Where I played whore to survive. Where I was drug from to be sacrificed.....Now even that's gone....No money, no home,...not another dress to wear....Free for naught." And she burst into tears of desperation.

A burly somewhat garbled voice emerged from the canvas shelter. "Then my dear Nadre, you are completely free to begin again. No questions asked. You have confessed to your sins. They are gone forever, thanks be to the Holy One."

Nadre sat up, stunned. Then she jammed her hands over her ears to block out Oros' words. "No! No!....You liar!......... I don't believe you!........ The Holy One demands retribution!..... The Holy One is slow to forgive. ...And now you deliberately torment me with your so-called .... Damn you!" She ran stumbling into the dripping forest, tripping over stones and roots in the darkness. With a heart wrenching cry of anguish, she threw herself through a thorny briar tree, from whence she sobbed until dawn.

Oros hobbled over to rescue her, but Rux persuaded him to wait: Nadre needed time to rid herself of the demons she claimed as her past.

The rain decreased its downpour overnight and began slacking off. Shortly after dawn Nadre limped to Oros' shelter, soaked, drained and yet somehow her demeanor appeared peaceful. Her face and arms spackled with blood and her bodice and skirt tattered beyond repair, and yet she smiled. A humble tentative smile, but a smile nonetheless, an authentic smile which she probably lost thousands of cycles ago. She pensively stood at the entrance to the canvass shelter.

"Come in. Come out of the damned rain." Oros welcomed her. "Its not proper that you should catch pneumonia nor go about naked. Rux, get some clothing from the saddlebags." He called to the skinny fellow trying to start the breakfast fire.

Neither set of clothes suited her well. Oros' tunic was too short, exposing her well-turned legs. And Rux's shirt was far too tight for her curves. But the combination of Rux's breeches and Oros' robe worked out sufficiently well to provide warmth and modesty, at least temporarily.

After washing and donning her new wardrobe, Nadre, with a stern gaze, removed the hobbling Oros from kitchen duties. He obeyed without further comment.

"I'm sorry." Nadre said quietly after breakfast. Her head hung low and her eyes would only study her bare feet.

"Apology accepted." Oros spoke in his most formal tone. Then he touched her chin, forcing her to see him. "Are you now free?" His voice full of compassion and empathy.

"I....I...I believe so." She stammered. Then she smiled, as her insight continued to throw off the past and its demons, as she realized what 'free' meant. "Am I supposed to have a new name?" She asked hesitantly.

"Good gracious, no!" Proclaimed the fat priest as he hugged her. "All you need is a new soul.....and that you have.....Of course, I heartily recommend surrounding yourself with a few well-chosen friends."

"Then I choose the two of you." She called out. And then she cried again, but these tears for the hope of the future. "Until your 'extremely special' trip is over, I shall travel with the both of you." She said with confidence.

"You know about the Quest?" Asked Rux.

"Quest?" Her face puzzled. "Quest means nothing to me. I'm just stating that I'm now part of your group, forever. We are a trio. ....Sorry if it didn't come out clearly....I guess I've still got a lot of rethinking to do."

"Rux will help you, it took him quite a while." Oros reported with a hint of one-upsmanship.

"Really. I never would have guessed." Nadre gently teased.

"I vote 'no' for the trio. Its bad enough having one person against me, now I'll have two." Rux became an actor. Sighing dejectedly, full of self pity, only to provide opportunity for the other two's enjoyment.

"I do have a modest question for you, Rux." Nadre cautiously asked, as she twined and inter-twined her fingers.

"Yes, my dear Nadre." Rux replied, pretending his best to be a real gentleman. "What is it that you require of me?"

Nadre stalled before asking. Then she rapidly blurted out. "Just how does that 'gift' of your's work?"

Rux laughed, shaking his head in disbelief. "AH, you are indeed a bold one." He said approvingly. "However, what you require I can't provide for you." His tone became sober. "The particulars of the gift are between myself and the giver of the gift. That is a solemn contract which, under great penalty, I can't disclose.."

Nadre's countenance dropped. "I'm sorry." She apologized. "I have no desire to place your life in peril."

"Then you assume too much for yourself, Nadre." said Oros. "The fact of the matter is that only Rux controls the gift. The responsibility is his, not yours. You may see yourself in the uncomfortable role as tempter, but you can never remove his responsibility. We are each responsible for our own gifts."

Oros looked deep into Nadre's eyes. "Do you comprehend that there are significant limitations to your responsibility?" He asked in the manner of a wise old grandfather.

"Then I'm not responsible for what happens?" She asked innocently, but with insight.

"She's beginning to realize she's not the Holy One, Oros." Rux smiled at the blushing Nadre. "Congratulations!"

Towards noon, Oros found the location of Krucik's castle on one of the confiscated maps. It provided a path to Haaf North, approximately eighty miles due south. It also presented a foreboding notation: the castle could be reached via a tunnel from the north. The tunnel's entrance began near an unidentified river, located downstream from a volcano. Oros kept this latter information to himself.

Nadre violently objected to Rux's command to start breaking camp. In her self-assigned role as nurse and physician, she forbade Rux, with all manner of horrendous threats, that he would not move until the Oros' wound stopped draining. Actually, Rux had little choice; Oros' earlier activity caused the infected wound furnished him with both an irrational stupor and some dreadful hallucinations. A priest envisioning toothed flying rabbits gathering to eat him, was not travelling anywhere. Even Rux, who remained rather adamant about getting to Haaf North promptly for 'professional treatment', relented when Oros' hallucinations escalated. Such a high-handed attitude placed Rux at odds with Nadre, who now only communicated to him with rough glances

After three days of morose silence, Nadre did speak with Rux, apologizing for her lack of manners. Rux awkwardly responded with a dimwitted explanation of what he really meant. Nadre listened a patiently as anyone else, but suddenly she burst into laughter at his preposterous explanation. In response, Rux delved into a self-pitying silence which Nadre gently terminated with a kiss on his cheek.

Oros' hallucinations completely disappeared on the forth dawn, simultaneously with the sun's first showing in as many dawns. The vibrant shafts of light, piercing the overcast sky, were most welcome. They allowed cleanup from the night's filthy downpour. It rained mud. The rumbling to the north did little to encourage a restful sleep. As Oros ambled about the campsite in the late afternoon, devouring whatever his chubby fingers could grasp, Rux took leave to explore Krucik's castle. Leaving 'Nurse Nadre', as Rux had taken to calling her with some amount of affection, in charge of the overweight priest. He mounted his Striper and set off at a gallop across the wheatfields.

The soaked brownstone walls, at least those which still remained as testimony to the once proud castle, steamed as the sun pulled moisture from them. That scene, compounded with the ash filled puddles and the charred beams presented Rux with a sense of the unreal, the mysterious. For, in spite of the evil being cleansed from the castle by fire and water, a haunting evilness remained. It bothered him. Rux thoroughly enjoyed a simple life of black and white, a life as clear cut as his divine gift.

He tethered the Striper at the former kitchen entrance, anticipating a walk to explore the inside of the chapel. He wanted to know if the altar still stood. It would be a positive sign that the evilness he felt perhaps was just in his mind. He carefully maneuvered his way through the fallen debris as he headed towards the chapel. He heard a soft rustle off on his left. As he turned to see it, a rock bounced off the back of his head. He careened headfirst into a dirty puddle, unconscious.

"Check him for a dragon tattoo!" Called a strong voice. "Then tie him up. Its time we got some answers about what's happened here."

The vast majority of southern Haaf was nothing but a gigantic quagmire. Fluz Marsh dictated exactly what occupations the people had and what demeanor they carried, as well as influence their activity and productivity. Unfortunately, the marsh's natural power, being too hot and humid in the short, insect infested summer to actually farm and being nothing but a thick ice sheet in the long sun-never-rises winter, kept most of the few folk who lived there rather unoccupied. Two major exports stood out as significant: story weaving and sending young people north to work in the crowded cities. Those who chose to remain in the marsh stayed as fiercely independent as their illiteracy allowed. They were Haafian in name only. The people preferred to form bands of territorial families.

This society Jabbi did not enjoy, but as part of his assignment laid down by the Council almost twenty cycles ago, the luxury of choosing left long ago. The time easily passed for three hundred cycles.

Jabbi traveled solitaire, posing as an itinerant poet. Such fellows found welcome in every pub and tavern, for whether or not their verse had any quality, their visitations became profitable, at least to the establishment owners. And in a land riddled with absolute dullness, a crowd was guaranteed. Furthermore, even suspicious swamp dwellers usually opened up to a drunken poet. Jabbi quickly realized his real task lay in ascertaining the truth from the swampers. But as superstition ran untamed in these parts, separating truth from fiction added to this difficulty.

The boisterous crowd finally left. Both moons had risen and set all ready. The stench from the wildweed cigars claimed the atmosphere in the bungalow-type tavern. The so-called poet rented a small loft for the night. The beer guzzling swampers invited him to continue for another evening, but only if the topic the poems and stories centered upon 'dragons'. He had a half day to concoct some rubbish to put before them. Perhaps it would be worth it, for some peasant challenged him about the dragons, bragging that an old man he recently fished with, told an extremely different story.

Jabbi finished his tankard, said good-morning to the innkeeper, and stepped up into the loft. As he pulled the ratted and stained curtain, he noticed the innkeeper, whose sleeves were rolled up for scrubbing dishes, bore the tattoo of a flying dragon. No wonder they wanted to hear more dragon fabrications, Jabbi dully thought as he nodded off.

"There's a old man here." The innkeeper yelled up the stairs to the loft where, despite the multitude of bedbugs, Jabbi actually got some sleep. "Claims you be late for fishing."

Jabbi yanked his breeches on and practically fell down the coarse wooden steps on his way to the door, boots still in hand. From the back corner, a strong resonate voice beckoned him.

"Come and sit, poet. The fish aren't ready for us yet. Breakfast is." As he continued stumbling to the table, Jabbi found himself elated by this fortunate change of events: the Elder arrived.

As Jabbi awkwardly sat himself, the old man spoke. "You've changed since last we met, poet."

"I guess I have, old man." Jabbi acknowledged, somewhat embarrassed by his present disguise. "I guess I have."

"Now,.. about this asinine 'dragon stuff'?" The old man began, keeping a watchful eye on an overactive innkeeper. "Seems you've been telling folks that they fly?" The leading question deliberately attracted the innkeeper, as it was meant to.

"That is what I said.... Everyone here last night will vouch for that."

The old man became contemptuous. "And just how do you know this?"

"I suppose you're going to convince me that you've actually documented a flying dragon?"

"I saw one land in Krabo....... It landed right in front of the Council

Hall building." Jabbi caught the game fast and pretended to be defensive about his experiences.

"You sure did, poet. But only in your windswept dreams. Or maybe you got one of them far fetched imaginations, stirred up with plenty of cheap booze." As the old man continued his mockery, the innkeeper continued to wash the same table, never missing one nuance of the conversation.

"Innkeeper!" Shouted Jabbi. "Get us some good ale over here! And don't be taking all day about it."

The dirty shirted man brought two flagons to the table and arrogantly slammed them down. "Anythin' else you be wantin'." He snorted. His demeanor resembled a beast. His new 'flying dragon' tattoo still swelled.

Yes." Said Jabbi, focussing his eyes on the tattoo. "Any man who wears this tattoo ought to know something about them." He grinned at the Innkeeper as if he possessed some erudite knowledge. "Look here old man," Jabbi continued as he pointed to the Innkeeper's tattoo, "that dragon is flying. This man knows I speak the truth."

The dense Innkeeper rapidly swelled with self-importance. He grabbed a chair from the next table and sat. "Dragons fly very well." He proclaimed with an air of intelligence. "Dragons live in the north, at the top of the world, where it's always hot."

"See, old man." Jabbi gloated. "Even he knows better than you."

The burly Innkeeper rubbed his mammoth hands together, a smirk running from ear to ear. He looked absolutely ridiculous, so sure of his dragon knowledge, so sure of his responsibility in this feigned argument. Jabbi bit his lip to keep from laughing at the Innkeeper, now perched on the chair, his hairy gut protruding over the top of his coarse linen breeches, just waiting to pounce upon the next the essential details that he alone could adequately supply.

"Well, Innkeeper." The old man reverently asked. "We humble ourselves before you. Let us hear about the truth, the dragon truth." He then emptied his half filled flagon and positioned himself in front of the Innkeeper. "Sorry we caused you any problems before."

"Don't worry about it." The Innkeeper snorted in a self important manner. "I'se been listen to many who comes here ta drink. They claim a dragon flies into the swamp, lookin' fer virgins ta eat." He laughed so hard the solid wood chair split under him. He grabbed another and continued his lecture. "'cept they ain't no virgins in the swamp." His overwrought delight about this cultural manifestation caused the demise of yet another chair.

"Please, good sir, continue."

"I recons the dragons don't return cause they starve down here."

"Probably so." Jabbi dryly commented. "But then, you did see for yourself these dragons 'fly' into the swamp? We need to convince this old man."

"I needs bee's honest with ya. I didn't seed nothin' 'cause I bees workin'."

"Then where did you get your information?" The high eye-browed old man testily asked. "I do presume an expert to properly enumerate his sources."

The mental capabilities of the Innkeeper jostled and strained. It showed in the wideness of his bloodshot eyes. He sat there, quietly pretending to think.

"Tell us, my good man, how did you come by your evidence?" Jabbi rescued the illiterate slob.

The big oaf suddenly swung out of his stupor, greatly relieved. Then he leaned over the table, frowning. "I ain't supposed to tell ya that." He fearfully glanced about the empty room, as if something invisible might be spying on him. "I can't tell ya no more." His anxiety robbed his voice.

Jabbi wanted to give the Innkeeper a bit more pressure, but the old man interceded. He spoke quietly. "Somethings need to remain secrets. I respect a man who can uphold such a contract." The Innkeeper's face calmed down and he relaxed a bit. "But, if I might be so bold, tell us about your tattoo. I doubt if that's a confidential issue. After all, the beast stares us in the face." The bewhiskered ancient one pointed to the Innkeeper's forearm.

"A..A....A ..yes," The dimwitted Innkeeper, caught totally off guard, bewilderingly replied. He took a moment to catch his bearings and then spoke. "This is for safety. The dragon people, especially them real 'pale ladies' who put them tattoos on, tells us it means we're safe when the dragons come again......" He smiled wisely, at least to himself. "Don't need to take any chances, ya know."

"Well put, my big friend." Jabbi smiled. "But what about us? Are we safe? Or do we need·a·tattoo also?" Jabbi pretended to sound worried.

"I'd take ya there myself." He said proudly. "But I'm fixxin' ta work all night......But you can go there yourselfs."

The rambling directions produced by the Innkeeper, lead the two men to a squalid wooden shack some four miles into the swamp. Rancid smoke drifted from the shack, suggesting the burning of peat. Heavy brown canvas half-covered the two small windows and the undersized door. The men decided to wait until the second moon for their unannounced visit.

In the course of waiting, a small crowd of half drunk swampers gathered about the shack, all asking for protection. Three delicately built dark haired women, wearing overtly revealing apparel, emerged from the hovel, responding to the men's requests. The women voluntarily pranced before the delighted howls of the swampers, exposing even more of themselves. This continued until most of the men sank into an uneasy slumber, as if their local ale had been drugged. Then the women donned their discarded blouses and set to work, first robbing all money and other valuables from the stuporous men, and only then, utilizing the crudest of hot needles, began the tattooing process.

At that juncture, Jabbi suddenly wondered why he and the ancient one hadn't been spotted. They stood not more than thirty feet away from the wooden hut and in full view, but everyone present ignored them.

"Ancient One." Jabbi whispered. "Why haven't they discovered us?"

The answer returned at normal volume. "Because we are invisible to them."

Jabbi's brows knitted themselves tightly, believing and yet, simultaneously, disbelieving. However, the old man's words proved correct, no one paid them any attention. "But then they'll hear us." He stood nervously, overwrought by this new reality and the immanent peril of being discovered.

"I doubt it." The old man spoke casually. "They hear only the wind and the birds. Follow me. Let's see what's inside their home." He rankled his nose at the selection of his last word, quite disappointed he selected such an irrational term.

Quite deliberately, the Elder walked Jabbi through the drunken swampers and the women, pausing to smile at the terrified Jabbi who just didn't comprehend walking through a crowd as if their existence was merely a vaporous type fog. When they walked into the wooden house to the dismal interior, Jabbi almost fainted.

"Hold on, my son." The Elder firmly albeit gently commanded. "You'll get used to this."

Jabbi shook his profusely sweating head. "Never, never, never. This just isn't right...This isn't possible."

"Nonsense, my son. You certainly can't just ignore the truth. Its goes against the Holiness Code." The Elder began exploring the smoke clogged interior. "This is my gift." The elder said shortly, explaining himself. "I'm sharing it with you."

"Damn it!... No wonder no one can ever find you!"

"And that makes you angry?" He spoke while turning pots upside down and rummaging through some filthy garments. Inside an ornate silvered canister he discovered more of the same filmy, albeit delightful, garments the women presently adorned themselves with. "Help me examine this place." His stern tone persuaded Jabbi to obey.

Jabbi explored the woven baskets near the doorway. Their unusual construction showed remarkable skill, the weave so tight as to be waterproof. He gently grasped the handle and pulled off the lid, a decision he immediately regretted. Four large orange diamond-backed adders shot from the basket and sunk their deadly fangs into Jabbi's arms. Or so it seemed. In truth, the vicious adders plunged through Jabbi and bounced off the packed dirt floor and from thence, hurriedly zigzagged their way out the door to freedom.

A stunned Jabbi watched the illogical scene with mind-boggling bewilderment. "Damn!" Is all that he shouted.

"You'll have to change your language, you realize." The Elder commented while continuing to upset the entire room.

"I have no reason to change my language. It's about the only defense I have."

"Your disguise isn't a defense?" He offered in highly amused manner. "I assumed you'd be most grateful for this gift of total invisibility."

"Damn! I don't even know exactly what it is or where it came from or why I have it." Anger almost erupted within him. "There's an awful lot of things that need explaining." He demanded of the slightly built Elder.

"Yes, there probably are." Came a staid reply. "But you better get used to it........ Its your's to use whenever you desire."

Jabbi yelled 'damn' again, simultaneously as the pale women returned to their shack, now recklessly strewn with everything the Elder dug out of boxes and bags. One lady stood right inside of the petrified Jabbi as she stripped and then searched the shack for her tattered robe.

"You filthy pigs." She spit at the others. "I leave for a while and you use the cabin to take on what? Maybe three dozen drunken swampers? No wonder you can't walk right!"

While she maintained her haranguing, the Elder dragged the blushing Jabbi through the wooden wall and into the swamp grasses. "Now settle yourself. You've seen plenty of naked women before."

"But they also saw me." He defended himself.

"Then maybe you should count your blessings." He said with a smile. "She was pretty, wasn't she?"

"And you're supposed to be an Elder?" Jabbi put a particularly hard edge on the last word.

"Yes, and so are you."

Jabbi's mind began fluttering away again, back to the state of bewilderment, as it strained to its utmost to deflect the newest unasked for message. The Elder's strange utterances weren't to be taken seriously, he persuaded himself. Nevertheless, the edge of the message bore deeply into his soul, as if buried truth became uncovered. He and the wizened old man, still invisible to everyone else, slowly walked back to the inn. The fact that they walked through most people, that they heard every word of their mundane yet intimate conversations, that they espied some of the usual 'adulterous' meetings of the community meant nothing to Jabbi when compared to the intense inner struggle of his whole being. Finally, as they reached the dusty main street which passed in front of the Inn, Jabbi exploded with a shout.

"Damn it! Damn it!" Then he faced the Elder. "We're not going any further until YOU clear up a few of these damnable mysteries."

"Ah," A nonplussed Elder responded. "So, you've finally come to your senses.....I was beginning to believe the others committed themselves to an erroneous decision."

"And just what does that flippant remark mean?" Challenged the reddened-faced Jabbi.

"Just that the possibility existed that you weren't thoroughly investigated before we choose you." His attitude remained nonchalant and unemotional.

"So the Elders go about spying on all of Haaf." His cynicism exposed itself. "Don't you have anything better to do? Why is it that we should revere all of you?"

"That reverence is on your part. We never asked for nor commanded it."

The unwelcomed insight struck too close to home for Jabbi; his stomach knotted. He staggered to moss covered stump and slumped, his hands covering his paled face. The Elder found a nearby stump for his table and a rock to sit on. From his robe he pulled out some day-old bread and a wedge of rank smelling cheese and from his sack he managed to produce a small flagon of red wine and two battered tin cups.

"Care to join me. You're probably hungry." He said without looking at Jabbi.

Jabbi stirred, just slightly.

"Come now!" The Elder spoke brightly, and with authority. "Time to end this introspection garbage. There's too much you have to learn before I die."

Jabbi stood and straightened himself up, thinking he appeared half presentable, at least too himself. He then ambled to the table. "Good Elder, why me? Why not Baste or Blue Turtle or Vosnob? Their credentials far exceed mine. And their experiences..."

"They are all ready Elders...But, just who do you think extended you the call? ....I know," The Elder proclaimed with a stinging sermonette. "A bunch of ancient do-gooders sitting about making inane proclamations that have, at best, nothing to do with the real world.....You worry me, Jabbi." He said with a kindly smile. "Do you believe the Holy One ignores his own people?"

Jabbi's bewilderment momentarily returned. A cup of red wine in his face returned him quickly.

"Sit and eat!" The Elder demanded.

"I'd rather have tasted the wine for myself." Jabbi noted, wiping his wine-stained face clean. The shock brought him about, however. He found a log, picked it up, then dumped it directly in front of the Elder. Jabbi sat on the log, his robed arms crossed in front of his chest. He glared at the innocent looking old man, who merely continued to eat his lunch, smiling all the while. "So this is how the pieces fit together." Jabbi proclaimed as if all creation demanded to listen. "First, you Elders, select me to join you." He paused, tentative.

"So far, you're correct." The Elder mumbled, his mouth stuffed with bread. "Continue." He said placidly.

"Then you provide me with this gift that makes me oblivious to everything and everyone. A gift I don't even know how to use."

"And you didn't ask for any instructions either..... You somehow think you're above asking?" The white-haired old man dryly intoned. "Its time you put your faith to work."

"I believe I'm about to hear the axiom repeated...No... I'll repeat it. I quote; 'As the Holy One, Blessed be His Name, gives all good gifts as He alone chooses, it is our personal responsibility to acknowledge the value of the gift by using it correctly.' end quote."

"Wonderful." The Elder pronounced blandly. "Now, just what does all of that memorization actually mean?"

Jabbi's anger reignited, "Damn all this stuff. I want no part of it."

"Who allowed you a choice?" The Elder spoke, wiping his hands off after putting the food away. "Come, we need to get back. You're beginning to bother me. I presumed you'd be mature about this change. Instead, I find an advancing degeneracy."

"I'm not moving from this spot."

"Don't be so sure of yourself, after all you don't even know how to remove yourself from invisibility." With that, the old man delicately gestured with his fingers.

A thick, strangely dry fog-like atmosphere rapidly encompassed the two. As it moved, twisting into an unnatural vortex, Jabbi cringed with fear, unable to utter a single word, while the white-haired old man kept moving his fingers in delicate patterns. Then, even faster than the fog-like atmosphere had encompassed them, it vanished.

The immaculately clean stonewalled room appeared familiar to Jabbi; the Chaplain's quarters at the High Striper barracks in Pinduala.

"Well Kloshic," Vosnob smiled. "Its about time you arrived." He looked directly at Jabbi, who stood fearfully shaking, totally ununderstanding. "We have a lot of work to do."

Jabbi, without a word, fainted away, slumping onto the cold stone floor. Vosnob, with the aid of the Chaplain, drug him into a comfortable chair.

The smell of salt water blowing in from the Upper Sea woke Jabbi with a start. Or was it the warmth of the early morning sun that bored in through the window? He really didn't know and, with the multitude of confusing and conflicting thoughts incessantly pounding in his head, perhaps the answer was irrelevant. A thunderous banging on the door momentarily curtailed his garbled thinking.

Vosnob strode into the room and seated himself. "Good morning, Jabbi." He spoke much too cheerfully for the half-asleep totally confused Church Knight.

"Maybe to you." He shot back with a snarl. "Will you kindly explain how I, rather, we got here." He then demanded.

"Its called 'relocating'. Might take you all of three breaths to learn how its done. But then you'll have to practice for a while. I certainly don't relish the thought of removing you from inside a castle wall."

"Thanks for the encouragement!" He tossed off his blanket." After breakfast." He anxiously suggested to Vosnob who had begun to delineate the day's itinerary.

"After breakfast. Then, I promise, in spite of what the Elder may have shared with you, that I'll be ready......I hope."

"Interesting."

"Why?"

"Kloshic claims you were a model student. A most promising Elder is how he described you, Jabbi. Are you telling me the old man lied? And who would lie on his death bed?" Vosnob, obviously amused, just shook his lean dark brown face. "After breakfast?"

"Yes."

The meeting commenced on the flat stone roof above the Chaplain's quarters, the same place where Brey began her recovery. Jabbi, now with his wits partially about him, as promised, was joined by the Chaplain, Vosnob and Kloshic. The stressfully independent Blue Turtle swept in a few moments later, surrounded by that thick dry fog which caused Jabbi much anxiety. However, the warm sunshine was preferred over the cold frozen ponds of the dismal Fluz.

"You did send him to find me." Kloshic began the meeting. "He actually did quite well. Fast pick-up more than anything else." The Elder then proceeded to retell, with some ludicrous embellishments, the story of their meeting at the inn and the journey into the swamp.

"Anyway," The old man finally halted his monologue. "The final analysis leads me to believe that the Southerners aren't particularly decorating themselves with Haafian patriotism."

"What a surprize." Blue Turtle sarcastically mumbled.

"You're starting so soon?" Vosnob jumped Blue Turtle.

"No reason not to. There's better things to do than worry about those swampers. They were excluded from the last war, so they have no history of the real situation. Its only natural that they protect themselves from something that might destroy them."

"You mean the dragons?" Questioned the Chaplain.

"Yes, even though its not possible for a dragon to fly that far."

"How can you be so sure? What if the journey was accomplished in several shorter jaunts?" Jabbi asked. "If they were able to fly into Krabo?"

"Good point." Vosnob noted. "It is possible. But now everyone is watching for them. The element of surprize is long gone. And the Light Striper can eradicate them." He drew in his breath, contemplating his next words. "I'll triple the garrison at Poldu and also at Brakki."

"We did that a while back." Blue Turtle stated flatly. "And the Light Striper of the Islands has increased its patrols. There is no sign of any increased activity."

"What Light Striper of the Islands?" Queried a mystified Jabbi.

"Didn't anyone tell the guy anything?" Denounced a falsely angry Blue Turtle. His smirk told the story. "Let's get this new Elder the information he needs to get to work. I've got to be in the village for supper."

With that usual abruptness, the Yldian launched into a dissertation of the 'will'. The 'will' as formulated by concentrating the mind on what 'total invisibility' is, in direct relationship to the environment, produces the effect for those to whom the gift has been bestowed. The ability to be completely oblivious to those surrounding you, to the point of actually walking through them and other solid objects, remains the fullest expression of the gift. This, stated Blue Turtle, is exactly the experience that Jabbi 'enjoyed'. At other times it might only be necessary to 'invisibilize' one's voice, or one's person. Even this gift belonged to few. The most useful and used element of the gift was translocating.

"The 'will'", According to Vosnob, who now picked up the lesson, "Formulates an aura about the person creating it. Other persons or things could be included in this aura, but only if they are deliberately willed there."

"Then I could hide an entire army?" Jabbi considered out-loud.

"No one has ever had that much strength, my son." Replied the Chaplain. "Though there is no valid reason for excluding such a possibility. The difficulty is the constant focussing of the 'will'. It takes the greatest of efforts and when terminated can often leave you exhausted. The gift does have a price to it." The Chaplain stated with a sense of weariness, the weariness of experience.

The statement went by as the Chaplain turned to the other dimension of the gift: relocation. The focal point of this variation of 'invisibility' rested with the 'will'. The mechanism for the 'transporting' remained a divine mystery, impenetrable to all persons. This adamantly required a perfect mental visualization of the intended destination. Any incorrect details might set one down in the Upper Sea or a raging volcano. Such a scenario visibly frightened Jabbi; the others found it most amusing. The arched eyebrows and the 'I've-been-there' glances added depth to their self-effacing laughter.

"It appears that I'm joining a stranger club than the one I've left." A somewhat defensive Jabbi offered.

"But you aren't leaving anything." Vosnob said with a smile. "You'll continue with whatever you were doing, just like the rest of us."

"Ah," Blue Turtle acknowledged. "The price one pays for supreme elevation."

"Such sarcasm is most offensive, Blue Turtle." Quipped the well mannered Baste. He still blew off the dry fog as he spoke. "Congratulations, Jabbi." He extended his hand to Jabbi who then found himself wrapped in Baste's massive bear hug.

"Congratulations." He repeated. Then he disappeared, leaving a floundering Jabbi hugging dry fog. "Welcome to the world of modern communications."

"That really wasn't necessary, Kloshic." An unamused Jabbi spoke.

"But the next part of your journey is." Commented the Chaplain. "You'll be out of circulation for a while. But only we'll know that; everyone else knows you're searching for the wispy old Kloshic. Who, as we all know, can always be found fishing."

Kloshic gently maneuvered his fingers, causing a toad to drop on the Chaplain's bald head, providing Jabbi with his best laugh in a few days.

"My, but we're touchy these days." Responded the Chaplain as he, with a few almost negligible finger movements, transformed the toad to a sunflower. He turned back to Jabbi. "You'll be in the mountains for a few months, learning to properly utilize your new gifts."

"And," Added Vosnob, "You'll be studying the volumes of Prophesy Scriptures."

Jabbi's face was bleak. "Why me? No one is capable enough to discern the meaning of that collection."

"But now we know more of the Truth." Explained Vosnob.

"No, actually it was before you were willing to admit more Truth existed." The tall Yldian deftly corrected those who adhered only to the written word, denying the power of the Spirit. "And we all recognize the Holy One rescued us at the last battle."

"Oh, Shut up!"

"Yes, master Vosnob!" Snapped Blue Turtle, with an air of superiority. "Far be it from me to cause you any anxiety."

"Don't you have a meeting waiting for you?" Vosnob coldly questioned.

"But this is more fun, even without Yganak."

"So I've noticed....... You never know when to quit."

"I don't need to. After all, you are the Elder Elder." His face became one of complete smugness.

"Meeting adjourned!" Declared Vosnob with a stamp of his booted foot. "Jabbi, time to go. As for the rest of you, two cycles until our next meeting, provided we don't run into any more of the damned one's surprizes." With that, both he and Jabbi, wrapped in the dry fog simply vanished from the room. "I'm glad the book work went to Jabbi." Commented the Chaplain to Blue Turtle. "My eyes just can't take that garish script anymore."

"I agree." Replied Blue Turtle as he left in a cloud of dry fog for his supper meeting.

Chapter 7

Luuft's severely battered face, plastered with thick dried blood, allowed him to recognize only pitch-black. His stiffened swollen body refused to move. His once capable ability to concentrate refused to function. In the never-ending blackness he vaguely remembered the flatboat being thrust into the air, somehow. Then bits and pieces, fragments of the experience of flying through the air, along with Deep Owl, Jelkio and a few others also littered his unsteady thinking. These detached and disoriented thoughts jabbed into his unsettled mind. Then he slumped again, unconscious, into the heavy pine branches where he originally landed.

Mid-day's bright blinding light became his next recollection, the first time he'd seen any difference in his environment. This time, his arms moved. They moved painfully, thoroughly bruised, but, at least to his initial examination, nothing seemed broken. However, below his waist, nothing moved or even felt injured: only his upper half functioned. Luuft slowly peeled the dried blood from his face, only to re-open the gash over his right ear. Only then did he recognize himself suspended some fifty feet above the rocky ground. And only then did he realize the precariousness of his perch: one swift ripple of wind and he'd bounce off the boulders underneath him.

An excruciating right turn of his head provided him with an uphill view of the black-sided and barely steaming volcano. It lay about four hundred feet away, its top a huge gaping maw, now deadly quiet. So was everything else. The steep slope, littered with large boulders and a few bramble bushes, gave mute evidence of the explosion. He shook when he saw the motionless bodies of two Yldans some fifty feet from the volcano's summit. No one could have survived that landing, he painfully thought, actually not wanting to know the truth. He painfully jerked his head to look in the opposite direction. There he discovered the massive pinetree thrust itself forward as the first of an entire thicket. Maybe thirty trees he reckoned to himself and maybe, he continued thinking, others might have landed in them. On that note of exhaustion and feeble hope, Luuft returned to a semi-conscious state.

He awoke against a black sky, though the two moons shone bleakly through the overcast. He had some feeling in his feet, they pulsed, full of a remarkably beautiful pain: he wasn't paralyzed. Below him something or, more preferably, someone, stirred. He thought he heard the sound of voices, at least two. But he wasn't sure if he recognized them, or if this was the beginning of his journey to Paradise. Then again, he thought, better to die in the pinetree than at the hands of renegade Haafians. Anyways, he couldn't call to them; his voice didn't work. Once again he succumbed to an exhausted sleep.

The tree's abrupt swaying woke him from his stupor. He thought that he might fall, but he couldn't move. Branches began to bobble about him as someone or something attempted to climb the tree. He forced a terror stricken raspy throated yell from his parched and swollen mouth: a gurgle emerged.

"He's still alive!" Shouted Deep Owl, whose climbing brought him within a few feet of Luuft's perching branch. Joyful shouts from the ground responded; one of them female. "But he's in pretty bad shape." He called down after he reached the semi-conscious Luuft. Softly inching himself out towards Luuft, Deep Owl proceeded to wipe Luuft's face with a wet rag, dripping some of the life-giving liquid into his parched and swollen mouth.

Luuft responded with a frantic, desperately fearful clutching action which sent both he and Deep Owl on a perilous slide through the heavy branches of the pinetree. Deep Owl managed to free himself by jumping into a side branch.

"Catch him!" Cried Deep Owl. "He's sliding out of the tree." As he quickly descended.

As the terrified Luuft brushed by the tips of the bottom branches, four pairs of bruised hands grabbed him. They immediately placed him in the shade. This time, before blacking out again, he did recognize Jelkio's worn, but smiling face.

When Luuft finally awoke again, another two dawns had passed by, so Jelkio explained to him. His new home was a small cave near a fast moving stream. The entire campsite, located in a deep ravine, provided a needed respite from terror of the flying flatboat and the ensuing havoc. However, no campsite provided any respite from the enormous grief he felt. For all he could tell, only the six of them survived. If only he might speak. Still unable to, his frustration level quickly reached its peak, forcing him into rank despair.

Jelkio, her face and arms black-and-blue from bruising, came and sat beside him. "Its about time you started to come about." She said without any trace of sympathy. "We lost everyone, you know. Its just the six of us. And we can't even get out of this damned place until you can move." In spite of her initial remarks and attitude, tears gently flowed. "Don't", She said softly, "You go and die on me. I've lost three all ready. And Deep Owl isn't too steady yet......Live, damn you." She sobbed uncontrollably, covering her hands with her face.

Luuft reached out, hands and arms quivering, to comfort her. He, as well as the others could now understand her, though she spoke with the a heavy accent.. A while later, as a deep purple darkness crept across the sky, the others returned, lead by a shaven head Deep Owl. Luuft stared and hurt himself with a laughter that refused to emerge from his insides. Even Jelkio retained a bit of a smirk. The three Yldans brought some fresh fish and some wild berries.

"So," Deep Owl commented dryly. "You really don't like the new hair style. I thought you weren't so narrow minded." He smiled wickedly at Luuft. "Actually, Jelkio and I had a rather nasty argument concerning the hair....."

"It was a miserable, hateful fight!" Jelkio summarily corrected the bronze skinned Yldian. "And if I hadn't cut it off, you would have bled to death." She continued with a sure sense of herself.

"But Qill," He corrected, "Actually performed the stitchings on my shredded scalp. That's what stopped the bleeding and kept my precious brains from falling out."

"And the most honorable Qill is a multi-talented shaman. And one of your people. What did you expect?"

"Just some beautiful young lady to patch me up." He murmured with a hint of lustiness. Presumably Jelkio blushed, but the bruises prevented any evidence from giving her away. Qill and the rest smiled. "And Qill is obviously from another tribe. He only has one name."

Luuft could not fail noticing the deliberateness of the social games. They conveniently drew their attention from acknowledging their frailty. Their battered physical conditions and the hopelessness of the present situation, to say nothing about their extensive grief over the loss of close friends, left everyone mentally and spiritually exhausted. Some things would be dealt with at a later, more secure time. Not content to be an observer, Luuft tried to pull himself to a sitting position, but rapidly found himself slumping into a heap.

"Take it easy." Said Qill as he rushed forward to prevent him from smashing his face. "In a few days you will begin to move better. Now," He motioned for some berries. "You will eat these. Without food, there is no healing. And you can swallow the smashed berries."

His voice had a stern edge, demanding full compliance to a shaman's wishes. Luuft ate and swallowed the berries, almost two cups worth. Then exhausted, he returned to a deep sleep.

The trout baked over a large red-hot stone. The meal filled the belly, but left much to be desired, especially as they silently contemplated their meals back in the 'civilized world'. Brewed herb tea, served in damp clay pots provided the other menu item. The clay tasted stronger than the herbal tea. Even so, warm food did much to displace the dismal atmosphere surrounding them. With minimal quiet conversation, the five drifted off into an uneasy restless sleep.

In terms of a sun which separated day from night, the morning never actually arrived. Colossal thunderheads carved their way slowly across the dawning sky, causing it to retreat. Then came the pounding, blistering wind-driven torrents of rain, moving like ranks of soldiers against the trees and boulders. Incessantly, without a hint of mercy, it toppled the life-saving pine trees and rapidly created an earth-carving demon from the placid trout filled stream.

Five survivors fearfully watched the malicious storm, somewhat secure inside the shallow cave. Luuft, breathing easier for the first time, solemnly slept at the rear of the cave. Qill's smirk indicted a rueful appreciation of the paradox, even if no one else could. Deep Owl moaned about catching cold because of his shaved head, while Jelkio complained about a need for a bath.

"Well, my lady." Kofe sarcastically yawned. "I don't care much about a bath, but if you want to resemble Deep Owl, just stand in the driving rain. She'll take both the dirt and hair off of you."

"Damn fisherman!" Retorted the unamused Jelkio.

"Just an idea." He laughed. "And I really thought you enjoyed that trout last night. You certainly ate enough." He pretended to be hurt.

Jelkio moved to clobber Kofe with a fish, but she was physically restrained by Nooy, Kofe's silent and rather invisible companion.

"Look!" Nooy pointed Jelkio in the direction of the now restless Luuft. "Get him something to drink." He told her.

Jelkio's startled countenance indicated both worry and hope. Luuft managed to sit himself. His reddened face dripped with sweat from the excruciating effort, even as it shone with success. A round of hearty applause rang out from the others, echoing throughout the cave. Luuft nodded his black-and-blue head in cheerful acceptance, then steadied himself by leaning against the cave wall.

"Berries?" He half mumbled, half gurgled.

Luuft remained up after eating. His struggle to regain his old self took the group's attention away from the raging storm. Qill reminded Luuft that the longer he could stay up, the quicker the liquid would disperse from his lungs. Luuft grinned and cautiously swallowed a few more berries.

"Those berries have something mixed in with them, don't they?" Queered a suspicious Jelkio.

"Now, perchance, why would you say a thing like that? You're going to disturb these tender feelings of mine. You don't want that on your young and innocent conscience, do you?" He sweetly bantered back to her, trying to emulate her accent.

She leaned over and kissed the old man on his whiskered cheek. "Thank you."

"You're giving me some wrong ideas young lady, especially since these grey whiskers haven't been kissed in a long time."

"Liar." Kofe disdainfully pronounced.

"Well," The Shaman retracted. "My beautiful wife doesn't kiss my cheek. She hates the whiskers, she does."

"Then cut them off." Kofe injected. "Or don't you want to lose your Shaman badge?" He became deliberately obnoxious, attempting to bait Qill.

"Maybe I gave the berries to the wrong person after all." He countered. "Of course, I'd put a mixture in your's to increase intelligence." His caustic remark brought laughter from the group. Even Luuft managed a weak chuckle.

"Ha!" Noted Qill. "The medicine works all ready. Tomorrow he shall talk."

"Then I'll need ear plugs." Kofe said dryly.

The vicious wind storm which drove the rain abated towards evening, though the rain itself continued. During the drizzle, most sought to explain their situation. Luuft, being more of his usual insistent self, contrived to change the topic by scribbling on the dry dusty floor of the cave.

"How are you in such good shape?" He composed with a shaky hand.

"Look!" Quipped Nooy. "I do believe his writing ability has improved. What say you? Shall we answer his somewhat earnest query?" He teased. "Or shall we continue on our way?"

Deep Owl, pretending to be thoughtful, suggested, "Until such time as we can't walk away from him, perhaps it would be well to oblige the bossy Haafian."

While this discussion didn't conform to his desires, Luuft did accept the current perspective of his attitude. He even ventured a smallish scary smile.

"The question boils down to this: why me?" Said the Shaman. "He feels a bit put out because he's lost a day or two while living in the pinetree."

Luuft gravely nodded his head; admitting others could be right proved most difficult for him.

"Luuft," Qill began. "We all, almost all of us, landed in an overgrown thicket of rhododendrons. It broke our fall far more gracefully than the pine tree did. We ended up bruised and stiff, but on the ground and walking. We spent two days searching for others. We found most of the flatboat crew, crushed when they encountered the rocky slope." He paused, his voice heavy with pain. "I'm not quite sure how we located you, no one thought to look in the trees. The branches caught you, however, your spine received a severe jolt. When it settles you might walk again, then again, perhaps you won't."

Luuft's gaze turned an agonizing whitish color. His face became flush. He fully understood the grey-bearded Qill's words.

"I wish I might extend a better prognosis." The Shaman sighed. "But I can only tell you what I know. Let the Spirit be at work within you." He reverently suggested as he closed the discussion.

A slowly nodding Luuft accepted the Shaman's verdict. "Thanks." He scrawled on the cave floor. Then, his meager energy expended, he reluctantly retired to the cave floor, asleep before his head hit the damp floor.

Jelkio quietly whispered a strange sounding liturgy from her seat next to the cave's sheltered entrance. The rest paused to listen, there being a mysterious, yet kindly rhythm to the chant song. With her long blue arms held out before her, and her countenance in complete incongruity with the present situation, one might believe that the Queen's Lady-in-waiting transcended her environment. However, this trance-like quality lasted but a few moments. Jelkio returned to the immediate only to find the others staring at her. All too quickly her blue face turned a whitish color.

"I'm sorry, My Lady." Qill apologized for the rest. "We had no intention of intruding upon your person, nor do we desire to denigrate your worship."

"I...I was just praying for healing." She stammered.

"To the god who-has-no-name?" Deep Owl questioned.

"You making fun..... of me?"

"No, my Lady." He politely responded. "But if your god refuses to allow you to know his name, then how do you know where your prayers go?"

"Its simply a matter of faith for us Taths. We believe our god without-a-name knows his people. He has not abandoned us, in spite of our ancestors' act of unfaithfulness." Her positive tone wasn't that of some theologian dictating from an extravagant stone tower, but from her heart. "We were rescued from the Evil One." She offered as proof.

Deep Owl appeared perplexed. "Rescued you for what? You are the only one left....... And we are hardly secure."

"I'm not sure I have any answer for you." She honestly admitted. "But our journey is not yet ended. Perhaps my part in our god's plan is to find the commonness which has the power to bring our peoples together.......I really don't know................. It's just a guess."

"And a rather intuitive one at that." Qill enjoined. "I would approve of such theology. It makes sense."

"So if it not be logical, we throw it away?" The self-proclaimed antagonizer Kofe interjected.

"And what good is any theology if it isn't useable?" The Shaman challenged without blinking.

Deep Owl, however, felt as if his non-existent feathers were being ruffled; god-talk spooked him.

"Score one for the old man." Nooy said to Kofe. Then he picked up the conversation. "Maybe this isn't the right time, Jelkio..."

"My Lady." Deep Owl corrected him.

"Do you have a problem? You always need to recognize she's a lady?" Nooy's grin belied a bit of lustiness which embarrassed Deep Owl. "Maybe the Shaman better have one of those coming-of-age talks with you." His smile grew. Then he turned to Jelkio. "What shall we call you?"

"Jelkio is my name." She returned Nooy's smile.

"Then move this 'thing' of your's along." Blunt were Deep Owl's words, which Nooy totally ignored.

"As I was saying,....... before being rudely interrupted." Nooy continued. "I'm curious. I know you were captured by the Kyykki and their so-called friends. But how did you come to be captured? We never even heard of Tath. Nor did I ever see such pretty blue ladies afore."

Something within Jelkio enjoyed the complements; her face brightened. That could be noticed even as the twilight sky pushed the torrential rains into intermittent drizzles. She adjusted herself and straightened her shoulder length blonde hair.

"As you wish, Nooy." She said pleasantly. "But the story is not so long nor complex as you might imagine. I hope you won't be disappointed. Tath is a vast flatland, a steppe, running from ocean to ocean. Ice caps and a few cities border the northern ocean. The south is divided from the rest of the world by the Dark Lands, as you call them."

"There is a whole country north of the Dark Lands?" Deep Owl found himself perplexed at himself. He had shut himself off to the notion that most of the territory was well-known. Even his campsite on the cliffs, existed with the belief that only a few miles to the north was the end of the world. This Tath country was completely unknown.

"Why do you find that hard to believe? And," She quietly smiled. "What reason do I have to lie?"

"Forget the dumbfounded one." Vented Qill. "Please, continue with our education."

"Thank you, Qill." Jelkio paid deference to Shaman Qill before returning to her narrative. "Our country is the opposite of these mountains, valleys and volcanoes. We have very few trees, and where trees grow, so meander the sluggish rivers. We tend to ignore the rivers, however. Too many mosquitoes, too many swamp 'things', and far too many people."

"You share the land with others?" Deep Owl finally exposed his real interest in learning about Tath.

"The swamp people, as we call them, river people as they call themselves, are a lost people. When we were forced from our original land, because of our lack of faith, some decided to begin anew, without our god. They created an entirely different ethic to live by, but they have no god. They still consider any god to be capricious and dangerous. Our ancestors rightfully confined them to the land adjacent to the rivers. Both groups are to remain separate."

"I thought maybe the difference was more like that between the Yldans and the Haafians. Being a godless people is beyond comprehension." Deep Owl interrupted by thinking out loud. A scowl from Kofe brought him about. "Sorry, my Lady."

"We are not a godless people, as you well know." She spoke deliberately to Deep Owl. She turned to speak to the others. "We are a seminomadic people; we travel during the dry season with our herds of sheep and goats, living in yurts."

"Begging your pardon," Kofe disrupted her narrative. "But sheep? goats? and yurts?"

"Sheep and goats are our animals of sustenance. They provide us with milk and cheese and wool and skins, even tallow for our candles. Yurts are akin to your.......... tents? Except they're round, about thirty feet in diameter, maybe twenty feet tall in the center. The straight walls allow for a lot of room. Outside, the yurts blend into the tall grasses, inside, they're more beautiful than most... palaces?....or so I've been told.....I've never really seen a palace."

"When we get away from here, I'll show you the King's palace at Krabo." Luuft muttered from his corner. All heads turned towards him. "I've been listening, I confess.....You know, in my whole formal education, no one ever mentioned any of this before. The universities are going to look more stupid than ever. Imagine, the north isn't hot anymore. The Dark Lands merely divide two peoples. This flat land we live on just got bigger."

"Who said its flat?" An indignant Qill spoke out. As all other elements of the sky are round; the moons, sun, the stars, why not this world we live on? Why should it be the exception?" He challenged Luuft. "What do your people say?" Qill asked Jelkio.

"We've never thought about it." She nervously exclaimed. "This is something I've never even heard about. All our time is spent trying to return, to recapture our god's blessing, so we can return to the valley you saw from above."

"Relax." Kofe told her. "New ideas aren't going to destroy any of us. The use of bleach proved that." He rubbed his hands together with a sense of deep satisfaction as he remembered the episodes before they rescued Jelkio, Tiello and Queen Sjura. "But, from how you speak, your people are not so numerous as our peoples are?"

"I believe that assumption true. Our tribe has only twenty thousand people and we are the largest of the tribes."

"How do you travel? You did not mention Stripers or Massive Blues?" The here-to-for absent Nooy entered the conversation.

"Stripers and Massive Blues? These I am unfamiliar with. We travel by Istelles....We use them to fly to our destinations. If that's what you mean?" She spoke with an honest openness.

"HA!" Luuft triumphantly grunted. "This is just a silly story for a rainy evening....... Imagine, flying? Do your people have wings like the Evil One's dragons?"

"No, we use Istells."

"That is the second time you've used the word.....And just what, if anything, is an Istell?"

"About four hundred feet across the wings and one hundred feet in length...... Most are white, at least ours are. Some smaller reddish ones inhabit the frozen north."

"Sounds like a big chicken to me." Retorted Luuft, all too smugly.

"Can you ride one of your chickens? Ours carry people everywhere. They even guard the land, with ....what's the words....troopers.... riding them. And they can glide for almost a whole day." She proudly presented. "This I know to be true, my father runs a hatchery."

Qill thoughtfully gazed at her, then turned to the irritating Luuft. "Think for a moment. This lady as absolutely no reason to trick us. She's telling the truth.... That's the bottom line for your book-limited faith, isn't it? If it isn't written, it doesn't exist." He paused to observe Luuft's reaction. "And you had the gall to impugn the university? Hypocrite!"

But Luuft didn't hear, his mind wandered off somewhere, as if unanswered fragments of the past still retained possibilities. Slowly and deliberately he spoke to Jelkio. "These Istells?"

"Yes."

"Do they, perchance, fly over the great swamp at the other end of the land?" Luuft braced himself for an answer that could free the original group of spies. He had an explanation for the shadow that followed and watched them.

"I am not of the.....what do you say........ military." Jelkio answered sadly. "And I know of no swamp....... What you suggest is possible............. Istells range far and wide across our land.....and maybe into yours as well. Queen Sjura would answer your questions." She stopped short, realizing her mistake: Queen Sjura was gone. Jelkio had yet to properly mourn her, yet alone deal with the extraordinary circumstances that would render the funeral service impossible. Jelkio sobbed into the evening: Qill moved to sit beside her.

The jabbing brightness of dawn had everyone up early. The damage executed by yesterday's storm proved extensive. The rhododendron thicket splintered into twig-like shards, only two or three of the huge pine trees still had boughs. The trout stream ran brown with dirt and debris as it flooded out its usual narrow channel, acting as a vengeful demon, striking and demolishing everything it surrounded and touched.

Without food and water, Qill and Deep Owl decided to break camp. Once off the volcano, they believed, a better opportunity to find food and clean water existed. Luuft, against his arrogant stubbornness, found himself lashed to a makeshift travois. Throughout the entire morning his bitter cursing and other irrational behaviors continued unabated. Kofe and Nooy, who were assigned to pull him, desperately attempted to ignore him.

Around midday, the group paused for a break at grassy knoll. A bubbling spring provided water, and also supplied the needed instrument for Nooy's and Kofe's revenge. Luuft found himself receiving a cold bath, one from which he extricated himself with difficulty and a much sober mouth.

The swollen stream began to recede, enough to permit an easier journey downstream by hiking along its soggy banks instead of hacking through thick underbrush. Another few miles brought the fatigued group to the juncture of two streams: the new one made its entrance into a modest sized pool via a splendid fifteen foot waterfall. The ground's rockiness gave way to shallow soil, hardy trees and grasses. Evidence of small animals found about the pool brought Nooy to life: soon they would eat. With their physical conditions all ready deteriorating, and with the area potentially habitated by food sources, Qill called for the day's stop. Luuft's assigned duty placed him by the pool, with a fishing pole, while Kofe and Nooy sought out other game as well as saplings suitable for weapons. With maximum effort and just a fragment of flint, Deep Owl and Jelkio started the fire.

That evening's feast, consisting of freshly roasted fish and rabbit, raw fruits, and herbal mint tea, provided the positive encouragement the exhausted group required. Prior to sleep, Deep Owl placed the other Yldans on watch duty. This unknown region could easily conceal some nasty unwanted surprizes.

The following dawn's brightness, filtered by the trees and the soft wind, found everyone except Kofe, soundly sleeping. Another shift at guard duty, he figured, didn't matter that much to him. By mid-morning the others regained their feet, and with another feast, were not entirely refreshed, but headed in the right direction.

Consequently, Luuft now posed the major problem for the group; he had feeling in his feet, however, his legs refused to respond to any stimulus. No actual improvement occurred since he slid from the pine tree. His usually overt personality took on shades of self-doubt and despair. While no one had yet spoken of his critical condition, he knew he severely taxed their energy and hindered their rescue and survival efforts. This unknown territory, obviously, wasn't the optimal place for an invalid. Luuft, realizing his severe limitations, literally tore his mind apart searching for a solution, which he disguised by quietly fishing the rest of the day.

Nooy and Kofe disappeared downstream immediately after their mid-morning feast. Both wore wide eyed grins and spoke in 'coded words'. Deep Owl confided to Jelkio that the two were up to one of their ludicrous projects. He witnessed them at work in the past, especially the project involving a 'powder' to throw rocks into the air. Half the village burnt down. He relished laughing as he retold the story. He felt a great comfort when he noticed that Jelkio enjoyed the story as well. The spidery, grey bearded Qill, on the other hand, stomped off for a bath when it became apparent that the campsite of last evening would be the same for this evening.

Jelkio butchered ten rabbits to roast for supper, though she had no idea of what a live fully-furred rabbit looked like. Nooy and Kofe's animal traps served the group well, however, their silly grins remained firmly intact. Luuft's fishing produced results as dismal as his emotions. Qill added his wild carrots and some tubers to the meal. A long circuitous walk in the meadow above the falls had quieted his anger, encouraging his appetite.

"We started a conversation last evening we actually didn't finish." Qill spoke to Jelkio.

Both moons now firmly beamed in the lightly clouded night sky. Their position in the heavens indicated to Luuft that the group might be farther south than anyone realized before. Because Jelkio promptly acknowledged Qill's invitation, Luuft stuffed his observation in the recesses of his mind and promptly forgot about it.

"I'm not up for another theology debate." She muttered ungratefully.

"No, my dear," Qill's tone cleaved close to being apologetic. "Theology is not the issue for the evening. I'd rather have everyone participate by keeping the topic less esoteric." He shot a smirky grin at Kofe.

"I'se be da stu-u-pi-dist!" Kofe retorted with a menacing grin. "Best bees care-ful. May-be I'se kin not eben 'member ya name. Ya jist ma be Kyykki." He waved his newly-fashioned stone tomahawk in the night air.

"Shut up or I'll put a spell on you." The Shaman retorted.

"OOOOOO! I'se bees scared." Kofe acted the role of the fool almost too well. Qill threw a rabbit bone at him.

"What is the topic?" Jelkio interrupted the carrying-on with a matter-of-fact voice.

"We've never heard the story of how you arrived at the dungeon inside that damned volcano." He said. "Would you care to share your story with us?"

"All depends." She replied in a quizzical tone.

"Depends on what?" Deep Owl asked.

"On whether or not there might be just the minusculest amount of sobriety among certain members of our group." She eyed the still grinning Kofe through the thin smoke of the campfire.

"Yes 'im." He broadly smiled, doing his best to be oafish.

Jelkio began to giggle, then caught herself. Once, twice, she began the story, then stopped. The giggles simply refused to quit. After the third time, her story began in earnest.

"The three of us, with an escort of twenty flew....yes flew...Luuft, its true.....on the Istells to the edge of the southern steppe, where the bald mountains begin. In a small valley there our people built a temple to our god. It's built at the spot where our god denied us re-entry to our homeland. The building is simple: a block with windows cut into the greenish granite sides and a small shaft in the ceiling that aims our vision towards the sacred mountain within our homeland. .....Anyway, only royalty, Queen Sjura, and us...."

"So you are royalty. I should have thought as much." Luuft interrupted.

"I am." She answered shortly, and then rapidly returned to the story. "We had gone to pray. It usually takes us three to four days. We stay by ourselves. The Istells and the escort stayed on the steppe, guarding us from a distance....Though nothing ever happened before...... On the second day of our vigil, something wretched dropped through the shaft. Sweating and burning, we ran outside, only to be gagged and tossed about like wheat sacks. Then we were blindfolded...and carried by something big ugly and hideously smelling...."

"Kyykki, I'll venture." Luuft's voice bounced from the shadow.

"As you call them....The next thing I remember is living in the dungeon. But none of us knew where it was nor what it was. Our captors spoke Haafian, like Luuft. Some spoke a guttural demon speech. But because of Queen Sjura's ring, we knew what they said. They worshipped an evil god. However, they treated us kindly, though we were never allowed to go anywhere without an escort. We never saw the Evil One, but his assistant, the one Sarg finally killed, regularly interrogated us... Then after almost three years, you came to the rescue, answering our deepest prayers..." She paused, as if to relive those moments again. "That's my.... excuse me, ..our story..... Rather uncomplicated."

"Actually," Luuft continued interjecting his comments. "It tells us that the Evil One designed to ransom or concoct some type of deal with your people. If the ugly bastard captured you and threatened to kill you, then your people would be neutralized. His Kyykki became free to attack us in the south. Ingenious really."

Jelkio did not buy Luuft's reasoning. "No, the bastard, as you rightly call him, could not attack north. His troops....the Kyykki, require both dampness and warmth. Neither exist on the steppe. What would he want with our land? His plan was something else."

Kofe murmured. "The damned one wanted a wife. Its that elementary. He needs to look and act respectable. Right?" He held out the question for anyone to reply. An ignoring silence reigned for a long embarrassing moments.

"Clarify part of your story." Deep Owl finally petitioned Jelkio. "Returning to your story.........." "What is a 'year'?"

"Our way of keeping time. A year lasts four hundred days...or dawns, as you count time."

"When the two moons act as if they are required to start their identical trip through the skies again!" Deep Owl exclaimed as if he discovered a fortune in jewels. ...."And then your country, Tath, is ruled by women?" He continued.

"Yes...... How intelligent you are." Jelkio teasingly proclaimed before returning to the original topic. "But then, years are a whole lot smarter than using only cycles." Her voice full of royal superiority.

"People, 'fer dis gits ta be trub-bul, I'se gittin ta sleep." Kofe coughed to hide a giggle, threw a couple of logs on the fire, and curled into a ball.

"How cute." Jelkio flatly commented.

Kofe belched a loud 'good night' to the rest.

The following morning's repeat breakfast of fish and fruit did not diminish the tranquillity the group felt. It arrived as an unasked for blessing, yet one that compelled the group, to remain encamped for the day. As became their habit, Kofe and Nooy immediately disappeared downstream, this time under the pretense of the pool being overfished by Luuft.

The depressed Luuft refused to even move from the back of their lean-to, preferring to pretend to sleep. With an excess of time strangely available, Jelkio took advantage of the luxury by climbing to the pool above their cave to wash the few tatters she called clothes and to bathe. Deep Owl watched the camp and, with Qill, planned ahead for the next step of their unconventional journey.

"Water is going to be the easiest way to travel, especially for Luuft." Deep Owl said. The two were well beyond Luuft's listening range.

"That's not the issue. The man is extremely depressed by his injury. Perhaps he might even try to commit suicide." Qill said.

"You aren't serious?"

"Indeed, I am. He's a warrior. He's proud. He's well educated. And those slanted eyes of his tell you that he's quite aware of his loss." Qill had prepared himself for the worst.

After a few moments of striving to pull some semblance of thought together, Deep Owl quit. "What plan do you have?"

"He isn't dead yet." Qill corrected. "Stay in the present." They walked further away from camp, but remained within sight of the lean-to. "We'll head downstream tomorrow morning, provided the weather's half-decent. A raft, large enough for us and with a chair or brace for Luuft, will head us to the Black Water. From there we can skirt the shoreline until we're able to make contact with a Haafian city."

"That's going to be Haaf North, I think." Deep Owl not overly sure of the geography. "But there are probably smaller villages closer to us."

"It doesn't actually matter, does it?"

"I guess not. Your plan is what we need. Somewhere to begin. Something to show us a way out of here. Maybe even the extreme possibility of accomplishing the original mission."

"My, but we can be excitable." Qill smiled dryly. They returned to camp, arriving approximately the same time as did a freshly scrubbed Jelkio. "Another alluring woman has joined our entourage, I see." He appreciatively announced to any who cared to listen.

"The fresh pine smell coming from Jelkio's direction caused Deep Owl to excuse himself. He'd return later.

"O' I presume you'll return after a bath. I wouldn't want you to embarrass yourself either."

"Quiet, you cynical old man." Deep Owl grumbled over his shoulder as he walked around camp and then climbed to the pool above the falls.

"Where's he going?" Asked Jelkio almost innocently.

"Just someplace where people can't smell." Qill sarcastically allowed.

"My goodness." Jelkio half-blushed. "Whatever might this world be coming to?" She flashed a broad grin at Qill and they both laughed.

A stomping noise downstream caught their rapt attention. Qill drew his bow while sending Jelkio to the recesses of the leanto, next to Luuft. The noise now included grumping sounds and a few curse words, causing Qill to quiver his arrow. The camp clowns were about to make their grand entrance.

"Come on out, Jelkio." Qill called. "You aren't going to believe this."

Stumbling and kicking through the underbrush off the side of the stream came Kofe, followed by an equally well-laden Nooy. The stout pole stretching between their shoulders sagged from the weight of newly-tanned and sewn garments, their back packs bulged with who-knew-what.

"Put the pole down gently, you big dummy." Kofe bellowed.

Nooy promptly bounced the end of the pole off Kofe's doubledbraided head. "That should fix you, boss man!"

"What's all this?" Jelkio looked at the furs in amazement.

"We dummies bees buz-zy mekkin some de cloths." Kofe deliberately slipped into the accent that repulsed Jelkio. "Dems ya bees wearin' all but keeps ya nik-ked." Then he produced a false blush, causing Jelkio to become rather self-conscious. She desperately tugged at her ragged clothing. "Ser-ry, But ya need ta try dis on. We promise not ta looky." He slyly grinned as he reached for a well tailored dress, produced from rabbit skins, of course. "We sorta had ta es-ti-mate yer size, but'n Nooy sez it fits."

Jelkio, red-faced and flustered, grabbed the rabbit skin dress and dashed for the thicket. Deep Owl coughed loudly and two tailors did indeed turn their backs to her, delightfully smiling all the while. When she reappeared, it was to the raving revues of the two tailors. The dress fit well, reaching to mid-calf.

Except for pulling on a pair of the rabbitskin breeches, Luuft kept to himself, hiding in the shadows of the lean-to. Early the next morning, slightly before the sun's dawning, he found himself rudely awakened, hoisted up and plonked down on the travois. Despite his uncomplying behavior, and the cascade of unbelievable curses, Nooy and Kofe trudged downstream with their hyper victim. Qill, Deep Owl and Jelkio followed behind, carrying the clay pots and dried rabbit in the backpacks. After a harsh mile of trudging through and around dense thickets and masses of jagged raspberry bushes, the trek abruptly ended at a large quiet pool which. At the edge of the stony beach sat a well constructed raft, large enough to hold the entire group. A chair frame rose from the middle of the raft. That's where they surreptitiously dumped the now hoarse Luuft.

"Well, Deep Owl." Smiled a proudly beaming Kofe. "What do you think?" Both he and Nooy took an overly theatrical bow as the others arrived.

Deep Owl surveyed the raft. The stone tomahawks produced evenly rounded grooves, to which vines were wrapped to hold the whole contraption together.

"Well done." He announced with a very pleased grin. "Well done. ...But how is the stream?"

"It gets about twenty feet wide and probably around two to four feet deep. We can pole to the sea. We can even fish while we're underway."

"Just how far downstream have you checked this out? "Jelkio asked with more urgency than curiosity.

"Maybe two miles?" Nooy glanced at Kofe for confirmation.

Qill spoke. "You're anticipating the arrival of some rescuing Istells, perhaps?" He looked directly at her.

"Yes." She said with firm conviction. "Our rescue is shortly at hand."

"Then may the Holy One be praised." The Shaman quietly responded.

"And may our God be praised as well." Jelkio added.

Although the stream followed a course laid out by a drunken snake, they made excellent time, due to the expert poling of the two 'redeemed' clowns. Mid-afternoon found them leaving the safety of the forest for deep and heavy grasslands. Now the lightly clouded blue sky half blinded them. For Jelkio, however, it was time to scan horizons for evidence of the four hundred foot Istells. This remained her hope for rescue, in spite of the fact that no one actually knew just where they were.

The first moon rose before the sun's light died, cut off by the volcanic mountains behind them. It provided a blood-red sky peppered by wispy black-bottomed clouds. The thickening atmosphere presented a foreboding which generated anxiety and tension among those on the raft. Meanwhile, the stream straightened a bit as other, smaller streams joined with it. Then, immediately around a sharp overcut bend, the raft suddenly spun and bounced through a rapids and into a darkwater creek.

"Everyone all right?" Qill half shouted.

"Keep the noise down." Deep Owl retorted with some indignation. "We don't know who might be out there."

"Yose bees rite." Quipped Kofe. "Dem mom-sters kin come ta et us."

"Et?" Said Jelkio, perplexed. She found learning the Haafian language difficult enough without Kofe's clowning. Now she had to decipher the utterings of Kofe who deliberately butchered the dialect, if only to deliberately torment her.

"Gob-ble up. To place some-tin in de muth." He most gallantly smiled.

"Thanks." She said. Then making a devious dive, she knocked Kofe into the water. Her next sentences, entirely in Tath, severely denigrated the sopping Kofe simply by their emotional impact.

"You won't translate that, will you?" Asked an apprehensive Deep Owl.

"I'm not sure you could handle it." She haughtily suggested.

"Give the Lady some room." Qill cautioned. "And get the big dummy back on board. Who knows what just may 'et' him, seeing that he's playing 'fish bait'."

"Trouble ahead." Stated a heretofore quiet Luuft. He pointed to a well-used tow path on the far shore. "Looks like that might be how the flatboats get to the volcano." He surmized.

"Then we best find a secluded spot for supper and sleep. And no fires tonight." Ordered Deep Owl as he steered the raft into the muddy bank opposite the trail.

"Not yet." Said Qill as he pushed the raft back into the slowly moving current. "We'll tie up back along the next stream we come to. No one's going to be traveling this late in the day."

"Kofe will go reconnoitering the neighborhood." Nooy volunteered.

"And you'll be right beside me."

"I'm glad that's settled." Deep Owl replied. "You two will leave as soon as we camp and have supper."

The two Yldans glared at each other.

A few more miles of poling brought the raft within sight of a small well-used docking area. The neatly stacked piles crates and casks indicated recent activity, perhaps the load waited to be pulled up to the volcano. The real towpath began here: downstream the tall grasses and bulrushes claimed the debris strewn shoreline. From the docking area the ground rose quickly, as if to protect itself with a wall, or, to keep others from whatever lay on the other side. A well-worn waggon path ran obliquely up the rise and disappeared.

"That's where you two are headed." Deep Owl pointed to the waggon path.

They nodded and poled faster, having seen evidence of an emptying stream about a quarter mile below the docks. It actually proved to be a large protected eddy. Being almost three hundred feet long, surrounded by tall pines, Qill called it 'camp'. Camp became a lean-to one hundred feet back from the water, beyond the reach of mosquitoes and other pests. The sun finally disappeared, allowing the second moon a chance to light the world, however dimly. Supper consisted of the dried rabbit and fish plus a luke-warm tea Jelkio made from some herbs.

Much later, as Kofe and Nooy rested from swimming the creek, the acrid smell of wood smoke crept down from the rise. Cautiously moving off the waggon trail and moving through the tall grasses, the two reached the top of the rise. In the far distance, maybe five miles away, flames burning red and blue shot like evil fingers into the night sky, as if trying to free itself from the source of its fuel.

Instead, the conflagration met with absolute failure; the heavens opened a downpour which diminished the two scouts' vision to a few feet. They watched, frozen on the muddy rise, as the elements of water and fire fought their battle. In the midst of their observing, a thunderous blast came from the inferno's source, thrusting a huge ball of fire into the heavens like a shooting star. Then the fire slowly died. It punished the area with a blanket of debris laden smoke and an acrid smelling air, contaminating everything.

A dreary second dawn rose upon Kofe and Nooy as they navigated the swollen creek on an old driftwood log. The rain still fell, though it no longer pummelled the ground. Now it descended gently and sweet smelling, as if to purify the atmosphere. At mid-afternoon, as best as anyone could tell, Kofe and Nooy reported their findings to the camp.

"So you think it was some kind of large building?" Deep Owl reflected on their report.

"Maybe a couple. With the torrent, I couldn't make out to much detail."

"Then maybe it was just a big hay fire?"

"Couldn't be. We recognized the outline of some huge structure." Nooy responded.

"Ha." Came a terse muffled sound from the lean-to. Luuft raised himself up on an elbow. "We just finished our mission. That building had to be Krucik's mansion. There's nothing else out this far north."

"That's got possibilities." Deep Owl thought out loud.

"No possibility." Luuft remained irritated. "I know it's the right place....There's a large keep at the end of the chapel. The mansion house is separate. Its all constructed of local brownstone. Maybe that's what exploded. The rock tends to collect moisture. Just add intense heat and you have...."

"A great big blast?"

"I never realized how intuitive you were Nooy." Luuft sarcastically countermanded the interrupting Yldan. "Anything else you want to add." He said caustically. Then he screamed, throwing everyone off balance. His non-functional legs suddenly snapped up, striking him in the chest as they contracted. He rolled to his back, using his arms to force the legs away from him. Qill grabbed his ankles and pulled. That became effective only when Deep Owl steadied Luuft's shoulders. The seizure lasted, seemingly, for an eternity. Luuft, drained of all strength, collapsed.

"What happens now?" Jelkio asked desperately. Tears flooded her bluish face, running down her cheeks. Luuft's continual and unrelenting day-to-day torment eroded her stamina.

"We'll keep him warm. I think the dampness might have set the seizure in motion....He'll require complete rest for two days."

With those few words, the Shaman set the schedule. Deep Owl would cross the creek with Kofe and Nooy as soon as the weather permitted. In the meantime, everyone simply watched the rain drizzle through the pine boughs, creating miniature streams on the forest floor.

That drizzly evening, with the two moons shrouded by thinning thunderheads, the conversation turned its way, once again, towards the theologizing which had been a continual piece of their journey since the rescue of the Tath ladies. Luuft initiated it by his first comment since he woke.

"Why me?" He whined.

"Why any of us?" Qill rephrased the question. "And, yet I'm not prone to believe that's even the correct question. Perhaps this: why not me?" He looked at their faces, darkly shadowed by the night and light given by the campfire coals.

"Speak for yourself, old man." Luuft spat out acidly. "I've received what I've earned. The past caught me." He sighed miserably and continued. "Its just a matter of time until your past catches up to each of you." Even this acidic remark carried the tone of self pity.

"So, the Holy One delights in tormenting us for not being perfect. No wonder prayers don't get answered. He's too busy meting out a specific punishment for a specific sin for everyone in creation. Makes me wonder why the Holy One bothered to create us in the first place. We never were perfect; never can be perfect; never will be perfect. We can be faithful; we can live with the intent to do our best. But to be free from sin? Never."

"Thanks for the sermon, Qill." Luuft said haughtily.

"I prayed you were listening." Deep Owl's judgmental tone cut as a razor would, tearing a gash in Luuft's self-pitying refuge.

Luuft replied by repositioning himself, noisily, on his back. From that position he easily avoided everybody.

"I recognize that you are struggling Luuft. That is rather commendable." Qill's tone changed to one of some 'little' compassion. "By tomorrow, you'll have reassessed your situation." He forwarded his remarks as a suggestion.

Jelkio abruptly cut into the discussion, reorienting the topic. "You spoke of creation." She said with some hesitation. "Can you tell me more?"

"Its rather simple." Kofe said seriously. "Before anything was created, both what we can know and what we can't, there existed only the Holy One. In His own time, He decided to create..."

"How?"

"Out of nothing." Kofe casually noted. "He just said 'apple tree', and there were apple trees."

Jelkio shook her head in true incredulous disbelief. "I don't understand it. Creation from nothing?"

"Gives you a rough idea of His strength and power, doesn't it?" Deep Owl added.

"Actually, it gives me very little." She paused, as if she might have stumbled into some theological nightmare. "Our story is different." She attempted to correct the awkward situation.

"There is much room for discussion, and just as much room for the 'created' to hypothesis what God has done, my dear lady." Qill had a way of putting her at ease. "From what we've shared so far there appears to be no rationale for killing each other over our religions. Our Gods do not seem antithetical..."

"Damn heresy!" Shouted Deep Owl. "There is but One God."

"And have we enough evidence to know that Jelkio's god is not actually the same as ours. Does the Holy One always appear the same to everyone?

Do you forget that you are a Yldan, lead by the Spirit and not by the Book? Yet it is the same Holy One? Speak, am I in error?"

Deep Owl put his head between his knees, as if to block out any more of Qill's all-to-penetrating sermonizing.

"Ye bees r'mindin' me of a 'lil boy." Mocked Kofe. As if to prove Kofe a liar, Deep Owl straightened himself and tried to stare down everybody. The peculiar result resounded in uproarious laughter from the rest, and, following a few moments of red-faced embarrassment, laughter from Deep Owl himself.

"De truth dun maake ya free, liken a bird." Mused Kofe, wiseman of the clowns.

"I suppose you're right." Said a more balanced Deep Owl...... "Jelkio, I apologize for interrupting you. This is not proper."

"Accepted." She said with a hint of a bemused smile. "Sometimes you can be so polite." She adjusted her seat of pine boughs and renegotiated with the rabbit skins as to how the dress should properly fit. "Our God," She reiniated her original statement, "created everything from what was."

"What was?" Qill's face wrinkled in puzzlement.

"At the beginning, what was....was intense, massive chaos. It had no purpose, no goal, no form. What was....was lost. Our God, whose name remains deliberately hidden from us, brought this chaotic mess into order and purpose. Our God rendered what was lost, found....Its that simple, Kofe."

Kofe was caught off-guard; his smile weak and somewhat stupid. "I think I heard you. But Haafians believe we put order into things and give our lives purpose."

"Perhaps you think too highly of yourselves." She said forcefully. "Can you turn a pile of ashes into an Istell? Does your life mean anything without having your God be apart of it? Or," She said grinning, "Did you create yourself?"

"I believe Kofe overstated our position." Qill apologized. "We do have concrete boundaries, of which Kofe summarily ignored. What he actually meant was that the Holy One has given us the blessing of freedom. We are to choose, to decide and then, decide again. Our freedom also calls us to personal responsibility."

"Then we are much the same, Qill."

"Then, your God-without-a-name permits you both responsibility and choice."

"Yes. Isn't that obvious? You saw the paradise which once was our home. We lost it because we choose the pathway of irresponsibility." Jelkio spoke with the sadness of endless ages which preceded her.

"Your sadness is great, my Lady." Qill tone resonated empathy for the Queen's Lady-in-Waiting. "Must you carry it? You did not commit the sin."

"It is the sin of a people....an unfaithful people." Soft and melancholic her voice rang. "When our God deems our penance suitable, we will be called home. Until then, we wander on the steppe and northward across the frozen tundra."

"I find that grossly unfair." Now incensed, Deep Owl spoke as self-proclaimed judge. "Responsibility is placed upon the individual, not the society. When the perpetrator is gone, his crime is also gone....removed."

"Not quite accurate, my son." Qill's relaxed tone automatically denied Deep Owl's penchant for the dramatic overkill. "Might I digress for a moment?"

"Please." Though he did not mean it.

"The War ended before you were even conceived. The War began due to our reticence to combat evil. Vosnob is one of the few left who fought that war. Are we not still fighting that war? Isn't this mission part of that war?" Qill quietly walked back to the lean-to's roofline, allowing Deep Owl some time to collect his thoughts.

Jelkio asked, "How long has the War been fought?"

"Just about four generations.....too long." The Shaman acknowledged. Kofe's and Nooy's heads shook in agreement with the grey headed shaman.

"But," Protested Luuft from his protected cover, "You Yldans didn't pay much of the price. Haafians did the majority of the fighting."

"And is that not true only because there are about forty to fifty Haafians to one Yldan?" The rebuke came quiet and dignified.

Once again, Luuft' responded by simply rolling on his side, towards the back wall of the pine boughed shelter.

"Therefore," Jelkio returned to the topic. "Your sin has also been carried throughout the ages. Perhaps we Taths take the whole concept more personally. After all, our ancestors were personally asked to leave the paradise."

"And we pay for our sin against the Holy One in a more indirect manner. You are a rather astute theologian, Jelkio...... We must pursue this further, but not tonight...... There are a number of items I must attend to before sleeping." With that, he silently strode into the shadowy darkness of the pines, strolling to the eddy's shore. Perhaps he spent that night in prayer, no one knew for sure. He felt both deep relief and an unnerving remorse during the emotion laden conversation. Some items bordered on heresy, yet the Spirit had involved itself. All were more than reasonable causes for meditation. A new world, because of Jelkio, commenced opening itself to those who would hear it. Qill heard: and elation and dread filled his heart. He choose to ask for a sign, the most concrete one possible, for he believed himself weak and not up to the task given him. As the blackness of the foggy evening turned to a dryer charcoal colored sky--the variety that arrives before the brightest of cloudless days-- Qill still awaited his answer as he sat by the eddy. The Holy One would answer, he was positive. But he also humbly conceded, deep within his mind, that he had no power to force an answer. That belonged only to the Holy One. As the first passive orange streaks split the dawn from the night, Qill anxiously prayed only for patience: that and nothing more.

The blindingly warm sunshine promoted a more cooperative attitude within the group, at least for the morning. Even the recalcitrant Luuft moved himself to a sunny spot. The main difficulty lay in fording the creek. After some intense conversation, more like a 'polite' argument, the trio went fishing instead. Jelkio supervised the campsite. A pensive troubled Qill meandered throughout the campsite, through the forest and then down to the eddy, where Deep Owl's prowess as a fisherman all ready furnished them with an enormous supper, but the Shaman said nothing and his face betrayed little other than tiredness. Even by supper his countenance hadn't changed, and he refused to eat.

"Don't worry so much." Deep Owl replied to Jelkio about Qill's fasting. "Fasting is part of his spiritual journey. It has something to do with searching for answers."

"Then Qill isn't sick?"

"Hardly. He's hungry and tired. But fasting is the Shaman's way. Only they truly comprehend deep spiritual things."

"That's where his wisdom.."

"Yes, that's the original source of his wisdom and the wisdom of all our Shamans for that matter." Deep Owl explained.

"Then they are your priests?" She thought out loud.

"………Well,…. yes, though I've never thought about them as priests. But, the function is probably the same. Though the Haafian priests are much more formal and highly educated." His inflection clearly indicated a depreciation for the latter.

"Are we biased today?" Luuft tried to provoke a fight.

Quick on the uptake, Jelkio interposed herself in the matter by deftly changing the subject. "What is this thing called 'book'?"

Luuft's rude laugher thoroughly embarrassed Jelkio. Her bluish face transformed to a glowing white, which caused her even more misery.

"Damn you, Luuft!" Yelled Deep Owl. "You have the manners of the…"

Qill remained firmly planted between the two antagonists, his arms motioning them to 'silence'. Then he glanced at the despondent Jelkio, her face still glowing, bidding her to continue. Wiping her tearful face with a rough handkerchief made from her old dress, she slowly began to compose herself. Qill's hardened stares silenced Luuft's infantile behavior and, simultaneously defused Deep Owl's entrenching wrath. Jelkio turned her back to the abated fray, tidied herself up a bit and then turned back around, ready to begin.

"I thank you for your kindness, Qill." She spoke quietly. "Luuft, you shall owe me an apology...a public one. And when you decide to give it, remember that I DO NOT need to accept it. I find you TOO offensive these days." And she turned from him to Deep Owl. "As I began a while ago, what is a 'book'?"

Qill smiled, pretending to be totally neutral, as Deep Owl fumbled and floundered for a way to begin. His awkwardness showed in his disorganization. Being semi-illiterate, the lady-in-waiting, placed a difficult task before him.

"A book...Well its something one needs to read....read to understand what's in the book..Some books are about animals, others are Holy books, and other instruct us....Like how to do finances or how to build a castle...."

Jelkio sat down on some pine boughs looking bewildered and perplexed. "So, books, whatever they actually are....are worthless unless one also has the ability to read them...What is 'read'?"

Deep Owl also sat, to collect his mismanaged thoughts. This frustration of not communicating bothered him. It was not proper, but it abjectly interfered with his Yldan dignity. Then, perhaps through the mysterious ways of the Holy One, the essential concept he desperately needed, suddenly arrived. With a most unYldan smile, Deep Owl proceeded to draw characters in the dirt, surrounding them with a rectangle.

"This is what a page looks like." He looked at Jelkio to discern whether she understood: the answer was negative. "Pages are made of animal skin or paper...Forget about paper for now...When we take a goodly number of these skins and put them together....by sewing...we call it a book."

Jelkio's blue face gave absolutely no hint, even vague, of comprehending.

"Now, on each of the skins, which we usually refer to as pages, there are characters written there. The characters are used...to formulate words... and the words are put into sentences....all to tell us..to tell anyone who reads it exactly the same thing."

Jelkio's countenance began to change. She smiled, politely. "A book is a collection of all types of things. You make marks on skins so you don't need to remember much, but it forces you to understand the complicated markings. Is that correct?" She asked in a most understated manner.

Nooy and Kofe burst into a fit of laughter. Jelkio started to blush again, more hurt than embarrassed this time.

"No!" Called Nooy, attempting to apologize. "You just upset a whole way of thinking..... Which is worse, learning to read or learning to remember?" His words broke off as he laughed again. "Some's o' us can't do neither....and we still get by pretty good."

"Someday, someone will explain this to me in terms that resemble ideas that I can grasp." Jelkio, exasperated, valiantly sought a way to gracefully discontinue the topic.

Deep Owl politely ignored her. "See these 'markings'?" He pointed to the characters he had drawn within the rectangle.

"Yes."

"Each one has its own sound."

"Yes."

"When we put the sounds together,........ they form the words we pronounce.....Look here...See what I wrote? Now, I'll have Kofe read it for you." He motioned and Kofe ambled over, took a glance at the words and returned to his seat. "What did you read, Kofe?"

"The words say, 'The Holy One'." He proudly stated.

"I didn't know you could read." Muttered an astonished Nooy.

Jelkio gasped and shook her head. "That's too frightening...to read." Qill nodded in tacet agreement. "It is!" She explained. "It robs one of privacy......... It can equalize everyone. Those who read know the hearts of others."

"Only if they write the truth." Luuft grumped.

"Shut up!" Kofe and Nooy yelled simultaneously.

"You don't have books in Tath?"

"Isn't that rather obvious, Deep Owl?"

It was his turn to be embarrassed. "Indeed, Jelkio." He disparagingly admitted.

"Is not that bad, is it?" She teased. "OR, maybe it is. You men folk are quite unpredictable."

The dusky colored morning proved a better time for traversing the creek. Since yesterday, the muddied water dropped several feet and slowed considerably. The sky shown a bit dimmer than the previous day, due to the multi-layered cloud cover. After breakfast, the trio swam across the creek, using a piece of driftwood as a raft. The docking area, untidily dismantled by the flood waters, showed no signs of any recent visitation. Spreading out downstream from docks, the trio slipped and pulled themselves up the soggy slope of the weed covered rise. Utilizing only hand signals, they proceeded towards the sight of the conflagration. As the weeds and grasses gave way to another pine forest, one that straddled the rutted waggon road, faster progress ensued. At midday, by a fern laden brook a few feet from the waggon road, they paused for lunch.

The fresh pine smelling forest received another insult. The damp acidic odor of burnt wood lightly gusted through the forest from the south. Its pungency practically ruined their lunch, for something more than burnt wood invaded the smell, something evil, something foreboding. With the meal terminated, trekking resumed. Another deeply forested mile posited them at the edge of a wheat field, near a forgotten dilapidated stone wall, now overgrown with shiny green-and-white vines. Beyond the field, rising starkly as an appropriate monument to an unknown fire demon, stood the ravished ashen skeleton of a once proud and haughty castle. Perched precariously upon four slender stone pillars, all black and encrusted with debris, balanced the roof of the keep. With its battlements still in place, the flat roof resembled a ghastly crown balancing upon an invisible head. A flame-gutted roofless two storey structure stood apart from the keep while another large building, at the foot of the keep, was strewn with ashes. Its stout outer walls, burnt and broken, denied evidence as to its function.

After a diligent search of the wheat field and the surrounding area, the Yldans concluded that no others dwelled in the near vicinity. However, because of the expanse of open territory from the decayed stone wall and the 'supposedly' Krucik's mansion's ruins, they decided to wait until dusk to explore further. They settled in for a semi-restful afternoon, taking turns at being 'on guard duty'.

Soon the boredom of doing nothing provided the incentive to change their former plan: they would crawl to the scorched brownstone ruins now. Crawling, strangely enough, went faster than anticipated. Once at the two storey building, they gasped. Protruding through the burnt wreckage of broken timbers they saw the charred bones of more than twenty individuals. The gutted building yielded little evidence to ascertain the identity of the incinerated persons.

Deep Owl motioned for the three to gather. Drawing with his finger on the ash covered ground, he sent Kofe to the right side of the keep and Nooy to the left; he would back them both up by staying to their rear. As a smoky haze clung to the interior of the structure, obstructing clear vision, the advance demanded a deliberate slowness.

Suddenly, as they entered the dark cavernous edifice, the soft gallop of a Striper sounded out. Kofe froze, backing himself into the nearest corner. Nooy grabbed a filthy stone and quietly dropped to his knees under the cover of a huge half-burnt ceiling truss.

The Striper stopped at the edge of the same structure. The delicate sounds of one being deliberately silent came from the rider. His presence, extremely powerful and strange, gave away his location, though he could not be seen. Soft footsteps brought the intruder closer to the holocaust. Nooy watched the thinnest person he had ever seen coolly stop and begin to spy out the corners. Believing himself spotted, Nooy hurled the stone, tumbling the thin man to the debris strewn floor, his head landing in a dirty puddle.

"Check him!" Deep Owl's strong voice called out. "Then tie him up. Its time we got some answers about what's happened here."

Deep Owl ran to the fallen intruder before the others extricated themselves. He quickly pulled the unconscious soldier from the puddle. "He's a Haafian."

"Wonderful." Kofe grunted. "More traitors. Just kill him and we'll move on."

"Maybe later." Deep Owl returned flatly. "This one's going to put some pieces together for us....... Qill has just the right mixtures."

Nooy and Kofe removed the unconscious Haafian outside. Deep Owl brought the Striper around. "Luuft happened to be right. This is ...or was... Krucik's mansion. Nooy, take the Striper. Get word to the others and bring them here. Luuft knows the way home from here." Some hopefulness welled in his voice. However, he still realized that the mission still lacked completion.

While Kofe galloped the Striper to the docking area, Nooy searched the saddlebags and started laughing. In his hand he held a book, a large leather bound volume. Deep Owl failed to see the humor and concentrated on binding the soldier's head. Another search of the saddlebags produced two official-looking documents. Without a Word, Nooy gently handed them to Deep Owl.

"Damn it all anyhow!" Deep Owl groaned disparagingly. "This is the King's seal!" He yelled holding up the smaller of the two leather bound scrolls. He stuffed it under his arm and glanced at the second one. It was all ready opened. He unrolled it and read aloud.

"To whomever reads this, the King's official manuscript, given to Rux, Gifted of Special privileges.

Greetings from your King.

The bearer of this document, upon proper identification, is fully privileged to any and all necessary items that he may request. Upon the mark of his ring, full reimbursement for same shall be provided from the King's treasury."

He drew a deep breath before ending. "[signed] THE KING."

"We're in a bit of trouble?" Kofe grimaced.

"I expect we could be. Its a matter of crisis management."

"What's this 'gifted'?" Kofe sounded disquieted.

"If I recall....And I'm not sure that I do...It has something to do with how he protects others."

"You want to explain that in Yldan."

"Where's his weapon?

Kofe checked everywhere for a weapon, nothing appeared. "Maybe he left it on the Striper." He plaintively suggested.

"And a warrior shows up here unarmed?" Deep Owl knitted his brows as a worried look crossed on his face. "I believe we're looking at the man... this Rux...who fired this place...and everyone with it."

"And when he wakes up, we're next." A doleful noise emerged from Kofe mouth. "Hit him over the head again. We'll get a few miles between us before he wakes."

"You really aren't serious?"

"You bet I am. We both saw those bones sticking from the rubble."

Rux's coughing immediately suspended the conversation. Kofe held a stone, ready to slam it on Rux's bandaged head. Deep Owl rolled the skinny soldier over on his back, pinning his hands under him.

"Are you Rux?"

"Who vant know?" He barely produced the words.

"Are you Rux.....the Gifted?" He repeated slowly and loudly.

"Not deaf!"

Are you Rux...the Gifted?"

"Could be, maybe not." His eyes focused on the Yldan bending over him. And then he caught sight of the one holding the stone. He moved to release his arms, but was too weak. "Let me rest."

"Then you are Rux?"

"Naturally..." And he fell back into a semi-conscious state.

Deep Owl stared at the thin bony Rux, a vague expression of regret marking his weathered red face. In Rux lay their way out, but they almost killed the 'gifted'. He waited impatiently, pondering some thoughts. Isn't it a bit incomprehensible that ordinary Yldans should be able to incapacitate such a unique person? Maybe the fellow lied; few indications marked him as a warrior? But then, this Rux, who actually confirmed his identity, carried nothing one considered to be a weapon. And the scrolls from the saddlebags, who knew if they weren't stolen? He waited, crosslegged, next to the semi-conscious Rux, conjecturing a reasonable answer for this peculiar man. Hopefully, he'd conceive of something legitimate before those across the creek arrived.

"Come and eat!" Nooy half whispered. Deep Owl, plunged into his meditation, heard nothing.

Nooy shoved a piece of bread into his tranquil face. Without a word, Deep Owl, reached up, grabbed the bread and rapidly finished it off. "You planning on being a statue for the rest of the day?" His voice sounded weak and rather uncertain, as if this deprived environment tormented him.

Deep Owl slowly shook his braided head. "I don't think so." He ventured casually. "I'm just trying to formulate all the pieces into a coherent story."

"And what be so difficult?"

"First, is this actually Krucik's mansion? If not, where are we? Second, who is this man? Rux? Or someone pretending to be Rux? Thirdly, I can't believe he's out here by himself. These men usually guard extremely important persons. But who is being protected? And what side are they on?"

"I mean no insult, but aren't your fanciful notions taking you away from reality?" Nooy continued. "I'm inclined to believe that you just might overwhelm yourself. That's not going to help us."

"Keep your presuppositions to yourself." Deep Owl arched his eyebrows and put a finger to his lips...."Listen."

Nooy instantly picked up the sound: animals walking through the high grasses, heading directly to where Rux originally posted his Striper. He clambered up the broken wall to spy. An ugly twisted beam broke, causing him to topple seven feet to the burnt earth. His muffled scream immediately brought the animals around the side of the building.

Deep Owl gasped at the invaders: a fat Haafian atop a Massive Blue being chased by a tallish footsoldier. The soldier ran poorly, but with a maniac determination to keep up. Another Striper cantered along behind. Then, simultaneously, each group caught sight of the other and, uncomprehending the immediate situation, froze.

Slowly, the soldier moved next to the Massive Blue. The two moved towards the Yldans with deliberate slowness. Deep Owl rose and stood in front of Rux's unconscious body, partially hiding it. Nooy pulled himself to his feet only to trip over a board and fall again.

As only one Haafian appeared armed, a sword dangling from the trooper's hand, but in an awkward, unskilled way, Deep Owl risked raising his hands. The fat fellow on Massive Blue also raised his hands and kneed his mount forward. The soldier at his side swung the sword, only to have the fat man wallop her on the shoulder, which spun the sword in an ungainly arc into a charred debris pile. The Yldans glanced at each in disbelief.

"We bid you no harm." The fat man called from fifty paces away. He kept a hard grip on the soldier's shoulder, even as he dismounted, giving the clumsy fool the Massive Blue's reins. He walked forward, palms stretched open.

"Nor do we bid you harm, if you come in peace." Deep Owl called back, his tone flat and firm.

"We have to examine the conflagration's results. We watched it burn from afar." The fat man ambled within twenty paces. "Not much of a beautiful mansion remains, does it?"

"That's close enough, fat man."

Oros turned and threw a quick glance at Nadre, then returned just as rapidly to answer the Yldan, "I pray you haven't insulted my colleague."

"I wasn't talking about your colleague."

"Then is there someone else about?" Oros monotoned. Nadre bit her lip and lowered her head.

"Am I talking to a dunderhead?" An aggravated Deep Owl shot out.

"A dunderhead?" The monotone droned along. "Haven't seen one of them since......about three ...four dawns ago."

Nooy immediately replied. "Just what did he look like?"

Deep Owl glared, his face livid and Nooy dropped his head in embarrassed shame.

Oros stood still, totally ignoring the Yldan problem. "He's about this tall." The fat man reached his hand over his head while standing on his toes. "And if you turn him sideways, he'll disappear. Maybe you've seen him? .....Oh, he's not too bright, hardly remembers his name sometimes."

Deep Owl refused to take the bait. "Haven't met anyone fitting that description, fat man." He paused. "I think you've seen enough of the ruins."

"But I haven't even begun." Oros droned again. "And what might the King say if I came back empty handed, because of two Yldans?"

"I'm to believe that this is your mission? From the King?"

"I have papers." He yawned and sat down on a stone. "This is tedious, isn't it? There's not even a lousy stool left in Krucik's mansion to sit on.... Shall we continue, or do we need to wait until your friend returns with the reinforcements?" The fat priest caught the Yldan off-guard....

"......I congratulate you on your perceptiveness."

"Oh," Oros yawned again, "Not me, the fat one, behind me...Can't use a sword worth a damn, though." Nadre kicked him in the back.

"OUCH!"

"Serves you right, insulting me like that." She tried another kick, but Oros grabbed her foot, tumbling her to the scorched earth like a sack of potatoes. As she ungracefully descended, her tunic hood dropped away, revealing the beautiful woman. Half mortified and half embarrassed, she yanked the hood up and over her head.....but too late.

"Well now, that explains the most bizarre sword-swinging I've ever seen." Deep Owl smiled and chuckled, which, in turn, brought the flush in Nadre's cheeks to a redness that thoroughly triumphed over the Yldan bronze. "Now, fat man, be polite and introduce the dear Lady to me and my friend."

"And to whom, exactly," Oros stretched the word to its furthest limits, "Shall I be introducing the Lady, such that she is, to?" While framed to pass as a question, his words carried a wariness that everyone detected. "And, before I allow that, can you tell me if my good friend, who lies directly behind the two of you is dead or sleeping again? ....He sometimes just thinks he can sleep anywhere or anytime, that's simply how his disease manifests itself.......You haven't touched him, have you?" His face lit up with a tinge of mischievous vengeance.

Deep Owl calmly inspected the fallen Rux. "Rux still breathes." He said coolly, disinterestedly.

"Then you have indeed come into contact with him." Oros raised himself from his seat and lumbered towards the two Yldans. "Do not fear, I need to see if you've caught the disease. It's overtly contagious, you understand."

Nervously the two watched as Oros ambled closer. He stopped a few feet from the two. "Aha!" He squinted, his puffy cheeks forcing his eyes to all but disappear. "Aha." He repeated.

"Aha?"

"Aha...Yes." Oros shot back, then he plunged between the two men to bend over the unconscious Rux. Before the startled Yldans realized the change in the situation, Nadre, perched on the Massive Blue, stood over them, bow ready.

"Gentlemen, you treated me with a falsehood, Rux obviously damaged himself as he fell. Examine the lump behind his skull." He smiled gently and turned about. "My name is Oros, a common priest of the Holy One." Then he waved a stubby fingered hand at a tense Nadre. "That is my beloved daughter. You may call her Nadre........ I give you my permission."

Nadre followed Oros' lead extremely well, nodding demurely and yet properly, to both Yldans. She lowered her bow and quivered the arrow. As she slid her leg over the Massive Blues' rump to dismount, Nooy, bright and beamy, moved to assist her. Even to her own surprise, she allowed him to help.

"How is Rux, 'Father'?" The final word rang acerbically.

Removing some small pouches from the saddlebags, she began to wrap the welt on Rux's skull. The lazy breeze momentary shifted, blowing her sun-streaked blonde hair into Rux's face. He sputtered and coughed, then fell back to sleeping.

"Where, in heaven's name are your manners?" Oros reprimanded the two Yldans. "Who are you?"

"We're Yldans." Deep Owl replied, trying to retrieve control of the situation, not yet realizing the former situation didn't exist.

"No!" Oros exclaimed in mock surprise.

Nooy lost what little composure he retained. "YOU!...You, You, You ...." His countenance likened to one who suffered from disparaging dreams and visions.

Nooy's face went white. He shyly glanced at Deep Owl, who wagged his braided head at the irrationality of the entire conversation.

Distraughtly, Deep Owl finally replied to Oros' original question. "My name is Deep Owl. Perhaps you know my mother's brother. His name is Blue Turtle."

"Well met, my friend." Oros quit the game and became serious. "I certainly know your esteemed, but crazy uncle. Many stories I….But who is your friend?"

"That strange person is Nooy." He answered distressfully.

"But he is a good stone thrower." Oros stuck up for the downcast Yldan. "We watched from across the way." He interjected the explanation rapidly. "Nooy?....Then you're from the northern tribes?"

"Yes, Oros priest." He stammered.

"Just Oros."

"Yes."

"Obviously," Oros began tentatively, "You are not on the evil one's side. Or else we'd all be headed back to some volcano. The question is, what are all of you doing here? Your appearance is significant, especially since you arrived from a northern direction. How exactly did you circumnavigate the Dark Lands?"

Deep Owl found himself overwhelmed by the hypothesis thrown out by the corpulent priest. Actually, it mattered not so much if they were presuppositions or conjectures, for Oros targeted the situation precisely. While this uncanny trait belonged to most Shamans, Deep Owl never expected the secular, book educated Haafian clergy to do more than conduct the liturgy. He felt irritated with himself, he should know better than to buy into prejudices. He stood in silence. "I apologize." He spoke sincerely, eyeball to eyeball with Oros.

Oros grinned and his fat bounced as he squished the daylights out of Deep Owl with one of his famous bearhugs. "Apology accepted." He informed Deep Owl as he bounced him up and down.

"Enough, Oros!" A not-pleased Nadre protested. "This is embarrassing."

Oros dumped the breathless, but grateful, Yldan onto the blackened earth. Nooy hastened to his side, his face a mixture of mirth and confusion.

Nadre moved to support the semi-rousing Rux, whose moanings touched a soft place inside her heart, a part that while healed, had yet to venture into growing.

"You've missed the whole thrust of Deep Owl's journey!" Oros joyfully informed her.

"What journey? The Yldan hasn't told you anything." As difficult as it might be to accuse Oros of over-stating his case, Nadre's face became incongruous: once again she became distraught with her own uncomprehending.

"But he did journey, for he contradicted none of my statements. And no Yldan would allow a lie to be told upon him." He then stared at the huffing Deep Owl. "Is that not correct?"

"Indeed, and, except for the various details and their consequences," He coughed. "You are basically correct. We invaded to Dark Lands, to map them actually. Somehow..."

"Grace, it is." Nooy corrected.

"By Grace we end up at Krucik's burnt mansion."

"Well, if you were but a few days earlier, you'd have seen Rux do the place in."

"We saw the flames from the creek bank." Nooy said. "But who killed everyone....those soldiers?" His nose twitched.

"I did." Rux garbled, leaning on Nadre for support. Though his vision hadn't returned to normal, he immediately recognized his assailants as Yldans. "You guys are good." He off-handedly commended them. "I never sensed the rock coming....But that's exactly why it worked."

Night crept in so slowly that only the dwindling campfire's light caused the yawing to begin. The long tales of each party, questions and all, drove the fascinating conversation along. Neither party found itself too willing to believe, or, in a few instances, even understand the other's story. Dragons and lakes teeming with tadpole-like Kyykki, as well as a priest attempting a Quest to solve the theological difficulties of the

'White Eagle' and a trooper whose sole weapon is his fingers, these things stretched imaginations to their maximums bordering on incredulity. By nightfall the two groups had merged into one, eating and swapping their stories about a small campfire.

"Oros?" Called Nadre, "You getting too old to stay up late?" She teased the balding fat man.

"No." He respectfully returned. "I'm just a trifle worried."

"About what?" Nooy sounded alarmed. He stood, bow in hand.

"Please Nooy, its a different type of concern."

"Oh." He said. His disappointment actually showed. Returning to his former seat, he asked. "What then?"

"I believe that with all this conversation tonight, with all the incredulous and alarming things we've shared, that we may find ourselves not believing each other. I'm fearful of that."

Rux unpolitely dumped his remaining herbal tea over Oros' balding head. The ensuing laughter proved Oros' concern too dramatic, and unrealistic.

"Listen, Old Man." Rux added. "This is the first 'good' evening in a very long while. ...Don't spoil it."

"Thank you, my confessor." The cynical tone grated on Rux, but, having used all his tea, he quietly left the urge for revenge dissipate. "Deep Owl, when might the others catch up?"

He thought before answering, creating a silence filled only with the chirps and creakings of the night insects. "Because Luuft needs ferried over, and I don't know if Jelkio swims, I'm not sure.....Maybe we should meet them at the docks."

"Not a bad idea!" Nadre almost squealed. The idea of another woman about delighted her. "When do we all start?"

"We'll break camp at dawn?" Deep Owl conjectured in a strained way, being unsure of how much authority he now carried.

"Sounds good to me." Oros announced. "Just one problem."

"What's that?"

"Nadre has seen too many 'blue women', none of them ...."

"They started out as...." She defended herself.

"The point is, Jelkio is a Tath."

"SO!" Nadre, hands on hips, stood defiantly leaning over the priest, readying herself to harm him.

He smiled up at her, pensive and quiet. "Its like I mentioned this afternoon, all Taths are naturally blue....I didn't want you to become alarmed."

Nadre dropped her hands to her sides and kissed the priest on the top of his head. "Thanks!" She said. "But I CAN handle the situation." She announced with pride.

"We'll see." Rux dryly commented. His rebuttal, in the form of a swift smack to his cheek, arrived instantaneously, to his chagrin and the Yldan's laughter. Having reclaimed her besmirched dignity, Nadre wrapped herself in a blanket and entered the lean-to.

Until daybreak all, excepting Nadre, took turns with guard duty. The night's dramatically gigantic star patterns set against deepest darkness, and the soft warm wind shoving clouds across the sky, allowed for a needed restfulness.

The welcoming at the docks proved utterly embarrassing for Jelkio. The rabbit-skin top of her dress split out during the swim, causing her to remain well-hidden behind the raft until Nadre could locate something to fit her. Oros' extra large robe wrapped about her nicely, but, being that she put it on while still in the water, the soggy brown garment clung to her curves like a second skin. She still felt and looked naked. Nadre came to defense, demanding the men 'go first'. Then she quickly robbed the Striper of his saddle blanket.

"Prying eyes is what them types have." Nadre lectured the men savagely without venturing to ask about Jelkio's position. "Now be watching yourselves, not this lady. Where be your manners?"

Saga of The Light Striper

The men obeyed, rather amused. A surprized Jelkio kept quiet. Her bright eyes never strayed from this brownskinned lady with beautiful blonde hair. Never before had she even envisioned such. Nadre's bluntness and her commanding attitude caused Jelkio simply to observe.

Later, as the story of the two group's meeting added itself to the story of the additional three members, a sense of completion existed, even though everyone realized Haaf North mandated a sizeable journey. The waggon road did promote a sense of enhanced security, if only because its grass lined ruts lead towards civilization. The increased size of the group added to these feelings.

Qill, the thin Shaman, strolled in his damp smelling rabbit skin clothing with Oros: they lead the party towards the gate of Krucik's demolished and God-forsaken mansion. Within moments their conversation turned to professional and spiritual things. Such conversation, more inherent to their personal needs than concern over food and other of life's necessities, claimed their lifestyles.

Luuft, in spite of all that transpired, declined into a state of deepest depression, caring for naught, connected to nothing. Even his contentiousness fell to the power of the depression. The Yldans gently tied him into the saddle of Rux's Striper. The Massive Blue, as Nadre demanded, went to the ladies. The menfolk, as only proper, would walk. The other Striper carried their supplies. Jelkio found herself admiring this brown-skinned lady.

The evening's encampment rapidly unfolded into a pleasant meal of cooked vegetables and rabbit stew. Rux erected a separate tent for the two ladies. Oros decided to examine Luuft.

"You may." Qill gently protested. "But I think you shall find that little more can be done, especially in these primitive conditions."

"Oh," Said a detached Oros, "It's not that I doubt you. The Holy One forbid. I am well aware of what you Shamans possess, in terms of gifts, that is. Simply call it my professional curiosity." Then he whispered into Qill's. "I'm surprized he's even still alive."

Qill modest a look of satisfaction graced his face. "Thank you."

"I'll need about four of you. And Qill, I'll need you to assist me." Surrounding Luuft, curled again into his now familiar fetal position and sleeping, Oros gave orders for Luuft to be turned on his stomach and stretched out. Then he and Qill would examine Luuft's spine. Commands are usually easier to give than complete; not only did Luuft propose to wake the dead with his moaning and glib remarks, but also his leg muscles had tightly contracted, allowing Kofe and Rux to believe they were breaking his legs as they pulled them out from under his chin. Much, much later, the semi-straightened Luuft, finally quiet, lay before them. Jelkio, now dressed in a quickly retailored priest's robe, pressed hot compresses against his quivering leg muscles. Using his stubby fingers instead of sight, Oros, beginning with Luuft's neck, firmly pushed and massaged each vertebrate.

Qill watched intently. "I've never witnessed this before."

"Probably not, its rare. But it can be effective." He spoke calmly as his fingers continued to probe Luuft's vertebrate at the mid-back area. "So far, I can't feel anything out-of-place." He mumbled. A full-sounding "AH!" came from his mouth a few moments later. "Put your fingers here, Qill." Oros grabbed the man's bony wrists, placing his thin fingers along the lower back. "Feel the vertebrate? Tell me what you discover."

After many quiet moments, with everyone watching, anticipating, the Shaman more-or-less confirmed Oros' findings. "It seems, but I'm not certain, that two of the bones," He prodded where of he was speaking, "Are far out of any type of alignment....Is this what is causing the paralysis?"

"That's my conjecture. Seeing that the spine connects all the body parts together, its been hypothesized that a misalignment will disconnect the body's coordination."

"Such as producing this paralysis?"

"Perhaps." He solemnly replied, his real attention being the vertebrate's non-alignment. "Now, two men at each extremity." He called. "Pull slowly and gently, I'll inform you when to hold perfectly still............... Qill, you place your hands on the lower bone."

"To what end?" Qill sounded somewhat mystified.

"As the spine is stretched, we'll have room to reposition the two bones....move it gently back in line with the one below it. I'll do the same with the other bone....Then once we have them aligned as best as possible, the men will slowly release the tension...."

"What then?" Asked Jelkio, definitely worried.

Oros commented. "I don't mean to be glib, but there is no way of ascertaining the results until after the realignment is performed."

Jelkio, with her hands over her eyes, turned, stumbling into Nadre, who gave her a strong affirming hug. "The ugly guy's kind of special to you." Jelkio nodded her head, which snuggled on Nadre's shoulder.

"Ready?....Pull!" Some anguishing snapping noise reverberated, then stopped. "Now, HOLD!" He commanded. "Qill, slowly twist the bone....I'll wait until your fingers are out of the way."

Sweat, in rivulets, popped from Qill's forehead and ran off his chin as he gingerly manipulated the bone. "I think its in place." His voice tentative.

"We'll double check after this other bone is moved." He worked at his re-engineering of the bone as he spoke. "Qill, I believe the bones are as good as we'll get them....Let the pressure off the arms, slowly......Now, same for the legs."

With a gasping, the four relinquished their duties. Luuft's body remained limp, though he finally cursed again. His miserable attitude retained its fatalism and resentment, but that too, indicated a positive change from his detached lethargy. Luuft's ramblings of abject hopelessness ran continuously into the night. Finally, with the help of Nooy and Rux, Qill rammed one of his sleeping concoctions down his throat. Excepting those on guard duty, the warm starry night, once again, provided rest for those whose limits had been mortally tested.

Whether the new day began with Luuft's yelling or the bright sunshine, not even Kofe, who had duty at the time, really knew.

"My legs are burning! I can feel them burning!"

"How long might that continue?" Qill asked.

"I don't know, Qill. Its just a sign that something is functioning again. Thus, in spite of his protestations, it is good news."

"I'm not sure I'm comprehending."

"Ever sit on your leg for a long time?" He didn't pause for an answer. "When you begin to move, the leg hurts something terrible. It also indicates that the leg is returning to normal. It can feel again. It will bear your weight again."

Qill simply smiled: he understood. "Even so, I'll allow him to eat and sleep, else we'll never get underway."

"Agreed." Oros was satisfied. "Tie him to the Striper."

After many miles, following a light breakfast, the group paused for lunch. The waggon path picked up a sinister appearance: trees hung over the path, weighed down with ugly growths of vines and mosses causing the path to darken dramatically. Birds and other animals which played in the dense forest just a quarter mile back, were noticeably absent. The strange vegetation within a few feet of the waggon path defied identification. What might it be, so foreign looking, so ugly and putrid smelling?

"Another trap."

"What did you say, Kofe?" Called Nadre who busied herself tending the small campfire.

"The forest is a trap."

"That's what you think, or what you know?"

"Neither. Its something I feel." He tried to explain.

"Well, I'll test your 'feeling'." With that she carelessly tossed a smoldering stick into the canopy above the waggon path.

A horrific sickening yowl, more felt than heard, rang out from the vines as the hot end of the stick seared them. Then, almost faster than eyes can discern, other vines, moving like leaf disguised serpents, surged in to crush and otherwise devour the stick. Within a few blinks of the eye, nothing discernible remained. The vines continued prowling, moving to and for, opening and closing the canopy above the waggon road to the bright mid-day sun, still searching for more victims.

"Holy One, protect us!" Oros prayed loudly.

Some of the others stared in awe of the monstrous greenery. Kofe, noticing the same vines also loped on the ground at the edge of the waggon path, took a hot brand to another vine. It winced back into the dung smelling undergrowth before he even touched it. Startled, he jumped back, just as a vine from above dropped a sticky noose about him. Other vines rushed to join in, facilitating his capture.

Screaming for his life as his feet left the ground, the others turned to see his futile struggling. Rux noticed that five vines, dangling from the canopy and under great stress with their burden, stopped moving, as if to wait for reinforcements. Rux, his fingers together, sent a bolt of lightening into the clenching vines, severing them like a broad axe through tallow. Kofe dangled a moment in mid-air, then plunged six feet into the high grasses of the waggon road. Deep Owl and Nooy rushed to pull the tenacious vines from him.

The viney forest screamed. It was an evilness comprized of terror, completely unknowing of defeat. The severed vines dripped red, thick red, blood red sap. The sap produced a nauseating stench; one of death and decay, of vileness. Then, as if to verify the theology of the Holiness Code, the other blood-sucking vines attacked the wounded ones. The overhead canopy became a turgid morass of twisting, winding and devouring green serpents. No one in their right state of mind could consider these things 'vines'. But the lesson, now exemplified, exonerated itself: evil is self-destructive, feeding upon itself.

Paradoxically, the mounts seemed oblivious to the wretched scenario, serenely chewing on the grasses of the trail. Luuft, drugged into sleeping again, also missed the terror. Jelkio and Nadre wiped Kofe off with an astringent that helped his blood to clot faster. His shocked demeanor wore off, and he fainted.

"Damn this place." Nooy murmured.

"That can be arranged." Rux allowed with a wicked grin.

"So that's your gift?"

"Yes..... Shall I use it again?" He placed his hands together.

"NO! STOP!" Qill yelled. Rux hesitated. "It is not needful to destroy the vines at this time, especially as we must travel through them. They know we offer pain and not food. I believe we shall travel in peace."

Rux deliberated; the suggestion adequately dealt with the vines, but it did nothing to avenge this friend's pain, nor did it recon with his sense of justice. Then he raised his fingers.

"Knock it off, Rux." Oros bellowed. "Save it for later."

Reluctantly he dropped his hands. "You owe me."

"How long is this damned vine filled tunnel?" Deep Owl asked, anxious.

"How can we know?" Came Oros' curt reply.

"Then let's move now, I'm not crazy enough to sleep in this God forsaken tunnel." Walking between the ruts of the waggon path, staring at the ground, tomahawks at the ready, they literally ran through the viney tunnel.

Early evening brought them to a large clearing, one showing signs of much use, there being a well-stocked supply of wood and several plank-built shacks. From the clearing, the same deadly vined path twisted off to the south.

"Check around for booby-traps." Ordered Deep Owl. "We've had enough surprizes for today."

A thorough investigation showed the inviting shacks to be vine infested. Another shack retained remnants of various dry goods, all spoiled by the damp. The last vestiges of food ended up as supper, such as it was;

old bread, a few pieces of dried rabbit and cold herbal tea. Due to the circumstances, the consensus of the group kept any fire from being started. The same consensus also placed a double guard for the night, this time the women volunteered and were accepted with little discussion.

Luuft ate some bread then slept stretched out, complaining that his toes should wiggle, but they didn't. He further mentioned that he felt no pain, though he wasn't exactly sure what Oros did to his back.

Shooting stars and both moons made for an interesting sky; at this juncture in their journey simply surviving removed any poetic notion to a far, almost forgotten corner of their lives. Even for Jelkio, a stranger to this land of Haaf, even their survival until the end of the following day, was as much as her heart could carry.

Their breakfast of stale bread and tea was rudely interrupted by the sounds of waggons and coarse shouting. The party scurried for cover. Because of the vines, this maneuver necessitated moving back along the tunnel path. Oros, dressed in his priestly robe, remained seated about the fire circle. Rux flanked the right side of the incoming tunnel, Kofe and Nooy covered the left.

The ruckus increased; individual voices barked commands. The regular creaking sounds of the waggons ceased. An advance party crashed through the tall grasses of the path. As they rounded the bend, the three troopers, casually swinging broadaxes against the grasses, halted in their booted tracks. Oros stood and waved to them.

"Ho! Priest!" Shouted the lead trooper.

"Come and have some tea!" Oros smiled as he called back to them.

"What the hell are you doing here? This is not your property." A surly arrogance backed his accusing words.

"But this is part of the Holy One's creation. It belongs to all his children." Oros deliberately sermonized the men.

"Wrong stupid priest!" The helmeted trooper yelled as the three stormed across the small clearing, broadaxes raised. "This land belongs to another lord, the God of the Dragons!"

"Then I must assume you really don't want any herbal tea." Oros said flatly as he set his cup down. Simultaneously two black fletched arrows pierced the backs of the trailing men. They silently crashed face first into the grassy turf. Their leader, enraged by Oros' preaching, never saw nor heard his men fall. He did see Oros sweep his robe open to draw his sword.

"Just drop the sword and turn around." Oros commanded the mounted soldier.

The trooper smirked, the odds still ran against this arrogant fool. Then he looked around for his men.

"Yer mens be sleepin'." Nooy drawled in his atrocious accent.

"Sleeping forever,.... in hell." Kofe added. His arrow pointed at the arrogant trooper's heart. "Now, you'll apologize to the priest you insulted."

The trooper commenced an ugly reply, then toppled in a heap. Without further words, they dragged off the trooper, and stripped him. Nooy became the new trooper. The other uniforms, being bloodied, were tossed out-of-sight.

"Shall we invite the others to join us?" Nooy asked Oros while he indicated the southern path with his finger.

"As soon as you lose the bow. Quite out-of-place, you know."

A toss of bow, followed by quiver and Nooy readily marched to the waggons and troops waiting around the bend. Rux pursued, keeping close to the deep shadows. Nooy hailed the mounted leader from a distance of some three hundred feet.

There was no mistaking the silver-black dragon embroidered on his red tunic. With his gloved hand, he motioned for the waggons to move forward, slowly.

Rux, now far ahead of the others, launched himself into a shallow ditch just off the main path; its dry grey dirt blending well with his tattered clothing. All four waggons moved by, three loaded with tarpaulin covered supplies, the other carried a 'cage' full of intoxicated 'blue ladies'. Rux anxiously bit his lip when they proceeded by. The rear guard amounted to an undisciplined platoon on foot. More of their effort went into deriding the ladies, than protecting their cargo. Obviously, this vine-guarded territory posed little threat to the so-called dragon god and his followers.

The skirmish began as soon as the quick-witted leader realized Nooy, his braids sticking out like black wings, wasn't included in the advance guard.

"Attack!" He screamed to the four other mounted men who rode behind him.

He turned and ran to the campsite, the mounted troopers gaining. The Yldans waited until the troopers cleared the corners, then fired. Three of unsuspecting men rolled from their Stripers without a word: the fourth threw his broadaxe, hit nothing and fled back to the waggons. Cursing all the while, the rear guard fast-marched beside the waggons, responding to their leader's final command.

Rux, in an exaggerated performance, strode to the middle of the waggon path, behind the rear guard. "Where do you think you're going?" He called up the line.

Half the platoon stopped. They turned back to meet the intruder. Calmly Rux waited until they cleared the waggon, then, with one savagely slashing motion of his fingers, the troopers collapsed on top of each other, dead. Next, without a word nor a thought towards revenge, Rux demolished the 'blue ladies' and their cage with a ball of intense heat, immediately rendering them 'ashes', leaving the waggon and team unhurt. The teamster threw a curved dagger at Rux, jumped from his seat and darted into the undergrowth. Rux anguished more from his tormented cries than he did from the dagger's gouge in his right thigh.

One mounted trooper and half the platoon reached the campsite, totally unaware of Rux. The explosion from the waggons suddenly alerted them. They were surrounded; vines along the sides, the Yldans and company in front, and who-knew-what behind them. The teamster's harrowingly frenzied screams only added to their anxiousness. A terrified team of Massive Blues stampeded through their red tunicked ranks, scattering the troopers. The waggon careened sideways through the campsite, flipping over and skidding into the harnessed team. Bones crunched and snapped.

Seizing the moment of confusion, the half platoon charged across the same open area. Arrows brought five down. At close quarters, intense hand-to-hand combat ensued. The last mounted trooper charged into the tunnel, trampling Qill. Luuft desperately flung himself at the Striper's hind leg as it galloped past him, catching a neck shattering blow from the iron-shod hoof, while hurtling the rider into the deadly canopy above. Within moments, the bloody skirmish ended. The last red-tunicked trooper fell.

"So be it!" Deep Owl disgustedly yelled. "Another one headed for hell."

Rux pulled around, driving the second supply waggon. "No one left behind me." He said flatly and then cursed under his breath. He bled from the thigh wound, his breeches dark red to his ankle. "Maybe these supplies ...." He stopped short, staring at Luuft. He saw the grotesque angle of his neck. "Wait here!" He shouted, especially at the two ladies. He climbed down and limped over to Luuft. Before anyone else noticed, he gently moved Luuft's head back to a normal position and held it there.

"I'm sorry." He haltingly informed the others as they came running over, "But Luuft is dead."

Silence, silence broken only by the wind gusting through the overhead vines. A sacred silence reigned for a long time after Rux spoke. The badly bruised Qill neglected his wounds as he too contemplated the ugliness of the skirmish and the price it cost. The ladies wept openly, resting on each other's shoulders.

"There are many questions I demand answers for." Deep Owl sullenly threatened no one in particular.

Rux swallowed his struggling sense of remorse, as usual. Not as commiseration for the 'blue ladies', their judgement being precluded by their choice, but that same incessant battle with his 'gift'.

While the nervously twitching vines prowled for other food, the men prepared Luuft's body for burial. The two Massive Blues, dead of hemorrhage, were quickly buried with those bodies of the traitors, what few they located. The broken waggon, minus its cargo of food stuffs, became the wood for the campfire as well as Luuft's funeral pyre. The three remaining waggons formed a rough triangular fortress with the six Massive Blues and the six stripers tethered along the waggon tongues.

"This is the water we were given!" Jelkio exclaimed as the ladies randomly searched the supplies. "I recognize the red square on the barrel."

"Then from Haaf North come supplies for the damned one's experiments...... There, so it seems, his followers dare to wear his uniform..... Has the whole city sold out?" Oros, upset at the find, delineated a worst case scenario. "Perhaps, we should head in another direction once we clear this infernal forest."

Jelkio took a rather dim view of such unwarranted speculation. "And I suppose you know everything?" She taunted him, eyes blazing hostilely. "Shut up, you old fool!"

His head peered over his belly to explore his usually hidden feet, his face burnt. "You are quite right.....I have no reason to burden you with my own foibles... I am sorry...We have enough to do as is."

"Apology accepted." Rux muttered. His brusqueness touched off something inside of Jelkio; she sobbed openly, uncontrollably.

"Damn you!" She pounded her fists on his thin chest. He wrapped his arms about her, holding her firmly but not hurting her. "Damn you and this whole thing...this ...this idiotic journey."

"And why is it damned?" Rux spoke calmly, trying to meet her gaze. She continued to fight him. "What is the burden that you hide?" He half-accused the beautiful blue-hued lady.

Her hands suddenly paused from their intense hammering. Her

tear-filled eyes met Rux's understanding gaze. "Since we began, every new friend I've made, has died, usually trying to rescue me. And I'm left alone. ..." Her crying recommenced, but her pounding did not. Rux kept a firm hold on the lady, perhaps as a bridge to helping her, perhaps to convince her that he also knew what being different and alone meant, perhaps both. "Luuft was the last Haafian......... Sarg and Vauk and Brey, killed by the damned volcano....and over twenty Yldans with them, including our Queen Sjura and..." Her sobbing returned, breaking off the story.....the pent-up grief...her sense of being a stranger, an outcast whose skin color relegated her as a stereotyped evil-worshipping whore...All these uglinesses that blighted her life. "And ...my best friend, Tiello.....Everyone is gone!!!!!" Finally, out of tears from the sobbing and out of energy, Jelkio suddenly realized Rux kept her from falling over, moreover, there existed no signs of rejection or judgement in his face or his encircling arms. She learned her head on his chest, sad, emptied and thankful.

Oros, aided by Qill, began the funeral service for Luuft as the first streaks of dusk oranged the blue-grey cloudless sky. He was dressed, as best as possible, in the uniform of the Light Striper, most of material coming from the waggon's cargo. With his broadaxe long gone, Nooy asked to substitute one of the tomahawks. Oros nodded, tearfully appreciative of the gesture.

Memorized funeral liturgy from Oros, prayers from Qill and a blessing, in the Tath tongue, from a tearful Jelkio, comprized the service. They stood silently as the flames claimed Luuft's remains.

That evening they told stories as they sat inside the waggon fortress warmed by the flickering shadowy light of the evening cook fire. Such fellowship brought a new dimension to the group. Luuft, like many heroes before him, created a stronger community by his death.

Among the multitude of treasures found on board the waggons, none more pleased the ladies than the discovery of beautiful ornate gowns, not too dissimilar from the ones Jelkio wore while incarcerated in the volcano.

With a number of alterations, Nadre, who was bustier and taller than the blue skinned Jelkio, produced a dress almost as provocative as the one she wore back at the tavern. All of this, occupying the early morning, forced the men into furnishing an edible breakfast. If one enjoyed fresh eggs, slabs of ham and hunks of dark break with strong tea, then breakfast, attested to by the ladies' smiles, they succeeded.

Before mounting up, the men re-armed themselves with the oldstyle crossbows and well-worn swords found in the third waggon. Three cases of new steel speartips were also found along with four stacks of ancient round shields. The bundles of blood red uniforms with the embroidered silver-black dragon became food for the predatory vines, which made little distinction between living and innate objects in their hideous scavenging. The workmen's clothing, however, was immediately appropriated to replace the rabbit skin breeches as well as the tattered rags of Rux and Oros. No size fit the too tall and lanky Rux. His newest outfit rendered him much akin to a scarecrow. However, with knee boots pulled up, his appearance improved to that of a country simpleton. Rux quickly became deaf to the snickering about him.

They moved out in quiet. A mournful emptiness still dug at their insides. The need for vengeance coursed through their minds and emotions. They still journeyed in the midst of an evil foreboding land. They entered the vine-laced tunnel from which the damned one's troopers, just yesterday, emerged. Rux turned in his saddle. With rapid movements of his fingers, he split the vined canopy at its apex. The bolt of bluish lightening sundered the green ceiling, causing each side to cascade in upon itself. The unheard, yet deafening rage of the vines startled the party. In the dizzying sunlight that now claimed the tunnel's floor, the party watched in horror as the severed vines, bleeding their red blood-like sap, were devoured by those still healthy vines which bordered the sides of the trail.

Rux smiled ruefully. "That should keep anything from following us." He spoke to no one in particular.

"Actually," Qill commented on the deadly vines from the waggon where Nadre deliberately placed him." This reminds me of the old wisdom saying.."

"That evil is self destructive." Nadre mocked, poking him with her elbow. "I've heard it enough."

"Don't be so testy." He shot back. He grimaced from the bruises suffered in being ridden down by the Striper....... "And you're wrong. The saying is this: 'When it finds no food, evil dies.'"

"I find little difference between the sayings."

"I suspect you don't." Qill did not reproach her, but seemed indifferent. "Perhaps 'tis just as well. Too often we find ourselves not fully examining our 'supposed' wisdom."

Jelkio, riding next to Nadre, shook her head at the conversation, her long hair wrapping about her blue face. "It is not incorrect for a lady should reprimand a Shaman." She said, her eyes staring at her slippered feet. "In Tath, they would whip you for such disrespect of one that our god called to serve Him." She hesitated, as if to continue, but remained silent.

Nadre, always used to besting someone in a game of words, now became utterly embarrassed; Jelkio cut her to the quick. She berated herself, aloud, for having offended the Shaman. Rux looked on, amazed and bewildered by this too often rough-and-tumble lady.

"I.... did not mean..... to offend." Nadre stammered for almost a dozen times, in spite of the fact that Qill forgave her at least two dozen times.

"Nadre!" Rux's voice sternly ploughed through her remorse. "You are forgiven!" He gently met her eyes with his gaze, one that reminded her of the events of a night not to long ago. "You are forgiven." He spoke softly now.

She half-smiled, half-wept, reflecting upon the truth Oros and Rux extended to her: a tormenting truth that finally she allowed to set her free. "The prison is gone." She whispered.

"What did you say?" Asked Jelkio, puzzled.

"Just something from the past, something I dare never forget." She inclined her dark face towards Rux, knowingly. "Thanks." She mouthed to him. Rux bowed, awkward as can be, from his prancing Striper.

Deep Owl and Nooy performed as the advance guard, galloping out-of-sight on their newly gotten Stripers. Kofe and Oros drove ahead with the other waggons, where Rux had tethered the extra Stripers. Rux dropped far to the rear, mainly in order to rebandage this wound. The gentle rhythmic swaying of the waggons sent the bruised Qill to the land of dreams, and Nadre slumped, resting her head on Jelkio's shoulder, forcing the inexperienced Tath to hold the reins.

However, she welcomed this challenge, if only as a diversion from her hidden sorrow: she still could not weep for her dead Haafian love. Her heart refused to acknowledge the truth.

A shallow stream provided for the solitary stop of the day, and that simply to rest and water their mounts. The sunny day, with a dusky hue, blew thin clouds across the wide sky, for, except for the volcanoes behind them, the forest ran level before them. As they pulled into another campsite, one almost identical to the one used last evening, Deep Owl and Nooy stood by a small cooking fire. Supper boiled in the pot. Rux, arriving later, expressed his concern over the site, there being three other exits, two heading almost due south, the other in an eastward direction.

"We'll be taking the east road. It leads most quickly to Haaf North." Deep Owl sketched out tomorrow's traveling with the others.

"But how safe do you find it?" Rux endeavored to sound trusting, but failed.

"The vines are gone. The road joins the main road from the Battle not but ten miles from here." The reply cautious.

"Then you rode that far?"

"Yes." Deep Owl smiled. "The road is well-used. We'll find travelers on it, mostly merchants."

"Yep." Nooy chimed in. "Tomorrow we'll sell this stuff to those going back home. That should cause a stir when these old weapons show up."

"Very plausible idea, Nooy. You're more devious than I thought." Qill laughed. "I wonder how the Evil One going to repay those merchants he considered bought and paid for. Imagine, selling 'his' ill-gotten gain. Certainly will be difficult to hide his damned army from the Light Striper."

"Glad to hear that you approve." Nooy commented as he drug a package from a saddlebag. "Here!" He yelled, tossing the package to Rux. "Thought you might appreciate something 'fitting' to wear into town."

Warily, Rux opened the package, disclosing clothing most appropriate to his stature. His weird smile aptly acknowledged the gift as well as the joke behind it. "Thanks, perhaps I just might owe you one, ...some day." His eye brows twitched meaningfully.

There existed a 'something' in Nooy that often caused people to underrate him. Even in his cute, unabashed attack upon Rux's wardrobe, followed by his gift of properly fitting breeches and an extra long blue tunic more than balanced his words, leaving poor Rux in a state apoplexy. That this came so natural, so innocently, impressed Jelkio. She found herself a bit too interested in the Yldan and pulled back, slightly shaken.

"You not finding this funny?" Nadre queried, noticing that Jelkio didn't laugh with the others.

"A..A.. No!" She hurriedly lied. "Actually I ....I found myself thinking about something else." She quietly confessed.

Nadre reached out and put her arm over Jelkio's bare shoulder. "I find myself doing that sometimes too. ..There's so much going on...Its hard to find a place to fasten yourself...Or a person..." Mumbled Nadre, thinking not of anyone, but of her former life in the south, in a time before she became a criminal. Suddenly she smiled, forgiveness covered all of that life as well, according to Oros. She felt free, but this time she would control her freedom.

Evening conversations died away as, one-by-one members of the group drifted off to sleep. Qill slept in the waggon, despite his violent protesting. The expansive campsite, being too wide for the vines, allowed the double moons' pale light to reflect off the wind rustled leaves. This painted a wondrous silent peaceful show for everyone. Nooy blew some beautiful soft tunes on his carved wooden flute. The camp's tranquil atmosphere brought dreams of the far past. Except for Jelkio: from across the campfire, she only pretended to sleep, choosing to study the flautist instead.

Ten miles to the main travel road, it was. Another ten placed them in the confines of Haaf North. The journey, however, deliberately transpired over the course of three days. Their military hardware sold well, but they offered it only to those heading towards D'Ka or south. The Yldans, though not common in this eastern area, were accepted as merchants.. They sold the workmen's tunics cheap enough that even a poor farmer afforded one for each of his raggedy children. The poorly made and badly used swords required the greatest salesmanship, until Kofe demonstrated they worked well for harvesting wheat or chopping weeds.

Meanwhile, Jelkio found herself alone, tending the campsite some fifty feet from the road. Her blue skin endangered the entire group. On one level, this separation enraged her, even if Nadre, whom travelers refused to buy from, became a regular visitor. On an other level, she thoroughly enjoyed their concern for her safety, and, to a significant degree, the solitude assisted her in processing the past. Part of her soul hurt deeply: Would she ever see the vast steppes of Tath again? Would she ever be with her family again? What about Queen Sjura? How would the people know what actually happened? For three tedious days, these dismal questions and their tenuous answers, if they might suffice to be that solid, constantly nagged at her.

Per planned routine, Rux and Oros meandered into Haaf North the evening of the first 'merchant's day', posing as a couple of drunks. Port cities' taverns happily accepted anyone with a few coins, just as they usually supplied information to those who cared to listen. Haaf North was no different. Examining the great deep water port from a rise, most everything appeared normal. A number of other things presented themselves as extraordinary.

The noise of the port city, even one with high granite walls broken by three huge towered gates which echoed and amplified the commotion, was definitely missing. Obviously, at least one or two major 'doings' in the port city ran amiss. Thus, instead of entering as two drunks, they rode in as two monks. If stopped and searched, their mission concerned the immediate delivery of the scrolls and papers found at Krucik's mansion.

They entered the city, pausing to bless great numbers of people, most whose grip on reality, Oros assumed, had somewhat departed. Eyes vacant and staring, without a sense of hope. Common everyday people, those who worked the wharves and manned the ships and the storekeepers, all shaken and grabbing at whatever benefits the Holy One might offer. Rux almost felt as if he reigned as some type of hero, a thought he definitely abhorred.

A quick look about Haaf North showed an abnormally subdued mood: double guards posted at all intersections, mounted patrols clinked along the cobbled streets watching for signs of trouble. Taverns, even at this early hour, showed signs of closing. Few windows on the first floors remained open, in spite of the gentle breeze coming off the bay. The merchant's tents pitched in the square, what few existed to contest for the always cramped space, stood emptied of goods as well as buyers and sellers. The usual party-in-the-square, with drunks and pickpockets, and the 'popular ladies', all nonexistent.

As Rux and Oros turned their silver and black mounts towards the wharves, a patrol of Light Stripers approached them.

"Docks be off limits, priests." An unidentified voice spoke. "It be too dangerous for ye. Please head back to the abbey."

Before their mounts could turn to obey, the Light Striper patrol encircled them. Rux stretched and then moved his fingers together. Oros, extremely fast for his extravagant bulk, kicked him and shook his head: 'no'.

"I've not seen the city so somber." Oros spoke, glancing about him to locate the patrol's leader. "What is happening here?"

A veteran trooper, reins in his left hand, the other sleeve blowing in the wind. Rux caught himself staring.

"Lost it at the last battle." He said. "I bee'd infantry then. Damn if this arm didn't cost the bastard god six of his own."

Rux abruptly pulled his eyes away.

"Don't go feeling sorry, priest. This is just part of being a trooper." He acknowledged forthrightly.

Oros face twisted in consternation. "Say those words again..."

"The names Jed. Sorry for swearing." His contrition showed. "I don't mean the bastard god part though. That's true. We all heard the Holy One say so himself, right after the battle."

Oros' face completely warped itself, shattered by disbelief, riddled with the unknown. Rux started to speak, then realized nothing came from his mouth.

"AH!" Said Jed. "We've seen these faces before. Happens to them that not been listening very much these days." Rux and Oros exchanged glances as Jeb, motioning with his right arm stump, headed the patrol in the direction of the abbey. "Well, I guess its my responsibility to catch you priests up on a few things. Mind you, in spite of what them other high-up priests been worried about since the Holy One spoke, I'm just telling you the truth....nothing added."

The trip to the abbey became a mind boggling enterprise for the two priests. The humble, yet proud Jed, step by step produced the most detailed account of a battle ever spoken. Jed stopped the entire escorting party, out of reverence, as he quoted the Holy One in regarding the other, the damned Evil One. "Bastard!" Jed called him, then spit on the ground. "The Holy One's son or not," Jed noted with more than grim determination. "I'm willing to settle the debt with him, personally .....very personally."

"Your arm?"

"No, skinny.."

"Rux, the name is Rux."

"No Rux. I explained that before." Jed irritatingly shot back. "You weren't listening. The missing arm is part of the job. It happens." He splashed the cobblestones with spit before continuing. "My men, half of my platoon fell to his new Kyykki. Them and their spears. This happened afore the Holy One arrived."

"Sorry." Rux said slowly.

"At least you be honest. That I can appreciate, especially from a priest." The rest of the patrol chuckled.

"And so now there's a cliff dividing the Dark Lands from Haaf?" Oros struggled to change the topic.

"OH...It be hugest thing I ever saw. And with a new lake at the bottom....well them Kyykki got stuck in the hot north, nowhere else for them to go." His toothy smile flashed. "The Holy One reached out for us believers and just ripped the earth in two. Afore that is when he told the bastard to keep his place. ..But I fear there's more worser times coming." Jed commented matter-of-factly.

Both so-called priests, realizing the new danger--danger to a people this trooper couldn't comprehend--said quiet prayers. Even so, prayer could not and did not stabilize the multiplicity of new thoughts brought by the straightforward Jed. Oros stood in awe of the simple concrete faith of Jed. Such devotion brought up feelings of a much younger, less worldly Oros, one unblemished by time and society, one who refused to recon with the concept of compromize. And the more he fumed about Jed, the worse he felt about himself. The group rode on in silence.

The large greystone abbey rose as a squarish structure, built as much for defense as for worship. In this respect, it differed little from the rest of town, for the city, now with some thirty thousand Haafians within her confines, had been rebuilt after the Battle. Even the newly dredged harbor permitted adequate supplying should a siege begin. Streets and intersections became straight and wide, wooden buildings disappeared.

Looking up, Oros noted a white marble chalice, some six feet tall, mounted above the abbey's iron-gated entrance. While it recognized the sacredness of community and communion for the believers, the chalice signified one of the few differences which set the abbey apart from other similar structures.

The mounted patrol paused on the light cobblestone street while the brothers labored to raise the heavy iron-gate. Or, perhaps, it took so long because the brothers detested being bothered. Their scarcely hidden self-righteous comments angered Oros, who hadn't even been addressed yet. Nor were his papers asked for. Oros' stomach ran queasy, full of a dreadful suspicion, he carefully motioned to Rux, 'be ready.' Rux nodded.

"Jed, you never finished explaining to us why you escorted us to the abbey?" Oros spoke as the gate slowly rose. "What is the situation?"

"You don't know." He looked surprized. "But then you just arrived." He explained himself to himself. "Well, I might alarm you but, our townspeople, at night, been ending up dead."

"Not dead." Kicked in another trooper. "Murdered, by 'somethings' wearing hoods. ....Ripped limb from limb, and not a drop of blood found in any of them....And anyone is fair game, old, young, rich, poor, it don't matter."

"When did this start?" Rux asked, sighting up the abbey.

"About a half a cycle afore the last cargo ship arrived...maybe some ten plus three dawns?" The other trooper answered, asking his fellows for some confirmation.

"That's about right." Jed drawled.

"How many Haafians been butchered?" Rux pressed, still examining the immediate environment.

"Many fifty plus some."

"Yea!" Croaked another voice. "But we gots reports of more in that be missing. ...It be an evil thing happening."

Just then, a burly bald headed monk ducked under the half-raised gate and approached Oros and Rux. Strangely, he carried a spear. "What you two be wanting?" He growled. "I'm the Abbot. No one told me about any visitors." He held out his dirty paw, expecting Oros and Rux to dismount and kiss his greasy ring.

Instead, Oros showed him a scroll. The King's stamp and seal visibly imprinted upon it. The Abbot moved closer to see, then stared at the scroll, impatient and absolutely unmoved.

"So," He smirked. "You have a sealed scroll. What's that to me?"

Oros moved quickly, before Rux acted upon the Abbot's obvious incompetence. "Dear Abbot, its merely a letter I am to read to you, and the congregation, written by the Council of Elders."

"Who are the..."

"Ah, I'd love to hear what the holy ones say." An excited Jed interrupted.

With a rapid twist of his fingers, Rux collapsed the Abbot. His ring hand tightly clutching at his heart, he slowly tumbled to the cobblestones, face flushed and barely breathing.

"The Abbot's stricken!" Yelled one of the monks still wrangling with the gate.

Jed and two other troopers hit the ground almost before the Abbot did. Rux danced his Striper to the gate, blocking any interference from the other monks. Oros waved another document, this one giving him access to whatever he needed.

"Can you read Jed?" Oros yelled down from his mount.

"Enough, if I have to."

"Read this, then bring the Abbot to the barracks for treatment." His voice unusually firm. "Quickly, before he dies."

While two troopers put the burly Abbot over a Striper, Jed read the

King's note. His face whitened with a tinge of embarrassment. "I'm sorry." He saluted Oros

"We are at your disposal, SIR!" He boomed in his most military voice.

"Wonderful!" Oros blasted. "Let's get him to the barracks before he dies." Oros turned his mount to follow the lead trooper. "Rux, watch the rear."

"Done!" He quipped, as his Striper kicked the first monk who began to protest. "Let's move out!" He bellowed while cutting the rope holding the gate. Giving his mount the spurs to the flanks, he caught the patrol within three blocks.

"How far to the barracks?" He called to the nearest trooper.

"Only a quarter mile, Sir!"

Rux smiled at the formality. "Thank you, son."

The streets and intersections being previously cleared of townsfolk, they galloped to the castle-like barracks within a few moments. A quick call from Jed allowed them to gallop into the center court unimpeded. As the wooden gate swung shut behind them, a foot patrol formed up to meet them and another patrol mounted up, ready to leave.

Shortly beyond the middle of the night the Abbot finally coughed up some information, His resistance to the concoctions Oros liberally borrowed from the Yldans had been formidable. But he finally gave way, finding it most difficult to explain away his blood-red tunic with the silver-black dragon embroidered upon it hidden beneath his priestly robe. And, no longer could the sweating arrogant fool negotiate his way through the myriad of questions Oros pumped down his thick throat. His confession arrived in bits and pieces: he was never a monk, Krucik bought him the position and paid for Church building as well. He, bloated with self-importance, was a 'most important' merchant shipping 'whatever' to Krucik's mansion.

"Furthermore", he blabbered on. "My clerical position places me above the law."

"Not anymore." Jed blurted out angrily. "Sorry." He said, forgetting that a Captain of the Light Striper being present.

"Quite all right, Jed." Said the white-haired man. "That's exactly what I be thinking."

"Yes, Sir."

"Well, Oros." The Captain caught Oros' gaze. "What next?"

"I think, from information a lady provided me, that you might be able to end the city's terror this night."

The Captain smiled. "Go on. I'm beginning to see why the King gave you the letter."

Ignoring the final comment, Oros slapped the Abbot's paled face. "Wake up, you fool!" Then he tossed a flagon of water on his face. "Time for another question." The limpid configuration on the 'phony' Abbot's face bore no more traces of opposition.

By the Grace of the Holy One, only a few people witnessed the Abbot's confession. If his blurred words were true, half the garrison belonged to him. He laughingly bragged about how well paid they were. His money to pay the men came from recruitment of young ladies for the troops. His laugh at this point became a hideous rasp, which raised the hairs on one's arms.

"The troopers are the demon lords, leaders of the greatest army Haaf will ever see." The filthy Abbot reveled in his confession. He suddenly sat up, glazed eyes seeing that which remained invisible to the others. He called out. "Yes, Master, I am here!" Sickening glee filled his face as he reached out to an unknown 'something'. A cold chilling darkness swept through the room, coalescing just before the Abbot's upraised hand.

"Behind me!" Oros demanded of everyone. "It's the Evil One!" He flapped his chubby arms wildly as they scrambled to obey him. "Don't say anything!" He cautioned, his eyes never leaving the solidifying evil-spewing shadow.

The Abbot weeping, knelt before his horned and scaled master, who unmercifully yanked him up by his broad shoulders, his three-clawed hands, drawing blood.

"You bungling idiot!" Snarled the evil one. "You know the penalty for failure!" And with those grating words, the slime-covered fangs of the evil one opened wide, biting off the still smiling Abbot's head. He promptly gulped and swallowed it, dropping the headless flopping body to the stoney floor.

Then he turned to Oros, blood flying from his fanged maw as he bellowed. "And who are you to stand before the ruler of the world?" He spitefully challenged. "Bow and live!" He demanded.

Oros, shaking like a willow tree in a thunderstorm, braced himself and then spoke. "So, you are the son of the Holy One?"

The demon-like beast, caught off-guard, stepped backward. "And who provided that lie?" He sneered, yet a sense of unstableness existed.

"Your esteemed above-all-else-in-creation Father, our God. He did so at the last battle, where He further divided your damnable property from the rest....Perhaps you have forgotten?" Oros' voice began to ring righteousness.

"You forget who I am?" He shouted, enraged enough to shake the building. He stomped forward as if ready for another meal.

Oros met him eyeball-to-bloodshot eyeball. "And you forget who our Protector is." He said flatly. "Perhaps Our Father should show up, where then will you be? You are far beyond the limits set for you." Oros' sermonized. "In fact, you have no protection here....and we don't want you here." The fat priest stomped his foot. "Begone!"

Clawed paws dug into Oros' shoulders, drawing him near the evil one's mouth. "Even a gifted one can hurt you here." Oros spoke loudly. The motion stopped as the evil one squinted in disbelief and profound arrogance. Then, as Oros slowly lifted from the floor, Rux side-stepped him bringing his fingers together simultaneously. A pure blue streak of lightning sawed through the evil one's scaly wrist faster than a blink of the eye.

Oros dropped to the floor along with the evil one's severed green bleeding paw. The wounded bastard, howled as the green blood shot from his stump. Instantly, he returned to shadow, and disappeared, leaving the room reeking of hell.

"Maybe now you'll appreciate your gift, Rux." Oros moaned from the bloodied floor. Then he passed out.

Chapter 8

Since the catastrophe of the King's inspection of the New Knights, the sickly man remained secured with the best physicians in Krabo. This illustrious group of eight tended the King day and night. He was never without two of them. Under their dutiful care, the King had all but disappeared from sight.

Next to the King's seven room suite, the Captain retained an office that doubled as bedroom and sitting room. From his small office the administrative rulings and orders originated and were disbursed. Below these third floor rooms, in the great High Council Hall, the usual deliberations of merchants and nobles had fallen off.

Since the last battle, the New Knights received new recruits, all from the nobility, of course. Baste began to work from a merit system, creating an elite 'light guard' from serf volunteers. He wanted to mount some phalanxed trained infantry on Stripers.

"Strictly an experiment," Baste explained to Vosnob. "We don't know what the bastard will show up with next."

Vosnob responded with a muted nod, for, in spite of the success of the New Knights of the Light Striper and all the innovations they skillfully utilized, he wrung his hands in unhidden desperation. "Do whatever you believe correct." Vosnob answered Baste flatly.

The Captain turned from gazing out his window. "Listen, Vosnob, I'm as aware as anybody about the negative way you see the Holy One's intervention at the battle. You believe its a divine omen signifying that we are too weak to defeat the bastard. On the other hand, the Holy One's appearance answered questions we struggled with for the last fifty years: we finally know who the enemy is.."

"Most certainly," Vosnob interjected. "That's why we can't defeat him....we are now fighting a god...... Mortals don't win battles with gods........ Its impossible." He tossed his huge callused hands into the air. "Its impossible." He quietly muttered.

"Are you so sure?" The Yldian Elder, Blue Turtle, commented as he materialized on the padded chair by the window. "I was of the notion, erroneous as it now is, that only the Holy One was uncreated'. I don't believe the bastard is 'uncreated'; no more than my own son is uncreated..... Now, damn it!" Blue Turtle smiled obliquely. "You dare to tell me this is nothing but a lie. The bastard and the Holy One are equals."

This last statement caused a stir among those gathered, including the two last-to-arrive Elders, namely Oros' real father, the totally disarming Kloshic and the invariably independent Chaplain from the garrison at Pinduala.

"Say your piece, old man. We've heard heresy before." His grin showed bright teeth, but hid his green tinted slanting eyes.

"I'm not sure who is the l enemy, sometimes!" A visibly irritated Vosnob shot back.

"Answer the question. Its still fishing season, you understand."

"Yes, oldest man." Vosnob mumbled, hinting at some little disrespect. "Damn!..... I don't have a cute, concise answer. Its more that I feel the worst is yet to come.... And that we aren't going to fight the Kyykki too much longer."

"True enough." The Captain stated. "That's all ready been anticipated........... And we're preparing for that eventuality."

"Get to the real issue." The Chaplain pushed, impatient. "Is this so-called bastard, 'created' or 'uncreated'?"

"We supposed to vote on this issue?"

Vosnob tossed a full goblet of wine at the pernickety Baste. "This is not a voting issue...Can't any of you get serious for a few minutes?"

Isn't this the very issue we sent the honorable..."

"And fat..."

"Thank you for that needless addition, Kloshic." The Captain politely suffered. "...Oros on a Quest."

"And we really haven't heard from him for over ten full cycles, have we?" Blue Turtle posed the real biting issue.

Oros and Rux, as far as anyone could ascertain, disappeared after leaving a few dead 'goons' in a small village to the far northeast, a town far removed from their assigned destination. A village whore 'supposedly' disappeared at the same time. Beyond that, nothing of their trail survived.

"No, we haven't." Vosnob despaired openly. "Nor have we heard much from Sarg."

"But we have!" Baste corrected. "That's why we've located as many of the Dark Land's lakes as possible. With the newest catapults, thanks to Wygga and Gath, we're tossing bleach almost a half mile."

"And how long ago was that message?" Vosnob charged.

"Some eight cycles ago." His voice somber. "Nothing since."

"That's why I'm worried!" The angered Commander pounded his fist on the polished oak table. "We just don't...."

A pounding knock landed on the Captain's heavy iron banded door. Instantly the Elders faded to other destinations. Their weekly conversations to be resumed later, perhaps when the two moons rose, about a half dawn away.

Answering the pounding, the Captain yanked the door open. "What do you want?" He shouted into the physician's beet-red face.

The thinnish, long featured man stammered, shaking in his long baggy sleeved robe. "Its....the...the....thhe...Kig...King..."

"And what about the King?" The Captain held the physician by the shoulders, exposing dragon tattoos on his forearms. The Captain could not see them. "I'm waiting!"

Still stammering and now intimidated, his coarse vocalizations became bright and high pitched. He's....talking about.... about..." He suddenly stopped. "Just....fol..low." The Captain loosed the whiny physician. The fellow bounced to his feet, immediately pulling down his sleeves. He motioned the Captain to follow.

Once inside the guard-posted door of the King's suite, the head physician cheerfully guided the Captain to two other physicians waiting in the next anteroom. There sat the King, dressed in his usual sleeping robe. His countenance, bright and energetic, belied his physique. It portrayed a man weak, fleshless and listless; a grotesque living skeleton. The Captain pretended not to notice this paradox, just as he usually pretended the pretentious physicians didn't occupy most of the third floor.

"Captain," Called the King in a voice not quite his own. "Come closer."

The Captain provided his King with a perfunctory bow before seating himself to the right of his King. He waited in silence, studying the physicians' clouded and absent faces. Something very wrong, perhaps evil, lurked here.

"Now," The King spoke too perky. "Don't you think I'm beginning to recover?" He spoke knowing the answer. "Well,.... don't I look better?... I'm feeling much better."

"Yes, your Highness." The Captain said politely. "This is the most animated you've been in since....well...since you inspected your New Knights."

"Who?" Queried the King, a frown of bewilderment transplanting his recent sickly smile.

Before the Captain had opportunity to edge in a word, a heavy set physician with big fleshy hands answered in a southern accent. "Ah!" He proclaimed magnanimously. "The King is able to question now? He IS getting better."

The King smiled childishly at the empty flattery, his eyes glittering. He turned to the Captain. "Perhaps, in a few days we'll go riding?" The voice again, unnatural.

"Yes, your Majesty, if that is your desire."

"Splendid!" He gleefully clapped his hands, dangerously teetering upon his heavily cushioned seat.

A physician, dressed in an unusual red colored robe, bent over to assist the King, exposing an arm decorated with a dragon tattoo. The Captain thanked the physician for his efforts.

"It is but my honor to serve my King." The man announced unemotionally.

"I'll bet." The Captain thought to himself.

"Ah!" The southern voiced physician announced with some ceremony. "I believe the King has had enough excitement for this day.....Thank you for coming to visit, Captain."

"I welcome your invitation at any time, your Majesty." The Captain said calmly, rising to leave the anteroom. He did not appreciate the unsolicited escort to the hallway, verbally noting such as he shook the two physicians from his elbows.

Once re-ensconced in his one room office, the Captain propped his feet on the window ledge, settled back into his padded armchair and drew out his long neglected clay pipe. He fumbled about the desk drawer searching for some tobacco, stuffed his pipe unceremoniously, and striking his well-used flint, lit up, encasing the office in a pale blue cloud. That finished, he sat back to ponder his visitation with the king. Why was it so contrived? How sick was the King? Or, more likely, how were these so-called physicians keeping him sick? As he puffed on, he recognized this issue demanded an exploration from the bottom up. Just who were the eight physicians? Who assigned them to the King? He remembered the red dragon tattoo, but thought it would explain itself when the rest of the pieces fell into place. A long while later, the pipe burnt itself out, allowing the room to become visible once again. Shortly afterwards, the Captain headed out for an early supper.

Still tumbling through his unorganized thoughts, the Captain passed by the hollowed and burnt wreckage of Krucik's stable, turned right at the next block and entered a seedy-looking tavern. The candle and lamp-lit interior exposed a crowd of technical workers ruminating over the boring record keeping work of the government. These were literate men, often wiser than those administrating their respective departments, and more-often-than-not, they knew it. This nondescript tavern formed their unofficial headquarters. Here lived the subtle plotting and intrigue that often saved the high-and-mighty from themselves. Access to such knowledge is why the Captain often occupied a seat off to the side of the bar.

After piddling with a steaming bowl of onion and barley soup, and a flagon of ale, a thin-nosed gentleman with eyeglasses, an ever present occupational hazard, fell in across the planked table, spilling half his tankard. The Captain smiled as he clanked his mug with that of the second secretary of the documents' department.

"You're looking a bit too well."

"Why not Captain? Since you've taken over, its been easier to get things done. We're betting that its the military way you handle things; no politics involved, you know." The man's voice rang with the heavy bass accent from central Haaf.

"Yes, I believe I do know. But without the politics, isn't the job a bit boring?" The Captain gently steered the conversation to the point, too much time in the tavern might jeopardize him.

"Hardly," The man gurgled as he swallowed. "There's still a lot of funny business with material headed to Haaf North. We have a trace on the load of 'junked' shields heading that way. Bought by a merchant who turned out to be the Abbot!" He whispered, eyes bright and glittering.

"Keep on it, my friend." The Captain's tone business and quiet. "I have another task for you. One that may take some digging outside your department. Might you handle it?"

"Handling it is the easy part. What's in it for me?"

"Another trip to the lodge by the lake."

"For six dawns?"

"Six dawns."

"What's the assignment?" He swigged down the last of his ale and stared at the Captain.

"Eight physicians currently torment the King. I want to know who they are, where they come from, any connections they have with any nobility or merchants. I also want their qualifications documented.... Easy enough?" The Captain picked up the mug and drained it.

"See you in three dawns, same time."

"Agreed." The Captain left via a rear door, leading off the alley. From there to the market place and then, guardingly retracing his steps, returning to the one room he improperly referred to as 'home'.

The King did recognize the Captain, someone he knew for he first time in ages. Now he struggled with the raging turmoil within his mind. For dawns on end, never sleeping at night and always under the scrutinizing eyes of the 'Great Physician' and his cronies, the King's mind and body relentlessly fought off a multitude of concoctions deemed 'medicinal'. Now he began to bring himself back from the brink of the 'endless nothing', as he called it. An 'endless nothing' of no thinking, no dreaming, of nothing but dark waves permeating his drugged brain, never ceasing and changeless, yet powerful enough to drown any and all vestiges of who and what he ought to be, by virtue of the Holy One's gift. The recognition of the Captain birthed the King's last desperate hope.

The King had plenty of highly rated visitors claiming miraculous cures. Some actually did work, as long they and their concoctions remained sequestered with the King. Once gone, the old, vile elixirs returned, usually in double strength. And, who could know of any change. The physicians and their assistants were above reproach, their loyalties unquestioned, and their reports to the High Council, full of hope. More time was their eternal request. Then the King would be fit to rule once again. Until such time, the King found himself--de facto--a true prisoner, unable to perform as he had been called.

Perhaps, as a certain small voice inside his muddled and strangled brain suggested, something might happen. If not, then there existed another way to rid himself of the barbarians surrounding him--monstrous heretics who boasted of the Holy One's eminent downfall, and of their rise to glory under the coming order--a forty foot fall out his bedroom window.

A dazed smirk stayed on his face, that of a simpleton. Now it became the King's ally, allowing him to posit some ideas, struggle to concretize them, and to find some of his long lost dignity. When he was elected King, the High Council adequately supported his physical needs with a full medical staff. He now saw this insidious maneuver was designed to ruin the country from within. Had their trickery worked? The King knew not. His last true recollection was of the beginning of the New Knight's inspection. After that the dark waves never ceased their fiendish intentions to incapacitate him.

Until this time, that is. The King struggled mightily against the elixirs, reframing his thoughts. Why, out-of-nowhere, did the Captain arrive? The King had often tried, even demanded, that others be summoned. Deviously creative excuses refused each summons before, so why this change in the routine? Was the Captain suspect as well? The more he struggled with the mysteries and evil deceptions which enclosed him, the more the waves blew against his thoughts, until finally, they left him stuporous once more. Hope against hope: the King succumbed to the concoctions, sitting as a stone carved statue until the break of another dawn.

The gift of 'thought travel' as Jabbi renamed it, quelled any ideas he entertained about living safely. It terrified him to the innermost depths of his soul. One small detail missing from his destination and he just might end up caught in the middle of a tree, or hanging in midair or, the Holy One forbid, in hell. One blessing he dearly appreciated came in learning that each Elder had an identical cell room in each of the major cities. Just remember the city's name and then project himself there. Conversely, he soon realized, traveling to aid another in an unknown environment proved impossible, One could not travel where one never had been before. Even accurate descriptions given by others mattered not, for how one person delineated the spot to be transported to might contain a few errors or a misjudgment, or a misinterpretation, all possibly fatal. Jabbi figured he'd rather take his favorite Striper or, just maybe, one of those thousand foot long birds some folk around the monastery had recently been chattering about.

His continuing education proved the high point of his confinement at the monastery. The cadre of learned doctors set upon this novice with something just short of vengeance. Jabbi attacked whatever they threw at him with such a devouring energy that he, within a matter of two double moons, found himself almost at the head of the students. While the word 'student' both troubled...more likely embarrassed him...it also structured his stay and goal at the monastery. The fact of his 'calling' to the position of Elder seldom elated him. It functioned more to weigh him down, especially when he pondered the responsibilities that were guaranteed to become part and parcel of his future. There remained within him a gnawing inferiority, a doubting which questioned not only his call, but his real ability to fulfill that call. Thus he strove for a perfection never meant for any mortal. His despair materialized in his evening prayers.

"O Most Holy One," Jabbi anxiously prayed, tears of fearfulness and self-remorse dropping from his newly bearded chin into his cassock covered knees. "Why is it that I am here? There are many others who suite your Holy purposes better than I. The burden given to me is well beyond my capabilities...."

"And you may shut up." A hooded monk sitting in the corner calmly ordered. "This self-pitying routine is not excusable, nor is it productive. Furthermore, you are telling the Holy One, Blessed be His Name, that he is ignorant of who you really are. Quite a presumption on your part, isn't it?" He waited for Jabbi's answer.

"Yes...." Jabbi stuttered. "Yes...you are correct.....But..."

"'But' is a non existent category. You know that by now. Stop the self-defeating games......Live by grace." Mysteriously as he had announced himself, the monk took leave.

Jabbi could only imagine that he had spoken to one of the Elders he might never meet face-to-face. Contrary to popular belief, not all Elders met together to pass judgments and issue decrees. Another twelve circulated throughout Haaf, posing as very ordinary types of persons. Their calling made them part of the working class society, close to those whom the Holy One sought to help. The few that Jabbi encountered impressed him with their unswerving devotion and their down-to-earth practicality. He also found them unnerving. He was unwilling for all of this to be 'proper'.

During the relatively empty evenings he took it upon himself to discover the monastery. By the way the sun reflected upon the chapel tower, some four hundred feet high, but still below the ancient forest trees which surrounded it, he believed he was moved east, east beyond the lake. The endless ancient forest which formed the neighborhood consisted of huge dark evergreens. They rose as a jagged sky-pointed fence. The white stone buildings of the monastery wove about their trunks. Never had a tree fallen to the axes of the builders. This respect for the Holy One's creation, Jabbi learned, derived from the Yldans.

Incongruous as it seemed to Jabbi, the Yldans had indeed built the monastery. That history, etched upon the stones inside the chapel library and upon skins in the Upper Library of Ancient History, undeniably stated these facts. As usual, when he encountered the truth about the preconceived notions he brought with him, Jabbi felt his head swim. Then he felt the tides of his own meager and erroneous scholarship strive to drag him under. Only with the astute guidance of the Abbot, a Yldian who might pass as Blue Turtle's twin, did he remain afloat.

Following a pattern set down in Creation, the monastery formed a series of interlocking ovals and circles. The ten immense towers, signifying the wholeness of creation, were gracefully circular; their white carved stones forming a beautiful paradox against the blackness of the tree trunks. The walls bent and swayed about the same trunks, often hiding the location of other walls as they meandered about the forest, but somehow getting one to the correct tower.

Except where torch flames scorched the walls, the monastery's interior also was white, a harsh blinding white properly symbolizing the Holy One's righteousness and purity. But nothing on the bas-relief carvings which adorned most sizeable walls ever even hinted at the prospect that the Holy One had a son. In spite of the authenticity of reports from the front, Jabbi remained baffled by this problem. Which story, which evidence should be true? His muddled head, so he told himself, would burst before such a divine mystery might be resolved.

In a trance-like state, Jabbi wandered through two towers and up higher into a third, not quite aware of his journeying. Then, some six flights up, as he turned a rounded unwindowed corned, a quiet authoritative voice called out to him. Jabbi stumbled.

"Get yourself up, Jabbi." The voice called out from behind him.

Jabbi obeyed, pausing to dust off the knees of his robe. He hesitantly turned about to see the Abbot sitting behind a large stone desk studying some parchments. The wooden doorway to the Abbot's study obliquely entered the hallway directly behind Jabbi. Unless he faced the opposite direction, the passageway was all but invisible.

"Yes, Abbot."

"What brings you to the fifth tower?" He sounded a bit amused, as if he knew the answer but wanted to see how Jabbi handled the situation.

"This is the fifth tower?" Jabbi faced flushed. "I'm sorry. I will be leaving."

"But no one gave you that permission."

His face went white. "I had no permission to come here to begin with...."

The sentence protruded awkwardly upon the scene, as if a confession. "I'm not even sure how I got here."

"I shall assume that you walked."

Jabbi stood silent.

"Well?"

"I guess I'm wandering about looking for answers." He sounded like an errant school boy.

The Abbot pushed a darkened-with-age parchment towards him, motioning for Jabbi to enter and sit. "Then you have stumbled into the right place." He said quietly. "Do you know where you are?"

"High in the fifth tower, somewhere?"

"That somewhere is the Library of Ancient Prophecy. You have heard of it?"

"Yes." Jabbi's voice filled with awe.

This, the repository of the Holiest of the Holies for collections of the oldest sacred writings, thoroughly overwhelmed Jabbi. The very fact that the Abbot personally invited him into the library aroused his anxiety. Yet another part of him, one a bit more detached from his emotions, proclaimed this as his true destination.

"Yes." He reiterated with awe, gazing slowly up and down the shelves bursting with the very documents people only spoke of in hushed tones. "Yes, this is the place." He said firmly, almost joyfully.

"Then you are happy to have found the place?"

Jabbi, squinting to read the titles across the room, completely missed the question.

The Abbot raised his voice. "You are happy to be here?"

Startled, Jabbi almost fell off the wooden armchair. "Ah..a...a. Yes...... There's something special about this room....These writings in Holiness."

The Abbot peered down at Jabbi, a murky twist of a smile upon his thin red face. "You find the room AND its contents comfortable." He stressed every word, speaking slowly.

"I do. For some odd....maybe not odd....reason I do feel comfortable here....Just a bold hunch. .Forgive me if I am out of line, Abbot."

The thin man raised his arm, meaning for Jabbi to continue.

"There is something I must do here, isn't there?" Jabbi sat back in the chair, almost cowering, expecting a sermonic barrage for his unjustified impertinence.

The Abbot smiled thinly, then openly and finally laughed so loud as to become irreverent. He stood and moved to Jabbi's chair. With a smile so broad as to square his thin face he whacked Jabbi on the shoulder.

"Ah, my son." He sighed beautifully as if a load upon his heart now dissolved. "I have been waiting for you."

Jabbi dashed from the library and tore down the hall.

"Return as soon as possible, there is much to labor on here." The Abbot called down the hallway, still laughing and gleefully smacking his bony hands together. "Finally," He said to no one and yet everyone, "The one who can find the answer has arrived......Thank you."

Two mornings later the Captain received another unexpected invitation from the King. As with the former visit, the dutiful physicians encircled the sickly King. The King's face, especially his eyes, seemed more intense this time, but nothing else appeared different. Jabbi, after kneeling before the King, accepted the seat the King offered him. The head physician had to move. He did so quietly. However, Jabbi caught his eyes for a split moment: hatred filled them.

"I have heard that my New Knights behaved and fought well when they met the legions from hell."

"Well put, Your Majesty." The Captain responded. "You have received the truth."

"Good." He somewhat mumbled. "Sometimes I think I'm fed only good news......As if I'm too weak to handle anything." The King's unsteady gaze fell on the Captain.

The Captain simply nodded his head.

"Now, Captain," The King began carefully. "I have an errand of some importance to me, one that requires your assistance."

"If possible, Your Majesty." While Jabbi spoke, the physicians nervously twisted and then untwisted their overly pale hands, waiting to pounce, should the King furnish them the slightest mundane excuse.

"I have little doubt that you'll be able to accomplish the errand....... As I find myself in delicate health, proven by the existence of these physicians, I also realize that I'm not about to be traveling."

The physicians collectively sighed. The Captain ignored them.

"Therefore, I want you to bring three or four of those New Knights here....to my chambers."

"Yes, Your Majesty. That shall be accomplished quite easily."

"But we shall examine each knight. They might be carrying some disease." The head physician spoke with a tone showing his annoyance with the King.

"But, of course." The Captain and the King replied simultaneously.

"Good." The King shouted, almost, for a cough arrested his delivery. "I want to hear the story of the battle first hand. Not filtered through some damned scribe!" "How soon might the knights...?"

"Your Majesty." The head physician pleaded. "Such a visit is beyond the exertion I recommend for you."

"Damn you, Baltee." The King shot back. ".....You'd rule out breathing as too strenuous for me.....Anyway!....I'm still the King!"

"Yes, Your High-ness." He politely garbled while cursing under his breath.

"Captain, off with you. See that I received my visitors as soon as possible." The King smiled, swooned, dropping off his chair to the carpeted floor. "Damn doctors, can't even catch me when I fall.....See the incompetence I'm forced to live with."

The Captain ducked out the doorway and into the hallway before the physicians reorganized themselves. In his well-executed faint, the King communicated an unspoken message to the Captain: the physicians must go. The Captain immediately dispatched the King's wishes to Baste. He then opened his desk drawer and propped his feet against the narrow window. Now it was time for his pipe. And, by supper on the morrow, he'd have the answers he needed.

Jabbi spent the better parts of two dawns recomposing himself. He ran, and for it he dishonored himself, embarrassed himself, and for no reason. Even the Abbot showed true kindness towards him, yet he ran. He seriously considered leaving.

Without warning, a thin wizened old man appeared in his cell. "What's this self-pity stuff? I never saw any of this while we roamed the wilds of the half-frozen swamps."

"Kloshic!" Jabbi exclaimed, embarrassed by his own thinking.

"You expecting a dragon?"

"Might be a quick way to end all of this." He pouted.

"This isn't very acceptable." Kloshic detachedly noted. "What's the problem?"

"I don't belong here." He tried to present himself as a victim.

"And what asinine dolt gave you that idiotic piece of advice? The Abbot?"

"No."

"Ah....Then my hunch is correct....."

"......That I'm the asinine idiot."

"Couldn't say it better myself." He smiled aggravatingly rueful. "Now its time for business, Jabbi. In the future, you'll have plenty of time to pummel yourself for not being the Holy One."

"I NEVER claimed..."

"You have. Each and every time you berate yourself for some ridiculously insignificant imperfection. What a problem you have!" Kloshic snickered.

"Shut up!"

"Finally!.... Are you ready to begin work? Turn that anger into something a bit more useful than self degradation?"

Jabbi sat back on his cot. Kloshic brought up the stool and sat on it. "Well?"

"I don't know."

"Maybe you aren't supposed to know. After all, this is your schooling, isn't it?"

"I..."

"You lose."

Without taking either the time nor propriety to knock, the Abbot burst into the small cell, catching Kloshic's stool with the corner of the door. Kloshic lost balance and fell backwards into the Abbot, who also fell. Jabbi desperately tried to conceal a grin as he reached to pull the men up. He broke into a fit of riotous laughter. "I'm sorry." Jabbi vainly tried to regain his composure. He failed.

"I guess we deserved that." The Abbot said to Kloshic.

"Speak for yourself, most Reverend one!" Kloshic snorted, not too well pleased at having lost ground in his discussion with the recalcitrant Jabbi.

"Damn!" Cursed the Abbot. "Now I have two sniveling brats to tend to." He deliberately grabbed Kloshic's stool and sat. "Now Jabbi," Said the Abbot tersely. "You will listen and obey....."

Kloshic moved to the window ledge and sat there, out of eye sight. Jabbi gathered himself at the foot of his straw filled mattress, pensively awaiting a judgement. The Abbot gently kicked the door shut.

"Now then," The Abbot's stern gaze honed in on Jabbi's very soul. "I'll come directly to the point." He folded his thin well-worn hands. "Elders take certain vows most of Haaf is ignorant about. One of those vows concerns a pledge to devote ourselves to the study of the present Scriptures given by the Holy One."

"Present?"

"Indeed, this is not the first age for people. Peoples come and go. The Holy One is the only constant....Can you follow?"

Jabbi nodded his head. "Then there are other Holy Writings?"

"Yes."

"I can't believe this!" Jabbi exclaimed, shocked. "Why should we not use all the Holy One has provided?"

"You think us stupid?"

Jabbi said nothing.

"First time for everything." A mirth riddled voice floated in from the window.

"Shut up, Kloshic." The Abbot said. "We have obeyed the traditions handed down to us, Jabbi. The writings of the past were deemed too dangerous. We know those ancient peoples, using the Scriptures to defend themselves, actually exterminated themselves."

"Then the legends of white people with huge weapons and 'tree clouds' are true."

"There is truth within them, yes."

"And yet this history is hidden from the people. Shall we condemn ourselves as the white peoples did?"

"That's exactly the point, Jabbi. We need to know their story, especially their Scriptures." The Abbot became fearful, as if treading upon the forbidden.

"So, you Elders who took the vows, want to dump this responsibility upon me. ...I'm the sacrifice to the Holy One's wrath." Jabbi flinched at the thought, then gulped deeply. "Suppose I refuse?" His voice arched.

"Then we perish." Kloshic whispered flatly from his window perch.

"He is correct." The Abbot agreed. "Within our present Scriptures we can't account for this 'bastard' who not only claims to be the Holy One's son, but wasn't denied that preposterous label by the Holy One Himself..... And to this revelation there are thousands of eye witnesses."

"I am familiar with the stories from the front. I've asked myself the same question: Who is this 'bastard'? Who would turn against his own Father?" Jabbi muttered soberly. "Who then has the answers?"

"We believe they are in the ancient Scriptures of the extinct peoples..... Their 'received' words were collected into one single volume, The Holy Bib-le."

The low-ceilinged, smoke filled tavern, found itself a bit more crowded than usual. The Captain considered himself fortunate to occupy the corner seat where he observed the comings and goings of the eclectic clientele. As he finished his beef stew and a mug of ale, three troopers from the Church Guard blew in, all ready with a few too many drinks in their bellies. They slammed down at a table near the Captain and ordered a round. The ham fisted tavern master served them, but not until they received his lecture on 'respectable behavior' and the fact that their Commander, the Captain, sat at the next table. When they turned to verify the tavern master's words, the Captain just nodded, his eyes as cold steel. The armed trio instantly transferred to another table, one at the far side of the room.

Shortly thereafter, but before the local fiddler commenced his blunt political melodies, the Captain's contact drifted in through the side door and sat down. His features showed signs of strain and he was winded and sweating.

"There's not much time." He gasped. "I've been found out."

"Shall we leave?"

"No, it'll be safer here." Though he surveyed the drinkers as if one might be the assassin.

"Then move along. What have you found out?"

"Krucik was behind it all. He bought the jobs for the head physician and two others. None have any of the usual credentials ---in spite of what the records show." The man leaned forward, borrowed the Captain's mug and sucked a long hard draught. "Furthermore....."

Even as he spoke the Captain suddenly caught the man by his shoulder and dropped him to the floor---a broadaxe split the chair where he sat. As the clerk drew himself up under the protecting table, he heard a soft agonized moan, then a red-cloaked figure dropped onto the floor next to him, a dart protruding from the middle of his back.

"Get the other three!" The Captain yelled at the Church Guards. The damage was all ready finished. The two other assassins lay dead and a third one struggled against the sword balancing on his throat. "Bring the fool here!"

The trio of truly sober Church Guards dragged the chunky man to the Captain's table, his hob-nailed boots clanking the entire way.

"Do you recognize this man?" The Captain spoke both to the informer as well as the Guards.

"I've seen him in the records department." The informer dusted off his clothing as he studied the man. "Yes, he works there."

"Why have you come to kill this man?" The Captain demanded of the fellow while the rest of the overly curious customers grudgingly left, thanks to the urgings of the tavern master's large swinging broom.

The man refused to answer, even when the guard applied pressure to his arm. He spat on the floor. "I will tell you nothing!" He arrogantly bellowed.

"I though as much. Then I shall let you go." The Captain motioned for the man to leave.

He started for the door, walking backwards, then stopped. "There's devilment here." And he froze in place. "What's the game?" He demanded.

"I don't play games. But I know that when your type fail, you might as well be dead. And I won't have to lift a finger, will I?" The Captain and the others smiled, but not pretty ones. "I'll just let the word out that you gave us some information and that you betrayed these dead fools...betrayed them to me."

The immediate bleakness of the man's stricken face showed that the Captain's words reached to their intended goal. "Well, do you wish to live or not?"

"Captain," The informer interrupted, his voice choked. "Check the man's arm. If I'm not mistaken, you'll find something most interesting. In fact, you'll probably find the identical markings on the others."

"What markings?"

"Dragon tattoos." The informer rallied to smile triumphantly as the assassin's face burnt a bright red.

A guard ripped open his captive's sleeves with his sword. A bright dragon tattoo covered his left forearm. So too for the dead assassins.

"What have we here?" The Captain inquired as he studied the captive's arm. "Signs of a secret allegiance. And not extremely original at that."

The man spit towards the Captain: one of the Church Guards thumped him in the stomach, doubling the prisoner over. He puked on the floor. Standing back a bit, the Captain mulled over the newest facts. He didn't care for them, this conspiracy endangered the nation. But, should this become general knowledge, the ringleaders and the path to reach them might vanish forever. He sat down and finished his drink.

"Put the fool in the anteroom." He ordered. Then he called across the room to the tavern master. "Is your wife about?"

"I'm sorry Captain, I didn't hear you." He called back, raising up from his sweeping.

"Ilty!" The Captain spoke louder, an edge on his voice. "Ilty, your wife, is she about?"

He hurriedly sauntered into the kitchen, returning with a lissome blonde woman. She wore the apron of a cook and carried an ugly saw-bladed cleaver in her hand. While her face, dark with bright greenish eyes, was beautiful, her state of mind wasn't.

"I'm just starting to cut up the cow." She complained to her husband who pulled her by the arm. Then she saw the Captain and the three bodies on the floor. "Should've known you'd be part of this mess making." She half teased. "Problems? And you require my help." Her high voice portrayed a note of insider knowledge, as well a bit of friendly taunting.

"Indeed." The Captain flatly acknowledged. "Can you reach Vosnob tonight?"

"Are you going to butcher my cow?" She bargained, hands on hips.

"If I must."

"You must!"

"Then you need to be off." Before she left, the Captain spoke with her in private. Vosnob would reach out to the other Elders, letting them know of the depths of the conspiracy as well as the marks of the 'red dragon'. Vosnob and the other Elders would formulate strategy. That was the easy part.

Wrestling within himself concerning the spiritual dimensions of the 'red dragon'--that part, he realized meant the end of restful sleep for a long time. He remembered seeing the tattoo on one of the physicians attending the King. How many more had reached similar levels of power and trust within the government? He dreaded the thought.

Ilty nodded her head, silently agreeing with the Captain's assessment of the new developments. She would leave momentarily. Then she rose, kissed her husband, who knew she'd be gone for a while, and returned to the kitchen.

The captain returned his attention to the informer. "Can you leave tonight?"

"How about the family?"

"They'll go with you." He pulled a parchment from his belt and began to write. "You've been re-assigned to the Church's castle in Buda. So says the King." The Captain smashed a signet ring into the wax he dripped on the document. "You'll leave tonight, through the underground. The family will follow on the morrow." He handed the document to the informer and nodded to the guards.

Quickly they tromped across the tavern floor from the door of the anteroom. "Dispatch a few non-uniforms to escort him and his family to Buda......Check everyone for tattoos. You handle it your way."

"Yes, Captain." The senior guard snapped.

"And put a close watch on the fool. I want a daily report."

"Yes, Captain. Is that all?" His thin face bore a trace of a smile.

"Get these 'things' out of the tavern."

The senior guard motioned for the two others to dispose of the corpses. "Make it appear as an ordinary brawl."

"Bring the fool back in."

A moment later the failed assassin stood before the Captain, pale, reeking of vomit, his chin held high. The Captain lifted his empty mug in mock salute to the bulky tattooed man, then clunked it upon the table. With a bit of flippant whimsy he stared at the man. "Well, there's nothing else we need from you. Boot him into alley. ...We'll take bets on how long he survives."

Screaming both curses and fantastic deals, the two guards hauled the chunky man away and threw him across the alley into the garbage.

Seated in a hidden-away hallway stuffed behind the Abbot's office, being shelved from floor to domed ceiling with the most rare and esoteric volumes from ancient and, extinct civilizations, Jabbi pondered away at the translating of the Bib-le. While the difficult task both bothered and bedeviled Jabbi, the real issue arose from the Abbot's absolute insistence that the book 'must' render answers to the present theological dilemma: where and what is this 'son of God'. Once such facts were ascertained, then the downfall of this 'evil' son, pursuant to the Holy One's dictates, of course, his 'evilness's' permanent demise would be at hand. However, in the candle lit days and nights he spent poring through the fragile ancient manuscripts, Jabbi found little that confirmed the Abbot's predictions.

He played in the dry dust littering the stone desk with his fingers. This Eng-gel-ish language stumped him once again with its ungainly and erratic spellings. Obviously, the text he used wasn't the original, the different versions confirmed that fact. But then, he was afforded no other options. He stood and walked about the table, there barely being enough room for such exercising in the narrow hallway. Once he tried to walk outside but the Abbot had guarded the only doorway.

Pressing his tired fingers against his forehead, Jabbi began to summarize for himself what he found so far....so far that might aid their theological dilemma. First, and not surprizing, the Holy One, from the beginning, announced himself as Creator of all, visible and invisible. This creation process of the world seemed to him a bit truncated, stuffed into only seven days. He thought it best expressed the faith in the Holy One as Creator, rather than in the exactitudes of the 'how' of creation. More importantly, this Bib-le denied any creation of lesser gods. The Creator stood alone in this book of beginnings: Gen-nee-sis. The only other consequential references he noted concerned 'beings' the Holy One deliberately sent to give messages to his 'called people'. Not a one of these 'an-gells' received status, not even a name. Jabbi found multitudes of evils listed in the ancient texts. These appalled him, made him wince. But these evils were created by people, not an evil god. In all cases the Holy One remained faithful, but his 'called people' often rejected Him. Jabbi dismally shook his head, wondering how long ago this transpired, for things seemed little different these days.

When he finished with the writings of those who spoke for the Holy One, yet were rejected by the very people to whom the divine message aimed to save, Jabbi cried. The weight upon him was unbearable. His soul gave way to despair, for those very words he translated readily belonged to his own people, the Haafians. Yet, even in those desperate writings, no mention of an evil son of the Holy One showed itself. Rather, the people promulgated their own evil. The Holy One brought the judgement, true and fair to all creatures.

Only a few dawns passed since Jabbi's rough translation was finished. Now, a Holy Council, attended by all who resided at the monastery, restlessly sat in the great stone spanned dining hall. A flustered and disturbed Jabbi, sitting off to the right of the Abbot, found himself the most unlikely 'most-wanted' person, even though most of what he had to say in his speech later on had been leaked. At last, the Abbot rose and introduced Jabbi, acknowledging his holy gift for translating as well as his intense diligence in finishing the tedious work within so short a time period.

As the polite applause died, Jabbi rose, bowed to the Abbot, then to the other auspicious dignitaries and finally to all others. With hesitant steps, he moved to the lectern, his white knuckled hand crimping his copious notes. He cleared and re-cleared his all ready cleared throat, then with a weird resolve, he simply tucked the notes into the wide sleeve of his robe and began to talk.

"The Abbot's kind words notwithstanding," He began. "I find I have little to offer you....perhaps nothing at all."

A gasp of consternation rose from the floor. The critically honed eyes of the dignitaries spared him not. Only the Abbot stayed the course without emotion. His fist pounding upon a ceramic plate returned order.

Jabbi continued. "My 'given' responsibility consisted of a two-fold nature: to translate an old holy tome of an ancient civilization called the Bib-le, then I was tasked to search for answers to our present theological dilemma..... That is, who and what is the evil son of the Holy One?...." He paused, as if gathering up some new found energy. "My translation of the ancient scriptures--to the point where I terminated my endeavors--denies any reference to a lesser evil god---lesser by virtue of being 'son' and not an equal. Even in the sequences of the Holy One's creating, there is but one Holy One---there is none beside Him." He glanced to the Abbot, who had all ready risen to speak.

"Jabbi, I commend you for your diligent work. You do, however, leave us clearly in a predicament, a crisis of faith, if you will."

A swelling of sighs and nodding filled the cooler evening air.

The Abbot raised his hands for silence. "By myself," The Abbot recommenced with a slight air of superiority. "I translated the rest of the ancient book of scripture. Two thirds of this book are considered the Old Test Ment. This is what the honorable Jabbi has translated. What he has not seen is the last third of the scripture, called the New Test Ment." Jabbi, eyes down, missed the ugly grin offered by the Abbot. "As the name implies, 'new' signifies a starting over. But, before I share my findings with you, I need to ask Jabbi to sit....... I thank you for your earnest labor in translating. I had hoped that your findings would back mine. That is, the Old Test Ment providing hints about what is found in the New Test Ment. Actually, Jabbi has confirmed my translating work." He stopped then, allowing a humbled Jabbi to seat himself. The Abbot wore a smile from ear to ear.

Moving himself to the now empty lectern, the Abbot posited himself behind it. "The Old Test Ment ends with the Holy One sending many messengers to bring people back to him. The world, then as now, stuffed itself with sin. The New Test Ment begins with the Holy One, as a last recourse, sending part of himself to earth: ostensibly, his son."

A gasp squeezed out from the gathered clergy and others.

"At first, all went well. This 'son', named Jes-sus, taught fairness and truthfulness as the Holy One's way for us to live. He healed the sick, raised folk from the dead."

Another shock wave of gasping filled the dining area. The elated Abbot paused.

"Then, for some reason, this Jes-sus rebelled, going so far as to claim that he and the Holy One were and are equals. Then this Jes-sus took it upon himself to announce that he alone was the entrance to the Holy One's kingdom. Thereby usurping power not belonging to him...."

He deliberately waited for the impact to settle in a bit deeper. Self-satisfaction barely hid itself under his heavy eyelids.

"Listen to the rest!" He commanded. "The people and the righteous clergy of his day recognized this Jes-sus as both liar and heretic. As was only proper for the devout people of the Holy One, they rose up and ended this evil one's career by killing him."

The crowd, excepting a few too puzzled to be bothered with such emotionality, stood and clapped, viewing themselves as the righteous part of the story.

Holding his translation over his head, the Abbot continued. "So, we do know who the evil one is: this Jes-sus. ...The scripture tells us that as he died, he cursed the Holy One, threatened to return and destroy all those who refused to believe in him. Furthermore, he somehow escaped from the stone-locked tomb where they buried him."

Now the crowd hushed itself into an eerie silence as the result, the impact of the Abbot's translation dug into their souls; the once cool air replaced by a humid frightening fear.

"I fear my friends," The Abbot continued to artfully manipulate his audience. "That what arises is a battle between gods. An old one and the new one....... But then, that is my humble opinion." His comment elicited more than a few nods. "In order to provide you with enough information to move from the story to a theological proclamation for the people, I have asked that copies of my translation be given, once produced, of course," He smiled. "to all of you for study."

He immediately stepped away and disappeared to his chambers, leaving the room a quagmire of questions and half answers. Jabbi slid out a side door banging into Kloshic. They glanced at each other, both shaking their heads in disbelief. Kloshic grabbed Jabbi's hand and the two vanished.

So seldom used these days, the dusty confessional booth, that it provided the perfect escape for two Elders. Luckily, the privacy panel had long ago been removed, otherwise Jabbi's person would have been divided. Kloshic, anticipating a verbal reaction from an irate and obviously confused Jabbi, plopped his hand across his mouth, stifling a shout all ready there. Jabbi relaxed and then bit Kloshic's thumb. He groaned as he bit his lower lip.

"Quiet." He hissed as he shook his pounding thumb.

"Where in the Holy One's name are we?"

"In a confessional box....I didn't think you'd recognize it." In the dusty, spider web filled darkness, it was impossible for Jabbi to see the gleeful smirk of revenge covering Kloshic's face.

A strange wind-like noise prevented Jabbi from uttering his ugly reply. An excited woman's voice squealed from the far corner of the confessional.

"AAAHH!" She said, being unprepared to find visitors in her spot. All then when quiet. "Who is here?" She finally demanded, breaking the silence.

"Just me, Ilty." Kloshic replied, rather lazily.

"Damn it, you scared me to death, Kloshic. What are you doing here?"

"Escaping from the monastery. The Abbot's turned traitor and a fool." He spoke softly, but a bitter anger showed itself. "And showing off the new Elder."

"Oh!" She exclaimed. "I received the news a while back. Just didn't have much time to pay a visit. The Captain's got me running errands."

"What errand brings you here?" Jabbi spoke up.

"I'm looking for Vosnob. This is the second city I've checked. Is he here?"

"I really can't say, we just arrived a few moments before you did."

"And just where DID we arrive?" Jabbi demanded.

"Haaf North. In the old chapel, as I recall." Kloshic replied, a bit irritated. "Time to go. Seems we both have jobs to do. Standing here in the dark ...."

Ilty opened the door before he finished the sentence. The chapel, this one belonging to the clergy, unlike the large one found on the first floor, ceased to exist. In smoldering torchlight, the group now viewed, first hand, the total depravity of the Evil One. From the blackened sooty ceiling hung blood red banners depicting a silver-black dragon. The carved marble altar, smashed into thousands of fragments, lay under a crude and massive statue of the Evil One himself. Cruel and hungry looking, half person, half reptilian with folded bat wings, it pompously sat upon the altar's remains, a chalice crushed in its taloned grip. An open fire pit, well used, was dug into the floor before the statue. Evidence of sacrifice showed everywhere, though none in the group chose to discuss the horrid matter.

Leaving the abomination behind them, they quickly rushed out the side on at the street level, only to be knocked about by a patrol galloping around the corner.

"What's the rush at this time of evening?" Jabbi asked tersely, readjusting his wind blown clothing.

"I'm not sure, but the direction taken leads to the barracks." Kloshic replied. "That might be the best place for us. Who knows, maybe even Vosnob is there." He grinned at Ilty.

"He has to be somewhere." She brusquely replied. "Let's get moving. Its about a mile walk." Without waiting, she strode boldly across the street and headed towards the barracks. The men followed obediently.

Two intersections later, the rapidly moving trio found themselves surrounded by a mounted patrol. The patrol leader studied the unarmed persons for sometime, juggling in his mind what type of visitors these might be. They fit none of the descriptions provided by the Captain of the barracks, nor did they present themselves as being dangerous. But why did they ignore the curfew, placing themselves in danger? Finally, he brought his Striper, this one almost totally silver, before Kloshic.

"Whats be-in yer busness, old man?" His accent much akin to that of a non-swamper from the south.

"We're heading to the barracks, my friend. We heard there's trouble about and we arrived too late for a room." Kloshic pointed to the empty streets, made even more desolate by the first floors of the taverns and shops being shuttered tight. He paused, reining in the Striper. "You know about the 'blue ladies'?" His face strained nervously as he glanced up and down the streets.

"All too well." Jabbi said slowly. "All too well."

"Can you all ride double?" He asked quickly.

"All except for my sister." Jabbi explained.

The young bearded patrol leader gallantly swept down from his silvered Striper. "She'll ride mine. The rest of you can double up...." He waited until the three were saddled. "Let's move out! To the barracks!" He jogged along side Ilty's cantering mount.

An atmosphere of tension pervaded the barracks. Guards stood at the ready, double patrols with extra crossbows and torches moved into the streets after a thorough inspection. Jabbi considered they might be launching an attack against the 'blue ladies', but kept it to himself.

The Captain of the Barracks and the Chaplain, the trio accidentally discovered through the ramblings of the custodian, might be available later. All he actually knew concerned cleaning up a mess in the 'downstairs'. Something about unexplained visitors making too many problems at the worst times and he definitely was too old for all of this. With his damp mop and ragbag he sauntered on down the hallway, in no particular hurry.

Until an officer could be obtained the trio continued in the friendly custody of the patrol, wasting time with small talk as they sat in the guard room annex. The three exchanged quizzical glances as they observed the departures of raiding parties. If the patrol that brought them to the barracks knew anything, which seemed dubious from the expressions on their faces, they kept quiet.

Much later, an exhausted and thankful Rux passed by the hallway to the annex. Ilty, half-nodding off to sleep, caught a glimpse of his lanky frame. "Rux!" She struggled to cry out, but only yawned.

Kloshic identified the familiar figure as well. "Rux! Hold up!"

Rux paused from his long striding and turned, peering down the hallway and into the annex. "Who calls?" His face showing signs of uncertainty; his voice fatigued.

"Its me, Ilty. Kloshic is here too."

"The night gets even more stranger." He mumbled to himself as he briskly walked to the annex. "Ah, Ilty. Good to see you again." He spoke as he about crushed her in a bear hug. "You too, Kloshic." He reached for the old man's hand as he casually plopped Ilty into the padded bench. "Who is the stranger?" He lied, grinning at Jabbi.

"Very funny." Jabbi said. Then, as became his abrupt style, he immediately changed the subject. "Where's the fat guy you're supposed to be protecting?"

Rux slammed his fist to Jabbi's angular face. It was deflected by Ilty's faster moving arm.

"Something's very wrong." She said. "Better bring us up to date. This quest is still of the utmost importance." She then presented Rux with his own arm.

Rux shook his head. "Oros was attacked and wounded. He's downstairs under heavy guard."

Jabbi's facial expression became his apology. "What happened? How seriously is he wounded?"

Kloshic suddenly went pale. "By the Holy One...." He gasped and stuttered. "The Evil One did this!..................... Didn't he?" He gasped again, Jabbi rose to keep him from falling over. "The damned creature knows of the Quest."

"That's pretty much the story." Rux let out dolefully. "He showed up at the...."

"Chapel." Kloshic interrupted. "We personally saw how the turncoats welcomed him....desecrating the altar and all."

"I don't doubt your story, Kloshic, but the truth is simply that the attack took place here........ We were trying to interrogate the Abbot....the 'late' Abbot." He corrected himself with a touch of ironic self-satisfaction.

"Why the smirk?" Ilty demanded. "Rux?"

"Sorry." He jumped. "No smirk. Just a cover up. .....Damn!" He swore. "It's still terrifying. The evilness, the emptiness and depravity.... the coldness."

Kloshic, breathing a bit more regular now, nodded his head as if to agree. "The damned thing is always closer than we want to admit." He shook his head in disgust. "I sincerely wonder if he hasn't bought out the nation."

"Just its mercenary leaders." A cynical Rux spat out.

"And the King's so-called physicians." Ilty added, causing the others to focus upon her.."....Yes, that's what I'm doing here. Well, partly. I still need to locate Vosnob...to share the wondrous news with him." Disgust covered her brown face.

"Looks as if the pieces are beginning to come together." Jabbi announced as he rubbed his hands together. "Perhaps," He cautioned, "We ought to be more selective about where we discuss these matters."

"You'll make a good Elder yet." A smiling Kloshic observed.

After a brisk eat-and-run meal, Rux and Ilty met Jabbi and Kloshic. They forced themselves to visit the scene of the evil one's appearance. Both walked away afflicted and unnerved, still remaining unaware of Rux's single slice, and the consequent wounding of the damned one. Rux, strong-armed by the wispy thin Ilty, paid a visit to the wounded Oros. They found him sitting up and, as usual, stuffing his face. No sooner had they shut the door to the third floor room when the other two barged in, still not quite back to normal, and Kloshic puffing heavily.

"If I knew what room you'd taken," The spidery old Elder yelled at Oros. "I'd have gotten here without a heart attack." He gasped out even as Jabbi stuffed him into a padded armchair.

"Well, I'd shake your hand too, you old geezer, except I'm not allowed to move this shoulder." Oros eagerly parlayed with Kloshic.

"If you weren't so damned fat, they wouldn't need to support your arm like that." Came the terse reply.

Except for Rux and Jabbi, everyone smiled, Ilty snickered.

"Someone want to share this with us?"

"If these two cantankerous old men don't fight, then one of them is dead." Ilty answered between a couple of sighs of relief.

"Times wasting." Muttered Kloshic. He stared at Oros. "Glad to see you made it."

"Thanks." Oros muttered in return. "But Rux is the one on the cutting edge."

"And what kind of stupid riddle is that?"

"Tell the old fart, Rux." The red-faced Oros requested.

"Actually, I don't remember too much." He shook his head slowly, an inexplicable bleak look on his face, re-living the horrendous event. Then Rux just stopped, until Oros walloped his back side. "I cut his damned hand off." He shot off the words so soft and fast that no one would catch them.

"You wounded the Evil One, Rux?" Kloshic's voice wrapped itself in pure amazement. "The Evil One is one-handed!" He began to shake for joy, then abruptly changed his mind. "This is another stupid joke, isn't it?"

"Calm thyself!" Oros demanded. "There's a sick man present who needs peace and quiet."

"Oh', shut up!"

After Rux went through the episode about the now one-armed Evil

One, things settled down, or almost did, for Kloshic kept intruding with his snickering about the 'now' one-armed evil son of god. The pieces of their stories began to assemble themselves into something useful for the Haafian situation. However, before Kloshic took it upon himself to summarize their meeting, the next day arrived and with it breakfast and a special message for Rux. He received it quietly in the hallway. He re-entered with a broad twisted smile, decisively cutting off Kloshic's initial remarks.

"What now?" He shot out, exhausted by both the intensity of the night and its agenda.

"The nights are safe again in Haaf North." He yawned. "They've dealt with the 'blue ladies'.

"Dealt?"

"As in dead and gone."

Ilty's face glowed, offended at the slaughter. But then, she found herself being reprimanded. She had not experienced even one of the 'blue ladies' who sold themselves to the Evil One, let alone tangled with their other heinous adventures. She bit her lower lip. "I stand corrected, but I find nothing worthy in killing all of them."

"And there is nothing worthy in the killing at your tavern?" Kloshic appraised her, though politely.

"But they were men."

"And that has absolutely nothing to do with the Evil One. He'll scrape up followers from wherever slime exists." Oros added. He started on a sermon

"Time for the summary!" Kloshic crashed Oros' speech. The two snarled at each other. "This is what we now know, however tentatively, to be true. The damned one must be created. He is not truly an uncreated god. While far more powerful and deadly than any mortal, the bastard can be injured. And, if injured, then the damned thing can possibly be destroyed."

"True enough...though time will tell." Oros gently added.

"It will be up to the Captain and Vosnob to supply the tactics to implement the information. Is this our agreement?" He slowly went about the room, seeking nonverbal endorsement from each. "Good." He then cleared his hoarse voice with a drink of tea. "We affirm that the one-handed damned one has been diligently at work, deceiving Haafians and buying willing souls. That's the reason for the King being so deviously attacked. In sending the clergy to the people, he attacked the tap root of the evil one's support: the people's ignorance. Now the King is barely alive, unfit to govern......That is,.. ...until the physicians are sent here, post-haste, to provide care for Oros, whose sickness definitely resembles that of the King's."

"I think the lure will work." Jabbi interjected carelessly.

"The summary?" An unamused Kloshic silenced Jabbi. "Then, the normal inspections throughout the Light Striper will be commanded by those whom Vosnob knows personally. We'll gain a better idea of the numbers we're fighting afterwards....... Might be facing a damned civil war."

"Skip the local commentary!" Oros snorted at Kloshic. "Show me your arms! Maybe you have one of the dragon's tattoos."

Kloshic answered nonverbally: he stuck out his tongue.

"As for the Quest, we seem to have a partial answer. From the work of Jabbi in translating, and then from the Holy One himself, and then from the Abbot's commentary, which seems rather concocted. Finally, the entrance of another god, that of the Taths. This is extremely fragile, tenuous territory. Jabbi will locate and translate this newer testament for us, while Oros and Rux....along with your Yldan friends will visit Tath." He gulped some more tea, slobbering the front of his tunic. "Am I still on track?"

"First time for everything, old fool."

"Shut up!" Ilty yelled at the foolishly smiling Oros.

"Finally, Sarg is reported as missing."

"Sarg and all the rest." Oros corrected.

"So be it!" Snapped an angry Kloshic. "I'm sorry it had to turn out this way. .... But now its time to spread the news."

"After I get a little rest." Ilty said. "Back at the tavern." With a small dry dusty cloud swirling about, she disappeared to her tavern. Jabbi and Kloshic would find Vosnob. Oros and Rux were assigned to bring the rest of their party to the barracks, though Oros found himself on bed rest, physician's orders.

According to the King's physicians, the Captain's visits had severely weakened the King. Thus, for the next four sunsets, the King found himself a prisoner of his medical staff. He had, however, explored newer ways to handle the mind-eating drugs they fed him. Puking on the head physician was one of his more delightful ones. His other favorite sorely stretched the limits of the physicians, He played the Prophet, totally out-of-his-mind with denunciations of the bastard Evil One. But, so that he might remember exactly what the 'Spirit' had made him preach in these moments of divine ecstasy, he mandated the physicians to write, verbatim, each and every word he uttered. Later, after he recovered from the preaching by taking a long nap, the physician of his choosing read the 'sermon' back to him. The physicians dreaded this assignment. But the King is the King. The Truth both nauseated and condemned them.

Towards sunset of the fourth day, the Captain burst into the King's suite unannounced. A platoon of the Church Guards stood behind him, dressed for battle. The derisive nature of the arrogant physicians disappeared immediately as the guards surrounded them. The Captain held a rolled document bearing the stamp of Vosnob.

"Sorry to be bothering you." The Captain announced to all in a breezy manner. "But," He instantly turned hard. "I have a message from Vosnob that will require your well-acclaimed talents to work elsewhere."

The head physician went livid and shook his fist in the Captain's face. The rest acidly stared at the Captain, their overt haughtiness barely under control. The Captain ignored them, motioning instead for a lanky older guard to gather up the medical accouterments which occupied the tables in several of the other rooms. His motions were a clumsy, if not plainly indifferent, to the fragile nature of the physician's healing tools.

"Damn!" The head physician swore. "Stop that. You have no right."

"But he does, my friend." The Captain bluntly asserted. "Vosnob commands all of you to be in Haaf North as quickly as possible. These guards will escort you. Stripers await you outside the Council Hall.... You'll be leaving momentarily."

"This is preposterous! We are not to leave the King's side! This is our sworn commitment!" He tall man argued, barely keeping his anger under control.

"Yes and No."

"What asinine word game do you play?"

"No game. When the welfare of many exceeds the welfare of one, even though it be the King, the many come first. You know what your oath is." He handed him the note written by Vosnob.

He scanned the paper, as if to find an excuse. "It says that two Church Elders have come down with the same illness the King presently manifests. The Abbot of the city believes the illness might be contagious, endangering the clergy as well as the city's population. We are forthwith commanded to leave for Haaf North. Vosnob is sending his personal physician to care for the King until we return.....The signature," He announced caustically, "is genuine." He savagely crumpled the order.

"You are ready to go?" It really wasn't in the tone of a question, but of a terse command. "Time is wasting....Church Elders are a most valuable asset.....May the Holy One be praised for His gift to us."

The physicians almost vomited on the words, yet tending to two Church Elders presented itself as not the worst trade-off possible. Apparently, to their relief, their true identities remained undisclosed. They gave up the King,--- but then, he could never recover---but secured two Church Elders, that should please their unholy master. With an ungracious huffs, they grabbed cloaks and stomped out and down the marble stairs.

"Where's our waggon?...And where's our driver?" The burly southern accented head physician demanded.

"You'll ride Stripers, just like us." Answered the Guard's leader, the same lanky fellow who jammed the medicines into a few sacks. "You obviously did not hear the Captain."

"What's your name?" Baltee cursed. He jabbed his bulbous finger at the Guard's leader.

"Yganak."

"Well then, Yganak, know this!" He barked. "We aren't going anywhere until suitable conditions are arranged for us." He clamped his arms together about his chest.

Yganak pulled his curved sabre, and, with one quick downward flick of the steel blade, sliced the front of the tunic off the man. He stood there shaking, white belly hanging out, his arms still folded above it. The troopers smiled quietly.

"I'm the one in charge." Yganak admonished the white-bellied physician. "None of you have any military rank...... Furthermore, until I've handed you over to the Abbot, you'll do exactly what I say, when I say. Am I understood?" He stared, waiting for an answer.

"And what if we refuse?" He arrogantly replied.

"It's called insubordination. You'll hang for it." Came an indifferent reply. "The choice is your's... and........ rope is cheap."

The physicians, with much assistance from the troopers, gamely struggled to mount up. When Yganak swung his arm to move out, two physicians, still unmounted, were drug to the outer gate, ropes about their feet. A few more disciplining episodes leveled the head-strong idiotic physicians to a relatively tolerable degree. Yganak commended them for their new attitudes, after all, he reminded them, their journey just began.

"'Frustrating and nonsensical! Frustrating and nonsensical!' That's all he's said for the last three mornings. I'm exhausted just listening to the big oaf talk. And then he begins that never-ending sequence of pace-and-stop, pace-and-stop." Queen Sjura found comfort within the women's tent; comfort and enough ears to listen to her recurring travails with Sarg.

Sarg's characteristic demeanor had not changed, but this new environment had. He now saw the green valley as the ultimate in prisons. This, their well-watered and game-filled valley, the valley that saved them from dragons and the Evil One, the valley which allowed them to physically recover, became the valley which they would never leave. The valley's walls became slippier each day. At present, they resembled little less than polished glass, impervious to any breaking, cutting or shaping. Even Sarg's 'gift' backfired, his deadly cutting beam ricocheting off the wall, almost slicing him in two on the rebound.

Vauk later attempted to explain the properties of angles to him, but his effort proved futile. Sarg didn't need a lecture and he wouldn't endanger himself or others with another attempt, even if he understood the properties of angularity. These dawns furnished no consolation for Sarg.

Blue Turtle ruminated with Sarg concerning their desperate situation. The worn-out party had only been able to rest but a sixth of a day. Each time they rested, the ground began to drift and sway beneath them, like a rug being gently pulled out from under one's feet. Their constant journeying left them always in the middle of the valley. The company's efforts to reach the southern end were valiant. They were also quite in vain. The faster they moved, the faster the land receded. When they headed north, the valley's land flow reversed itself.

Resting beyond a sixth of a day became a signaling for dragons and the Kyykki to leer from the top of the cliff. Yldan scouts got no further ahead of the rest than two miles. At that point some invisible barrier shoved them back towards the others. This proved true even when scouts traveled north and south simultaneously, both Yldans came rolling back to camp, unhurt but exhausted.

An increasing drudgery appropriated their lives. They became enslaved to depression in trekking nowhere. Hopelessness surrounded them. Brey became one of its first victims. Perhaps her depression tied in with the loss of Luuft, or perhaps with her own near-to-death experience, or even memories from the ghastly realities of the past moon cycles. In any case, at present, Tiello found herself being both sister and mother to the diminutive Haafian.

No longer did the moons pass overhead, just periods of darker and lighter yellowish-grey broken by skeletons of once-huge blossoming clouds. A drizzling commenced, one that not only brought the humidity to unbearable levels, but one that refused to quit. Food stuffs that once allowed at least for one 'good meal' spoiled with mold. Dampness prevailed, actually, it conquered. Mildewed clothing began to rot, leather boots fell apart. Then, a soft wet snow began to drift down into the valley. Temperatures plunged below freezing within a day. This valley of safety, with hungry dragons now passively gazing down from the cliffs, had become a tomb---an icy, foodless, half-living nightmare for those trapped within its bitter confines.

As of yet, no one had died. However, Sarg knew the impossible conditions would quickly change that. They were at the mercy of the Evil One. At best they would buy time, hoping against hope that the Holy One heard their prayers from the pit. Instead, another skeletal demon, this one silver hued instead of black, hailed the group from the safety of the cliff's upper rim.

"I bring you greetings from my Master." He intoned with belllike hollowness. "My Master who controls even the weather." He now leered, taking into consideration the desperate state of the survivors. "Would you like the 'nice' weather to return? Would you enjoy being dry and warm again? How about a 'nice' rest in a valley where land doesn't move? What do you think?" Having said as much, all things instantaneously returned to what they originally were.

The demon floated down into the valley.

Sarg, fronting the entire party, with the exception of Sjura who stood beside him, met the demon as he touched the valley's greening floor. Sarg filled with righteous indignation. This demon's visit, he speculated, meant only trouble. Thus, some type of vindication--probably his last, he thought--was mandated.

"I hope you appreciated what my Master has done for you." The demon hollowly intoned, hinting at something yet to transpire.

"And what is the price for this change?" Sarg replied, cutting into the demon's speech. "Your Master isn't known for his generosity."

"Then I'll not waste time." The silvered demon leeringly smiled, exhibiting a nasty set of dagger-type teeth. He wrapped his red-black cloak about him, found a pocket and pulled out a formal looking document. "I'll leave it to you to read it to the rest." He tossed the rolled parchment to Sarg.

"Still can't read, can you?" Sarg quipped as he caught the paper.

The demon 'smoked' in darkest anger at Sarg's sarcastic remark. Nevertheless, Sarg took his time in examining the document's contents. He then passed it to Sjura, who pretended to read it. She transported it to Brey. And Brey it delivered it to Blue Turtle.

"You think me a fool? I need an answer." Demanded the impatient demon.

"Not quite our usual ugly self today, are we?" Sarg snapped back. "You'll have an answer when we've all studied the mandate. Unlike you, we fully intend on reading the perverse document."

"Its not a mandate!"

"Then what do you call it?"

"An honorable agreement." His 'smoking' increased, blurring his skeletal face.

"'Honorable' isn't in your damned Master's vocabulary."

"You go to far!" The demon snorted, flame shot from his mouth.

"You learned a new trick. I didn't think it possible...Let's see, that raises your filthy carcass to the level of a frog... Congratulations!" A grinning Sarg, full of pent-up cynicism, faced off with the demon. He rubbed his hands together. "How long do you want to live, stupid?" Queen Sjura grabbed his arm, but he pushed her back.

The demon drew his sword. Its hilt was of steel, but the blade of pure blue fire. "Your time to die!" He bellowed as he charged.

Sarg quickly quartered him. Then focused his fingers to turn the slimy green parts to ash. Lastly, he took the parchment from Tiello. "Anyone want to sign this?" Everyone shook their head: the negative reply was unanimous. "Vauk, burn the damned thing!"

With much gusto, Vauk struck his flint. The document existed only as a flaming torch, passed from one member to another. The note of triumphant rejoicing rapidly quieted. The weather suddenly degenerated into a blustery winter storm.

"If this be the end, we shall meet it with our dignity intact." Sarg spoke quietly and earnestly to the group.

"And we have lived in faithfulness." Added Queen Sjura. "I only pray..."

"And your prayers have been heard, Sjura." The voice sparkled of vibrant life, of wholeness. But it could not be located. And as the voice continued, the valley returned to life. "I am here to return you home."

Sjura fell to her knees, pale and trembling, Tiello following after her. With her head to the ground, the Queen spoke apprehensively, yet with a nervously shaking happiness. "My Lord and My Master. Thank you."

"Thank you!" Tiello blurted before passing out.

Sarg and the others stood in silent bewilderment, insecure of the mysterious happening.

The bold crystalline voice spoke again. "I am witness to your faithfulness......Now climb to safety!" Though a command, it permeated their souls as a pleasant invitation, one that renewed each wearied person the moment they responded. Within an instant, the ragged band had been rejuvenated.

A rainbow appeared, touching the earth in front of them. The upper end wrapped itself in a voluminous white cloud. Delicate and fragile it appeared, as though the slightest breeze might tear it asunder.

"Sjura!....Rise and lead the people." The voice emanated from the cloud. Its tone portrayed Holiness.

Sjura allowed Sarg to help her to her feet. "This is your god?" He said, believing that it was.

"Indeed!" She smiled. "Let's get out of here!" She called out. "Follow me." Without hesitation she strode to the rainbow and climbed. The others could see her feet through the transparent banding colors. Most were frightened and a few not entirely convinced. Past trickeries placed doubts in their minds.

"Move out!" Sarg commanded. "This is our rescue."

With mixed feelings, most obeyed. Tiello grabbed a few Yldans by the arms, pulling them up the rainbow. Sarg brought up the stragglers.

An ugly, anger filled voice rang out. "This is my valley! You shall not leave!" It thundered, shaking the rainbow bridge.

"Climb faster!" Yelled Sarg. "The bastard's returned!"

The winds picked up power, but the rainbow swayed no more. Neither did the Troopers feel the wind, even as they passed by the rim of the cliff and looked down, some seventy-five feet to the valley's floor. Fearfully they traveled on, walking on air--solid air---following the example of Queen Sjura, going ever higher entering the cloud itself. A sinister wind raged and howled, but the Troopers remained unaffected, protected by the rainbow.

Suddenly unleashed, the dragons swarmed at the rainbow, only to have their belching fire reflected. Kyykki began clambering up the rainbow.

Sarg and two other Yldans fought with them. Quite easily, most lost their balance, falling to valley floor below. Once past the valley's upper rim, those Kyykki still climbing dropped to their deaths. The rainbow no longer existed below the rim anymore.

The damned one finally appeared, launching lightning bolts at the rainbow. After another series of hits by lightning bolts, a crack appeared in the rainbow. The Troopers groped and crawled up the collapsing rainbow, no longer secure, but fearful of the doom-bringing lightning.

The crystalline voice spoke again. "You have no power here. Begone before I slice off your other arm."

"I have the power here!" Barked the Evil One.

"You have nothing unless 'someone' signs your contracts. We know that without them you are nothing." The voice of Sjura's god remained firm and steady.

A solid block of lightning ferociously blasted through rainbow, severing the bottom portion. Sarg and the two other Yldans suddenly found themselves hurtling to the ground.

"That's how much power you have, you mongrel." Bellowed the Evil One gleefully. He looked up from the ground, gratuitously awaiting their deaths.

A hand-like cloud reached out, gently enfolding three, then delivering them inside the cloud. A most horrified Sjura clung to Brey. Upon seeing Sarg, Sjura ran through the cloud room's mists into Sarg's arms. As he held her, tears of joy streamed from his face.

"Away, foolish one." Commanded the righteous voice of Sjura's god. "Your power is limited. Even I can best you. Flee before I become angry with your inane stupidity."

"My day is yet to come!"

"Yes, I believe you used that lie during your last failure on the battlefield......And Krucik and Baltee......shall I continue?"

"Damn you!"

A titanic eruption detonated just below the cloud room. The vaporous room rattled and shook, light turned to darkness and back again. The tenants dropped to the floor, sliding and rolling as the cloud bounced and skittered in the yellow-grey sky. A moment later, calmness returned and their cloud room thinned out, permitting a view of the land, three thousand feet below.

Joy and fearfulness, wonderment and befuddlement, anger and peace, all these and more paradoxical feelings raced through their beings. They did not fathom the cloud room sprinting through the air, leaving the 'safe' valley far behind. They held onto each other, each nervously re-assuring the other that everything would turn out well. They hoped.

As quickly as the cloud room raced across the sky, it dropped into another valley. This valley they saw from high above, on a cliff, where they witnessed a magnificent waterfall feeding it. The cloud returned them to the very valley Queen Sjura once claimed as her homeland. In the midst of a flower-filled meadow, the cloud room vanished, leaving the shaken and thankful group in a new environment.

"You are safe here." Came the voice of the still hidden god. "Sjura, bring your people home." Again the voice commanded, but it resonated within her heart as a gentle invitation.

Tiello, overjoyed, hugged Blue Turtle until he almost fainted. Sjura, feeling more than overwhelmed, simply gripped Sarg's hand while staring at the ground. Vauk meandered through the meadow, frozen in a dream.

Brey broke the unreal, the unnatural silence. "I'm hungry." She mumbled, only to find everyone staring at her. "Well, I am.. ..When 's the last time we actually ate a real meal.....I'll tell you. It was the night we camped on the cliff over the waterfall......You remember how long ago that was?" She stammered defensively while pointing to the well known landmark high above them.

At first, no one answered. Then came a snicker, then a nod and another, then the first laugh. In the end, even Vauk jumped from his dazed mood into the joyful present. Finally, most admitted to being hungry.

"Good. ...I'm delighted to see you adjusting to your new surroundings. ....I apologize for the rough trip. But, everyone is safe." The voice of the unknown god rang out, mysteriously, speaking directly to the heart. It disguised itself so as not to be identifiable as male or female.

"Do not waste your time attempting the impossible... Just accept that I am....And that I did hear your prayers...And you are safe." This god correctly read their minds. "Whatever needs you have, especially food, dear Brey, will be well accomplished in just a few moments."

A most embarrassed, flush faced Brey, knelt and said, "Thank you, Queen Sjura's and Tiello's God."

"You are most welcome. Your forthrightness becomes you, as long as you don't over do it, of course."

Sarg and Vauk laughed, causing Brey's face to burn with consternation. These two knew her too well.

"Sjura, bring this Sarg to me........I'm near the rock by the creek."

"Yes, Holy One."

"No."

"No?"

"No. I am not the Holy One. I am simply god, god of the Taths. No more, no less."

While Sjura vigorously attempted an apology, the god of the Tath's words instilled themselves into every listener. Here a grand mystery existed, partially solved, and partially mixed up. No person could make much sense of these divine ways, though it was their nature to try.

"Do not worry, Sjura. I will not change my mind. You will bring the people home............But not by yourself..... Do you love this·Sarg?" The god abruptly changed course.

"Yes, I do. But...."

"But he is a serf. And he isn't blue" The unnamed god paused....."What if I transform him into blue and make him a real prince?"

"No, please!" Shouted the Queen. "Then he would no longer be the Sarg I love."

"Truly spoken." The god's voice sounded amused, yet satisfied. "And Sarg, you are not one of my people....I will not compel you in any way.... But I do hope you respond to the Queen's love."

"Are you suggesting ....."

"Perhaps....Colors and royalty count for little....Love counts for much."

"I didn't dare think I could love her....not as a wife...... that is."

"What say you?" Sjura spoke in Sarg's face. He could not avoid the confrontation.

He stammered and blustered long enough to have everyone laughing, everyone except Sjura, that is. She refused to remove her hands from his tunic and her nose from his nose.

"Then you'll marry·me?" Sarg finally blurted out, his face blushing beyond belief. Sjura stood silent, transfixed.

"Relax, Sjura. You both have my blessing." The hidden god announced. "Answer his question, Sjura?"

"Yes." And she kissed him. The din of laughter, hooting and crying rose and then faded.

"Hold hands." The god gently requested. "I've always wanted to do this." There was heard a joyous chuckle. This was not quite in keeping with traditional ideas concerning the nature of god, especially for those from Haaf.

"Do what?" Asked a still not-quite-exactly-with-it Vauk.

"I'm going to marry them, of course." And so the god of the Taths did.

Then the god without-a-name appointed Tiello and Brey to establish a camp until the newly-wedded returned. The god gave one other suggestion. Everyone should remain in the valley until the arrival of the Istelles.

Chapter 9

"Isn't it time for a rest?" Baltee, arrogantly bellowed. Three long dawns in the Striper's saddle left his are aching. His superior attitude diminished somewhat, though not enough to suit the Church Guard.

"Not until we reach the next outpost!" Yganak yelled over his shoulder. His blue tunic flapped in the dusty breeze as the platoon with its addition of physicians cantered along under a merciless sun.

"Damn you!" Baltee returned. He fumbled with the reins, not yet comprehending that long flowing gowns worn by physicians proved hazardous while mounted. Being adverse to anything acknowledged as work--or that which required effort, as in sweating--did nothing to bolster his pathetic image with the Troopers. As the gown flipped, covering his face, another trooper grabbed his reins. No precious time would be wasted on these traitors.

Yganak ignored this cursing episode, just as he did the hundreds of others which came and went during their expedition to Haaf North. His only respite came during the evening stays at the military outposts along the road. There, he left the garrison Troopers in charge of the physicians. Such nightly stopping also allowed Yganak to inspect each barracks and send runners ahead. That evening, following the typical 'trooper's meal', Yganak called for the usual inspection. Most problematically for Yganak, a few troopers with the red dragon tattoo existed within the ranks. After a short discussion with the Staff Master and the garrison chaplain, such Troopers found themselves locked under the keep, awaiting court martial.

Peddlers and cattlemen, moving their goods along the cobblestoned Haaf Bay road, removed any sense of boredom from their journey. Yganak found himself a more than simply curious when he espied serfs carrying old battered round shields. When they paused for a lunch break, more for the hard-run Stripers than for themselves, the lanky commander sent four Troopers to discover the source of the ancient weapons. They each returned with a battered shield.

"Where did you get these?" Yganak asked without looking up.

"Couple of kids, down the road a piece, Sir." Snapped one of the four Troopers. "They sold them for three stone. Said they bought them from some Yldan peddlers. They are living out of their parked waggon."

"And where's this waggon parked?" Yganak looked up. His suspicions raised. Not many Yldans travel this far east, and those who did were seldom traveling salesmen.

"The waggon's on the east side of the next garrison, shoved up against a grove of trees.....And, there's a woman with the Yldans, a Haafian. ...The kids said she's a real good 'looker', blonde hair and all."

He shook his head thoughtfully, strangely bemused by this oddly constructed peddler's group. He grasped at nothing, just wispy enigmatic pieces that didn't fit together. "We'll be stopping by tomorrow for a visit." He told the Troopers. "Just don't tell the physicians."

"Yes, Sir!" Came the Troopers' reply.

"Anything else?" The commander mentioned as the men began to mount up.

"Well......We did see some red tunics on a few people. Tunics seemed strange..."

"Strange?"

"Yes Sir....Like the serfs removed something from the front. I could see the stitching outline, it wasn't faded underneath. Just like what happens when my wife takes these stripes off an old tunic....brighter color underneath."

Yganak put this additional thought with the other disjunct ones. He needed more time. "Thank you, Raff.... Let's ride!" The commander tore off down the river road; something about this little episode made him extremely nervous. He had an inner demand: solve these perplexing mysteries.

Another uneventful evening passed at the next outpost, uneventful except for Yganak, that is. He spent much of the night rambling about the parapets and staring at the two moons from the roof of the keep. Sleep eluded him, and, realizing this, he thought to discover answers to the mysteries they would meet on the morrow. Who were the peddlers? Raff spoke truthfully, but Yldans with a Tath woman simply refused to make sense, especially when that fact was tied to them marketing old weapons. And if they also secured an access to red tunics with dragons embroidered upon them, are these peddlers hostile? Were they a trap? A way for the evil one to reclaim his derelict physicians? He gratefully accepted a stone bench seat from the last watch detail on the keep. As the new dawn shot orangish fingers into the cloudy grey sky, he fell asleep.

Raff gently awakened him for breakfast. "Sorry Sir!" He nervously spoke. "You need to be up for breakfast. Its a bit late as it is, Sir!" He helped the stiff and somewhat groggy Yganak to his feet and lead him down the stairs.

"Thanks Raff." He groused, not intentionally meaning to be abrupt.

"Yes, Sir!" Raff said.

"Sorry Raff, I don't mean to treat you so rudely."

"No offense taken, Sir!"

"I appreciate that." Yganak paused at the bottom of the steps. Turning to Raff he continued. "I fear this is not a good morrow. Have the men ready for action. If anyone needs a crossbow, make sure they get one. And plenty of extra bolts. And add three pack Stripers loaded with extra provisions. And .... if things get intolerable, the physicians are expendable."

"But Sir!" The muscular black bearded Haafian protested. "We are assigned to escort them safely to Haaf North."

"I fully understand, Raff." Yganak replied softly, not wishing to be overheard. "But the fact of the matter is simply this. The physicians are traitors, in league with the damned one."

Raff shuddered, from fear.

"Its true enough....Check their arms. You'll see a flying dragon tattoo firmly imbedded on each of them. Moreover, the Captain has evidence showing that these physicians deliberately poisoned the King."

"The Captain has evidence?"

"Yes." Yganak sadly smiled. "Yes he does.....Now, this latter conversation."

"Yes Sir!"

"You never heard it....Understand?"

Raff nodded his head and then disappeared to carry out Yganak's orders. Yganak headed to breakfast, not that he felt hunger, just the opposite, but with his feeling for the day so negative.....He forced himself to see the truth. You can't fight without energy.

The extra Stripers slowed their pace and caused a few questions, especially from the saddle-sore physicians. Yganak turned his mount to confront their incessant bitching. "This is the way it is. Tonight we'll be camping out. I suggest that should answer all of your questions.....Is that correct, Baltee?"

"As a matter-of-fact..."

"Excellent!" Yganak nudged his Striper forward, ignoring the frustrated man.

Late afternoon brought the baggage laden platoon to a single lane stone bridge which crossed a shallow forty foot wide creek. Shade trees, mainly birches, shaded the other side of the bridge. The light breeze and billowy clouds seemed to belie Yganak's earlier feelings.

"Any time allowed for some fishing?" A Trooper yelled to Raff.

"Have you secured the other end of the bridge?" Raff shot back.

"No, that hasn't been done."

"Then neither is any fishing allowed....See to the bridge!"

The Trooper, along with two others, crossbows at the ready, gently spurred their Stripers up onto the bridge. As usual for this northern part of the country, everything had the concept 'defense' built into it. The single lane bridge, with twin three storey towers rising from its mid point proved no exception. The troopers stopped, studying the towers. A movement at the windows showed them occupied.

Then a voice hailed the trio from the top of the tower. "Who is it that wishes to cross?" The accent of the red-tunicked soldier at the top identified him as a southerner.

"We are the Church Guard." The Trooper answered as politely as possible, considering the circumstances.

"We don't recognize no Church Guard about here....Be off with you." And then he commenced cursing. Simultaneously, the Troopers heard the galloping of Stripers in front of them.

"Time to teach these heathens a thing or two?" Queried the trooper to the right.

"Only if you can hit him."

There was a twanging noise, then a yell, followed by a man dropping off the tower's parapet to the cobblestones below. His body slowed the approaching Stripers. About twenty-five men decked in red tunics, swords drawn. The narrow bridge prevented the attackers from riding more than three abreast. The crossbow man galloped off to alert Yganak: the other two troopers would buy some time. At less then fifty paces, the crossbows fired, the single lane bridge clogged as two more casualties crowded the lane. The panicky red-tunicked soldiers blundered into each other, exposing their inexperience. The two Troopers safely made their escape.

The physicians, dismounted, cluttered the end of the bridge, But they moved quickly to let the Troopers through. In two ranks, the platoon gathered behind the physicians, Yganak, crossbow in hand, positioned himself squarely in the middle. The galloping stopped as the attackers came within eighty paces of the Troopers. A tense foreboding quiet ensued. The Troopers quietly called out their personal targets.

A red cloaked man, both gloved hands in the air, rode forward. Within easy talking distance, he stopped. "You have offended us." He suggested in a nasally toned voice. "Why is it that three of my men are dead?...I demand justice!...Give me their murderers!"

"But you have no authority......And you belong to whom?" Yganak replied, almost relieved that his misgivings about today were correct.

"This is our bridge!" The reply, curt.

"This bridge belongs to those citizens of Haaf and to the King."

"That sick old fart...."

"You shall clear the bridge, immediately." Yganak raised his hand, when he dropped it, the platoon would fire.

"Hold, my good man." The red cloaked one suddenly changed his tune. He smiled brightly, revealing a mouthful of broken teeth. "How about a deal? You get the bridge. I get the physicians."

"Why might you want them? They don't even have proper credentials. They are just a bunch of lazy hired lackeys."

The stunned physicians turned to stare at Yganak, hatred shot from their squinting eyes.

"No matter. Someone wants to talk with them."

Terrified, the physicians turned to stare at the red cloaked man. He spoke directly to them. "You incompetent fools were well paid....... But you failed."

"I have no reason to make a deal with the Evil One, nor any of his idiotic stooges." Yganak leveled his voice.

"Then we shall take them by force......You'll see another squad of my men to your right... That makes the odds definitely in my favor."

His words were true, from the shadows advanced some thirty red-tunicked soldiers, a majority on foot. Once in a defensive angle, they stopped.

"Shall we deal. You can have both your lives and the bridge... Just give me these worthless potion-makers and we'll disappear...You don't loose any men." A smile glinted across his deeply wrinkled face. He knew something. "Yes, Yganak, I know you............. Surprized?"

"Yes." He answered, then changed to another topic. "And what guarantee do you give?"

"My word."

"And your word was given long ago, as a member of the High Council. There you swore to uphold the King and your country."

"You are much too serious, Yganak. These days of Haaf are soon about to end....As are those who decide to remain with the old King and the old God."

"Obviously, I'll require something beyond your word. You, I can not trust."

He flung his red cloak around before responding to Yganak. "Then I will remain with you until the sunset... My men will escort the physicians to our camp....How do you like that?....... Me, your honorable hostage?" His countenance bore the look of a man who just concluded the world's greatest swindle, and got away with it.

Caught in the middle, their miserable lives on the line, the physicians panicked. The Church Guard refused to allow them to retreat, unless they wished to be trampled underfoot. One ran to the red-tunicked leader, begging on his knees for mercy. A moment later, his head rolled down the bridge ramp, coming to rest at Baltee's feet. He flushed white and puked.

"Hreenki." Yganak said calmly. "This deal needs to be concluded before all of your hostages die."

"I agree." He replied while casually wiping off his sword blade. "My Master will need proof we captured these moronic drugdabblers........We have a deal?"

"Yes." Yganak replied, his slanted eyes narrowed. "I believe there is no other choice."

Hreenki guided his Striper off the bridge, placing himself in the midst of the Church Guard. His mounted men, swords drawn, unceremoniously tied up the physicians, trussed them over the saddles of some empty Stripers, and galloped away. Loud cursing permitted Raff to trace their journey. Once across the bridge, they took a sharp right and then north along the stream. They're heading directly into the Dark Lands, Raff thought to himself.

The other contingent of red-tunicked men, apparently upon a pre-arranged signal from Hreenki, suddenly charged. Swiftly, the bolt from Raff's crossbow echoed on Hreenki's balding head, sending the unconscious man to the cobblestones. Then the Trooper's crossbows sang, bringing down the mounted troops. A quick charge with their infamous double-headed broadaxes flying collapsed any lingering resistance. What few survived to surrender proved to be southerners also, mostly illiterate men from the swamp.

"I think ya breaked 'is neck." A Trooper offered to Raff after examining Hreenki.

"Better his than ours." Raff replied rather dryly. He finished inspecting the ropes binding the prisoners together then dumped Hreenki's slackened body over a pack Striper.

Yganak sent four men, dismounted, to explore the twin towers. Waiting their return, everyone ate a cold meal. Off to the side, Yganak confided with some of those who discovered the round shields and the red tunics. They confirmed his evaluation. The prisoners used the old shields and still wore the tunics. Whoever sold these items to the serfs obviously didn't know how stupid their actions were. Which also meant these peddlers certainly couldn't be in league with the Evil One. However, one mystery still stood. Who were these peddlers? And just what, exactly what did they believe they might be doing?

Yganak absentmindedly accepted some cheese and a mug of ale. So deep into his mystery, he only noticed them when he attempted to mount his Striper. If anyone noticed his embarrassment, they kept quiet.

The three troopers returned, carrying the fourth. "The towers are empty, Sir. But Lanf, ees not so good. Got stabbed in the shoulder. Lost a lot of blood."

"Can he make it to the next outpost?"

"I dont rightly no, Sir."

"Raff, check him out."

In an attempt to save the Trooper's life, Yganak ordered the platoon to camp in the towers for the night. Raff spent the night utilizing what few medicines were available, even so, like Yganak, he realized he only bought time for the Trooper. Yganak, finally secure enough to take a break, curled up on a cot and fell asleep, exhausted.

Morning arrived late, the slow drizzle preventing any sense of the sun's rising from reaching the eyes of those encamped in the towers. Raff saw to the Trooper's regular duties. Yganak, still a bit weary, spent the morning being idle. That, of course, was his perception. Raff declared he went fishing, or, more exactly, drowning worms. During these late morning hours Lanf died, surrounded by the other Troopers. Before continuing on with their journey, Yganak conducted the funeral service. As the last flames from the pyre died away, the Church Guard silently mounted up. They had a score to settle.

A strange quietness invaded the platoon as they rode through the steady drizzle. The new, vicious reality set in. The old enemy, the soulless Kyykki added to itself Haafians, men of their own kind. This change weighed heavily upon them. The old black-and-white warfare became grey as the afternoon. The skirmish at the bridge, and the death of a fellow Trooper stamped these new issues into their souls forever.

That night, after the drizzle ended and the thinly threading fog set in, the platoon silently rode past the next barracks, making up for lost time and permitting Yganak to reach the peddler's waggon by sunrise. There, within a half day's ride of their destination, Yganak believed his mysteries would be solved.

A deadly blinding sun tore through the early morning fog, returning some life to the weary Troopers. With justly warranted anticipation they goaded their tired Stripers forward, hoping soon to dismount for breakfast.

Even Yganak wore a less bleak smile. He too wished for a break, the opportunity to unravel these bothersome mysteries.

Dark smoke wafting above some mature willows seemed to indicate their overnight sojourn was about to end. Then, dusky red flames shot up through the willows, immediately redefining their intended destination. Muffled cries could be heard as well as cursing, all in Haafian. Raff immediately sent a squad ahead. Unfortunately, the overwork from the night's traveling permitted them to move only slightly faster than the rest.

Crossbows at the ready, they proceeded along the cobblestone road towards the rapidly increasing inferno. The screams and cursing had disappeared, leaving only the roaring of the flames.

Responding to the squad's distant hand signals, Raff spread out the remaining Troopers. Yganak stationed himself next to Raff who co-ordinated the platoon's movements from the line's center. A few moments barely passed before the Yldan peddler's campsite, what charred evidence remained, came into view. Two troopers had dismounted, exploring the still hot and smoldering waggon and its environs. They signaled back that no persons were found, either dead or alive. Some blackened and hollowed out round shields lay in the embers of the waggon. Tracks indicated a goodly number of mounted men had been involved, with larger hoofprints ascertaining that the Massive Blues, at least three teams had been present.

"I hate mysteries." Yganak mumbled as he dismounted. "Secure the area." He commanded. He retreated into mumbling again. "Maybe six Massive Blues, but only one waggon....That makes no sense."

"Perhaps, it does, Sir."

"Raff?"

"Yes, Sir....It could be that the other waggons and their contents were stolen. That explains where the Massive Blues went. And perhaps, the Yldans we wanted to meet."

"And this done by those damned scoundrels we encountered earlier."

"Yes, Sir. We know the Evil One doesn't have much regard from those who disobey him."

A Trooper, one who had investigated the rutted road heading north from the campsite, excitedly flagged his arms. "Quickly!" He yelled. "Another campsite.....And a beautiful creature."

Indeed she was, blonde hair, rounded eyes and healthy blue skin. A fearfulness showed itself in her eyes, but she stood, erect and proud. Her gown, though torn and mud smeared, did not prove her a peddler, but added still another burden to Yganak's enigmas.

"We've all heard about these 'blue ladies' before. This one isn't going to kill anyone else." A Trooper raised his crossbow.

"Put it down!" Yganak snapped angrily. "She isn't one of them. Look at her! She carries herself too well. She is of another race........ No pointed ears, no slanted eyes."

"Another race?"

"I don't know what else to tell you, Raff....If the Holy One created Haafians and Yldans, why not others?" Yganak preached. He dropped his broadaxe to the grass, and began walking towards her, arms open, palms up.

The beautiful lady recognized the broadaxe as well as the Light Striper uniform worn by Yganak. "You...are Haaf?" She smiled as she nervously spoke in halting Haafian.

Yganak stopped and smiled in return. "Yes, we are."

"I am Jelkio." She spoke softly. "I am from the Kingdom of Tath."

"I am Yganak." He spoke slow and distinctly. "These are my men."

"Will you hurt me?"

"No. We are honorable men, bound by the laws of the Holy One."

"I have heard of your Holy One.......I will trust you, Ya-gan-ick."

The Troopers began to relax, Jelkio's whole demeanor disarming their tension. Raff ordered a meal prepared and the Stripers attended to. Camp was called for the day.

Yganak offered Jelkio a seat near him so they might talk. Raff soon arrived with tea for both of them.

"Thank you, Rall." She said.

"Raff, Lady Jelkio." He politely attempted to correct her.

"I am sorry." She sputtered. "Only three double moons ago, as you tell time, I did not know that you people, Haafians, existed...That is when Sarg and his company of Yldans rescued us................" She stammered to a stop. Her emotions, once again, were in an uproar.

Meanwhile, the name 'Sarg' overwhelmed the tired Yganak. "You know the 'Sarg'?" He posed the question as neutrally as possible, though inside he felt himself ready to explode.

"Yes. ..He is a great warrior....He found us locked in the vallkane-now. He saved us.... He died when it exploded....Along with Queen Sjura." Her eyes filled full of tears.

Yganak, well aware of Sarg's clandestine mission, unexpectedly felt the pain of another loss. This Tath, whatever exactly she and it were, could not have dreamed up such a story. The pieces of Sarg's mission fit together too well, unfortunately.

"How are you here?" Yganak tried to keep his vocabulary as simple as possible. She certainly understood Haafian, but he had naught an idea of what 'Tath' might be.

"Some of us ...made it through the explosion... Nooy and Kofe and Deep Owl.and Qill.......Luuft died helping us against the devil-men." She wept again. "Then we met fat Oros and Rux and Nadre. And came here."

Yganak easily shed his agonizingly wearied body and mind as this incredible story unfolded before him. He desperately prayed about untangling the mystery: the Holy One chose to give him an excess. He chugged his tea and called for more. Raff arrived with a plate of bread and cheese as well. Both Jelkio and Yganak ate in silence.

"How do you know our talk?" Yganak posed, hoping to draw more information from Jelkio.

"You mean 'language'? She gave him a smile which forced an immediate blush, though being polite, she did not press her advantage.

"I'm sorry. I did not mean to insult you." Yganak apologized. "I simply wished to hear more of your story and of what happened to the Yldans you traveled with."

She finished her tea before responding. "After we met Oros and Rux and Nadre at Krucik's mansion...They burnt it down, you know.. ...We traveled here, through people-eating vines and an army ... They killed Luuft." She covered her tear-streaked face with her long blue fingers, sobbing.

"I didn't know." Yganak gently placed his large hand on her shoulder. Jelkio looked up and wiped her eyes.

"Thank you." She smiled melancholy. "We then came here, with the three waggons we captured."

Yganak held up his hands as if to say 'enough!'. So many pieces came flying at him. He felt overwhelmed by the knowledge of this stranger from an unknown territory. Yet, fascinatingly enough, he believed her. He shook his head in a futile effort to clear it. He didn't recognize himself: intrigued by someone, a female even, whom he didn't know, yet believed. He wasn't too secure with this newness.....Or had he fallen into a well-prepared trap. He shook his long-haired head again.

"I'm the one who needs to apologize." Yganak said. "This is all a bit much for me."

"You've never met a Tath before, have you?"

"Obviously not." He nervously shuddered.

"Your Sarg acted pretty much the same way. Queen Sjura had his head swimming. Maybe you Haafian men are all the same?" She winked and then caught herself. "Not true. Brey and Vauk were very different personalities....people....different."

Yganak just listened, dumbfounded. This lady even knew all the people on the 'secret mission'. Except Brey must be Breel. No females belonged to the Light Striper.

"Sir!" A familiar voice called to Yganak from the campfire. "Shall we rest, Sir?"

Yganak, engrossed within his own world of speculative thoughts, heard nothing. Jelkio answered for him. "Camp and rest. We'll find the others later tonight."

Raff saw that Yganak appeared to be sleeping. He called for camp to be made and placed sentries. "Thank you, my Lady."

Yganak snapped to. "You know where your friends are? Why didn't they capture you as well?"

"They were poorly organ-zed...no leader." She said. "They were also angry...stupid....I had the camp to myself during the day. 'Blue Ladies' have...ev-vil....ev-vil....."

"Reputation?" Yganak offered.

She nodded and continued. "They carried off the Yldans....Tied behind some white-robed people."

"Damned Physicians!" He growled. "How do you know where they went?"

"It's the same path we came from." She stated matter-of-factly. "You rest." The firmness of her voice indicated this was not a suggestion. "There is no need to res--que...save, my...er..our friends now. Soon they are forced to stop." She spoke knowingly.

How?"

"Rux cut the people-eating vines. They cover the path. They can't get more than....."

"Enough." Yganak said. Yganak realized his supply of authority had emptied itself. "I'll get some sleep." He said softly.

Yganak slept exceedingly well; pleasant, even intoxicating dreams entertaining him. Raff, as second in command, now also unofficially behind the take-charge Jelkio, placed camp in order. The Troopers attentively listened to the stories that Jelkio shared concerning her country and her perilous journey. The most logical and literal thought she lied; Istells? Couldn't be? A country north of the dark Lands? Heretical! Others, however, enamored by the gracious lady, sought to draw closer, asking perplexing questions which, potentially, might embarrass Jelkio.

Raff suddenly became her guardian in these manners, severely limiting the potential of the double entendres. The larger moon now hovered above the diminutive entranced group. A sputtering of wind through the willows and the aroma of well-cooked food firmly displaced their exhaustion. None expected rest and relaxation until reaching Haaf North. Now it arrived most welcomingly, albeit without the original 'guests'.

Jelkio paused her narrative for a moment to sip the herbal tea. She sputtered with it when she saw the two 'extras' materialize behind the row of seated Troopers.

"That's no way to greet some old friends." Came a deep rounded voice.

The surprized Troopers immediately surrounded the odd looking pair: their deportment far from friendly.

"Its my friends, Oros the Priest and Rux." Jelkio urgently yelled. "Don't hurt them!"

The commotion roused the sleeping Yganak. He came to with a start. "What's going on?" He demanded in a half-slumbered voice, so out-of-character that the Troopers turned away from the newcomers. He stamped his bare feet, and stood, forcing his way back into the land of reality. "Well?..... What seams to be the problem?"

"Visitors, Sir!" Raff quickly responded, his broadaxe in hand. "Jelkio claims to know them.....A fat priest and a skinny...."

"Rux and Oros." Yganak forcibly interrupted. "Give them something to eat. And send them over here... Jelkio too."

"Yes, Sir!"

Finally collecting himself, he called the newcomers plus Jelkio and Raff to conference with him. His blunt invitation couldn't be refused.

"Seems you two have a strange way of showing up when least expected." Yganak muttered into his tea mug after everyone had been seated.

"And why should I disappoint you?" The portly Oros returned, his eyebrows just twitching for a verbal competition.

"Not now, Oros." Yganak scolded. "We have work ahead of us."

"You mean the morons who stole your Physicians?" Rux taunted, catching an elbow to the ribs, gratuitously donated by Jelkio.

Yganak, threw his mug across the campsite. "So, tell me what you've done? I'm almost afraid I'll..."

"Shut up!" Oros gruffed. "We've done you a favor....And one for us as well....Some of our friends were also hauled away." Oros came close to being contemptuous.

"Actually, we had no other choice." Rux casually re-entered the conversation.

Jelkio thought his demeanor transmuted; Rux seemed more alive, more vibrant. Perhaps he had finally come to terms with his 'gift'.

"Nadre, Kofe, Deep Owl, Nooy and Qill needed rescued. They are the Evil One's 'wanted list....But you all ready know that." The thinnest of smirks momentarily crossed his face, one overlooked by all except Jelkio. She squeezed his bony hand, and smiled at him...a proud smile. He merely nodded in return. "Anyway, our people should be here at sun-up, with the waggons. Everyone's doing fine."

Jelkio, as a grateful acknowledgement of an answered prayer, grabbed Rux in a huge hug, knocking him off his seat and into the grass. She landed on top of him and planted a kiss on his mouth. He wrapped his arms about her and returned the kiss.

"I should have known I could count on you. Nadre said you could do most anything." She whispered into his ear.

Had it not been for an overly loud and pietistic remark from Oros, the embrace would have continued indefinitely.

"How can you explain what happened, my dear Rux, when your mind is far from the intended topic?"

"Maybe I don't give a damn." He grumbled as he gently moved Jelkio to the side and sat up. "It shouldn't take long to finish this." He whispered to no one but Jelkio.

Jelkio, realizing her impetuousness left her royally undignified, especially while tumbling to the ground, now slowly adjusted her gown. Deeper inside, she wondered if Rux received an erroneous message from her; she merely wanted to thank him for the rescue effort. After all, Nooy ....yes Nooy, she reminded herself, was safe. But Nooy, she jarringly reminded herself, had not the slightest idea of her feelings for him.

With a brilliantly rash idea in her head, she stomped over to the trail, She would wait for Nooy. And the rest of her friends as well. This time everyone was returning alive. She uttered a sincere prayer of thanks to her God for their deliverance.

"Jelkio!" Rux called after her. "Aren't you interested in the rest of the story?"

"I have an idea of how you operate." The blonde replied flippantly. "Besides, everyone is safe.. That's all that matters to me." She walked on, beyond hearing distance. The gory details and their impact, she willingly let the menfolk enjoy.

"Yganak," Rux began, his voice sour. "We arrived at this campsite as the morons headed down the waggon path. From recent experience, Oros and I knew they wouldn't get far. They thought they succeeded, in spite of the demise of their illustrious leader." Rux curtly bowed towards an embarrassed Raff, who communicated nothing in return. "Towards evening, they camped and got drunk on some physician's concoction." He paused, grimacing. "We could not save the physicians." He announced rapidly, desiring to plow through the details of their judgement.

Oros, noticing Rux's reluctance, picked up the story. "The traitors found appropriate punishment. Their deaths came at the hands of those who supposedly saved them. BUT, they were saved only so that their real master, one of the Demon Lords, could deliver his justice: death to those who fail. Ultimately, as the Holiness Code declares unto us, 'Evil is self destructive.' It has no mercy, no grace."

"In short," Rux cut through the sermonizing. "The damned doctors were disemboweled and then roasted on spits, still alive." He looked over to Oros, then returned to the subject. "The Demon Lord feasted on their raw entrails."

Gasping and gagging noises suddenly flooded the camp as Troopers allowed the abject horror and negation of Haafian ethics to reach them. Any passing thoughts of a victory celebration were vanquished by Rux's blunt details. The ultimate wisdom of the Holiness Code apprehended them as never before. Book knowledge translated itself into real day-today living. The gruesome reality of true evilness no longer lay undisturbed or disguised. Now it was inseparable from their duties as Troopers of the Church Guard, and not as an abstract ideal. Once their noises subdued, Rux continued.

"The Demon Lord wished to present our friends as a gift to his Lord, the evil one himself. Therefore, they were unmolested, including Nadre." All attention focused upon Rux, akin to cats waiting to pounce upon their prey. "The Demon Lord ended his life in purification."

Even Yganak drew back at this oblique reference to justice.

"Just speak in plain words, Rux. I'm not prepared to ferret out your cute riddles."

"As you wish."

"I'll finish the story." An also irritated Oros broke in. "The damned Demon Lord vanquished in the same flames that claimed the physicians. After Rux quartered him, that is." Another queasy gasp kept Oros from continuing. "The other traitors are scattered throughout their campsite, dead....Our friends are bringing all remaining provisions and equipment with them. Two waggons full." The fat priest sat down, indicating the story's end.

The Troopers stared at Rux, suddenly realizing he was the 'one' who had the awesome 'gift' they heard rumored about. Yganak silently wept, head bowed. The escalation he desperately wished to avoid exploded upon him. A civil war erupted about him, forever blurring the easy demarcation lines between good and evil, black and white. Yganak sighed heavily. His comfortable old world died before him. Retreating from this new repulsive reality became tempting, even tantalizing, but freedom existed only in the truth. In spite of his inward struggle, Yganak knew he would not desert his tradition nor his God, the Holy One.

Rux, in the meantime, meandered through the questioning Troopers, and out to the waggon trail, intentionally finding himself beside a quieted Jelkio.

"I'm sorry." He finally blurted. "I didn't mean to take advantage of you, my Lady."

"My Lady?" She sounded surprized.

"Indeed." He said most soberly. "I've watched you watch Nooy."

"You what?" A tinge of anger crept into her voice.

"I also watch everything else."

"I know." She sighed slightly. "Its that damned 'gift' of yours." She enunciated with more anger. Then Jelkio turned to him. "I'm angry at myself. I haven't the honesty you have." She confessed.

"Yes, my Lady." Rux said softly. "Nor does Nooy know."

"I need to become truthful before I hurt more of the people I care about."

"Even I might appreciate that." He smiled before wandering back into camp, searching for a mug or two of ale. Jelkio, her long blonde hair streaming about her anxious face as the breeze fluffed its way by, stood alone, awaiting her love, her Nooy, who had the dutiful right to know her feelings for him. She stared down the rutted waggon path for a long time. Then, as if driven by some chastening demon, she suddenly hiked up her long dirty gown and sprinted down the path towards the should-be coming friends. Rux watched her leave, his heart aching as well. Grabbing another mug of ale, he slowly started after her.

Instead of securing Jelkio's safety, Rux bumped into a bewildered Jabbi and the rather cantankerous Kloshic. Both had relocated off to the left of the waggon path, leaving the breeze to dissipate their customary dry fog. Rux studied their tight faces, their appearance wasn't deigned for a celebration.

"I suspect you'll want Yganak and Oros to join us." And the thin protector walked back to camp, head bowed. If any day had been designated to deliver to him the ultimate in hardships and heartaches, this must be it. So Rux brooded as he kicked his way across the campsite.

"Jabbi and Kloshic want a visit." He said while tapping Oros on the shoulder. Oros turned, glimpsing the two off in the shadows. "Bring Yganak." Rux morosely called as he kicked his way back to Jabbi.

"Seems this isn't your day." A typically sarcastic Kloshic announced.

"Only because you've brought more good news...Like Haaf North has fallen to the Kyykki."

"No, only about ninety percent." His wrinkled face drew up to examine Rux more closely. "Your heart hurts." His tone quite sympathetic and open.

"Yes. And, damn it, nothing I can do will fix it."

"You're much wiser than I ever gave you credit for." Kloshic sagely replied, a hint of lightness within his deeply set eyes.

Rux forced a twisted smile in return, a smile rendered in dejection, straight from his heart. "You know the others are safe? That 'bunch' of renegades and their Demon Lord are dead, along with the King's Physicians?"

"Sounds as if you've been extra busy." Jabbi noted. "Time for you to take a vacation."

Rux looked away.

Oros and Yganak rounded the copse of willows. Neither presented evidence as to their state of mind, and that included any anxiety. The quintet stood quietly in the shadows, each readying himself for the next blow.

Jabbi broke through the foreboding silence. "Haaf North belongs to the Evil One." He muttered and slurred his speech, forcing out the unwanted truth. "The Church there recapitulated into the damned one's camp as have most of the Light Striper....The few faithful are headed our way before nightfall. Along with any civilians who desire to leave."

"And they're just going to walk away from the fortress?" Rux asked, incredulous.

"No. The new Abbot is even more of a demon than his dead predecessor." Jabbi answered softly, painfully soft. "I'll assume they'll allow the Faithful leave, so long as all their worldly possessions remain behind.....Then, when the waggon road narrows for the swamp, they'll be ambushed, massacred. Any who might survive will be murdered by the 'Mounted Reds' as they now portray themselves." He laughed, but not funny. "Ironic, isn't it?" He queried no one in particular. "We have a civil war under our noses...And we were stupid enough to believe we only need fight those damned frog-faced 'things' from the Dark Lands."

Yganak put a hand on Jabbi's shoulder and met him eye-to-eye. "Then this is why the Holy One has placed us here at this crucial time.....There will be a massacre....But not one of the Holy One's faithful!" His voice resonated with infuriated determination. Righteous indignation swept through him, eclipsing his depression and any other feelings. "We will stand and fight!" His voice softened. "I'm assuming that your information...."

"We stole it before we left." Rux interrupted. "And Ilty is taking it to the other Elders."

Yganak groused before resuming, something about Rux irritated him. He didn't require such distractions now. "What military equipment do the waggons carry?"

"Some fifty old style crossbows. Plenty of swords, but poor quality. The shields are gone." Oros answered.

"How many bolts?"

"A few barrels full, but they're old. Don't expect too much accuracy from them."

"How many faithful Light Stripers can we expect?" Yganak's questions refused to stop as he assessed and then re-invented the upcoming battle. He paced the campsite, commanding Raff to have the platoon battle-ready, half dismounted. Then he quickly strode to the waiting circle of friends. "How soon can the waggons arrive?"

"Should be soon, I hope." Answered Rux anxiously.

"Will the men be able to join in the battle?"

"Not Deep Owl. His injuries have caught up with him."

"So I can count on three more." Yganak made it perfectly clear that he relied upon these additional men.

"Maybe four or five." Rux returned, straining to look past his shoulder to the soft steady treading of the Massive Blues. "Waggons coming!"

"Four or five?"

"Don't think you're so important that the two ladies will comply with your traditional obligations….I'm warning you… Don't even think about forbidding them to fight. They've been victims, now its catch-up time." Rux elaborated. "Time of justice…" He studied Yganak's face, ready to lecture him about true righteousness if the leader exhibited any signs of misgiving.

"I've lost this one, correct?"

"That the smartest answer I've heard from you in ages." A smug-faced Oros quipped. A sword appeared from his brown robe. "Tell us the strategy."

The group encircled Yganak, both apprehensive and relieved. He breathed deeply then spoke. "There are well over two thousand Troopers against us and the civilians. I'll assume only a few hundred will be sent to massacre the unarmed civilians and faithful Light Horse Troopers… Unfortunately, we number fifteen. Therefore, I'm proposing first, an ambush, then a holding action at the tower bridge until Jabbi brings us reinforcements from D'Ka."

"I'm not leaving until after the fight."

"I didn't give you a choice, Elder or not...Time is essential.."

Jabbi vanished before Yganak finished his sentence. "Some Troopers just might arrive earlier than the obnoxious Commander ever thought." He vowed to himself as the cloud of dry fog inundated those remaining.

Yganak cleared his throat. He outlined the next day. Group one, headed by himself and the dismounted Troopers would strike from the east, coming behind the ambushers hidden in the swamp. The ambushers would be forced into the open. The troopers would remain concealed. Group two would head up the road with the waggons, posing as Striper traders. Rux would ride ahead to locate the faithful Troopers, sending them to re-arm at the waggons. Those Troopers along with the mounted men would manage a slow retreat to the bridge, protecting the civilians. At sunset, but prior to the two moons' rising, everyone was to gather at the tower bridge. They would hold there until reinforcements arrived. Yganak paused, waiting for any comments.

Rux coughed.

"Out with it." Yganak ordered.

"You done forgotted de ladies." He rudely mocked.

"Actually, I haven't." He brusquely retorted. "They can choose whichever group they want. Your injured Deep Owl stays in the waggon, however. Heroics are not an invested priority. Staying alive is...."

Finally, the waggons turned the corner past the copse of willows, a joyous Jelkio riding next to a white-faced Nooy, her arm about him. His strangely twisted countenance and curled smile told the entire story to Rux. His own heartache instantly returned. He grabbed the reins of the first Striper he located, swung into the saddle and rode to explain the plan to Kofe.

Qill jumped into the rear of the waggon to unload the armaments.

Nadre bundled up the vividly protesting Deep Owl, wrenched the reins of the Striper tethered to the waggon gate and rode to Rux, her face bore the mask of impenetrable determination.

"Time for justice?" Rux casually noted as she drew near.

"More like revenge." She said tersely. "This time...no more, ever, shall I be the victim!"

"Good." He said simply. "Would you like to ride with me?" Without waiting for her answer, Rux tossed her a crossbow. "You can use it?"

"Want to be the first to find out?" She cutely beamed.

"I'm looking forward to this....Maybe we'd make a good team."

Nadre, caught off guard by the remark, momentarily hesitated with her Striper. What, exactly did this 'gifted' bag-of-bones intend. She had little time at present to deal with the issue. Squeezed elsewhere in her thoughts, it would be contemplated later. There was a battle to be fought. It came first.

Rux galloped ahead, hoping to locate Jed. He believed a one-armed Trooper would stand out in the escaping masses. More specifically he thought, Jed would be at the rear, attempting to organize a counteraction. However, in being unarmed, it meant suicide. Jerking his Striper about, Rux cantered back to the waggons where he untethered an entire file of Stripers. Then, with Qill and Jelkio's assistance, the mounts were outfitted with swords, bolts and crossbows, all dangling from the pommels.

Nadre caught up to Rux, righteously taking half the mounts from him. "If I turn to the left around the bend, we'll reach the Troopers quicker." Is all she said.

"No." Rux answered. "You head out towards the bay, off the waggon road. There's less danger of an ambush there."

"I actually thought you didn't care." She hurled the phrase at him. Then the truth hit her: she lied to herself. And now he knew it.

"But I do care....I think." He muddled through his reply. "But maybe not as you might think." She never heard the last sentence. The clankings and clattering of the waggons destroyed all others noises.

From the cobblestone road Rux watched the masses of disorganized civilians stream towards him. All appeared empty-handed, just as had been anticipated. Within a few moments, he spotted a group of some forty blue tunicked men at the rear of the multitudes. Many carried the elderly, others worked to keep them people moving and together. The final tall Trooper, standing alone between the multitudes and the fortress-city walls, raised a crude banner, a black chalice upon a white sheet. Bolts shot at him from the drawbridge gate.

"That's Jed!" Rux barked. "I'm going out for him!"

Tying the reins for all other Stripers to his saddle, Rux kicked his heels into his Striper's flanks, galloping to rescue Jed. Deftly using his 'gift', he gently shoved the driven multitudes to the sides, cutting a straight line to the faithful Trooper. His heart sank as he rushed through them: despair, disbelief, shock, utter hopelessness claimed their dirty, tired faces. The fatalistic, believing they knew the future, duly accepted their onerous fate. They slumped to the ground casting off their few belongings to anyone in sight. Rux sickened on this act of faithlessness.

To his right, sturdy dockhands cursed their new lot in life, demanding only a few clubs to wreak revenge. Rux drew back on the reins, shouting at the dockhands. With maligned smiles, they jogged off towards Nooy's waggon. Another thirty for our side, he thought.

Another moment late a dumbfounded Jed was in the saddle.

"Give me the banner!" Ordered Rux, who promptly left it fall. "I'll make you another one....Grab the sword!"

As many Troopers mounted, they turned, trotting out of firing range only to meet Nadre. She comfortably sat in her saddle, surrounded by almost twenty blue-tunicked Troopers, all mounted, all well-armed. Another twenty, dismounted gathered about, still unarmed.

"Share the weapons!" Nadre yelled.

Obediently, the mounted Troopers tossed crossbows and swords to the rest, never once questioning the authority of this unknown Lady.

"Form up to receive cavalry!". Jed barked.

An inverted albeit ragged wedge appeared, swordsmen and crossbowmen alternating. Jed, sword over his head, stood in the apex between Rux and Nadre. The other mounted men covered the flanks. Red-tunicked Troopers slowly entered the field, masses of them deliberately forming the standard three lines. Arrogance showed in their demeanor.

To their immediate right, anguished screams from the swamp suddenly filled the dusty air. The petrified civilians came to a complete halt, terrified of the noise. Then as if of one solitary mindset, they suddenly turned, rushing for the narrow cobblestone road. Disorganized and smashed together, they presented the very target the Mounted Reds wanted.

Jed's blue eyes froze on Rux, necessitating an explanation. "Well?"

"We split up our forces. The ambushers in the swamp received justice."

"A few less damned traitors." Jed smiled. "We'll take out some more shortly."

"More than a few, Sir!" Came determined, hopeful words from a Trooper on the left flank. "Turn around, Sir!!"

His ever-widening eyes beheld a positively bizarre vision. Civilians added themselves to the wedge, the dockhands stormed across the small field armed with poles, swords and crossbows. The half-platoon of Church Guards emerged from the swamp having fashioned rough-cut birch lances. They stayed to the shadows, waiting for a flanking opportunity. Further back, the two waggons blocked the narrow road from the Mounted Reds. Nooy and Kofe, waited, at the ready. Jelkio stood waving, crossbow in hand. In the chaos, few paid her any attention.

War Tubas blew violently: the charge began.

Yganak and his men appeared at the edge of the field, his halfdozen men stampeding the Massive Blues towards the on-coming Mounted Reds. Then Yganak grabbed one, hauled himself up and charged, lance in hand. His men immediately followed suite.

The War Tubas rattled the ground once more: two ranks, instead of the usual one, now charged.

"Choose your targets and wait!" Jed instructed. "Dockhands! Step into line!" Now he yelled, faithfully determined that this 'last stand' count for something. "We fight for the Holy One! Blessed be His Name!!"

At four hundred feet, the crossbows fired, leaving torn holes in the red tunicked line. Armed only with broadaxes, the Mounted Reds suffered heavily. Twice more the crossbows twanged. Then the Reds hit the line, angry and savage. In the carnage that followed, no quarter was taken none given.

Rux deftly ducked a crude swing of a broadaxe, then decapitated the Trooper. A blue tunicked Trooper kicked the body from the saddle and mounted up. Nadre aimed at a priest wearing a dragon helmet. He died clutching the bolt in his chest.

Even so, the wedge slowly retreated towards the waggons, where more civilians waited their turn to fight. Yganak's small group, now reinforced by the rest of his platoon, surprized the second charging rank, rolling them up to mid-field. Then the sheer numbers of Mounted Reds pushed them back into the wedge.

"Nice day to die, Sir!" Jed shouted over the din to Yganak.

"No, Son." Yganak yelled back. "I'm here to live." He scanned the battlefield. The immediate situation lingered in dreadful precariousness. "Reform at the waggons!" He studied Rux. "Give them something to remember us by!"

Rux smiled and cantered his Striper away from the retreating and reforming wedge. Nadre, crossbow reloaded, followed him. He scanned the field. The second line had passed through, causing as much damage as the first. The third mounted line, now walked forward to finish off any survivors. With deliberate strokes of his long-boned hands, he dispatched the middle of the third line. He felt a thud and landed on the grass, a red tunicked man landed on him, Nadre's bolt through his skull.

"Stand up!" She called. "I'm not reloaded." She swung her crossbow to fend off a broadaxe cut. The crossbow splintered, Nadre crashed to the ground, blood on her scalp and draining from her ears.

Rux rolled and simultaneously fired, slicing both trooper and mount in two. Furious he stood, mowing down the now charging line as a sickle cuts the dry wheat stalks. Then he fired again. Anything red went down. Then he cradled the unconscious Nadre, unaware of the battle anymore. Through the vicious combat he wandered, dazed, still carrying Nadre.

"Over here!" Screamed a female voice, Jelkio's. "Bring her to the waggon!"

Silently, oblivious to the butchery about, Rux obeyed. "She's dead!" He cried out as he handed her limp body to Jelkio.

The weary Tath examined Nadre, but her face revealed nothing. "Make her life count for something." She somberly told Rux. "Make it count!" She demanded.

The next empty mount became Rux's. Utilizing the Massive Blue as a plow, he diligently proceeded to cut down anything red. Once free of the sickening melee, he meditated, gathering what strength still existed within him. He concentrated until sweat poured from his angular face, soaking his tunic. His fingers poised together, launching an ethereal shaft of sparkling bluish light towards the fortress-city's monumental east gate. Blinding everyone who beheld it, the immense solid beam struck the east gate as an arrow shatters a pane of glass. Huge fragments of rock, particles of warped twisted iron, splinters of gigantic oaken beams and of renegade troopers, hurtled high into the mid-day sky.

For a singular awesome instant this physical cloud of debris suspended itself in a silent sky. Then with a ferocity which only the Holy One possessed, the debris slammed into the city, gutting homes and warehouses, firing the marketplaces. Instantly, supernaturally, Haaf North existed as an incendiary. The scorched fortress city continued to smolder and burn.

Unfeeling, and beyond exhaustion, Rux collapsed atop the Massive

Blue, incognizant of the battling behind him. The Mounted Reds died everywhere. They had nowhere to retreat or hide. The vengeance of the former city residents allowed for no survivors nor mercy for their wounded.

Rux awoke to the grimmest of realities two evenings later. Yganak looking peaked and worn, kneeled beside him.

"Thank you." He said too soberly. "We, though few, are safe.... Haaf North is deserted. Actually, it's completely destroyed."

His own questioning thoughts, confused and muddled. Yganak's sentiments meant little. "Nadre?" He questioned earnestly. Then his bandaged head fell back upon the blanket covered grass. He turned his head right and then left. All that existed were the wounded and those who attended them.

"We lost half the platoon." His voice soft, almost choking to let the aching words out. "The Yldans are well and Jelkio..."

"Nadre?" Anger rose within him at Yganak's evasion. "Damn it!" He cried out in grief, trying to sit up. "Tell me of Nadre!"

"She's alive, not well.....just barely."

"Take me to her." He demanded, struggling to his feet, finding himself unable to balance. Oros jammed his shoulder under Rux's arm, steadying him. Rux's vision cleared and fogged again. "Thanks fat man. Good to have something sturdy to lean on."

"Perhaps, perhaps not." Oros shot back. "After all, you'll have to trust me....entirely."

"Just get me to Nadre." He ignored the retort, having only enough energy for one goal: Nadre.

The field of wounded covered most of the field. The path to Nadre doubled upon itself, there being no real paths. At one point the two passed by a newly dug cemetery. Rux shut his swollen eyes, pretending he observed nothing.

"Lying to yourself won't help our situation." Oros reminded him. "Almost seven hundred graves...and that's without counting the Mounted Reds."

"Just get...me....to Nadre." He groaned, his weakened body throbbed with a nauseating pain.

Nadre lay under one of the waggons, covered with a blanket, a soaked compress hid most of her head. Her face, clear, serene, and flaccid, caused Rux to heave. He flopped himself beside her. "What happened?" Tears flooded his eyes and dripped on Nadre.

"The scum who splintered her crossbow lived long enough to cleave her scalp." Jelkio replied, as pained by Nadre's condition as she was by Rux's. "She's my friend." She said, sobbing.

"She took a blow meant for me." The difficult words slowly rose from Rux. He shook his head, endeavoring to comprehend her illogical actions. Perhaps he refused to acknowledge the truth. Perhaps he found himself too stupid to realize what Nadre saw in him. He sat quietly, openly weeping as he touched Nadre's bruised shoulder.

Jelkio sat with him for a long while. Oros left, returning to his priestly duties of comforting the wounded, making sense of the carnage, pulling the ragged collection of survivors into a community. The huge man was exhausted, but his responsibilities outweighed the exhaustion.

Jelkio sat with Rux. They quietly prayed, each to a different god. But each prayed for the same healing. Jelkio shook her head. "You truly don't know, do you?" She gently inquired of Rux. "This is too different for you, isn't it?"

"What?" His voice terse, anguished. "She's dying....And for what?" He moved his hand from her shoulder. ".....I don't know."

"She loves you."

Rux did not reply. He remained motionless until after the moons rose, still Nadre did not respond. During her final rounds for the night, Jelkio gently pushed him over and covered him with a scraggly blanket. He slept beside Nadre.

As one convinced that he best benefited others by doing the least expected, Kloshic gave no thought to removing himself from Haaf North.

He stood with the jubilantly cheering populace as the Mounted Reds paraded out through the thirty foot thick east gate. No Demon Lord presented himself as King, yet. However, a too familiar face preached to the infatuated multitudes. Kloshic instantly recognized him. The Abbot from the monastery where Jabbi and he escaped. Kloshic figured the Evil One brought him here. No matter. His life was forfeit. Kloshic swore at the Abbot's new clerics. The man wore a hooded crimson robe decorated with a silver-black flying dragon. Kloshic swore again.

Kloshic mumbled to a Trooper standing along the main right-of-way. "What be diss celebrashun?"

"Another moron from across the bay." The Trooper sarcastically acknowledged to an overdressed merchant. "Well boy, it's this way. As the Holy One refused any questions directed to Him, he proved himself dead. Just like the old Abbot promised us..."

"That's correct." Added the smugly featured merchant. "So we got a new God. All business...No more of this damned mercy shit, no more forgiveness shit...No more sick and weak people to be responsible for...Hell with them if they can't produce enough for the new God." He laughed self-righteously, complimenting his Trooper friend. "All them damned weaklings left a while back..."

"Yep, them sure did. Even my platoon leader went. Sorry to see him leave. I always thought Jed had some sense, some potential."

"But now yoos be seain ta truth." Kloshic inferred. "Only ta wise end ta strong survive."

"For a newcomer, you catch on fast, boy." The merchant mocked, smirking. "But, I warn you. If you aren't tattooed afore the evening, you're liable to find yourself impaled." His fat finger pointed above the east. There on lances, hung the bloody corpses of a few hundred city dwellers. "Most are those confounded priests and their families. All refused to bow to the new God....Like I said," He pompously sprouted. "This new God loves perfection and obedience."

"Where da ya git der tat-toe?" Kloshic nervously interrupted.

"End of the street, go right." Stated the Trooper in a cold matter-of-fact voice. "But first you got to promise allegiance to the new God....Only then can you get the 'saving mark'."

"All rit." Kloshic mumbled. "But what be diss new gods name?"

"God's name is Ashuwa."

"A-shoo-waw?" Kloshic repeated. "Be it mean some 'tim?"

"Supposed to be 'destroyer', as in cleansing, so said the old Abbot."

Kloshic left before the merchant finished. He considered his newest self assignment. He must dismantle this new Abbot and his heinous theology. Such overtly blatant disregard for the Truth would not go unpunished. When the war Tubas blasted forth the second time, the Abbot, with two robust bodyguards, disappeared from the east gate landing. Just as quickly, Kloshic vanished in a haze of dry fog. The frenzied crowd never took interest.

Knowing full-well that the Abbot's traitorous identity lay concealed from the Church, Kloshic relocated to the Abbot's private historical library. Jabbi never knew of it existence, it being hidden behind the other bookcase in the narrow office. Its contents included several versions of the sacred writings of the ancients, a volume know as the New Test Ment. More valuable than that, the Abbot's private diary lay open on the stone podium. Kloshic judiciously packaged it and several copies of the former into a waterproof sack, then hurriedly relocated again. His destination: 'Nowhere', the only place of guaranteed security for the present time, though the most dangerous place in all of existence.

His dry fog hung in the air when the Abbot materialized moments later. Angry cursing oaths emerged from the camouflaged library, frightening more than a few curious novices. The Abbot froze with fear, the missing volumes spelled his execution by Ashuwa. When he realized the diary also vanished, all hope left his life. The Church knew of his defection to the Evil One.

Shortly thereafter, as the ancient bookcase was opened, a gruesome stench greeted the priests. The Abbot lay on his back, a silvered dagger through his heart, Dragon tattoos were still burning the flesh off his forearms.

As the screaming shriek of the Abbot's soul passed through 'Nowhere' on its miserable journey to Hell, Kloshic decided to release himself and rest in his cell at the Monastery. He slept thankfully that night, after spending much time in prayer. Obviously, he now realized, the elder whose demise had been predicted was the heretical Abbot. He smiled at the pole in the corner. Fishing days still lay ahead of him.

END OF CHAPTER 9

Chapter 10

Vosnob anxiously paced the parapet of newly finished observation tower of the castle. Its haunting panorama of bleak yellow-grey terrain spotted with deep-red boulders caught the eye. That bleak landscape was punctuated by gaped-mouthed volcanoes, seething incessant steam clouds and ash. Neither of these meant much to Vosnob. The fact that the land lay five hundred feet below the newly formed polished granite cliff, that brought him amazement. That the cliff was constructed by the Holy One Himself brought him a sense of security and a renewed faith.

This dawn found Vosnob wrapped in issues that only provoked his sense of fairness and ethics. Persuaded he must find an answer to correct the internal strife which exploded upon Haaf, he kept to himself in prayer and meditation. The boundaries, the assumptions he once found familiar dissolved before him. Was he a foreigner in his own land? His imagination implied this to be true. He slammed his fist into the palm of his left hand in disgust.

"You trying to play god again?" Came a cheerful feminine voice behind him. "I thought you gave that up?" Ilty, her pale blonde hair streaming in the breeze, dusted herself of the dry fog cloud even as the Commander spun about to attend to his surprize visitor.

"Ilty?" He exclaimed with some relief.

"I certainly hope so."

"How good to see you." He continued, back on balance. "Though I may not be so inclined towards the messages you bring." He sounded apprehensive.

"I worry about you. Sometimes you portray yourself as lost, as if the Holy One just......disappeared."

"To be honest with you, I do feel that way... I'm not prepared for a civil war, spiritually or emotionally...It's difficult to even believe that its happening." Tiredness thinned his face.

"But why do you believe that you have to do everything all by yourself?" She said sternly. "Is there no one who, excuse me, isn't there a group of persons to assist you?"

"Nope! No Way!" A cynical old voice critiqued as his relocating dry fog dispersed. "These military folks takes things far too seriously. We don't even exist."

"Just what I need. Another judgmental pest."

"Well, then, you don't have anything to complain about." Kloshic waved a bony finger up in Vosnob's unsmiling face. He raised up on his toes, pushing his crooked nose into Vosnob's unyielding grimace. "Sit yourself down, Commander Vosnob!" d. "I've got some good news....as in pleasant information. .... just for you."

Perhaps unconsciously, Vosnob obeyed, abdicating his position for the time being. Ilty quietly crossed the stonework parapet and sat next to him. He tried a smile, but a smirky grin was the best he produced. Ilty giggled and gave him a hug.

"And you're a happily married woman, Ilty!" Kloshic sarcastically mocked her.

"And you're nothing but a jealous ole bag-of-bones!" She returned with some exaggerated body language, causing both Vosnob and Kloshic a bit of restlessness. "You two are embarrassed!" She laughed. "Ah, I see the two of you aren't familiar with tavern antics."

"Enough!" Vosnob groused. "What's this 'good news' you tout?"

"Well, before Rux, with the divine assistance of the Holy One, devastated Haaf North, I visited the city.."

"You went back?" Ilty cried out.

"I thought that's what I said." He scratched his long whitened beard, simultaneously examining her. "No, I don't believe that you're deaf." He finally concluded.

"Get on with it!" Vosnob's restraint on his irritation slipped.

"All right!" Kloshic shot back. "Inside, the people yelled and cheered for the new Abbot. One wearing a crimson tunic with a sliver-black flying dragon embroidered upon it... Well, after a sorry excuse for a sermon, he disappears. ...But I recognized him as the Abbot at the Yldan-built monastery."

Vosnob shook his head. "I can't even begin to comprehend such blasphemy, such perverseness." He said very slowly, wearily.

"Then you better learn." Kloshic admonished. "Anyway, I beat him back to his private library, where he hoarded the volumes of the ancient's scripture, namely that New Test Ment he utilized to make Jabbi look the fool....I stole the volumes before he arrived. I also stole his private diary...."

Vosnob glanced up, hesitantly, hopefully. "And now we have the information to 'clean house'."

"Almost."

"Almost?"

"You can't believe that one Abbot held all the power?"

"Why not? He was an Elder, correct?"

"Unfortunately.......... Makes the rest of us a little suspect, doesn't it?" Kloshic walked a small circle then returned to the topic when no encouragement came. "Actually," He re-geared his stance to one of reflection. "The other Elders thought I was the next to die. I agreed. The Holy One always informs us when one shall die, so we might select and prepare another."

"Jabbi." Said Ilty.

"Yes. Our twelve were lead to believe he would replace me." His tones softened as his personal examination deepened. "Jabbi is a good Elder, he'll even become a better one.....But that's not exactly the pertinent issue...... The Holy One does control the universe, too often we just aren't capable of seeing it.... That's why we are the created, and not the Creator...The Holy One knew the Abbot had defected,........ had apostated,..... had turncoated us......... We were the unknowledgeable ones."

"Will you tell me something I don't know." Vosnob frustration carried through on his wearied voice.

"On his way to Hell, the Abbot's soul passed by me as I secreted myself in 'Nowhere'."

Ilty shrank back, her face flustered. "That's most unwise. You might find yourself trapped there forever."

"But I didn't." He cheerfully responded. "And that's the end of the matter... ..Almost.....Understand, I had the ancient's volumes of sacred scripture,........ and," He smiled almost too gleefully. "I had his personal diary, the volume covers more than a thousand double moon cycles."

"So, even if you couldn't relocate from 'nowhere', the Abbot's career effectively ended. His usefulness to the Evil One ended, and with his subterfuge among the Elders and the novices revealed, left him completely...."

"Extraneous to the entire situation." Kloshic hurriedly concluded Vosnob's remarks.

"I feel sorry for him." Said Ilty. "Apparently he refused to consider the truthfulness of the our Scriptures: evil is self-destructive."

"I completely agree...... And therein lies our hope."

"You might wish to unpack your single line theory. I'm not prepared for any mental testing today."

"Just this!" Kloshic poised himself as if to deliver a sermon, then nervously paced the parapet rubbing his bony hands together. Finally, he settled down, his wording slow and deliberate. "I haven't shared this with anyone before....You can critique my opinion.... Because evil is self destructive, that also reinforces the idea that it literally feeds upon itself. Hence, contrary to popular wisdom, there is no honor among thieves. Rather, thieves tend to be cutthroats, not only of the general populace, but of each other. This also recognizes and affirms another axiom relevant to our crisis: evil, if it can find no other target to destroy, must, of necessity, destroy itself. Do you follow so far?" Nervous fingers betrayed Kloshic's apparent mastery of their predicament.

"This territory's been covered and re-covered. What makes it so important now?" A puzzled Ilty questioned.

"Up until now its only been words! Now we must act on those words." Kloshic's old wizened voice cracked with anxiety. "Its time for all the faithful in Haaf to migrate." He stopped there, waiting any reaction from the Elders.

A guard interrupted the trio while they contemplated the incomprehensible blueprint posed by Kloshic. Vosnob immediately sent him to prepare a supper for three. While the plan's simplicity allowed for the theory to be understood, its logistics were totally mindboggling, unthinkable. Something about the plan remained enticing, perhaps its profound logicality. Somethings bothersome remained as well: it had never been tested.

Their hot supper of noodle soup and cheese with ale and hot tea, was preceded by guards delivering a table and three comfortable chairs. Excepting the minimal comments concerning the meal, an uneasy silence reigned.

"This is beyond what we three might decide. Nor are we empowered to enforce such an all-encompassing decision.....I will call for an Elders' meeting before moving any further."

"You are referring to all twenty four, I assume." Ilty offered for clarification.

"Twenty three." Kloshic corrected.

"No, twenty four, unless Jabbi doesn't count." Ilty continued her argument.

"Indeed. We'll need all the guidance possible."

"Then you will proceed with my theory?" Kloshic sounded weak.

"You expected me to laugh at you, right?"

Kloshic refused to reply, instead his mind wandered through the incredulities of his theory, especially because he was taken seriously.

"Let's meet here, ten dawns hence. Kloshic, make sure Jabbi has his translations with him....And let him re-examine those translations of the Abbot."

The quiet dry fog left behind provided Vosnob with a brief moment of internal quietude: perhaps an answer did exist. At least there existed 'something' concrete to examine.

As the Chaplain noted and then emphasized by underlining in his personal logbook, the past double moon cycle concluded with fewer than half the outpost scouts reporting in. At present, no viable explanation existed for their disappearance. Because the flying dragon's tattoo put the traitors away, desertion was eliminated from the problem. Actually, no flying dragon tattoos showed themselves in Pinduala. Naturally, tattoos existed among the sea-going Light Striper, some rather lewd but no dragons.

Those scouts who did return, he scribbled, presented slight evidence for believing anything might be amiss in Zuda Marsh. Nightly noises increased, especially sounds of 'plowing' through the jungle. But morning's light provided paltry assistance in securing evidence of any tracks or damage to the jungle. That is, the Chaplain wrote, unless those who discovered the source of the racket were those who did not return. Then he discovered the answer. He wrote it quickly, dipped his quill into the ink well, then secured his name and moon cycle stage to the page. With a sinking feeling in his stomach, he left his second floor room in the stone barracks to locate the Staff Master as well as the Wharf Manager.

Two blocks south on the wide avenue leading to the merchant's quarters, the Chaplain found his old friends exactly where he expected them, at the Hog's Head Tavern. He joined them at their table and ordered supper. The high beamed room with its narrow shutters opened to the salt-tinged breeze allowed for a most pleasant atmosphere in the normally stodgy pub.

"You're running a wee bit late, matey." Announced Ushver, an overly muscled deeply tanned Yldan, who managed the wharves since the rebuilding of the city.

"Does the ridicule come from the Yldan or Haaf side of the family?" Countered the Chaplain.

"I would never insult my dearest Mother!"

"Then it's a Haafian insult....How boring." Then he laughed along with Ushver and Tubt.

Tubt leaned back, his stocky arms resting on his broad stomach. "Coming late is a bad sign." He acknowledged, squinting his eyes. "Better tell us what's going on."

"I believe the Kyykki are coming sooner than expected." His bluntness stirred both men. "Something larger than we can imagine is coming our way."

"Why?"

"Because, Tubt, the scouts who return are those who stayed closer to the reed swamp. Those who disappeared, explored the jungle itself."

"Why attack here?" Ushver questioned. "Pinduala is specifically constructed to halt them. That's no secret, especially to the damned evil one."

"True, as far as it goes. But, we are lightly defending the line to the west of here; most troops are stationed along the central escarpment."

"The divinely raised escarpment." Added Tubt, as he saluted with his mug.

"Yes." Consternation broke across his face. "Can we move along!"

"Urgency doesn't become you."

"Shut up!" He yelled at Tubt. "Perhaps you've had a bit too much ale tonight."

"What if I did?"

"Then I'm wasting my time. The line needs reinforced, yesterday!............ AND..... we need those new weapons." The disgusted Chaplain rose to leave.

"Sit down!" Barked Tubt. "Yer supper's coming.... And don't be so sanctimonious with us."

The Chaplain turned sideways on his chair, pretending not to listen. Even if their agenda didn't synchronize with his, his pride refused to surrender to such antics. "Can't you understand the danger we're facing?" He quietly mumbled.

"We sent orders out three dawns ago to cover your concerns." Tubt smiled wickedly. "Have a drink." He said nonchalantly.

The Chaplain, finding himself sabotaged, ate supper without another word. Perhaps supper cleared his head, it actually mattered not, but after he scraped his apple pie from the plate, he apologized.

Ushver laughed. "I'm glad you are concerned."

The Chaplain gulped, stifling his mouth. "Just get me up-todate." He grumbled.

"Baste is sending half of the mobile artillery. We also plan to receive about a third of the New Knights, not the newest regiment, but veterans from the cliff.......... Finally, some newfangled outfit is headed our way." Tubt titled his head in mock amusement. "They're supposed to be those phalanxers, but now Vosnob's commanded a regiment of them to be mounted." He mealy-mouthed the whole concept, as he usually did for the nontraditional augmentations to the military.

Ushver lived at the other end of the spectrum; he thoroughly enjoyed new contrivances, especially when they protected his sea-going troopers. "Your attitude continues to degrade your abilities. ...And why is that so?.... Because you recurrently are in error." The half-Yldan pointed his finger at the staid Tubt.

"You're getting a bit too personal with this." He challenged.

The Chaplain utilized this opportunity to cut in. "So, then you want to return to the old crossbows, to forget the bleach, to melt down Running Cloud's razor wire?"

"Shut up!" He roared, causing the other patrons to pause and stare. Embarrassed, he chugged his tankard of ale.

The Chaplain pursued his train of thought. "This idiotic newfangled outfit, such as you would proclaim it....just who did Vosnob appoint to command it?"

"Some young fool." He slammed his tankard down, calling for a refill.

"And I'll bet he even has a name." The Chaplain deliberately mocked.

"Ayhn!" He pounded out the single syllable name as if he were cursing.

"Ah." The Chaplain ungraciously sighed as he learned back. "That young upstart with the reputation for achieving the near impossible with uppity nobility."

"The one who held the line with infantry at the 'cliff'." Tubt thoroughly enjoyed edging in a few barbs of his own. "Who'd ever believe that a new idea might not only have merit but also succeed."

Ushver chugged the recently-arrived tankard, the white foam drenching his pointed chin. "Can we terminate this damn game?" He entreated earnestly, but with a white-faced anger. "I agree, Chaplain, our situation is precarious, even with Vosnob's reinforcements coming. ...We have over five hundred miles to guard....And absolutely no one can identify what exists in the Zuda Marsh.."

"Not entirely true, matey." Responded a tall bare foot Light Striper, one who carried a cleansing salt aroma with him. "We got bigger problems than you can imagine." He motioned for two tankards of ale and grabbed a seat.

"Invite yourself, Ellom."

"Thought I just did, Ushver." He winked brightly, crinkling the deep sea-faring lines on his bronzed face. He tasted a swig of the ale and then set it down, the foam forming a puddle at its base. "Never thought I'd witness the day when the high-finned sharks had too much in their god-forsaken stomachs." He almost whispered, as if the scene carried the weight of the truly unbelievable.

"What exactly are you mumbling about?" Demanded Tubt.

"The Kyykkii," He swore. "They're swimming around Pinduala. Thousands and thousands of them."

"Impossible!" Ushver pounded the table.

"Tell that to my crew.........We quit when the ammunition ran out... And then we collapsed from chopping them into shark food. ...You keep thousands of them damned toad-faces from clambering up the gunwales..."

"You really are serious!" Ushver, obviously shaken, thundered.

"That I be." And he swallowed most of the tankard. "They cannot be slaughtered fast enough."

"So, the attack is from the sea?"

"I believe only part of it. If they surround Pinduala, the western corner of the nation is effectively out-of-business. Them buggers will simply ignore us and rampage through the western coast and into the Haafian plain."

"Unfortunately, the scheme is strangely logical." The Chaplain thought out loud. "Surround us, and the door opens wide to the country.... Sickening, isn't it?"

"In view of the fact that we cannot support two fronts simultaneously, ... yes........... Damn it." Ushver's bushy eye brows knit together in intense concentration. He fidgeted in his seat. "Just give me a moment.......Its not quite that simple, I feel a missing element....Can't figure out what it is....."

"Have another drink, maybe that'll loosen up them boulders 'tween yer ears." Ellom eloquently suggested.

With a nod, he literally obeyed Ellom. Slamming the tankard down on the counter, he gasped for air, then spoke. "Why, do you suppose?" He eyes beamed a bit out of focus. "Why do you suppose that the Kyykki decided to conquer Haaf by swimming around it? They've never attempted swimming before....Why?......And why not just throw their idiotic frog-faces through our rather defenseless border?........" He scanned the others for their answer, no matter how tentative. To his wondering dismay, quietude reigned among those gathered.

Within an instant, Ushver's enlightened disposition melted into disgust. "I'm almost ready to swear that the three of you are brainless."

"It takes one to know one." Tubt challenged. "Now, just get to the heart of the matter. What's the solution to the Kyykki invasion?"

"I'm doubtful that you puddin' heads can understand it, but its certainly worth experimenting." Seeing seriousness re-appear on Ushver's face, the trio listened. "As I understand the Kyykki, they are inferiors, depending upon numbers for their success...... By their natural predispositions, the Kyykki are denied the cold and the dry...You gentlemen still following me?" He asked cautiously.

"We're well versed in biology." Replied the Chaplain wearily. "Please, move along!"

"Well, between the Zuda and D'ka is nothing but plains. And, during this harvest season, those plains are naught but torrid and parched. Its a natural defense against the damned frogfaces.. And that's the reason why they took to swimming." Assured his of competent analization, he bellowed for another tankard.

"Your logic is quite improved, except the fact that; number one, when the harvesting ends, the winter rains begin and, number two, the newest edition of the Kyykki do survive the ravages of Haafian seasons." The Chaplain, like other Elders, was privileged to an inside corner of the latest information.

Ushver, habitual as usual, openly despised those who kept ahead of him, or so he claimed. Nevertheless, extremely conscious of the Kyykki's attack on the ships, he bit his lip, redressing his mental map to include the additional pieces the Chaplain provided. Within moments, he integrated the newest material. "Then," He commenced. "We have a different situation. The Kyykki probably will wait until close to the winter rains before challenging us on the plains....The only benefit we reap is that, until the beginning of their onslaught, we have the luxury of dealing with their attacks one-at-a-time."

"Some dubious luxury." Ellom slurred, speaking as he swallowed. Then he planted his tankard in the middle of the table. "But that does nothing to rectify my position. We're all ready under attack. Another half moon-cycle and they be at the wharf."

"And that is the frustration I feel.". Tubt began pensively. "They call the shots. Everything we've planned is defensive, and they know it........ They can beat us because we are content to placate them instead of eradicate them....Its time for a new aggressive strategy." His mood escalated, becoming defiant.

"Stupid heroics!" Ushver blasted Tubt. "The overwhelming odds against us prohibit that approach........"

"So, we gradually succumb to the idiocy of the present out-dated strategy? I refuse to believe that... In fact, with the incoming reinforcements from Vosnob, we can attack the Kyykki....Attack and win!" Tubt proclaimed. "And here's an outline."

Finally aware of the attention they attracted, the somewhat discomfited quartet retired to the barracks. There, in the Chaplain's quarters, Tubt outlined a well received strategy for launching an offensive against the Kyykki. The Chaplain relocated himself to seek Vosnob's approval. The dry fog produced by his actions still hung in the air when he returned, a thin smile on his boxy face.

"Vosnob gives us his blessing. However, he does remind us to be as cautious as possible."

"What else did you expect him to say?" Retorted Tubt.

The Chaplain wisely ignored Tubt. "He also mentioned a meeting to be held nine dawns from now. All Elders are required to attend, so I'll not be able to participate in the invasion as I had intended."

"Not just some 'simple' meeting, be it, matey?" Ellom asked, his voice upset.

"I wish that it was....Unfortunately, the topic is one I'm not at liberty to disclose."

Ushver rubbed his hands anxiously. "But I'll wager that our plans might significantly impact that meeting."

"What gives you that idea?" A suddenly surprized Chaplain countered.

"Only that our new strategy deviates from the past by some hundred eighty degrees." He announced smartly. "It's never been attempted, perhaps never actually thought about, and totally unexpected, especially by the Evil One."

A salute of clanking tankards ended the evening's business. They scheduled the following morning for turning their logistical nightmare into a workable offensive.

To others, he appeared, actually was, more maligned than ever before. Since the 'Gifted One', dismembered his arm below the elbow, Ashuwa, constantly raged and fumed. Any he encountered, he dis-membered and then devoured. Consequently, those who brought him reports never left with orders as to how to proceed. Their blood, a wretched and sticky yellowish-green substance, besmeared the blackened walls of his cavern high in the volcano, its acrid fumes and intense heat slowly baking the random left-over parts of his victims.

Finally, utilizing one of his lieutenant's arms, Ashuwa grafted the arm onto his own stump, even as the petrified victim watched. Once accomplished, Ashuwa tested his new arm by dangling the screaming lieutenant over one of the flame holes which pierced his habitation. Satisfied with the arm's strength, he dropped the scorched corpse down the flame hole. As he bellowed with insane hysterics over the success of his new arm, the volcano shook approvingly, scattering black dusty soot throughout the Dark Lands.

The monster continued, lavishing bestowing a multitude of curses upon his father, the Holy One. For once, his punishment for his action sat the battle of the cliff, contributed no pain or frustration. His banalities towards the Creator were exactly the truth. So too were his predictions of how this 'father' would be tortured, prior to becoming his feast, that is.

As his agony-spurred energy waned a bit, a minuscule amount of rationality crept into Ashuwa's mind. Where were the hordes of Kyykki he sent into the Upper Sea? Had they captured Pinduala? Where were the messengers? And his lieutenants? His slanted bulgy eyes glanced about the gore-filled room. He indifferently nodded, knowing full-well what had become of the emissaries sent to him. He ruefully laughed, then wrapping his cape about him, stomped off to his throne room.

Time for an accounting of his invasion orders was at hand. How many of his lieutenants and other leaders still existed? Soon he would soon know and then recruit more.

Quite unexpectedly, Ashuwa discovered his throne room awash in pornographic reveling. Porehote and Haadd, naked from the waist down, cavorted with Wakin, their mother. She, as usual, was drunk. Ashuwa, not really caring if he was noticed or not, watched from the debris filled doorway. Wakin, in the ancient days when gods and goddesses were plentiful, claimed possession of the moon. In the days of the single moon, Wakin's beauty inspired whole civilizations to worship her. Now, the puffy-eyed hag, bent from the weight of her ponderous breasts, sought pleasure from any and all providers. And few survived anymore. Her ashen colored skin and the jowls split by curving canine fangs, as well as her insatiable sexual appetite killed off too many lovers. So she trained her sons to satisfy her. In the repugnant process, she transformed both into eunuchs; her nibbling being well-beyond lustful passion, more akin to an uncontrollable disease.

Not being able to conquer his punishment of truthfulness, Ashuwa let it be known that his tolerance with slobbish Porehote and imbecilic Haadd ended. Jumping between their mother's well-spread knees immediately ceased. "Be damned, you three!" He thundered, sending a sprinkling of pebbles and ash tumbling from the black ceiling.

"Finally, you've come to claim me again!" Wakin smiled delightedly through her thick, fang-split lips. Without another word, she hurtled her boys against the rough volcanic wall, cracking their heads. Then, grabbing the threadless garment she usually wore, she delicately wiped off her nipples.

"No, I haven't."

"You're such a damned liar!" She said with the sweetness of dust as she launched herself upon Ashuwa, knocking him over. "Oh, but you aren't enjoying this anymore." She grunted as she clutched him, jamming him into herself. "But I don't really care, DO·I?" Her smile became vicious and she drooled in his leathery face as she pumped herself on him. "While you ate the messengers," She teased her victim. "I took on a whole company of your Haafians. All in one afternoon, to be exact.... Now they're all eunuchs!" Her riotous nauseating laughter brought another dusting of ashes.

With a mitigated vengeance, Ashuwa clutched her fatty belly with his reptilian clawed hand. As green-slimed blood dripped through her flared nostrils, Wakin most eloquently argued, pleaded for release, for mercy.

"Your pronounced vileness has perpetrated itself far too long." The Evil One confuted her earlier exclamations. "You are nothing more than an arrogant, wanton whore." He said unemotionally. Then, while extolling her virtueless, demented, self-gratuitous and undisciplined life-style, Ashuwa ungraciously tossed her across the garbage strewn cavern floor.

"I don't understand!" She complained. "You always enjoyed me before..."

"Its MY punishment....It messes with my mind...I've become a contradiction."

"Don't take it out on the Moon Goddess!" She haughtily proclaimed in the best self-deifying voice she still retained.

"A goddess is only as strong as the number of her followers." He quipped maliciously. "The Creator reclaimed your throne eons ago."

"Damned usurper!" She spit. "His time is yet to come!" She angrily vowed. "I never abdicated! I never sent a resignation!"

"And nobody even cares!" Ashuwa stood over her slumping carcass, his foot on her flabby stomach. He stomped her twice. "Do I have your undivided attention, you whoring bitch?"

"Careful, you degenerate bastard........... Like it or not, I'm indispensable for your so-called 'master plan'." Her face drew up, a ball of puss requiring a lancing. "I'll not be victimized by your temper tantrums." She challenged him from her lamentable position on the floor. "I can be more stubborn than you. ...And don't forget for one moment that you will prevail without my mastery over the Haafian women."

She suddenly kicked high and lurched her body to the side. Ashuwa's balance on her stomach gave way to a stumbling splatter on the cold ash covered floor. When he looked up, he noticed his lieutenants surrounded him, their faces a coarse indescribable mixture of unabated lust and bewilderment. "You want the damned bitch?" He asked them scornfully. "Then have the pervert....I'll send for you when I am ready."

"I knew you still love me." Wakin gleefully yelled as the unpretentious lieutenants graciously knelled before her spread legs. "Thank you, O divine one!" She excitedly called as Ashuwa stormed from the room.

In a chamber at the volcano's rim, one clean enough to eat in and one of the smattering of rooms with a modicum of rough furniture, Ashuwa sat enthroned upon a seat constructed of Haafian bones. His lieutenants sat three steps lower about a plank table. Provocatively unclothed 'blue ladies', standing in the shadows, eagerly serviced the table and its exhausted and sore tenants. Ashuwa, consumed by his unknowing of the results of his previous orders, paid little attentiont.

Unredeemed, vengeful and 'bought' summarized the attitudes of those seated at the table. Full half were new, due to Ashuwa's recent appetites. At the table sat Porehote and Haadd blabbering like idiots. Four other members consisted of the 'newest breed' Kyykki, who could verbally communicate, though in a primitive way. They did not respond to the 'blue ladies' invitations. The remainder of Ashuwa's lieutenants were overanxious Haafians. They remained afraid to consummate the 'blue ladies' obscene offers.

Far deep within himself, the Evil One moaned and screamed, the unremitting truth he was forced to constantly live with grasped him even tighter. "Look!" The voice of unremitting truth proclaimed. "Can you seriously believe these incompetents will allow you to conquer the Holy One?" The words 'Holy One' totally incapacitated him.

The numerous incongruities between his goal and the means to achieve it racked his brain. He sat as a statue, oblivious to the orgy at his feet. Finally, he thought, if I must deal with the truth, then I shall also free myself from the lies that defeated me at 'the Battle'. With that idea, hideous sense of actually prevailing emerged, he grimly smiled. Waking from his self imposed trance, he pounded the tablet: time for his meeting to begin. "Where are my six demon lords?" Ashuwa demanded.

"He doesn't even know he ate them." Haadd smugly whispered to his brother. "And he's supposed to be our god."

Too occupied with bouncing a bare-bottomed 'blue lady' on his lap, Porehote heard nothing. Ashuwa's clawed foot first sent the woman crashing into the wall where her neck produced a horrific 'popping' sound, then as his foot continued forward, it drove Porehote into an undisciplined heap on the floor.

"No matter that the demon lords are gone." Ashuwa said flatly. "Where are their replacements?"

"My Lord....?" A nervous Haafian spoke.

"Go on!"

"They are leading the Kyykki into the Upper Sea. At present, Pinduala is but some fifty miles to the south...Others still conceal the dragons...And the rest continue with the commands they received from you ten dawns ago." His voice quivered while he awaited his fate.

"Well done, Haafian."

"Thank you, My Lord."

"And this be your reward: to lead the Kyykki through the Zuda to Pinduala. You will invade from the west, separating that damned city from the rest of Haaf. Then, after the city is demolished, burnt to the ground and the inhabitants impaled," Ashuwa softly gleamed. "You'll then march on D'Ka."

"Yes, My Lord."

"Any questions?"

"Yes, My Lord."

"Ask!" A short tempered Ashuwa thundered.

The man's voice quivered as he attempted to obey. "Will the forces swimming in the Upper Sea join to invade Pinduala? And will they assist destroying D'Ka? And...."

"Will I provide you with dragons?" Ashuwa brusquely added.

"Yes, My Lord." The Haafian anxiously stared at his folded hands, refusing to let his eyes meet Ashuwa's.

"What you ask, I shall provide." He replied in his most magnanimous manner, taking upon himself a god-like quality.

"Yes, My Lord." Sputtered the Haafian. "May I present a proposed manifest and a strategic plan for your divine approval?" He cautiously chose his words, exerting no pressure on Ashuwa.

"All will be ready on the morrow?" Ashuwa's eyes gleamed fierce.

"All will be 'provisionally' ready, My Lord, awaiting your blessing." The Haafian corrected himself, staying as far from Ashuwa's authority as possible.

"And should I chose not to bless it?"

"Then, I shall substitute your corrections into whatever parts of the total plan you deem appropriate, My Lord."

Ashuwa, wickedly smiling, sat back on his Haafian bone chair. "I like you, Haafian. There is much the others here might learn from you."

The Haafian simply smiled at his still folded hands.

Ashuwa, in a deliberate effort to obliterate Porehote and Haadd, placed them under control of the Haafian. He encouraged the two to redeem themselves, making their mother justly proud of their accomplishments on the battlefield.

A Demon Lord and two Kyykki were assigned to reclaiming the Paradise Valley from Sarg and his companions. Their attack would be launched from the escarpment where the waterfalls commenced. Experimenting with a new tactic, this force numbered equally of Haafians and Kyykki. Two invasions at once, Ashuwa enjoyed that idea. He'd catch everyone off-guard and separated.

The truth continually urged Ashuwa to remove obstacles which denied his goal. He could no longer lie to himself about their usefulness. Ridding himself of the two moronic blabbers became important. Their hideous mother, though a one-time goddess in her own right, also, required a quick thrust into oblivion.

Following his abrupt dismissal of those gathered, Ashuwa retired to a quiet fissure in the volcano's molten skin. This, in turn, lead to a small balcony overlooking one of his breeding lakes. The dragon's entrance lay a few hundred feet below him. With his scaled ulcerated back against the volcano's slope, he gazed eastward, recognizing his kingdom of darkness, hopelessness and emptiness, was exactly that. No longer could he falsely persuade himself otherwise. The truth precluded such an aberrant perspective on his kingdom. He would have no more of it!

As he contemplated these festering thoughts of truth, Wakin, strode through, fragmenting Ashuwa's personal time and space. You must keep the boys here!" She demanded, flouting her short skirt and opening her vest to show herself. "It is far too dangerous for them to be on a military expedition."

"It is time for your incorrigible sons to earn their keep." He said slowly. "To this very date, they've only performed for your perverse needs."

"But you enjoyed it as well." She angrily countered.

"What I enjoyed has nothing to do concerning the truth. In fact, I intend to use the truth to set myself free from this Hell."

"By sending my innocent babes off to their deaths!" She waved a fat stubby finger at him.

"I need to begin somewhere." He nonchalantly retorted. "Best to rid myself of excess baggage before setting up my new kingdom."

"So that's what you really think of us?"

"Yes," He muttered, having more than enough of the inane conversation. "And that's the truth."

"The Holy One did curse you, didn't He?" She exclaimed incredulously, wanting to succor Ashuwa in her ponderous breast.

"In reality, the 'curse', as you label it, is both promise and penalty."

"Damn it! You're jealous of the big oaf. And that's the extent of all this invasion shit!......And the only thing it will accomplish is getting my sons killed!"

"Perhaps then, my jealously is justified." He said flatly. His face tensed, filling with animosity. "But you, you fat assed whore....You degenerate goddess of dead worshippers."

"You will never insult me that way!" She yelled even as her hand swung to strike his face. Bones crunched as Ashuwa intercepted her slap. He twisted the arm, Wakin dropped to her knees in front of him. In desperation she reached to fondle him. He unhesitatingly crushed that arm as well.

"Insult?" He laughed derisively. "It's no less than the truth...Or is the truth beyond your comprehension?" He gaped uncompassionately into her injured face.

She met his gaze, eye-to-eye. Then Wakin spit at him. "See if you comprehend this truth....You bastard!....You'll survive only as long as you as you remember your proper station...You forget, O damned mighty one, that you are far less than the Creator!"

"I am His son. I shall rightfully remove Him from His throne... As sons replace their fathers." He sneered.

"You slimy, pathetic fool...You're only a son to Him as we all are His children. ...He is the only pre-existing..."

Unwilling to deal with another truism, Ashuwa's pent-up rage compelled his actions. In a painfully slow sweeping motion. Ashuwa pulled Wakin over his pointed head, her blubbery body dangling, her torrid face writhing in abject horror. Then, finishing the motion, Ashuwa threw the moon goddess against the volcano's lower slope. A few unamused dragons watched her carcass bounce and then careened into the poisonous breeding lake. A quieted Ashuwa stood silently as her anguished cries and curses burst from the carnivorous slime. Then the wretched crying suddenly stopped, followed by its equally horrid echo. The lake's surface immediately returned to a counterfeit calm.

Ashuwa retraced his steps, walking back into the depths of his volcano. "One down and two to go. And that's the truth."

"That's one of your problems, Sire." The Captain critically appraised the King. "The old drugs stopped only five dawns ago. The new ones have yet to take hold. You're still more than five stone underweight. You shake and shiver. Look at your skin! It is not a ghastly, unhealthy white?.....And, with all due respect, Sire....There is no way in creation that you are going riding today."

The faint blink of hopefulness faded from the King's face as the Captain's blunt remarks gripped his soul. "Damn it, Captain, how soon until I can become a 'real' person again?"

The King's question directly articulated his present dilemma. He was at that agonizing stage between sickness and healthiness where one single thing or event might kill him.

"I've been quite foolish....as a King." He abruptly stated. "Idealism doesn't carry one too far....I should've kept the White eagle vision to myself....Used it to draw my energy from as I ..."

"Are you digging your grave?" The captain asked indifferently.

The King laughed easily. "Perhaps I am....At least we might take a walk....outside?"

"No, that remains restricted territory...But we can head to the roof."

"Again?" He moaned. "I'm sick and tired of the roof. And what, pray tell, is so exciting to see?"

"Am I to understand that you aren't appreciative of the mounted dragon skeleton in the courtyard? I'm shocked!" The Captain mocked, grinning from ear to ear.

"Perhaps you need to shut up!"

"Then who would you have to verbally abuse you with irrational and mundane....."

"Shut Up!" Called a callous voice from a fast gathering cloud of dry fog. Oros' rotund outline instantaneously appeared. "Enough of this nonsense!.....Sit.. Please, Sire." Oros smiled.

"And I was beginning to think about the guards cleaving off your disrespectful head." The King replied gamely. "You've become much of a spoilsport."

"Perhaps." He laughed. "However, I do bring some serious news. The Full Council of Elders will meet in five dawns."

Both men stared at Oros, a goodly measure of disbelief wrinkled their faces. After a long moment of silence, the two seemed to fall upon the identical insight. They began to laugh. In direct acknowledgement of their misguided convulsions, Oros stomped his sandalled feet.

"Forget the ruse, Oros." Snickered the Captain.

"It's the truth, Captain." Oros said without changing his composure.

"But the last time the full council of Elders was summoned, was before either the King or myself..."

"Was born." Oros concluded the Captain's statement. "I am well aware of that, as are most of the Elders, who, likened to yourselves, have never convened as a Full Council."

The King nervously paced the small room. "I'm just getting back on my feet and the country is falling down about me." He muttered to no one in particular.

"What an optimistic fellow." Oros commented weakly.

The Captain's impatience wore thin. "Get on with it, Oros. What is the meaning of this 'convening'?"

"A shocking proposal has been put forth. Haafians will migrate to Tath or somewhere until the evil here destroys itself."

"You aren't serious!" The king shook his head in disbelief.

"They are." Oros' answered. "Based on the theological principle that all evil, when it has nothing to feed upon, feeds upon itself. The plan is to expedite the Evil One's remaining time by eliminating his targets... Starve him to death, so-to-speak."

"So we just...just leave everything....the entire population."

"Almost, no one is to be forced to leave... Those thousands who all ready defected will remain."

"And what is this 'Tath'?" The King requested angrily.

"The land north of the Dark Lands." Oros responded, trying not to further aggravate the stressful situation. "That's where Jelkio's from....I believe you two have received updates from Yganak on this matter."

"Yes!"

"I'm just making sure I'm not getting ahead of myself, Sire."

"I'll let you know when you are."

Oros exchanged worried glances with the Captain. Sick or not sick, this King began proving himself another obstacle.

"Now what about the Istells?....I don't believe them...in,." The King continued.

"We didn't expect that you would....Their existence comes too close to your dreams, even to the point of dumping it on its head....... No one cares to re-formulate his visions."

"Precisely. ...So why must it be?"

"Because its the truth...And we live by the truth." Replied the Captain.

"So, now it's two against one! And I thought my prison days ended."

"Since when does any King have freedom?" The Captain's remark came bursting through. "Let's get you back to the truth. I'm inclined to think that Baltee's concoctions are still running through your brain."

"That's not the issue." Oros cut in, abruptly re-aligning the topic. "The council convenes in five dawns hence. I will personally deliver you, Sire, to the council of Elders. There you can present an alternative plan, if you so desire. And there will be one issue to arbitrate before the migration issue. Jabbi is finishing the translations of the Ancient Scriptures for us. Kloshic's thievery is paying off beautifully. The past works of the Holy One, especially those before...."

"The idiocy of the past peoples exterminated them all." Interrupted the Captain. "We know all about that. No reason to repeat the scenario, is there ...Sire?"

The King refused to answer, instead he left the room, slamming the wooden door behind him.

"See you in five dawns." Oros shot out to the Captain. "And may the Holy One bless you both." He vanished, leaving the peculiar dry fog swirling about the room.

The Captain plunked himself down at the desk. Slowly he readied his pipe and then lit it. Five dawns is a long long time, he said to himself.

The refugees from the once inhabitable port of Haaf North crowded the shore road to D'Ka. Yganak, with assistance from the surviving Light Stripers, brought a semblance of order to the retreat. Riders were sent ahead, a large rear guard under Raff's command kept vigil at the stone bridge, other able-bodied persons were posted on the sides of the slow moving company of destitute families, merchants, bankers and craftsmen.

Yganak, without much thought, gave in to the demands of the dock workers, placing their contingent and the sailors in front and to the bay side of the road. If another attack commenced, these hotheads demanded first crack at the enemy. Having witnessed them in action, unorthodox as their methods were, and recognizing his primary responsibility to defend the former citizens of Haaf North, Yganak, acceded to their wishes.

Out-of-sight in a waggon carrying the wounded, Rux, nursed the still unconscious Nadre. Her breathing returned a healthy regularity and the swelling on her head decreased rapidly, yet she lingered in the nebulous dimension between this world and the one to come. Rux gently comforted her limp form, covering her ashen face with tears and kisses. For the present, Rux concentrated only on Nadre, having little interest in any happenings beyond the confines of the waggon.

Jed, due to the temporary loss of Rux and Raff having command of the rear guard, found himself promoted to Yganak's primary aide-de-camp. Being used to a more active and active military style, he adjusted poorly to Yganak's musings and theoretical explanations. Why Yganak just didn't 'do it' far exceeded Jed's straightforward approach to dealing with life. However, Jed's insistent demands for action prodded Yganak from melancholy.

Yganak managed to move the city's survivors from the battlefield to safety beyond the stone bridge. Though hungry and suffering from dreadful personal losses, Vosnob's second-in-command, kept the five thousand or so city dwellers from pandemonium. Religious services were held the first three nights, Burials were proper and the stones erected. All foodstuffs, including those of the Light Troopers and what provisions the waggons carried were equally shared by everyone.

Towards evening of the fourth dawn, just before the half-slumbering

Yganak usually called 'halt' to the day's march, a Light Striper Trooper, galloping through the crowds, rudely awakened him.

"Sir!" Snapped the trooper.

"Yes!" Yganak responded slowly, trying to gain focus.

"Sir! There are three Church Guards who desire to see you."

"Is there any reason why this is so important?" He snapped. "After all, doesn't just about everyone want to see me?" He rhetorically muttered.

"I can't actually answer that, Sir!" The Trooper looked puzzled. "But these have just floated in from the bay. They claim they escaped as the city exploded. They also claim battling the Kyykki north of the city and being saved by ...." The trooper stuttered to a halt.

"By what?" Demanded a fully alert Yganak. "Tell me the whole story, Trooper!" He impatiently adjured the man.

"Sir! I have no intention of being disrespectful, Sir!" The rattled Trooper proceeded. "But, their story is extremely dubious. Sir!"

"Let me do the judging, son....Tell the story."

"Yes Sir!...They were saved by a huge white eagle....One that killed the Kyykki..."

"Bring them here immediately! Wait!..Did any of them provide you with a name?"

"Yes Sir!" Responded the Trooper. "He claims to be a platoon leader. Name is Treh!"

"Interesting. Most Interesting." Yganak softly smiled.

"Sir?"

"Nothing, Trooper. ...I'll have supper with these three tonight. That is all." As the Trooper galloped away, Yganak thought back to the King's proclamation, to Oros' Quest which was and remains intricately tied to this fellow Treh, and to his own forebodings prior to the city's devastation. Meeting this Treh might be exactly what the Holy One intended for this misguided believer, Yganak thought to himself. And for that he felt thankful, thankful and relieved.

Yganak moved his supper meeting to a dense copse of willows that grew along the muddy bank of a stream. The 'waggon of contagious illnesses' parked not more than twenty paces away. Being quarantined from the 'in exile' community, it proved a satisfactory haven for Jelkio, the recovering Deep Owl, Nooy and Kofe. Only Qill made himself known to the refugees. He was a shaman. He had much work to do.. All of these, including Rux, Raff and Jelkio received a formal invitation for supper.

Even so, Jelkio hung back in the shadows while Treh commenced to narrate, with overly lucid, albeit truthful, additions from the other two surviving platoon members. Nooy studied Jelkio's facial expressions as the report continued. Fear and horror narrowed her oval eyes when Treh detailed their ambush at the old campground. Later, they widened as he systematically described their miserable journey to the Dark Water coastline. Then, as the Church Guards described the miracle of their survival, the arrival of the Great Avenging White Eagle, Jelkio turned more colors than the rainbow produces. Her quiet patience swiftly reached its limits. She unexpectedly spoke out, startling everyone.

As her graceful blue form silently emerged from the shadows, Jelkio sustained herself as a startling revelation to some of those gathered. Their initial glance had, unfortunately, become commonplace. They only saw her as the horror, one of the 'blue ladies'. Her healthy beautiful physique and her dignified royal bearing quickly squelched that erroneous conception. Nooy, her Yldan escort, gently cradling her hand, also aided in quieting the supper guests. This most unusual couple presented themselves as something held in awe.

"Good Sir," Jelkio began in her highly accented Haafian. "You tell a story in which an Istell dove upon the Ky-y-ki."

Treh, caught off-guard, mumbled his reply. "Yes.....Ah, ...Ah, the Great White Eagle dove upon the Kyykki, picked up some in his talons, and then dropped those frog-faces on their own kind. The Kyykki were most fearful of the Eagle's shadow."

"And well they ought to be." She returned rather sternly. "But," Her tone softened. "The birds are Istells, not eagles. No bird is larger than the Istell. Your eagle may run thirty feet from wing tip to wing tip. An Istell measures four hundred feet."

"My lady," Asked an awe-stricken Treh. "How is it that you know these Is-tells?"

"They are our transportation in Tath." Jelkio smiled at Nooy, acknowledging that the evening would be a very long one.

Comments and verbalizations of shock and denial bounced through the supper party. Those with more Tathian knowledge supplied it to the disbelievers. Nooy found an oaken stump large enough for Jelkio and him to share. Jelkio watched in fascination as the conversations departed from the original topic, dissolving into a complete morass.

"Welcome to the southern world." Nooy wryly whispered to Jelkio in Tath. She gently squeezed his hand in reply.

Evening became night long before many of the Haafian assumptions of the world were properly affected. The entire company stood in awe of Jelkio, in whom and perhaps unwittingly, they saw hope.

As she began to perceive their intentions, however well-meaning, Jelkio nervously voiced her disclaimer. "Friends," She called to those gathered. "I am not of another world, just of a northern country. I am mortal, like all of you, the time will arrive for my death, as it did for my mistress, Queen Sjura, and my friend, Tiello." She paused as the grief of her loss did. "I am not a goddess...... I have no answers for your salvation........ I don't even know if I shall ever see the steppes of Tath again."

Yganak, who had been unusually silent for most of the moonless night, stood to speak. "You are most correct, Jelkio....Accept our humble apologies, please. These times are ones of grave desperation for us. We ache for quick, simplistic answers. Forgive us for putting that burden upon you. We have no right..."

"Forgiveness is bestowed." Jelkio gently cut in. "I shall aid you as the gifts my God shall allow...... Our enemy is a common one.....I have also thought....if Tath were not a land of steppes and cold, our land would also be under attack."

"My Lady?" Raff politely paused for recognition. Jelkio nodded. "Is it not possible to travel back through the Dark Water to find your Istell?"

"That's exactly what Oros' Quest was about, or did you forget?" The rough voice came from a haggard Rux, who strode into camp more than half-drunk. He plopped himself next to Yganak. "Besides, if you'd been listening instead of yapping, you'd realized the bay is no longer useable."

"Explain yourself." Yganak sternly ordered He motioned for a mug of tea for Rux.

"Just listen!" He cursed.

At first, they heard only the inconsistent wind, pushing itself in from the bay as it did every night. Then, a slow irregular beating noise became barely audible. The group stared at each other, attempting to make sense of the increasing vibrations. Within a few moments, the entire encampment heard it. The very ground vibrated, throwing many off-balance. A tuba abruptly summoned all men to their battle positions surrounding the camp. Now the sound turned to a dull buzzing, then more akin to thunder in the near distance. Towards Haaf North, strange blustery streaks of lightning shot down at the all ready desolate city, causing a multitude of explosions.

"What in hell's name it is?" Yganak demanded as stood to take his place with the troops.

"Just sit yourself down." Rux said flatly. "Its just the dragons. They've flown in ......to control the city.....Haaf North is now Dragon Town." He laughed, still half-drunk. "I doubt if anyone will navigate through the bay into the Dark Water... What the Holy One established with the Cliff, the damned Kyykki leader just swapped for the northwest coast of Haaf." His dismal assessment rapidly infected others in the group. Whatever hope Jelkio's revelations initiated suddenly died, negated by dragons.

"It's JUST the dragons!" Yelled Treh. "I ought to bust your head in!" He moved to smash Rux with his fist.

"Don't even try!" He leered. "I might be drunk, but I'm still faster than any of you." He dropped his head, ungracefully rolled from Yganak's side and lay sprawled in the weeds, dead to the world.

"I jist loveses dees truthful opty-mist-stick guys." Kofe's sarcastic remark shot by with that barbaric accent that caused most to snicker and Jelkio to flinch. "Yep, wid dees guys, wees got more en-ju-mees, den de e-bill one's gots dem froggy-faces."

"Then these..dragons..... don't bother you?" One of Treh's men snapped, incredulous.

"Noper, sure don't." Then Kofe dropped the hideous accent. "You see, dumb ole bleach kills dragons. Eats their guts right out. Nooy and I, and Qill witnessed it ourselves before we reached the volcano and rescued this pretty lady." And with that he soundly kissed her on the lips, leering at Nooy. Before the 'Ahs' faded, he addressed his pleased audience. "Never listen to, let alone believe, a drunk."

"Well and good." Yganak pronounced to end the session. "But our current situation calls for us to deliver these people to D'Ka. And to get them there safely...Within a few dawns or less, these dragons will be flying, making forays over this land. ..Raff!"

"Sir!"

"Get word to the rear guard. ...They are to leave immediately. They will follow us, about two miles back....Oh!...Take them any bleach you can find.. Have them stuff dummies with it."

"I understand perfectly, Sir." He tilted head, exposing a weirdly appropriate smile.

"I thought you might."

"I never once suspected that governing would prove so easy." Brey said to Tiello. "Nor did I ever believe that menfolk would actually obey."

"Perhaps it's all gone to your head." Tiello replied as she pushed her blonde hair behind her neck where she fastened it. "After all, we've only been in charge five mornings. ...And then, in Tath, we women are normally in charge....And then, our God, our divine rescuer, declared that we are in charge..... Perhaps our God had a bit more to do with our positions here in Paradise Valley then you give our God credit for."

Brey, a bit frantic, blushed, embarrassed by her own words. "I'm sorry. I had no intention of denying the power of your God....I only meant to suggest that never before have I witnessed such a co-operation between men and women....I mean I had to pretend to be a man to enter the Light Striper.."

"Yes, I recall your dour story." Tiello replied teasingly. "I'm also sure that my God will not explode you with a bolt of lightening.....I think." She presented the still flushed Brey with a little crooked smile.

Sarg and Queen Sjura were sequestered at some unknown spot in the valley since their 'divine' wedding. Therefore the handful of Yldans, under guidance from the women, began constructing a fortified village. With the pointed stockade fence and the long houses clustered about a central public space, it looked identical to the village where Brey stayed before entering the Dark Lands. Wild game and fish were plentiful, and with the wild fruits easily within reach, a tranquillity unknown for quite some time now began to nourish the survivors.

Loneliness, a legitimate complaint, soon became one everyone agreed upon. In this Paradise Valley, no one had the usual relationships enjoyed in the past. Families and friends, lovers, wives and children, the hometown villages, the festivals and customs were all missing, leaving most survivors with an edgy emptiness. Safety could not replace the need for true community ......not in the long run. As the mornings wore on, even Tiello and Brey felt this weight upon them, and helpless to combat it.

The newly-wedded sought out a single story cut-stone cabin which, the God-with-no-name suggested to them, stood beyond the third ridge of trees and then in the midst of huge evergreens. As small as Sarg thought the valley to be, they ended up sleeping under a huge oak on their first night. However, Queen Sjura, returning from a bath at the stream, gently persuaded Sarg that sleep would wait. The morning sun caught them snuggling in each others arms, their nakedness exposed to the dawn. Breakfast, and a journey of less than a mile, set them in front of the stone cabin, to the chagrin of Sarg.

"Why are you so distraught, my husband?"

Sarg had to think for a moment, then he smiled broadly, giving his wife a bear-hug. "That's true, isn't it?"

Queen Sjura pulled back from the hug, her face bore a puzzling smile. "Are you feeling all right?"

"Yes!" He smiled, grinning from ear-to-ear. "I'm married....to you!"

"Yes." Her face took on a stranger look.

"Don't you understand? I'm not alone anymore...Its so wonderful. So beautifully strange."

"I think my husband is going crazy."

"And you would ruin my happiness with caustic remarks?" He mused. "No!" He loudly continued. "You will not ruin my happiness....You are my happiness, My Queen, my lover, my wife."

Sjura began to weep, tears flowing towards the corners of her proud smile. "You make me so happy also, my husband....You've never spoken this way before."

"You don't care for it?"

"Indeed! But...."

"But,...... I never did before....I know." He lowered his head, unwilling to let his eyes meet hers. "I didn't think I could dare to....In my mind, you .."

"Forget the Queen and serf routine, Sarg." She lifted his head, focusing directly upon his doubting face. "I love you...You love me....And my God married us.....What more approval do you need?" She smiled gently, then hugged him. "This happiness is more difficult than spying, or leading the Yldans or killing dragons, isn't it?"

"You're....you're.... not... supposed to know....... that." He stammered to her.

"And why not? I *Am* your wife....And that's just part of my responsibility to you."

"And what's the rest?" He thought out loud, not meaning to.

"That depends." Sjura quickly responded.

"Depends?"

"Depends on whether or not there is a goodly bed inside this cabin."

"I think I understand."

"It's about time."

She opened the cabin door, exposing the three rooms, bath, kitchen and bedroom. All spotless and bright, all inviting, especially as the wind played through the soft curtains and the mid-morning sun splashed dappled lights on the whitewashed walls.

"Perfect!" She exclaimed, while dragging Sarg into the cabin and slamming the door.

From a discrete distance underneath a copse of sassafras trees, not more than two hundred paces away, Kadima, a radiant blue Tath and her husband, a mystic Yldan called Feathered Goat, stood hand-in-hand, silently observing their new charges.

"Beautiful, isn't it." Feathered Goat whispered to his pregnant wife.

"Reminds me of long ago." She said flatly, but her teasing eyes gave her away.

"So, my lack of romance is how you received this stretched belly?" He teasingly replied, squeezing her long fingered hand.

"I'm not sure. Perhaps you might try a bit more..."

"Ah!" He announced somewhat triumphantly. "You did enjoy my efforts....That makes me happy."

"It certainly should!" Kadima returned to feathered Goat, who gazed as the royal couple entered the cabin. A certain mischievous visage drew up his features into a look Kadima too easily deciphered.

"No!" She reprimanded Feathered Goat. "You shall not disturb them at this time...As our God commanded, after three days we shall gather with them....Now come, the children are waiting."

He moped as they headed towards the cliffs. "It would have been fun."

"As if you didn't have enough to do all ready." She teasingly snapped.

During the evening, the silvered white cloud, a perfect replica of the one which brought them safely to Paradise Valley, suddenly appeared. It rolled away the dusk with its resplendent brilliance. Though, paradoxically, this same brilliance blinded absolutely no one. Instead, its inherent spiritual warmth, a perfect kindness, attracted the Yldans and their leaders to the voluminous sphere resting just outside their compound. Silently everyone gathered in nervous anticipation before the cloud.

"Thank you for attending." The god-without-a-name softly called from the slivered cloud.

"We are humbly honored by your appearance." Tiello spoke. Then she submissively bowed before the cloud, touching her forehead to the ground.

"Get up!" The unnamed god ordered. "This bowing tradition leaves much to be desired....I do not wish to communicate with someone who has their head in the ground and their rear in the air..... Is that comprehensible?" He paused. "Actually that's not a very polite way to communicate with anyone, is it?"

Tiello immediately stood, flushed with self-consciousness. Even Brey giggled at the god's perspective on obeisance.

"Tiello, please do not be offended." The nameless god spoke, almost laughing. "Mine was the poorest choice of words and I did choose the poorest of moments to express my wishes." In spite of the apology the nameless one's chuckling continued. "Actually, Tiello, you look excellent from every angle." This time the unnamed god cackled hard enough to disperse part of his cloud.

The Yldans stood frozen, shocked far beyond belief concerning the manners of this god. This is far too personal, too direct for any of them and mayhaps, not holy enough for a god. Being attuned to the Spirit, the Yldans accepted a Holy One who reached out from afar with that same Spirit, unwilling perhaps to soil himself by touching the created. Now, once again, they were face-to-face with an unknown god who delighted in personal, even joking conversations with his people. The Yldans looked askance at each other, full of puzzlement, wonder and a bit of dread. This god, who had clearly proven himself, forcibly yanked the Yldans from their comfortable traditional theology.

"My Yldan friends," The unnamed god solemnly addressed the group. "I am very different, perhaps, from the Spirit who usually directs you. Your minds speak to me of confusion and bewilderment. ...Let it not be so... Simply allow me to earn your respect, I ask no more."

"You not do demand or constrain us to worship you?" A dubious Yldan voice anxiously put forward.

"No...I have the Taths...And they are quite enough." The lilt in the nameless one's voice caused Tiello to flush. "Sorry Tiello, but you are aware of the rambunctiousness of your people."

"You speak truthfully....... ..However, this truth is somewhat embarrassing."

"But it will prove itself useful in the near future."

"Of what do you speak?" Shouted another Yldan.

"Please, I am not deaf....... At least not yet." He snickered. "Does a god age?" He paused, the comment caused the god to reflect. "I'll work on that another time."

"Yes, My Lord." Tiello acknowledged.

"Returning to the subject: my demands of the Yldans. Only that I be allowed to earn your respect, nothing more nothing less. The Holy One, blessed be His Name is your god, not I. And should you recall the recent past, I choose to rescue you from Ashuwa."

"We remember...and we...I...am most thankful and humbled by your blessing." The speaker, the Yldan who almost crashed to the ground with Sarg, tearfully replied. "You have my respect, Mighty One....But, I know of no Ashuwa."

"My apologies, my friend, Ashuwa is but the newest name claimed by the damned one...The Evil One.......Now, I sense a deep emptiness, a loneliness within most of you....Allow me to make a proposition."

"Please, continue." Tiello said, her blushing finally gone.

"Shortly, your Sarg and his wife, Queen Sjura will return...Oh, what a wonderful surprize they're headed for." He laughed, but left the Yldans mystified. "Inside joke." He offered as an apology. "When they return, the War will be raging in full force. Ashuwa is attempting to invade the northern part of Haaf. He desires D'Ka as his new capital city...Not that I blame him, his volcanoes are dreary hideous dwellings, especially when they smell like rotting Kyykki dung."

Now, a few of the Yldans laughed along with the unnamed god. Then a dreadful silence reigned as the impact of the Kyykki's invasion hit them. Their very task, the very mission they volunteered for, now proved itself worthless. They never finished their task, and now time had run out on them. This unnamed god, hiding within his silvered cloud, aptly skewered them with their failings.

"I do not make it a habit to read minds...However, I am sorely troubled by the punishment you batter yourselves with...At the dire risk of sermonizing, allow me ask you this basic question: why do you fault yourselves? Have you not done the best possible as you struggled with the adverse circumstances which beset you?.........Then why punish yourselves?"

"Because others will die."

"Others are always dying."

"But these shall die because they had not the opportunity to use our discoveries." Brey continued her argument with the unnamed god.

"And just how might you actually know this to be true?"

"We alone are the survivors. Our findings, the maps produced by Sarg, the ....."

"Yes, so you have assumed, my dear Brey." The nameless one's said flatly. "But by what evidence, what proof do you offer to confirm your failure?"

"Only that we are here...and the information needs to be with Vosnob." Brey offered.

"No!" Tiello urgently interrupted. "Something is hidden here, isn't there?" Then, realizing she spoke rudely with her god, she became distraught. She reverently bowed. "I apologized, My Lord." She professed most earnestly.

"Rise, young one. You are wiser than most." The god delayed speaking, as if re-assessing Tiello. "Yes, there is more here. Assumptions usually prove us foolish...."

This time Brey flushed with embarrassment. Then, as if hit by a bolt of lightening, her composure abruptly reversed itself. "We aren't the only survivors!" She exclaimed exuberantly. "That's true!" She spoke directly to the pulsing cloud. "Isn't it?" She lowered her voice, a subtle confession of her presumptuousness.

"You are most correct." Announced the nameless one with the mirthful voice. "There are other survivors from your expedition. Obviously that is 'good news'."

"Why....did..di... didn't you tell us?" Brey stammered, almost overcome by her emotions.

"You didn't ask before." The nameless god said without apology or snugness. "Perhaps you know these persons; Qill, a Yldan shaman, Nooy and Kofe his associates, one of my daughters, Jelkio, and a fellow named Deep Owl."

The effect of those names thoroughly stunned the small group. Boundless joy existed for those named. Relationships were automatically reformed. A sense of accomplishment took root. Yet, too many were not named. The community shed tears for both groups, common tears that brought a closure.

"Are those names.....everyone?" Requested a broken voice from the Yldans.

"They are." The nameless one replied gently. "I am sorrowful for your losses. But you have not failed, even now your information travels to Vosnob." And with a sudden abruptness, the silvered cloud vanished from sight, leaving the group to attend to their victories and losses.

What most thought to be the middle-of-the-night found everyone seated about the log fire in the central yard of the stockade. A desire for sleep entirely evaded them. A grand ceremony of stories, both new and old, each recalling the lives of those mentioned and those unmentioned lasted until the orange streaked dawn. Vauk, his slanted eyes reddened from tears, tenderly held Tiello's hand while she acknowledged her deep feelings for Luuft. He continued to hold her as her tears drenched his tunic.

A regular, soft beating noise reverberated throughout the valley. Tiello looked upward, almost in desperation. The Yldans followed her lead, especially as the sound grew louder, and the beating noises suddenly disharmonious.

"The Istells are coming." Tiello said quietly to Vauk. But in the silence, everyone heard.

Just then bolts of fire shot down from the sky. Vauk realized Tiello's error. The dragons attacked. But the Yldans had no defense. In spite of their prowess, it would be the luckiest shot in the universe to stop a flying dragon. Nevertheless, without too much cursing, the Yldans along with Vauk, Brey and Jelkio stood in defensive positions upon the stockade wall. Jagged bolts of fire poured down upon the enclave to consume it.

Then, mystically, the death-dealing bolts serenely reversed themselves, exploding in the fanged mouths of those dragons who spewed them out. More than ten headless dragon corpses dropped out of the dawn sky. Shortly thereafter, realizing the futility of their attacks, they stopped.

The sky went grey. The party looked up to see a massive dragon flight. They counted over five hundred of the evil, foul-smelling beasts snorting their way south. The end passed overhead even as the bright morning entered Paradise Valley.

"Sorry I left so brusquely." Said the unnamed god. His cloud ship suddenly materialized just outside the stockade's main gate. "Its not that I am incompetent, but the damned dragons took to flight before I prepared for them.....Obviously, these eleven never knew what hit them.......How shall I put it: 'Destroyed by friendly fire'." The god laughed, then stopped quick. "That's not so funny to you, is it?"

"We thank you for your protection, nameless god." Vauk said, manipulating for more information.

"And I shall remain nameless, thank you, friend Vauk." The god snickered. "I bring you a few presents. Look behind you."

Walking across the valley towards the compound was Queen Sjura, but with another Tath woman and two children. Sjura waved. The others responded, albeit hesitantly.

"Now, my friends, look to the east.... High to the east."

There, in the not-to-far distance, appeared a bird shaped cloud. As it drew closer, its true character revealed itself; an Istelle. As if summoned by the expansive cries of the group, the Istelle circled, flying ever lower. The four hundred feet of wings floated through the air more than they beat at it. Then as it made a steep bank, the observers noted two men riding the huge bird; the first appeared to be a Yldan and the second, a completely terrified Sarg. A quarter mile from the stockade, where Queen Sjura and her new entourage waited, the Istelle softly landed.

"And," Announced the unnamed one, loud enough to refocus the gathering. "I have a final surprize for you.... They're a bit terrified yet. ...The ride was rather....bumpy. ....The dragon fight,....... you understand."

And with that, a door-like projection of the cloud opened. Tumbling out, faces scared stiff and disbelieving, came families and friends, the entire Yldan village upon the cliff, now arrived in Paradise Valley.

"Have an enjoyable reunion!" Shouted the unnamed god above the joyful hubbub of the tumultuous gathering. But even then, no one paid any attention. In the midst of the unabating happiness and confusion, the silvered cloud silently disappeared.

END OF BOOK ONE THE SAGA OF THE LIGHT STRIPER

Volume 2

Selected Readings from the Holiness Code

As you are created in the image of the Holy One, Blesssed be the Name, remember then; you are brothers and sisters of each other.

The Wise live by the Holiness Code, others simply know about it.

Evil in any of its forms is an abomination to the Holy One, Blessed be the name. Severe shall be the judgement of those who practice it. And great shall be the reward for those who stand against it.

Take caution in your judgments, only the Holy One, Blessed be the Name, knows the entire truth.

Only by living by the truth shall you remain free. The path of truth is most difficult.

The path leading to the future is never a straight one.

Truth grows from personal integrity. Integrity arises from true humility, amd humility is born when one recognizes one's place in creation.

Evil, which thoroughly delights in deceitfulness, promises without a struggle.

A fool will trust only that which is himself. The wise take heed to the guidance of the community.

Think not to impose your personal observations upon another, thus making his burdens heavier.

Knowledge of the Light and the Darkness is not the property of the created. Rather, the responsibility of the created is to remain faithful to their Creator.

Evil shall destruct and die of its own greed. For when its finds nothing more to devour, it shall starve.

Study the creation, the handiwork of the Creator, Blessed be the Name. Carefully note theat the Creator appreciates differences.

At the End, as at the Beginning, there is the Holy One, Blesssed be the name, who is with us even now.

Chapter 1

Quite appropriately, inebriated Rux slept through entire next morning. Now, his head incessantly pounded: too much ale the night before. He remained at least partially in control of his facilities, especially his mouth. Glancing upwards, by the sun's positioning overhead, he surmized it---midday. The waggon his colleagues unceremoniously dumped him into continued it's jarring ride eastward.

Something must be very wrong, he thought. Massive Blues were not meant to gallop. His clogged mind began to function a bit clearer. Rux realized the retreat to D'Ka had become profoundly earnest. Soon the dragons would commence their avenging flights. What right had he to lie in the waggon, as useless a dead Kyykki? None, absolutely none, he screamed to himself as he rolled over the tailgate and dropped to the cobbled road.

The landscape changed dramatically since last evening. The Light Striper reinforcements arrived and deployed as a rear guard as well as flanking. Massive Blues stood hitched to 'dragon waggons'. A total of four, he counted. Hardly enough to withstand the onslaught of five hundred vile-tempered flying creatures.

"Ho! Master Rux!" Called a familiar voice far to his right.

"Nice to see you about."

"Good to see you also." Rux muttered, his mouth dry and pasty. He glanced over at Jed, whose optimistic presence only grieved him, especially as he noted Jed's empty sleeve bouncing about in the breeze. "Do you have an extra Striper? And, the Holy One preserve me, some water?"

"Both are available." Jed motioned to a Trooper. "Bring the sobered one a drink and a sturdy mount."

The Trooper saluted most properly, then obeying a commanding wink from Jed, emptied his canteen over the Rux. Fortunately, few persons enjoyed his overly-detailed expletives. The revitalized Rux then realized his waggon constituted a defensive position in the rear guard.

While laughter ensued, Rux cleaned up his ragged appearance, then clambered up the largest Striper he'd ever ridden. Moreover, its colors were delicately muted, as if a bluish dye imbedded itself upon the entire animal; the usual razor-sharp demarcations between the silver and the black simply blurred into each other. Also, the Striper's four pronged antlers existed as but twin points, curled behind the ear then forward under the eyes to protrude menacingly above the creature's snout.

"All right!" Yelled a disparaged Rux. "What exactly is this animal?" As if to reply, the beast swung its head around to stare down its mouthy rider.

"Its a half-breed." Jed said nonchalantly.

"A WHAT!"

"Half Striper, the sire…and half Massive Blue." Jed smiled with a sense of false distress. "I actually didn't believe the combination to be so difficult to ascertain."

"WHY?" He roared. Rux, who not quite finished struggling with his hangover, was in no mood for something strange and new. "What is the sense of all this?" He demanded. "Just because something is possible, doesn't give us a rationale to produce it."

"Quite true." Agreed Jed. "However, this new breed carries the armored knights well, and their speed is almost doubled. So too the speed for the war waggons. And, irregardless of which of the three one chooses, their antlers all form deadly combinations."

"How exciting." Rux sarcastically groused as he whipped the reins across the half=breed's hairy neck. Then, jabbing the mount with his heels, he galloped off, leaving Jed alone with his observations concerning experimental animal breeds.

Locating the hospital waggon proved more difficult than Rux anticipated. When he recognized that too much transpired for just one evening's worth of a drunken stupor, Rux asked a few questions. A few answers later, he ascertained that he had, in fact, lost an entire dawn. Angrily cursing, he ferreted out each waggon, desperately searching for his lost Nadre. He, he found Yganak first. Oros rode next to him, his huge frame bouncing amicably upon one of the half-breeds.

"Look who awakened to the light of another glorious day." Oros smiled broadly as he delivered his stinging barb.

"Why, it is Rux!" Exclaimed Yganak, gesturing wildly with his arms so that none would overlook Rux's appearance.

"I just love you gentlemen." Rux raspingly choked, though his volume caught the ears of many Troopers.

"We wouldn't have it any other way." Oros gently replied. Then, as Rux fell alongside, Oros directly switched content. "We expect the dragons at dusk, when we'll be handicapped by the sun's setting..... You up for a fight?" He whispered.

"Where's Nadre?" Rux ignored the obese priest's question.

"Safe and.....from what Vauk hinted, asking for some skinny drunken fool." Yganak enunciated, a trace of mirth piercing his staid military demeanor. "She's riding in the lead waggon."

Unamused and yet thankful, Rux spurred his mount forward. The lead waggon was almost a mile ahead of the rear guard. As he galloped through the masses of civilians, ragged, filthy and completely destitute, he puzzled at their freely flowing tears. In his single-mindedness to reach his Nadre, he heard nothing of their appreciative cheering.

On approaching the lead waggon, Nadre waved to him from the tail-gate. With her blonde hair covered by a make-shift bandage, Rux almost didn't recognize her. He jerked the reins hard. The mount stumbled to a dirt-digging halt behind the waggon. An awkward leap deposited him beside a beautifully smiling Nadre.

The Captain's task of restoring the King to his former right-minded condition refused every effort. Each time the King appeared to have recovered, something else went wrong. The frustrating situation revolved about a peculiar phenomena; when the King's mental abilities waxed strong, his physical body wasted away, and vice versa. This precarious unbalancing of mind and body claimed the King. While he no longer felt the injurious effects of the traitorous physicians, he remained incapable of ruling over the country.

Yldan shamans had been summoned to the High Council Hall in the hope that their potions might rectify those utilized by Ashuwa's physicians. Even with samples from the Evil One's concoctions, no medicines the Yldans produced yielded a substantial difference. At best, they formulated a new tea-like substance that saved the King from the severest aspects of the strange illness.

Several of the Brothers who first helped the King with his "White Eagle" vision also arrived to help. These Churchmen found themselves as powerless as the Yldans. Prayers and ritual eased the King's anxiety, but did not prevent the diabolical illness's resumption. The Brothers hypothesized that the elements used in preparing Ashuwa's so-called medicines derived from the Dark Lands themselves. There too, they haplessly concurred, lay the antidotes.

During a hotly contested evening meeting, the Captain found himself pitted against both the Yldan shamans and the Brothers. With regard for the King's personal integrity and a concern that the nation have a more stabilized leader, the Captain proposed that the King abdicate. The countering forces voraciously denied this, maintaining that the King, simply as a national unifying symbol, could adequately fulfill this role in his present condition. After all, the Brothers claimed, the King's illness and absence had yet to impact the populace. Heated claims, proposals and counter proposals carried the discussion into the early morning. Nothing solid existed to present to the Council of Elders. Furthermore, the King had yet to be consulted concerning this meeting.

The contestants were so involved with their opinions that none witnessed the dry fog enveloping the room. As it dissipated, a rather perturbed Jabbi observed the discussion from the corner of the room. He still went unnoticed, a fact that might be later used against this less-than-reasonable assemblage.

"Good Morning!" Jabbi challenged from his corner, startling all those gathered in the room. "I said, 'Good Morning!'"

It took a few moments before the assemblage regained their composure. And when they did, Jabbi found himself the target of their collective hostility. The cantankerous din expanded beyond respectable levels, even in the worst of the taverns. He held his arms up for silence. After a long grudging moment, the group granted his request.

Animosity still shown in the Yldans eyes, and the Brothers nervously fidgeted with their guilt. Jabbi waited before speaking. He sat and propped his feet on the wooden table and pretended to smoke a pipe, causing the Captain to laugh at the caricature.

"Shall we begin?" The Captain queried of those gathered.

"We shall!" Jabbi announced with authority, even as he blew pretend smoke into the air. He brought his feet from the table with a crash. "Tell me," He asked as he sternly gazed at each one, "What is the meaning of this ridiculousness?"

The hushed room provided few clues for the perturbed Elder. Finally, the Captain, now emulating Jabbi's caricature, spoke as he too puffed an imaginary pipe. "We don't know what to do with the King."

"Why not?"

"Because we want him both replaced and still running the country....... ....simultaneously." The Captain continued puffing his non-existent pipe. "But mainly because we refuse to compromise. Some here think such a conception is inherently evil."

"I understand." Stated an unamused Jabbi. "Then is wasting time NOT reaching any conclusion is also a blessing from the Holy One?"

"You aren't serious." Choked one of the Yldans.

"Why not?"

"Its too ...too... preposterous."

"And isn't this stubbornness of yours' just as preposterous?" Smiled Jabbi menacingly. "How much longer will your pretensions feed the whiles of Evil One?....... How much longer will the damned one enjoy the time we grant him by NOT reaching a conclusion?" He paused to inhale on the imaginary pipe. "I wonder what the Council of Elders will think about this matter. ....They might wonder if this is deliberate."

A shock rippled through the Brothers and then the Yldan shamans. The Council of Elders was ancient and its power beyond thinking. Jabbi calmly rested his booted feet back on the table. "Time is short!....The Elders have convened all ready........... But do I send them no answer?"

The room grew heavy as the responsibility for the King's future as well as, perhaps, the country's future fell upon the shamans and the Brothers. The heavy wooden door flew wide open, exposing the King, robed and stooped, but smiling.

"Why have I been eliminated from these discussions?" He shamed them. "Is my incompetency that oblivious? If so, then why didn't anyone suggest abdication to me?" His astuteness paralyzed the group. "I'll tell you why. You've forgotten to whom ultimate allegiance is due..... I'm just another person. Certainly the Holy One used me for the benefit of the nation, but that time may have ended........ And why not?........Substantiated rumors tell us of Istells, Eagles of Victory as I view them....... Does this not replace my usefulness? ....Are you afraid that my improperly interpreted vision will invalidate the rest?"

No one moved, but sideways glances about the table proclaimed much, especially anxiety. The group stumbled.

"Sire?" Asked Jabbi forthrightly. "Do you have a suggestion?"

"Indeed...I AM·THE·KING!" He chuckled. "My suggestions are Law...This meeting is dismissed...I will remain King...But I ORDER the Council of Elders, along with those deemed essential to handle the administration of the country, to rule in my stead until the present crisis is ended....At such juncture, I will meet with the Council to abdicate. IF my present condition is not improved....And if it is, then I know whom to thank." Hoarse coughing caused him to sit.

The Captain gave him a tankard of water. Soon after, the King summarized his mandate, concluding with: "Is everything understood?"

At this juncture, no one dared to argue, or even question the King. His forcefulness and his demeanor paralleled that of his famous Council Hall Address. That he grasped the significance of his office as well as the nation's future was a moot issue. One-by-one they assented to the King's command.

"Excellent!" Commented the King, smacking his hands together. "Then, before I place it 'officially' before the people, I have but one question: Jabbi!"

"Yes Sire."

"Tell me, has the Council of Elders been infiltrated? Compromized?" Though some seemed horrified, the King was deadly serious.

"To my knowledge, they are, at present, secure from the damned one's influence.....at least directly........I think."

"A rather tentative answer." The King mused. "But it is a believable one."

"Thank you, Sire."

"This meeting is adjourned." The King suddenly stammered, his limited energy spent. As the Captain returned the weak monarch to his quarters, Jabbi left quietly, leaving only the dry fog to acknowledge his attendance.

Vosnob did not appreciate the 'late-arriving' Jabbi. He nervously paced about the entrance to clandestine rendezvous, his thick fingers intertwining and then disbursing randomly.

Jabbi spoke as soon as he recognized him. "Vos..."

The distinguished Elder immediately cut Jabbi off with a quick finger motion across his throat. Jabbi responded with quirky smile, half worried, half unsure. Vosnob motioned for Jabbi to translocate. First, Jabbi studied the heavy wooden door behind which the other Elders knelt in meditative prayer. Within the cramped chamber, they readily acknowledged their weaknesses as mortals, as the created, requiring the Holy One's assistance in order to guide the nation through its partially self-wrought turmoil. The need for forgiveness permeated their supplications.

Jabbi made a gesture with his hands. 'Where to?'

Vosnob shoved a ragged scrap of paper in his hand. Jabbi translated himself to the Abbot's library of ancient Holy Books. Vosnob smashed him into the stone wall when he appeared a twinkling later. After rising to his feet and dusting himself off, Jabbi proceeded to complain.

"Keep it quiet." Vosnob sternly admonished. "Even the walls are listening these days." He angrily muttered.

"Might you explain just a BIT of what's happening?" Jabbi demanded. "First I receive the most difficult set of directions I've ever seen. Then after you've gotten us all gathered---and inspected---you send me off for more information. Only to, once again, re-direct me to another out-in-the-middle-of-nowhere secret rendezvous." Jabbi's brown face began to flush white with his consternation. "And now you demand I exit the Council meeting without ever showing......."

"Here's your explanation." Vosnob said.

Jabbi crossed his arms over his chest. "I'm listening."

"One of us is a traitor.".

"Such has been suggested by others, the King even mentioned it." Jabbi replied coolly. "But, what evidence can you provide?"

"Nothing tangible, absolutely nothing I can present to the Council."

"We're dealing with one of those 'Holy Hunches' you oftentimes receive?" Jabbi lost his antagonism as the impact of Vosnob's confession struck home. "......This is....isn't what ...."

"It seldom is." Vosnob corrected. "As the Holiness Code directs, however painful the consequences, we are mandated to abide by the Truth. In that is our true freedom." He grimaced. A traitor this well-placed, this so-close-to-the-heart, this is totally unheard of. It almost gutted him. "No longer is anything untainted by the damned one." He angrily muttered.

Jabbi moved forward, saying nothing. He deeply felt the Chaplain General's anguish. Then Jabbi backed away and slumped in the corner, immersed in prayer. Vosnob stood, shaken to his soul by this insidious invasion. If ever his age showed, it was now. The usual vitality, spiritedness and humble sense of purpose seemed withdrawn. To Jabbi, the Chaplain General looked akin to a living corpse. Jabbi impulsively threw an ancient tome at his leader. It thudded on his chest, knocking him into a case of dusty volumes. He stared at Jabbi, not in indignation, but in sorrowful questioning.

"Why?" He uttered as a whisper.

"Why not?" Jabbi answered disdainfully.

Vosnob managed a weak smile; a bit of color returned. "This isn't time to pity one's self, is it?"

"No, my dear friend, it certainly isn't." Jabbi spoke sympathetically. "But, we both are prone to this weakness, aren't we?"

"Indeed, ...indeed. ...Perhaps it is to remind us that we are not in charge after all....Sometimes I ..."

"Enough of this self deprecation. It isn't needful, unless you are the 'pretender' to the Holy One's throne." Jabbi's mouth rounded out at the corners, producing a 'tweaked' smile.

Vosnob laughed briefly then sat himself at the stone table. "The traitor....bothers me."

Jabbi stood. "I doubt if I ever could comprehend such."

"Would like me to return this volume?........ Across your thick cranium?"

"Actually...No." Then he sat across from Vosnob. "Any hint or suggestions as to who might be the traitor?"

"I have desperately tried to remove you from the listing." Sarcasm dripped from each syllable.

"I pray you didn't strain yourself."

"I didn't, thank you." He rubbed his longish face with his hands. "Time to change the subject....A traitor is most serious business. ...Some I trust implicitly...Ilty, Baste, Kloshic, Oros, the Chaplain.."

"Did you trust the 'damned eternally' Abbot?" Queried Jabbi. His question arose not from finger-pointing, but from a concern that the damned one might actually 'buy' the Council of Elders.

"Difficult is your question, because I am reluctant to answer truthfully."

"Still pretending to be perfect?"

"No." He answered wearily. "Its just that everything is so heavy for me....My errors destroy people needlessly."

"I suggest that if the people of Haaf were so disgruntled by your incompetency, a great rebellion would have sent your soul to heaven long ago........Get your head straight, Vosnob!" Jabbi reeled back, his words sterner than intended.

"Might you desire this position of dubious honor?"

Shamefacedly, Jabbi shook his head. "I'm sorry."

"And so am I." Confessed Vosnob. "But that's where I'm trapped. I've no idea how to restart, how to correct."

"Is that your responsibility?" Jabbi rose and leaned over the table, going eye-to-eye with Vosnob. "Is that your responsibility!" He repeated.

For a moment, silence reigned. Then Vosnob sighed and squirmed on the stone seat, his facial colorations retreating and advancing rapidly. Suddenly, this too quieted. Vosnob regrouped himself, becoming the determined Chaplain General Jabbi recognized.

"No." He announced quietly, eye-to-eye with Jabbi. "It isn't my responsibility ....We shall proceed with our plans as if nothing is amiss...

This will permit the traitor to become elated with his or her success. Perhaps that will trip him or her.... Also, in faith in the Holy One, I place the future of Haaf. ..."

"Well spoken, Vosnob." Said a less anxious Jabbi. "Well spoken.....Our faithfulness to the Holy One, and not to ourselves, must prevail."

"Indeed." Muttered a disgruntled Vosnob. "We should have remembered that from the battle at the Wall....How short our feeble memories tend to be....Are you ready to return?"

"In a moment." He paused to survey the ancient library. "Is there anyway this can be preserved, intact? There is more here that what we now observe. Hidden within this library are more secrets. I can almost hear the volumes scream to me."

"And I thought I was about to ...."

"Can we close this off?" Jabbi brusquely interrupted.

"After the Council meeting concludes, we'll return." He aptly bargained, wanting to quickly return.

"Let's be going."

Leaving the ancient library filled with swirling dry fog, the two Elders immediately translocated to the exact anteroom they recently vacated. Their arrival, with the quiet continuing seemed to guarantee their absence had not been noticed.

"Are you ready?" Jabbi shot a cautious concerned glance at Vosnob.

"As ready as I can be." He replied tightly. "The Holy One will provide." He said with mixed emotions. "The Holy One shall provide!" He repeated to himself. The words ringing with greater confidence than previous.

"Keep believing." Jabbi slowly opened the door to the cloistered group of Elders, not desiring to intrude upon their prayerful meditations. Not wishing to embarrass himself by arriving later than his instructions demanded.

His respectful entrance proved unneeded. A blinding light glowed from the center of the roof. Underneath it, suspended in mid-air, slowly rotating by his head was Attriv, eldest of the Elders. His deeply lined hands still clutched two curved daggers. One dripped blood. His toothless mouth vibrated with silent screams. His beady eyes bulged, distended with holy terror as he futilely struggled to complete his carnage.

Frightened for himself, Jabbi grabbed the door frame, preventing Vosnob not only from entering but also from seeing the crisis within the Elders' chamber. Peering about the room, Jabbi discovered the Elders pinned against the outer wall, speechless as they stared at the unnatural spectacle.

Jabbi rapidly counted sixteen. "Where were the others?" He yelled out at the mesmerized group, more alarmed than frightened now.

His yell broke the silent tension. Vosnob ploughed through him, striding into the center of the room. A transparent vengeful smile strapped itself to his face, only to be instantly destroyed when he saw the plight of the hapless Attriv. In spite of the bloody carnage committed upon the Elders, Vosnob's sympathy went to the one who now existed beyond all hope.

Suddenly, the hopeless Attriv began to radiate as brilliantly as that powerful force which held him suspended. His daggers rattled upon the marble floor even as his features disappeared into a blur. He twisted faster and faster. Then, as his brightness blinded the entranced Elders, he expanded and exploded, white sparkles of flame deeply gouging the walls and ceiling. The uniform sparkles also struck the Elders, only to harmlessly drop to the floor. Those sparkles which struck the wounded and the frightened, the confused---healed them immediately.

The singular ethereal light high in the ceiling intensified its brilliance, forcing the Elders to cover their eyes. Then it began emanating pulsing bursts of peace-giving luminescence, establishing an atmosphere of divine tranquillity. Fear and disorientation quickly dissipated underneath the vibrant pulsing globe. A strong not-to-be-denied voice spoke to their minds. Baste, now standing towards the center of the chamber, instantly recognized it. The Holy One addressed the gathered Elders from the now descending globe. It dimmed enough that all might view it. All Elders fell to their knees, cognizant of the Holy Visitation.

"Fear not, my Children." The Holy One spoke in a solemn yet joyful tone. "Rise! There is much I have for you."

All obeyed immediately, though a touch of confusion tainted their thoughts. Standing in the divine presence of the Holy One could be dangerous, especially for those 'gifted' with the Eldership. They knew too-well their faults, their sins, their cover-ups. Righteousness was not a concept they dared claim. The aged Vosnob found himself a pace away from the pulsing orb. He stood transfixed, paralyzed.

"Peace, peace to you, My children." The Holy One now spoke plainly from the descended orb. "Have no fear. I bless you with My forgiveness.... Make yourselves comfortable, please.. Even you, My dearest Vosnob." While the Holy One's voice acknowledged no dissent from His dictates, it also allowed for a hint of pleasurable mirth, especially in regards to Vosnob.

The aged warrior's mind extended well beyond its normal self. He struggled to pull himself together, but to no avail. He remained transfixed by this Holy encounter, perhaps because of his close proximity to the orb.

"Vosnob!" The Holy One spoke.

An orange tendril of light swept out from the orb, encasing Vosnob from head to foot in a pulsing transparent cocoon. The transparency immediately disappeared, leaving the overwhelmed Elders gazing at a Holy Mystery. Their minds desperately cloyed with the thought of Vosnob's fate. They knew the lore concerning those who ventured too close to the Holy, either deliberately or inadvertently. Every documented case terminated exactly the same way: 'An unsolvable Holy Mystery. Complete disappearance of the individual. May the Holy One have mercy.'

How much time elapsed before Vosnob reappeared no one actually remembered. No one really cared. His new presence stunned everyone. The Holy One recast his person to that of a young man, except for his eyes. There the aged warmth and depth of wisdom remained. However,

Vosnob stood paralyzed, as if his new form, clung to him most incorrectly. Murmuring commenced among the out-of-balance Elders as they attempted to bring sensibility to the Holy mystery before them.

"Peace! Peace, My Children." Words half-spoken dropped in the air as all turned the attention to the Holy One. "I give you Vosnob. He has served me well. His honesty deserves recognition. I have provided for him..... Behold your Head Elder, and now your youngest Elder."

A collective gasp issued from the others. The mystery unwound only to engulf them in another example of the omnipotent power of the Holy One. Without thinking Ilty reverently bowed, the rest quickly followed suite. Vosnob stretched, then wobbled as he realized his new form didn't function like the old one. He sauntered over to the nearest chair and promptly dumped himself into it.

"I have imparted to Vosnob messages for all of the kingdom. Heed them and instruct My People to obey them... More than just their lives are at stake, their souls are in danger of being sold and destroyed....That is what happened to Attriv. His existence, in all its totality, is expunged, eternally."

The concept of complete non-being stupefied the gathered Elders. What could ever so be permanent, negatively permanent? To never have been, when once one was? When from the collective memory of the community, the name is erased? If the concept horrified, it also had been aptly demonstrated.

A single pulse emanated from the softly glowing orb. In its aftermath, no one remembered the missing Elder. Counting to twenty three was easy. Putting a face or name to the missing Elder was impossible. Nothing except nothing remained concerning the missing Elder. As they later discovered, there were usually twenty three Elders serving at one time. Naught remained of the 'missing' Elder in the records or documents. Everything concerning such an individual was divinely expunged.

The voice of the Holy One returned. "Listen to me: prepare yourselves for the future and its awesome complexities. The unpredictable shall become

Saga of The Light Striper

the normal. The unexpected shall become usual....And creation shall be torn asunder...I shall be with you. ...Peace." As wondrously peculiar as He arrived, the Holy One took leave, instantly vacating the Elder's chambers.

After a prayerful silence, the now 'venerated' Vosnob spoke. Catching even himself off-balance, Vosnob's strong tones hadn't been rejuvenated. He wheezed and then coughed. "I must suppose that had the Holy One, Most Blessed be His Name, reinvented my voice, then hardly anyone would recognize me....Such wisdom is truly divine." He sighed, leaning back into the chair. Immodest giggles from Ilty caused him to realize the stupidity of his erstwhile comment.

"I apologize to all I have unthinkingly offended." He drawled with a hint of a smile. "I'm not sure I understand any more of this than you." He addressed the others from the chair. "Except that I am exhausted, as you must be. Therefore, prior to commencing our meeting, we break to eat and relax."

The chamber overflowed with dry fog before the venerated one finished his sentence. Jabbi sat in the far corner, opening his sack of dark bread, cheese and a flagon of ale.

"Bring a cup, young fellow!" He gently taunted Vosnob. "Looks like you might be hungry."

"Some things will never change!" Vosnob muttered as he strode to the corner.

"Thank the Holy One for that security." Jabbi almost soberly admonished the 'new' Vosnob. The young warrior simply claimed a chair and a cup of ale.

Celebrations lasting three dawns are quite a rarity, but that's exactly what transpired in Paradise Valley. First, the God-without-a-name descended into the camp delivering some three hundred friends and family members of the Yldans. Simultaneously Sarg and Queen Sjura returned from their hideaway to their wedding reception. Sarg arrived straddling an Istell. His color drained to nothing for fear of falling through the clouds. Kadima, the Tath wife of the Istell master, casually trekked into camp with Queen Sjura. Kadima's youngsters followed quietly behind, somewhat frightened by the numbers of people, even though most had the bronzed coloration of their shaman father, Feathered Goat. Miraculously, enough foodstuffs, housing and other necessities appeared to keep everyone satisfied.

The Tath women, in a quiet copse of birches just beyond the camp's perimeter, gathered to thank the God-without-a-name. Brey joined them, not so much to worship, but intrigued by a god who presented himself as a person. During their silent prayers and soft rhythmic hymns, Brey watched, astonished, as 'the cloud' responded with a twinkling of miniature lightnings. There is a special closeness here, she thought to herself, that is nonexistent with the Holy One. The 'why' of this escaped her. However she briefly considered the fact that the company of women might have a bearing on her perception. She then shuddered, ashamed of herself. How dare she feel so insubordinate to the Holy One.

This fourth evening, Queen Sjura lead the small group to the copse of birches. Her face beamed more brightly than most brides, but she excused herself from that with a nod to the happily embarrassed man whose hand she held. Vauk, and Feathered Goat also attended, both acknowledging the rightness of thanking the God-with-no-name who saved them. 'The cloud' awaited them, full of miniature rainbows. With the exception of the Tath women and their husbands, the rest slowed, apprehensive of the altered condition of 'the cloud'.

"I see that some rather enjoy lightning instead of rainbows." The voice of the God-without-a-name spoke in his usual optimistic lilt. "No matter! There will be both." Immediately 'the cloud' sparkled with rainbows that broke then shattered as lightning does. "No need to offend anyone over such a trivial matter.....Please, come closer."

In an unflattering lock-step, those whose anxiety kept them behind the Taths, suddenly caught up to the rest. When they bumped into Queen Sjura and her entourage, most everyone laughed. A light laughter erupted from 'the cloud', further embarrassing the stragglers.

"Your God is most unusual." Sarg whispered to his wife. "Not very god-like."

"But that's just the way I choose to be." Replied the God-without-a-name. "And don't be alarmed..... I don't intend on banishing the Queen's husband."

A flushed Sarg bowed meekly, his giggling wife catching him in the ribs with her elbow. "I....I...did not mean to offend."

"I know your heart, my son.....Just as I also know the paradox which you chose not to reveal even to your wife."

Sarg instantaneously pulled back, half expecting the wrathful hand of the God-without-a-name to slam him into eternity. Queen Sjura unroyally tumbled back, landing on her rump. Her hand still firmly clenching her husband's. She stared up at him with a touch of horror in her eyes.

"Just what have you done?" Her voice pained.

Sarg slowly regained his usual composure, then placed his case before everyone. "My thoughts, owned by no one except me,.... my dear Sjura is not involved,.....concerned what I perceived to be the inconsistent nature of the Tath God." He said flatly. Seeing that his statement did not connect with most of the group, he added. "Before us is a most gracious god, perhaps one too close to his subjects, perhaps too personable. His subjects have few regulations and nothing written. He molds himself to bring his people closer to himself. It is clearly demonstrated that this nameless god does love his Taths...."

"Thank you, Sarg." Confirmed the nameless God. "You are correct in what you say.... I have no desire to be other than what I am. Conventionality.... Well, I simply have little use for it...But, that is another aspect of myself we can explore later..... Please, continue. Some still don't quite follow your line of reasoning."

Nervously, Sarg continued. "In spite of the picture I've just constructed of the Tath god, it clashes, in a most puzzling fashion, with the god who evicted his people from their home simply because they wished to know his name.....And now, without any warning, they are commanded to return." He drew in a heavy breath, still expecting punishment. "To me,...... this is capricious...nothing less." He stood, expecting the worst, but knowing he fulfilled his duty to be truthful.

The small group said nothing. Queen Sjura, unsure of what she heard, rattled by the implications, stared at 'the cloud' and then back to her husband, and then back again. The tense hesitant moment lingered on. Only 'the cloud' exhibited signs of life. It's continuous patterns of flashing rainbows providing evidence of the god-without-a-name presence.

"You are 'bout the gutsiest person I've ever known." Feathered Goat whispered to Sarg. "And that's a mighty high compliment, especially for a Light Striper."

"You have that uncanny ability to read my mind." The unnamed god's voice pierced 'the cloud'. "I don't really welcome that."

"But we all have our gifts, don't we?" Feathered Goat bantered back as if conversing with an old drinking buddy.

"You could choose to use it more carefully."

"What? Should all these thankful followers be denied the truth?"

"Perhaps not....Then again," He laughed a most person-like guffaw. "Then again, if I allow the truth out, I may not have anymore followers."

"Sometimes one must take that risk." The Yldan shaman replied. "You could learn from Sarg."

Everyone stood, aghast and gaping at Feathered Goat's seemingly uncivilized treatment of the nameless god. His wife backed away from him terror stricken.

"You are correct." Laughed the nameless god. "I'm always learning. ...Just consider it as part of growing up....But then, Sarg is correct. I am capricious,

I have abused my freedom as a god...... After all, I bow to no one.....That is an inherent danger I wrestle with."

"That's unfair." Murmured Queen Sjura.

"And so I am, My Lady." The voice sounded more sobered, less offhand than before. "I have made mistakes...that allowed the damned one, Ashuwa, to grow in strength..."

A gasp erupted from those gathered. What god, of any ability, would disclose his faults to his people? What kind of god would admit immaturity? With such a declaration, could any god even hope to retain a people for himself? Awaiting further disclosure from this less-than-experienced, this capricious, this strange god-without-a-name, those gathered stood as statues. The second of the moons shone overhead before he spoke again. Alerting the congregation, the illumination from 'the cloud' pulsed rapidly, then burst into a thousand miniature rainbows. The following revelation astonished and frightened even the Taths.

Standing some seven feet tall, but thinner than a willow tree, with arms outstretched, stood the nameless god. Resplendent in a knee length silvered robe, and surrounded by a glistening orange aura, he reminded some of an ancient knight caught in the dawn's sunlight. Out of respect and fear, the entire group backed away, leaving only the royal couple and Feathered Goat and Kadima before the incarnated god.

"Please, be at peace." He spoke slowly, his words not fitting his mouth. He spoke both Tathian and Haafian simultaneously. He motioned for all to sit, a most unusual, if not self disrespectful, gesture for a god. Nonetheless, everyone obeyed.

"Thank you....I will begin where I must: attempting to rectify the past....I evicted my people....from this valley, actually, in that time...the valley contained the majority of the Dark Land...I did it... Me....a self-serving god..." The silvered god paused, scanning for congregational responses.

"What sort of god are you?" Vauk gingerly asked. "I am at loss as to what has or is happening."

"Yes." Came from the god's contorted mouth. "I am one of the survivors....Your own Holiness Code contains the following statement: 'I, the Holy One, shall be the first god. You are called to obey me.' Is this not accurate, Vauk?"

Vauk rocked for a moment, his hands scratching his long braided hair, his slanted eyes closed in deep thought. "You, O God, are not so young then...You were before the last civilization.."

"Yes, in your terms I am ancient....But the last civilization, had they been that, would not have destroyed themselves...But their story has no bearing here tonight....I desire to make perfectly clear to all of you, Yldans, Taths and Haafians, that I am one of those gods noted in the ancient Holy Books as existing,...... but not necessarily worth worshipping....Perhaps you can see that precise truth very clearly now." His voice resonated with a sadness, not of self-pity, but of remorse for his failures. If anything, the god acknowledged his faults, bringing forth a full confession before the congregation. "I have not been the god I should have been, Queen Sjura, Kadima, Teillo....... Pettiness is one of my faults...My pettiness, which did rule over me, caused your expulsion from the valley....Then, as I gloated over my power, the 'unbelievers' left me and settled along the frozen rivers in the north. They deserve no punishment nor reprisal from myself or your own subjects, Queen Sjura."

At that, the Queen froze with misgiving. Throughout her reign she took pride on 'keeping the heathens in their place'. Those apprehended outside their swampy river basins were promptly arrested and imprisoned until their useful days declined. Then she commanded the transgressors be returned, as a burden to their families. Now Queen Sjura realized her own god, through his own capriciousness and self-interest, brought an unwarranted exile and division to the Taths. Her blue-tinted face went red with unhidden rage. Her righteous anger firmly centered upon the nameless god.

"You play games with us!" She roared at the silvered figure. "How dare you mock your highest creation!" She sucked in her breath as Sarg held her shoulders. "How dare you let ME believe I was faithfully doing YOUR will?"

The nameless god kept silence, allowing the Queen to vent her righteous anger. Her outburst even surprized Sarg; he thought he knew the strength of her determination. The god spread his arms to speak as Queen Sjura. She sobbed on her husband's shoulder. In spite of his genuine confession, the unnamed god received little sympathy and little support from those gathered. They followed the Holy One. They expected better from a god. They demanded consistency, stability, and honesty. This nameless god needed to be ignored during the past and now. Such were the sentiments shared by the Taths.

"You may walk away." The god announced rather slowly. However, this time, his enunciation, regardless of the language, matched his facial expressions. "It certainly would not be the first time." He did not beg, nor manipulate, just a statement of fact.

"Have you not defeated yourself?" Asked Vauk. "What is a god without a people?"

"Yes, I have." The god softly replied to the first query. "Gods without people resemble lost souls, floating along in 'nowhere', bereft of any future, and unable to escape the imprisonment of 'nowhere'.

"Perhaps that's exactly what is needed for incompetents." Snarled a completely disillusioned Sarg, his high standards openly displayed. His wife gaped up at him, her eyes bright with fear. He placed a firm hand on her shoulder. "If he didn't destroy one of his own subjects who screamed at him, its doubtful he'd try to hurt me." He smiled at his wife. Then he shot an angry glance at the unnamed god. "You are familiar with the Holy One?" He requested.

"Yes....yes,.... indeed." His lowered voice rang with humility.

"Then you know this territory is not off limits to him?"

"That is true."

"What is it that you desire of me?" The undeceiving voice suggested to Sarg.

Sarg thought for a moment. He needed to be careful. "A testing." Sarg answered squarely, knowing the god's response would set the predominant path for the near future.

"This 'testing' has been required of me in the past." The god replied forlornly.

"Well we might believe...Your history probably is somewhat hypocritical, rather erratic, self-centered.... Still, you have not responded to my question."

"I will abide by a 'testing'." Came a somber statement, followed by silence.

"Then let us get to work. ...As a god you have recognized that a battle surrounds us. In fact, you rescued us from the damned one, Ashuwa, with your 'cloud'....We are most thankful for that."

"You are most welcome...Your wife's faithfulness did shame me into action."

"All well-and-good." Sarg brusquely commented. "But now you must act upon your own initiative...You must act in behalf of your people,............ should any still exist."

"There are many!" The nameless god defended himself.

"Then you shall call them together." Sarg informed the god. "Furthermore, you will convince them to become a nation again, even the outcasts and the faithless ones. ..Then as a people, with you as their CHOSEN god, Tath and yourself shall join with the Holy One in defeating the damned one."

"Do.you.know what you are asking?" The god responded with some agitation and unhidden hesitation.

"I mean for you to act as a god. Nothing more, nothing less." Sarg stood his ground, though with much discomfiture, knowing the god could simply disintegrate the entire camp. "I also know that if you do not have a people, your living quarters in 'nowhere' won't be entirely satisfying."

"That is truthful."

"There is more." Sarg quickly added. "Tell me about the seven rings of translating powers."

"I did not create them." He said unevenly, as if something else needed clarified. He paused and Sarg patiently waited.

Sjura wrapped her arm about Sarg. The awestruck congregation, Vauk excepted, stood frozen as the verbal confrontation headed another direction.

"Nor did I create the Taths." The god off-handedly blurted, perhaps believing that no one listened.

The entire congregation focused their bewildered ears and minds. His orange aura shrank to nothing. His arms twitched. His rounded chin dropped to rest on his chest.

Vauk accused before Sarg could stop him. "You have lied. You deserve nothing from us....'Nowhere' is for you.....The sooner the better!" He bombasted the god.

A pointed finger rose, launching a bolt of light. Vauk caught it squarely in the chest, knocking him through three rows of people. His tunic burnt where the bolt struck him. Brey and Tiello rushed to him, finding him breathing but unconscious.

"You vicious incompetent!" Brey screamed at the silvered god. His orange aura had returned. "Bully ...That's exactly what you are!"

"STOP!·ALL·OF·YOU!" Sjura demanded as respectfully as possible.

"You forget that I AM a GOD." The angered unnamed god retorted. "I will have respect."

"Only IF.... and.... WHEN..... you earn it!"

"Queen Sjura," Gasped the nameless god. "Even you?"

"Yes." She inaudibly mouthed, then spoke loudly. "Enough is enough..... If our people had had a written Holy Word, you would have been forgotten long ago......And you know that, don't you?" Her voice rose to become accusatory.

"I shall not deny the truth."

"Then you will heal Vauk.......Then you will obey my husband, knowing full well you are not more powerful than his God, the Holy One." Sjura continued, her queenly demeanor never showed so impassioned and resolute before.

"And if I should refuse?" The god tested her.

"My people shall desert you, and turn to the Holy One. And if you destroy us, you shall not have a people anyway....Should you wish to exist with the living....." She never finished her threat. It wasn't necessary.

After anxious moments of hesitancy, the god-without-a-name acquiesced to Queen Sjura's demands with a subtle nod of his head. Vauk immediately regained consciousness. Those gathered beside him breathed a sigh of relief.

"You are ready to earn your godship for the Taths?" Asked Sarg.

"Yes." Came softly from the god's mouth, no contortions marred his speech, regardless of the language. "Might I present you with a gift?"

Sarg paused, tentative. He wasn't up for any more games. He bought some time. "To whom are you speaking?"

"To you and your Queen."

"Is this some foolish attempt to alter the course of your testing?"

"No." He replied quietly. "Simply a way to unravel a mystery for you....To place....to create...... a better...an improved.... perspective on our situation."

"Go on." Sarg allowed.

"Scouts sent by your country reported sighting a brownstone castle near the shore of the Dark Water, towards the end of the valley."

"Yes?" Sarg answered, puzzled. He knew nothing concerning this venture.

"I should like to return it to you." Said the unnamed god. His smile wasn't big, but it genuine.

"Go on." Sarg repeated. "You know my distaste for mysteries."

"Sarg, that castle belonged to your father..... Excepting for its coloration, due to age, nothing about it is changed. Its the same land and castle Kracik stole from Haaf shortly after the Battle. However, the damned one had so inflicted his blasphemous depravity upon it that even Kracik refused to live there..... His brownstone is some eighty miles away. Its now burnt to the ground."

Sarg crumpled to the ground as the news sunk in. Never, in all his prayers, did he actually believe that one day.........

"It is true, Sarg....As soon as we end this meeting, I shall rebuild the place for you and your family..."

"Family?" A frowning Sarg, looking up from the ground, tried to understand. Sjura smiled radiantly at her husband. "You...You're........ pregnant." He stammered to her amusement.

She tightly hugged him, squeezing the life out of him. "I thought so, but I wasn't sure....Its my first...Our first." She quickly caught herself. "Thank you." She whispered in his ear, her tone both devilish and delightful.

"Does that mean we can't practice anymore."

Queen Sjura pulled back to study her husband's brown face. He hid it in the folds of her apron, not wanting her to examine his proudest smile, at least, not just yet. Sjura played along with the game, for all of two breaths. Then she stood, dumping the ecstatic Sarg on the cool night ground.

"Do you love me?" She demanded, embarrassing him before everyone.

"Yes." He stammered. "Yes, I love you, my wife and mother of our child." And he twirled her about, both of them landing on the grass laughing like children. Applause from those gathered abruptly terminated the lovers' merriment. The Queen flushed as Tiello and Brey gently helped her to her feet.

"I never thought you had it in you." Vauk remarked smugly as he yanked Sarg to his feet. "Wait 'till the Light Striper hears all this news... Your reputation.."

"Enough." Sarg snarled through clenched teeth. His smiling, twinkling eyes gave him away, causing Vauk to cackle. "Shut up!"

"Yes SIR!" Came the caustic rejoinder.

Sarg sought to regain focus on the god-without-a-name. The god hadn't moved, though his countenance shone with the 'I-got-you' smirk. "Had to ruin her surprize for me, didn't you?" Sarg reprimanded the god.

"Well, there are some things even bungling, incompetent gods can do well." He said indifferently.

"Perhaps so..." Sarg reflected a bit, then refocused. "Thank you for my wife, my unborn child....and the return of my father's property....I appreciate your gifts."

"You are most welcome." The god hastily provided, striving to create some sense of godliness about himself.

It was, the unnamed god thought, much easier before the new world. In the old days, a god's faithfulness meant little. He just had to provide answers to prayers and petitions once and a while. Now, 'non-existence' stared at him eagerly, as if it desired to readily consume him. He gulped as the fear stilled his body. A mortal demanded his full, stable and consistent behavior....not for himself, but for a people he usually forgot. He knew about those 'other gods' who refused to act as what they were. They constantly moaned throughout the 'no time, no place', 'nowhere'. He had absolutely no inclination to join them. He feared non-being more than he feared being a true god.

He squared himself to face Sarg. "Allow me to backtrack a bit."

"Go on." Sarg allowed for a staid permission.

The nameless god winced, then spoke quietly, but with a sense of power. "You asked me about the power of the seven rings. They have but two uses. First, as you recognize, they can translate any and all languages for the wearer. Second, they are of great benefit to me...At least five of them are. Two are either lost or destroyed, eons ago...My benefit is that the rings transmit to me everything they contact." It desperately grieved him to expose this last item, for it compromized what he might do.

Sarg's slanted eye's pierced the god's. "You,.... therefore had the power to save, to heal, to protect...countless times.... Yet you refused to act upon your opportunities......You even ignored Queen Sjura's pleas for rescue when she and Tiello and Jelkio were confined beneath the volcano by the damned one.......Well?"

"I did nothing...Yes, I knew well of their plight...The damned one even dared me to stop him..."

"You cowardly bastard!" Vauk blasted.

"He had power...to kill me." The unnamed god sadly commented. "It was easier for me to hide...."

The god's confession eroded more of the insignificant respect of the Yldans. Vauk continued to adumbrate the god while Brey, who once portrayed the victim herself, found a bit of sympathy for the nameless one. Queen Sjura, unwilling to have conflicting loyalties, began to search the depths of her queenship, whether her people's god or the people themselves were of more importance.

Sarg continued with his relentless testing. "If nothing else," ·Sarg commented to those gathered. "We know this god refuses to lie to us...I suspect that is a beginning." He turned towards the god and took a few strides, stopping when the two separated by a sword's stroke. "Our Holiness Code states that 'The truth shall set you free.' Do you believe that?"

"I do." The god announced firmly. "I remember hearing it for the first time...eons ago." He paused, slightly, cocking his head. He was not comfortable with the truth. "However, words are easy........... Deeds which verify the words are not."

"And I would agree with that statement." Then, after twisting his hands together, an action which made the survivors tensely anxious, Sarg brought about another refocusing. "Then you agree that these Yldans you brought here and the survivors are completely separable from your goal of binding the Taths into their old nation?"

"Yes. I so agree."

"But this is opposite of your original intention for them. Am I correct?"

"You are." The god's voice manifested a raspy quality. He desperately battled for control.

"Is it not true that you intended to use these most gracious Yldans to form a new people for you?...Is that not the rationale for presenting us with Feathered Goat and Kadima?"

"Yes!" Anxiously replied the god-without-a-name.

"That plan is terminated." Sarg stated. "This is the new plan. Queen Sjura and myself will remain here in the valley....All others who desire to leave you shall return safely to their chosen destination. Then, and only then, you shall gather the Tath Queens and whomever else is required. That body will direct you concerning further actions demanded to bring the people together....... as well as establishing a force to destroy the damned one...Is this understandable to you?... Remember, not only are these gathered witnesses for your response, but also the Holy One listens."

"The Holy One listens." The unnamed god repeated Sarg's statement verbatim. "I understand fully and I pledge myself to the quick fulfilling of my testing."

As the first glimpse of the dawn slipped by; the sheerest of orange-grey streaks advancing upon the black night sky, the nameless god departed. As a testimony to his return, his 'cloud' waited just outside the camp. Most of the Yldans headed to camp, there was much to discuss. No one had ever taken on a god before. Sarg carried his exhausted wife back to the campsite, though, in his mind, no clarity existed as to whether she suffered more from lack of rest or the tortuous decisions she alone would make for the future of Tath. He silently prayed to the Holy One that this unnamed god might somehow, perhaps with the Holy One's assistance, begin to act as a god should. He smiled as he tucked his wife in and then cuddled next to her; how beautiful the future might be if even part of his prayer became reality.

A lightning storm of intense magnitude blew away the tranquillity of mid day. From the west, wherein lay Sarg's ancestral home, the lightning not only slammed into the earth from the sky, but also a red-tinged lightning leapt from the ground. A huge luminous cloud hung above the valley where the castle stood, much as a vulture hovers about his not-yet-but-almost-dead prey. Great slashes of light from the stone castle cut away chunks of the luminous cloud. As parts of the cloud dissipated into the mid-day sky, the intensity of its lightning blasts intensified. The Yldans and survivors watched with intrepidation, fearing for themselves if this unnamed god failed in his attack. As the unnatural battle wore on, their anxiety abated as the reddish lightnings slackened.

Finally, a most peculiar shooting star, traversing a due north course, slammed through the cloud. The gathered people pulled back, awed. The astounding projectile restored the cloud as it passed through on its unerring course to the castle. Then, not but some five miles to the west, just outside Paradise Valley, rose a gleaming white castle. Its immense size far dwarfed Krabo. Then, as if to further accentuate the castle's greatness, the barren filthy lands about it transformed their ugly blackened brown to lush verdant green, with pastures and forests instantly appearing.

With mystified awe, those gathered were overwhelmed by what transpired. Never had mortals directly witness an immortal god working, creating. Never had any witnessed such a decisive end to the unholy. More than the usual simple respectful fear arose within them. There emerged a new hope, reborn within them. Along with hope, a holy purpose underlined by clean distinctions between the Holy and the damned took root They witnessed the ultimate power of the Holy. Now they readied themselves to respond to it.

An unearthly, ethereal wind blew down from the white castle, instilling a sense of urgency as well as correctness within them. As those gathered struggled to put all they observed into comprehensible language, the god-without-a-name suddenly returned. Burn marks marred his glistening silvered form, his orange aura, however, gleamed brighter than before. A smile of success and wonderment clouded his face.

"I have begun my testing, Sarg." He announced quietly.

"We have witnessed your first attempt to reclaim your godship. You have encouraged us....Personally, I thank you for the return of my father's castle." Sarg replied as stately as possible under the extenuating circumstances. He found it difficult because he didn't want to remove pressure from the god.

"You are most welcome. But I only conducted the battle. In Truth, however, the castle you can barely see is not your father's.'"

"Then...?" Queried a puzzled Sarg.

"All the newness belongs to the only One who can create."

"The,...I think it is called....'a shooting star'....was the Holy One providing for his people." The nameless god added. "He has been merciful to me....I shall not be negligent of my responsibilities...my testing."

Sarg felt himself flush with embarrassment, not from what the nameless god said, but from his doubting. He mentally kicked himself for not believing the Holy One would actively participate. Such sin ought to be punished, he thought. An elbow to his ribs brought him about. Sjura gently smiled at her perfectionistic husband, wordlessly teasing him. Sarg regrouped quickly. "That is good. You have accomplished an excellent beginning. ....But are we to presume you have an alliance with the Holy One?"

"I dare not, I will not, presume anything for myself." The nameless one said modestly, anxiously attempting to extricate himself from such a relationship of dependency. "His aid arrived and aptly finished the job. I did not ask for his assistance, believing that my 'testing' required all of my strength and wisdom. To ask for outside aid....I refer to such as cheating."

"I think I understand." A surprized Sarg admitted. "Perhaps I have too sternly judged you."

"Rather doubtful." He said ruefully. "You know little of my history........ Let us simply agree that I've accomplished the first task of my testing."

"So be it." Smiled a presently mollified Sarg. "Your past history is of no consequence anymore.......Consider this is your new beginning..... And........ if it pleases the Holy One to aid you, Blessed be His Name."

"Indeed." The god returned the smile, then looked about. "My next task is to return any or all of you to the place of your choice...... Who wishes to return?" He called to those gathered.

The god-without-a-name's 'cloud' easily accepted all those who chose to return home or, per previous agreement, wherever the cloud's occupants desired. Knowing they returned to villages and kinfolk, most left whatever they brought for the benefit of those who stayed.

Sarg almost chose to leave, his written reports to Vosnob and his multitude of maps had yet to be delivered. Queen Sjura, using her royal imperative, delegated the reporting business to Vauk. Sarg conceded after a bit of an argument. Vauk's return was expected within two sunsets. The nameless god accepted this as another testing. He accepted full responsibility for Vauk.

A few farewell waves of hands and the cloud shot off through the blue sky like lightning. The handful left, Sjura, Sarg, Brey, Tiello, Feathered Goat, Kadima and their two children, spent a quiet night at the encampment discussing the future move to the 'Holy' castle.

As they slept, an obnoxious armada of five hundred dragons silently flew over the encampment. Their goal: to claim the port of Haaf North for the damned one, Almighty Ashuwa. Their reward: anything that existed in the Haaf Bay. Much later they swept down upon the devastated city of blackened walls and nonexistent buildings meeting up with the other dragons already there. Little did dragons care for much beyond a good perch and food. Even ruined Haaf North provided that much. Orders to destroy survivors and those fleeing went ignored. The 'belly' came first, even before the commands of the damned one. Besides, as they discussed among themselves while navigating through the cloudy night sky, the weakly two-footed creatures could be disposed of at anytime. They were of little consequence.

From high upon the cliffs, where the beautiful waterfall commenced its tumbling into the valley below, the Demon Masters huddled. They silently watched the majority of their intended victims depart in the 'lightning cloud'. This disturbed them more than the damned one's command to 'Kill everyone! Let no one live to tell the story!" Punishment awaited them for allowing the 'cloud' to remove Ashuwa's victims. But by destroying the remaining they might be redeemed.

As the sun faded, but before the double moons' light could give the Kyykki hordes away, they scrambled down the rugged cliff. The combination of slipperiness, of fresh pure water and the Kyykki's inexperience of cliff climbing created numerous casualties. Irregardless, when the cool dawn rose, over a thousand stood at the foot of the falls, about three miles from the small encampment. Littering the ground behind them, lay the broken bodies of the dead and wounded, which were habitually ignored, if not eaten. The Demon Masters fast-marched the horde towards the encampment. There was no loud doumy-doumy preparation. Had it not been for the putrid stench natural to the Kyykki, their attack might have been a surprize.

Forewarned, Sarg alone stood before the stockade's door to welcome the invaders. Feathered Goat, per hurried plan, disappeared into the scrub forest to the north of camp. Sjura, flanked by Brey and Tiello, watched from just inside the door. Sjura stood close enough to provide aid in translating.

"Halt! Halt! You insolent trespassers!" Sarg yelled at the advancing horde. When they refused to acknowledge his command, he immediately unhitched his double-bladed broadaxe.

One of the four Demon Masters walked forward. The horde stumbled to an awkward halt. He spit out a jumble of words, then tested the air with his forked tongue. Using his pole axe, he made some incomprehensible maneuvers, then with amazing, surprizing accuracy, threw the weapon at Sarg. The pole axe grazed Sarg's left arm, then vibrated as it dug into the soft dirt. Sarg's instinctive reply left the Demon Master clutching the shaft of the broadaxe protruding from his scaly chest.

At a signal from other Demon Masters, the Kyykki stumbled forward. A huge shadow suddenly covered them. Then a boulder smashed the line's center, thrusting mangled fragments of green slimed bodies into the air. The fragments rained down upon the ranks, causing the attackers to slip, faltering.

Sarg placed his fingers together, pointing them at the cliff, some fifty feet below the waterfall's source. "For the Holy One!" He shouted boldly as a bolt of lightning shot towards the cliff.

The explosion rocked the valley, scattering rocky debris into the air. The stunned Kyykki turned about, looking behind them. In slow motion, an immense cube of granite separated from the cliff, forever changing the creek's course. Another boulder obliterated the right side of the Kyykki horde. Sarg slashed through the left flank with a razor sharp bolt of light. The fleeing survivors found themselves wrestling with the Istelle's attack.

Feathered Goat glided the Istell in just outside the stockade's door. With a wave to his wife Sarg climbed up and tied himself to the huge creature. With a few strokes of its two hundred foot wings, the two airborne men headed for the cliff.

"Circle to the right." Sarg said to Feathered Goat. With a movement of his foot that touched the right side of the bird's neck, it banked towards the cliff. At a forty-five degree angle, Sarg went white with terror. Feathered Goat grinned to himself.

"We need to slow."

"What for?" Asked Feathered Goat.

"There's a tunnel that divides the creek, allowing the water to provide a hidden transportation route. ...Need to destroy it!" Sarg's anxiousness made him shout.

"Only on one condition." Feathered Goat demanded, turning his head to yell into Sarg's whitened face.

"What's that?" Sarg asked nervously.

"Quit yelling in my ear!"

With a sickly grin, Sarg responded almost too quietly. "You have a deal."

Their flight produced fantastic explosions as the Istelle glided by the mountain ridge which covered the tunnel. When the immense dust clouds settled, Sarg and Feathered Goat examined the leveled mountain ridge. They slowly glided by the waterfall. Its force easily doubled, causing the falls to shoot out beyond the rocks, digging a hole at the base of the cliff. Satisfied that the tunnel no longer existed, Feathered Goat glided the Istelle to the encampment.

Brey awaited their return. Her anger showed. "You left survivors!"

"I presume then that there are no more." Sarg stated matter-of-factly. "After all,.........you are a Light Striper.... We have a reputation to maintain."

"OH!" She screamed. "Shut up!"

"Things are returning to normal around here." Sarg said to Feathered Goat.

Chapter 2

"Ashuwa acknowledges you as the biggest incompetent that ever 'partially' existed." Haadd loudly berated his benumbed, worn-out twin brother.

"Only that after you?" Came the sneering response from his twin, Porehote.

"You're the shiftless slop who is keeping the attack from its schedule." Haadd, sweating profusely due to his grotesquely obese physique, angrily responded. "You know the penalty for failure,........ or have you forgotten that also?"

"You'll die long before I will." Porehote shot back with a hint more acid. "And ....Hopefully with a hell of a lot more pain. May Ashuwa grant my request, and ......may it take an abysmally long time as well."

"Mother always overrated your kindness." He sneered back.

"You erroneously assume that Mother never thinks beyond having something stuck between her pimply legs."

"Shut up your ugly face...." The younger of the twins spit. "She's all we got....And don't you never forget it."

Porehote deliberately forgot this insult. His physical exhaustion extended well beyond anything he ever knew. Yet he lasted almost four sunsets since leaving the protection of Mother and the volcano. This expedition was the most difficult obstacle in his life. He felt proud of this singular victory. Wisely though, did he keep it to himself. The Demon Masters supposedly assisting him never took a break, never sweated. The Haafian leaders never showed, content to run the invasion from a distance. Secretly, he believed, everyone ridiculed him, and rightly so. He had no concept of warfare, of geography, of leadership, even of simple survival skills. He only knew how to keep Mother satisfied....Well, at least if he realized the bottom line, he thought, then he was one step ahead of his twin. The animosity between them grew and festered.

For his part, Haadd consciously withdrew from his brother. Not because his physical stamina was worse than his brother's, but because he intended to learn from the Demon Masters. He lived this ridiculous lie. The truth being that he neither observed the Demon Masters nor anything else that didn't fit his mouth. His goal stemmed from the damned one: conquer Pinduala and be rewarded. Thus he examined the hordes of the Kyykki, especially the newer breed. Then he watched as the Demon Masters organized everything and adequately handled the logistics of the operation. From his perspective, he merely needed to survive, nothing more, nothing less. Translated that meant: stay out of the way. In the deepest recesses of his febrile brain he rejoiced at his brother's 'pretending' to lead the forces. Soon he'd die in battle, a wondrous hero. ...Then he'd have Mother all to himself. Obviously, neither of the two knew of Mother's fate.

Following the desolate and arid valleys formed by the volcanoes, where the sun-baked ground became like stone, the innumerable Kyykki hordes trudged ever eastward. They headed towards the staging area, lumbering from one stagnant pool to another. Their intended destination being a shallow plain rising west, just above the Zuda Marsh. There, after a rendezvous of all the Kyykki as well as the promised dragons, the invasion would begin. The Haafian leaders were to make final adjustments affecting troop movements and timing. The rendezvous would also provide for an acclamation area. The stress from leaving the barren valleys to the marshy over-ripe jungle, required rested Kyykki. Even the Demon Masters had no intentions of stupidly sacrificing their soulless hordes by ignoring the effects of the environment.

The twelfth dawn began. The Demon Masters summoned both Haadd and Porehote to their council meeting. The slovenly bastards showed up late, further distancing themselves from courtesies the Demon Masters did expect from two outsiders. Amidst a semicircle of large gaunt-faced muscular Demon Masters, each standing according to his position in the hierarchy, the blubbery twins rightly felt uncomfortable. Nervously folding and unfolding their sweating paws, the two listened intently to battle strategies they could not comprehend. They wisely voted with the others, following the lead of the silvered and blood-red tunicked Head Demon Master.

In spite of their fear, the twins refused to run away. In truth, they were too exhausted to move much further. Moreover, they wisely kept their asinine remarks to themselves. They even earnestly pretended to understand the council's deliberations. They stood at attention, wearing their swords. What more could these Demon Masters expect?

"Porehote!" The Head Demon Master angrily thundered, causing the fat oaf to commence quivering. "Come before me!"

Lumbering grossly, a feminine waddle, Porehote crossed the circle. Coarse laughing surrounded him. Even his brother joined in, true loyalty bowed to group consensus. Safety existed in numbers.

"Yes?" He twittered in a squeaky voice.

His feminine cackling sent a few of the lesser Demon Masters tumbling to the ground in hysterics; this gross spectacle being more than they could handle. The Head Demon Master smirked wickedly.

"Before me, you uncouth slob! You degenerate piece of Kyykki dung! You filth from your Mother's filth!" Barked out the Head Demon Master. His eyes blazed with intense animosity.

"Ye....es.....sss." Chirped the blabbering Porehote. He stood but two paces from the towering Demon Master. Porehote found it impossible to see his feet But he stared at the chest of the Demon Master, too cowardly to meet the demon eye-to-eye.

"Show me that by which you so pleased the whore you call 'Mother'?" He smirked through his anger, his dagger teeth still red from supper's meal.

Porehote froze. Another Demon Master snatched off his tent-sized tunic. Naked, Porehote backed away as the Head Demon Master pushed his needle-like fingers into his overabundant belly.

"I think it not be much." Commented a demon standing on the side.

"Nor was that 'thing' called his 'Mother'." Shouted out another.

"How can anyone really tell! Look at all that blubber." Added a third voice.

Porehote remained frozen, whether from embarrassment or fear, he knew nor cared not. Defenseless, he stood encircled by the Demon Masters. Unwilling to think about a recourse for his precarious situation, he simply pretended it didn't exist. Nightmares go away in their own time, leaving no real scars, no real damage, he prudently thought to himself.

"Then remove the blubber!" Commanded another unidentified voice.

Suddenly, with a single stroke, a razor-sharp sword deftly removed Porehote's huge belly. He stared blankly at his immediate demise; his internal organs falling upon the dirt, green with red tinged blood pouring out. In horrified anguish, he grabbed for his non-existent gut. The Demon Masters laughed. In abject horror Haadd finally quit his giggling. He thought to run, but found Demon Masters gathered behind him. He wet himself.

"I still can't see what satisfied the whore."

"Then I'll show it to you." A blue gowned Demon Master laughed viciously.

Kicking Porehote to the ground, the Demon Master forced Porehote's thick tubular legs apart. With a flick of his sabre, the Demon Master sent Porehote's manhood sailing through the air, landing in the dust before his brother's feet.

"Recognize this?" He savagely taunted Haadd.

As the Demon Masters continued their roaring laughter, Porehote died, mutilated and abased. They tosssed his grotesque carcass to the Kyykki horde.

Haadd, terrified, for his own welfare, fell to his stubby knees, imploring the gathered demons for mercy. He bargained with outrageous promises, which greatly embellished the evening's entertainment.

"You would live?" Derided another Demon Master. "Then lick my feet." He laughed dryly, deadly.

Haadd crawled upon his hands and knees, but found it impossible to lick the demon's clawed feet without first resting on his more than considerable gut. He looked right and then left, then, with an ostentatious grunt, kicked out his legs. Before the humiliated Haadd crawled to the Demon Master's feet, two demons, brandishing a sharpened log, laughed with the rest as they impaled Haadd from behind. One hard shove and the pole went in behind his rump and then emerged through Haadd's huge stomach. He desperately clutched at the point as it passed by his twisted face, his eyes white with agony. What he giggled about when he joyfully tortured the 'blue ladies' now openly confronted him in his own death.

Numerous Demon Masters grasped the pole and while boisterously cackling, launched it into a waiting mob of screeching Kyykki. The impaled Haadd, twin son of the lover of the damned one, Ashuwa, shrieked. His body parts were ripped from him. He died alone.

"Now," The silvered and blood-red tunicked Demon Lord said. "Our entertainment is over. May we thank our God, Almighty Ashuwa, for his most fitting gift." A hearty round of slapping commenced and then absolute silence.

"This, then, is the battle plan...Listen well....Failure still means your death...and mine." His tone lost all of its resonating laughter. "However, our success is guaranteed....... The Haafian enemy is as knowledgeable and skillful as Porehote and Haadd."

Guffaws rang about the circle; these Demon Masters were all veterans. They recognized hyperbole.

"We must plan very carefully, with contingency plans as well...... Are we in agreement?" The Head Demon Lord cut to the quick. "Our recommendations will be examined by the Haafians. When they are finished, we'll attack, according to their plan. The onus of failure is upon them."

A nod of sharply featured scaly heads provided confirmation. Then, until the sun hazily rose, he barked commands to each and every one of his underlings. By mid-morning, regardless of the condition of the Kyykki, the ascent into Zuda Marsh commenced. So came the orders from the Haafian leaders, who actually changed nothing in the plan advanced to them.

"Somewhat commendable." Those two words formed the essence of Vosnob's reaction to the quartet's ambitious plan to counter-attack the Kyykki hordes which had recently entered the Zuda.

The Chaplain and Captain Ellom smiled quietly. Their remarkable plan fared better than they thought it might, the running commentary by Ushver and Tubt notwithstanding. Vosnob's calmness came from his 'new' self. However, he still had excellent experience in tactics. Challenges from others did not bother him. Vosnob strode about the Chaplain's quarters at the Pinduala barracks, his huge hands covering his ears. No one disturbed his concentration. While waiting for Vosnob to amend their plan, the four finished breakfast. Soon afterwards Vosnob posited himself on a heavy wooden chair; he faced the others at the table.

"There is great merit in your plan, especially in the concept of originality." He began, his tone serious. "However, the territory you would invade is fit for neither Haafian nor Striper....Even Sarg...." He paused as an anguished look of loss and despair momentarily clouded his bronzed face.

"Yes, Sarg." Softly echoed the Chaplain.

"Aye." Added Captain Ellom. "He'd be'ed an impressive one." He whacked his mug on the oaken table top. "Ta Sarg!"

"Yes," The soft spoken Vosnob allowed before returning to his assessment of the original plan. "It's suicidal to send troops into the swamp."

Tubt scowled. "Then you'll dump the entire plan."

"No, I have no intention of that." He sighed, a bit weary of the all-or-nothing attitude of the Staff Master. "However, I will permit an attack ...by sea."

"Now that's more like it!" Gleefully commented the Wharf Manager, Ushver. His wheeling and dealing directly contrasted with Tubt's concrete attitudes.

Vosnob ignored the comment. "We'll bring the entire weight of the Striper's Navy to bear upon the water-borne filth. The ships will clear the sea as well as keep the Kyykki on land."

"What kind of attack is that?" Ushver waved his hand impatiently.

"A delightfully damned good one." Captain Ellom interjected. "Its a matter of sending the po' devils ta hell thu' exhaustion. Once them devils learn they gots nowheres ta go, they jist drownds.."

"Fair enough, good Captain." Vosnob respectfully critiqued his friend. "But, you underestimate the Kyykki. Instead of swimming, they'll travel along the coast."

"So Pinduala's in for the fight of her life." The Chaplain bluntly stated. "I thought as much. .That's why I suggested we meet them north of the city, using that new ....Oh!" He cursed himself for having forgotten. ".... Those new Stripers...with the lances.....when you put the phalanx on....."

"We are familiar with the mounted phalanx...Seems they've chosen the name 'Lancer' for themselves. 'Lancers of the Light Striper' to be exact and formal about the whole thing."

"Well....why not use them?" The Chaplain continued, a bit of an edge to his voice.

"Settle thyself." Said Captain Ellom. "This be listen'ng time."

"Ayhn has too few lancers...They are still untried." Vosnob groused.

"Sorry....sorry."

"When the Kyykki are gone from the sea, they'll move south to Pinduala by land. Hoping that we'll still be out at sea. ....That is true.... But I seriously doubt that Pinduala is their goal. The Damned One wants Krabo."

"To rule a country of people." The Chaplain's voice rose with amazement, stunned by his own insight. "Then he could establish a bonifide claim to being a real 'god'.....Perish the thought."

"Aye." Chuckled Captain Ellom. "Hees gonna make ye future life miserable."

"This isn't funny." Snorted the Chaplain. "This is, however, a direct result of the Holy One's punishment. By being unable to lie anymore, the damned one realizes his hordes and his domain do not qualify him as a true god....And that's exactly what he wants...a real people."

Tubt pounded his mug on the table. "Shut up! We've got other than your hypothetical theology to worry about."

"Well put." Ushver murmured. "Can we move along?"

Vosnob coughed, a deliberate cough. As silence pervaded the chamber he began to speak. "The Chaplain is correct. The Holy One forces Ashuwa to move quickly, before the stench of his present kingdom kills him. The damned one's time is at hand. He either gets a people or he dies."

The others nodded their apologies to the Chaplain and Vosnob refocused their discussion. "To the east of the Holy One's Wall, a fortress of 'some' proportions is being built. It forms the anchor for a line of smaller forts that lead due south. These are built according to standards set after the Battle." He paused, eyebrows raised, wondering if he piqued the trio's curiosity.

Ellom spoke first. "You're herding the Kyykki south. South into the plains....Kyykki won't exist there too long." He smiled.

"But how do we know enough of them will die so that Krabo is actually secure from the blackened horde?" While he sat well poised, the tenor of the Chaplain's voice belied his nervousness. "After all, cutting through their own territory hasn't cost them too many casualties. They merely lumber from fetid pond to fetid pond. The 'long glass' on the tower provided that evidence....We'll be fighting fresh troops...not even ones hungry enough to act irrationally."

"Quite true." Vosnob replied without much excitement. "That's why the 'navy' will be putting the Lancers ashore to the north. And why the fortifications at Pinduala are being strengthened.. ...The goal is to drive them south...Then to isolate them on the plains. D'Ka is the farthest south they'll reach."

"Glory bees!" Captain Ellom proclaimed jubilantly. "If we keeps 'em away out 'en de plains, then we got's de damned ...."

"Perhaps," Interrupted an unconvinced Tubt. "The strategy succeeds only if all four parts hold firm. One city falls, one hole in the fortress line appears, and we'll need another..."

...."Place to live?"

"Not proper to interrupt, Ushver."

"Too bad.......... Besides, it's all theory. The assumptions are based upon the fact that we believe the damned one will proceed as usual, simply throwing his hordes into our weapons. Probably see more than the usual number of dragons as well. They've all ready moved into Haaf North....Or what 'was' Haaf North. Almost a thousand of the ugly things."

"I am aware that the enemy has encroached upon our sovereignty. But those dragons and a few demon lords can't do much beyond provoking fear...And how long they can maintain their desolated outpost is numbered by the next few double moons."

"Then the rumor is true: the city is being bleached...Another of the old man's contraptions I assume."

"No." Said Vosnob. "He's back at Pinduala. Gath remains near Haaf North. His efforts allowed the survivors to reach D'Ka safely." He smiled wistfully, knowing far more than he had revealed.

"Ye ain't be square wid us now." Commented Captain Ellom. "Ye needs bees tellin' de whole story."

"Are ye sure ye can handle it all?" Vosnob spun his pewter mug in his large hand, finally getting used to being young again, even if his appearance still rattled those about him. One look at Vosnob was close to seeing the Holy One.

"Best iffen we'd be'ed finding out." Ellom flatly responded.

"Well, for starters, Oros and Rux returned. Seems they arrived at Haaf North just in time to see the Abbot's execution before they and Ilty escaped..." A hush caused Vosnob to continue. "An extremely beautiful 'blue lady' is also among those rescued."

"And she's pretending to be one of us?" Sneered Tubt.

"Actually, she isn't. Though, I haven't personally met her....Maybe on the morrow."

"Well, what is she then?"

"A Tath."

"Ah, so the demon ladies concocted a fancy name for themselves. Won't help keep them alive any longer."

"Ye of little faith." Vosnob said slowly. "Taths are an ancient people. Perhaps with a history longer than ours. Strong blue, a healthy robust pale blue...not decaying blue,.. is their natural color. Their eyes are oval. Their Kingdom...excuse me, their Queendom lies to the north of the Dark Lands. I understand their territory to be vast, probably greater than Haaf." The Commander looked about. The trio stared at him as if he were insane. "And, you remember the King's white eagle? ....They're called Istelles and they run twice the size of a dragon." Vosnob smiled, quite delighted by all the good news.

"Ah!" Sighed the Chaplain. "This rejuvenating by the Holy One as injured your poor brain...You can't discern fact from fiction anymore...... Or....Ah, you're excellent.....You're just testing us, aren't you?" His voice hinted of doubt.

Vosnob took them all on, eye-to-eye. "Everything I've explained to you is the truth. What we imprudently believed to be true isn't true....The world is far larger than two nations, far more complex than two peoples plus a demon race...And far beyond my thinking as to how a nation can be run by a woman."

"We do pretty well without a King." A smirking Ushver noted.

"That's quite enough." Said Vosnob. "Do you understand the implications of having another nation north of us? We assume them to be neutral concerning the Kyykki. But," He paused. "Think of them being persuaded to join with us. Think of massive Istelles tossing dragons from the skies and smashing the blackened hordes with boulders dropped from the sky."

Captain Ellom thoroughly enjoyed himself, being part of the unknown navy allowed him privy to many secrets, especially when it came to devising weapons. "I must meet this woman."

"And you shall, all of you. I've slated a meeting for next double moon. We'll meet here." He relaxed in his chair, taking a long draught from his pewter mug. "The lady is a lady...as in being a princess. Her formal name is Jelkio."

The room suddenly froze, firmly encapsulating the five men. A small twinkling cloud descended upon the flat roofed chamber, disgorged a solitary passenger and flashed away as silently as it arrived. Vauk, still sweaty and shaking from his terrifying cloud ride, rested on the carved stone bench. Something about speeding above the land, watching the lights and the people, knowing that only air kept him from falling thousands of feet, totally paralyzed him. He traveled the way of gods and he was but a mortal. But, he said to himself, a mortal with a most serious mission. He patted the leather pouch with Sarg's maps and notes. Everything was proper. Gratefully able to stomp his feet on something hard, Vauk stood up and headed downstairs. He wondered how a stranger from the heavens might be received. Chuckling to himself, he knocked on the wooden door. The knock on the door released the spell, one the quintet never recognized, nor felt, nor suspected.

"We're not to be disturbed!" Barked a miffed Chaplain. "This 'was' supposed to be clandestine, wasn't it?" He whispered to the others.

"I bring you good news from Sarg." Said the voice.

Immediately everyone sat up.

"You are alone?"

"Indeed, Chaplain."

"And how is it that you know me?"

"Because I'm a member of a scouting party that resided here. We solved the mystery of the 'pale women' for you."

With a broad smile the Chaplain rose and yanked the door open. "Welcome, Vauk......I'm surprised to see you..."

"That's an understatement, if I ever heard one...Welcome, me boy." Captain Ellom stood and saluted. "Nice ta see you under more pleasant circumstances."

"Thank you, Captain." Vauk clutched the leather pouch tightly. "I am entrusted to deliver these to no one else than Vosnob, Sir!"

"Sarg's maps and notes." Vosnob said. "Sit down, please. Getting here must have been an ordeal for you."

"More than you might be able to comprehend." He smiled. "But you are not familiar to me, Sir.....And where is Chaplain Commander Vosnob?" Vauk stood quickly, believing himself deposited an erroneous place. He curse the stupidity of the nameless god. Vosnob wasn't present.

"I am Vosnob." Said the Commander. "My age, just recently, was dramatically altered by the Holy One."

"I have witnessed too much lately. Too much of evil magics and damned things which ought not to exist....How am I to know this is not another entrapment? Have you more proof of....."

"Would you believe the Chaplain?"

"Yes. We have worked together...These others here, Captain Ellom excepting, are strangers to me..........Perhaps the Chaplain and the Captain are actually prisoners."

Vosnob turned slowly on his chair, amused and yet agitated by Vauk. "What proof might convince you that I am Vosnob?"

Vauk slid closer to the door which just admitted him. "Would you answer some questions then?" He asked tentatively.

"Indeed, if I must." As Vosnob turned back in his chair everyone noticed that his color turned lighter. His voice sounded strained.

A nervous Vauk held his ground. "You must."

"Then be on with it."

He placed his hand on the door latch before replying, even though the Chaplain and Captain Ellom made gestures to the contrary. "When a secret mission, sent out by Vosnob, finally collected all its members..."

"Come on boy!" Vosnob's indignation showed. "They were Sarg as squad leader, with Luuft, a thin fellow named Briel and yourself. Now, according to Sarg's own documentation, this Briel became the first female to successfully join and remain in the Light Striper.....Now can we dispense with the rest of your inane questions and get to the matter at hand?"

"You're the Vosnob who blasted Luuft out prior to leaving for the Dark Lands." Vauk said quietly. He handed the leather pouch to the Commander and saluted.

"I apologize, Sir!"

"Please, enough of this.....Sit down." As he rummaged through the worn leather pouch, Vosnob suddenly pulled back, alarmed. "How did you find us?...And what of the others? ..Especially Sarg? ...Tell the story."

Thereupon Vauk undertook the longest narrative of his life. Beginning with Brey's disclosure of her real person and name, Breel. He continued with the voyage and the pirates and the unfortunate sinking of their small vessel. From thence he meticulously described the inland journey through the Zuda Marsh and the Yldan, Blue Turtle, who rescued them and brought them to the cliffs. His detailed reporting concluded, the first time, when he acknowledged the dragon's lair and their invasion of it.

"Sarg didn't take such chances!" Vosnob declared.

"Yes, Sir, he certainly did...Especially as there were no other choices.... We had the sole option of going forward....We actually didn't fair too badly."

Vosnob simply nodded.

Vauk accepted a mug from Captain Ellom before returning to his story. Ushver and Tubt sat stone silent, mesmerized by Vauk's reporting of a world that few could believe existed, a land where evil actually ruled, totally unopposed.

Putting his mug down, Vauk commenced with the rescuing of the Tath women, Queen Sjura, Jelkio, and Tiello. His description of their blue skin and oval eyes confirmed what Vosnob enunciated a few moments prior to Vauk's surprize arrival. But his version of the Paradise Valley, waterfall and vibrant greenery in the midst of the hellish Dark Lands, stunned everyone. In rephrasing Queen Sjura's explanation of the valley and its relationship to their strange god-without-a-name, the men became bewildered. Ushver threatened Vauk.

Vauk, his voice now raspy and raw, requested that he might continue on the morrow, seeing that his official assignment had nothing to do with the narrative. But for naught, Vosnob demanding a full accounting for the remainder of their mission. Outranked and overruled, Vauk bargained for another mug of ale before returning to his story. Vauk painfully shook as he shared the journey down the tunnel which caused the loss of Luuft as well as Tiello, Qill and many of the other Yldans. He stopped and wiped his eyes. Sharing the story with those who did not know it not brought his anguish to the surface again.

"You know they felt exactly the same way about you." Vosnob said slowly.

"I'm not sure I understand."

"Tiello and Qill....plus a few others...did survive...Luuft did also...for a while .... He died defending the party from renegade Haafians."

The time arrived for Vauk to be bewildered. He slowly rose from the table, trembling. Making his way to the arched window, he stared out across the fortress city. Silently he offered a multitude of conflicting prayers, believing the Holy One could make sense of his non-sense. He felt a strong hand on his shoulder, one which emanated empathy.

"Thank you." Vauk offered the Chaplain. Both returned to the table where Tubt, Ushver and Vosnob patiently waited. "Do you know the rest of the story, then?"

"Only according to what Qill and Tiello provided. I'd send for them, except they're a goodly distance from Pinduala." Vosnob offered.

"Thank you, Sir. ...Just knowing more of their story will bring encouragement to Sarg and the others...O' yes," He smiled wryly. "Sarg is going to become a father......... And he's married, to Queen Sjura. And he's been 'gifted'. ...But you probably all ready realized that from the story."

The Chaplain shook his head. "Not until now......Somehow none of this truly surprises me........At least not anymore." He sighed. "May the Mercy of the Holy One guide us."

"Which part?.... And why not, Chaplain?" Asked Vosnob.

"Haven't you noticed something special about him? Isn't that why he's headed up most of your dangerous escapades?...And now he's married, finally, to a queen....Does that mean he outranks you?"

Vosnob squirmed, and then laughed. "I can't wait to visit the old fool."

"You'll need to wait until Sarg's talkdown with the nameless god produces the required results." Vauk cautiously allowed. "That is, until all the Tath tribes have convened at Sarg's. Then until they decide to confront the damned one. And then, until after all the battles are fought and Sarg's kingdom is at peace...."

"You certainly aren't serious."

"Couldn't be more serious, Chaplain ...Sarg challenged Queen Sjura's delightful ..... yet horribly inconsistent god with his existence. Either the unnamed god begins to be a god or he'll lose every worshipper. ...And spend eternity in 'nowhere'."

"Whoa!..... Slow de bilge pumps down!" Ellom yelled. "Be time ta call this quits."

"On the early morrow, my friends."

A nod of weary spinning heads easily assented to Vosnob's command.

While the refugees were extremely vulnerable along the Bay Road, the dragons never attacked. This unusual maneuver confounded Yganak. Usually the damned ones swooped down upon the helpless. Now almost a thousand dragons kept a silent watch from their desolate perches at Haaf North. Certainly their threatening had a major impact upon the masses of refugees, but with Gath and his 'dragon waggon' machines entrenched outside the desolate city, their intimidation was balanced.

After allowing for a period of rest, Yganak ordered the refugees located south of Krabo. Vaal sent the Church Knights to relieve the exhausted Light Stripers, a gesture of true kindness that Yganak appreciated. Under Rux's intensive care, Nadre's recuperation sped along rapidly. Oros intimated to the Yldans and Tiello that 'love' was showing its supreme power. However, he also allowed, the first one to mention this to Rux might pay dearly.

Two dawns later Vaal arrived with his guard to personally escort Tiello and the Yldans, along with Rux and Nadre plus Oros to a private audience with the King. Tiello found no enjoyment in being bounced about like some 'thing'. The full extent of her anger exploded upon the unsuspecting Nooy. As a matter of self-defense the injured Yldan disappeared, causing Tiello's outbursts to increase. Only as the heavily escorted waggons left D'Ka did Nooy re-appear, and then with reinforcements, Kofe.

Both Yldans forcefully wedged their mounts in behind the Royal Waggon, against the protests of the Church Guard. They cantered along patiently, waiting for Tiello's acknowledgement of their presence. Shortly before the mid-day rest, Tiello tersely, in the manner of oafish royalty, responded via a messenger. She would speak to the 'commoner' for a brief time. The word 'brief' was underscored. Winking to Kofe, Nooy responded with a dialect that clearly offended the sensibilities of the messenger.

"We'se be 'vited ta bisit wid da blue prin-sess." Nooy yelled at the nearby guard, his voice carrying over to the bench where the Tath lady-in-waiting demurely sat. She flushed at the gritty sound of his voice.

"You may enter, but mind your manners."

Nooy barged through, leaving Kofe holding the reins to their mounts. He shrugged his shoulders when the guard talked to him, feinting deafness. The guard turned away, hopefully finding more enjoyment in the upcoming verbal battle than conversing with a deaf Yldan.

"Ga-day ta yer high-ness." Nooy yelled as he clumsily prostrated himself before Tiello. He bowed from the waggon's back gate.

She had little choice but to acknowledge him. Elevating her slender hand with a so-called royal gesture, Tiello bid Nooy to stand. "I thank you for the visit." She said in heavily accented Haaf.

"I'd not-not miss-sed dis fer all de jewels in Tath." He sputtered away.

"How kind of you." She gently smiled. Her pretensions were obvious to all watching. She might be a princess, but not one carved from the Haafian mold.

"It 'pears yer not be too con-fert-able in dees surroundins, my lady."

Tiello forced herself to look away from this 'peasant', away into the strained faces of the retainers and the guards. She shut her eyes, forcing their impolite stares from her mind. "This is most difficult." She confided to the peasant in Tath.

"Then, may-haps yer bees in-te-res-ted in udder thins'?" He graciously delivered her one of his irresistible twisted smiles.

She flushed, her bluish countenance deepening. Then she sighed.

"A diversion from this captivity?" Nooy returned in perfect Tath.

"Perhaps," She replied in Haaf. "The ostentatious company is very boring." A broad grin of satisfaction shot across her face as she witnessed the stylized 'offendedness' of her Haafian royal retainers. They stood, mute with shock at Tiello's criticism of their 'royal persons'.

"Aye." Nooy announced with another clumsily executed bows; all for the benefit of those gathered.

"Then, come sit." She motioned for Nooy to sit next to her on the bench, a highly irregular procedure. She anticipated something, Nooy felt it.

He scrutinized her, finally realizing Tiello had no rivals for beauty.

The long laced gown silhouetting her features, accentuating her long neck and daringly exposing cleavage atop the tight fitting bodice, emboldened him to continue his plan. Stepping nearer, as if to sit, Nooy ignored the painful noises emitted by the retainers. Then, in a swift movement, he dropped to one knee, unceremoniously tossed Tiello over his shoulder, leapt over the waggon gate and hustled towards his waiting mount. Tiello desperately clasped her hands to her chest, trying not to allow anything to fall out. Nooy placed her behind him and galloped off before anyone realized what happened. Kofe's suddenly bucking Striper refused to let the Church Guards follow.

The furious moments of running put the needed distance between the royal entourage and the escapees. Then, after some dizzying twists in the nearby forest, some jumps over briars, and two forded streams, Nooy permitted the Striper to walk. He grasped Tielo's hands, which fearfully clung to his waist. Relaxing, she rested her chin on his shoulder.

"Yer feelin' better?" He asked with the irritating dialect.

She bit his shoulder.

"Yes.... You are feeling much better....But do you feel safer?"

"Am I not with you?" She coyly whispered.

"I had hoped as much, my love..... But now you'll have to spend the evening with me....Does that bother you?"

"Should it? We've spent many nights together before."

"But there's always been company about....Now it's just ...us."

"Perhaps that's exactly what I've been waiting for." Then, as they rode deeper into the forest, she leaned into him, holding him tightly as she relaxed. "This is my commitment, my love," She said softly. "I'll never leave you."

As a red-sky dusk descended, Nooy made camp in hollow of willows fronted by a slow moving stream. The saddlebags contained enough provisions for three mornings, but Nooy decided that fresh fish were proper for their evening meal. Their first meal together-and alone--he nervously thought. Tiello had seen to the saddle blankets and prepared camp for the night.

When he returned with some fish, Tiello was brushing her hair, her tightly laced bodice rested elsewhere. He'd never seen her in just a simple petticoat, He lowered his head, a bit embarrassed.

"Do I not look pretty to you?"

"Perhaps too much." He looked at his feet. "You are...... so......beautiful."

"Then look at all of me, for all I am is yours."

As Nooy slowly raised his head, Tiello stood. Her petticoat fell to the blankets. Excepting her blonde hair, Tiello was entirely blue, head to foot. Nooy refused to look away this time. He tossed the fish behind him and rushed to embrace her. The single moon bounced a soft light off the stream when they finally broke away to wash and then eat their evening meal. The mid-morning sun discovered them still sleeping in each other's arms.

The Church Guards had long ago suspended their searching when they finally realized the nature of the 'supposed' abduction.

Irregardless of its location, stench is stench. Seldom does it dissipate, nor does it dilute when the wind blows. Much to the contrary Ashuwa thought. The damned breezes only locked the stench inside his volcano. Even HIS volcano had been violated, and then, HIS prisoners escaped, and then Sarg receives 'the gift'. Nothing ever improved, his kingdom was plagued by incompetence. Krucik didn't deliver as he promised. Then the moronic twins--they and their mother—useless beyond measure. And then, unexpectedly, from a slumber of countless eons, the 'spoiler' returned and his 'cute' cloud with him. Ashuwa, well aware of the nameless one's gimmicks, also knew it as the primary source of the 'spoiler's' strength. Without a positive, a true identification, the unnamed one's heritage went unknown, making it nigh impossible to reach the troublemaker----and kill him. Angrily, Ashuwa pounded the arm of his stone throne chair.

Under the impact, it splintered, showering the huge chamber as well as the Demon Lords surrounding him with razor-sharp shards. His fanged jaw opened wide as he launched a thundering bellow followed by a snort of fire. It incinerated two Demon Lords.

"Those two should have kept a respectable distance!" He screamed at the rest. Their ranks quaked with fear. "Leave, you damned idiots!.... Leave."

While the Demon Lords bolted for the exit tunnels, Ashuwa rose and walked across the solidified lava stream which once separated him from the filthy Kyykki. Gazing at the still viable Kyykki who inhabited his 'newly poisoned' lake, he raged at how deeply he had been violated. If war they wanted, then he'd provide the damnedest war ever waged. In fact, he smiled grimly as he pulled his blood-red cape about him, their damned war had all ready begun. Soon his hordes and the dragons would rampage Pinduala. Then, destroying every living thing in their path, his hordes would attack Krabo itself. D'Ka, isolated from the rest of the country, and then starved into submission, would become his first 'People'.

Such strategies brought him powerful thoughts of revenge. Feeling much better, Ashuwa, using his new Haafian hand, tossed his immature Kyykki a handful of pebbles. He roared with laughter as they fought each other for the assumed fodder. Returning to his throne, he earnestly began contemplating his final victory. He'd destroy the Holy One, and reign in his stead.

Most of the planning he accomplished that night. In the midst of the stench-filled torch lighted chamber, he scribbled detailed instructions to his minions concerning the final campaign. Towards the second moon's rising, Ashuwa demanded a full council meeting with his Demon Lords. Rather mechanically, they quickly responded by encircling his raised throne. In their collective ugliness, with their skeletal bearing and deeply sunken eyes only Ashuwa realized, and relished, their relentless drive to serve him. Conversely, each Demon Lord remained fully cognizant that his life depended upon properly fulfilling his Master's will. Certainly Ashuwa lavishly rewarded the successful--with anything and everything they might imagine. But in these present times of warfare, casualties among the Demon Lords often outranked the front line. Appropriately then, those now gathered watched as the few survivors from the failed attack on Paradise Valley were sacrificed to the lake-bound Kyykki.

Ashuwa turned from gazing at the feeding Kyykki. "Welcome!" He thundered. "I offer you the final strategy. With these plans, I will soon be more powerful than that asinine Holy One. ...You will each have a kingdom unto yourself, such is my gracious reward for your excellent services."

A perfunctory clapping followed, followed by Ashuwa blandly smiling at his pets.

"First, Paradise Valley will be taken. The entire valley, including the new castle far up river from the Black Water, must be destroyed within one double moon cycle. Before the putrid blue skin tribes are gathered the valley will be mine. Expect interference from the moronic god-without-a-name........ The Demon Masters at Haaf North will assist you with their dragons."

Again the perfunctory applause conveniently erupted.

"Thank you for your positive assessment of my plan. Does anyone care to offer any suggestions?"

The droning din of, "No, My Lord Ashuwa!" continued until Ashuwa himself raised his clawed fist for silence.

"Then, listen to the rest of the plan." He said.

While shifting himself into a more comfortable position on his damaged throne, Ashuwa wounded one of the 'pale ladies' chained to the throne's base. The woman cried out in pain. Ashuwa casually kicked her head across the chamber. The rest of her thin body lay chained, covered with blood.

"Now then, I continue." Satisfaction gleamed in reptilian eyes. "Never before have I permitted anyone to have a name, excepting myself. And I have enjoyed many names....Now,.. I have changed my mind..... With a name, the Kyykki and the Haafians will know and fear you, as they know and fear me....Why?..... ...Because I alone am the name-giver.... And names have power...... And more power is required to defeat the Haafians and their repulsive, insolent god...The day is upon us when ...SOON...SOON...I promise you, this Holy-One-piece-of-Haafian-dung will genuflect to me.....or Die!" He stood and danced about the throne's pedestal, gleefully kicking another 'pale lady's head across the chamber. Then he heaved the blood spurting carcass after it. "So shall I end the rule of the fecal-faced god of the Haafians!" He danced back into the throne. "I will choose only one for the honor of the naming. He will be great and victorious over my enemies... He shall devour their men and ....do whatever he will with the women and children." Ashuwa lowered his voice for emphasis.

A frightening glimmer in his eyes caused the Demon Lords to consider retreating a step. Instead, they wisely dug their claws into the stone floor, creating an unnerving screeching noise.

"Have I frightened you?" He sought to intimidate them by going eye-to-eye.

To the benefit of the Demon Lords, an out-of-breath Haafian requested an emergency audience. He spoke to the door man who relayed the message to Ashuwa. After listening, Ashuwa quietly and forbiddingly, summoned the Haafian.

"What is of such importance that you dare to intrude upon my Council?........... Out with it, Haafian!" He bellowed to the cowering prostrated messenger.

"Yes, yes, your Worship." Clambered the slovenly dressed Haafian. "As the damned Elders departed from their Council Meeting just a half moon cycle ago, only twenty three left the building."

"And what is that to me, you dung heap?"

"The list of the twenty three I bring you." He gave a dirty parchment to a lackey. Ashuwa ripped it from the creature and examined the list.

"There are no secrets here, you fool...You will provide better Kyykki food than you do messenger service." He descended the throne stairs to throttle the Haafian. After he watched the man's eye's pop and heard his neck snap, Ashuwa fed the carcass to his Kyykki.

The spy had recognized the wrongness, the grave error of the compilation, he did not know the reason why. Ashuwa failed to recognize the change as well. He ripped the listing of the twenty three to shreds and returned to his throne. To him, nothing changed, his spy remained an Elder.

"Now then," He directly summoned a reddish-silver colored Demon Lord. "You are my chosen....... You shall carry the power of the dreadful, fear producing name I have chosen....... You are to be called, henceforth, by all my subjects, 'Warmaker'.

A truer applause broke from the gathered Demon Lords as grim smiles appeared upon their skeletal faces, each truly thankful for being passed by. The chosen Demon lord prostrated himself before his Master's feet, whence Ashuwa touched him, bidding him rise.

"Bow to your chosen Master, Warmaker'.

Obeying Ashuwa, the Demon Lords dropped to the stone floor, in homage to one who had been elevated far above them. While the stilted ceremony proved successful, the motives behind their meek obeisance to this ridiculous 'Warmaker' weren't. Recognizing traitorous eyes among those below him, Warmaker promptly tossed three Demon Lords into the lake, alive.

"Let their screams be a remembrance." Softly he spoke. "I shall tolerate only as much deviation as my sovereign, the greatest god, Ashuwa."

Without word, the Demon Lords again prostrated themselves before Warmaker. Slowly they stood, each pledging personal allegiance to Warmaker, not unlike the pledge, long ago, they gave to Ashuwa himself.

When the pledging finalized, Ashuwa called Warmaker to stand on his right side. The others resumed their usual places. Due to their losses, their circle decreased. This both disgruntled and pleased Ashuwa; his Warmaker did indeed belong to the hierarchy.

"Warmaker will commence battle with Sarg and those witless idiots in Paradise Valley. By the end of the double moon cycle, the valley shall become MY pond, that my children, my nepes, may grow again....... My land shall not be permitted to contain invaders...... No longer shall hideous patches of dusty brown-yellow filth desecrate the Dark Lands,... MY LANDS! They shall be beautiful again!" He thundered. Debris from the ceiling rained upon them. Ashuwa choked on his words. Their truthfulness bit at him.

The Demon Lords stood silent, unwilling to confess that their Almighty Ashuwa confused them with his rhetoric. Then again, all that was required of them was dutiful obedience. Thinking proved an unnecessary burden.

"My Lord!.....And My God!" Warmaker saluted Ashuwa. "I do as commanded. The valley shall again be yours and those vile creatures who tread upon your dignity and eminence...Shall DIE!"

Shouts of approval greeted his remarks, as did silent thanksgivings that Warmaker would soon be gone. With a raised Haafian fist, Ashuwa declared silence. Then he thrust a frightfully grotesque curved sword into Warmaker's clawed hands. "Have fun with this!... You'll discover it not only cuts through Haafians and Taths effortlessly, but it will also cleave chunks of stone from buildings." He smiled.

"Your graciousness to your humble servant is most appreciated."

Ashuwa nodded. "When your campaign is won, more rewards shall be yours...Shall I save some women for you?.................... Some children?"

"Thank you, My Lord........I shall consider these things in the future..... At present, until the campaign is won, I must subject myself to fulfilling your goal. Self-indulgence is unwarranted.....Your commands take president."

Ashuwa quickly gazed at Warmaker, considering the truthfulness of his remarks, so unusual, especially for these times, so extremely rare this caliber of discipline within the ranks of the Demon Lords, even though he personally created them. "Do you choose to mock me?"

Warmaker, paused, stunned by the acidity of Ashuwa's remark. "No, My Lord... I do not mock you....It is but the simple truth. Should I have my thoughts elsewhere than that which you have commanded of me, then all my efforts cannot be invested in accomplishing your commands..."

"You are extraordinary,.... Warmaker...... However, you shall prove yourself upon the successful accomplishment of the valley's absolute destruction."

"Yes, My Lord..."

"Then go and prepare....Council meeting adjourned!"

As dense fog escapes through hallways and staircases to the lowest point possible, so did the Demon Lords. They exited the chamber, creeping down the stairwells into the excrement filled sub-levels of the volcano. There, they recklessly indulged in a multitude of debasing activities. The women chained there were subjected to the animosity rightfully due Ashuwa...and, now, to Warmaker. He upset the traditional balance. The rules changed. Now one had to accomplish, to be disciplined, to think. Anger rose within the group, a personal indignation, even a 'certain' discrete madness. The elimination of Warmaker created a dreamy illusion, one that would contain them until their cowardice might sufficiently be overcome to perform the deed.

Warmaker, secretly followed them down the stairwells He entered their subterranean cesspool, executing six of the Demon Lords. The grotesque sword Ashuwa bestowed upon him worked well. The rest took refuge in heaps of foul smelling debris and under a few newly created corpses. "I will uphold My Lord Ashuwa...... For if you destroy me, you destroy his plan as well. Give me but one excuse, and I will gladly exterminate the rest of you dung-brained morons." Warmaker said as he turned and strode from their filth-piled quarters.

Later, Warmaker, after claiming a windswept chamber high in the volcano for his own, sent for information. Maps and numbers of Kyykki and minor demon masters became essential for his succeeding. Also needing clarification were the number of dragons actually allotted him. Finally, he desired two small favors from a currently benevolent Ashuwa. First, an appropriate mount for himself, Ashuwa's foremost warrior. Second, a request for him to personally lead the forces. Assistance from other Demon Lords being redundant. And, most probably, the best route to failure. He would not fail

Sometime later, as time is ascertained by those in the Dark Lands, Warmaker had his audience granted. He carried himself well as he strode down from his perch to Ashuwa's throne room. And well he might, the information in his possession, in terms of maps and logistical concerns, gave him a clear edge over his enemies, both within and without the volcano. If his allotment from Ashuwa came close to what his figures suggested, then he victory belonged to him--and thus, to his Lord and Master.

Entering the now less filthy throne room, Warmaker bowed before his seated god. The ever-present 'blue ladies' had vanished. Warmaker wisely decided not to question their whereabouts. But, after rising, he did comment on the brightness of the throne room. Usually caked with vermin and slimed walls, it now shone with the dark luster of polished volcanic rock.

"I thank you for this most gracious opportunity you offer me." Warmaker said with his head bowed.

"It is only proper. If you have not the proper equipment to wage war in my behalf, then you cannot win."

"That is true."

"Yes, damn it!" He snorted fire. "Anything less than the truth, is beyond my present capacity......But when the Holy One discovers his people worship me....Then he will never again do anything....He shall be

DEAD." A thunderous pounding of his Haafian arm on his throne caused the fingers to break off. With an indelicate snap, he broke the arm off. Then, even as slimy red and green blood spurted forth, he asked Warmaker a question.

"How loyal are you?"

"I have pledged you my career and my honor, My lord."

"But is that enough of a testing? ...Words, merely words."

"But what might I have to present you, My Lord, that isn't your's all ready."

"I sincerely doubt that I... that even I would have chosen better words.... Come here."

Warmaker stepped to the dais of the throne. Simultaneously, Ashuwa reached forth, smoothly decapitating Warmaker's arm. After casually adjusting it on his stump, he gazed quietly at the stunned Warmaker.

"Your loyalty is tested, Warmaker." Ashuwa smiled at his new set of claws. "Hold forth your stump."

Without a sound, Warmaker obediently held out his dripping stump. Taking the stump between his two clawed hands, Ashuwa raked Warmaker's reddish-silvered scales forward. He then squeezed the scaly material and molded it. When he finished, he smiled, well-pleased with himself and with his 'Warmaker'. Warmaker studied his new set of claws. Slowly he twitched them, then grasped his sword hilt. He returned a smile to Ashuwa, being well-pleased with passing the loyalty examination and as a bonus, obtaining another set of claws which functioned as well as the original.

"You are surprised with me?"

"No,.....no, My lord." He paused. "And, to be honest, yes."

"You reason deeper than most, Warmaker. I believe I have chosen well. Your qualities will serve me well."

"Thank you, My Lord." He paused. "Might I ask a question of a personal nature?"

"You would ferret out my deep secrets?" Ashuwa's eyebrows raised in suspicion, his reddened eyes pinpointed to a deadly glower. "You have plans to conquer even me?" His entire color darkened in wrathful anxiousness.

"No. No, My Lord and My God....My question is actually quite harmless.....Should you deem otherwise, then you have no reason to answer........Is that not true?"

"Certainly.... But you will, henceforth, delete that 'word' from your vocabulary."

"As you command."

"I require you. Ask your 'question of a personal nature'."

Warmaker stood uneasily. "I did wonder, My Lord, in my state of ignorance concerning 'godly' things, as to why you simply did not create another set of claws for yourself after that wretched Haafian sliced your's off."

Ashuwa paused, his reptilian eyes narrowed as he engaged another battle within himself. He might continue lying to himself, but the opposite occupied all conversations with others. Warmaker's logical question actually embarrassed him. Ashuwa's answer simply lodged itself in the area impulsiveness, nothing less, nothing more. But this, he thought to himself, wasn't the 'godly image' he wished to expose to others. Nonetheless, he replied to Warmaker, he had no other choice. "I am your God, as such..... it is my prerogative to operate according to my own law." His words struck Warmaker with a tinge of reticence, as well defining 'the' boundary which one never crossed. "My freedom defines all that is required for my subjects to understand." He paused.

"I, your humble servant, understand that Almighty Ashuwa is free to do whatever, whenever he so desires....I believe that is what you explained to me, My Lord."

"You are then, satisfied?" Ashuwa nervously queried, still agitated with the incessant combating within himself.

"I am, My Lord. ....Thank you."

"You are here to request provisions for the campaign against Sarg?"

"I have but two small requests for your consideration."

"And those two 'small' items are?"

"Thank you, My Lord for granting me this audience....In order than your assault upon Sarg might be one which brings you glory and implants fear into all those who you shall later destroy..."

"Get to the point!"

"A....A...Yes, My Lord....I require knowledge of the strength and disposition of the types of troops I shall have at my disposal as well as information regarding the same for Sarg..." Warmaker trembled a bit.

"And your second item?"

"A suitable mount for your personally chosen warrior, My Lord .... One that spreads intrepidation and fearfulness throughout the ranks of your enemies." He quickly bowed and stood back from the dais.

"You intrigue me, Warmaker. I enjoy your planning, especially as it applies to preparing for the total annihilation of my enemies....A special mount for you? One that transmits fear?....I grant you both requests."

Ashuwa suddenly stood, descended from his Haafian bone throne to stroll towards the ledge which overlooked his lake. He motioned for Warmaker to follow. Together they stood, silently surveying the wretchedness of the Dark Lands, taking in the vile, oppressive atmosphere, the stagnant land's sterility--its dearth of life. Ashuwa realized his intolerance for this unbalanced, this deadened fragmented land. He despised that unremitting truth.

"Do you enjoy this land, Warmaker?"

Warmaker hesitated, unsure of the question's intent. "It's the only land I've ever known, My Lord."

"Yes, it is...You have nothing by which to compare. Consider yourself fortunate."

"Yes, My Lord." Replied a confused Warmaker. He had no way to comprehend the raging battle within his god.

"At one time, trees and flowers blossomed here. Once, the sky was blue and the rains and seasons, the years......And animals, by herds,.. and some solitary, ..roamed here also....Once, a time long before this time, I governed as god over such a kingdom.. many kingdoms, in fact....Now,...... this is all which exists..........and it is a damned absolute nothing compared to what I once had." Ashuwa's weathered face showed a hint of loss, a bit of sadness.

"What happened, My Lord?"

Ashuwa answered slowly, his mind dredging up warm memories from the ancient era. "In those ancient days, my kingdoms were beautiful, full of liveliness and vigor, full of color and music, of famous artistic accomplishments, both for the ear and the eye."

"And the Holy One destroyed it all to spite you, My Lord?"

Ashuwa's breathing stuttered to a choking halt. Yet another battle brewed inside. How easy to allow Warmaker the lie, yet that time officially concluded when the Holy One pronounced punishment.

"No, Warmaker," Ashuwa replied as if conversing with a child. "The people,... they called themselves 'humans' in those days, actually killed themselves.....They poisoned themselves .....with chemicals. They ruined their own environment."

"Quite stupid hew-mans, My Lord."

"Yes,...yes, stupid is precisely what they amounted to! And with their demise, I picked up their pieces and designed the Kyykki. Kyykki function well in the putrid, the cesspools. But now, the beautiful destroys my nepes."

"Yes,....My Lord." Warmaker murmured softly, feeling an anguish of unknown origin. It gripped at his heart and then slowly relinquished that grasp.

Ashuwa spoke little else. He remained at the ledge until the first moon's shadowy beams burnt jagged holes through the stench-laden vapors rising from the lake. Dismissing Warmaker, he returned to the throne, thinking about his illustrious past and how his Father's benevolent freedom allowed all humans to perish. This terminated his influence upon human history.

Even then Ashuwa protested this 'freedom' idiocy. Simply being created in the divine image of the Holy One did not accord the 'created' with wisdom for their freedom. Ashuwa witnessed his Father's failure as the humans disappeared. The old fool, accordingly, required removal from his high place. When he finally conquers his Father's Haafians, the imperfection of freedom would be obliterated forever....That time had started.

Flying with the wind, Captain Ellom's extraordinary fleet of ten double-hulled warships plowed northward for four dawns, their doubled sails stretched to the limit. The planks connecting decks served as stables for Ayhn's lancers, however the Stripers took poorly to the swells and windiness of the sea. Within the first dawn, the majority of the antlered mounts suffered from nausea and refused to eat. Captain Ellom noted in the ship's log that the only benefit of congregating the Stripers on the suspended decks existed in the ease in cleaning up the animals' enormous amount of manure.

Two of the ships carried further refined 'war waggons' of Wygga's devising. The ten light-weight waggons were widened to allow for a total transverse of all weapons. Five waggons were outfitted with heavier crossbows: ones proven effective against dragons. Three dozen double-hitched single-axle carts constituted the logistical transportation necessary for a quick campaign. As best as possible Ayhn trained his Lancers for attacking the Kyykki from the rear and the flank while they approached Pinduala.

To clear the shipping lanes on their return voyage, Captain Ellom reinforced his crews to the maximum, including the 'blessed' addition of tons of bleach power and barrels of extra bolts and arrows. To surprize the damned one, the fleet initially sailed east, past the 'hidden' islands, then turned due north. In this final day of their voyage, they now sailed west towards the northern peninsula of Zuda Marsh. The cry of "Land Ho!" rang out from the crowsnest.

Prior to the lancer's disembarkation, Ayhn's scouts reconnoitered an area about twelve miles into the Zuda. While waiting for their return, Captain Ellom secured rafts for transferring the lancers and their waggons to shore. Four dismounted platoons rowed ashore to establish a suitable base for the regiment. Less than a half mile inland the Troopers claimed a grassy knoll for their encampment. Nearby palm trees provided logs for their barricades.

Well after dusk, an exhausted scouting party galloped in. One Striper carried two lancers. Ayhn met them at the shoreline.

"Scouts reporting in, Sir!" Bellah, the red-headed corporal breathed heavily. "One Striper lost to quicksand along the northern beach......" He took another deep breath. "All the men are well."

"I assume then that you found evidence of the Kyykki?"

"Yes, Sir....We found plenty of their three-toed prints after we turned due south. ...We also found some carnage, parts of non-Kyykkian carcasses,.... butchered or tortured,....hard to tell..... then eaten by the blackened toad-faces."

Ayhn turned to face the sea, and then turned back to Bellah. His mind striving to place the trooper's report into perspective. "Might the Kyykki have rebelled against their leaders?" He asked of no one in particular.

"More akin to the Kyykki removing those who don't quite fit in. Those carcasses could have been Haafian."

"Yep," Added another of the scouting party. "Only if they be huge."

"You don't believe that's true? That traitors are with the hordes?" Ayhn asked.

"No Sir." Replied a less winded Bellah. "The other footprints we discovered had four toes, all webbed together...Those 'new' taller Kyykki, perhaps? But nothing we discovered had five toes."

"Perhaps." Ayhn said reflectively. "However, something greater then the taller Kyykki are required to field such an army....I need more details concerning these four-toed prints."

Bellah straightened his tunic, then initiated a proper accounting. "We triangulated our search, beginning with a seven mile leg running parallel to the inlet...It definitely seems endless. It might be the north end of the continent... Then we turned due south into the swamp, losing the Striper after about two miles. Within another three miles, we discovered the swamp, what was left of it, all mangled and stomped. A flattened swath of ruined swamp, almost two miles wide, headed south. But nothing stirred, no insects, no birds...nothing. The unnatural silence was deadly, overwhelming...After tracking along the edge of the path, we located a campsite....Circular, and planted in the midst of the Kyykki hordes........ A mostly-eaten impaled 'something' stuck up in the swamp like a pennant."

"That's the non-Haafian creature you described to me?"

"Yes it is, Sir." Then Bellah continued his report as the other scouts tended to their mounts. "From there we returned to the beach.....That meant tramping through four miles of the natural swamp....The place isn't fit for anything alive.. But I felt something alive.... didn't see anything, didn't hear anything...I felt it though, evil, powerful...like it allowed us to through, thinking we didn't detect it....We flew through the swamp, the Striper knew something was there...."

"They probably did, Bellah." Ayhn said rather absently, his mind focusing on a broader picture. "Tell me, did you smell anything? Anything other the usual obnoxious swamp fragrances?" A thin smile broke across his bronze face.

"Yes, I detected a 'fragrance'........I can't place it... Something powerful, nauseating.......very different."

"Was there a touch of something 'burnt'?...Perhaps a bit smoky?"

Bellah's bushy eyebrows twitched. "Yes..........Sickly sweet 'burnt' smell, it was."

Ayhn's countenance tightened as the implications of Bellah's report radically shifted his thinking. He walked away from the scouting party, leaving Bellah wondering if he was dismissed. When he saw Ayhn hailing an ensign aboard an incoming raft, he judged himself dismissed.

"Ensign!" Ayhn called out to the Striper laden raft.

"Yes, Sir!"

"Here!"

"Where is here, Sir?"

"To me, Ensign!"

"Yes, Sir!...Sorry Sir. Can't see too much. The sun going down against the water." A splash followed. A few moments later the soaking wet Ensign pulled himself from the rolling surf not distant from where Ayhn stood. A few strides later he stood before Ayhn and saluted. "Sir, how might I be of service to you?"

"What's ashore tonight, and what's yet to be ferried in?"

"Roughly half the lancers and mounts plus half of the wagons and their supplies."

"No war waggons?"

"No Sir...... We had orders to wait until sunrise, .Safety reasons, you understand."

"Normally I would, Ensign...But that order is nullified...Get the war waggons and the full crews ashore ...immediately."

"Isn't that too dangerous, Sir." The rather stymied Ensign said.

"It'll be more dangerous if we don't get the transfers done this night." His voice took on a slight edge. He refused to disclose the truth to the Ensign, for fear of panic. "I'll sent to a note to Ellom, requesting the change."

"Yes Sir."

The Ensign waited, shivering in the breeze as Ayhn scribbled a note to the Captain. Ayhn wrote the 'why' of his order, then sealed the note with wax. The Ensign waded out to the now unloaded raft, commanding the sailors to pull hard and fast for the return trip. Ayhn headed back up the beach, looking for Bellah.

Bellah, a man fond of his Striper, had a metal comb in one hand and a tankard of ale in the other when Ayhn located him inside the palm tree barricade. Ayhn watched as the corporal gently pulled the briars from the Striper's tail. The logs' shadow hid him from the encampment. He saw that everything was as it should be; double pickets, all mounted, supplies stored inside the barricades, no fires. As much as obeying the regulations satisfied him, Ayhn also realized that such precautions would be useless if the dragons decided to attack.

"Bellah, I need to speak with you." Ayhn called to the busy scout.

He quickly turned saluting with his tankard, smacking himself in the face. "Sir?"

Moving Bellah out of earshot, Ayhn briefly explained the dangerous scenario to him. He'd seen dragons at the Wall, but he figured that would be the extent of it. Now, in the darkness, dragons waited patiently in the Zuda. Like Ayhn, he realized their jeopardy without the war waggons.

After a brief conversation, Bellah gathered his scouts together. Moments later, the small patrol walked their mounts towards the Zuda. They carried quick-light torches to signal any signs of dragons.

Captain Ellom's eyebrows knotted as he read Ayhn's sealed report. Fighting pirates was one thing, but, like most of his Troopers, these dragons were an unknown commodity. He quietly ordered the fleet to prepare for battle. A small skiff sailed back to the outer islands for immediate reinforcements. The speed of unloading the lancers and their equipment doubled, even though Captain Ellom feared for the worse if the dragons suddenly attacked. Retreating to the ships was not an option. He sent a sealed note to Ayhn indicating his apprehension and requesting Ayhn to reconsider the debarkation.

Ayhn received the note after most of the war waggons reached shore. Ellom's apprehension matched his own, yet he believed the current situation could also prevent the Kyykki hordes from attacking Pinduala. Then he realized just how absurd his thinking had become. He opened the door to martyrdom, to suicide, both antithetical to the Holiness Code. He reconsidered his responsibility. He kept the present course with major modifications. First, he commanded underground shelters be constructed and camouflaged. Following that, all mounts received a coating of dye which matched the sand. Ayhn ordered all uniforms bleached, rendering them the sand color, an ugly mottled off-white. While the Troopers grumbled about working throughout the night, their muttering died when, shortly before dawn, Ayhn announced to them the presence of the dragons. He commanded that the encampment be concealed before the dawn. Everyone occupied the underground shelters, Stripers and war waggons included. When he heard reports concerning the inadequacy of space, Ayhn dispatched the entire lancer corps to dig harder and faster. As the Troopers frantically dug, a runner headed for the fleet with a message explaining Ayhn's rationale for their remaining on shore and the newest strategies he undertook to counteract the dragon menace.

Bellah and his men spent a nerve-wracking night deciphering swamp noises. That sweetly sickening odor noticed yesterday had vanished, replaced with the fumes of rottenness and decay. From their camouflaged positions three miles inside the Zuda, nothing out of the ordinary--ordinary for a repulsive swamp--ever appeared. For this Bellah felt relieved. He valued his life as much as anyone else. In the oppressive humidity of the afternoon, the scouting party carefully maneuvered its way south. With hardly any air movement and the boggy surface, their Stripers suffered greatly. With nothing to report, Bellah turned his scouts east. Another evening arrived before they returned to the hidden encampment.

By that time, half of the fleet sailed east, just out-of-sight. The other five ships rocked at anchor, standing in as the Lancer's reinforcements. Those at the encampment emerged from their subterranean homes as a golden dusk settled upon the shoreline.

Ayhn met Bellah as he galloped in. He spoke even as he swung down from his lathered Striper. "The Zuda appears clear, Sir!....Clear of the.." He instantly lowered his voice so as not to alarm the entire camp. "Dragons, that is."

"You saw no signs of them?" Ayhn asked, both troubled and curious. If the dragons had traveled on, then the attack upon Pinduala advanced a dawn closer, Ayhn thought. This meant another change in tactics for the Lancers.

"Nor any smells. We traveled south for five or six miles, but still no signs, ...except..."

"Except?"

"Except the Zuda lay deadly quiet, as if shocked by what devastated her interior."

"The Zuda is a living thing, so your assessment is appropriate, Bellah." Ayhn paused, carefully negotiating tomorrow's schedule via Bellah's information. "Get some food and some rest. And make sure that Striper of your's is well cared for."

Bellah, relieved of his duties, tiredly sighed. Then, without a word, obeyed Ayhn's instructions. Before dawn the Lancers began their invasion, heading south, seeking the whereabouts of the Kyykki and their dragons. Yet, if this secret lay exposed, another remained hidden: renegade Haafians commanded the blackened hordes as well as the dragons.

Chapter 3

Once again, the Captain and the King launched into another of their nonstop verbal confrontations. The issues, regardless of importance or timing, made little difference to the King. While the Captain disciplined himself to remain neutral as possible, the King, on the other hand, delighted in pulling out every tactical and emotional stop. This battle of wills rapidly caught the attention of the locals. They diligently pursued every tempting morsel, or, as the Captain later discovered, any figment of their imaginations. While this continued, the Captain gave thanks to the Holy One. The bottom line being that the King, once unable to remove his own crown, now had enough stamina to wage a verbal tirade for the better part of the afternoon.

This unconventional routine began shortly after Jabbi and Etan left. The Captain did not actually enjoy the verbal joustings, but he recognized their positive role in strengthening the King. At present, that responsibility of the Captain's progressed well. In fact, the following afternoon, the Captain planned to escort the King to the High Council Room. This would be the King's first public appearance since his review of the troops. If the King might just be able to persuade the locals that his health improved, then hope renewed. At least that potential existed, the Captain thought.

The past two double moon cycles witnessed the Haafians adjusting to a new life style. The clergy labored with the people more diligently than ever before as they brought the Holiness Code to each village. Since the Holy One manifested himself at the Wall, the Chapels brimmed over with the curious as well as the true believers. Few desired to be labeled as unfaithful; the Living God, the Holy One was too close. A living theology, somewhat like the spirituality of the Yldans, quickly emerged.

Nor did the merchants receive much rest. Krucik's death exposed too many merchants like himself. If not imprisoned or dead, the remaining merchants now competed with the serfs. The serf entrepreneurs now maintained the upper hand. In the quickly-formed vacuum, these adventurous persons established the new class, a fourth class of people in Haaf, ironically labeled the 'wealthy poor'.

As Jabbi sarcastically predicted, the nobility 'mystically' disappeared to their comfortable estates. This did not prevent the taxation officers from visiting, and it did allow their taxes to become realistic. For once, all their property fell under bureaucratic scrutiny. The Captain's friends in the governmental structures soon found themselves running their departments. Most head administrators who 'bought' their positions died under the broadaxe of incompetence. The Captain became 'hero' to the bespectacled ranks of bookkeepers.

These alterations within the country demanded a unifying voice. They also required a means by which to reorganize the economic and political infrastructure. Here the Church's influence was well established and the appearance of the Holy One only reinforced her leverage. But the Council of Elders report to the Captain carried no hint of a theocratic state. The 'created' required balancing forces in their lives. The tyranny of but one solitary voice ruling Haaf strongly sounded like a world dominated by the damned one. That portrayal of the country's future was to be denied at all costs.

The stronger, yet still weak King, realized he needed to be a stabilizing platform for the Haafs. Thus, on the morrow, at mid-morning, the King would speak in the High Council Hall.

"I pray you'll sleep well tonight, My Lord." The Captain said to the King. They ate supper together on the roof above the High Council Hall.

"And why should I? Three times the Yldan shamans will awaken me to require the state of my slumber....Does that sound restful to you?...."

"It is for your own good." The Captain replied without a trace of sympathy.

"Hardly, It's all for the country's benefit....And we both know it, don't we?" The King dumped his anger on the Captain.

"Mind your temper, My Lord. Another stuttering fit you don't need."

"Ha!" Quipped the King. "You're the person who doesn't need it. You don't pick people off the floor very well."

"Especially if they happen to be nobility." The Captain easily agreed. He ducked the tankard heaved at him, then laughed. "See, My Lord, you are regaining your strength, but your aim still needs some work."

"AND SO DOES YOUR MOUTH!" The King roared, laughing. "You accursed little hypocrite!"

"Majesty, your vocabulary increases. I'll pass that on to the Council of Elders."

"Actually, you'll inform them publicly, tomorrow. I've got nothing to hide."

"Thank you, My Lord."

"And you can stop that damned frivolous.."

"....polite speech." The Captain correctly finished the sentence.

The King stood, turned and slowly sauntered to his room. The Captain quietly finished supper, somehow feeling confident that tomorrow brought hope.

The Church Guards forcefully cleared a path for the King. His attendance at the Council meeting attracted crowds from all over the city. The central space within the Hall disappeared before dawn and now even standing room was non-existent. The few reserved seats in the chamber, with the exception of those designated for the clergy, became the property of those who occupied them. The old distinctions between nobility and merchants disappeared. The 'wealthy poor' sat wherever, tradition be damned.

The tubas heralded the King's arrival. The diverse gathering of persons quieted as the King, flanked by the Captain, Jabbi and Etan, appeared at the entrance of the hallway. Another chorus from the tubas and those gathered silently rose, straining their necks to catch a glimpse of their King. The Church Guard plowed through the ranks of those standing in the central area, escorting the King and his advisors to the dais.

If nothing else, the King looked like a king, carrying himself well, albeit a bit stuffy. His robes fit as did his crown. A new sword gently swayed at his side, never once scraping the marble floor. Once upon the dais, he slowly worked the untraditional crowd, his eyes intently taking on all gawkers. When one blinked, he smiled to himself, his confidence growing.

Deep on the left side of the gallery, some Haafian started the chant, "Long live the King." Before the original phrase worked its way to the ceiling, the entire Council Hall reverberated with the chant. "Long live the King!" As the volume increased, people began stomping their feet, the building shook and windows cracked. Rather than taking an increasing risk with the overly emotional crowd, Jabbi signaled the Church Guards. The tubas rang out, but their brassy tones converged with the cacophony. Jabbi, now nervous, signaled again. This time he and the King raised their hands for silence as the Church Guard quickly flat sworded the white marble walls. This 'ringing steel' pierced the tumultuous din. The people raised their hands, symbolically joining their monarch in requesting order and quiet. As fast as the chant multiplied, it died. The unnatural quiet rang in their ears. The Captain motioned for everyone to sit. They did.

The Captain separated from the quartet, moving to the podium. "Thank you for that glorious welcoming!...Your King appreciates it as much as he has appreciated your prayers for his recovery. He is here this morning to speak with you....I bid you to listen well........This time, these days, are resplendent with massive changes and with heavy challenges,... most notably, the Kyykki's intended invasion of our homeland... We have need for direction, for a unification of purpose....For these we look to the Church, She has provided well....But we also look to our King, who is also called by the Holy One, Blessed be His Name, to lead us into a new civilization, a new future for every citizen of Haaf............. Listen carefully to your King!" The Captain thundered the last sentence.

Moments later, the King slowly rose. A thunderous round of applause greeted him as he approached the podium. To Jabbi, this merciless intrusion upon his sensitive ears lasted much too long. The King, however, revelled in his people's appraisal, enjoying all of it. To him, it meant a forgiveness for his old self-serving ways.

The King raised his hand. A hush fell across the huge cavern-like chamber. He turned, acknowledging the clergy behind him on their raised platform. In return, they rose, extending the King a formal, yet gracious blessing.

"My people," The King began. "I personally thank the Holy One for each and everyone of you. Without your constant prayers, I should be dead by now." A round of applause and cheering broke out, nevertheless, without interruption the King continued. "You are fully aware of the details concerning my poisoning by the damned Krucik's 'bought physicians'. They now all reside in hell together. Justice exists!........

Another round of applause broke into the King's speech. This time he waited until silence reclaimed the chamber.

"My health, as you all are witnesses to, is much better,... though I shall not be joining the New Knights at the front in the near future... The poisoning I received derives from the Dark Lands and there lies the antidote, or so my advisors suspect."

"Now I must direct my comments to the present, our present. With justice bestowed upon the traitorous merchants, a new class has risen up to prevent our economy from collapsing, the 'wealthy poor'. May the Holy One bless you!..... And from hereon, any having the talents and ambitions to become a merchant are welcome. The class once known as merchants is now open to merit and those skillful enough to succeed...."

A gasp lunged forth from the multitudes. Meritocracy suddenly replaced traditional birthright. In the near past, this unprecedented monarchical dictate would have brought about a rebellion by the merchants. Society changed, leaving a hole in the fabric of Haaf which required patching. So, although the King's action was designed to secure the economics of Haaf, he nevertheless brought hundreds of thousands of serfs to his side, firmly indebted to him.

"You nobles have little to fear. But as you are firmly aware, your birthright now promotes you directly to the military. These perilous times call for a steadfast soldiery, one we praise for their efforts at the Wall......... The New Knights have proven themselves,........ at great personal expense............ I am proud of them!" The King paused during the shouts and applause. He caught his breath and for the first time realized how quickly his strength waned. Though this startled him, his iconoclastic exterior refused anyone else that knowledge. He vowed to continue the speech and to depart with true dignity, as befits a king. He silently uttered a prayer. "Now, I do not make these changes in our society lightly. Indeed, in making these changes I have followed the example shown by the Holy One at the Wall. That is, as the Holy One, Blessed be His Name, sought to save us by rending the earth, so I have sought to save Haaf by rending society so that our essential balances continue intact. We cannot exist without a merchant class. Yet this very class, to a significant degree, became traitors, selling their very souls to the damned one. What the damned one sought to destroy, I have tried to repair, following the example of the Holy One." As the people applauded, the King once again went eye-to-eye with them. He must be firm and strong, he told himself. His people need to see him healthy and strong. He raised his hand for silence.

"I am finished, for now....I thank the Holy One for the honor and privilege of being your King. I thank you for your prayers...Please continue and may the Holy One bless our nation." As he sat down, the people stood, cheering and applauding their king: the volume greater than before.

"I told you he could do it!" The Captain yelled at Etan and Jabbi.

"Yes, but what about the price." The staid comment from Jabbi quelled the Captain enthusiasm, as if it were premature.

True, the King properly exited the High Council Hall. No sooner did he arrive back in his chambers, than he collapsed into a semi-conscious state. As a bright cloudless day emerged from the drizzly dawn, the King lay on his couch, regaining strength. He spoke quietly. He was proud of the way he conducted himself and of the positive image he presented.

"Exhausted or not, I acted like the King I was called to be. Some of you just better understand that." He yelled from his cot in the adjoining chamber, then burst into ragged coughing.

The trio promptly invaded the chairs in the King's chambers, waiting for the monarch to continue. He obliged them, but on his own schedule. The Captain dawdled with his half-lit pipe, streaking the air with billowy bluish clouds.

"Put the damned thing away, Captain." The King muttered distraughtly. "I want to breathe....fresh air..... Understand?"

"Yes, My Lord." He mumbled, tapping the pipe on his boot heel.

"I'm just fascinated by your attitude, so positive." The monarch's sudden, unexpected sarcasm brought laughter from the other two. "And that will quite enough out of you two doubters." The King stately announced.

The two responded in quiet, deadly quiet. The Captain smiled.

"Jabbi, you will report to the Council of Elders concerning my appearance yesterday. Also, I'm inviting the Elders to meet here in four dawns. We need to develop a more cordial relationship."

Jabbi's bronzed face contorted, his pointed ears stood out, his voice hushed, a bit alarmed. "My Lord, do you realized what you ask?"

"I request something that hasn't been done before...That's not exactly new for me, is it?"

"Most certainly not." Etan said.

"Throughout this age, since its establishment by the Holy One, a great bond of trust has existed between the Council of Elders and the King, even when the King refused to heed the council's advice."

"Spare me the history lesson, Jabbi." The King barked. "Your fear is that once the members...."

"Once we personally know each other, the entire council is placed in jeopardy........Sorry for interrupting, but what you request is not granted....... It's simply too dangerous."

The King became livid, his face streaking with white and brown colors. His extremities shook, uncontrollable. Jabbi disappeared in a wispy cloud of dry fog. Etan bound for the door, searching for the Yldan shamans. The Captain moved toward the King with an indifferent attitude, having witnessed this situation too many times. Carefully he cradled the King in his arms, denying the monarch the possibly of hurting himself. Moments later, the seizure subsided enough for the Captain to stretch out the King on his couch. Two shamans arrived later, Etan hard on their heels.

"Leave him rest." The Captain said.

"Did he hurt himself?" The taller of the shamans nervously asked.

"Nothing is wrong...What energy he reserved for today's verbal battle, is gone."

In spite of the Captain's diagnosis, the shamans thoroughly examined the King, testing his breathing, monitoring his pulse and mixing a few of their potent concoctions. As they concluded, Etan draped a light blanket over the monarch.

"When he wakes, make sure he swallows every drop of the medicine?"

"You love to give orders."

"Ah, Captain, we are bored with your comments. Is it not possible to be more creative?" The taller shaman retorted with a smile.

"I really doubt it."

"Nevertheless...."

"He'll drink the poison even if I have to force it down his throat."

"And perhaps you will!" Smiled the shorter of the shamans.

The Captain played with his pipe, pretending not to hear. Etan conversed with the two as they took leave of the King's chambers. Then he slumped down on an arm chair, waiting for Jabbi to return and the King to show signs of improvement. He worried about the King's demand, the ramifications of such an agreement probably escaped the King.

Towards mid-day, Vosnob-the-younger, as he had come to be called, arrived with Jabbi in tow. The Chaplain General's demeanor clearly told everyone to carefully choose their words. Jabbi's countenance bore the marks of one having fought dragons single-handedly. Wordlessly, he slumped into a high-backed chair across the chamber from the Captain. Their eyes met for a moment, the Captain nodded and left the room.

"He quits before the battle's initiated." Vosnob stated bluntly. His remark must have been for his own amusement, for no one responded in any way.

The King threw off his blanket and stared at this stranger in his chamber. "Get this man out of here, Captain!" The King said with indignation.

The Captain returned to the room, a broad smile decorated his face.

"Don't even think of obeying." Vosnob challenged the Captain.

"You aren't much fun this day, are you?"

"Didn't know that was part of my responsibilities." Vosnob groused.

"You certainly didn't!"

"My King?" Vosnob responded to the oblique remark.

"Who are you and why are you here?"

"My King?"

"Damn it, soldier! Tell me your name!"

While Jabbi found a 'warped' revenge in the King's demands, Vosnob did not. He paced the room, puzzled about the situation. Was the King that far gone? Was this a contrived set-up? Or, had he missed something? His pacing settled nothing and actually exacerbated the situation.

"Captain, seeing this imprudent idiot can't answer a simple question, you answer it. Then throw him in the dungeon." The King said.

"Yes, My Lord." The Captain stumbled over this tongue to refrain from laughing. "As you so decree."

"Cut the gibberish formality....Who is the dolt?"

"Vosnob."

"And I'm one of those blue skinned Taths."

"He is, but you aren't." Etan said as soberly as possible.

Vosnob quit pacing. "I am Vosnob, My Lord." He bowed stiffly.

The King looked askanced, then peered through Vosnob as a jeweler examines the qualities of a diamond before cutting. "Take off the stupid disguise." He demanded.

The trio burst out laughing, compounding the King's problem and further annoying Vosnob. The predicament worsened. Vosnob sat down, his deep chin resting on his hands, the others wrapped in mirth and the King totally befuddled.

The Captain was the first to regain any semblance of composure. "My Lord, allow me to rectify this strange situation."

"Please?" The wearied King half-asked, mostly in desperation.

"Do you recall the report concerning the Holy events of the Council of Elders meeting?"

"That puzzling ....." He searched for the right word, "Jargon about there being only twenty three Elders, but none could remember nor discover why, either in any writings or from memory?"

"Yes."

"Then you recall the an unnatural phenomena mentioned in the same report?" The Captain proceeded cautiously.

"The Holy One appeared, giving great power to Vosnob."

"Do you recall anything else?"

"Damn it, man. Get to the point...Quit coddling me!" The monarch snapped as he stumbled up from the couch.

"The Holy One recreated....... renewed Vosnob. His physical body regained the vitality of one less than half his age, but his mind retained all the wisdom for which he is known and revered."

"Yes....." Came the King's impatient response.

"Well, that Vosnob sits in the corner."

"No!"

"Yes." The Captain reiterated. "Yes, My Lord, that is Vosnob sitting in the corner."

Vosnob slowly lifted up his head. His tired eyes peered at the King.

"The Captain tells the truth. I am Vosnob....And, now let us get on with the reason for this meeting...My patience is long gone."

"You are Vosnob...The Holy One re-created you, so-to-speak." The King's bulging eyes stared through the Chaplain Commander. "I simply can't begin to comprehend....to understand....even imagine in my dreams.....this miracle of the Holy One.....I apologize for my rudeness... This faith 'stuff' still is difficult for me."

"You are forgiven, My Lord." Vosnob said, biting his lip. "But if you refuse to believe this miracle, then how can it be possible for us to continue this conversation?"

"I believe." The King said unconvincingly.

Jabbi thumped across the chamber and stood nose-to-nose with the King. "Have you forgotten the Holiness Code?"

"No." He mumbled quietly.

"Then why do you act it?" Jabbi said straightforwardly into his face.

"I believe."

"I don't hear any real dedication....commitment." Jabbi responded like a Basic Troop Trainer.

"I·DO·BELIEVE."

"I'm not convinced that you are, My Lord!"

"I don't need convincing. Vosnob does. Ask him!" The King shot back.

"I'll take it from here." Vosnob interrupted. "Everyone sit!" The group complied with Vosnob's command. The Captain picked up his pipe and stretched out his booted legs on the table top. Vosnob ignored the action and the Captain's ingratiating smile.

"Whether or not you can handle the truth is not an issue of my concern." Vosnob said to the King. "My concern is with a meeting you decided to convene, a meeting with the Council of Elders."

Brooding in quiet, the downcast monarch felt compelled to answer, but the correct words--those of power--evaded him. This Vosnob had the power, and he became intimidated by it.

"You have nothing to say." Vosnob stated the King's position, then pushed on. "What you have proposed is denied. The council, as the name aptly connotates, has its membership: Elders. When and IF you are summoned to become one, then you'll be invited to the council meetings."

"But I am the king." He weakly protested.

"And that has nothing to with your request. The council, from the early cycles of Haaf, remains independent from the political realm....You must learn to trust the Elders."

"And just how do you propose that? I don't know any Elders. This is a mystery to me."

"So?"

"So I don't relish such things!"

"There is no choice in the matter. The Council of Elders will free Haaf from the grasp of the damned one....You need to know nothing else....As usual, you will be contacted when we deem needful."

"And that terminates the whole matter, doesn't it?" The King angrily snapped.

"Yes, My Lord." Vosnob said calmly. "You are but my King, not my Creator." He continued without apology, without castigation.

"Once again I play the fool." The King lamented.

"Why?" Asked the Captain.

"Because my request...has come to naught...again."

"Self-pity has no room in a monarch." The Captain replied. He thudded his boots to the floor.

"You made no request that I'm aware of, My Lord." Said Vosnob.

He glanced about the chamber, seeking confirmation in their nodding heads. Partially dumb-struck, the King realized the truth. Then, joining their consensus, he also nodded. "So be it."

"You are most welcome, My Lord." Vosnob answered the King.. "Now....Captain, walk with me to Vaad. I must be off."

The Captain joined Vosnob as he walked towards the door.

"I have yet to give you my permission to leave." The King cried out.

"Thank you anyway." Replied an indifferent, a tired Vosnob. He rounded a marble columned corner and hastily disappeared.

Desiring a respite from the King and the commotion, the Captain walked through the High Council room, now about vacant, down into the courtyard. He tapped his pipe on the dragon skeleton, smiling all the while. Then he meandered off to the tavern, hoping for some of Ilty's vegetable stew and information from the inside.

Having exhausted himself, Etan and Jabbi put the King to bed. Leaving the Yldan shamans in charge, Jabbi and Etan took leave to finish their respective labors.

The Haafian commander, surrounded by three dragons and a host of Demon Masters, and some other traitorous Haafians, barked out blunt commands. His attack through the Zuda kept pace with Ashuwa's quick-moving timetable, though at considerable risk. His Kyykki hordes had only a few hours for rest. Rations weren't part of the logistics. Ashuwa used the spoils of Pinduala as motivation instead. That did not make up for the thousands of dead Kyykki.

The land to the north, according to Ashuwa, teemed with unknown powers. His assigned attack route brought the Kyykki close to this dangerous border. Ashuwa reminded the Haafian commander that this land belonged to no god. Now that the horde turned south, the northern territory dropped from conversation and thought.

"Allow the unwanted who habituate there alone." Ashuwa had warned the Haafian. "Your responsibility is to deliver Pinduala, D'Ka and Krabo...... to me." The Haafian Commander smiled openly as he remembered the rest. "I shall reward you with a kingdom of your own choosing. But Krabo shall be my capital."

As the Haafian pursued alternative threads of thought, he constantly found himself reaching the same conclusions. He'd ignore any invaders on the northern shore. They 'could' be dangerous or, even worse, his delicate scheduling would be compromized. Getting Pinduala destroyed was all that mattered. The Haafian fleet, however, needed expunged from the sea. The capture of Pinduala demanded the termination of such a pernicious force. This is what Ashuwa commanded, and so that is what he ordered.

Before commanding the fleet to be destroyed, the bulky Haafian took refuge in his tent, pitched along the escarpment above the Zuda. There the rolling breezes refreshed him. No sooner had he propped up his feet, when three bare-breasted 'blue ladies' brought him a small table full of drinks and bread. One girl coyly raised her long skirt for him, inviting him to sample her wares. Another, in competition, dropped her thin skirt altogether, then smothered the Haafian in her loins. Within moments, a free-for-all commenced, lasting well into the evening.

Ayhn moved his Lancers further to the south that same evening. His movement of twelve miles went unnoticed. Ayhn camouflaged the new encampment as the old, excepting the War Waggons, which waited at-the-ready along the perimeter and four gathered as a core. Before retiring for the morning, Ayhn posted a triple guard and had the waggon crews sleep under their waggons. In spite of these precautions, he realized, his numbers would prove too few when the dragons attacked. The Troopers fostered no illusions about their enemy. They came to fight--to fight for their country.

Captain Ellom, his fleet slowly tacking just over the horizon, awaited the dawn. The Ensign Ayhn sent delivered his report earlier. Captain Ellom had a premonition prior to the Ensign's arrival, something in his lanky old bones made him fearful. Now it was confirmed. As the stars and the double moons shone, Ellom walked the bridge of his flagship. Anticipating a dragon attack, he issued orders well before the orange-grey dawn. Finally, he prayed to the Holy One. May the reinforcements arrive on the morrow, early.

In anticipation of an attack, the fleet dropped the drag anchors and furled all sails. From the holds came extra bolts for the crossbows and pitch for the catapults. Squares of hull planking were removed below decks, allowing for six additional crossbows to be discharged on both port and starboard sides. This latest addition to their arsenal provided some protection from the dragon's breath. Casks of sea water were hoisted high into the crowsnests as protection from fire. Captain Ellom anxiously paced the deck. This newly arriving dawn contained unprecedented savagery and destruction. While he readied himself for it, he could never fully prepare himself for it. Ellom accepted that as a fact.

The Haafian Commander, exhausted and sore from his evening of sensual frolicking, slept until mid-day. He awoke in a sweat. The enclosed tent, sweltering under the intense sun turned his civilized dwelling into a hell-hole. Kicking the naked 'blue ladies' out, he dressed himself and walked from the tent. The Demon Lords, having no orders, awaited him.

"Fetch the Demon Masters." He muttered angrily, knowing he'd have to push the Kyykki and dragons harder to keep on schedule. "And lock the bitches up until I call for them." He said as an afterthought.

Before he drowned himself with a flagon of ale, all the Demon Masters, brightly adorned with their rank-specific capes, appeared in a cloud of dank dust. Dismounting their dragons the Demon Masters approached the tent.

"Haafian, we are here." The glistening bronze-scaled Demon Master announced indifferently. Together the seven Demon Masters bowed stiffly in the general direction of the Haafian.

"Obliviously." The Haafian quietly muttered to himself. "Tell me your answer, Head Demon Master.... Off the shore lies a fleet of Haafian warships......... Presently, they kill each Kyykki sent south........ How many dragons do you request to destroy them?"

The Head Demon Master bowed. He clustered his subordinates together. Clicking and clacking noises erupted, then subsided just as quickly. Leaving the encircled group, the Head Demon Master walked towards the Haafian. "You have kept information from us."

"Only in accordance with the Almighty Ashuwa's commands. Those 'things' which are on the northern beach must be avoided."

"Ashuwa, the Almighty, is wise....Did our great Ashuwa tell you why we must not destroy these 'puny things'?"

"He said those from the north are unknown, therefore their power is also unknown..... Furthermore, we have orders to attack those who have offended our god....... These few 'things' on the shore will be ignored." The Haafian spoke with a sense of authority he never recognized before. Then he realized an awesome truth, Ashuwa's Almighty power dwelt within him, he wasn't actually running the invasion by himself. "You have what you need. Get me an answer."

"Yes, I obey."

Numerous clickings and clackings greeted the Demon Master's return. Their tone turned ugly as the Head Demon presented his new information. A deep green Demon Master raised his sabre. His scaled head rolled before he brought the blade down.

"What is your problem!" Roared the Haafian.

The Head Demon Master strode back to the Haafian's tent. His own sword dripping of greenish red-streaked slime. "The demon refused your explanation, Haafian. He did not believe you spoke for the Almighty Ashuwa.........He will trouble you no longer."

"I am pleased with your judgement........What reward might you consider suitable?"

"Thank you, Haafian....... Almighty Ashuwa commanded me to obey you. He knows you will lead us to victory."

"I choose to do the bidding of Almighty Ashuwa, as do you. We, however different, are of the same allegiance."

"That I affirm."

"Your reward?"

"One of the 'blue ladies', a healthy one, should it please you, Haafian."

"Granted...... However,...... your reward will wait until you have destroyed the Haafian fleet."

"As you wish." He said rather dismayed. Instantaneous rewards were more to his liking. His mind quickly re-enacted the deadly 'playing' with Haadd and Porehote.

"How many dragons will you require?"

"Because we will ignore the 'things' from the north, and because a spy reported but ten ships anchored off shore, twenty dragons will render the fleet incapable of destroying Kyykki in the future....As the current along the shore drifts southward, any survivors will be most welcomed by the Kyykki swimming there."

"You have a marvelous sense of strategy." The burly Haafian announced as he gleefully rubbed his hands together.

"Thank you, Haafian."

"Fly directly east, to avoid the northern 'things'. Then fly the coast to attack the fleet......... Return by the same path. Ashuwa will personally punish those who attack the forbidden northern 'things'."

"When shall we commence our attack?"

"At mid-afternoon. By the time you reach the fleet, the darkening skies will be to your benefit. Haafians see poorly in the darkness. Your dragons will not be easy targets."

"It shall be done." The Head Demon Master bowed stiffly, tossed his blood red cape about his shoulder and departed.

From his tent the Haafian leader watched twenty dragons ascend into the cloud-filled afternoon sky, each carried a Demon Master. He noted that if the humidity increased, a real danger of thunderstorms existed, presenting a potent danger for the dragons.

In single file they circled ever higher, their stretched leathery wings pounding at the air, scaly necks craning forward. They disappeared into the first level of clouds. Even higher above, they formed two parallel lines in a 'V' shaped formation. Saving their energy for the attack, the formation of dragons began a slow gliding descent. Moments later, the Haafian lost track of the dragons. He drained another flagon of ale and, refocusing his thoughts, called upon the Kyykki Demon Lords to report.

Intent on battle, an easy battle, the dragons lumbered through the sky unencumbered by any thoughts except that of discovering the fleet's location. Using the updrafts from the hot sands of the shore, they glided eastward and then to the north. Believing the fleet but a short distance away, they dropped for a low level attack. At one hundred fifty feet, their immense two hundred foot shadows blacked out the sun from the beach.

This strange phenomena wasn't wasted on Ayhn's scouts. Their mirrored signals quickly notified the camp of the impending shadows heading towards them from the south. The camp prepared to receive the attacking dragons--or whatever might be approaching. All heavy-duty crossbows were laid in with exploding heads and trailing lines, some with the razor-wire. Ayhn had the waggons select their targets. At best, they might get off two rounds. Ayhn decided to wait for a close range volley.

With less than a half-mile to fly, the scouts, being almost directly underneath the dragons, reported that the dragons watched the sea. They were unaware of the Lancer's encampment. Ayhn thought this most peculiar, and yet to his advantage. Believing the dragons preparing for a frontal attack, Ayhn ordered half the War Waggons to re-target at one hundred eighty degrees Those dragons surviving the first onslaught, would be shot from behind.

The Troopers, with a sense of fearful awe, watched as the slowly flying dragons headed towards them. Impossible as it seemed, the dragons appeared oblivious to the danger before them. Suddenly, almost at the last possible instant, the dragons desperately veered eastward, attempting to avoid the camp, their sharp banking maneuver exposing their vulnerable bellies to the crossbows.

These 'things' from the north stunned the unprepared Demon Masters. They appeared from dust, these northern 'things' Ashuwa forbid the dragons to attack. At once they veered off, recognizing the danger of a 'thing' which blended into the sand. Ashuwa's perfect judgement about these northerners made them flee.

No one told the War Waggon crews anything. They simply swung their crossbows east and fired, at point-blank range. The huge sucking wounds in their bellies tumbled half the dragons to the sand. Another few crudely dashed into the beach, their slimy innards pouring out, leathery wings torn to flapping ribbons. Noting his severe losses, the Head Demon Master, with a twisting thrust of his sabre, ended his own existence.

The survivors flew on, away from the Lancers, never once even looking back, never attempting to unleash their dreadful fire. They had, however inadvertently, disobeyed the Almighty Ashuwa. Such disobedience, in the span of a few moments, cost them all but six dragons. Ashuwa's punishment would cost the survivors their lives.

The Haafian fleet hadn't been sighted, let alone attacked. Gaining as much altitude as possible, the six continued eastward, searching for the fleet. They would finish their assignment.

Ayhn sent the Lancers to finish off any wounded. He made the command while still immersed in the incredulity of the skirmish. The officer corps didn't understand the dragons' avoidance either, nor their inattention to the landscape. Never had dragons been known to flee.

"We call these things 'miracles', Ayhn." The voice belonged to the Lancer's Chaplain, a rugged fellow who tended the wounded at the Wall, only to witness the Holy One heal.

"Yes, yes, we certainly do....Fourteen of twenty dragons down. We have ..."

"About less-than-serious wounded.......Crossbow strings broke, a couple of broken arms."

"Thank you, Physician."

"My pleasure actually. I feared for much worse."

"Is there any of us who didn't." Ayhn replied, still mystified. He struggled to reorient himself to the present situation. "Signal the scouts about the victory. Then send them forward to establish another camp. We'll move out when supper is over." Ayhn dismissed the officers, except for the Chaplain.

Ayhn, followed by the Chaplain, walked through the encampment, still struggling with the non-existent battle. "Chaplain, I have little difficulty with miracles, especially after the Wall." He tried to convince himself.

"What makes this victory over the damned one any different?"

"I'm not sure. But those dragons behaved unnaturally. They ran from the fight...... They refused to fight. ....It's as if they intentionally avoided us, even though they headed directly for us..."

"The Holy One functions in mysterious ways, Ayhn."

"Just skip the trite statements!"

"No!" He said with a smile. "But, under the circumstances, I am unable to offer you anything better. Perhaps, as we obtain more information..." He never bothered finishing the sentence: Ayhn wasn't listening.

As a murky, cloudy dusk arrived the surviving dragons found the Haafian fleet anchored well off the coast, far beyond where they were supposed to be. Due to a desire not to repeat the past, the dragons now flew separately. Shocked by what slowly rolled on the sea waves not ten ships, but twenty, the Demon Masters cursed. For this mistake they would pay dearly.

Obviously, the ships waited for the dragons. The furled sails and empty decks declared the Haafian readiness for battle. No matter, the Demon Masters committed themselves to a plan during their flight. To return meant death anyway. They each choose a ship to destroy. They grouped together, then launched a devastating attack. From a thousand feet high and a quarter mile distant, they dove down at the fleet. With wings tucked and head stretched out and claws curled underneath, they presented a difficult target as they barreled in.

Captain Ellom watched with horror as he realized the suicidal nature of the attack. His ships had no time to move. The only hope lay in the accuracy of the crossbow crews. A hundred heavy bolts jumped at the six dragons. Their deadly blades spread to kill the attackers. As the volley launched, the dragons dropped lower, the bolts whistled over their heads. Razor wire caught the right wing of the middle dragon, shearing off his left wing. With an agonizing roar, he shot a final gasp of fire towards the ships, then plummeted into the sea, smacking it like a board. The dragons swung to their specific targets as the second volley blasted forth, claiming another dragon. Belching fire, the dragons splattered the first row of ships. Then, without pausing, four huge hulks slammed into the decks of four ships. Three died before impact, their momentum carrying their two hundred foot carcasses onward. They slid across the decks and into the sea. One slammed into a hull amidships, the vessel snapped from the impact, the bow and stern launching into the sky.

Captain Ellom, white hands gripping the railing, yelled for rescue boats to be lowered. The battle was over. Three more of his fleet slowly sank into the sea, the first rank of ships battled fires and burning pitch. In disbelief Captain Ellom gazed at his fleet; so fast and furious had the attack arrived, so quickly and devastatingly had it ended. He studied the fleet's damages. Horrendous flames lit the early evening sky, reflecting orange colors off the low hanging clouds. Sailors screamed for help. Rescue boats, filled beyond capacity, bobbed in the choppy water. Water buckets in the crowsnests dumped their life-saving contents, then dropped into the sea for refills. The flames refused to yield.

Expecting a second wave of dragons, Captain Ellom sent out orders to weigh anchors. The least damaged ships sailed to the perimeter. All crossbows were restrung for the longest possible shots. Then Captain Ellom raised sails on his flagship and took the southern point. As the middle watch came and went, he remained glued to the bridge, definitely expecting a second wave attack. He could not afford the losses of the suicidal attack. However, that bothered him as well. Such a sacrifice on the part of the damned one's best warriors, made little sense, or maybe it did. Ashuwa followed his own rules of war. Even so, the appearance of only six dragons did not make much sense. His knowledge of this engagement contained many holes and he knew it. On the morrow, the fleet sailed south to connect with the Lancers.

Queen Sjura, even with her ever enlarging abdomen, which now hindered her walking and balance, couldn't recall a time when she felt better. She carried the child of her beloved husband, Sarg. Never had she expected such a family. Never had she envisioned participating in a battle between the gods, let alone encountering a god whose powers far exceeded anything imaginable He actually created from nothing. Finally, not only had she been blessed to view the valley home of the ancient Taths, she now carried the responsibility of uniting them and returning them home. These unexpected twists and turns of her life, and the pains and agonies they added, would have shattered her if not for the love of her 'gifted' husband. She chuckled to herself, now he even spoke the true language of the Blue People of the North, Tath.

Looking from the wooden stockade to the newly created glistening white castle in the distance, she sighed. While definitely beautiful, her yurt was home. Marble walls, most any solid wall, gave her that unwanted feeling of imprisonment. In this, she was hardly alone, having Kadima with her as well as Tiello. Tath women riffled at the very idea of being enclosed.

"Sjura," Called Sarg. "Are you packed?"

"Look at me and tell me I'm not packed." She teased, patting her stomach.

"Well, that's not exactly what I meant."

"I'm ready. Should be wonderful to spend an evening camped out."

"That's not the best for our child....You are taking too many risks."

"You sound like my mother." She smiled back. "Look at Kadima, she's proof everything is well."

"But you aren't Kadima...Royalty is used to a softer living than the others."

"So you claim!........ Nevertheless, I shall walk and if I can't walk, I have this most understanding husband to carry me."

"Carry 'us'." Sarg corrected his wife. "There are two of you, remember?"

Brey could not ignore their bantering. Though most uncharacteristic of Sarg, the change somehow strangely fit him. She found herself happy for this irregular hero. But their joyfulness and contentment for one another reopened a wound deep within her heart. She still despised her past, her old life. As a member of scouting party she tried to eliminate it from her life. In this, she failed, and she realized that truth. But what future existed for one bought and sold by Krucik? Keeping her head lowered, she tried disguising her agony.

Tiello, now caught between friendship with Brey and her continuing duties as the Queen's lady-in-waiting, recognized that she had been displaced by Sarg. Her role, at least her functioning within it, became erratic, scheduleless, and therefore, frustrating. But, with Sarg always about, and her Queen so elated and occupied with her pregnancy, she found no time to express her feelings. Those days ended with their rescue from the volcano. With Brey, however, she felt a close affinity, being at the bottom rung, and, being single. The latter problem they often discussed between themselves.

This group readied itself to move downstream to the gleaming white castle. As much as he grumbled about the raft not being properly loaded and balanced, it formed a thin veneer. Sarg's anger towards the nameless god continued. Vauk had not returned. Another promise broken, one less Light Striper for their journey.

"Sjura," Sarg motioned his wife away from the other women. "I need to talk with you."

"It can't wait?"

"I wish that it might."

Recognizing a slight 'edge' in his voice, Sjura stepped back towards the stockade. If he worried, she tended to worry even more. And when she worried, the entire group easily recognized it; her countenance became white. The ladies huddled as soon as they saw her coloring change.

"Sjura," The edge of his voice increased. "I know that you aren't responsible for the actions of your god. But," He paused, holding back his feelings. "He's breaking another promise. And this time Vauk's life might be in danger."

"Yes." The Queen's word rang firm and yet shaky. "That is true. I am worried...... I have expectations for him, especially since he is to gather the Tath Queens together.... I care for Vauk as well." She gave her Sarg a huge sideways hug. Though appearing humorous to the others, it was the only possible way to hug her husband until after her delivery. Then she whispered in his ear. "Quit playing the Almighty...The job's long been filled." While true, her tone rang with a teasing that normally settled him down. "Just relax, my dear."

"I truly wish that possible." He whispered. "My trust level for your unnamed god isn't very high....He's too reckless, undependable."

"But you still like him."

Sarg pulled back a bit, somewhat amused. "Does it show?" He asked reservedly, embarrassed.

"Only to me, you foolish old man." She smiled.

"I can't be that old, if I'm responsible for this." He gently patted her stomach. "It took a lot of work."

"Work!" Sjura replied with mock indignation. "And I thought you enjoyed yourself..........Well, if its work, then you can't do it anymore...... You are commanded to only enjoy yourself when with me....in private, that is." She added the final phrase when she realized their 'supposedly' private conversation was't. The Tath women felt the wrath of her steely gaze. They laughed anyway.

"There's not much respect for royalty in Haaf, either." Sarg allowed as an aside.

"And you'll live, Prince Sarg." Brey called from across the way.

"Shut up." Sarg muttered.

"Well, if that's how royalty treats others, they deserve no respect." Brey continued, not so much from wanting an argument, but out of wanting more in her life, something to quell her feelings of worthlessness.

"Careful." Sarg said softly. "You don't want to injure my feelings."

"Maybe I do!" Brey too quickly exclaimed.

Everyone turned and stared, waiting for the result of her explosive statement. They were all well acquainted with Sarg's current stressed state-of-mind.

"My dear girl, what you need---as soon as possible---is a lover,........ a dedicated,.... permanent lover.....one which you call 'husband'." The reply came from the Queen. Even though the Queen's sentiments arrived gently, almost motherly, Brey's face blanched.

For a moment she froze, then holding her hands over her sobbing face, she scrambled for the shelter of the stockade. Queen Sjura forbid the other women to follow. Instead, Sjura entered the stockade to personally handle this issue. Sarg joined Feathered Goat, who sat, amused by the spectacle, on the bank near the raft.

"Don't know if I can stand all this." The Yldan shaman said. "Too much excitement isn't good, especially for the children."

"You really worry about them."

"More like 'loving' them."

"Indeed." Sighed Sarg. "I've never been a father before."

"So I've noticed."

"This is 'pick on royalty afternoon'?"

"No, that be on the morrow.....This is annoy Sarg time." His face remained straight. "Anyway, your bid to royalty is rather dubious."

"Another joker, just what I need."

"No, you needed a good woman......... You received what you needed. Thanks be to the Holy One.....And you got the best lover that ever existed." He winked at Sarg. "Don't worry, Kadima's exactly the same......... Tath women are extremely affectionate. Relax, enjoy yourself, and never let me hear you use the word 'work' again."

"Another boss." Sarg said irritably.

"No, just another pain-in-the-butt Yldan shaman, who simply happens to be married to another Tath Queen." He readjusted himself on the bank, throwing a mischievous look at Sarg.

"Kadima?"

"I'm only married to her."

Sarg went silent, being aptly skewered by his own ridiculous remark. Inside, his head pounded. Iron plates clanging together made less pressure, less problem. Then anger crept up on him again. He never received an answer concerning the whereabouts of the nameless god. He walked on the stream bank whistling an ancient melancholy Haafian melody. The huge shadow of Feathered Goat's Istelle spun him off into momentary darkness.

Sjura apprehended the sobbing Brey, causing her to turnabout. She did so, but with great trepidation, responding to the Queen's authoritative voice than her words. "We shall talk, my daughter....Come and sit."

Without an argument, Brey obeyed. She sat. She listened. She listened to one having the wisdom to read her heart, to understand her hurt, her degradation, her loneliness. But she only listened with her head, at first, and with a multitude of barriers. Sjura never acknowledged any of this, she simply continued speaking as a concerned mother to her daughter. Little by little, Queen Sjura's words conquered her barriers, then moved in to conquer her heart. As the early evening sky began, Brey finally released her embrace on Sjura. Together they walked towards the raft, too late to begin their journey, but not late enough to miss supper.

A much lighter Brey, if not enlightened Brey, quietly ate supper surrounded by the others. Not much of anything was spoken to her or anyone else.

The lightning spackled 'cloud room' awaited them as they awoke to a drizzly day, providing another headache for Sarg. He couldn't wait to listen to a long line of excuses intending to deliver the unnamed god from responsibility. When the nameless god invited them into his 'cloud room' for breakfast, Sarg's indignation rose. The god scored first with the hard-to-refuse offer of breakfast.

Vauk met the still sleepy campers at the cloud's gleaming entrance. His enigmatic smile betrayed another traveler. Confounded, Sarg and Brey stared at the man who spoke like the Vosnob, but this young man standing before them.....

"Nice trick!" Sarg yelled at the unnamed god. "But it doesn't work. You are late.."

"This time you better allow yourself the gift of silence, Sarg." The nameless one replied nonchalantly. "Remember your own Holiness Code."

"Please calm yourself, Sarg." Said the unknown 'someone' impersonating Vosnob. "Vauk has brought me up-to-date on most of your adventures..

But your attacking the volcano and the linking of two separate cultures is well beyond anything ever done."

Sarg, considering something subversive about, refused entrance to the rest of his party. Deliberately ignoring the 'impostor', Sarg proceeded to concentrate upon Vauk. Certainly, Vauk appeared the same as before. His mannerisms and personality appeared to be the same, even so, Sarg remained suspicious. "Tell me Vauk, who are our newest members?"

"I don't think I'll tell you" He gruffed impatiently. "This stupidity of not trusting anyone but yourself..."

"Is exactly what I'd expect from Sarg in this most peculiar situation. I can sympathize with him, it's not often one gets the opportunity to be renewed. And, I also remember how scandalized you were, Vauk. Initially, your resistance..." Vosnob left the sentence unfinished.... "Actually, this 'testing' is one of those remarkable skills Sarg's renowned for."

Abruptly, Sarg turned, staring intently at this 'impersonator'. "Finish your remarks." Sarg invited the fellow. "What is my history?" He challenged.

The lanky Chaplain Commander began. If any hostile emotions stirred within him, they remained well controlled. "Before the first war, you were married. When the war obliterated your farmstead, you were in the south. .. Kyykki also murdered your family. Shortly afterwards you joined the Light Striper.... angrily volunteered...to be exact..... I'm the only one that's ever commanded you........ We fought together at the Battle."

Silence reigned for a moment.

"You are Vosnob." Sarg announced, though still taken back by his transformation. "But there's much you'll have to explain to me." He crossed the room and smashed Vosnob in a bear hug.

Before Sarg had the opportunity to prevent him, Vauk invited everyone to breakfast. With Sarg out of the doorway, they passed through, then stumbled at the sight of Vosnob, whom nobody recognized. Brey quickly withdrew from his offered handshake, only to bump into the hilariously laughing Vauk.

"What's so damned funny." She demanded. "First, you're three dawns late. Then,....well,...just who is the stranger?"

"My dear Brey." Vauk laughed. "You better salute our Chaplain General of the Light Striper, Vosnob."

"Right..." She responded. "As if I'm that stupid."

"You aren't, but I am.....Vosnob, that is."

She gasped weakly, then examined Sarg's face. He slowly nodded, telling her to believe. Her slanted eyes flashed downwards, her impetuousness embarrassing her. Then, instinctively, she saluted Vosnob. He saluted in return, a marvelously smirking smile covered his long face. Any opposition Brey retained, quickly dissolved.

"But how?" She twittered meekly. "You are older than my father."

"And I still am... Allow me to declare that my transformation is a true gift from the Holy One. Later, as time presents itself, I'll explain." He now smiled graciously. "I'm most happy you've survived................. Especially as I've never met a female Light Striper before." His voice resonated with the wisdom she remembered from her training cycles. "Vauk's physicianship proved useful, didn't it?"

"Yes." She demurred, slightly embarrassed by his concern and knowledge of her situation. "I really fooled everyone,... didn't I?...... And Vauk is actually a physician, licensed and all?" She shot off the questions so rapidly that no one understood her. Accepting her nervous blundering, she reiterated her questions articulately.

"Yes,...to both." Vosnob easily replied.

Sjura, bullied her way to stand before Vosnob, looking up into his eyes. Neither of the two flinched, yet within a moment, the two broke out laughing. Another moment passed, and the two leaned upon each other for support. "Is this not an improper way for royalty to become acquainted?" Queen Sjura laughed, speaking her best Haaf.

"I would concur with your judgement," Vosnob returned with a grin.

"However, it is doubtful that we can begin again. And, for the record, I'm not royalty."

Such a strange introduction initiated the emergence of the great alliance between two different peoples. As rulers, the two had much in common, especially with their concerns for the immediate future. Vosnob found himself outclassed in issues requiring a subtle, devious touch, just as he recognized that he was unprepared for a woman to reign over a nation. Much adjusting and re-educating occupied the morning. By mid-day, most participants suffered from headaches. Just too much transpired since Sarg's expedition began. It simply overwhelmed everyone. One exception existed: Sarg politely requested an audience with the nameless god, who remained strangely hidden throughout the morning.

The trio of Sarg, Queen Sjura and Vosnob, met the unnamed god by the creek bank. Dressed in the whitened robes and yellow sash of a Tath scholar, he stood on the water, fishing. His colorful appearance shown greenish this time.

"Don't be concerned about the new color, it simply confuses the fish. They don't know I'm here." He said offhandedly.

"This is your god?" A unabashedly startled Vosnob asked Queen Sjura.

"Yes....It is me!" Answered the god, giddy as once before. "Got you this time Sarg...Vosnob demanded I bring him. He drives a difficult deal, not unlike another Haafian I happen to know..... .....Anyway, that's exactly how the scheduling..."

"I know." Said Sarg. "This time I owe you an apology."

"Really, I never even heard you yell." The unnamed god spoke. He yanked fishing pole, exposing a line without a hook, then walked across to the shore

"You usually fish that way....without a hook?" Sarg asked almost judgmentally.

"You forget that I AM a god. I do this for the fun of it. I have little need for food."

"Quite true."

"We've talked much, haven't we, Vosnob?" The nameless one snickered as he changed into a yellow color that contrasted with a purple tunic, also changed from the white. "Do you like my outfit?" He inquired earnestly. "It's important to me. I must present myself better. Correct me if I'm wrong, Sarg."

"You are correct."

"Wonderful." He replied in a most ungodlike manner. "Ah, my favorite queen, you've expanded a few fingers worth since five dawns ago...And you are feeling well." He said assuredly.

"Yes, thank you." She answered kindly. "But, as my energy is spent carrying our child, may we, quickly, get to the business at hand. What about the gathering of the tribal queens."

The nameless one glanced at Vosnob, as if to explain away his noncompliance, then stopped. "I am behind on that schedule, only you and Kadima...."

"True, but when can I expect the others? Since you've been gone, we've fought off one attack."

"I have five more queens to contact..."

"......You aren't." Sjura interrupted.

"I am bringing even the atheists, provided they give me half a chance. I haven't contacted them in......I even forget how long."

"And you need every resource to save yourself." Sarg snapped sarcastically.

"I'd appreciate a bit of kindness from you, Sarg. We're going to be together for a long time, perhaps to the end of the age."

Confused, Sarg drew back. "Explain yourself, what's this jibberish concerning the 'end of the age'?"

"Look about you, Sarg. At present, three gods actively struggle for control of the future, your future,--my future,-- come to think about it." He laughed at his discovery, which those gathered found most disconcerting.

Then he continued. "Four peoples are also involved--well, actually three--the Kyykki qualify as moving dung heaps. Then a Wall is erected by your god. I renew and reopen Paradise Valley. With the blessings of two gods, you take Queen Sjura to wife. Me--a god--is commanded by you, Sarg, to gather together the Taths. The damned one, aided by Haafians, now vomits his blackened hordes into the south....Do you actually believe that when all this is over, the world will remain the same?.....Its changed all ready....We are the changers, whether we enjoy it or not. That's the truth."

Both Vosnob and Sarg studied the unnamed god. His logic bothered them. It forced them into another realm, far beyond their present situation. It also bothered them because the old, the traditions, the habits, were on the verge of being reinvented. But on the bottom, they were severely troubled because both of them had been through an 'end of the age' once before: at Battle.

It finally hit Vosnob. Underneath, hidden from the others, he sought an answer for the rejuvenation. The god without-a-name gave him the answer. A new world needed a new leader. Could he believe that the Holy One chose him for the responsibility?

Sarg's heart flew as he recognized his position as a 'father figure' for the transforming world. In just about everything he might imagine, he had firmly planted himself in the middle: mixed-race marriage, a kingdom between two others ruled by a woman, and a bizarre mixture of friends with which to establish this new world----and it existed exactly where his father dwelled. He hugged Sjura and patted her swollen stomach. She held his hand, adding to his resoluteness to weather this coming maelstrom.

"I believe you agree with me."

"Yes, whatever name you might have--god." Vosnob replied slowly.

"I agree. It's been happening all about us, but we never realized..."

"Speak for yourself, Sarg." Feathered Goat interjected. In true shaman etiquette, Feathered Goat simply walked into the meeting. As a 'holy person, he belonged everywhere and, paradoxically, nowhere. "It's time you become divested from your 'too close' proximity to the field of action. You need to acknowledge the larger picture."

Sarg gruffly responded.

Feathered Goat continued. "We here are the first families for a new nation...I hope you've realized that by now. This Paradise Valley will soon ignite into a beautiful rainbow of peoples from everywhere."

"There's only north and south...Only three peoples." Brey appended to Feathered Goat's prophecy.

"Only if you dare to believe that our piece of land is the only one in existence....Do you?...How long ago was it that we all knew for certain that the north was always hot and the south nothing but cold?....We remained ignorant of the Taths for..."

"Way too long." Kadima spoke loudly, scaring a few people. "Now get off your bottom, there's work to do. Your philosophizing can wait for another day.....when I'm not about." She smiled faintly and then turned and headed towards the barricade, the children in tow.

Queen Sjura asserted her royal authority. "Can we discipline ourselves long enough to establish a plan of action? The longer we wait to meet, the more time the damned one has to attack us."

"Well put." Sarg added. "Unnamed god, what provisions have you prepared?"

"I thought you'd never ask...... ." The nameless god drawled caustically.

"You asked me for some kindness, didn't you?"

"Yes, thank you....I will deliver those Tath queens and their entourages, as willingly consent to attend the meeting, at the safest place in the valley: Sarg's castle..... which brightly gleams in the yonder distance."

"Spare me." Moaned Sarg, his face noticeably pained, all feigned. The he abruptly changed direction. "Your plan is workable." His mind wandered elsewhere. "Can the castle logistically contain a few hundred people, with sleeping and food....and all the rest?"

"Ha!"

"Ha?"

"I've seen your castle, that the extent of my remark...Trust me, you'll be able to support an entire army for fifty of your double moon cycles with the rooms and provisions waiting there."

"But how?"

"You claim the Holy One creates from nothing....But you ask me how?....Sjura, this man needs more rest." The god-without-a-name's jovial recklessness returned. "Now, after the noon meal Vosnob is returned to wherever he desires.

> Then you-all
> will paddle-de-de
> down the creek-ee."

His ridiculous singing rhyme caused much groaning.

"In three days, I'll arrive there with whomever I can persuade.. I'll even be transporting Istelles .... Just a bloody warning to ye, mister." The god croaked out, just to further upset Sarg.

Per agreement, the nameless god departed immediately after the noon meal. Again, a terrified Vosnob clung to the intangible filaments of the cloud chamber. He would return, in force, as per agreement with Queen Sjura and Sarg.

Chapter 4

For once, perhaps the first time in his entire life, Nooy felt little compulsion to move. Entangled in Jelkio's beautiful blue arms he felt at peace, experiencing an intangible contentment. He rotated to his side and kissed her forehead, then snuggled his arm around her. She continued sleeping, a radiant smile frozen on her face. As he tightened his embrace, she tilted her head to return his kisses. In the silence of the dappled afternoon, with a lustrous sun slicing through the forest canopy, they made love, slowly, tenderly until the sun disappeared. Exuberantly enervated, the two lovers bundled even closer in their blankets as the cooler evening night air with its attendant dampness crept over them.

"I love you."

"Yes, Jelkio, you do." Nooy spoke in fluent Tath, without any aggravating accent.

"Do you mean anything by that?"

"Only that you have a special way to overwhelm me...."

"You care not for my love?" She gently teased.

"Just the opposite." He murmured as he rolled over on top of her.

She flashed her long eye lashes back at him. "Again?" She purred, wrapping her arms about his bronzed back and pulling him closer.

"Again and always." He whispered in her rounded ear. "Again and always, my love."

A splotchy daylight invaded the forest before the lovers decided to rise and bathe. Only then did Nooy realize that neither had eaten for a dawn and probably another half dawn. As Jelkio washed out their clothing, Nooy readied a meal of cheese, bread and wine and tended to their most patient Striper. During their meal, their discussion drifted towards future plans, especially ones a bit more organized than their escape from the King's myopic entourage.

"I need to take us one more step." Nooy nervously said.

"A riddle, my love?"

"No, I simply mean that it is not right that we live like this."

"Are you finally requesting..."

"Will you consent to be my wife?" He hurriedly finished the statement. "I promise to be yours as long as I live."

"Am I not your wife all ready?" She smiled coyly and planted a soft teasing kiss on his forehead. "I like that when you do it to me."

"Please," Nooy voice strained. "I must have our marriage be recognized. In our Holiness Code, there is no place for hidden lovers."

"Then you are proud of me!" She exclaimed as she hugged him.

"Of course I am............ Why should you think otherwise?"

"In Tath, men often have many lovers who are not wives."

"That is wrong, Jelkio...... I will have you only and you will have me only...And I want all creation to know I love you."

"You are serious?" She asked with some astonishment.

"Yes, yes, yes." Nooy repeated emphatically. "Do you believe that I could have spent two nights with you, making love to you and not want you near me forever?"

She sighed wistfully. "Some of your traditions are far more proper than ours. I shall enjoy being your wife forever." She smiled and kissed Nooy again.

"I'll try my best." He then sprawled out, resting his head in Jelkio's lap. After a short while, his face twitched.

"Is there something wrong, my love?"

"You will have to explain something to me. You are royalty, a true princess, like those on the waggon."

"Don't remind me of those arrogant windbags."

"The point is this, my status is far less. I am a free man, as are all Yldans, but I am an ordinary woodsman. I can lay no claim to anything beyond that."

"So what?"

"Can a princess marry a woodsman?"

Without warning, she pushed him off her lap into the moss, then dropped on top of him, smothering his dark face with kisses. "You simply remember one thing..."

"Tell me." He said as he hugged her and wrestled her over into the grass. The advantage now belonged to him.

"Only this, lover....We royalty can do as we so choose...Haven't you ever noticed that peculiar trait of ours?"

"So.....?"

"So...I shall wed you. Nothing more, nothing less. I make it a royal decree, a formal mandate......"

"Den I got-sez nuddin ta b' worried 'bout." He broke into his hideous Haafian accent.

"Exactly right." She smiled mischievously.

As they slept tightly wrapped about each other, the single moon sky, ominously clouded over with thunderheads. Waves of heat lightening raced towards them. Even as the increasing winds blew debris through their campsite, they slumbered on, oblivious to any impending danger. With a deafening wallop, a colossal thunderclap broke above them, followed by a streak of lightening that split an oak near the creek. They jumped from the covers as it exploded. Fragments rained upon them. A massive branch crushed their blankets. Nooy pulled Jelkio back into the shelter as far as possible, then positioned himself in front of her as a shield. She went white with fear and tightly clung to him.

The Striper fended for himself, having departed to the innermost regions of the forest as soon as it smelled the storm. Now prancing and pawing the moss-covered forest floor, the terrified beast desperately sought for a way to protect himself from the lightening and the driven rain. The Striper blindly galloped further into the wild timberland. After countless miles of twisting and turning through the underbrush, she tripped over a root and smashed into a tree. There, broken and exhausted, lost and alone, ...it died.

More quickly than it began, the violent lightning storm suddenly stopped. In its wake, the protecting forest lay as debris piles, wasted and mangled. The driving torrents continued pounding into the moss-covered ground, transforming it into a quagmire. The tranquil creek rose, challenging their once secure campsite. Its two inhabitants scrambled up a muddy uncovered knoll. There, huddled with their blanket and what few supplies Nooy fetched from the flooding creek, they waited out the storm. In spite of her nervous shivering, Jelkio dropped into an exhausted sleep, her head resting on Nooy's shoulder.

Much later, as the dim rays of sunlight battled the foggy mists, Nooy listened to the faint rustles stirring in the demolished underbrush. Immediately, instinctively he reached for his bow and fitted an arrow. Silently, he bundled Jelkio, softly laying her on the mud-caked ground. He motioned for her to remain calm, but due to the terror-stricken look on her face, he wasn't sure that she'd comply. He stood as another shadow in the foggy morning, to listen. The rustlings became more frequent and emanated from three separate directions. A wry smile claimed his face. He lowered his bow and gently pulled Jelkio up beside him.

"We bee's a jist a passin thru." Nooy conversed with the fog in his normal tone of voice. "De storm dun kill-ded our camp, gottez de Striper tooo...May bees yers all got-tez sometin' fer break-fast."

"Shut up Nooy and speak properly." Taunted the familiar voice, located somewhere to their left.

"Nope-er, Kofe."

Jelkio sighed with relief and hugged her Nooy. He kissed her hard and lovingly, stopping only when Kofe emerged from the fog laden environment. His huge grin evoked something between jealousy and true compassion with more than a hint of mischief added.

"Have you been spying about us?" Jelkio fiercely demanded. She spoke in Tath.

Nooy desperately attempted to control his laughter. "It may not appear the truth, and I apologize for smiling,...but no, we started after you when the towering black cloud blew through the northern plains."

"Well if you did spy, our god will repay you for your indiscretion." She threw the threat onto Kofe. "And if you did see, did like what you saw?" She deliberately teased, tossing away their soggy blanket. "And just who is 'we'?"

"I thought you figured that out." Kofe answered, his voice radiated with 'I got you'.

He yelped as her bare foot connected with his bottom. Two other voices, also familiar also laughed.

"Everyone in from the fog."

"Who put you in charge!" Demanded a feminine voice, speaking brusquely from the far left.

Moments later the reunion began. Rux and Nadre climbed up the muddied knoll. Re-introductions were prefaced with unspoken, unhidden smiles. These quickly embarrassed Jelkio. She tucked her blonde head under Nooy's slightly pointed chin and wrapped her blue arm around him. A sudden sharp breeze brought an uncontrollable shivering to Jelkio, she lost her natural blue.

"My dear," Said Nadre. "This pasty-white is definitely not your color. Come with me."

Nadre and Jelkio quickly slid down the knoll and stomped through some underbrush where her Striper nervously waited, his antlers slicing at some unidentified enemy. Smelling Nadre, the beast quickly calmed, allowing her to peruse her saddlebags for the appropriate clothing.

"This should warm you up right quick." She half teased in broken Tath. She held up a long riding dress, with a deep lacy bodice. "I'll bet he'll enjoy watching you take it off." She said knowingly. "Wait, you'll need some dry 'underthings' to go on first." And with that Nadre brought out the briefest set of drawers Jelkio had ever seen and a thigh length slip.

"What does 'it' really cover?" Jelkio asked, most intrigued.

"It's the revealing that counts. They like to be teased...I like to tease him." Jelkio confessed.

"You know a bit more about this than I do." Jelkio spoke as she donned the new clothing, admiring the enticing way each piece fit. "Nooy is my first lover."

"I had thought as much..... You are most fortunate... Rux is my last... Oros married us!" She blurted out, her face shined.

The two shared a long hug, then Jelkio confessed Nooy's demand to do the proper thing. Though she admitted that she would remain with him regardless.

"You, like myself, have a good man. Let your union be honorable and legitimate." Nadre said with conviction. "My past shall not be repeated by you."

"I thank you....You will come to the wedding?"

"What do you think I brought those clothes for?"

"You knew?"

"Let's say I suspected...... Yldan men are quite moral."

"But the underclothes?" She hesitated, a bit confused.

"For afterwards, when you've kicked out all your friends to fend for themselves."

"Sounds most appropriate to me." She returned, totally ignoring Nadre's feinting 'injury' as her mind raced into the evening: her first as Nooy's wife.

"Let's get some food." Nadre snarled, then laughed. "Time for breakfast. Then we're all heading west to locate 'the mountain'."

"Excuse me.";

"Oros, the fat priest, he's waiting a few miles away. He thought you two better make things proper before that thin waistline of your's commences to expanding."

Jelkio blushed. Nadre's bluntness scored a direct hit on a neglected target. Lovers usually beget children. Strange, until now, that dimension of her love for Nooy had entirely escaped her. "We better eat." Anything, she thought, to remove the thought from her mind. She thought again. What might Nooy think about children? She better broach the topic in the near future.

Breaking the fast together reminded each of the intensity of their relationships, created through hardships. Those relationships contributed to the two unions. Hope found allies and strength here. Their common history, especially as it engaged three races, demanded a brighter future.

"And that's exactly how the fat man obliges the future." Rux said. "By performing the weddings, he's pulling us together, and not simply by the bonds formed around physical love, but beyond that....And I hope he's still a priest."

As the laughter quieted, Kofe spoke. "I'd never heard you speak that deeply afore, you're beginning to worry me."

"Have no worries, Kofe. What you witnessed is a phenomena which exists between all lovers. It happens rather naturally when your personal world now covers two persons."

"Or maybe even more." Nadre's adorable smile caught her husband off-guard. He paled as the group's laughter filtered into the lifting fog.

"You aren't pregnant?" Rux anxiously questioned.

"I'll tell you when I am." She teased. "But, I will tell you first......in private." Her long eye lashes fluttered.

"Enough now," Kofe interrupted. "Oros be awaiting at the meadow. It's time these others," He lightly mocked. "Got married for those....."

"Hush your mouth!"

Nooy glanced at Jelkio, then to Rux, then returned to Jelkio, his thinking disrupted Jelkio's order. Trying to interpret the implications his head felt light and he slumped. Jelkio rushed to comfort him.

"Are you?" He queasily gasped into her rounded ear, but loudly enough that everyone heard.

"Not yet!" She responded.

Nooy promptly removed his head from her shoulder and lost his breakfast. After he quit shaking, he found Nadre staring him down; her gaze intimidating.

"Listen, Yldan woodsman," She said straightforwardly. "This beautiful Tath princess has chosen you over every other man in creation to be her lover, friend and husband.... Being a father comes with the package.... Understand?"

Plaintively, Nooy shook his head. Jelkio beamed radiantly at her husband-to-be. Nadre grabbed Rux's thin hand and lead him to their Stripers. Kofe, picking up on the hint, also left.

"Our Striper ran away." Jelkio called out.

"We brought an extra one." Kofe said casually, without looking back. "You'll just have to ride together. Actually, you do that quite well....You certainly impressed the Church Guards."

Oros, impatiently waiting in the meadow, greeted the party with his usual diatribe, which delighted everyone. Within moments he positioned each person for the ceremony. Nervously and proudly the two lovers stood more over than before the much shorter--and wider--priest.

"In case you are wondering about the issue of so-called mixed marriages...there isn't any such thing. People are people. The Holy One's plan demands only that the marriage union consist of one male and one female.....In other words, if Nooy decided to wed a Striper, that is forbidden. That is an actual mixed marriage.... Now, we are some four dawns behind our schedule. The King waits to meet all of you.....I'll bet making him wait was worth every precious moment, wasn't it?" He said to a blushing Nooy.

Following the wedding ceremony, which proceeded without many remarks from those gathered, everyone mounted. They rode west, catching the road, hopefully before sunset. The newlyweds constantly fell behind, too busy staring at each other. Kofe grabbed their Striper's tether and tied it to his pommel. In spite of nasty protests, the cantering Striper kept them with the rest of their entourage.

The eclectic group connected with the road shortly before dusk. While the women and Oros prepared supper, the others erected three tents, spaced rather distant from each other. They grinned about the obvious, but no one mentioned it. By mid-day on the next dawn, Krabo should be sighted, weather permitting. So prophesied the obese priest as four persons, broadly smiling, declared they required rest for the next dawn's ride. So, with the still setting sun lighting up their campsite, Oros and Kofe sat about the deserted campfire.

"Listen, if you roll over in your sleep ...."

"I promise to squash the life from you." Oros filled in the missing words.

Ploughing through the forest underbrush and the wind wrought debris, a party of five taller Kyykki discovered the lover's last campsite, ruined by the storm. Desperately hungry, they spent little time gathering information there, but continued deeper into the unknown forest. Following the vaguest of wind-blown scents, they turned due south and began their strange loping gait. Shortly thereafter, the five blackened spies discovered the dead Striper. Until they satisfied themselves with his flesh and bones, their mission drifted into obscurity.

The longer he listened to the so-called extraordinary troops and material which Ashuwa allocated for the invasion of Paradise Valley, the more indignation rose within Warmaker. Certainly, the Kyykki's numbers were almost unlimited, but they were also the nauseating derelicts of his Master's tampering with creation. He stood by, watching them parade, proudly-as-they-might, in review before the two of them. The majority of them hobbled, their legs being extremely weak or they had one Kyykki webbed-foot and one Haafian foot. So it continued for other body parts, the array of mix-and-match parts proved repulsive and sickening. Worst, it was an army without potential.

Seeing Warmaker's displeasure, Ashuwa pointed to the far corner of the cavern's grotto. With a great flourish, Ashuwa waved them forward. Warmaker smiled as he saw troops of the taller Kyykki advance.

"I present you with two thousand of these worthy troops, Warmaker. Make me proud."

"Thank you, Almighty Ashuwa. Your generosity is most helpful. For you alone and your glory, I shall conquer the Paradise Valley."

"Indeed you shall." The ominous tone of his words belied the indicated promise. Warmaker acknowledged the threat. "Now, I have two more gifts for you. Some twenty five Haafians and fifty dragons, most of them extremely energetic and more than willing to give battle."

Warmaker thanked Ashuwa but his mind swept to the real issues. Could the traitorous Haafians be trusted? How are young, inexperienced dragons going to benefit me? "My gracious Lord."

"Speak, Warmaker. What else might you require for the invasion?" Ashuwa's tone demanded he ask carefully.

"I appreciate your fine gifts, My Lord."

"Yes?"

"Might I be given time to adequately prepare them for the battle. This Sarg has cost you one invasion force all ready. He must not be allowed to repeat himself."

Reddish smoke poured from Ashuwa's finely pointed nose. "Yes, you are correct. The old tactics did not prevail...You, with extra time, can do better?" An indirect threat presented itself as Ashuwa slowly pronounced the last words.

"Yes." Warmaker affirmed as strongly as possible. "With proper discipline and training, this army will destroy your enemy, Sarg."

"How long do you require?"

"One double moon cycle, if you please."

"Granted."

Warmaker's ability as a strategist left much to be desired, if compared to the Haafians. However, Warmaker easily ranked first among all the Demon Masters. This position he maintained by eliminating all competitors, the way of operating he commenced when Ashuwa first promoted him. That burning desire to never fail, to never know defeat, pushed Warmaker to create a super loyal cadre of secondary officers. These fifty, a brutal combination of some Haafians, taller Kyykki and Demon Lords, had specific duties and goals. From this cadre Warmaker created the most disciplined force Ashuwa ever knew. Thus Ashuwa marked Warmaker for automatic dispatch once Paradise Valley was in his steely claws.

Warmaker's so-called training process consisted of eliminating the unfit from his attack force. Running through the volcanoes easily eliminated the majority of his defectives. With a force cut by almost one third, Warmaker's army moved with a speed slightly less than that of the regulars. Once he trained the dragons to fly either in direct support or as a diversionary maneuver, the second part of his strategic training stood ready. The third part dealt with the Haafians assigned to him. The Haafians were assigned to Sarg's castle, to infiltrate. The intricacies of this Warmaker gave to a Haafian named Garht, a one-time Light Striper with an unswerving grudge against the person who had him court-martialed ages ago.

When half the double moon cycle had passed, Ashuwa commanded Warmaker's presence in the throne room. The stern celebration proved an exercise for the god to re-assert his control over his general. It also served to clarify Warmaker's invasion preparations. Ashuwa had no intention of being blind-sided.

The throne room's brightness still took some adjusting. The volcano's inclining walls, now punctuated with huge irregular holes, allowed light to expose the true depravity of the chamber. Everything, from the sordid 'blue ladies' with their private parts painted orange, to the putrefying carcasses littering the cluttered floor, to the Haafian bone throne chair, now covered with some type of skin, was seen for its evil truth. The curse of the Holy One continued its invasion of Ashuwa's domain, though he had yet to recognize its full extent.

Ashuwa's Demon Lords formed a gauntlet through which Warmaker traveled to the throne, formidable and intimidating, deadly. Warmaker had no allies within this group. Drawing his sword, that gift from his god, he lashed through the musty air, exhibiting his expertise as he launched himself through their ranks.

"Nicely executed." Ashuwa commended him. "Obviously, you know the loneliness of being at the top."

"I am humbled by your concern, My Lord and My God."

"Indeed you should be. For as I have created you, so might I destroy you."

"That is ....correct." He quickly bowed, panicked that he almost used the 'death' word, as 'true' had become known.

"I thoroughly enjoy those who know their place....Lick my feet, Warmaker, they are filthy. ...They usually are after I've stomped a few of the darling 'blue ladies'."

He gulped, swallowed hard and trepidly crept up the dais, drawing near to Ashuwa's clawed webbed feet. With his blue forked tongue, he lapped up the clotted blood, clumps of flesh and bone and whatever other disgusting ingredients caked his Lord's feet. The other Demon Masters gleefully watched his humiliation, their serpentine eyes bulging with excitement. This depreciating action beckoned to their bizarre sense of justice. As Warmaker finally scraped the last morsel of garbage from Ashuwa's ankles, the god spoke. "It is not right that Warmaker be subservient to me? Is it not justice which declares that I must continually test his loyalty?" These seemingly fanciful questions he posed to the grinning Demon Lords, yet underneath lay the curse of 'truth'.

With much excited head movement and chanting they approved

Ashuwa's reasoning. Warmaker sprawled himself on the throne steps, silently waiting his death. Ashuwa raised both his clawed fists and silence immediately reigned. "You damned idiots are erroneous in your thinking." He sneered. "Warmaker has, thus far, served me faithfully, giving much and requesting little. He is the first to train the Kyykki. He will be my champion in conquering the damned Sarg."

Though he remained motionless, Warmaker felt a minute spark of hopefulness ignite within his blackened heart. Assuredly, he thought, his Master and Lord had more to say.

Ashuwa rose from the Haafian bone chair. "You on the right hand side," He sternly commanded. "Present to me what you bear most proudly?" He smiled hungrily.

Four held out weapons of great worth, usually gifts from Ashuwa. The others, in true lustfulness, raised their tunics high, exposing their most proud possession, their rounded bellies. With a sabre-like breath of flame, Ashuwa promptly incinerated their bulging bellies, leaving them gasping and trembling with a mixture of fear and rage. Death was close at hand.

"Losing your 'enjoyment' is a just MY way of rewarding those who lie to me." Ashuwa said indifferently as he sat down. "I shall not tolerate liars any more than I will the incompetent... ....Have I made myself understood?"

.

Their large scaly heads wobbled up and down in dreadful albeit truthful reply. Their thickly boned limbs trembled as never before. Greenish blood streaked with red ran from the groins of those Ashuwa torched. Even as the died, they stood as tall as the others. Smiling at his success in placing his fear within them, Ashuwa smacked his taloned paws together, creating a vivid display of sparks. He kicked at Warmaker, bidding him to stand.

"You are faithful, Warmaker. Every test I challenge you with, you succeed admirably."

"Thank you, My Lord. I request only to be your servant, to rid your valley of this scourge named Sarg."

"And, in due time, you shall." He smiled wickedly, gazing at those who felt his judgement. "For now, I question you."

"As you may require, My Lord."

"These wounded Demon Lords, did, in their blackened hearts, desired your execution. A similar case can be made for those not wounded. You are surrounded by enemies and treacherous fools, all jealous of your success.... What shall become of them?"

"My Lord, I am not a judge. I am simply as you have designated me, Warmaker, your First Named."

"You speak well, unlike these cowering imbeciles who wait only to pounce upon the mistakes of others."

Finally, from loss of blood and shock, one-by-one, the wounded Demon Lords crumpled to the floor. Ashuwa summoned the 'blue ladies' to roll their carcasses down the volcano's slope into the gaping mouths of the always waiting nepes. Ashuwa closely scrutinized Warmaker's countenance, watching for signs of emotion. Nothing materialized, leaving Ashuwa somewhat disappointed.

"You feel nothing, Warmaker?"

"No, My Lord...I accept your judgement. Should I dispute your judgments, then my faithfulness becomes dubious.......No, My Lord, how and what you judge is acceptable to me."

Ashuwa smiled, a devious twisted smile Warmaker found uncomfortable. It caused the leftover Demon Lords a great deal of consternation. Their breathing became forced and erratic, dense smoke drained from their nostrils.

"Acceptable is your reply,........My judgments are ended for Warmaker,.... I command the rest of you to the lower chambers. There you will pray to me with such utterances that I shall positively beckon to your persuasive pleas for mercy..... Am I thoroughly understood?" He snarled.

Those who still wielded their weapons hacked at their fellow Demon

Lords as they scrambled for the exits. Those available for prayer were fewer in number.

"Without the advantage of trust, which the Haafians and the Taths so highly prize, fear is the power I depend upon. Do you believe it effective?"

"So it appears to me, My Lord. I recognize the treachery about me. Fear either removes it or controls it. I have not the wisdom to discern which."

"'Tis a moot point which I have no intention of discussing." The loathsome god sat back on the throne, relaxed. "Now, Warmaker, explicate your battle plan...each and every detail. I do not intend on you failing me. That is forbidden."

Standing below his Master's throne, Warmaker presented each phase of his attack strategy. In return, Ashuwa nodded affirmatively or verbally lanced him. Ashuwa's favorite nepes being used as a feint demanded the most tedious explicating. Placating the irate god required the lightest touch and the most delicate wording. Sweating profusely, Warmaker accomplished the arduous task with all his body parts remaining where they properly belonged.

"And just how do you suggest that Garht and his ruffians invade Sarg's fortress?" Ashuwa's pace slowed to one of amusement. "Are they simply going to knock at the gate? And then Sarg will graciously grant them entrance?"

"My Lord, that is the whole idea. Garht and the band shall pose as refugees from Haaf North whose cargo ship floundered in the Dark Waters. They, the poor hungry souls, are all who survived a dragons' ambush. Sarg's own goodness will cost him dearly."

"Your Garht cannot gain entrance with lies."

"Your Lordship is correct. That is why the Haafians must be flown to Haaf North, to depart from there in a cargo ship. Once on the Dark Waters, I'll command a dragon to fire their ship. Those wretched few who reach shore, will tug most truthfully at Sarg's sense of righteousness."

Ashuwa interlocked his clawed fingers and wistfully gazed at the filthy sun-baked ceiling of his cavern. Entranced by his vision of ruling the Paradise Valley again, his needle-toothed grin developed into a raging laughter which seemed endless. With a sudden stomping of this fist on the Haafian bone throne, his laughter immediately ceased. "Yes, you plan exceedingly well, Warmaker. I am proud of you...You shall be my warrior, returning to me that which is rightfully mine."

"Thank you, Master."

"I have created a most suitable mount for you, as you did request of me...It needs but one additional component before I release it to you."

"My Lord?" Warmaker glanced upwards at his god, puzzled.

"Tell me your favorite color."

Warmaker paused a moment before reacting to the request. "Red, red akin to the Haafian's blood."

"Then it shall be!" He smiled and shot a beam of diffused light across the cavern's floor. It exposed the strangest beast he'd ever seen. "Do you not find it most suitable to instill terror in the Haafians?"

"It shall, indeed, it shall, My Master." Then Warmaker suddenly stopped. He stared at the awesome creature and then back to Ashuwa. "What is it, My Lord?" He asked pensively, almost believing he should know the answer.

The god laughed. "Since it is a singular beast, its name shall become its master's prerogative."

"I am truly honored, Master." Warmaker bowed deeply, then quickly returned to staring at newly created beast, his own singular creature of terror.

The 'thing' pawed at the cavern floor with clawed hoofs, hollow metallic noises rattled throughout the cavern. Its braided tail attacked the air, hissing and buzzing. Twice the size of a Massive Blue, in it's silhouette Warmaker counted two rapierlike horns, one located on the snout, the other between it's reptilian eyes. The biggest surprise occurred when the beast, summoned by Ashuwa, opened its leathery wings and gracefully glided to the dais.

"It flies quite unlike any dragon!"

"Don't get overly excited, its just an infant."

"How huge might it get, Master?"

"Only as large as it presently is. With this particular creation, size has nothing to do with age or ability." He said well pleased with himself. "Now what shall you call the creature?"

Warmaker almost ignored Ashuwa, his mind transfixed by such a wondrously terrible gift. "AH,...I'm not of yet sure, Master. Perhaps if I might be able to experience the unique powers you've provided the creature,...then the name could be an expression of your creative powers."

"That is thoughtful, but no." Ashuwa said, a drift of reddish vapor appeared from his nostrils. "The Haafians did that with my nepes...Now, I'm the only one who remembers to call them that."

Quickly and nervously, Warmaker bowed to the floor. From his position of obeisance, he spoke in tones of humility. "I ask pardon for my ignorance, Master....Such knowledge is well beyond what a general might know."

"A general doesn't need to know those things which have occupied the powers and time of the Almighty!"

"My words are confused, Master...I acknowledge that I know too little of your history, and therefore, of the injuries your perpetrators have inflicted."

"You are pardoned...... Recognizing the difference between your Creator and yourself is to your benefit." Ashuwa announced quite seriously. "Perhaps it will obtain a long life for you."

"As you command, My Lord." Warmaker looked up from his prostrating position.

"Get up and ride the creature. When you return I expect you to give me a name....A few more things, the creature breathes fire and its fangs deliver the most potent poison."

With a grateful bow Warmaker turned from Ashuwa. While circling his uniquely dreadful creature, Warmaker thought as to what their relationship should be. Ought the beast to obey through fear, or by reward for success? Warmaker choose the latter, simply because it placed the onus of any actions upon the creature, relieving Warmaker of such responsibility. Then he considered the practical side, he required an appropriate saddle, one which allowed him to be strapped in. Dragon riding provided no reason for such, due to their slower speed as well as their awkward maneuverability.

The creature sat passively while Warmaker secured a makeshift saddle just before it's leathery wings. Then he shoved a heavy bit in the creature's fanged maw, being careful not to nick himself. Strangely the creature hardly moved or took interest in Warmaker's preparations, though its large reptilian eyes followed his every move.

"You, beast, are My gift from your Creator, Almighty Ashuwa." Warmaker plainly explained to the creature as he patted its soft scaly hide. "Therefore, you shall act accordingly. As your master I command your moves. I will reward you for succeeding in your endeavors." He lied. The creature studied Warmaker carefully, testing him. "You are an intelligent beast, so......if you are hungry, nod your head."

The behemothic head bobbed rapidly, its twin horns whistling through the air.

"There are two 'blue ladies' behind the throne, the thin one is yours..... WHEN we complete the training. Do you understand?"

Once again the horns whistled and the reptilian eyes glared at its next meal. The terrified 'blue ladies', overhearing the conversation, went pale. The manacles about their necks kept them from escaping, but could not prevent them from committing suicide with a shard of earthenware.

"Beast, should you perform extra well, both 'blue ladies' are yours."

Fitting his jagged foot into a stirrup, Warmaker mounted the creature and adjusted himself in the makeshift saddle, making doubly sure his harness prevented his falling out. He gently tugged at the reins, the beast walked forward, a bit awkwardly as the claws constantly carved the floor. He jerked on the reins and the beast started a dizzying run around the vast cavern. The clumsy bounciness of his ride readily convinced Warmaker that his mount's true talents existed elsewhere. Wearied by the sloppiness of the ride, he pulled up on the reins, causing the creature to stop immediately. Warmaker ungraciously jerked forward in the saddle.

"Try that manoeuvre again and supper is denied!.... Understand?" Warmaker then cursed the beast.

The beast simply lowered its massive head, giving an ambiguous answer.

"Now, when I tug your reins, we'll glide around the cavern and then through the window and over the 'nepes' pond. I WILL negotiate the course....Understood?"

The massive head briskly moved up and down.

Warmaker yanked the reins, the creature reared up on its hind legs and jumped into the air simultaneously stretching out its leathery wings. The afternoon became occupied with turning, figure eights, appropriate landings and take-offs, all this inside the confines of the cavern. Then, with a sudden twist of the reins, Warmaker launched the creature through the window and out, over the 'nepes' pond. The sense of freedom he experienced made him a bit delirious, made noticeable by his erratic flying and the double loops which almost landed them in the swirling pond. The scare returned Warmaker to reality. In earnest, he coaxed the creature to great heights where ice formed on its wingtips, then to great dives. Later Warmaker experimented with fire-blasting rock formations to sand and turning copses of half-dead greenery to instant ash heaps.

Throughout the moonless night they flew together, often times crossing over the southern border into Haaf. Most importantly, Warmaker began a special bonding with the beast. The two flew as one, the creature almost able to discern Warmaker's command before the reins moved. As dawn's orangish streaks exterminated the blackness, the two glided into the cavern.

Ashuwa awaited them. "You have enjoyed my 'special' gift." He stated flatly. "It was to be expected."

"Thank you for the magnificent creature, My Lord." Warmaker bowed from the saddle, then dismounted to bow before his Master once again.

"A name?" Ashuwa demanded of Warmaker.

"I,... if you please, My Lord,..... humbly place before you the name... 'Windfire'." Warmaker spoke softly, hesitantly. For the first time he recognized a searing pain in his legs, a pain familiar to those who spend much time in the saddle.

Ashuwa withheld his response. He motioned to the exhausted beast. Obeying, the creature quietly clattered across the cavern floor to the place where the corpses still lay, their wretched blood clotted. Using its claws, the hungry beast immediately removed the heads and, after cracking the skulls, swallowed them whole. He finished by licking the floor clear of every last drop of blood.

"You will make sure that 'Windfire' is carefully fed in the future. His feeding will come even before your paying obeisance to me."

"My Master, I understand." Warmaker paused, fatigued. "You.. then have approved 'Windfire' as an appropriate name?"

"As I have spoken Warmaker." The god said sternly. "Now go, prepare your forces for the eminent attack on Sarg And his fortress..... My valley is to be mine forever!" He roared, causing dust and debris to rain from the cavern's ceiling.

Obeying, Warmaker took his leave.

Captain Ellom summoned the other ship's captains to his flagship just before dawn struck the sky. Even now, the battered flotilla raised sails and swung to a southernly direction, sailing some fifteen miles. The high-finned sharks, still circling the last sinking ship, voraciously devoured the remains of the suicidal dragons. They also feasted on Light Stripers who perished because of the dragons. Captain Ellom's hatred for the damned one intensified to the point of obsession. He shared this with his Chaplain.

"I share your agony over these losses, Ellom..... Not just good seamen were lost, but cargoes and ..."

"And the morale of our forces........Never would I have expected such a damaging encounter....Suicidal dragons... I've even heard that their riders died smiling..."

"Captain, did you seriously believe that, not being victorious, the dragon riders would have survived their master's wrath to fight another time?"

Turning away from the Chaplain, Captain Ellom walked slowly to the bridge railing. His weathered face, saddened and reddened by his anguish, tears upon the salt-stained boards. His weathered hands gripped the railing remorsefully. Silently he lifted up his voice in a desperate prayer to the Holy One; wisdom and strength he asked for, some particular way to comprehend, to make sense of the slaughter of a thousand good sailors. The Chaplain stepped forward, joining Captain Ellom at the railing, standing beside him. Together they prayed; together they mourned; together they witnessed the blazing sun burst out from the blackest of nights.

The five surviving captains, met for council with Captain Ellom in his stateroom just moments after the short dawn gave way to morning. This sober and staid group nervously waited for Ellom to begin, not knowing the direction of his thoughts. Also, not knowing when another attack might come, such a gathering of the captains was not merely unusual, but dangerous. Ellom lumbered in from the bridge, followed by the Chaplain. His face retained the stains from his tears, his hands trembled a bit as he earnestly shook hands with each Captain and shared a few quiet words with each. "Unfortunately, some are missing from our gathering." He slowly began. "I miss my friends, my colleagues....It's as if my family has been torn asunder.....These things I mourn. I can deal with the unfairness of life, of the horror of battle, but that does nothing to soothe my anguish." He turned to the steward, and requested a bottle of wine and glasses. "We shall celebrate our friends. We shall have a toast for them, all of them who lost their lives."

The toast came and went in reverential silence, the creaking deck and the wind pounding at the tacking sails being louder than the clinking of glasses. The Chaplain offered a benediction.

"There is still our mission. It is just begun." Captain Ellom sounded more like his old self, except for the lingering sadness. "As a fleet we are still quite viable. However, I prohibit any doubling until further notice. It is my fault and responsibility that we were not in such formation when the damned dragons attacked us." He stopped and wiped his face. ".... Unfortunately, we may have witnessed the newest version of attack...... As the Chaplain reminded me, the damned one loses no battles. Those who fail in their mission....." His sentence drifted off to nothing.

"Sir?"

"Yes, Captain.....speak,........................ you are among friends."

"Thank you, Sir." He cleared his throat. "I believe we can better protect ourselves from the dragons."

"I'd welcome your ideas......... A thousand casualties is far too many against the damned one and his legions!" Ellom replied.

Those gathered sensed the rise in Captain Ellom's righteous indignation.

"On that we are in total agreement....First, we keep the fleet sailing. The dragons are clumsy, not like the gulls. Moving targets will definitely be more difficult for them." One of the wounded Captains spoke.

Heads nodded in agreement, even Ellom half-smiled.

"Second, we need more dinghies on each ship. Actually enough to hold the entire crew. We can't stop a diving dragon committed to destroying himself by using our ship, but we can provide more adequate escapes for our men."

"We will." Ellom muttered heavily.

"Third, cancel the fires used for pitch, and triple the water carried aboard. Fire prevention must be number one priority if we are committed to dragon fighting."

Murmuring broke out. As of yet, Captain Ellom remained quiet, listening to the viability of the suggestions. Proposals and counter-proposals jumped about the Captain's stateroom creating a most nonprofessional ruckus. When Captain Ellom raised his hand the cacophony diminished. "We'll attempt all the suggestions, but in my prioritized order. The dinghies come first, then we need to increase the number of high-powered crossbows. Finally, I want you Captains to meet and set up a fleet-wide program dealing with the fire problem....... During this time the fleet will keep sailing. ...We still need to locate Ayhn and the Lancers. Just as we need more information on why so few dragons attacked us......... For now we are dismissed."

After the Captains left, Ellom slouched in his cabin. A knock on the door roused him. "What is it?"

"The reinforcements are in view Sir."

"Thank you.... I'll be on the bridge shortly." Nevertheless, he grabbed his battered jacket and bolted for the door, knocking the Ensign to the railing. "Sorry."

"I'm all right Sir."

Captain Ellom's spirit surged as he watched the second fleet come into focus.

Ayhn struggled with the difficulties presented by traveling along the beach. He had yet to discover the Kyykki's whereabouts, let alone pursue the blackened creatures. At best, the scouts reported the Kyykki remained some two dawns ahead, irregardless of the Lancer's pace. This 'army of the damned' left enormous amounts of evidence; the broken jungle, the unusable streams filled with filth, the gut-wrenching stench.

Ayhn acknowledged that his expeditionary force was in a quandary. The Lancers, per agreement with Captain Ellom, followed the shore heading south towards Pinduala, but the Kyykki now headed inland, moving southeast, as if to conquer D'Ka instead of Pinduala. Ayhn reckoned the Kyykki's route change as stupidity. With Pinduala left unmolested, her forces would harass the Kyykki in the flank. This provision remained true even if the enemy gained the headwaters of the Haaf River. In spite of this knowledge, until Ayhn regained communications with Ellom's fleet, the cities could not be warned.

A runner approached, his Striper's hooves beating softly on the sand, Ayhn pulled himself back to more immediate concerns.

"Sir!" he panting runner saluted.

"Carry on, Trooper."

"The fleet's been spotted...." He paused for a quick breath. "On the horizon, about five miles north."

Ayhn drew a heavy breath and left it out slowly. "As soon as possible, signal them with the mirrors. It's essential that they send extra water.... Signal that our encampment will be here, next to the hillock off to the right.......Also, tell them to alert D'Ka and Pinduala.....The horde is heading southeast." He paused. "Give my report to the first ensign who comes ashore." Ayhn reached into his saddlebag and yanked out his notes from the skirmish with the dragons. He wanted to know if Captain Ellom killed the others, or if he even saw them at all. If the dragons had been able to return with knowledge of the force, then they were in serious danger.

Report in hand, the runner sped away. Ayhn reined in the Lancers to construct the evening's encampment. Though their water supplies were almost nil, word of the fleet's appearance increased the Lancer's morale.

The following morning Ayhn walked the deck with Captain Ellom. The essentials of the dragon's attack had been discussed, and dismissed as complete failure. The fleet's loss, on the other hand, demanded a change in strategy. The Lancers must remain within signaling distance of the fleet. This, the two commanders conceded, hopefully negated any surprize attack.

"Somehow, suicide on the dragon's part does seem feasible." Ayhn said.

"It doesn't make it right."

"Agreed." He glanced out to the placid sea, mesmerized by the jump of a squat whale, a symbol of good luck, even though the concept of such was frowned upon by the clergy.

"Beautiful, ain't she."

"Indeed, Captain, indeed."

A short while later, refreshed by the salt-tinged breeze, the two commanders returned to the topic: the whereabouts of the Kyykki.

"I don't believe that the Kyykki would expose their flank by simply ignoring Pinduala. They're stupid, but not that stupid."

"Then what do you suggest?"

"What estimate is available concerning their numbers?" Captain Ellom requested, his mind far ahead of the question itself.

"Maybe a ten or twenty thousand...Probably more. They're traveling in such a narrow path, only a few hundred feet across, as if to disguise their true numbers."

"Exactly my point, Ayhn." He looked intently at the young commander. "I'm rather certain that the actual number is three times what you suggested.....Also, their way of traveling can disguise many other horrors."

"Dragons."

"Yes, dragons. Place them in the middle of the column and we'd never realize they existed as part of the Kyykki force."

"Then you believe that the port is going to be attacked."

"It's just a matter of time."

By the middle of the morning, the two commanders agreed to the following strategy. First, the fleet would sail for the port, adding their arsenal to that of the heavily defended city. Next, Ayhn's forces, after moving within ten miles north of Pinduala would maintain scouting duties, direct confrontation with the Kyykki to be avoided at all costs. Mirror equipped Lancers would penetrate the jungle until a full accounting of the enemy existed. Then the Lancers were to disengage and re-assemble at Pinduala. Captain Ellom designated three ships for this. With a handshake and a prayer, Ayhn returned to shore. Captain Ellom shipped off the last supplies to shore, and, towards mid-afternoon, raised sail for Pinduala.

Two long dreary dawns in the humid jungle thoroughly exhausted Bellah and his Lancer patrol. What the contemptible insects and other miniature carnivores did not bite or suck from the Troopers was duly compensated for by the lack of any direct sunlight. Negotiating the swamp-like jungle rather instinctively than by map-and-compass, Bellah's Lancers trudged in a southeasterly direction, more often than not, dragging their haggard Stripers behind them. Everyone breathed easier when the third dawn brought the patrol up a rise. There the mucky greenish soil gave way to partial grassland. The sun dappled ground and the cloud washed sky brought the Stripers energy. They bolted towards the grass as the top of the hill, in spite of the fact that the Lancers strongly pulled the reins back. Only the strong odor of Kyykki kept the mounts from galloping beyond the hilltop.

"Oh shit!" Bellah hoarsely gasped. He found himself gazing upon an immense horde of Kyykki plowing through a ravine not more than three hundred feet away. "Back away before they smell us."

Frozen with fear, the Stripers had to be cajoled into quietly backstepping down the hill. The six Lancers exchanged lances for crossbows. Their only salvation at this moment lay in the fact that the patrol traveled downwind from the blackened horde. As long as the nauseating stench forced them to gag and vomit, they continued in relative safety.

Bellah forced a smile as he contemplated this twisted paradox. "Hand me the 'long tube'. He whispered to the greenish complexioned Lancer to his right. The afternoon comprized itself of Bellah staring through the 'long tube' and then scribbling notes which a runner delivered to the mirror operator perched high in a palm tree below the hilltop. In the course of the afternoon, the patrol collected enough information to answer more than a few nagging questions. The stumbling haggard horde they spied possessed little energy. Bellah watched as the horde lurched and stumbled along, reinforced by the whips of the taller Kyykki. The weak and exhausted were trampled into the muck of what used to be a stream or creek; the endless three hundred foot wide swath of bobbing Kyykki insured that the fallen never rose.

In the distance, Bellah discovered other streambeds. Each, he presumed, stuffed to their breadth with parts of the same Kyykki horde. How shrewd, he thought, especially for the Kyykki. The polluted streams only tell where the horde was. By refusing to travel overland and outside the swamp, the telltale dust was not only removed as a witness to their exact whereabouts, but also excluded their need for any scouting parties along the perimeter. Finally, stream walking provided an ally for the Kyykki. It removed an essential element for Haafian life: pure water.

The mirrored messages deliberately ran one direction only. Bellah desired to return safely. As the first dragon came lumbering into view, looking disdainful for having to tromp through the mucky streambed and for carrying some partying Demon Masters, Bellah and his patrol rolled down the slope, running into the safety of the dense jungle.

At next dawn, just after a sudden hail storm, the patrol made it to the jungle's border. Exhausted and hungry, they gladly settled in for a quick break, and a time for the Stripers to unwind as well. Bellah signaled with the mirror to get a fix on the Lancer's location. He received nothing in return, in spite of the fact that other scouts were supposed to be posted at one mile intervals along the beach. Not in any condition to press the issue further, Bellah ate breakfast before considering the meaning of non-response.

As the hail storm suddenly quit, the putrefying odors of the Kyykki emerged from the jungle in great strength, causing Bellah considerable anxiety. Apparently, the damned blackened creatures plodded along through the night or maybe another horde marched directly behind them. In either case, the patrol sat directly in front of the advancing Kyykki hordes. The six Stripers, unable to withstand the stench without direct Haafian control, suddenly tore lose and bolted towards the seacoast.

"At least they didn't take much with them." Mumbled one of the Lancers.

"Do you think we can outrun the damned Kyykki?" A Lancer angrily challenged.

"We don't have any other options." Bellah announced. "Grab the canteens, your weapons and let's move out."

They jogged quickly in the shade of the jungle's trees, heading south. After a mile, a filthy, muddy stream caused them to pause. The Kyykki stench hung thick in the atmosphere about them. Then the splashy sounds of the horde tramping along the streambed became too obvious, too close for anyone's comfort.

"What now, Bellah?"

"Fighting them won't make any difference. Six against a few ten thousands. ....We dig in and watch the stupid beasties ramble by. .... Hopefully, we'll be able to signal the coast....If little else, this attack will not be a surprize....Quickly, dig in behind that briar thicket."

One hastily dug channel between the short trunks of the briars provided the entrance. Using knife blades as shovels, a hole large enough for six soon existed in the sandy soil. This they covered with their tunics, using their lances for support poles. In the space existing between the sand and their makeshift roof, they observed the landscape, diligently watching their perimeter. Bellah resumed sending mirror signals out to sea.

The Kyykki horde ignored the fact that anyone might be observing them. They traipsed right to the jungle's border without any advance guard nor any taller Kyykki nor any Demon Lords. They struggled to a halt as the intense sunlight bore down upon those in the front ranks. Their efforts were in vain: the momentum of those marching behind either plowed them under or forced them into the sunlight. Long before any taller Kyykki arrived to re-organized the horde, it had spread to over a mile in breath at the sunlight's edge. When those who reached the sunlight suddenly stopped, the others slid right and left until they reached the unwanted sunlight. This radical change in environments demonstrated a major weakness in the attacking horde.

In dumbfounded astonishment, Bellah grabbed the Lancer to his left and bent his head towards the sea. There, charging up over the dunes came the Lancers of the Light Striper, decked out in their bright dress uniforms. Each carried a small polished round shield that reflected light into the horde, confusing, blinding and frustrating them. At thirty paces, the first rank whipped their lances through the front rows of Kyykki, inflicting many casualties. The next four charges did exactly the same, but to a different portion of the Kyykki line. With undisciplined madness, the Kyykki horde plunged into the hot sand, accepting the bait of the Lancers. Keeping only a hundred feet in front the frenzied horde, the Lancers picked off the taller Kyykki with crossbows, then feigned another retreat.

Before the Lancers galloped from view, Bellah urgently signaled from their pit, 'Dragons follow the horde'. Without pausing he constantly flashed the message, stopping only when the first dragon's shadow darkened the briar patch. "Holy One be with our forces." He whispered.

"The Holy One be with our forces." Quietly prayed the rest of the patrol. "Amen!"

Only as early evening arrived did the patrol witness the end of the rambling horde. It numbered well past seventy five thousand, plus over a hundred dragons of all sizes, all headed due east, against the sun, into the sea. Their sandpit refuge transformed into a humid inferno, offering only rancid sweltering darkness to the six. Cautiously, they removed portions of their roof. The fresh sea air quickly revived them.

Silently they planned to leave at late dusk, hoping to find safety along the shore, some three miles distant. However, because of the meandering dunes, they knew nothing of what lay beyond the original charge of the Lancers. This made for much anxiety. As the six tossed off the last of their tunic-made ceiling, a soft rumbling noise interrupted their preparations. The ground quivered twice, then nothing. Bellah squirmed his way through the briars, then immediately jumped back.

"Someone important is camping to the right, just out of sight." He paused for air, gulping nervously. "The rumbling is a pair of little dragons, with some type of contraptions on their backs."

"For the damned one himself."

"That's quite doubtful......This must be one of his Demon Lords, the moron who just watched his horde attack the seashore."

An amused chuckle greeted Bellah's sarcastic appraisal.

"We have only two canteens of water left." Said a Lancer. "Another day stranded here might be our last."

"I just love an optimist." Countered another Lancer.

"Quiet!" Cautioned Bellah. "Listen."

The contraptions mounted on the backs of the juvenile dragons were command posts. They appeared to contain, judging by the different sounds, five to six Haafian individuals. A cadre of taller Kyykki surrounded both dragons.

"Just explain your failure to me....." Screamed a Haafian voice. "Just how did this northern corps get out of your so-called iron-handed control?"

"My Lord..." Begged a ragged-edged Demon Lord voice.

"You got one thing right....you moron-faced toad."

"My Lord," He repeated without emotion.

"I'll show you 'My Lord'!" The sound of a heavy sabre cutting a thick robe sounded. Then an empty thud, followed immediately by another. "Now throw the brainless...headless failure to the Kyykki....They must be hungry by now."

"Yes, Master." Instantly sprang from the voices of several Haafian lackeys, one of them female.

"Send me someone--something-- who will explain the slaughter of half the northern corps." The Haafian demanded.

A deeper voiced Demon Lord spoke. "The Kyykki were in front of us, as usual, plowing through the streambeds to make room for our dragons........."

"Tell me something I don't know."

"They stopped when the deadly sunlight caught them at the edge of the jungle."

"And you brainless dung heaps didn't have any taller Kyykki in the front to control their emergence onto the sand."

"No, My Lord....But soon after."

"Soon didn't come soon enough, did it?"

"We were ambushed by these Haafians."

"Certainly you were...A whole Haafian army can easily hide on the wide open beaches, especially ones with polished shields." The Haafian's tone increased in anger and cynicism. "The truth is that your taller Kyykki DID NOT control the horde....... The truth is that no leaders were in front of the horde!.... Not one of you ever imagined that a beach might be next to the sea!....SO, SO.......... The imbecilic hordes took the bait of a few hundred spear-armed glory seekers, didn't they?" The Haafian roared in disgust and anger.

"Yes,....... My Lord........And they ate quite a few." The Demon Lord quietly defended himself.

"So I heard....And fifteen dragons?... Explain their gutting to me, you idiot."

"The dragons flew over the Haafians, roasting quite a few. Then, huge spears launched themselves, by magic, from the ground."

"By MAGIC!" He screamed. "There is no magic.....only your damned stupidity!" He paced for a while, then tore into the Demon Lord again. "And ALL fifteen never returned.........The wounded were eaten by the horde....Is that correct?"

"Yes,...My Lord."

"Have him impaled through his thighs, then hang him up high. I always wanted a living flag........That's about all your kind is useful for, you stupid..." The rest of the sentence was muffled by the cry of pain.

Bellah stared at the faces of his patrol, though without the moons he was forced to move from nose to nose. Every face bore the makings of a thin smile. "Perhaps we did some good after all." Bellah whispered as he shook hands with each Lancer. "Now, shall we finish off the Haafian traitors?........This we vote on."

No blatant disrespect intended but the Council of Elders had no intention of ruling Haaf. Their responsibility lay in a much broader direction. With the latest report from Vosnob concerning his reuniting with Sarg, the Taths, the new country of Tath and Istelles, plus the current invasion at Pinduala and the disturbing unrest in the south, the Elders had all ready spread themselves as thin as possible. Even the addition of the twenty fourth member of the council was placed 'on hold' due to the current 'essential project' as Blue Turtle had nicknamed Jabbi's translation efforts. This translation was the sole agenda item for the morning's session.

Since his last attempt at presenting this material, Jabbi had thrown himself into this translating responsibility with a certain vengeance. Never again would his reputation be shredded. Those times of naiveté belonged to his past. To prevent another misleading presentation of the Ancient Scared Books, Jabbi conducted his research with two other Elders.

Gathered in their comfortable 'hidden' residence, Jabbi rose to speak. "Before the importance of the Ancient Sacred Books is disclosed. I must credit my two colleagues for their perseverance, tenacity and diligence. But most of all for excellent tea and wonderful company. They have honored me as I did not deserve." He turned and gestured towards Narganna, a lithe dark haired widow, and Fert, an old cripple with the incredible ability to almost be in two locations simultaneously. "Without these two persons, the work would not still continue." His gracious applause, quickly joined by the others, caused the two to rise and bow.

"Now," Jabbi began his narrative. "We commenced our research by obtaining as many documents as possible. Libraries throughout the nation, and possibly beyond," He shot a quizzical glance at Fert. "Were raided for any tangible assistance possible." Jabbi's curious choice of words raised a few eyebrows, to which he cheerfully responded. "We thought all three of us should simply march into every library, especially the private ones, and demand ancient manuscripts pertaining to the old world. But that particular style of operation deemed to call attention to our secret endeavors, so we simply 'borrowed' what we required. And, as of this date, we've heard no complaints....Not that we were listening.....And all has been as carefully replaced as it was borrowed."

The august group broke out in fitful laughter; an appropriate approval of Jabbi's methodology.

"The collection needed a space far larger than twice this room. We found the basement under the High Council Hall most congenial for our efforts..."

"And nobody knew you were there." Baste commented from across the room. "Good show."

"It is significant that never did an entire manuscript exist. At best, we managed to piece together chapters of the ancient books. This proved rather difficult, far more difficult than expected. It appears that the ancients circulated the Sacred Books rather freely, to the point where notations cluttered many margins and family trees, and wedding documents marked the entrance into the book itself."

Looks of disbelief leveled themselves at Jabbi, such a thing as annotating Sacred· Writings was tantamount to heresy. The Holiness Code could be copied for teaching and sermons, but never, never was the text to be marred with extraneous scribblings.

"Shall I go on?" Jabbi quipped. "Or shall we judge those of the past age.....as if they might care?" He smiled. As silence began, Jabbi started once again. "The different translations provided a multitude of headaches. The En-glish language used often had three or more meaning for the identical word, not too unlike Haafian. But, we had to establish the original context in order to ascertain the 'most plausible', 'most correct' wording."

"Jabbi," A disgruntled Kloshic called out. "Listen son, we trust you and Fert and Narganna......You are among friends......Busy friends.....Move to your conclusions........ We'll decimate your incompetent research methods later...."

Snickers and cheers greeted the old man's comments. Jabbi glanced at his research colleagues. They nodded in agreement with the other Elders.

"It's our final version that will carry the weight and impact of our findings, Jabbi." Narganna said softly. She blew Jabbi a gentle kiss, easing his frustration.

"That you accepted Narganna's little kiss restores my faith in you. Maybe you aren't made of granite after all." Ilty teased, embarrassing Jabbi.

"Well...no more wasting time......There is no complete book concerning this son of the Holy One called Jes-sus. The best we have are bits and pieces of chapters of three books that mention this Jes-sus: Mat-thu, Loo-key and Jon. We differ with the conclusions of the late Abbot, however. This Jes-sus did good, having the power of a prophet and healer both, even to the point of raising a friend from death.....Jealousy created his enemies and on trumped up charges he was put to death. Crucified, is the word used.....Has something to do with a peculiar barbaric style of execution by driving nails through the wrists and ankles and then allowing the victim to die slowly over a period of days... ....We believe this is horrid death could only involve the damned one.......The names of a powerful evil 'something', closely related to godlike powers, are given as sat-tan and dee-vill. There is no reason to doubt that the damned one existed in the ancient world ......But now comes the strange twist...this Jes-sus isn't dead long...three dawns.......Then the text is missing, but picks up enough to state that for another forty days this same Jes-sus remained here with his friends. Then the Holy One removed him to his personal abode for the purpose of ruling over creation...."

The Elders sat, waiting for Jabbi to finally end. He obliged them.

"Bottom line, the so-called son of the Holy One, as Ashuwa claimed for himself, who was publicly admonished at the Wall, is not this Jes-sus of the Ancient Sacred Writings......

"SO," Kloshic broached the conclusion. "We are no further along than before."

"Yes and no,.... you old greezer." The hoarse voiced Fert interrupted. "We have eliminated a possible contender for the title...That's something we never had before....Furthermore," He wheezed. "Perhaps it doesn't make any difference ....about who the damned one was, or what his history might be..... Our lesson is simple, we need to deal with the damned one as he is.... It is our own past dealings with him that will assist us to defeat him, the Holy One willing."

"For once I'll agree with ye..........It just better not happen again, you old clodhopper...." Kloshic sounded as nasty, but his eyes gleamed with mirth.

"Thank you, Jabbi." Said Vosnob. "Now, what plans do we create from this information, if any?"

By the late afternoon a consensus developed. It called for leaving the Ancients Sacred Writings to the scholars. For the present, they contributed nothing to aid the Haafian situation. These were texts of another age, long past, when the living God, the Holy One, did reach out to His people in totally different ways. And this, after all, is and always will be, the Holy One's prerogative, Blessed be His Name.

Chapter 5

"I don't think I'll ever like this castle. It's too big. And it's not very homey.... The walls are too hard...cold."

"Sjura," Said her husband, a bit flustered. "You've only been here for two dawns. Nobody understands this castle, especially me........ And it's supposed to belong to me."

"Us." Queen Sjura gently corrected.

"Yes, all three of us." He smiled as he lightly patted her ever-growing belly. "Seems Tath women move this birthing 'thing' along much quicker than in Haaf."

"It happens as fast as it's supposed to.......Sometimes I wonder about you."

"I'm glad you do." Sarg interwove his large fingers with his wife's and pulled her closer for a long kiss.

"Enough of that." Yelled Brey. "That's how babies begin, you know." She giggled, and twirled about, her long dress brushing the marble floor of the keep's roof.

"Maybe it's about time we commenced a bridal deal with some rich Tath prince for you." Mused Sarg as he rubbed his chin. "Then you'll learn the truth."

"Don't you even think such a nasty repulsive idea....I forbid it." Sjura looked Sarg in the eye, then winked at Brey, further confounding her. "Brey, you know exactly how babies are made, it's quite easy and a lot of fun."

Sarg blushed at the forthright bluntness of his wife. She quickly elbowed him.

Sjura continued her lecture. "The most important thing is to find the right man to be the lover and the father and the husband." Sjura stressed the last word. "Without that one not only trespasses against God but against oneself.... AND, all babies require two parents......Is this not correct, husband?"

"Ah," Sarg was gazing at the forest before the castle. "Whatever you say."

Brey giggled, then latched onto Sarg's unencumbered arm as they finished their stroll around the perimeter of the keep's immense roof.

Impressive, magnificent, overwhelming, opulent and extremely practical. These feeble words refused to convey the extreme awesomeness of the 'gift' castle. Most obviously, its construction was not that of the created, but of the Creator. Sarg's brief tour of the immense complex lead him to climb to the four hundred foot tall roof of the keep. The trio reached it by climbing through the castle proper. However, the last hundred feet of their climb were totally devoid of the solid marble-like material which made up the rest of the castle. Instead, a massively thick floor appeared upon which huge hundred foot columns shot up to the roof, whereupon another thick floor marked the height of the tower.

"I have no idea what the Creator intended when he constructed this keep. Why four hundred feet high and why should it be almost a mile in diameter?" Sarg asked of no one in particular.

"Might I suggest that its design looks towards another 'new beginning'?" Sjura smiled up at her husband, confident he'd push for her explanation.

"Yes, my dear, you know that I enjoy having answers instead of riddles, even divine riddles."

"Well, I might be erroneous, but...."

"But what?"

"This roof is a landing."

Sarg looked at Sjura then at Brey, whose countenance exhibited the same puzzlement as did her Commander. When he glanced back to his queen, she began laughing. Feathered Goat and Kadima, who just reached the platform-like roof, joined in.

"What's so funny?" Sarg rankled.

"Dearest Sarg," Feathered Goat began with his most ostentatious attitude. "You married a Tath queen who now delightfully carries your child. You strap yourself to my Istelle and we destroy the damned one's supply route........ And yet you can't comprehend 'landing'?........ You are a most curious person, especially for one with the 'gift'."

"Istelles will land here!"

"Sjura, hold on to this Sarg. There's hope for him yet." Kadima laughed.

"Istelles will shelter under this roof as well. Below that is the Council Hall and living quarters for over nine thousand persons.....What a novel concept, ruling a country by air instead of sending runners plowing through the streets."

"Yes, my wise husband. But there is even more." She lead him to edge of the parapet where they stood before a mirror-smooth retaining wall. "Notice the distance to the first wall. It's almost ten miles from here, encircling the castle with but three rather insignificant gates."

"A gate fifty wide by thirty high is insignificant?" Sarg challenged his wife.

"There's only three for the entire perimeter, that's what I'm getting at....It's an inherently impractical arrangement for a nation that moves by land....Only one gate for every twenty five miles of wall."

"That could also be interpreted as defensive construction. Walls are weakened by gates....And this territory is located next to the damned one's volcano." Sarg pointed to the east, where Ashuwa's massive volcano rose in the mist-laden distance. "Then, there's absolutely no reason why both interpretations can't be correct. This castle is constructed not just for these times but for the future."

"Indeed." An out-of-breath Vauk proclaimed. "Look to the west, where the creek re-connects, causing us to become an island. See the wharves down there? Large as any in Pinduala and certainly constructed better........... Appears to be the same material the entire castle is formed of."

A hazy shadow, one of enormous size, suddenly crossed the landing.

A moment later, Feathered Goat's Istelle made the first soft landing, terrifying all but the Taths.

"Ah, she's knows exactly what this building is for...And when the rains arrive, she'll probably ensconce herself below." Feathered Goat smiled proudly. "You realize, of course, that it will be awfully difficult for the dragons to launch an attack. The Istelles will be airborne well before those clumsy miscreations get within twenty five miles of here."

"And just how can you be sure of yourself?" Sarg demanded.

"Thou shalt not aggravate a shaman." Feathered Goat pompously quoted the Holiness Code. "Actually, the bird's vision is ten times greater than ours. From this tower, five or six Istelles are all we'd require for protection."

"Actually," Sarg stressed the word to the limit. "You mean 'detection'. A handful of Istelles won't eliminate the Kyykki hordes."

"O' great master, I stand humbly corrected." Feathered Goat mocked.

Sarg chose to pay attention to Sjura instead of the conniving shaman. Feathered Goat treasured nothing more than baiting him. Quietly they strolled around the perimeter again. Sarg choked as he attempted to comprehend this city, twice the size of his old capital and thousands of times more gloriously impressive, yet still immensely practical. How much the Holy One must care for him. His mind, his emotions could scarcely contain it all. As a few tears dropped unto his tunic, Queen Sjura drew closer to him. She too had small dark spots on her gown.

Something entirely original, frighteningly innovative began here. Two unequal gods worked together, different races had to rethink their world and their place within it. A new city state that would become the testing ground for it all. And, for whatever incomprehensible reason, Sarg found himself in the middle of it all.

Gathering about a table and benches formed of the same white marble-like material for supper, these pioneers discussed the implications of their responsibilities within this new territory. Having nosed about the grounds more than the others, Vauk absently commented that no Holy Space had been delineated. Considerable loud discussion immediately followed as the group wrestled with the significance of Vauk's observation.

Unexpectedly, Brey summed up the entire issue. "Both of our gods are allowing us the freedom to ignore or obey them. Coercion is not utilized here....We are to construct the Holy Places."

All slowly nodded in agreement. Brey's summation fit in perfectly with the 'new' times which were upon them.

"Now can we get some sleep." Brey argued with almost no one. The others had all ready started moving towards their respective quarters.

The group passed through the fifty foot thick wall of the keep and out one of the six towerless gates. Now, miles from the keep, some ramparts began exposing themselves. The dusky sun's rays mirrored the white walled keep. However, much remained hidden because of the immense oak, linden, and fir trees which hovered above other walls. Between the copses the grass grew thick and green, and cattails rose in the fresh water springs that bubbled not far from the cobblestone road. This was not unlike the vegetation outside the middle wall, except for one peculiar feature. The copses formed natural boundaries between three different geographical areas.

One third of the castle state was fashioned as the Yldan homeland, identical as it was to the forests and fast streams east of Buda Lake. The second third presented the impression of the mixed grasslands and tree lined rivers of Haaf. The third half, elevated above the other two, resembled the vast steppe of Tath, complete with its waving bluegrass and oasis.

All this they observed from the central keep the day before. They also noted each area had its own city. A miniature version of Krabo existed in the established star pattern, while the wooden encampment walls of the Yldans gracefully meandered from redwood to redwood, working concordantly with the creation existing there. Spiked wood palisades and rough-hewn granite gates identified the Tath village, replete with their traditional heavy woolen yurts.

"You've never seen a yurt. Now you shall. You'll find them rather conformable and cozy." Queen Sjura announced proudly as they entered the grassy and gravel paved compound. She tossed open the blanket covered door and entered. Then, before anyone followed her, she suddenly screamed. "By the nameless god!"

Sarg and Vauk plowed into the yurt, gently pushing Sjura to the wall. They paused, in shock, as fifteen regally adorned Taths gazed at them in puzzled wonderment. Brey and the others instantly rushed in, swords drawn, only to find themselves surrounded by the silent, rounded featured blue Taths.

"Queen Sjura!" Asked a most confounded older woman. "What is the meaning of this rude entrance?" The orange glowing ring that she wore about her neck pulsed with energetic activity. Deadly anger shot from her eyes.

Sjura pushed through her guards.

"And what is the meaning of your condition?" Her tone turned icy-cold, extremely judgmental, when she saw Sjura's well rounded stomach.

"I am the owner of this city." Sarg deliberately interrupted. "My wife and I bid you all welcome......Unfortunately, we were not aware of your presence here.....I am sorry to have kept such royal visitors from Tath waiting..." Sarg spoke in impeccable Tath, to delight and further confuse the tribal leaders.

Sjura moved up beside her husband, standing beside him even as he spoke. "Yes, Queen Isolo, this is my husband...Our child, all quite legitimate, I can assure you." She spoke soft but firmly and in perfect Haaf, causing a number of the easier-going Taths to laugh along with Vauk, Brey and the others.

Queen Isolo required the assistance of Kadima to translate for her. She did not believe the ring. This 'request', by the disdainful look on her face, further separated her from Sjura.

The nerve-wracking voice, all-too-familiar, laughed as he entered the yurt, via the roof, in his rainbow-hued cloud chamber. "Well, Sarg, I done did delivered....And on time, I must add."

"And boast." Sarg caustically shouted back in Tath.

"Be nice, husband!" Sjura smacked his hand, while the other Taths, including Queen Isolo knelt in appropriate humbleness before their nameless god. Horror showed on their faces as they noted Sarg's irreverent attitude.

Sarg reckoned that this Queen Isolo came close to being his equal, obviously not in size for she stood as tall as her girth, but in terms of power and influence. If the Taths were to cooperate with the Haafians and Yldans against the Kyykki, she was the one requiring some political enticement. However, at this juncture, Sarg's incomplete strategy kept him from any maneuvering. He was caught by surprize and he knew it.

"Up, everybody, up." The nameless god commanded from the rainbow hued cloud. "Time to commence our business...... Time is not exactly on our side..... The damned toad-faced hordes of Ashuwa are coming soon."

"As I had thought. He dares to claim a real name for himself.... It is the time for his ultimate invasion, isn't it?"

"Quite true, Sarg....His initial thrust is aimed at retaking this Paradise Valley....Are you prepared to meet his offensive? I trust you are familiar with the city. It's easily defended......"But you, have none of the Light Striper regiments with you. Nor the assistance of the air-borne Taths of the northern steppes."

"The Haafians shall be arriving as quickly as possible....... That information you are all ready privy to..." Sarg paused to consider another jibe at the unnamed god, but quickly reconsidered, recognizing his need for Tath allies. "And if we all are to survive 'Ashuwa's' onslaught, then we must become acquainted....Will you perform the honors?"

Sarg's request momentarily blindsided the nameless god. He stuttered. Queen Isolo straightened her red-striped gown, beaming from floppy ear to floppy ear. Taking their queue, the rest of her erstwhile company stood and made ready. Brey moved up beside Sjura and Vauk flanked her as Kadima shoved her way next to the queen leaving Feathered Goat to manage the children. The two broke free and dashed across the yurt's mossy floor. They slammed into Queen Isolo, unceremoniously bouncing her to the ground.

Seizing the awkward moment, Sarg walked to the fallen Queen. His willpower stifled his countenance. He truly felt like laughing. He spoke in his best Tath. "It would be mine honor, High Queen Isolo, to offer you my hand, if your highness should consider mine offer a proper one."

A white blush covered the queen's royal face, but she did not respond. She removed a handkerchief from her bodice and placed it in the palm of her flabby, short-fingered hand. This she extended to Sarg both as a testing and an insult. Gracefully keeping his mouth shut, Sarg knelt, one knee to the mossy floor, accepting the queen's testing. With some large amount of effort, the queen slowly regained her pre-eminent position in the center of the yurt. She immediately withdrew her hand from Sarg.

"I'm glad you did that Queen Isolo," Sarg whispered in her rounded ear. "Your hand got filthy from your fall. Thank you for protecting me from such contamination." He smiled and returned to Sjura, whose face almost burst with the most uncontrite hilarity. Luckily, Sarg's body clogged the line-of-sight between the two women.

"You have made acquaintance with the leading queen, Sarg. But I need to properly introduce you to her." The nameless one said seriously. "Queen Isolo, the gentleman who assisted you in rising is named Sarg...... He is one the Holy One's 'gifted' as well as a most respected spy and Light Striper. This end of the Paradise Valley belonged to his father, as such he has rightfully claimed it for himself and Sjura, his wife."

"How dare she marry some brown-skinned......"

The god's rainbows instantly transformed to red lightnings. "I MARRIED THEM, ISOLO." The unnamed one thundered. "Do you desire to confront me with your petty incoherent preconceptions? Is not Kadima wed to a Yldan shaman?.....Is your wisdom beyond mine?"

"No, no, no, no, My Lord." She shuttered as she shrank to the floor, kneeling before her god.

"O' get up!....Your theatrics are worse than mine. ...I hope I made myself understood..... Skin color is a gift of the Creator, who happens to have a proclivity towards diversity.....Will anyone challenge him?"

Inwardly, Sarg rejoiced in the new-mannerisms of the nameless god. Outwardly he kept a stolid, but not overly cold demeanor as his protection. He needed to keep the High Queen off-balance until he could ascertain which way she ought to fall. Sjura elbowed him right neatly, having caught the devious glimmer in his slanted eyes, one of those things wives learn quickly.

Within the brightly lit yurt, a happenstance due to the nameless god's presence, the formality of proper introductions continued well beyond reason. Sarg remembered why he detested those social gatherings his first wife drug him to. He quietly used the idle time to ascertain the dispositions of the Taths. Almost immediately he recognized that only four rings were present. Presumably not all tribes chose to return to the ancient homeland and to a capricious god from the distant past. However, just which tribes accepted the invitation? Furthermore, just why had they come? Curiosity? Faithfulness? Self-interest? Sarg relied on time to provide some answers for him, knowing that Sjura would have additional information.

"Now that we are introduced," The unnamed god declared in a weird high-pitched nasally tone. "Let us adjourn to the village circle for a feast."

Oblivious to the table spread for royalty, complements of the nameless one, Sarg, Brey and Vauk dispersed into the crowd attempting to listen and to gather allies from the overabundance of retainers attached to the three Tath Queens. Having fulfilled his promise, the Tath god, without a word or sign, vanished.

Much later, under the soft lights of the double moon, high in the empty armory of Sarg's keep, the small company gathered to compare notes. The Taths decided to reside in their village, each tribe claiming a yurt for itself, the central one belonging to Queen Isolo and her retinue.

Immense as it was, and being constructed of the same white marble-like material, the armory's atmosphere reflected a strange warmth, especially as no echoes nor hollowness intruded upon their gathering. Most noticeable, if not most disconcerting, was the emptiness of the armory. That, and the limited numbers of the Light Striper left the entire city open to attack. The importance of gaining allies within the ranks of the Taths became essential.

"So, Isolo is queen of the largest tribe who control the central portion of the country. Therefore, her territory borders upon the Dark Land." Vauk summarized the findings of the evening's discussions. "In spite of that, she is reluctant to commit any forces." He stopped, angry with the queen's stubbornness.

"She believes she has nothing to gain by allying herself with us. She thinks she's strong enough to hold off Ashuwa, especially since she knows the Kyykki can't exist on the steppes."

"And there she's absolutely correct, Feathered Goat." Brey added her observation. "She needs to be approached from another direction."

"How about using 'mixed marriages'?" Sarg caustically blasted into the queen's repulsive ideology.

"Husband, be kinder. She's quite old."

"If you wish....But I find her attitude repulsive.......We need to be pragmatic about this matter...The other two tribes are more willing to assist. The eastern tribe is willing because the Itsell Bay is being contaminated by the drainage from the Kyykki breeding pools. The fish and whales are moving farther out, almost to the sea."

"So, economics aligns them with us."

"Deeper, my friend." Sarg said to Brey. "Economics is their survival.

From what they said, shepherding went by the wayside quite a long while ago, some three hundred fifty years by their strange time reckoning...... Anyway, at present, fishing is their mainstay."

"But they don't have a fleet. Just a large number of skiffs. Seems the Istelles do the spotting for them." Vauk added.

Jelkio had been listening most of the time, now she sat, pensively gazing at nothing particular. Since their entrance into the yurt, she had remained silent. Even during the reunion at the feast, she kept herself in the background. "The Northerners shall come." She said almost too quietly.

"How do you know that?" Brey asked.

"Revenge is a strong motive."

"Please explain the mystery, Jelkio." Sarg said.

"Our tribe, along with the Northerners, worships at the same small building..."

"I remember listening to Sjura's story."

"Some from the Northern tribe arrived a few days after our capture. They found evidence of our capture and a few pieces of our guards.... As they sought to leave immediately, to warn the tribes of the unholy incursion, the Kyykki attacked. Only one survived, thanks to an Istelle. Their Queen and her entourage were massacred......" Jelkio began sobbing; Brey and Kadima moved to sit beside her.

Vauk unexpectedly cursed.

Jelkio suddenly looked up in greatest surprize. Vauk stared back at her, taken aback. His complexion went ashen, a dreadful acknowledgement that something hidden within him had escaped. "What is it you know?" She spoke shakily, between her sobs. "What secret......do......you...have!" She hesitantly, yet defiantly demanded. "What is this news to you?"

Unable to state the truth, the Haafian physician turned away, walking slowly from the armory. His head bent to his chest caused his appearance to emulate a man headed to his death. Jelkio threw down her handkerchief and ran after him. Grabbing his shoulders she spun him about. Putting her finger under his chin Jelkio spoke directly to him. "Tell me your secret Vauk!"

He stubbornly refused her request. In spite of her desperate pleading he kept mute. He shook and tears dropped to his tunic. Instinctively Jelkio wrapped her arms about him, pulling him close, her blonde hair pushing up his chin, her blue cheek resting on his chest. Arms dangling, Vauk continued impassive, totally unresponsive to Jelkio.

Sarg, still prone to penetrating mysteries, entered, uninvited, into the strange confrontation. "Explain yourself, Vauk!" He ordered. Though he bellowed the command, in the unusual and unfamiliar confines of the armory, he sounded no less loud nor more loud than anyone else. This brought a look of consternation to his face, as if somehow his controlling influence compromised itself.

"I heard you."

"Then speak your peace. We've been through plenty together."

Vauk gently hugged Jelkio, then just as gently removed her arms from his about his chest. Even so, she stayed close, paying rapt attention to Vauk's forthcoming explanation. Vauk slowly turned to face the others, a bit of a military bearing displaced his former shakiness. "Another story concerning the same episode exists....A Tath guard related it to me....He portrays a much different Isolo." He paused, and with difficulty cleared his throat. He grasped Jelkio's slender hand before continuing. "The massacre did happen. That much of the story is true. However, Isolo is the guilty felon who planned the entire massacre.....She is horrified that Sjura still lives....She watched as you, My Queen and Jelkio were captured....She had enough Istelles to prevent your capture, but she wants only to rule all of Tath...."

Jelkio's hand attempted to pull free, so she might run, but to no avail. Then she broke down, sobbing uncontrollably on Vauk's shoulder. This time he wrapped his arms about her, very gently, very compassionately.

"I had hoped to obtain more information before I announced my findings, especially as this queen appears to be the key to recruiting the other tribes .....Sorry Sarg."

Whether Sarg heard, Vauk didn't know nor did he particularly care. Unable to stand the silence, Vauk continued the guard's story. "Isolo had the second massacre 'fixed' to make others believe that the damned one was responsible ....It allowed for Isolo to obtain another ring for herself...." He lifted Jelkio's head until her eyes met his. "I'm sorry....It is not my intention to distress you."

Sjura's face went cold, cold enough to chill everyone in the armory. As she held up her hand, the orangish glow from her ring pulsed violently, almost blinding those standing nearby. Sjura, speaking in stern Tath vocalizations, began speaking directly to her glowing ring. Immediately, the pulsing ceased.

"I accuse you of betrayal, Isolo. On two counts I summon you to court on the morrow, here in the armory. You stand accused of the intentional invasion of another queen's privacy. ...." Her countenance grew darker... "And you are accused of murdering Tath royalty."

The intensity of the ring increased beyond painfulness. It became impossible to view. In such ugly manner did Isolo's response arrive, leaving no doubt that she heard the entirety of Vauk's 'different' story.

"This being the territory of my husband, you are forbidden to leave the yurt. An escape or any attempt will provide us with a guilty verdict; your life will be open to all who desire justice. ....Have I made myself understood?"

A blinding flash of orange-red light promptly answered Sjura.

"She and her entourage will not escape."

"I understand the trial. And, unfortunately, traitors as well. ....But what does this manner have to do with Jelkio?"

"Quiet, my husband." Sjura quickly regained her usual composure. "Jelkio's intended husband was a guard. He was murdered in the massacre.....Is that not the secret?" Sjura stared straight at Vauk.

He spoke softly, not to the queen, but to Jelkio. "Yes, I knew."

Jelkio hung her head and wept silently, her hand reaching out for Vauk to enclose it within his own. He started to, then suddenly stopped, then continued until his hand firmly wrapped about hers.

"I knew only part. I knew Jelkio had an 'intended'. That is your way. .....Only this day did I know the rest..."

Jelkio glanced up at Vauk, a witness to the deepest of his hurts and trying desperately to run from his narrowed, pained eyes. She allowed herself to grieve with him. As the tears rolled down his tunic sleeve, she spoke. Her words came as a confession. "It is true." She spoke directly. "My parents and his parents raised sheep on adjoining property. Even though they were from the Northern tribe, at our births, the marriage agreement was signed." She stopped to pull another handkerchief from her sleeve. "Such things are common. Both families benefited from the shared land.... Now the agreement is void."

An empathetic Sjura provided a different focus. "When we were first captured, the agreement went void, Jelkio. No Tath would expect us to return .....Furthermore, well...you tell the truth to this one who has loved you from afar....Go on!"

"How did....did...did.... you know?"

"Quit stammering Vauk." Said Sjura. "The only persons you fooled were male.....Brey and Kadima will confirm my observation."

Both ladies nodded, their serious grins penetrating Vauk's vulnerability. Now he stood mystified, staring at Jelkio. Now she carried the 'shattering' secret.

"Jelkio, tell Vauk."

She smiled glibly, stymied for the correct words. She reached for his other hand, finding it, she drew him a bit closer, forcing him to face her.

"The man, ...the guard, I never knew his name....I never knew what he looked like.....I wouldn't..Not until the day before the wedding.."

"You would marry a stranger." Vauk stated, mystified and confounded.

"To please my parents,.... yes." She murmured softly.

"But what do you say now, Jelkio?" Her queen seriously inquired. "And you, Vauk.....now that the truth bestows generous freedom upon your stifled soul?"

"Aren't you making a bit much of this, Sjura?" Sarg whispered to his wife.

"Have you forgotten your nights of soul searching, my love?" She smiled knowingly. "You were so confounded, the marriage proposal didn't come out right.....I had to assist you with it." She hugged Sarg, though rather awkwardly considering her condition, then gave him a kiss. Then she turned her attention to the confused couple. "I shall expect you two to begin sorting things out this evening. Have I made myself perfectly clear?"

"Most clear, My Queen." She stuttered, realizing she had to face her own desires. The safety of the family contract no longer prevented her from seriously considering other men. The present became as fearful as when their capture began, as fearful as when unknown Haafians entered their lives, as fearful as escaping the endless valley. Then, in the silence of the moment, she realized that if these other fearful histories of her life......she would handle another one.

"We are going to talk, Vauk.....I understand that you are ahead of me, but were hiding your feelings out of respect....You truly are a gentleman."

Vauk stood as if struck by lightning, fully embarrassed. Brey, sitting with Kadima, began to giggle. "She certainly must be talking about another Light Striper." Then she turned up the volume. "Be careful he doesn't play doctor with you....Although he's very competent."

"That's quite enough!"

"Yes Sarg."

"The court begins at mid-morning. Everyone will be present. Until then, good evening." With a mischievous pat to her behind, Sarg marched Sjura off to their empty suite of rooms where they camped out on the floor, again.

Slowly, those few present left the armory for parts of the keep they tentatively claimed for themselves. Brey, in spite of her remarks, now realized the tremendous difference between being alone and being lonely. She wondered if this existence had more to offer. Once, it promised better, once she dared to believe that a special person might be hers. But such happiness belonged elsewhere: Luuft was dead.

Last seen, Vauk and Jelkio stood as immovable statues facing each other in the dimly lighted armory, resembling unthinking fragments of stone more than their true confused and 'set-free' selves. Later, they moved to a window ledge, where their painful conversation hesitatingly began.

Court began without much ceremony. Isolo, raging with defiance, entered the keep with her full entourage. All had dressed to the imperial hilt, weapons included. The other tribes, knowing the essence of Queen Sjura's accusations, flanked the opposing parties. In Tath tradition their prescribed role consisted of being the jury and then, formulating a judgement based on a consensus of those involved tribes.

"I am not stupid, Sjura." The hatred glowed in her eyes. "I did use the ring to listen in....Every tribe present can witness to that fact....However, most queens aren't as capable as you." She sneered at those on the flanks. "It's an honorable way to compete, I should think."

"Your avarice convicts you."· Sjura calmly replied. "What need do we Taths have for an untrustworthy queen?"

Ignoring the challenge, Queen Isolo continued upon her own path. "Before any form a judgement, let them ask themselves if they have not also, at one time or another, abused the power of the ring.....I shall not be judged by those who are also guilty of my so-called crime."

"Then you expect me to judge, Isolo?" Countered Sjura. "That would be a welcome...."

"No such thing....you hideous bitch....ridden by a mongrel and bearing a witless off-spring."

"I've heard your depraved ravings before...And, as is attested to by these tribes, the wedding ceremony......"

"Yes, the nameless 'thing' you worship presided." Queen Isolo sneered.

"How dare you mock our god." Came a gasping voice from the sideline.

"The ignorant powerless dummy will survive."

She sneered again, causing Sarg to become apprehensive. Instinctively, he pulled his wife back step. With the vocabulary becoming more debased, he feared that physical actions could easily follow. Isolo now had some twenty guards with her, presumably they arrived early that morning.

"Now, you dubious mistake for a queen, I confront you with your lie. Your demeaning accusation of my being an accomplice in a murder is beyond..."

"Is nothing more than the truth......The Northern tribe, as per agreement, pilgrimaged to our Holy Place not less than a week after my capture...You had them murdered and deceived the others into believing the damned one deserved such responsibility.... Can you deny this truth?"

"It is not my place to deny nor claim anything. You dared to declare the onerous deed belonged to me....Now bring forth your witnesses to prove it." Her sneering grated with an uglier edge.

She pulled her enormous bulk up to almost look Sjura in the eye. Isolo's challenge to the group put them on the defensive, exactly what she wanted. Once she could prove that vengeance existed as Queen Sjura's motive, the court would sway any direction she wished. A ruthless confidence shone in her defiant arrogance.

The gangly guard who shared his story with Vauk broke through the flanking tribes and entered the inner circle. As if a bungler, he overstepped the perimeter where witnesses stand for testimony and entered the center. There he stood, scratching his head not more than an arm's length from either queen. Suddenly recognizing his intrusion, he backed off a few paces.

"As the survivor of the massacre, I give testimony." He began nervously.

"I understood there weren't any survivors." Queen Isolo said contemptuously, though nervously.

"I don't think I be dead, Queen Is-slow."

"Its Queen Isolo, you damnable idiot."

"Continue with your testimony, guard." Sjura commanded.

"I be in charge of the Istelles..... From high above I saw Tath guards enter our Holy Place, drag out bodies and behead them. The bodies, that of our Queen Maavi and her faithful retainers were carried over the hill, into the Valley..."

A horrified gasp from the crowd stopped any further testimony. Queen Isolo dropped her head, her guards tensed.

"Why did you not aid your Queen Maavi?" Sjura cautiously asked the anxiety-ridden guard.

"I did not see the damned villains enter our Holy Place....Only the dead came out....I could not bring them back."

"You are nothing but a paid sniveling liar." Isolo attempted to frighten the guard.

"No, you filthy whore,... gone to bed with Ashuwa and his pricey little promises of being 'Queen of the Northlands'..... You have had your day."

"How dare you,...you piece of dung." Isolo motioned for her guards to seize the witness.

The guard began glowing, transforming himself into the rainbow cloud. Isolo's guards froze, dreadfully aware of their error. The remaining Taths, including Queen Sjura, bowed in reverence, awed by the divine presence of their unnamed god and his newly acquired trait of being with his people.

"You are a powerless imbecile!" Isolo screamed in terror. A thin bolt of light shot from the cloud. It wrapped Isolo's jaw shut. She squealed in desperation, attempting to verbally defend herself.

"I've had enough of you, Isolo.....How low can you go on......... allowing

Ashuwa to use your blubbery body?..... Selling out your people for personal gain?"

"My Lord," A blanked faced Queen Sjura said. "This cannot be true. Its is well beyond reason, well beyond comprehension..... beyond treason even."

"But not, my dear Sjura, beyond greediness and a consuming desire for power." The nameless god replied sadly.

"Perhaps I understand. I am not sure how one of our own could...."

"Just the same as Haafians manned the barges inside the volcano." Sarg softly replied, gently bringing his wife to her feet.

"You may rise, my people....rise and listen. First, the rings shall be banned."

Another flash of light scoured the room searching for the rings, and, once located, removed all signs of life from them.

"Now we are much safer. Queen Isolo, with her greedy disposition, traded a ring for a fantasy...the bride-to-be of Ashuwa.....Nod if that is true." He sternly ordered.

Isolo slowly nodded, her faced paled and she trembled.

The Taths spit on her, even her guards ripped off their tribal identifications. Everyone backed away from her in disgust and anger. She was hideous both inside and out.

"I'm grateful your putrid influence didn't carry far. I'm proud that the majority of my people are above your abominable pursuits. I'm positive Ashuwa will be disappointed, perhaps enough to have you for supper... Your lying is remarkably counterproductive, my dear fat Queen Isolo. You have no friends and few sympathizers here ...Yes, my dear, you are terribly fat..........You actually should be ashamed of yourself... Unfortunately, your fantasy is....... disintegrated. The rings have no more power, and neither do you. I hereby remove your queenship. Neither shall any kin of yours ascend the throne.......ever."

The rainbow cloud sparkled for a moment then vanished as the unnamed god made an appearance in the form of a rainbow-hued Tath, complete with a blinding orange cape which pulsed irregularly. He then strode over to the frozen Isolo and personally removed her ring. Then, amid a stressful hushed silence, the god smashed the ring between his hands. After exhibiting the flattened stone and metal glob to everyone, he again placed it between his hands. An excruciating crunching noise pervaded the silence, a sound which did nothing to alleviate the tension.

"I apologize for the disruption." Said the nameless god, his countenance friendly. "But I am required to fix the broken, this ring is the first one." He held forth a gleaming silver band in his right hand with a new stone, deep blue with a faceted cut which produced rainbows all about the armory. "A bit too much glare, isn't it?" The god asked no one in particular. He touched it with his left hand and the rainbows shrunk to a finger's length. "Much better, don't you think so Brey?"

"I......I...Yes, ...My Lord." And she hurriedly bowed.

The god laughed, delighted. "Now before I transform the other rings, the Central tribe requires a new Queen. I have chosen one. One who maintains a sure sense of righteousness, yet is humble and caring. One who has been experienced with great injustices, but they did not break her spirit nor her will. I have chosen one who realizes that listening and compassion are part of governing, although her experience in this governing isn't much at present....... Enough said, I certainly don't wish to embarrass the young lady'." He chuckled at his own joke.

"Who might this new Queen be?" A retainer from the Queenless Northern tribe gently requested.

"It will be revealed shortly. First, however, this sack of lard is wanted.... by Ashuwa....Seems you haven't delivered any of the information he requested...." The nameless god reached out and clasped Isolo by the head. "Now my dear, tell the bastard all you know...... Because you don't even know your name anymore." For the first time the god exposed his anger. "Now begone!" He twitched his glowing fingers. Isolo rose in the air, terror claimed her face. Then, in a blustery mist, she vanished forever.

"She'll land on Ashuwa's Haafian bone throne chair, obliterating it by her weight...I score twice: no throne, no traitor."

Sarg shook his head and glanced at his sadly smiling wife. He sighed heavily, finding himself somehow drawn to this strange god and yet, still baffled as to exactly why.

"Guards and retainers of the Central Tribe, step forward."

All immediately conformed to the dictates of their god.

"Some here connived with the ex-soon-to-be-dead-queen to massacre innocent believers. You are found guilty and are hereby...................dead."

Six Taths silently fell to the marble floor, among them the Chief Officer of her guards and two ladies-in-waiting. Each lay clutching their hearts with their left hands.

"They proved unmerciful and heartless." The unnamed god declared. "They died as such, without mercy and heartless....In these days of gravest danger to our tribal nations as well as beyond, there is no room for such as those...I understand that all of you understand my sentiments." He said firmly.

A great deal of murmuring went on among the tribal groups as they considered their god's wishes. Most were predisposed to obey, though a multitude of questions abounded. There was a heightened awareness of their responsibility. They discovered a new relationship with their god. His trifling ambiguities of the past became the substance of ancient history. His willingness to lead them, to personally intervene for their benefit endeared them to him.

"You are pleased."

"Indeed, my Lord." Replied Sarg.

"Your Holy One indeed chooses excellently in passing out the 'gifts.'"

"I am grateful. Thank you."

Such bizarre conversation made little sense to the tribes. No one sought to explain it, but it did much to cement the relationship of the Haafians and the unnamed god.

"Are we agreed upon a course of action?" The god queried his tribes.

"We fight this Ashuwa!" Proclaimed an older woman from the Northern Tribe. "He will be punished for crimes against your faithful people and my sister, Queen Maavi."

"Then you are the next queen, Queen Kullia."

A rousing cheer echoed through the armory, followed by more as each tribe, in turn, committed itself willingly to the conflict. As such the atheist tribe from the swampy waterways and marshlands regained its rightful place. Finally, the Central Tribe was called upon to reply.

A young retainer reluctantly spoke for her tribe. "We find ourselves unworthy, My Lord. We...."

"The unworthy are departed...Well, they're dead." He glanced at the corpses littering the floor. "How do you answer?" He asked gently.

"We desire to join with the rest of the tribes, My Lord. But we have no one......"

"For a queen." Chuckling to himself the nameless one completed the sentence. "Then if I proclaim your queen, your answer is a willing 'yes?."

"Indeed, My Lord...We only hesitate because we have no chosen queen....And we earnestly refuse to repeat the past."

"You are wise for such a young one....I promote you to first retainer to the new queen.... Do you like that Kinanna?"

"My Lord!"

"Good. Its settled then."

"But who shall be our new queen, this woman you spoke so highly of?" Kinanna pleaded.

"Yes, it is proper that I should name her.......Brey of Haaf is your new Queen."

Bellah's daring plan of attack proceeded quietly and efficiently. The traitorous Haafian and his flunkies, including a few Demon Lords and the 'blue ladies' partied into the early hours of the morning, exhausting themselves Believing themselves secure between the two slumbering juvenile dragons and far distant from the Kyykki carcasses littering the seacoast, they ignored standard protocol. Not one sentry had been posted.

Waiting just outside the enclave's perimeter, Bellah's Lancers swiftly eliminated stragglers and donned their vibrantly colored robes. A Haafian female, as drunk and as undressed as others, fell with a bolt protruding from her bare chest, oblivious to her own demise. As the orgy's noise became subdued, half of Bellah's Lancers crept towards the nearest dragon, keeping downwind of the fifty foot beast. The others invaded the canvass pavilion rising between the two dragons, the sight of the orgiastic partying. Silently, except for three high-pitched twangs of the crossbows, the first dragon commenced an eternal sleep. At five paces the crossbows' bolts burst through its iridescent eyes and into its feeble brain. As it began to lifelessly sprawl, the beast slid into the pavilion, disrupting Bellah's exterminations.

Muffled cries arose as a few Demon Masters rose to drunkenly confront their executioners. A deep blue colored one, clutching a pole, rushed at Bellah, tearing his arm open. A Lancer gutted the creature before he disrupted any more of their attack. The combined noise from the two events woke the second dragon. She casually peered about, sniffing the pervading scents of the campsite.

Bellah and his Lancers, frightened by the rousing dragon, began retreating towards the seacoast, the creature roared and then stood. The pavilion was smashed into the ground, trampled by the half-awake dragon rushing to her strangely silent companion. Rapidly aggravated by lack of response, the creature first gently touched the dragon's shoulder. The dead beast fell on its side, puddles of greenish blood covered the earth under its revolting head. Realizing her companion dead, the frenzied beast stomped and flattened the campsite, further obliterating any survivors. Then, uncontrolled and without her rider, the beast ravaged the camp, incinerating countless Kyykki. Wild with rage she dashed about, smashing everything she collided with, setting fire to the rest.

Within a few short moments, the entire Kyykki population along with the remaining Demon Lords, loped towards the commotion.

"My friends," Bellah yelled through the increasing din. "We've accomplished our mission....More than we ever thought possible."

"Then let's go home!" A Lancer yelled back, his last words. A taller Kyykki speared him even as he spoke.

The others fled towards the pavilion in order to escape being trampled by the curious and ignorant hordes. Another Lancer tripped on the long robe removed from a dead traitor and died quickly as the uncaring and unknowing horde pounded him into the ground.

Cursing, Bellah strode up to a Demon Master. "What's the meaning of this indiscipline?" He screamed into the fanged-faced beast. "Get this blackened heap under control immediately or I'll hang your stupid head on a pole."

The Demon Master looked twice, shaking its head, quite undecided about what action to take.

"You dung heap!" Bellah screamed at the impassive Demon Lord. "You want to explain this riot to the Haafian Lord?" Bellah swatted his scaly leg with the flat of his sabre. "Move or die, you wretched piece of dung!"

Sensing this Haafian meant business, the Demon Master forced himself into the fray. In single file, Bellah and the other three Lancers followed closely. The horde slowly parted before the Demon Master. They moved faster after the beast used a taller Kyykki as a pathway clearing weapon. The compacted horde swept in behind the Demon Master as soon as he passed, requiring the Lancers to continually fight, defending themselves from being crushed, slicing right and left at the Kyykki. The endless fray began to diminish when the Lancers descended to the shadeless beach.

Battered, bruised and bleeding, and still surrounded by the enemy, the four desperately sought for a respite as the first streaks of the red dawn pierced the starry sky.

Demon Master!" Bellah hoarsely yelled at the creature directly in front of him.

Without words, the Demon Master turned, tossing the taller Kyykki carcass, his weapon, across the beach. Greenish slime covered his entire scaly hulk, along his legs and his arms deep gashes dripped a disintegrating mixture of redish-green slime, his massively jawed head slumped forward as he attempted to focus on his Haafian master. He swayed, then groggily lurched backward, landing on his back, his battered chest heaved twice, then quit.

"Never figured I'd live to see the day when I'd be thankful for a Demon Master." One of the Lancers drawled.

"Nor me." Another added.

"I am as astounded as the rest of you." Bellah shook his bearded head. "No one is ever going to believe this..... It's just not natural."

"Shut up and drink! We've a fare way to travel before we're safe."

Bellah shook his bearded head once again. Security existed as a 'sometime' thing. Even at this moment, as the last of the Kyykki loped by them, his instincts clutched at him. "Follow me." Bellah called over his shoulder. "The longer we stay here, the fewer of us there's going to be."

Due to exhaustion, the three Lancers dropped to the sand, ignoring Bellah and passing the last canteen. Recognizing their limitations as well as his own, Bellah took a swig from the canteen. The dawn's light outlined the beach before them, exhibiting a multitude of trampled and wounded Kyykki, victims of the Lancer created chaos. The silent eeriness, overshadowed only by the distant wash of waves, returned the unforgettable memories from the Wall. In spite of the hellish surroundings, hope remained.

"What supplies are left?" Bellah asked.

"One canteen full and a bag of bread."

"We gots three crossbows and the swords."

"And dees 'funny-boy' robes." The Lancer spat on the sand and began removing the translucent gown.

"Keep the stupid thing on....When we're in safer territory, then we'll discard them."

"You be da boss." He said, readjusting the bulky garment. "But, Bellah, how you thinkin' we gets outa here."

Bellah's uncharacteristic silence disquieted the trio. They became more nervous as he studied the beach, the quickest route to safety, and then studied the palm trees that established the edge of the safety zone. He chewed on a piece of dark wheat bread, feeling it lump up in his undecided guts. Two Lancers all ready died during the scouting. The trio were not insensitive to Bellah's discomfiture. They too lost their companions, but akin to most Light Stripers, blamed no one for the loss. It came with the job. As a grey-skied morning finally broke through the low hanging cloud cover, the partially rested men, noticed Bellah's changed composure.

"Our personal safety is the primary concern. What disruptions we created in the enemy's camp will place a high price on our heads...."

The men smiled, appreciating their newfound reputation.

"Well, if we be heroes, so be it....Comes with the territory."

An uneasy pause followed, broken by the impatience of the Lancers. "Well," Came a chorus of voices. "What's the plan?"

Bellah outlined both plans which fermented in his mind. To rush though the sands to the safety of the waiting fleet was one option. However, it entailed the fleet being near enough to aid them quickly, for even during the night the Kyykki and the dragons would be searching for the quartet. It also implied 'out running' the enemy to the shore, about two to three miles on foot. Option two called for a trek northward, along the palm tree line of demarcation. Using the same for cover, travel during the daytime became possible. Once beyond the Kyykki's reach, they could more safely cross the sand to the shore. Sooner or later a ship would pick them up. Bellah recognized that neither option provided much chance of survival, especially since their dwindling supplies and loss of the mirrors exacerbated their precarious situation. Bellah allowed the men to debate the merits of each option.

"Bellah, I believe we need to head north...Charging across the sand is suicidal."

Two other heads nodded in tacit agreement.

Bellah responded quietly. "Let's get moving....Who knows how long the Kyykki....." The rest of sentence disappeared in the noise of equipment readjusting.

Late afternoon arrived and disappeared before the surviving Demon Lords regained some sense of control over their blackened hordes. By then, the extensive damage caused by the rampaging dragon was confirmed. The Haafian leadership lay smashed, one dragon dead by Haafian boltsand great numbers of their Kyykki forces randomly dispersed throughout the jungle.

A blue-scaled Demon Master, flanked by another four, took control of the situation. Originally, he placed fifth in the line-of-command. Originally he commanded a detachment of taller Kyykki held as reserves until Pinduala's walls fell. His ferocious Kyykki were to exploit the breach and hold it. He planned on using this tactic to save himself.

"Last day," He began his address to the Demon Masters and Demon Lords. "A few dead Haafians, both our allies and enemies, made us a mess...To save selves we press onward. Using the shaded sand during the daytime and then darkness we'll force march southward to join the rest. The dragons will fly. They will protect us from another attack....We break camp now." He turned and headed southward, followed by the other four.

The forced march began, a march that would end only after Pinduala fell. The blue-scaled Commander sent no dispatches to the forward units and none to Ashuwa. The original plan would continue unchanged. If the reserves could cover for the dead Haafian leadership until after the fall of Pinduala, then what transpired didn't matter.

Until the mid-day's scorching sun halted the massed Kyykki, they marched fast enough to regain their losses of yesterday. With dragons flying reconnaissance above allowing the march to continue unhindered. As soon as the sun disappeared over the palm trees, their forced march recommenced.

Bellah's scouting party moved steadily northward, taking extra precautions against an enemy that totally ignored them. That first evening, they dug into the sand attempting to find drinkable water but to no avail. With empty canteens, the environment became the true enemy.

"We'll rest and then move by night. Its cooler and there's a breeze.". Bellah suggested.

"We gone move to the sea?"

"Don't think we can risk it yet. They'll be looking for us."

A cackle rose from the oldest Lancer. "We killed their officers. Nobody did that afore, I bet....Now, I wants ta live to tell me kids the story."

"As if they'll ever believe you, Ruet."

"Ya jist wait, mister.....When your old enough for family." He snorted in response.

During the next two dawns they plowed steadily through the sand, still heading northward. While the beach remained empty, shadows of enormous size occasionally darkened the beach. The exhausted Lancers raced to the palm trees. Delirium, due to dehydration, became a recurrent visitor, forcing the Lancers to invest valuable energy in fighting 'nothing'. Even so, on the fourth dawn the quartet continued struggling northward, this time in conscious belief that the sea and subsequent rescue lay immediately before them.

An unexpected thunderstorm at mid-day revived the four. With thankful prayers in their hearts, they stood amidst dancing threads of lightning, feeling life spring back as the water drenched them. Then, wringing out their soaked tunics they filled their stomachs and then their canteens. They lay in the drizzle of a brief aftershower, enjoying the cool wetness and the refreshing northbreeze. As they physically improved, their delirium abated. They suddenly realized the safety of the jungle's edge lay over a mile to the west. Wet sand lay about them in every conceivable direction; protection from the dragons and the blistering sun was non-existent, and probably had been for quite some time. Bellah desperately tried to ascertain their present location, but with rain clouds, he got nowhere.

"We're alive,.... but lost." Bellah said flatly.

"One from two ain't the worst." Ruet reminded everyone. "Let's get to the trees before we be spotted."

A few grunts confirmed his advice. The sand, packed by the rain, for once provided a stable surface for walking. They reached the palm trees without further incident and decided to recuperate there. On the morrow, their northward trek must continue. Bellah believed that after that it would be safe to head east to the shore, on the provision that no more shadows spread themselves across the sands.

The softly beginning morn brought more changes for the hungry quartet. After a difficult mid-day's hike, the lofty palm trees gave way to miniature firs and the sand to rocky soil, their once dependable protection thus disappeared. The terrain's elevation increased throughout the morning, but no one recognized the difference until a sharp screeching noise from the north caused them to seek shelter in some rocky clefts. The discomfitting noise continued sporadically throughout the late day. Its source remained unknown. It originated and terminated high in the northern sky. And, whatever 'it' might be, sounded far more powerful than any known dragon.

"From this ledge, all the ground slopes downhill, except if we turn northwesterly." Bellah said after taking a swig of water. "No Haafians ever been here afore. There's nothing similar to this in our learning."

"Big deal!...... We don't learn much 'bout no dragons either." Ruet caustically offered. "But ain't this be what's a scouting party's 'bout, Bellah?"

"I suppose..... And we're the first Haafians to come this far north."

"That does little good for me stomach. And I don't scout much too good if I starve."

"Don't be to bragging overly much. You just might scout better iffen you be dead.....A lot less noise ta scare the animals."

"Quiet!" Bellah whispered. "Watch....over there!" He pointed at the northwestern sky where a huge, even from the distance, bluish-white 'something' careened gracefully through the air.

The 'something's' grace automatically labeled it as 'nondragon'. Its movements resembled that of the large red-tailed hawks that freely roamed most of Haaf. The creature's diving and gentle sweeping motions, grandiose, bold, but far from reckless, mesmerized the four Lancers. As a chilly dusk descended, the men searched the darkening sky for more signs of the huge beautiful creature.

"There's enough dry wood about....If we build the fire under the ledge, we should be safe enough."

"Beat's freezin' to death." Ruet climbed from the ledge, paused, then slowly raised his crossbow. No one had the slightest inclination as to what his target might be, but all immediately prepared for a fight.

TWANG!.............THUNK!

Ruet turned to look down at the alarmed Lancers. He laughed. "I gots us some supper......Jist don't know exactly what kind of animal it be."

"You sure it's dead?"

"Yes,..... O Master Bellah." He said in his most obnoxious tone.

"Then bring it back....Quickly!"

Once roasted, the furry horned creature tasted good, but a little strong, not unlike most wild animals. It stood only three foot tall. With its antlers and thin legs it resembled a miniature Striper. Its thin rust-colored hair and its pointed split hoof showed it to be another type animal altogether. That and a few wild onions provided the best meal in over six dawns. Back when they lived in another world.

Another shrill screech as dawn's initial rays of sunlight battled the darkness, tumbled the men from their rocky ledge shelter. The closeness of the thunderous noise stunned the Lancers. Ruet gingerly peered over the ledge, his crossbow in hand. Long moments passed as he studied the sky, his hands twitching nervously. Then he slowly returned.

"It be circling overhead, 'bout half mile high." He whispered. "We been spotted." He lamented.

"But is that good or bad?" Bellah responded quickly.

He mumbled something and then gazed out of the crevice. "I...I don't know what you mean."

"Think for a moment! Is this creature friend or foe? What have we heard about such a magnificent bird?"

"You referring to the visions of that muddle-headed King. The one who can't hardly walk, let alone think?" Ruet shot back sarcastically.

"You don't believe the King's vision."

"No more den I believes that dragons swim the sea."

"Then you certainly have a better explanation for the creature than I."

"Noper, I sure don't, Bellah." Despondency settled on Ruet's deeply lined face.

Rather than continue the fruitless discussion, Bellah crawled to the ledge. In vain he searched the crimson-purple streaked dawn. The bird, the King's white eagle, had disappeared. Disappointed, he reluctantly left the ledge. "The King's white eagle has disappeared."

"You mean Ruet's seeing things."

"Not at all. The endless sky could be the greatest place to hide."

"Never thought about it that way."

"We're going after the white eagle." Bellah abruptly announced.

"Why?" Demanded Ruet.

"Because it can kill dragons." Bellah's brief answer shocked the trio into action.

Moments later, in the tall dusky shadows of dawn, the Lancers started their journey northward following the stoney ridge. Animals paths intersected with their stumbling enough to teach them to use the paths. Once done, their speed into the unknown realm of the white eagle increased measurably. With the sole exception of the over-eager Bellah, the anxiety levels of the others escalated. Nonetheless they followed, watchful and wary, somehow confident about Bellah's order.

This was and is the nerve-wracking life style scouts claimed as their personal domain. This uniqueness set them apart from other Lancers, other Light Stripers. An inert pride existed within the elite group, a pride fostered by deliberate risk-taking, over-achievement and, more often that their stories might mention, sheer stupidity. As they slowly descended from the ever-rising ridge, these thoughts passed through Bellah's mind.

"Hold!" Ruet called from his position as point man.

"What's the story?"

"Come and looky....at this strange mountain....Gots a hole in its middle.....Akin to a rotted tree."

True to his description, off to the south rose an immense blackened cone. Trees had established growth at its bottom and clumps of pale green weeds cluttered the steep sides. A crevice let the later-day sun to penetrate the hollow core.

"What be this?........ Another part of the King's vision?"

"No." Bellah's voice cracked. "That's a volcano.. ...This is a feature of the Dark Lands......Sometimes these things spit melted rock and ash....That rotten egg-smelling odor at the Wall came from one of those volcanoes."

Ignoring the educational lecture, "Dark Lands" were the only words actually heard by the Lancers.

"We're in the damned one's territory?"

"Probably not...From what I've heard, nothing grows in the Dark

Lands. No animals nor vegetation can exist in the filth there. But that don't mean that we aren't far from it, either."

"Then explain the ...vol...cane...no." Ruet asked.

"Maybe I can't. ...Maybe the white eagle reclaimed part of the damned one's domain....Maybe these death belching cones wear out."

"And maybe the white eagle lives in it." Though Ruet caustically fashioned his remark, Bellah accepted the perception as a realistic possibility.

"Maybe you're right. Even a white eagle has to nest somewhere."

"Does that mean we're going to the volcano?"

"We're still headed towards where we first saw the eagle."

Bellah assumed point duty and headed off down the rocky slope. The others followed at fifty foot intervals keeping their crossbows at the ready. The twisting animal trail lead haphazardly in a northward direction. Soon the ancient volcano dropped from sight. Scrubbish pines established themselves as the primary vegetation on the rocky slope. Hopefully, the mixed pine and fir forest below would provide some security as well as some food. Shortly before entering the forest, the now familiar screeching noise blasted---almost on top of them.

Frantically the Lancers tumbled down the slope, wickedly bouncing off scrub pines and rocks in their desperate rush for shelter. The huge bird's shadow immediately passed over them and continued onward, disappearing to the west. The strange silence which surrounded them at the ridge top quickly returned, except now the elements of surprize and security belonged to the past. The capabilities of the 'white eagle' astounded the men. It roamed the skies as if invisible, exposing itself only to re-assert its authority over earth dwellers.

Only three of the quartet arrived at the safety of the tree line. Ruet angrily moaned from somewhere far up the slope, hidden from their view by a boulder. The trio climbed to rescue him, hacking their way through bramble patches that moments ago they rolled through. Ruet met them as they encountered the boulder, his left leg, below the knee, dangled at a most painful angle. The bone protruded through the skin.

"Lay him down." Bellah quietly ordered.

Against his strenuous protests, the two Lancers managed to land him on his back. Bellah ripped open Ruet's trouser leg and examined the injury. Before Ruet realized what Bellah planned, the bone setting was finished. A yelp of pain, a crunch of bone and it was over.

"I'll wash the wound and splint it once we get back to the tree line."

Around the small campfire, the four conversed concerning further scouting. Ruet's leg required medical treatment beyond what Bellah could offer. Getting him to safety became their new mission.

"Then as the morrow arrives we'll continue down through the forest. Hopefully we'll find water."

"And another of those animals that Ruet killed."

"Sure beats eatin' dees weeds."

The long night proceeded with agonizing slowness, violently interrupted by unidentified screeches, snarls and bellowings which frustrated everyones' attempt at sleep. It did keep those on guard duty awake. In the dimmest of the dawn's light, the Lancers broke camp. Ruet was lashed to a travois, much to his mouthy consternation. Bellah hammered away at the dead pine branches blocking their pathway.

The ancient forest appeared empty, silent now. Its immense brown-barked trunks reached over three hundred feet into the heavens. The heavens were obscured from the Lancers' view with their deeply arching branches. Nothing but a hand's breath deep of ageing pine needles littered the forest's floor, giving Ruet a rather comfortable ride. At what they guessed to be mid-day, Bellah called for a rest. While the slope lessened dramatically, the forest itself continued endless, never-changing, convincingly protecting herself with eternal sameness. Surely, no Haafian ever passed this way afore, not even the legendary Sarg. The joke created a needed diversion from Ruet, whose leg swelled to twice its normal size; whitish puss oozed from the wound.

"This forest be endless....No wonder there's only the huge white eagle.. ..Nothing else could ever survive."

The forest, stretching high into heaven and horizontally, steadfastly refused to answer them. A quiet mysterious atmosphere pervaded these woodlands, a sense of purity, of true peacefulness, a sense of the 'holy', which sent shivers through each of the men. In its unabashed pristiness, this pine forest belonged to something higher than these exhausted Haafian Lancers. As quickly as possible, their journey would recommence.

"Continue down the slope, a stream should be at the bottom." Bellah allowed.

"The word 'should' bothers me...Nothing here is as we know it."

"Yea, I know." He shouldered his bag and grabbed an end of the travois. "Let's move on."

Ruet continued in a groggy daze most of the afternoon, unaware of his degenerating condition. Though no one mentioned it, either Ruet received proper care within another dawn or he'd die. The leg had to be amputated.

Through the dimly lit pine needle covered forest they continued. The direction became less and less clear, for the immense woodland now flattened out into an endless plain. All the Lancers saw were millions of look-alike brown tree trunks, nothing more nothing less; no birds, no animals, no insects. Out of water and food, their speed dropped to a rough stumble, then faltered completely. Physically drained and lost within the confines of this 'supernatural' forest, the trio fell into a trance-like restless slumber. The concept of time fell into oblivion while their spirits struggled to regain strength. The hope which fueled their endeavors just a few short dawns ago, drained away.

When Bellah finally woke, the forest lay in the darkest blackness he'd ever witnessed, though the restful, secure atmosphere still stood in command. For the first time, he felt a breeze, a flitty, teasing wind, but a wind nonetheless. Slowly he felt around in the darkness, attempting to locate the others. Only then did he realize he felt renewed. Thirst and hunger had vanished. He felt strong, but had not the slightest idea as to why.

He rose and fell over the travois, dumping himself on top of Ruet. The wounded Lancer never moved.

"May the Holy One take you into his kingdom." Bellah sighed, realizing that nothing else was to be done. Then he bumped into something soft. His right hand picked it up, Bellah puked when he recognized the 'thing' as Ruet's left leg, his good leg, half eaten. In utter horror Bellah contemplated his loathsome deed. What he knew to be true, he actually could not comprehend, so abhorrent, so unholy. In spiritual anguish he cried out for release from his abomination. Long afterwards, when his searching did not locate the other two Lancers, he again cried out for mercy. Then he fell into an exhausted slumber.

When he awoke, he had no strength. An empty stomach blurred his thinking. The mid-day sun shot hazy shafts of yellowish light to the needle carpeted floor. Using all his strength, Bellah pulled his sword, rested the blade against his chest, and fell forward. As he died, Bellah acknowledged a 'touch' from beyond. The honor of the Lancers of the Light Striper would continue without blemish.

Chapter 6

For two single moon cycles the dragons at Haaf North flew infrequently. Their tactical forays east proved incoherent. So read the reports received by the King. The dragons kept the entrenched Light Stripers on constant alert. Totally aware of the Light Striper's weaponry, they delighted in teasing the machiners. The Light Striper's response, one backed by Baste, was to tunnel towards the city, placing crossbows in underground bunkers.

Identical reports reached Warmaker just as he placed the next piece of his invasion plan into operation: the transporting of twenty Haafian 'turncoats' to Haaf North. Their arrival coincided with Warmaker's command for three hundred dragons to attack the Light Striper's battlements and then turn to attack across the bay, destroying the fishing hamlets and securing most of the coastline. One hundred dragons were to attack the coastline first. In the immediate confusion, Warmaker expected the Haafians to arrive in the port, use one of the freighters docking there and sail west towards the Dark Water, all without any interference and without the Haafians noticing.

The dragons attacked late in the afternoon, forcing the Light Stripers to face the blinding sun. As soon as scouts noticed the blackened sky, the War Tubas sounded. The tunnelers, their efforts incomplete, rushed back to the ramparts, readying their weapons.

Jed, Yganak's aide-de-camp, quickly thanked the Holy One for his release from 'paper work' duty. With the King requesting Yganak's appearance in Krabo, along with Treh and the two other survivors, Jed reluctantly received the command. A recovered Deep Owl and Qill had responsibility for the second rank of crossbows while Raff continued faithfully in his specialty; protecting the rear.

The dragons used a new formation, attacking at three levels. The first flight, flying in dense order, flew twenty feet off the ground. This allowed their fire a greater opportunity to cremate the Haafians. The second group, almost two hundred in number, flew at several hundred feet in an open order. From past experience, the Light Stripers knew these dragons waited to exploit weaknesses exposed by the Light Stripers. The third group, never seen before, flew well above the usable range of the most powerful crossbows.

"What about them?" Jed asked Deep Owl. "Think they're heading inland?"

"No, they don't have any reinforcements. The further inland they go, the more the advantage is ours, especially with their slow speed."

"Anything that can outrun a Striper isn't slow."

"I was thinking about those Istelle birds...Remember Treh's..."

"Suppose you think about knocking a few dozens of the damn dragons from the air." Jed muttered angrily. "In a few breaths we'll be able to fire."

"And this time they'll not bounce through the bulwarks. The stakes and ribbon wire will gut them long before they can reach us."

"But we've not been attacked by this many afore."

"Commander, you're just going to have to learn to trust us Yldans.... Its actually not that difficult, you know." Qill smiled and turned away. "Prepare to fire the bleach canisters!" He paused and looked at the oncoming dragons. "Fire!"

In soaring graceful arcs, sixty ten-stone weight burlap canisters of pasty bleach charged towards the oncoming dragons.

"Fire!"

Another round jockeyed through the air before the first round located any targets.

"Crossbows...Fire!" Jed yelled and swung his arm, signaling those on the flanks.

Like a horizontal windstorm, the bolts pierced the air, some spinning ribbon wire behind them. Others, launched to intercept the second group, whistled as their deadly serrated blades burst open.

Half a breath later, the skirmish began. The dragons in the second rank, however, gained altitude and flew onward. They turned, banking south, following the bay's curvature. Then barely two hundred feet before the first bulwarks, the bleach, bolts and dragons collided. The impact tossed mortally wounded dragons over earthworks with uncontrolled, unfocused flames darting everywhere. Others touched down and lumbered in to confront the crossbows. Over half, painfully decorated with the pasty bleach, careened into other out-of-control dragons. Savagely wounded dragons littered the staked fields in front of the bulwarks.

The few survivors swiftly ascended, gathering with the second rank, refusing to regroup for another attack, even though the Haafians saw Demon Lords riding the dragons. At this moment, between a victory cry and reloading, a second low flying group approached the bulwarks from the northwest. Behind them, but partially hidden from Haafian view, another congregation of dragons quietly landed within the desolate confines of Haaf North.

"Damn." Jed cursed under his breath. "Reload! Fire when ready!"

A few desperate rounds sped towards the incoming flight. Being juvenile dragons, they attacked with abandon and recklessness. Their voracity swept the few survivors through the first line of bulwarks by sheer momentum. Many died of broken necks as they slammed into the crossbows. Scorching everything before them, a final few cleared the second line of defense. None reached the third line. Their surviving Demon Master riders, screaming loathsome oaths, died unquietly as pincushions.

Reloading came automatically, the Light Stripers waiting another onslaught from the congregation which entered Haaf North. The wounded manned the engines, while others struggled to repair five obliterated engines in the first line. There, most effort went to removing the dragon carcasses.

"Qill, what's the count?"

"We have some thirty five dead, three times as many wounded."

"Get them on the waggons! Send a dispatch to Raff for reinforcements."

As Jed turned around, he saw the dragon's newest strategy: smoldering fires dotted the coastline. Every fishing village sent dark smoke into the sky. Raff's rear guard launched a last long-range volley at the disappearing congregation. With a vengeance, he cheered as a few disemboweled dragons collided with the blue-green waters of the bay. Others joined in.

"What do you make of this, Deep Owl?" Qill asked as the violence of the skirmish settled.

"I'm not sure. We've never battled these 'babies' afore. They're too reckless and inexperienced,........ but exactly the type I'd use to penetrate a heavily fortified line."

"Just my sentiments." Jed added as he dismounted and climbed up the parapet. "Except, the order of flight made little sense. The penetrating attack arrived after the second and third waves passed....Usually it's the opposite, so the following ranks could take advantage of the hole punched by the others."

"Agreed."

"So how do we explain this?"

"As a simple diversion....Look at the burning villages. That's the original target, not our line....."

"Only partially correct, Jed." Qill interjected thoughtfully. "Two diversions ....Remember that congregation flying into the city...The suicide assault by the 'babies' happened at the same time...I doubt if it's a coincidence."

Jed rubbed his stubbled chin. "Yes, something else. Something bigger is happening......Quick, send mirror signals to Haaf West and Haaf South!"

"You don't think..."

"Why not? Their flight around the perimeter of the bay will put them directly inline to assault both cities...It's the next logical step to securing more territory. .....We become isolated if they succeed."

"Would you be serious."

"I am quite serious, Deep Owl." Jed said bluntly. "Pinduala is under attack. Think about it for a moment."

Deep Owl paced the planked floor of the frontline fortification, his mind over-working. "Then we must capture their base. If we capture Haaf North, then the dragons are isolated."

Jed grinned, a bit of a savage smirk on his face. "They haven't realized we can take the offensive, have they?"

"Wait a moment, you two." The Yldan shaman stated authoritatively. "This is no little unplanned skirmish. Once you re-conquer the city, you have to keep it.....We'll meet after supper." He left to visit the wounded.

That evening the King chose to introduce Jelkio to his court. That is, to the regulars attending the specially called High Council meeting. Even Treh and the other two survivors were put off until the morrow, but as heroes who first witnessed the Tath Istelles, they were hurriedly extended a special invitation. The entire Church Hierarchy gathered as had those few nobles not participating in the New Knights. The merchants and craftsman, as well as the new 'wealthy poor', all self-serving as usual, also demanded an audience with Jelkio. Dreams of fantastic new opportunities lay before them.

However, Jelkio had no intention of obeying any King who didn't have the common decency to request her presence properly. "I am not some piece of property.......Just who does this King without a name think he is?.....Our god without a name?" Jelkio huffed her way through the heavy furniture on their fourth floor suite. The next rooms were relegated to Rux and Nadre. Oros and Kofe occupied rooms at the rear of the High Council building, even so, they clearly understood each Tath word that blistered through the hallways.

"Even so, the banquet is in your honor....The first Tath to ever visit Haaf."

"And it should have been Queen Sjura." She angrily rejoined.

"And she'll be coming as soon as possible....And Tiello."

"I know!" Her voice instantly switched with her attitude, soaring high. "My Queen and my best friend.....Everyone's alive!...The Queen is expecting!"

Nooy laughed.

"What's so funny?"

Nooy's bronze face went white. "Can't tell you." He muttered, his face staring into the rug.

"Oh," She smiled at him, not so cutely. "You're imagining the two in bed, aren't you...?" Then she laughed also. "Never thought the day would come either...About time we had an heir to the throne.....Then SHE could give this "KING" something to think about."

"I'm not sure this King will live that long." Rux dryly commented from across the room. Through the open window he acquainted Nadre with the geography of Krabo's extensive shopping district. Her eyes got too large for Rux's comfort.

"I'm still not going." Jelkio reiterated. "The ignorant bum deserves a lesson in proper manners."

"Now you're talking about all men." Nadre eagerly chirped in.

"Seems my sense of humor is becoming part of you." Rux commented as he kissed her.

"It's much more than that and you know it." She whispered in his ear. Her teasing rudely ended as a stern knocking shook the wooden door on its iron hinges. No one bothered responding. The knocks repeated, much louder.

"Come in, Jabbi....and bring the Captain and Etan with you." Rux yelled at the door.

"Would you care to unlock it?"

"I certainly would." Jelkio answered in pretentious sounding Haaf. "This quarters is mine."

A huge, desperate sigh originated from behind the door. "My dear Jelkio."

"You have that much correct, 'King'."

"Please be kinder, I have an excruciating headache."

She quickly released the lock. Slowly, passively, the King made his entrance. His frail body reminded Jelkio of a man twice his age. Her heart softened. "I shall, your Highness." She said temperately.

"I understand you've refused the 'stuffy' ceremony in the Council Hall." The previous evening, with reports of Tath and Istelles, Sarg and Treh's tail, the old man simply listened. Now and then he posed a few oblique questions, but allowed nothing to indicate his true demeanor. Today, because of his sarcastic remark concerning the sideshow in the Council Hall, Jelkio discovered herself warming up to the King.

"I'm merely thankful that we both recognize the truth." She spoke in slow careful Haafian, accenting words properly, lest the King consider her vulgar.

The wizened King smiled, a sad understanding smile. "I have no need for sideshows either, especially as it would place you in a position where everyone can beg, borrow or steal from you."

"Then," Jelkio paused, confused. "Why was I summoned to appear?"

"It's called 'royal protocol'....Damned royal protocol...I have a bunch of old flunkies who instruct me as to what is supposed to be proper....... However," He coughed loudly, an expression of deep pain shot across his face....... "They're so rigid in their interpretations that even with such a monumental event as the acknowledgement of another nation, yours, my dear Jelkio, they dare not think of what 'your' royal protocol might be...... ....Anyway, I dismissed the whole obnoxious lot of them.......That's why I'm tardy....."

"I didn't......"

"Quite all right my dear Jelkio." The King smiled much broader now. "The flunkies are busy explaining their failure to those gathered for tonight's absolute nothing." He almost laughed. "Including the pompous clerics."

"Please, your Highness, sit for a while."

"Are you sure you want the company of a dying man?"

Jelkio rapidly changed shades. So did the others; stunned by the King's forthrightness. For a long moment, silence occupied everyone's thoughts.

"Come on now!" The King stated as he propped up his feet on a large cushion. "It's simply the truth. The Holiness Code demands we state the truth so we can be free.....To the point, the goon squad Ashuwa bought to be my so-called physicians have aged me quite far beyond middle-age.....I really am an old man...Nothing can be done about it."

Jelkio took a seat on the padded couch next to the King. "I'm sorry." She sadly spoke while holding his hand.

"I appreciate that, your tenderness and concern....It will be needed in the New Era."

"You promised to forget those words." Oros spoke from across the room, his pudgy fingers wrapped meticulously about a metal tankard of ale.

"The King may change his mind." Nadre shot a menacing look at the bulging priest.

"I can see why the Holy One wedded you to Rux." With this remark the King efficiently made an ally with the strong-willed woman. "Now you must listen."

All those in the room, regardless of what they thought, slowly formed a circle about the monarch. Oros grabbed the first chair for himself, while the husbands first seated their wives. The Captain, Jabbi and Etan slid a carved benched across the thickly carpeted floor. The King's words darkened the atmosphere considerably.

"Now then." The King thrust his 'official voice' upon his friends. "I'm not up for any game playing." He stared at Oros and then at the Yldans.

"Any reason you pick on just us three." Oros said.

"My 'kingly' prerogative."

"Just thought I'd ask, didn't realize you'd be so touchy." Oros muttered.

"This is the end of the age. How can it not be? Our knowledge is rendered obsolete by my visions. Istelles are my White Eagles. Taths might become our newest allies against Ashuwa.....And don't pretend you haven't heard the word before....The Kyykki have stretched their borders, surrounding Pinduala...... and dragons roost at Haaf North. Sarg becomes a ruler with a beautiful Tath Queen.... so Vosnob assures me, a 'new' Vosnob, mind you........Another country where the Dark Lands are supposed to be...And Tath, a country far different from ours lies just north of the Dark Lands.....Excuse me for repeating myself..." He suddenly began coughing. His handkerchief spotted blood expectorated from his throat. Then he commenced to wheezing and lost his breath. He fainted. Just as suddenly he regained his normal self, sat up, continuing his speech. "This age of the Kyykki against the Haafians is over. The world has grown immensely larger these last ten or so double moons......It won't retreat....Furthermore, there is another god involved.... Mysterious, independent type...and refuses any name or title..."

"That's how it's always been, King." Jelkio said. "With a name the mystery dissolves and...perhaps, some of the power."

"Quite true." Oros agreed. "Even 'the Holy One' isn't a name, though we tend to think otherwise.....But your point is well made, in spite of my personal reservations, the New Era is well upon us.....With a new people to populate the world..."

"What 'new' people?" Rux interrupted.

"Those whose parents are Taths and Haafians, dummy." Jabbi interjected.

"Still, we think in too narrow terms......We've begun an age of radical exploration, beginning with the Quest."

"Yes, Oros, we all remember your Quest....And all it really accomplished was Rux and Nadre's marriage.....Which is something I did not ever believe could happen....Congratulations

Rux smiled at his dark-haired wife. She gently kissed his cheek. Then he rose and bowed towards the King, Nadre quickly followed his lead. The King painfully nodded in reply.

"And congratulations to you, Jelkio and Nooy. Though I confess I knew neither of you until last evening...........However, Nooy's reputation for abducting a woman supposedly guarded by the Church Guard did precede him,........ much to their chagrin." He paused, wheezing for breath. "I'm thankful Oros took upon himself the burden of establishing morality in these relationships." The two husbands blushed while their wives sat even taller than before. The King's insightful charm wasn't wasted.

A subdued knock brought the proceedings to an immediate halt.

"Bring the supper in." Jabbi called to the door.

The heavy wooden door opened slowly, the slightly built maid using her rump to push it open. She carried a large tray covered with the usual white cloth. Just as she pivoted to enter the chamber, four armed men, dressed as Church Guards, burst through the door. The maid screamed, slipping to the floor, a dagger plunged in her breast. Slicing and hacking at anything in their way, the death-spewing quartet rushed for the King.

Etan yelled and kicked the door shut. The Captain stood, a formidable obstacle between the intruders and the King. Jelkio threw herself on top of the King, while Nooy stood before her, dagger ready. The Captain deflected the first strike with his arm, then dropped to his knee, capturing the leading invader. A no-quarter-given wrestling match ensued. Meanwhile, two invaders toppled Kofe and Jabbi as they pressed closer to the King. Rux cut loose just in time to save Nadre from a sabre thrust. Nooy took a cut below his ribs and then imbedded his dagger through the attacker's throat. Simultaneously, an attacker behind him tossed Jelkio over his shoulder and headed for the door. The remaining Church guard hacked the King with his broadsword. Etan, grabbing the maid's serving tray, deflected the first blow from the huge fellow carrying Jelkio. The kidnapper never delivered another as Kofe and Nooy skewered him from two directions. He ungainly dropped to the floor on top of the screaming Jelkio. Rux ended the life of the King's assailant by eliminating his armored-covered head. Oros terminated the wrestling match by whacking the Church Guard on the head, denting his tankard.

Hearing confusion in the hallway, Jabbi rushed for the nearest crossbow while Etan readied his sword. Nooy rushed to his wife and pulled her free. She screamed and then fainted when she noticed the blood dripping from his tunic. The King's butchered body lay on the couch, his stomach sliced through, his left arm splintered by the hacking. Oros gripped the King's lifeless hand as he offered prayers for the dead and wounded.

"Let us in!" Yelled a strong voice from the hallway. "There are intruders throughout the Council Hall!....The King needs protected!"

Unexpectedly, they burst through the door. Vaal, in the lead, almost received a bolt for his efforts. Jabbi's bolt thudded into the door.

"What the.....!"

"Your invaders reached us first.....The King.... is..... dead." Was all the Captain managed.

Rux shook his head, his arm gently wrapped about his sobbing wife. "Three are dead. We have a prisoner......The room is secure."

"Take no other prisoners!" Vaal angrily commanded the squad behind him.

Angered by the grizzly scene, the squad of Church Guards responded with a terrible vengeance as they rushed back down the staircase.

"Get a physician for Nooy!" Kofe roared at no one in particular. "He's bleeding to death."

Before the next dawn, Vosnob presided over a meeting of the twenty three Elders. The unbelievable news created a downcast atmosphere, in spite of the holy effervescence which still illuminated the secret chamber. Painfully, both on a professional and personal level, Oros lead the Elders through the ritual of mourning. While it served to focus the twenty three, it provided no relief from the shock and the grief.

After several moments of personal prayer, Vosnob stood to speak. "The King is dead." He said tersely, barely holding his own emotions in check. "He lives no more. Nor is there a new King ready for coronation.....Ilty has some other information to share." He dumped back into his armchair.

Ilty, at the far end of the table slowly stood to speak. She wiped her eyes; her blue apron streaked from her tears. "We knew that Ashuwa bought many Haafians....The southern territory finally announced its independence from the north, though it has no army to back its claim...We need to prepare for war with these traitors...for the murder of our King." She stopped to wipe her eyes again. "Our spies in the South, especially the Fluz Marsh territory are keeping us abreast with the latest news....So far, they don't know the King is dead."

"Neither do most of our own people." Baste bluntly critiqued.

"Quite true, my friend." Ilty responded softly.

"I apologize Ilty." Baste replied politely, then immediately continued. "The old days are leaving us....too quickly. We are rather unprepared for the new...." He paused, searching vainly for the correct wording.

"The 'New Era' is how our late King described what is coming. We are, so he truly believed, in the midst of the birthing of the 'New Era'.....Our responsibility is to guide, to control, to grasp the opportunity to provide for a more secure future than the present."

"Then you believe, my fat friend, that 'Ashuwa' must be exterminated, not simply fenced in."

"Yes, Kloshic, the damned one must be exterminated."

Baste stomped his heavy fist on the oaken table. "Dreamers! We cannot kill an immortal...a god....Even the 'gifted' will not best Ashuwa."

"Don't break the table." Jabbi interjected. "There's enough things which require fixing all ready.....However, returning to your former statement, I will politely disagree. A god without a people will perish, drifting off into the 'nowhere'. Our responsibility is to deny Ashuwa any followers."

"That's easier said than accomplished." Vosnob said. "Yet it is, in my judgement, the route we embark upon. It can't be any more difficult than relocating the entire nation."

"With that you've explained the mystery of the Holy One's work." The Chaplain from Pinduala barracks declared as he rose. "My friends, our prayers are answered...What other explanation can exist for this transfigured, transformed Vosnob? I understand that the Holy One obviously ....."

"One opinion...is one opinion." Oros cautioned his friend. "We better not allow ourselves to become carried away with the King's murder....Let's put him in perspective. He initiated this 'New Era' with his vision. This lead to him being deliberately incapacitated--the damned one's revenge--. However, before his death, the 'New Era' had open with the Quest I have yet to finish, but was actualized by Treh's scouting patrol and Sarg's venture into a new world--Tath.....All the damned one stopped was our King....He has no power to stop a divine vision, nor a new future."

"Even so, good fat friend, you have to allow a divine space for Vosnob. The Holy One does absolutely nothing without meaning, without purpose."

"Even if the receiver isn't ready to believe that truth." Blue Turtle added from his corner.

"It's just so wonderful to be surrounded with such supporting friends." Vosnob muttered.

The Elders divided into smaller groups for breaking the fast and further discussions. Within these informal confines an outline for the future, for their survival, slowly came into existence. Elders reporting from around the nation guided them through the present dilemmas. All future planning began on the current reality. These truths, irregardless of their painfulness, prevented any ill-conceived ideas from rooting. As a bleak mid-day burst in upon the Elders, Vosnob called for a final reporting and subsequent vote.

Boisterous noises, much dissension and chair scraping acknowledged Vosnob's request to commence the afternoon session. But it did not imply that Vosnob's request would be complied with in the near future. A huge fist slammed the table. No one escaped its vibrations. The refocused Elders quickly turned to Baste, the erstwhile 'slammer'.

"Shall we come to order." Baste commanded softly.

Everyone immediately acquiesced. Baste's penchant for doing all things properly brought a calming orderliness to the group. The clearing sky and moderate temperature helped establish a more positive atmosphere. A flurry of air followed by a dusting of dry fog signaled another arrival of the Chaplain from Pinduala. Being that his foremost responsibility rested in his presence with the Light Stripers at the besieged port, he was continually in-and-out throughout the morning.

"I'll receive your latest update afore we begin planning for the future." Vosnob said to the lean Elder.

"Thank you, Vosnob." He began. "Not much has changed. The port is surrounded on three sides. The Lancers are within the confines of the city, manning the machines. Ellom loses one to two ships per dawn to the dragons, but supplies are adequate. The Kyykki attempted to invade further south, but faltered because of the climate as well as their stupidity."

"Your voice tells me you haven't exactly told us everything." Kloshic observed.

"Quite true....It seems that Ayhn's last scouting patrol exposed a massive force of Kyykki and dragons, all camouflaged by the jungle. ..The Lancers attacked them on the edge of the jungle. The ignorant beasts tore across the hot sands of the shore. The toad-faces never quit their attack, as if they were leaderless...The whole division self-destructed, except for the fifty or so dragons...These caused numerous casualties."

"What else?"

"Two and three dawns later, signaling mirrors from far north of this battle told of a raid that eliminated several traitorous Haafians responsible for this Kyykki force....The scouting party then disappeared, presumed missing.... That's how I logged it all."

"Then, for the moment, Pinduala is secure?"

"For the present, your assumption is correct."

"How dangerous is the southern rebellion?" Vosnob quickly changed course to keep up with the time table.

"We've covered this territory thoroughly all ready, Vosnob."

"I have a responsibility to insure a common understanding of the present situation. With the Chaplain leaving and returning because of his other responsibilities and with a few other Elders traveling to ascertain the validity of some reference points, I make few assumptions about what we've covered." Tightly reined anger tinged Vosnob's words.

"The southern rebellion is a mish-mash of the usual malcontents, lead by a number of 'pale ladies' and promises of ruling over the North if they follow the way of the flying dragon."

"You mean the way of Ashuwa?"

"That name is unknown to the swampers. To them its not even heresy. They simply view the dragon's way as easy opportunity. The flying dragon promises riches and power and the death of the merchants, the clergy, the royalty and the bureaucrats."

"Haaf South is under attack from the dragons of Haaf North. The dragons learned to keep a respectable distance. However, any Light Striper force leaving the city's defenses will be easy prey to the dragons." An Elder from the besieged port added. "But no one in the city sees any need to worry about the swampers.

"True, however the southerners neither have a force to send northward nor can dragons delineate between Haafians. Like Pinduala, the situation is that of stalemate." Baste, whose homeplace lay in the swamp's fringe, affirmed.

"We are attacked, viciously, on all fronts and I'm hearing 'stalemate'. Please, someone, explain this. Personally, I only see losses, tremendous loses and open rebellion.." Doesn't a 'stalemate' indicate an equality of forces and determination?...... Is this the New Era...'stalemate'?" Ilty's comments were launched from her heart. She knew the country had new circumstances to deal with, and Haaf was not ready for it all.

"I quite agree, Ilty." Said Vosnob. "These stalemates are but temporary, neither side will allow for a non-victory. Even if we decide for a war by attrition. ....Listen to me. I offer a proposal..... Let the present stalemate continue. It prevents the damned Ashuwa from opening another front. Instead he'll pour countless Kyykki and dragons against his current targets, hoping that sheer volume will accomplish our destruction...... From my perspective, I think Ashuwa firmly believes that if one city falls, his blackened hordes will rush through, plundering all of Haaf."

"He has no concept of secondary defenses?"

"He does, my friend, but those Demons he raised to lead his blackened hordes cannot. Such conceptualizing is well beyond their abilities. That's the primary rationale behind his bribing Haafians to serve him."

"Like Krucik?"

"Unfortunately, and those Haafians killed by Ayhn's missing scouting party." Vosnob answered before plunging into his plan. "Now, with the stalemate's deliberate continuance, which is our secret, we pursue two other targets.. "First target; all traitorous Haafians. Monetary rewards will be given to those who report and help convict Haafians guilty of treason and heresy. This will keep the opportunists very busy and traitors very inactive. Those found guilty will be exiled to the Dark Lands."

"Vosnob, get serious."

"I am serious....All convicted traitors will be given a long rope to descend the Wall....I'm sure Ashuwa has a perfect reward for his abject failures." Vosnob raised his hand, inviting any comments or rebuttals. Actually, he wished for some, making such impacting policies bothered him. Part of him recognized it as the price for his divine rejuvenation, another part of him simply wanted to vanish. To his consternation, not one Elder responded. "Am I to believe that the Holy One has not influenced any other Elder to comment!"

"I comment." Oros gasped as he gulped his tankard empty. "Good plan." He smiled cutely, his beady eyes disappearing under the fleshy folds of his high cheeks. "Now relax."

Vosnob shook his head and sighed. The Elders laughed.

"I suppose I'll have to offer you the second..."

"You certainly do...We don't have any desire to be idle."

"Shut up Oros!"

"Yes, My Lord!" And he brought his tankard to the table with a resounding bang, splashing the final gulp of ale across the table. Laughter once again resounded in the chamber. The man-mountain cleric's sense of absurdity brought welcome respite. Even the perfectionistic Baste smiled. During the lighthearted interim, the Chaplain decorated the Elders' chamber with dry fog as he continued his rounds with the city-under-siege. As Vosnob raised his hand to signal a restarting of the meeting, a smoking and singed Chaplain returned.

"Stupid old man!" He muttered, not realizing that everyone was within easy earshot.

"What stupid old man are you referring to?" Several of the Elders responded simultaneously.

"Wygga....Wygga....Wygga....Who else?" The Chaplain sighed, exasperated from his last visit. "Wygga and another of his damnable inventions."

"Care to tell us about it?" Ilty queried, more mischief than genuine curiosity in her mind.

The Chaplain ignored the request, concentrating on brushing tar balls from his singed white hair. Then other Elders joined with Ilty in demanding a full report of his 'experience' with the newest of Wygga's inventions. With his plethora of ingenious inventions and positively uningratiating slandering of the Haafian language, Wygga created an atmosphere of awe within several circles in Haaf, the Elders being one.

"Tell us about Wygga's newest invention." Ilty called once again, teasing him with her long eyelashes.

"Quit that, Ilty...You're a happily married woman."

"I didn't think you knew....I have no more secrets." She professed to swoon, then laughed.

"I do owe you one, my dearest." He fumbled about, face blanched white by Ilty's mannerisms. He forgot she worked the tavern.

"Go on!"

"Yes, My Lord.....Vosnob...I believe."

Vosnob reached his hands towards the iridescent ceiling. "Dear Holy One," He loudly complained. "Why me?"

A few snickers rebounded the chamber, while others settled themselves for a more serious time. Vosnob began regaining control over the less-than-serious Elders. "Undoubtedly, we'll all have to listen to the entire 'Saga of Wygga, part three hundred, before I'll be allowed to introduce my second component to end the stalemate."

"Very true." Ilty said, almost thoughtfully.

"Very well then." The Chaplain threw off his smokey traveling robe. "Wygga suggested that dragons might be their own worst enemies. He witnessed them shooting fire into everything the machiners zipped through the air...Even simple, harmless bales of straw burst into fireballs whenever one soared near a dragon. Therefore, so Wygga reasoned, we might kill a few more if we gave them something more lethal to blow their fired breath at."

"Fair enough." Said an interested Baste. "What did our 'hero' concoct?"

"He dipped air-filled skins in tar. Once the tar coagulated, he launched the ball towards the dragons...It worked too well....Once the dragon perceived the object, the damned thing blasted it with fire.... This ignited the tar and because the skin exploded....something about hot air expanding, I didn't understand it all...Anyway, the skin-and-tar ball exploded into large fragments of sticky, burning tar. These landed on other dragons, causing them horrendous pain...Flying out-of-control, one dropped too close to me"

...Wygga, however, just said, "It be a funny hapinin."

A hearty round of applause greeted the termination of the Chaplain's story. Uncharacteristically, the Chaplain bowed to all present.

"To my second point...for your serious consideration." Vosnob no longer cared to ascertain the Elders' readiness. He continued. "We shall reinforce Sarg with as many Light Stripers as possible for two purposes. The first is to establish a secure base within Ashuwa's own backyard. This will throw him off balance. The second purpose is to support any and all assistance the Taths might provide...I do believe that the clumsy dragons stand little chance against the Istelles..." He grew quieter at the end.

Jabbi immediately yanked out the maps which Sarg produced and hung them from the glowing marbled wall. The route of Sarg's original party, the volcanoes observable from the Yldan village, the interior of the damned one's temple headquarters, as well as the route through the Endless Valley were shared with the Elders. The final map provided a glimpse of the Paradise Valley, with special notations in the upper right corner concerning the construction of the main fortress as well as the outer ones.

Driven by curiosity the Elders rushed to examine the maps. They proved almost unbelievable as they described lands and countries which weren't supposed to exist, especially the small map of Tath, a country clearly north of the Dark Lands. Discussions began in earnest as to how the Light Striper could reach Paradise Valley, especially with its isolation. It was surrounded by the hideous environment of Ashuwa's, including the Dark Water and blocked by the dragons' capture of Haaf North.

Vosnob and Oros talked quietly while everyone perused the maps. Both men sketched out possible invasion routes. Soon Baste entered the discussion as did Jabbi and Kloshic. Almost magnetically, the preliminary planning dialogue pulled all of the Elders into a concentrated session. Within the quiet atmosphere, their wondrous talents and skills composed a 'collective' invasion plan. Recognizing a unanimous consensus, Vosnob expunged the idea of voting from his mind.

"This then is our plan: Jabbi will, with the aid of the Captain, continue the administration of Haaf, the Elders from the southern parts will guide the Church Knights in ferreting out the traitors and instilling the fear of the Holy One back into the population. Kloshic will administer that component. That will be cause for Ashuwa to worry; as his friends just 'disperse'."

"But not enough to end any stalemate."

"No, but neither is the southern uprising any more than a diversion away from Ashuwa's plan to conquer the Haaf Bay area."

"Go on, old man." Oros drawled. "I'se bees gittin hun-gary."

A number of Elders winced at the horrendous accent; Vosnob frowned. Ilty tossed a tankard, missing the huge priest by the thumb's breath.

"Sarg's mapping is commended. From it we gain entrance into Paradise Valley, but a difficult one. A Light Striper expeditionary force, led by Rux and Oros and Captained by Jed will move into the forest north of Haaf North, utilizing the waggon path. Once the route is well established, an outpost will be maintained at Krucik's old brownstone castle…..at least what's left of it. Meanwhile, five of the younger Elders will translocate to Sarg's castle. Their mission, with or without the assistance of the Taths, is to secure a southern path connecting Paradise Valley with our forces. Reinforcing Sarg is half of the goal. We must have a secure supply route from the bay to Paradise Valley. To provide a diversion, the fleet from Poldu will sail northward. Hopefully the dragons……." Vosnob's speech wandered off. He sat down to rousing applause from the others.

"Then, the Holy One be with us. Let us conquer these damned forces of darkness!....Let the 'New Era' begin with truth, justice and wisdom!" Oros grandly announced. His fellow Elders shook their heads, ignoring his stilted posturing.

"But let love and compassion be within our hearts at all times." Ilty added with a serious smile.

Vosnob looked up at the standing Elders, a sense of satisfaction, ignited within his heart, a smile upon his face. "Let's get moving."

After four dawns of incessant attacks, Pinduala's dragon carcass-and-sunken-ship clogged harbor began impacting life within the besieged port. Supplies took an extra two dawns to reach the stone warehouses located just off the wharf. The wounded spent two extra dawns awaiting release to the Outer Islands for recovery. High-finned sharks roamed the inner harbor and docking areas as never before, searching for chunks of dragon and everything else that moved in the water. The thirty foot sea monsters attacked smaller sailing craft. Captain Ellom assigned four ships to tow the carcasses to deep water, but the Light Striper's annihilation of the dragons far exceeded their capabilities.

Diseases from rotting dragon hulks took a toll on the population. Even Yldan shamans had no experience with the malignant gasses and perverse fumes emanating from the beasts. The diseases traveled faster than wildfire throughout the city. A new proverb reverberated about: 'A live dragon is better than a dead one.' The deplorable truth of the proverb could be seen in those who bore the puss-filled raised sores on their skin. The black patches, if not continually lanced, rapidly bore holes into the bone, causing death by hemorrhaging. Haafians coughed up vile-smelling mucous which drained their strength. The infirmary swelled beyond capacity within four dawns of the first attack. Now the sick and wounded occupied the chapel and two of the stone barracks. Ayhn placed the port under strictest quarantine.

"We're stalemated!....... Shit!" Tubt muttered.

"That also means the Kyykki ain't going nowhere either." The Chaplain calmly replied. "So, maybe that's what we're supposed to be doing."

"Care to explain yourself?"

"If the toad-faces are concentrated here, if their responsibility is to devastate Pinduala, and if this is all the strength they can muster, we're doing quite well...... Furthermore, being occupied here, they aren't attacking D'Ka."

"Makes sense, I guess." Tubt murmured quickly. He glanced down at the nearly empty market place, then back up the alley. There he studied a Light Striper squad hacking another fallen dragon into transportable pieces. "Quite ingenious, don't you think Chaplain?"

The thin wizened cleric turned. "Yes, the Kyykki eat anything we toss at them, even 'bleached-out' dragon meat.....notice how they never understand.... even when the deception is repeated and repeated.....I'd almost believe their operating from a plan Ashuwa designed eons ago."

"Their stupidity bears that out, it's been two dawns since we tumbled the last demon off a dragon.....Just them taller Kyykki. Doesn't make a lot of sense."

The pair spun about catching Ayhn as he rapidly ascended the staircase. He carried a 'long tube' in his hand. "Can't quite remember how I survived without this wondrous devise."

"You mind explaining your outlandish remark."

"We're not battling against persons, but perversions rendered by Ashuwa.... They are soulless, hulks made only to destroy. The Kyykki are valueless to their god, except for the fact that they do have the potential to secure his goals.....And if there are enough of them, they might succeed."

"Thanks for the warning." Tubt's facial expression tinged with sarcasm. "Maybe I finish my 'last will'."

"Can I have your two storey house?" Ayhn seriously asked as he studied the horizon through the 'long tube'.

"Will you two shape up!" The dominating voice of Vosnob caught them by surprise. For once he truly looked distinguished, probably because a new uniform was imposed upon him, one he would wear for the King's funeral a few dawn's hence.

"What an impression you make! Maybe enough to catch you a wife!" The Chaplain returned.

"Just how did you get here?" A worried looking Tubt demanded. A Tubt determined to receive an answer.

"I wouldn't believe me if I told you the truth."

"Try me!"

"I thought my way here... I thought to myself, 'I want to be on the Chaplain's rooftop in Pinduala. I want to be there in two breaths."

Tubt leered at Vosnob with a most inscrutable stare. "You tell a very poor lie, Vosnob." He said soberly.

"I did not expect you to believe me, remember?"

"You aren't supposed to lie."

"He didn't lie." The Chaplain said. "I believe the man, after all who knows what gifts are disposed to this 'transformed' old man."

"Yes, that could make sense....But don't expect me to tell this to another...I'll not be threatened for lying."

Ayhn fixed his vision on an innermost grouping of the taller Kyykki. He missed the entire 'Vosnob' episode. Within a cluster of the taller Kyykki stood a dozen long-robed demons thrashing their clawed hands about wildly. "They're only a half mile away. A well-aimed bolt could ruin their damned conference."

"Well, Lancer Commander, get it done." Vosnob smiled at the startled Ayhn.

"Yes,...yes Sir!"

"Lighten up, Ayhn."

"Yes.." He suddenly realized an incongruity. "How did you arrive here.....?"

"You really don't wish to know." Tubt quickly interjected, rescuing his friend.

"What's happening out there?"

"The Kyykki, are receiving orders from the demons. They need to do something before their toadfaces starve...I expect we'll be greeted by a saturation attack."

"I'm not connecting with your thoughts."

"Yes, Commander." Ayhn explained how the front line Kyykki ate the poisoned food the Light Striper tossed to them. However, those Kyykki just arriving, had not eaten since their campaign began. Now starving because the denuded swamp offered nothing edible, they trampled thousands of other Kyykki simply to die from the 'bleached' dragon chunks. "They have a unique tendency to be their own worst enemy." Ayhn smugly concluded.

"Count your blessings."

"Double notch the tension!" Ayhn yelled at the machiners stationed on roof across the street. While they removed the hexbladed bolt to adjust the tension, Ayhn leaped down the staircase, dashed across the street and up to the roof. The well-tuned crew replaced the bolt before Ayhn arrived.

"You can get me a half mile?" He inquired with great expectation.

The crew chief briefly conferred with the others, then turned to Ayhn. "Sir, it's rather doubtful, especially with the wind coming at us."

"Let me show you the target, then you reassess."

"Yes Sir."

Ayhn directed the crew chief to the northeast, where the demon continued thrashing their arms about. Ayhn passed him the 'long tube'.

"Always wanted ta try one o' dees." He proudly announced as he clumsily attempted to focus on the group Ayhn explicitly designated. With a few helpful comments from his Commander, the crew chief soon grasped the 'long tube's' mechanics. "Praise be de Holy One!" He exclaimed. "We gots ober ten demons dancin' and prancin' over there!" He returned the 'long tube' to Ayhn and readjusted the flight angle of his machine.

"Remove the bolt. Use a double bladed head."

"Then you believe you'll strike."

"Maybe yes, maybe no...There's a lot 'o variances dat must be considered...Weight and wind be the biggest...And de distance....Half mile really be pushing de limit."

"Give it a good try." Ayhn commanded.

With the bolt removed from the machine, the crew chief tightened the tension another notch. The machine groaned, ready to explode. The crew became nervous. They knew of machines exploding under too much stress and a few exploding without prior warning.

"Replace the bolt......very carefully...and then off you go." The crew chief gruffly ordered his men. "N' you be leavin' too Commander.....Only one needs be takin' da risk."

"I'm staying....You set up the shot.....I'll release it."

"You're leaving, SIR!"

"I'm the Commander. I ordered the shot. I'm responsible for it!" Ayhn returned.

"Then I won't fire....Too dangerous!"

"I'm firing, Chief."

The burly fellow wandered over to the huge crossbow, resighted the machine and tightened the screws, locking everything in place. The machine creaked again. Then he yanked a line from his apron pocket and tied it to the release pin. He then tied another line to the initial one and walked to Ayhn. "You'll be over the wall....When I tell you ta fire....Yank hard and fast,....Then cover your head, this machine's gonna 'plode."

"Where are you......"

"Right here, waiting on ta wind." He returned to the machine and made a number of minor adjustments.

Ayhn stood at the top of the staircase, watching intently the casual expertise of the Chief. Absentmindedly he fumbled with the line tossed to him.

"I'll be needin' yer 'long tube', Sir....Then you be with da others.....Jist yank hard n' fast when I'se yell 'FIRE!'...Now, ya gots da line....move out, Commander."

Ayhn. passed on the 'long tube' then dropped down the staircase. He twisted the line around his nervous fist. His stomach nauseated him. He despised this power which sent Light Stripers to their deaths. It mattered little to him that the Chief received the command as 'doin' his duty', a phenomena common within the ranks, a phenomena Ayhn knew personally. Nevertheless, he grieved.

"Keep ready, Sir!" The Chief's strong voice sounded over the wall and into the street where the rest of the crew gathered with Ayhn. He untied Ayhn's line and placed a stone on its end, then he tied his own line to the trigger mechanism.

"Sir, I'll manage the line, Sir!" A crewman offered. "Its my responsibility, Sir!" He reached out and unwound the line from Ayhn's gloved hand. "Can't yank right with gloves, Sir....Da line might slip...Throw off the aimin' somethin' terrible."

Meanwhile, the Chief had been utilizing the 'long tube' well, examining the physical beauty of a local barmaid bathing two houses away.

"At the ready!" He yelled and slid the 'long tube' into his jacket. He glanced through the sights once more, tested the wind with his finger.

"PULL!" He bellowed as he dove under the huge machine.

SNAP! POP!....................Pfffffttt!..

.......CRACK!

.... BOOM!

The massive metal arms of the crossbow shot high in the air as splinters of twisted oak rained down on the crew and on the vacated Chaplain's roof. The moment the cacophonous explosion ended, Ayhn rushed up the staircase followed by the crew. In awe he watched the bolt arc from the ruined machine towards the prancing demons. The crew traced the bolt as well, watching it descend upon the demons. The bolt hovered motionless in the air, then unmercifully plunged to earth, bouncing once before slicing through the demons, then skidding as it tore off a dragon's wing.

"Think we gots a few killed!" A crew member called out.

"I 'spected as much!" Another declared a bit more jubilantly.

"Sir?" The third member questioned Commander Ayhn.

"I really don't know how many we got. Too far to see exactly from here. I need the 'long tube.'"

"Iffen' yer be movin' ta help, Commander Ayhn can have the 'long tube'." The Chief's sounded from under the machine's frame, now covered the splintered oak and deformed metal shards.

A quizzical smile splashed across Ayhn's face. The crew, without comment, tossed the damaged machine parts aside. The Chief, rather clean appearing, crawled out. He stood, dusting himself off and then returned the 'long tube' to the Commander.

"Did I worry for nothing?" Ayhn's voice tinged with a bit of resentfulness.

"No Commander," The Chief answered with a knowing grin, exposing a few missing teeth. "Sometimes our protection don't work....And there be too little space for da whole crew."

Ayhn quickly focused his 'long tube' on the newly created commotion among the demon leaders. "Excellent shooting!" He grinned. "Excellent!... About three, maybe four demons are gone......One dragon serious wounded. You certainly got a good fix on what you wanted."

"Yes, Sir...... ....Thank you, Sir."

"When the machine is recommissioned, Chief, you and the crew are entitled to an evening off." Ayhn blandly stated as he headed for the staircase. "I suppose one of you recognizes the young lady with the towel wrapped about her...She's waving this way."

An embarrassed gagged silence reigned until Ayhn was long out of earshot, then the Chief laughed hard enough to bust his gut.

In Garht's repeating nightmare he once again argued with Master Warmaker, a master who knew absolutely nothing of preplanning or Haafian. Most remarkably Garht survived his disagreeable encounter with the obdurate demon. 'How stupid this maniacal 'thing' is.' Garht found himself thinking again. 'He refuses to understand that Haafians are not going to travel to Haaf North without adequate provisions.. He can't comprehend that we are different from his toad-faced legions.' This indeed formed the core of the argument. Garht refused to travel without enough food, weapons and other provisions for the nineteen Haafians under his command. Even though Warmaker expressed knowledge of their journey to Sarg's fortress castle, he believed it possible without more than a loaf of bread and a sword. Only by convincing Warmaker that no proper sailor ever sailed without adequate provisions, lest he be doomed to failure if the weather worked against him, did the creature alter his orders. Garht recognized that surviving Warmaker meant his success because the jealous Ashuwa would destroy his victorious demon.

Shivering and sweaty, Garht rose from the straw batting and went to the tower window. At one time, this had been the Abbot's suite, now it housed more rats than anything else. Two dawn's ago he and the others gloated as the dragons reaped havoc upon the fishing villages, now he dwelt in a devastated port piled high with mucus dripping dragon dung. He gradually adjusted to the gut-retching stench, but not to Warmaker's asinine promise that a ship awaited.

Looking down to the wharf, he gazed at a dozen blackened hulks silhouetted by the brilliant single moon. Nothing in the harbor would ever sail, some lunatic called Rux was culpable for that. Yet Warmaker vehemently claimed that an undamaged ship... He shook his head. Warmaker's so-called well-engineered plan? A faultless design to destroy Sarg and glorify Ashuwa?........ Certainly!....And he was the damn Holy One.

Indignant, he slammed about the room, waking everyone. Within moments the room filled with cursing as the sleeping Haafians tumbled into the new dawn. Grabbing some food for himself, Garht headed for the market place to confer with the Demon Lords. The others could scrounge for themselves.

The dimly lit streets made dangerous by the debris, cast fanciful shadows on broken walls and empty doorways, not too different from their rooms at the volcano. Garht passed along without concern. His solitary motivation being to prolong his existence. That meant complying with the idiotic commands of his master, Warmaker. Without a ship, he'd request dragons to further the Haafians journey along the bay and northward along the Dark Water coastline.

Munching on bones of unknown origin while they meandered throughout the marketplace is how Garht found the Demon Lords. They walked by him with indifference bolstered by innate stupidity. If not for the fact that they alone controlled the dragons, he'd readily 'bleach' all of the slovenly bastards. He prudently tucked that in the back of his mind. He fortified himself to bargain with these 'creatures'.

"Yer dragons be hungry?" He queried no particular Demon Lord.

"So what if they be?" Returned a large grey-blue demon.

"Maybe I know the best fishing spot." He put out the bait.

"Plenty fish be in the water." The same demon pointed a clawed finger towards the bay.

"Plenty dragons die from 'bleach'. No dragons to execute Warmaker's plan ......Good way for you to get dead.....We all know about failure." He grinned, exposing his blacken teeth. His simplistic commentary attracted six other demons, exactly what he hoped for. Success and food were the key concepts these scaly dimwits actually understood. Garht used them well.

"Tell of fish...food place." A yellowish demon demanded.

"What have you to trade?" Garht responded.

"Got 'blue ladies'....You like to stick them?"

"Your 'blue ladies' are almost dead....Use them for your own supper." His chuckles were joined by a few others.

"Dragons are dying...Many of those who blasted the coastline didn't return.....That means plenty more work for those left. Can they do it without food?....Think for a moment."

A thin black demon responded. "The flight of many dragons isn't over...The flight across the bay is long.....They will rest before returning.."

"IF they return, will they not be hungry?..... Will you feed them 'bleached' fish?.....Will you jeopardize your lives? Warmaker despises failure."

"You have plan?" The black demon offered testily.

"I know where 'good' fish live....That is all."

As the demons pulled into a huddle, Garht reached for his loaf of bread and his wine bottle. He'd wait most of the forenoon, but he had nothing else pressing. He listened in on their broken conversation. They swallowed the bait, but they wanted to offer as little as possible to retrieve it. Nothing new about this approach, he thought. When the noon sun revealed the true ugliness of the god-forsaken port, the demons finally approached Garht.

"Where are fishes?" Requested the black demon. He posed himself as their leader. He would play hard, no compromises, no deals.

"You know the rules, nobody gets anything for nothing. What do you offer?"

"Your life....You may keep it."

"You kill me and Warmaker's plan fails....You will also die, at Warmaker's convenience....What do you offer?"

"Tell us...you want?"

"Just a ride for myself, the Haafians and our supplies."

"How much time?.....When you give location for fishes?"

"Location I give you...personally, after all is delivered. The fishes will all be yours and we Haafians will be on our way.... That's something you might enjoy." He laughed along with the demons. The deal was sealed.

By following mid-morning six dragons slowly flopped their leathery wings eastward along the windswept shore of Haaf Bay. Garht and his

Haafian companions plus their supplies boarded the beasts at first dawn's light. That soft light now scorched both dragons and Haafians as they quietly traversed the cloudless sky. As the coastline turned northward, Garht directed the dragons to follow. Their destination lay beyond the northern mountains which separated Haaf from the Dark Land.

As the blazing sun leaned westward, the Haafians caused the dragons to fly lower. The ruins of ancient fishing villages, with their immense carved stone wharves required detailed examination. Garht's shipwreck story required knowledge of this desolate coastline. Outside the third deserted village the bleaching bones of a few hundred Kyykki covered the stony beach, as did innumerable tracks of some huge unrecognized animal. The black Demon Lord, a supposed expert in living creatures, admitted his ignorance but placed the dragons on alert.

When the evening shadows appeared, created by the ancient volcanoes that now tottered, eroded into the battering waves of the Dark Water, Garht signaled the exhausted dragons to land. Here, quite incongruously and most significantly, a beautiful blue-green river emptied into the brackish foul-smelling Dark Water. Where the bleakness of the arid and ugly scarred terrain surrounded them almost constantly since they turned northward, before them lay a verdant ribbon of life.

"We camp here for the night. Your dragons are finding much fishes in the river." Garht said to the black demon over supper. "From here, we separate."

"Where is easy fishes place for dragons?"

A fast moving shadow passed over the small encampment before Garht answered. It swiftly darted into the afternoon sun streaks.

"It not be friend." The black demon stated, rather unnerved by the episode.

"One shadow against six dragons and their skilled riders. Surely you aren't fearful?"

"Garht not too wise…Better to use fear to live than foolishness to die."

"Well put, demon." Garht said apprehensively. "My apologies."

"Where be our fishes?"

"You'll discover them on your return trip....To insure the safety of my men and myself, I'll have explicit details when you leave on the morrow."

"We leave before sun be gone....This place is....is not good for me or dragons." He signaled for the feeding dragons to return. "Live up to your part of deal.....or I eat you Haafians for supper." His devilishly wicked smile greatly afflicted Garht.

"As you so desire, Demon." He softly replied. "Do you remember where we turned northward to follow the coastline?"

"I remember well."

Garht flinched at the unfriendly tone. "As you fly home, instead of following the coast, where it turns east, you fly south for three miles.... There is the greatest fishing ground along the coast."

"Should you be foolish enough to lie about plenty fishes, I return to eat everyone of you."

"I have no reason to lie......... You were faithful on your part of the deal, I will be faithful in mine.....May your traveling to Haaf North go well."

The black demon nodded as he grabbed a scale and dropped himself on the neck of his dragon. Motioning the others with a wave of his clawed fist, the fish-stuffed dragons slowly ascended into the hazy blue evening sky. Circling twice to gain height, they banked and headed south, flying their traditional double line pattern.

"The damned beasties be gone. Post the guard and let get us some sleep. Tomorrow we begins to play 'shipwreck'." Garht ordered.

"In a long moment. It's good smelling out here. No more damned dragons and demons....They not be natural." Commented one of the men.

"Its jist a relief ta be rid of them....Can't trust them toady 'things'." Another Haafian added to the open commentary.

Garht, aware of their precarious situation, finally terminated their discussion. "Listen carefully!" Indignation colored each word. "We entered this contract with Ashuwa to control the valley. Be careful what you say. The valley is worthless to you if you become.. 'dead'......... Furthermore, our journey as shipwrecked sailors has just begun...If we can't convince Sarg............."

Gradually, fewer and fewer bothered with Garht's diatribe. Their true allegiance belonged to wealth, something they never had, but something they expected shortly, in great amounts. Any god be damned, except the one which controlled their upcoming fortunes.

The six dragons slowly winged by the ancient wave-eroded volcanoes, utilizing the updraft from the Dark Water to save energy. The fading sunlight slashed through the volcano's aged crevices, constructing irregular patterns of shadows over the stony beach and the low flying dragons. From within the volcano's hollow core, three pairs of huge steely blue eyes monitored each wing flap. The Taths riding just behind the long necks of their Istelles nodded to each other. In single file, the trio left the sanctuary of the volcano through a split in its back and, with powerful sweeps of their gigantic wings, rapidly ascended to where the air remained a brilliant blue. Then, silently gliding on the winds, the trio closed in on the lumbering dragons.

Three huge shadows blasted forth from the highest heavens. Their hooked talons snapped the necks of the second file of dragons like twigs. The black demon twisted about, his vicious sword raised high. He only saw a flickering of white wings stretched wider than imaginable, gliding back into the volcanoes, the dead dragons dangled from their talons, their demon riders smashing into the rocky shore.

Panic seized the remaining trio. Urgently pushing the three dragons further from the coastline, the black demon felt no safer, but he believed a surprize attack less possible. The dragons ascended where the sky still clutched the blue. Here, he and the other demons nervously observed the sky for silhouettes. Instinctively he knew these huge creatures and the massive prints he examined near the Kyykki bones belonged together. Moreover, they recognized him. They attacked him at will and without warning. Fear gripped the black demon. He spurred the dragons further out to sea.

The sun's finishing rays purpled the evening sky. Then the Istelles purposely exposed themselves to the dragons. In banking ovals some four hundred feet above the dragons, they warbled their low-pitched battle cry, deliberately alerting their lumbering enemy below. In abject fear and trembling, the black demon watched the long-necked creatures mock him. Dead dragons still dangled from their talons, as if they weighed nothing.

The fierce anger which raged inside the three dragons since the first attack now belched forth in long sweeps of blue-red flame. The nimble Istelles banked left, dropping the dragons, then shot into the heavens, far beyond the dragon's range. The tumbling dragon carcasses collided with their enraged flame-throwing kindred. SNAP! The leathery wing broke as the falling carcasses broke it in two. All four beasts dropped uncontrollably into the Dark Water far below.

Turning from the stressful sight, the black demon fearfully pulled his mount up. The Istelles followed him. He turned, charging the Istelles, his dragon searing the air before them. At four hundred feet, the Istelles separated. The dragon cooked empty air. Suddenly, an enormous serrated beak slashed out, gripping the screaming demon. Then it cut the demon in two. Instantaneously, the dragon dove and rolled. As he pulled out of his clumsy maneuver, an Istelle flew directly for him, talons stretched out for the kill.

The Istelle Riders of the Eastern Tribe, not having fought dragons before, played cautiously and experimented. Fiery breath could topple any Istelle. But dragons flew poorly. Surprize and speed won the battle. Their report would produce useful tactics for killing dragons.

The lone dragon painfully, fearfully lumbered through the night carrying his similarly terror-stricken pale green demon. No time for the easy fishes; the Demon Lord, the great Warmaker, must be warned of these terrible creatures and of their incredible power. The battle for the heavens had commenced.

Chapter 7

The single moon had long disappeared when Warmaker received his summons from a seething Ashuwa. Half-asleep he forced his clawed feet to shuffle towards the raucous clamoring and the constant bellowing of Ashuwa, his god. More cautious than anxious, Warmaker stopped and carefully peered into the darkened throne room. Ashuwa's uncontrolled madness all ready decimated the Haafian bone throne: its jagged splinters covered the hall. Other larger fragments protruded through five or six of the 'pale ladies'. In horrendous agony a few continued to breathe. Numerous Demon Lords stood silent along the partially opened wall, bone fragments impaling them to its volcanic surface, their bloody limbs grotesquely decorated the floor along with their slashed out entrails. Warmaker trembled with fear as stood in the entrance way to Ashuwa's throne room, his scales rattled.

"I smell you Warmaker!" The god thundered. "Come forth!"

Very hesitantly, Warmaker proceeded forward at the slowest possible speed, his reptilianesque body poised to flee.

"Come forth!". Ashuwa repeated. "Had I wished to destroy you, I would have done it by now."

Not entirely convinced, Warmaker nevertheless approached the open edge above the volcano's lake where his master anxiously paced. At five long paces he deliberately stopped and dropped to his knees in obeisance. His wondrous sword loudly clanked on the dirty stone parapet.

"Get up, Warmaker....You are useless to me while you grovel."

"Yes Master." His sword chimed against the stone floor once again, creating an onerous sound. Warmaker saw that sweat and blood, mixed with the innards of the hall's victims entirely covered his master. However, his robe and smock were untouched, as if he replaced the originals. His vertically slitted eyes bulged and his nose flared over his high bony cheeks, flames emerged with each breath. Warmaker never remembered such a distraught Ashuwa. He shuddered as he thought about the source of all this rampaging.

"The moronic Tath god dumped one of my most effective spies one me.....Her fat-assed entrance utterly flattened the throne chair." His voice cracked as he spoke angrily through the flames roaring from his mouth. "The Taths will die in their frozen wasteland!.....I will have my revenge!"

"Yes, My Lord." Warmaker said, totally confused. Who are Taths? But he was far too fearful to ask. Survival counted the most to him, he'd pick up the knowledge somewhere else.

"I have been betrayed by the Haafians!" Ashuwa bellowed. Smoke poured from his noset.

"My Lord?" Warmaker trembled, did Ashuwa know something about the twenty who recently disembarked from Haaf North?

"Not your Haafians!.....The ones who led the attack on Pinduala!......... They refuse to respond to my emissaries, none have returned."

"My Lord!" Warmaker exclaimed with much personal relief. "No one would dare betray you."

"So I also thought, especially since I granted them the entire city of Pinduala when they had conquered it.......The attacking continues, but their Haafian Masters are not to be found anywhere....My Kyykki fight a stalemate, their substantial numbers reduced by Haafian ingenuity. Their technology progresses faster than I can produce my nepes." He smashed his hands together, the sparks momentarily lighting the shadow filled cavern. "Don't stare at me that way!........ You clearly recognize that is the truth, like it or not!" His voice angrily thundered again, causing debris and ash to drift from the ceiling.

"My Lord, have not the spies returned to you either?"

"I HAVE RECEIVED NOTHING!"

Warmaker awkwardly dodged the falling rocks and wobbled to keep his balance as the entire volcano swayed because of Ashuwa's roaring. He immediately realized his survival depended upon being out of Ashuwa's immediate reach and rectifying the precarious situation at Pinduala. Without considering any other options, Warmaker prostrated himself before his master.

"My Lord." He uttered almost too quietly for his god to hear.

"Speak, I command you....And get up off the floor!"

"Yes, My Lord." He straightened up his dust and debris covered uniform and fumbled to adjust his sword. "Might I request a favor?"

"The northern invasion is fully stalemated......and you...you bastard think only of.... a 'favor'.....?" Anger rose in Ashuwa. He stepped forward, ready to render Warmaker as nepes fodder.

Warmaker also stepped back. "My Lord, I ask permission to locate the missing Haafians......To end the stalemate at Pinduala." He retreated another step.

"That's a different type of 'favor', isn't it?" Ashuwa smiled vilely.

"Only should my humble offer be pleasing to you, My Lord."

"I'm damn sick of your 'humility', Warmaker." Then he turned to watch the dawn begin flooding the volcanic landscape with bizarrely twisted and fascinating shadows. "Have you the unique ability to be in two places simultaneously, Warmaker?"

"No, My Lord, I have no such ability."

"Then how shall Sarg be destroyed if you are in Pinduala?"

"My Lord Ashuwa, the invasion of Paradise Valley is on schedule. Even as we speak, Garht and his nineteen are sailing from Haaf North to the Dark Water where the dragons will shipwreck them."

"And what about your other forces?" A menacing tone directed Warmaker to be exceeding clear, specific and truthful.

"The more able Kyykki, guided by two Demon Masters and all the taller Kyykki are slowly moving along the northern borders to surround Sarg's domain...The others wait until I signal a frontal attack on his castle fortress.....Even now, they remain but a handful of Haafians, Taths and Yldans."

"Have you forgotten they collapsed MY supply tunnel? Have you ignored that Sarg is 'gifted'? And what about the significance of the Istelles?"

Warmaker felt the pressure; his robes went damp with slimy sweat, causing his silvered reddish scales to gleam. "That is why I need to wait for Garht and his men to reach the castle..... Murdering the defenders from within will save us many nepes and dragons....And one Istelle against the fearless youngsters you graciously allocated to me...."

"Your answer is well considered, Warmaker."

"Thank you, My Lord."

"I grant you three dawns until you report to me again. You are committed to ascertaining the whereabouts of the Haafians, the status of the battle and make recommendations you believe needful. However, you will not issue any commands unless you find yourself in peril.....Have I made myself perfectly clear?"

"You have, My Lord." Warmaker almost smiled at his victory. "Windfire and I will leave immediately."

"Begone then. I have much to contemplate before you return." With that, he stepped over the rocky wall and marched down the slope to visit his nepes.

Warmaker quickly assured himself that Windfire had eaten, then saddled the creature. As one solitary being, they rapidly ascended into the bright dawn sky and headed for Pinduala, using the scattered clouds for cover. He would return to Ashuwa the 'hero', so he decided for himself. He refused to share the fate of the other Demon Lords and Masters. After all, he righteously thought to himself, 'I alone, among the thousands of Demon· Lords, have obtained a name'.

The reprehensible circumstances concerning the King's death spread throughout Krabo faster than gossip. Along with the horrible news traveled facts appertaining to an unequivocal positive relationship between dragon tattoos and worshippers of the damned one, Ashuwa. Righteous indignation ripped through the city, forcing citizens to wear sleeveless tunics and gowns for their personal safety. The following drizzly dawn, the Church Guard gathered some three score and five persons from stone walls, fence posts and flagpoles, all lynched, and each bore a vivid dragon tattoo. The citizens' wrath showed no mercy.

Oros had returned from the Elders meeting. Jabbi remained with Vosnob for the purpose of directing the reinforcement contingent. Ilty, half-way across town, served the noon meal to Rux and Nadre. Rux's reputation limited his movements within the city. Scores of well-wishers followed him everywhere. Ilty, however, continued to enjoy her anonymity and her freedom.

Neither had sympathy for those who deliberately sold their souls to the damned one. That was discovered when Ilty shared a cup of tea with the newly wedded couple. And, before their meal was over, Ilty offered the free-spirited Nadre a waitressing job. Irrespective of Rux's protestations, she gladly accepted.

"A wife has her part do to as much as the husband." She smiled at Rux, then kissed him.

"These places are not exactly the safest." He murmured as a poor response.

"With you about, who would dare?" Ilty teased. Her eyes shone bright, not unlike how he remembered Nadre when he and Oros met her at the tavern.....For some odd reason, those moments seemed to belong to another time.

"Besides," Ilty continued, "With the King's royal funeral in two dawns, I'll need all the waitresses I can secure."

"I'm not about to win this argument, am I?"

"My dearest, I simply love how quickly you learn."

"You can be here for the evening meal?" Ilty quickly interjected before Rux recovered from his wife's oblique compliment.

In spite of Nadre's obvious victory, Rux did adhere to his previously made promise: they shopped all afternoon. Nadre actually bought very little, but had the penchant for trying on every single garment she admired. While Nadre returned to their suite at the High Council Hall fully invigorated, Rux, carrying a number of boxes for Nadre and two for Jelkio, stumbled up the marble steps, exhausted.

While to two women dallied about with the new purchases, Rux took leave to discover whence Oros and Etan had found some refuge. After much asking he located them in a small room under the elevated platform belonging to the Church Hierarchy. The two contented themselves with talk about past adventures, ignoring the presence of the King's marble coffin.

"Have the last seat."

"Thanks Etan.....Doesn't that box bother you two?"

"Should it?.........Twas sealed a while back......We're just the guard."

"Then the populace won't ever see their King again?"

"No, its better that they don't........All ready the news of his murder is creating more murder........ Even the Church Hierarchy looks the other way."

"Isn't this what we used to call 'righteous justice', Etan?"

"Justice is maintained through a series of procedures designed to at least permit the accused to defend himself or herself.. This vigilante atmosphere declares everyone guilty, check for the facts afterward....What about some of the mariners? ....They usually have a few tattoos."

Rux found himself in no mood to lose another argument. "But I've never seen a mariner with a flying dragon tattoo." He protested.

"The mobs don't examine the tattoos....A Striper, a high-finned shark, a flying dragon.....all the same to the mob....That's not the justice we Haafians have expected from ourselves." Oros said.

"Maybe that's the justice that the swampers might understand. They are responsible for this 'civil war'."

"Only to a limited extent, my friend." Said Oros. "Seeds of discontent were sown in the swamp ages ago...For our part, we've encouraged their second-class citizenship by refusing them nobility as well as education. We've made them the jokers and idiots of the country....Now we pay for our national stupidity."

Rux quit the argument. Recognizing that Oros wasn't about to concede anything, with a gesture of his hands Rux signaled his surrender. He joined the two in retelling the old tales, each being a critic for the other.

That evening the Church Hierarchy moved to quickly finish their extravagant arrangements for the royal funeral, allowing no room for common clerics such as Oros. However, the Council of Three, using the Captain as their spokesperson forbid the recalling of any ex-nobles from the field. Instead, each Regimental Chaplain would receive formal written instructions concerning the Ritual of the King's Funeral. Later that evening Etan further amended the Church Hierarchy's laborious notations by allowing the Chaplains to use the ritual as conditions and/or circumstances dictated. Riders armed with the Church document galloped through the outer gates as the third dawn since the massacre cracked the sky.

Before breaking the fast, Jabbi had a visitor, an unknown Elder. He maintained a small grist mill on the southern outskirts of the city, just to the side of the main thoroughfare. The location provided vital information since the building of Krabo.

"We have a problem you better deal with quickly, Jabbi." The young barrel chested man said as the dry fog blew across Jabbi's desk.

"And its not with the Church Guard either, is it?"

"No, they've reined in the vigilantes pretty well, except towards the south, without Baste's iron fist more than the usual number of heads will roll."

"Not much we can do about that, unfortunately...But come, your information......."

"Extremely early this morning a trio of middle ranking clergy, administrative types, rode by in a waggon headed south........ I thought it be unusual because of the King's funeral on the morrow and the visitation planned for this dawn......... Anyway, their sleeves were down, as if they didn't care for their own safety.......... Again, I thought it must be the coolness of the dawning that made they take such foolish chances..... But nobody had yet risen."

"That sounds suspicious to me, my friend....Clergy are stuffing Krabo, not leaving....... Especially since this is their first respite since the King compelled them to leave their monasteries."

"And not all saw fit to bless the King in a proper manner for his messing in their private affairs."

"You are implying that traitors exist within the Church?........ That rumor has been circulating for quite some time......We just aren't sure who or where they are."

"Then I'll settle the mystery for you, Jabbi." The barrel chested man proclaimed as he finished off Jabbi's tea, using Jabbi's mug.

"I have a feeling this is worth the last of my tea?" He smiled, his curiosity obviously piqued.

"The three cantered by the mill, then turned off into the forest glade, a dangerous spot for an early time. I followed on foot. They dismounted when they reached the water but appeared nervous. After a while a score of the 'blue ladies' entered the glade from the opposite side.......... The two forces knew each other well. They exchanged a number of articles I couldn't decipher, then separated...... The clerics are back in the city, breaking the fast at Ilty's tavern."

"Then I will have them apprehended immediately."

"Careful, this need not be a public lynching. Make arrangements for a quiet ambush. Their capture will be more beneficial than their traitorous carcasses."

"You are quite right." Jabbi slumped back in his chair. He needed some excuse to send the clerics down a back alley, one that, by decree of the Holiness Code, they dare not refuse. "I'm thinking, no priest could refuse to hear the confession of a man condemned to death?"

"The Church Hierarchy has no tolerance for such...."

"I thought as much....Therefore after relating our quiet ambush to Ilty, you shall be the condemned. The alley is two streets west from the tavern, turn right for another block."

"That's a dead-end street."

"I sincerely doubt that the clerics know that." He laughed along with the grist mill owner. "I'll have the Captain secure plain clothed guards about the bawdy house next door."

"And the 'blue ladies? We can't just let them melt into the backwoods of the eastern mountains."

"How do you know that's where they're headed?"

"Just a hunch, from knowing the direction of the road. The clerics might have more information." He smiled.

"We'll send a few Yldans after them, but their ambush is for keeps, not capture."

"I'll not be loosing any sleep over those 'demon ladies'. Their antics at Pinduala are not forgotten, nor are the stories coming from Oros' adventures."

"Just don't suck up all that miss-mash, my friend...."

"Don't get so uptight Jabbi...All that book learning keeps you from reality." The Elder smiled wryly. "I'll wrap this up by noon. I've got three waggons of wheat to process." His dry fog blew through the room before his words finished.

Jabbi located the Captain and notified Ilty, only to be reminded that another Elder allready assumed that responsibility. Though embarrassed, he stayed for breakfast, scrutinizing the three clerics in the darker corner. With their hoods raised, he was forced to use his imagination as he attempted to generate a picture as to what they might look like. It hit him like a thirty stone weight; they looked like the Abbot! Yet, he assumed the Abbot acted alone. This erroneous assumption provided room for the Abbot's colleagues to flourish. No one sought to look for more traitors among the clerical ranks. The answers to such mysteries lay in capturing the trio. Therein was the problem, Jabbi thought as he finished the last of his fast meal. As he rose to leave, a raggedy serf girl, maybe nine seasons old, burst into the tavern.

"Help me! Help!" She half-cried, half-wept.

Ilty's robust husband came around the bar to confront the youngster. "What be you need help for, young lady?" He said in a rather fatherly tone, as he held her by the shoulders.

"They's be stringing up my....my father....." She cried.

"He's being killed?"

"Yes, help me....."

"But why they be stringing him up for?"

"Dumb tattoos." ·She stammered out bluntly. "Dragon tattoos."

"I understand..... Is he a traitor?"

"Jist a stupid old idiot who got drunk and don't know how they git der.......Now the merchants' helpers are goin' string him up..."

"Not a proper way to die." The tavern keeper glanced about the smoky room. "Best we gets more helpers over there as soon as possible.....Some Church Guards and some Priests."

"Priests?" The girl shook her head, uncomprehending.

"Priests to satisfy your father's need to repent afore he is strung up..... The Holy One wants no one to go to hell, especially them that not be so smart..."

With wondering eyes the girl stared at the burly tavern keeper. As a warden of the back alley culture, she lived the rough unsavory side of life.

Instinctively she realized that father was as good as dead, but the tavern master held out a hope she'd forgotten.

"Then I will have my father go to Para---dize." She loudly confirmed her feelings. "He gots not much good nor brains, but he'll be a peace..... Where do I finds a Priest?" She asked the tavern keeper.

"They're sitting in yon corner....They'll go with you, I'm sure. It's their responsibility to the Holy One....If someone requests their assistance afore they die, the priests must go." He stood and gazed across the room. "Isn't that correct, Priests?"

A coughing sound emanated from the corner, the three striving to ignore the situation, pretending not to hear. The tavern master and one of his cooks approached the Priests' table.

"You all heard the youngster's story....You planning on obeying your vows?" His polite tone caught the attention of the audience. His body language aptly reminded the Priests they had no room to connive or bargain.

"Tis the story of a frightened urchin....How are we to know if such a 'thing' could even tell the truth?"

"And how do you know that you won't go to hell for refusing to discover the truth?"

The atmosphere tensed as everybody waited for the Priests' reaction. Clearly the street waif ruled their hearts, but would the clergy deny their Holy responsibility or not. The three huddled for a moment, whispering too quietly for even snatches of their conversation to escape.

"We are ready to leave..... However,... being that these parts of the city crawl with the uncouth and worse, we will have an escort.. an armed escort."

Loud, undignified booing rose from the audience. The clerics drew back, frightened. The girl gazed at the trio, hope still covering her dirty face.

"Very well," The stoutest of the three plaintively said. "We will follow the girl....Let us go quickly, before hell obtains another soul."

The three clerics reluctantly herded themselves out the door, following about five paces behind the youngster, continually glancing over their shoulders. After three blocks, the girl led them down a filthy alleyway where clamorous cursings added to the troubled morning air. Suddenly she disappeared, leaving the clerics dumbfounded and irritated. Just as suddenly, burlap sacks enveloped the clerics' heads and ropes restricted their movements. Before any of the three yelled out, a swift blow to the head knocked each one senseless.

The dozen serfs surrounding the clerics doffed their raggedy attire to reveal the Church Guard uniforms. The few onlookers rapidly dispersed behind shuttered doors and windows, wanting to know nothing concerning this discrete incident. However, their curious eyes never left the fallen clerics. They came angrily bounding from their hovels when the sultry breeze caught the baggy sleeve of the priest's robe, revealing a flying dragon tattoo.

"Gimme the damn traitors!" Yelled a half-drunken man who claimed to be the alley's bossman.

"Sorry, my friend, that's strictly against the regulations. These prisoners are headed for the gallows,........ AFTER their trial." The squad leader returned, his sword drawn as a warning to the gathering mob.

"We'll have the trial fer ye!" The man shot back. "Then wees hangs 'em.....No cost to anyone and wees be doin' our civic dooty."

"You have no such authority...and I shall not relinquish such authority to you."

"Supposin' we take it fer ourselves." He argued.

"That's a stupid move. Is your life as worthless as these damned dung heaps?" He raised his sword, with half the squad following suite. Those gathered suddenly quieted. "Head for home, we'll let you know when their hangin' comes.....Promise me you'll all attend?" He said smiling as the squad backed out to the main street.

The questioning took place under the High Council Hall, in one of the less-known rooms some three floors below ground level. Jabbi presided over the clerics' interrogation while Etan acted as scribe and the Captain maintained strict order and respect. Each of the clerics, now robeless, stood stretched against the stone wall. Their identical tattoos not only exposed their traitorous disposition but also furnished the starting point for Jabbi's questioning. Hints of defiance flashed through their glazed eyes at the beginning, but after a half day of standing the trio began to settle. When Jabbi returned to the prison chamber under the High Council Hall after dark, the hungry and thirsty clerics appeared ready to bargain. Rux and Oros, along with Vaal joined him for this interrogation session.

"Tis not proper that clerics be spoiling themselves." Vaal needled the chained trio. "Sets a poor example for the rest of us serfs, and you lose your credibility .....maybe even your lives." The final words were delivered into the gaunt, yet aggressive faces of the three.

Per standard procedure, the Church Guards maintained their post outside the barred door. The Captain lit his pipe and propped his booted feet on the banister while Oros sipped from his ubiquitous tankard. Etan began his transcriptions as Jabbi asked his initial question.

"The fact that each of you bears the 'sign' of the damned one, precludes an innocent verdict. Whether or not guilty means your death by public hanging is totally dependent upon your helpfulness............... Have I made myself understood?"

The three traitorous clerics remained stoic, perhaps waiting for a more lenient deal. Rux, meanwhile, began toying with their manacles, heating them with an almost invisible beam of light from his seat next to Etan.

"What are you doing!...... Something is torturing me!" Yelped the first of the priests.

"You want to play tough by refusing to answer, we play tougher."

"Our Master will save us!" He stammered in a painful defiance.

Oros smiled gently, then fixed his stare on the priest. "Just like he saved Krucik and his son.....Even invading dragons who catch us by surprize, fail dismally in the efforts to please the damned one."

None of the clerics moved, but sweat dribbled down their arms from Rux's tampering with their manacles. Their false bravado, slowly but surely, began to dwindle. Oros' truthful remarks bit deeply.

"Even now," Jabbi continued. "The entire Church, Hierarchy and all, is being searched. Before this dawn is ended, this chamber will be wall-to-wall,...stuffed with priests needing hanging. Some I fully plan to hang, others will meet Ashuwa face-to-fang."

"You have no such power." The third priest stated quite belligerently.

"There are Istelles which will carry you over Ashuwa's volcano, then simply 'drop' you into his courtyard. Should you survive the mile fall----mind you, dragons can't fly that high----you will be greeted by the damned one himself....and we are all aware how lenient he is with 'failures'."

With no forthcoming replies, Rux heated the manacles a bit more; their color slowly changed and they began to smoke. At this particular stage, Rux terminated the beam. All three yelped and cursed, especially at the Holy One. Their bowels finally gave out, and they messed themselves. Their shackles forced them to occupy the same space as their 'mess'.

"Pretty much as expected." Said the Captain. "They'll be brave, attempting to gain merits for their endeavors before confronting the dung heap they refer to as god."

"You shall not curse our great god!"

"But,... I have!.. And the idiot refuses me battle, fearful that he'll lose.....Even now he's condemned to telling nothing but the truth....Which means if you signed on with the loser before the 'Wall', then your entire agreement, a monumental lie, is more than nullified." He smiled at the arrogant priests, who now refused to look upward. "You three clowns really aren't too intelligent, are you?" His baiting produced desperate silence.

However, they slowly, pensively studied each other, not to acknowledge their defeat, but which might become the initial betrayer. Time moved with an extremely slow deadness, a pace the accused did not control. A pace which all ready placed them far behind their schedule. This factor Jabbi was well aware of, but kept it for future reference.

"This is the verdict." Jabbi announced suddenly, startling most everybody. "One of you will hang on the morrow, the other two shall 'drop' in on the dung heap you worship.....Now, I am a very fair gentleman, therefore in the privacy of this chamber you three will determine who gets off easy:..the hanging."

Jabbi turned, opening the heavy wooden door; the Church Guards snapped to. The Captain, Oros and Rux followed, acting indifferently so as not to reveal anything to the guards. Vaal waited for Etan to gather up his scribal supplies, then slammed the door and locked it twice, using two sets of keys. Much later, a personal guard composed of those who helped him defeat the dragon, were posted to 'watchdog' the regular guard.

Sometime after dawn, Jabbi, Vaal and Rux reentered the clerics' prison chamber. This dawn showed a different side of the clerics. Yesterdawn they plied their game with haughtiness and arrogance, this dawn, they hung limply against the wall. Their physical endurance and commitment to Ashuwa vanished, leaving behind clergy devoid of hope, clinging to the vaguest notion of personal preservation. Their perspective about living lay exactly where Oros predicted: self-preservation.

Vaal commanded his guards to fully awaken the clerics. It required three buckets of icy water. "Remove their shackles." Vaal ordered. "These 'women' aren't about to attack anything. ....I've always marveled how this ash-heap god enlists the worst possible...."

"We'll deal with that subject later, Vaal." Said Jabbi. "Right now these persons have a decision they must share with us...... Who receives the gallows and, the others, a quick trip to their moronic leader?.....Stand, my friends, this is no time for cowardice."

Painfully the men tottered to their feet, yet none would look up. Their iron fetters left black-and-blue marks and blisters from rubbing, but no burn marks. They shivered because of their mid-morning shower; their dripping tunics smelled fetid.

"What say you faithful servants of the ash-heaping god?" Jabbi requested. He turned to Vaal. "Ash-heap....I believe I've added another word for our vocabulary...Ash-heap-ER, that's exactly what he does."

"Can we accelerate this judgement process, Jabbi?" An impatient Rux interjected. Having been up all night and with Nadre waiting the tables most of the night, he had expected to sleep in. "Your rapturous enjoyment with 'words' will wait."

Jabbi arced his eyebrows in mock indignation, though he followed through on Rux's brusque comment. "What is your verdict?"

The arrogant loudmouth of the yesterdawn groaned then spoke in an almost inaudible croak. "We....ha--ve made our......judge--ment."

"Then OUT WITH IT!" Vaal slammed the words against the three, engendering much fearful shaking.

The cleric paused to suck some water from his soaked tunic. "We," He said less hoarsely. "All wish to live....Whatever you ask." He dropped to his knees, begging.

"That was not your assignment!" Jabbi yelled.

"We have much information that is useful....You may have it all."

"Suppose you have nothing I don't all ready know?" He taunted.

A slight hint of hope emerged from the man's filth-streaked face. "The Kyykki hordes invading from the swamp are lead by Haafians from Poldu." He smiled as if he just gained his life.

"Old news isn't helpful, cleric! These Haafians are dead, thanks to a small scouting party."

The man tore at his clothing with both hands. Two guards rushed to restrain him.

"And those women...the 'blue ladies' you rendezvoused with on the south side of Krabo....all hang from the gallows as of sun up this dawn..... Is there anything you REALLY have to offer?"

The renegades, perhaps for the first time in ages, squarely faced the truth. In unison, the heretical trio shook their heads, affirming a negative answer.

"Then who is to be hanged?" Jabbi demanded more than asked.

"Milloway is the weakest. He will hang." Said the fist cleric, still kneeling.

"So be it!" Snapped Vaal. "Guards, hang this Milloway just after lunch............. Send an acknowledgement to his family."

"Are you forfeiting their property?" Rux asked Jabbi.

"Only if they were acquainted with his treason and did nothing to stop him."

Milloway belched hard, spewing blood throughout the chamber. After his arms were refastened with manacles, the guards marched him upstairs and then into the courtyard to await his death. The vivid sunlight forced him to the ground quicker than did the insults from the crowd.

"You two priests will remain here until the Istelle arrives. Then arrives your judgement. ....I strongly suggest you clean up this 'ash-heap'. Jabbi stated and walked out along with his companions.

Once up to the third floor, Rux questioned Jabbi once again. "You actually believe an Istelle is coming here?"

"Just a matter of time before Istelles fly between here and Sarg's valley, or whatever its called......The Istelles shall come." He spoke as truly convinced.

Brey, overwhelmed and shaking stood gazing at the Taths, the Haafians and the Yldans. Everyone was stunned. The nameless god, without first consulting her, publicly pronounced her the new queen of the Central Tribe of the Taths. Never before had a yurt full of such prominent leaders of Tath been so deadly silent. Brey, nervous as never before, ran through thousands of questions in her mind. Then boiled them down to a select few: What business does a Haafian have being queen of Taths? Will I be accepted? Why did this god-without-a-name choose me? What qualities do I have that can compare me to Queen Sjura?

It was hardly inconceivable that the gathered Taths, Yldans and Haafians might be asking themselves similar questions. Why would an unknown foreigner be chosen over other Taths? What does this mean concerning our future, especially if we're in the midst of mobilizing for war?

Anticipating these very questions as well as a confrontation concerning his own leadership, the nameless god initiated the conversation. "I begin by reminding you of the traitorous queen of the Central Tribe who almost started a civil war amongst the tribes……. This damnable action I condemn and those who decided to attempt it will be severely punished…Does everyone understand?"

Heads bobbed up and down: some Taths backed away from the Yldans and Haafians. At this, a flash of angry fire burst in the yurt; everyone froze again. "Listen well!" The god-without-a-name continued. "The old age is now fading rapidly. Our Tath isolation due to the desolate lands of the damned Ashuwa is effectively ended. The Yldans and Haafians are here. We will not deny the truth….And this truth demands we rethink our ideas of citizenship. Does it have to do with color, or place of birth? What places shall we assign to those of mixed races such as Queen Sjura's 'almost here' family?" His light and enlightened statement cultivated some laughter and lessened the tension. In other quarters it raised more than a few eyebrows. "…..and Queen Kadima's children?…. Where are they to fit in? Even as I change my color, so too shall citizens these initial days of the New Era…. Why should it make any difference? Color has absolutely nothing to do with leadership nor faithfulness. The Central Tribe is all too aware of this significant truth…." He looked at everyone, eye-to-eye before moving on. "So, do they want a true queen, one whose heart and soul are prepared for the demands of the New Era? Or do they wish to crawl under the rock pile, where Ashuwa will destroy them all?"

A tense silence, full of anguish mixed with hope, gripped the entire assemblage. Caught off-guard by their nameless god, the Taths had to rethink their ideas, their history, their culture. Their future lay in the hands of their god.

"My Children, you must realize that in order to survive you must change, not unlike my recent transformation, which is why I am still your god........ Had I refused to change, you Taths would, in fact, be a godless people."

This reality surprized most. Their god spoke from personal example. In fact, as seemed most uncharacteristic, he now led his people through personal example. Truly, this day in the history of the Taths marked the beginning of a New Era, whatever that might be.

"Listen to me, my children....I did consent to the marriage of Feathered Goat and Kadima. Furthermore, I did myself wed the Haafian, Sarg to our Queen Sjura.....Mind you, in both cases royalty is married to commoners. And I shall bless their children with special gifts, that the evil which now confronts us, will one day be entirely vanquished."

A thin old Tath, bluer than most, butted his way to the front. Once there, he stiffly bowed to his shining god. The god waved a ribbon of dancing light.

"I represent the river tribe, we who are known for ignoring you since the Day of Sorrow, the day of our departure from Paradise Valley."

"You speak truly. Have no fear, old man, for you returned to me exactly what I did properly deserve.....nothing. I regret my capriciousness and the great damage it produced. Tribe fighting tribe, brother against brother, because of my selfishness. I have repented. This shall be no more. When we battle against ourselves, we allow the damned one to increase in power and destroy our territory....... Even now, the great eastern bay is polluted by runoff from the volcanoes."

"Master,..... I did not come to hear your confession, but such knowledge brings much.... credibility to your name....er'....to your person," He corrected himself. The thin representative of the River Tribe spoke carefully, as if what he heard was incorrect. "We are most pleased and humbled by these strangely wondrous turns of events. ......We did come, may it please you, to rejoin with our people to battle the damned one........"

"You are truly accepted, old man. ALL of you desiring a tomorrow..... shall be my people.......And it is solely in this spirit that I declared Brey as queen.....With all due respect to her, for I did not speak to her on this significant matter beforehand, I now simply request that she seriously consider the offer of queenship of the Central Tribe of Tath."

Brey blanched whiter than white, thoroughly embarrassed. "I...I shall .....consider, most earnestly .....your offer, ...My Lord. I shall pray the Holy One for correct guidance in this matter."

"I strongly suggest that without some help, some sign from the Holy One, that you do not answer."

"Thank you." A more composed Brey spoke. "But I shall require a blessing from the Central Tribe as well....I refuse to be an imposition upon them."

"Spoken like a true queen." Sarg muttered loud enough for everyone to hear.

"And I quite agree." The god without-a-name gently responded.

Feathered Goat's Istelle unexpectedly passed low over the yurt filled village, crying in long loud tones, then swooped away. Sarg, Vauk and Brey bolted for the door, followed by every other warrior. Jogging to the first defense wall they quickly climbed to its top. Nothing moved, no enemies stormed the gates. The westwardly blowing wing gave no hint of the usual Kyykki stench.

"The Istelle witnessed something farther out. Maybe at the log fortification." Vauk ventured.

"Perhaps,... or it's possible that they're moving west, using the gullies along the northern mountains."

"It's simply been a matter of time before they would attempt another attack....This valley and castle must really embarrass the damned one." Brey added.

"Yes, your queenship." Vauk mocked. His crude comment required a disrespectful response. Brey's unexpected swift kick to his rear almost tottered him off the ramparts.

"Are you two 'children' prepared to defend this place?" Sarg brought both of them about, instantly. "Wonderful! Brey, locate Feathered Goat and have him reconnoiter the northern mountains....Vauk, take half the warriors and scout the barricade....Take no chances, understand?....Brey, then join Vauk to scout the northern mountains."

Vauk nodded affirmatively as he and Brey descended the staircase. "And you?" Vauk called up.

"I'm taking the Tath Queens to the castle, along with a sizeable bodyguard.....Remember, they have yet to fully commit to defeating the Kyykki."

"And you have no orders for me, I suppose?" The god without-a-name laughed as his vibrant form hovered in the air a few feet above Sarg's head.

"You are definitely earning respect....Perhaps I was too hard on you."

"No, Sarg...not true. I'm the one who owes you. I now recognize that one more day of my self-gratuitous inaction meant another step closer to oblivion. ...Actually, by being who I am, my power has grown....What you said is verified."

"What is it that I said?"

"That a god's endurance and power is positively related to the number of worshippers.....Mine are increasing speedily."

"Then I congratulate you....But Brey?" Sarg sought to end another of those mysteries he detested.

"Some things call for patience, Sarg, others call for immediate action.... Let's get to the stockade!"

Ignoring the puzzled expression of Sarg's face, the nameless god instantaneously formed the 'cloud' about Sarg, reached out and grasped the distraught queens along with their entourages and flew them to the castle. Once the queens were safely delivered, Sarg re-entered the cloud. Hovering some twenty feet above the keep, Sarg gasped. Less than three miles away the dusty terrain transformed into a shiny black moving mass over two miles wide and one deep. Flying over the horde in open formation ten dragons criss-crossed the eastern end of the valley, incinerating whatever existed.

"So, the attack's begun!"

"Certainly looks that way." Mused the unnamed god. "But no one seems to be commanding."

"Nothing new about that, is there?"

"Except that a rumor designates a Demon Lord as commander-in-charge....'It', I understand, even has a name, a most peculiar change for my adversary."

"Therefore we have to deal with one more mindless frontal attack aided by ten dragons." Sarg's immediate concerns did not border anywhere near the god's philosophical ones. "Somehow the odds are against us."

"You don't believe that we can handle this moronic mess? Where has your confidence fled, my good man?"

"This isn't very funny....The leaders of your Tath tribes are depending upon us, to keep them secure."

"And you doubt that your castle cannot withhold these barbaric masses? Strange, as I perceive it, anything the Holy One creates is also holy, sacred....It's doubtful these slimes from Ashuwa's cesspools could survive the purity."

"So we do nothing?" Sarg demanded, his thinking a bit confused.

"No, we'll have some fun."

Sarg landed softly on the parapet while the god without-a-name spread out his arms-of-vivid-light over the ground before the rushing Kyykki hordes. Using the ground as a rug, the nameless one drew up the earth, a full ten feet deep, and simultaneously yanked it out from underneath the blackened horde. Then, as the airborne terrain buzzed with purifying light, he shook it, tumbling all remaining Kyykki to their deaths below. Once he ascertained that no Kyykki carcasses polluted the terrain, he dropped it on the masses of survivors.

"I've never seen such a victory." Sarg gasped. "In less than a moment you actually buried the entire attacking force....The territory must then be holy?"

"I'll assume you're complementing me."

"ASSUME!" ·Sarg yelled. "You did quite well!.......Excellent!..... No one ever anticipated that beautiful 'irregular' tactic."

The 'rug' of terrain measured some four square miles, terminating quite near the volcano's edge where Queen Sjura first gazed upon her ancient homeland. Now the three hundred foot waterfall dropped and spilled from moss-covered rocks and splashed into a pristine pool surrounded by immense and graceful trees.

"That's how this valley once looked."

"This is....temporary?" A puzzled Sarg asked.

"No, but until the War is over, this territory shall witness more fighting."

The terrifying sight of the earth rising up to consume them made the ten dragons dive up into the clouds. Thus concentrated, they focused their attacking fire upon the wooden stockade surrounding the yurts. The solid wood splintered into burning fragments when their initial blast struck, knocking some defenders from the rampart to the ground.

"Let's get out to the wood stockade!" In a breath, Sarg stood on the stockade wall, now infuriated by his own idiotic complacency; he had forgotten about the ten dragons. Placing his fingers together he aimed at the cluster of dragons. They blasted again, before Sarg commenced, taking out the empty cabins.

A yell for help--in Haafian--caused Sarg to turn. He knew the voice: Vosnob. Rushing to the central community building, now violently blazing, he kicked through the ignited door. Putrefying acrid smoke poured out, denying him access to the building's interior. "Here's the door!" He yelled into the blazing structure. "Come towards my voice!"

Before he finished his last shouting, the nameless god sucked the fire into the sky where it simply dissipated into nothingness.

"Thanks!" Sarg yelled the unnamed one as he dove into the smoldering structure looking for his friend. Off to the right, where the kitchen used to be, he discovered five Haafians. Each had soaked himself with water, but was singed nonetheless. Realizing another blast from the dragons would end their lives, Sarg smashed through the side door into the main compound. He fired and rolled and fired again. Explosions ripped the sky as four dragons forcibly swallowed their own fiery belches. The dragons' third combined blast sent him spinning into the air. A twinkling cloud instantaneously settled about him as he began the deathly drop to earth. He shot twice more from the cloud, slicing leathery wings and decapitating two dragons. The remnant retreated in a vicious panic, beating for the volcano's safety with all their might. They barely started before Sarg destroyed them all. Still blasting away at the distant volcano, the 'cloud' dropped the 'gifted one' in the main compound. A round of hearty applause surprised Sarg.

"Well done!......... Well done!" An uncharacteristicly emotional Vosnob shouted. "Well done!"

"Youthfulness has really ....."

"Quite enough, old friend." Vosnob interjected. "Now help me get these five to safety at your castle."

"No real hurry, Vosnob....But you entirely missed the massacre."

"Finishing off those dragons wasn't a massacre."

"There were only ten, young ones who are often blindsided by targets that actually return fire."

"Explain the massacre then." Vosnob groused.

A brilliantly glowing being approached the six Haafians. Five struggled not to retreat. "Sarg, allow me to explain the massacre."

"Most certainly, My Lord." He smile broadly.

Vosnob and the five others, the latter shaking violently, stared incredulously at the strange being. Sarg casually straightened then dusted off his tunic, disconcerting the others. "Allow me to introduce to you the god of the Taths." Sarg related to the others in a rather pompous way. "He is as Vauk described him to you: powerful, different and almost too close to his people, especially if you think in Haafian theology."

"Your truthfulness overwhelms me, Sarg." The mirthful voice of the god again portrayed himself as rather incompetent. He turned to the newly-arrived Haafians. "Good to see you again Vosnob, though I expected you, with all the stress to have aged a bit more." He chuckled at the inside joke. "I'm pleased that such is not the case."

Vosnob bowed his head in respect. "Your bearing continues to be quite unique, Nameless One."

"I thought as much also." The god laughed merrily. "You just missed a rather one-sided battle."

"I thought we were in the middle of it."

"Dear Elder, you survived a dragon's breath. The real attack began at the volcano where approximately five thousand two hundred four Kyykki initiated an asinine frontal attack on our stockade."

"Approximately?" Vosnob smiled.

"Counting walking dung heaps isn't a pastimes, Vosnob." Then he abruptly switched subjects. "As god of the Taths I had the responsibility of gathering the tribal leaders. They are deciding whether or not to become Haafian allies."

"How long might that take?"

"Perhaps by the end of this day. The queens and their escorts are safely ensconced in Sarg's castle. And you'll be overjoyed to know that Brey is a queen...almost."

Vosnob's eyebrows fluttered a bit, his mind swirled. Once again things happened which went beyond his experience. This nameless god both intrigued and frightened him, but he failed to pinpoint the 'why' of his paradox.

"Must you think so much?" The god without-a-name gently queried.

Vosnob did not respond; he could not. His soul reeled, baffled by this 'god'; his personality and his demeanor.....Is this actually a god?

With a florescent reddish beam of light surrounding him, Vosnob landed outside the stockade ramparts overlooking the newly reborn acreage, a wondrous sight equivalent to the lush vegetation surrounding the castle, depreciated only by the carcasses of the fallen dragons. The nameless god stood beside him.

"But a few days ago, as we compute time, this was identical to the territory surrounding the Kyykki's cesspools: totally uninhabitable. This same territory then was inundated with the Kyykki you 'had' to have me count. Those 'things' are buried......I didn't realize it at the time, but their rotting corpses will produce fertilizer...."

"You are a go...." Vosnob didn't catch himself in time.

"Yes I'm a god, like it or not....." The god hummed a tune that bothered the beleaguered and profusely sweating Vosnob. "Yes, I extinguished all those blackened toad-faces in less than a minute......Does that verify my godship? And I carried you on a lightbeam, and brought Vauk to you in ...Pinduala?.... Your cities look too much alike to me. Bottom line, Vosnob....It's up to you to believe, especially since I all ready know who I am."

"Thanks." He said dourly, but with much humility.

"You'll get over it..... Sarg did, but I'm not sure if he arrived at that stage before I married Queen Sjura and him or not....Doesn't really make any difference."

"Probably not."

"Cheer up, you're beginning to sound too much like Sarg."

"Unjustifiable comparison, don't you think?" Then Vosnob caught himself again. "I apologize, My Lord....Something isn't right with me."

"To the contrary, Vosnob." The god without-a-name continued. "The truth is the Holiness Code.........Truth is as embarrassing as it is often hard....I allow you to be free with the truth, after all,.... I'm the source of your embarrassment."

"I'm supposed to believe that?" He snorted, then apologized.

"Figure it out for yourself........ Meanwhile, I do not know the reason for your most perilous journey......... Translocation is extremely dangerous." A blinding flash of light passed and extinguished; the Haafians plus Sarg found themselves in the main armory of Sarg's castle: the god without-a-name had disappeared.

"Welcome to the castle, friends!" Sarg's voice rang in echoes throughout the mostly empty space. "This is one of our major problems; no weapons."

An Elder examined the sparkling white walls and the high arched ceiling; even with only one torch lit in the middle of the chamber with the polished reflecting its light, one could easily see everything.

"Are you sure weapons won't defile this castle, Sarg?"

"Interesting point, friend." Sarg knew the names of these two Elders were not his to learn, lest he ever betray them. "But when the Holy One created this castle and the surrounding territory, I don't recall any provisions laid upon its usage except for demolishing Ashuwa's realm. Whatever is required to defeat Ashuwa directs the manner in which these buildings will be used."

"Fair enough." The unnamed Elder responded. "But how long will Ashuwa wait until he attacks you personally? That is, as this unnamed god personally destroyed Ashuwa's horde, is it not reasonable to assume that the damned one will respond in kind?"

"And destroy this castle and its property?" A light dignified female voice surprized the six. Five stood quietly, rather perplexed; the language was Haafian but the accent totally unfamiliar. The voice continued. "What the Holy One created is far more powerful than the damned one's ability to destroy." Queen Sjura gracefully as possible entered the chamber from the far side; the other Tath Queens, 'designated queen' Brey excepted, were in her company, their retainers having been dismissed for the rest of the day.

As the five queens passed by, the five Elders deeply bowed. Everyone present knew this meeting could lead to momentous decisions for the New Era.

While the queens gathered their flowing gowns and silently took seat on the stone benches, Sarg whispered to Vosnob. "Exactly what are you doing here?"

"I wondered when you planned to ask that question....What's this gathering of about?"

"I asked you first...Besides, royalty has the prerogative."

"What confounded nonsense are you talking about?"

"My wife's a queen.remember?"

Vosnob paused and stared at Sarg. "I forgot...My apology."

"Most certainly."

"We came to ascertain how reinforcements might arrive safely. Rux and Oros are on their way to Krucik's old castle as we speak. From this end we must determine a route that avoids your 'never ending' valley, but connects to this castle."

Sarg nodded, but replied relative to Vosnob's question. "These queens haven't met in ten of hundreds of double moon cycles. Now they gather to decide whether or not, of one accord, the nation will become our ally, and, under what specific terms and when."

Vosnob's countenance strained. "This is extremely serious." He swallowed hard. "But where are those leaders and clergy who render the decision? Maybe I could persuade them."

Sarg laughed out, causing Queen Sjura to flash him an inquisitive glance. "What have I misunderstood this time, my beloved?" Her soft sarcasm hid itself in the musical brightness of the Tath language.

Vosnob raised his eyebrows when Sarg replied in kind. "Vosnob is very curious, ruling queens are new to him."

She raised her blue face to meet Vosnob eye-to-eye; neither flinched. "Good man, trustworthy." She smiled, almost ogling. "You haven't changed from the last time we met."

"Dear wife, mind your manners!........We have a more important 'problem' that requires attention before we begin...."

She stopped pouting for a moment. "What is it?"

"Vosnob doesn't realize that you queens, without additions of Clergy and merchants, make the ultimate decisions." Sarg answered in Tath.

Her face paled as her brows knitted together. "Allow me a few more minutes." She returned in Tath.

Sarg nodded and returned to Vosnob. "You better learn Tath, that's just a suggestion, of course, Chaplain Commander."

"Stranger and stranger.....this whole scenario." ·He mumbled to himself, primarily.

"Next time then I'll refuse the scouting expedition." He said quietly, though a bit edgy. "Listen, the queens have asked for another few minutes."

"What's a minute?"

"The Tath way for counting time. A minute equals maybe thirty breathes. The rest of their system is quite likable because it's logical and consistent."

Ignoring Sarg's description, Vosnob continued. "Why do they ask for additional time?"

"They aren't sure if they can seriously deal with a male leader." Sarg flatly stated. "They find males too inflexible, too conventional and too willing to damage or destroy. And usually, too lazy."

"Pretty intelligent ladies, very impressive."

"That's probably why I married one."

"Yes, the beautiful one very much 'with child'."

"That's correct." He said modestly, almost embarrassed. "My beautiful wife, Queen Sjura, Royal Head of the Western Tribe. The others are also queens representing the majority of the tribes. One queen, determined to be a traitor, left her throne open: the god without-a-name elevated Brey as Queen."

"She's not even Tath....This is outrageous!"

"And so too is the New Era.....Brey has not accepted the queenship pending advice from others." Sarg paused. The queens began seating themselves for their formal announcement. "You did bring a message of 'good will' from the King?"

"Unfortunately, the King was horrendously murdered. We have a civil war in the south."

"Wonderful.....Just have something ready....... We don't need embarrassing issues at this juncture."

Vosnob reached up his baggy sleeve and pulled out a parchment, one embossed with the King's cipher. "Prepared by the Committee of Three. They've actually administered the country since the King took ill."

"You can fill me in on all the wonderful details later."

Queen Sjura raised her left hand, signaling for silence and the beginning of their meeting.

"We, as we finished our deliberations under full view of the battle raging to the north, did witness the sudden appearance of several unknown Haafians. For the victory we give thanks to our Tath god, who truly demonstrates his concern for our welfare. To the visitors from Haaf, please be seated. You are welcomed to this auspicious meeting..........Sarg, will you introduce the representatives from your country, Haaf."

Following her lead, Sarg turned to the gathered queens. Dear Queens, I introduce to you the Chaplain Commander of the Light Striper. He represents our country and King. He leads the forces which defend Haaf from the damned one."

Vosnob rose and politely bowed. "I bring you greetings from the Committee of Three, who presently guide our country until the new king is selected." He paused as Sarg translated for him. "Our King's funeral is to be celebrated two dawns from now...."

A hushed murmuring rippled through the row of queens. Anxiety filled their faces. When they quieted, Vosnob continued. "We recognize this moment as one of greatest importance. We have wished to meet you since we received information from Sarg regarding your country of Tath and of course, the Istelles..."

Some laughter greeted his final remark; Taths seldom thought of their Istelles as 'special'. Sarg quickly explained this cultural disparity with Vosnob. Receiving the news with the greatest openness possible, Vosnob nobly smiled at the queens. He unrolled the parchment. "Might I obtain your gracious permission to read."

A few head nods secured his approval. Being unfamiliar with the written word, some gossiping commenced among the queens.

"These written words of ours are strange to you, as your Istelles are strange to us." Vosnob related before reading the parchment. "Nevertheless, both are of great benefit to each of us...Perhaps we might understand them as a blessing of our mutual friendship."

His explanation settled the queens. Vosnob read the standard hyperbolized greetings to the queens, making sure to substitute 'queen' for 'king'. Then he began the body of the letter. "Due to the tyrannically evil activity of the damned one who calls himself 'Ashuwa' we find ourselves confronted by a demonic force which clearly intends to bring our way of life to naught. We strongly believe he will not be satisfied with only our country, but will definitely attempt to subdue Tath as well. Having absolutely no desire for Ashuwa to succeed, we humbly ask the 'queens' of Tath to consider their participation in his defeat, knowing that Haaf will render herself into the service of Tath for the similar purpose of defeating the evil which now separates our countries and our futures."

Following Sarg's awkward translation of the portentous language of the document, the queens spontaneously applauded.

Queen Sjura stood to reply. "Thank you for your reading....I hope that is the correct wording....We Taths realize that the days of old are gone..... Our god has returned to lead us, and we have been graced by the presence of your country's citizens. The queens you see before you are the rulers of Tath...Is this not much different from Haaf?" Sjura smiled as she spoke. "Do not be alarmed, consider the difference a blessing."

"I appreciate your concern and wisdom, Queen Sjura." Vosnob replied.

"We have concluded that we, as the united tribes of Tath, shall endeavor to assist the Haafians in their battle against the evil Ashuwa...... We firmly expect the Haafians to assist us in return... We must make it clear however, that the Central tribe, being without a queen, did defer its vote until a new queen rules there."

"I am most appreciative of your intentions concerning a uniting of forces to conquer Ashuwa. I also appreciate your openness on the matter before the Central tribe. Queen Sjura. I find it most refreshing for the soul......Might it be appropriate to suggest a few possible ways of beginning our venture together?.. I could begin with the other reason I stand before you today."

"Of that we are all ready familiar, Vosnob....Vauk did bring and share with us an outline of your proposed plans...... Hopefully reinforcements are flying to us."

"They are indeed, but by land. Flying is something we are not acquainted with,........ yet...... We are attempting to locate and secure a route from Haaf to Paradise Valley. Holding this territory is of the utmost importance to us..."

"As it is to our god who defeated the last attack and your god who 'somehow' created this castle. With the gods co-operating, it is hardly correct for us to defer."

Though her words were truthful, the very idea of the Holy One co-operating with another god, explicitly brought his faith to the forefront, boggling his mind with the incomprehensible. The New Era, full of promises complemented by numerous problematic issues kept some doubts in Vosnob. Nevertheless, Vosnob realized there could be no returning to the old times.

"Might it be proper for us to send a delegation for your King's funeral?" Queen Sjura suggested with the nodding approval of the others.

A mighty 'thump' on the upper parapet startled the five Elders. Bewildered and frightened, they jumped.

"Feathered Goat has returned." Kadima softly said in Haafian. "Come, new friends. It is time to meet an Istelle."

Excited as little children, the five Elders, without waiting for a formal dismissal, bounded up the wide shining staircase. A brusque wind struck them as they reached the open area under the great parapet, slowing their progress to the uppermost level, but not their enthusiasm.

The queens, profoundly delighted by the Haafians' energy and inquisitiveness, returned to their yurts for a meal and to discuss their options with their advisors. Obviously, the men of Haaf were quite different from those of Tath, at least in the areas of motivation and leadership.

As incomprehensible as it could be, Vosnob froze solid at his first glimpse of the Istelle. The gigantic beast was yawning, a massive maw that could easily swallow a barn, and Vosnob almost ran into it. Never had Sarg witnessed such an enthusiastic Vosnob fall prey to his own emotions. Yanked from harm's way by Feathered Goat, Vosnob could only stare and murmur, trance-like. "The Istelle is 'stupendous', 'impossible', 'unconquerable', 'unbelievable'......

An unintentional benefit of the yurt is that everyone is forced to sit in a circle. The idea of 'prominence' is not central to Tath thinking; equality is, at least among those who rule. Even the newly re-established River tribe sat on the circumference and not behind it. They discussed their future plans.

Following worship in their respective villages, the two groups subsequently converged upon the castle's lower porch, shaded by huge elm trees. The atmosphere tensed when Feathered Goat reported that Brey, Vauk and the scouting party were not visible. At dawn Sarg would send out another patrol.

"The consensus of we queens is this: five Istelles will fly tomorrow to Krabo for your King's funeral. Their route through the mountains is one Sarg mapped for the Light Striper's use. Five more Istelles will fly forth to Tath with news of our decision while ten shall guard the mountain passage way from the dragons....We hope this anticipates your current needs." She spoke in Tath using Kadima to translate. "We are expecting the additional Istelles shortly."

Vosnob responded using Sarg to translate. "We appreciate your most generous offer of assistance. We have just learned that your beautiful Istelles are not too numerous. Therefore your offer does indeed humble us."

"We thank you. This is an acceptable beginning."

"Yes, Queen Sjura." Vosnob replied through Sarg. "In return we shall, if possible, send two regiments of the Light Striper to Tath."

"We intend to open up routes for trading as well...We believe this will be possible when our maps become updated...Is this appropriate?"

"Inasmuch as our countries are uniting to defeat Ashuwa, there is no reason not to pursue other mutually advantageous strategies as well. Perhaps the more we combine our resources, the better the New Era will be."

"I agree with your insights. Shall we consider the matter closed?"

"We shall...Since we have no 'papers' such as your's, our agreement shall stand on the strength of these witnesses here gathered.............A hug will finalize our new venture." Queen Sjura smiled willfully; Sarg looked away, grinning from one pointed ear to the other.

"If that is what your tradition requires." Vosnob announced soberly, stoically. Hugging a very pregnant woman made him unbelievably nervous, though he could not ascertain why. Sjura's embrace caused everyone except Vosnob to grin; he barely touched her, as if she were too fragile. Before releasing him Sjura whispered something in his ear. Vosnob's face went white, then bluish and his breathing rough. He sat down. Sarg demanded to know what she said to the Chaplain Commander.

"I simply told him the truth. He's a very handsome fellow who needs a good wife."

Sarg's laughter over the incident lasted until the next dawn when the five Istelles, lead by Feathered Goat, circled upwards from the castle and glided towards the southern passage way through the volcanic mountains. Their 'V' flight pattern ascended into the cumulous clouds and disappeared. Sarg then organized a scouting party of Taths and Haafians to search for Brey. High overhead an Istelle floated. Vosnob left as well; he had secured another ride with the unnamed god. Before flying off, Sarg informed Vosnob that his maps might be incorrect: Sarg was able to ascertain that the castle Krucik stole was now the castle, but he didn't recognize the brownstone castle that Rux and Oros destroyed.

Even though Windfire flew at three times the speed of the dragons, her flanks bled from Warmaker's continual kicks to her ribs. The slight bond between them did not allow for kindness. Warmaker had a single goal for which his mount provided the transportation, nothing more, nothing less. The pair traversed the desolate volcanic valleys until the Zuda Marsh appeared. At this juncture there was no mistaking the route of the Kyykki hordes. Their route, devoid of all living things and emanating the wretchedest of scents, presented Warmaker with the easiest tracking assignment possible.

By the beginning of the evening, Windfire circled the lumbering dragons who made up the rearguard. Once his elongated shadow dropped upon them, a deadly panic ensued. It caused a stampede that effectively stomped out a thousand of the Kyykki who had yet to reach the front. While Warmaker attempted to ferret out a few Haafian commanders,

Windfire filled his stomach with five or six of the wounded Kyykki. Finally realizing the Haafians did not occupy the rearguard, Warmaker flew Windfire within sight of Pinduala, hoping to observe the Haafians effectively directing an assault upon the port city. Again, he saw nothing but the usual full frontal attack. The stupidity of the tactic enraged him, especially as over half their efforts dealt with climbing over their own heaping mounds of the dead and the dying.

The Light Striper, he hatefully conceded, had their strategy organized well. As the Kyykki stood at the top of their carcass composed mountain, the bleach and bolts of the Haafian machines tumbled them backwards down their grotesque mountain. A battle of desires instantly raged within him; part to destroy the Haafian machines and lead the Kyykki into the city, part of him, on the threat of a most painful death, to find the ignorant incompetent Haafian commanders. Not yet having had the opportunity to defeat Sarg, he turned, ruthlessly wrenching the reins and dove for the sixth line of attackers. There he spotted a number of the Demon·Masters. Windfire's sudden unexpected dive towards the Demon Masters caused them to panic worse than the dragons. They foolishly swung their huge swords in the air, slicing one of their own on the down stroke.

"STOP!" Warmaker bellowed as his mounted skidded to a claws creeching halt in front of the terrified Demon Lords. "STOP THIS NONSENSE!... .....IMMEDIATELY!"

Recognizing Warmaker, but not his mount, the Demon Masters were more than somewhat hesitant to obey. All ready they carried on the siege of Pinduala without proper authority and without informing Ashuwa of the Haafians' demise. Now, apparently, this creature of Warmaker came to punish them. Almost as a single unit, they slowly backed away, forming a tight square against the beast, weapons remained at the ready.

Warmaker slide off his wearied beast, his clawed feet dripped of Windfire's reddish-green blood. However, his sword remained sheathed. Seeing a terrified look frozen on many scaly faces, he approached the group slowly, leaving Windfire behind him. For the first time he felt the tortuous salt breeze, the lack of humidity seared his parched throat and lungs.

"Where is something to drink?" He hoarsely called out.

A ripple of relief passed through the Demon Masters. A canister of water quickly reached Warmaker. He punched a hole in the lid and showered himself with the warm acrid contents.

"From the 'nepes' pond. "·Warmaker commented. "Not a bad refreshment at all."

"We are happy to serve you, Warmaker, personal envoy of Ashuwa."

"So be it, Yellow Demon Master." Warmaker said coolly. "Where are those Haafian commanders?....Ashuwa has not heard from them, nor does he know if they committed HIS plan to action."

"We attack each new dawn, drastically wearing down the city defenders. We have reinforcements, ready to kill. The Haafians have difficulty receiving anything because we have clogged the harbor."

"You have wasted dragons, nothing more!" Warmaker thundered. "The attacking is the same usual self-defeating frontal format. You waste the Kyykki for nothing!"

"We are besieging the city as we were ordered to, Warmaker. We are following our orders very carefully. Ashuwa depends upon our obedience to his ......"

"I know very well about obedience..........Now where are your superiors?" Whiffs of reddened smoke curled about his angered face.

Silence reigned throughout the gathered Demon Masters, all refusing to speak. His patience quite thin from searching for the Haafians, Warmaker impetuously slammed his fist through the scales of the Yellow Demon Lord. He opened his fist grabbing the Demon Master's innards. With a bone-crunching shriek, the Yellow Master collapsed as Warmaker held up his dripping innards. Petrified, the others became fearful as Warmaker proceeded to jam the innards into his fanged mouth. He laughed as the Yellow Demon Lord slowly died.

"Are you hungry, my pet?" Warmaker called to Windfire. "Have this one." He ungraciously kicked the mortally wounded Demon Lord in his mount's direction. A final desperate muffled yelp buffeted the air as Windfire crushed the demon's pointed skull before swallowing it. No one moved nor breathed. Warmaker made his position all too clear.

"NOW, WHERE ARE THOSE DAMNED HAAFIANS?" The stench-filled breeze almost carried his unbridled rage into the city.

Instantly the Demon Masters bowed low, their skeletal noses touching the earth.

"Get up, you foul dung heaps!"

Slowly, cautiously they obeyed Warmaker's command, ever watchful for the opportunity to escape this confrontation. Warmaker advanced a few paces. The Demon Masters retreated a few paces.

"Stop! I command you to stop!"

They obeyed, stumbling over each other: Warmaker kept his distance.

"Where do I find your Haafian commanders?" He growled. "Why is my question so difficult for you?...... Why should it cost you your lives?...... TELL·ME!"

"If it please you, Warmaker."

"No, it doesn't please me, Orange Demon Lord.....I should have had the answer long ago......Continue!"

"Our Haafian Masters died horribly, murdered by other Haafians."

"Are you telling me that some Haafian commanders were traitors?" His countenance remained severe but his hoarse voice betrayed much incredulity.

"No, our Master's Haafians were loyal to their deaths. From the details, and there were extremely few because the dragons stampeded and stomped most everything into the muck.,........ We believe that a mighty force of mounted Haafians surprised our Haafian commanders during one of their 'parties'."

"And there are no survivors I might interrogate?"

"None, Warmaker."

"And how long ago did this disaster befall the invasion force?"

"Eight dawns past." The Orange Demon Master answered pensively.

"Why did no one of you morons seek to inform Ashuwa concerning your decimated leadership?"

"The Haafians controlled everything except the attacking Kyykki and dragons.... Those we controlled according to the orders the Haafians gave us."

Ashuwa was not going to be pleased by this devastating turn of events, Warmaker thought. As the bearer of bad news, Ashuwa realized his own life lay on the line. To survive he would have to yank defeat from the Kyykki hordes, but that meant breaking his word to Ashuwa. The burden of the eastern invasion, though he was not personally responsible for it, fell with the greatest weight upon his shoulders. "I am to understand that the Haafians refused to share any of the invasion plans with Demon Masters."

"No, Warmaker, but the foremost Demon Lords died when the Haafians overran the campsite with their great numbers and surprize."

"Then all of you are second and third ranking ......"

"Yes," The Orange Demon Master lied. "We are far removed from those who make decisions."

Warmaker suspected the truth, at least a major part of it, is what he heard. To press further, he thought, would jeopardize his own life. Better to assume and live. "So, if no one has the power nor permission to make decisions, how is it that the Kyykki attack Pinduala?"

"We continue to operate by the final set of orders were given....We have obeyed to the letter."

"The invasion degenerated into stagnation, the Kyykki being the biggest losers."

"To the contrary." An old faded blue Demon Master responded softly. "We are winning, the Haafians cannot venture forth and as the Kyykki swim into the harbor, their resupply lines diminish. It's only a matter of time before they dwindle due to starvation........ Then we trample over their walls and feast."

"And how accurate is that information? What is your source?"

"From the dragon riders. We keep an eye on the harbor traffic, Warmaker.....We are told that fewer ships arrive and that the city streets are usually empty."

"You believe that only one explanation is possible?"

"Indeed, for our Kyykki are zealous in pressing their attack, constantly keeping the Haafians from resting....It's only a matter of time before the city falls." The old Demon Master pressed his confidence just enough to maintain his credibility.

"You survive because you play a good politician."

"I shall graciously accept your compliment."

Pushing this interpretation any further would only hurt himself, so Warmaker deliberately changed topics. "How long will your suicide attacks continue?"

"Until we are commanded to discontinue them or move southward, as was in the original plan. However, no Haafians commanded us to move into the northern plains of Haaf."

"I ·understand." He said indifferently, his head spinning from their innocent stupidity. Instinctively he recognized that another dozen or so of the insane frontal attacks meant the end of the eastern invasion force. The defeat of this massive force did nothing to bolster Ashuwa's goal to have his own people.

"Do you have the power to change something to make it better?" He suggested.

"We are doing our best with what we have."

"We are not!" A younger black Demon Master contradicted the old one. "The same plan goes nowhere because the enemy is ready for us..... We always attack the same way at the same time. The Haafians tell time by our attacks."

"Then you might do better." Warmaker deliberately paused. "And your Haafian commanders did not prohibit that, did they?"

"No................."

"Then, is it wrong to use their orders? Are you not to conquer the city?........... Are not your standing orders to conquer Pinduala?"

"Yes, Warmaker, we are listening to your wisdom." The orange Demon Master responded eagerly. "We are then to 'adjust' the Haafian's commands to succeed?"

"What say your colleagues?"

A discussion immediately commenced, often punctuated with threats. One disconnected scaly head sailed by. Just as quickly, a rousing cheer sounded from the Demon Masters, telling Warmaker that a consensus had been reached.

"How then do you answer?"

"My lord Warmaker, we dare not contradict the orders we received from the Haafians. In keeping with their intentions, that is, to conquer Pinduala, we are comfortable in adjusting our tactics to achieve victory."

"Then you must do so, lest our Master, the Great Ashuwa, think you fail him by repeating the same attacks, which only provide a stalemate.... Ashuwa demands a victory.....I shall shortly leave to report directly to him. New commanders shall be sent forthwith, but until then, destroy the city. I am well aware that you have a schedule to keep."

"We are humbled by your visit and advise."

"I gave no advice......... You received no advice from me...... Do you understand?" He said bluntly. "I asked only questions to clarify the status of the invasion force.......... That is what Almighty Ashuwa requested of me.....I take leave!"

Windfire immediately rose and sped westward, Warmaker had gathered enough information to satisfy himself. The third ranking Demon Masters argued about what 'adjustments' they should make to conquer Pinduala.

Chapter 8

It never happened before……nor will it again…. All of Haaf and Tath later called it 'The Time of the Great Heavy Darkness'. There will not be a reason that creation that will comprehend, only the price of out-of-creation meeting.

An impenetrable oppressive darkness immediately cloaked all the land, like a box trap springing upon its unwary prey. One breath the world as usual, the next breath nothing but thick weighty darkness covered everything. The high midday sun disappeared as did all other natural lights; not extinguished, but as if wrapped, blanketed by the same thick heavy darkness that physically sprawled across the terrain. Thicker than any known fog, denser than clouds, the substance required brushing off. Immediately, absolute chaos broke forth.

In Krabo, Vaal immediately placed the terrified and panicked city under marshal law. The Church Knights instantly cut-off access through the city gates, torches were lit, but the absolute darkness refused to allow their flames to shine beyond a hand's width. Those caught outdoors found refuge in the nearest house or tavern, where the hearths alone defied the mystifying darkness, at least to the distance of three hand's breadth. Around an open hearth in the High Council Hall in a misty light, the fearful clergy anxiously gathered. Explaining this 'supernatural' darkness was beyond their experience and knowledge, yet the populace would soon demand answers. Ilty's tavern closed its doors to all, there not being another half-space for just one more Haafian. She thought to translocate but then quickly changed her mind, with the evilness she sensed behind this darkness, who knew what else had been altered.

But the capital city did not rest, specifically because of the people arriving for the King's funeral. Keeping them safely indoors became the major problem for the Church Guards. Keeping them from fighting with each other quickly became the chief occupation of every tavern owner. However, as soon as Vaal discovered that the vast tunnel network under the city remained free of the darkness, all essential administrative work and guard duties, now doubled, proceeded as usual. Though he commanded secrecy concerning the tunnels, Vaal knew he battled time until the locals discovered the truth. He believed most Haafians would soon live in their basements.

"Only the Stripers and Massive Blues aren't terrified." A nervous trooper reported to Jed. "They simply think it's night."

"That's about the only relief out here."

"Yes, Sir." The trooper mumbled. "Ah....no Sir."

"Try again, I'm certainly not following your logic."

"Underground, in the tunnels....well, this 'stuff' won't go below ground. From the tunnels you walk up into it."

Qill and Deep Owl hadn't finished their pressing attack of Haaf North when the darkness enveloped all three defense lines, leaving Raff to fend for himself in the rearguard. Now, some lengthy time after the windless darkness dropped, Jed steered into another course of action. "Why not put everyone to work underground?" He suggested. "It's less fearful, and, being that the dragons can't manoeuvre either. It's a safe course."

"We've got nothing to lose. A tunnel to the city wall with disguised weapon pits is definitely to our benefit." Deep Owl agreed.

"No one benefits by doing nothing. Fear is the more deadly enemy. This 'darkness' does not kill, but what it hides--might."

"If it hides anything, Qill." Jed said. "Send everyone to the tunnels to dig in shifts. By constantly digging for two or three dawns, should there ever be another one, we'll be close enough to undermine the city wall."

"I like your ideas, but try not to share your confidence with too many others." Qill said to Jed as they talked almost nose to nose. "We'll cut a perpendicular tunnel for picking off the dragons roosting on the wall."

"Let's get moving then....For all we know, this is an evil ruse to catch us off-guard....Who knows when it will lift."

"Then we've established a motive to tunnel faster than ever. If we make the most of this opportunity, then we have a better chance of regaining the city." Deep Owl called over his shoulder. He felt his way out the door.

The dragons and their Demon Masters could barely discern their pointed noses. Even dragon flames disappeared in the thickest of darknesses. Having little potential to comprehend their situation, and even less inclination to move in any direction which might jeopardize their personal safety, the mission's success notwithstanding, the current occupants of Haaf North did nothing. Fearful of what the darkness might use to attack them, Ashuwa's defenders froze.

In Paradise Valley, Sarg sent word that everyone should move into the keep, where the hearth fires continually battled at the encroaching darkness. He anxiously awaited the queens' entrance because, like everyone else, he recognized this as an evilness which probably carried other evils hidden within it. The Tath's arrived, finally and without injury. Kadima led them, guards, entourages and queens, bound together with short ropes, feeling their way along the cobblestone paths.

Having little discernible recourse and no reason to move, the Istelles perched on the parapet nestled in for a sleep. As the thick darkness effectively muffled noises, any attacks would come as an unwanted surprise. In spite of this, the Istelle riders kept as best watch as they might, even extinguishing their torches so as not to aid any enemies.

"Ash Heap is behind this!" Queen Sjura declared when, except for the scouting party, everyone shuffled in. She held tightly to her husband's arm, fearful.

"I suspect this is the worst he is able to do."· Sarg replied with an easy confidence, one that belied his true feelings. "After all, this valley and castle belong to others, us, gifts from two gods. Ashuwa cannot compete directly against them, so he targets us....As best we can, we need to be prepared for any eventuality. Gathered here we know exactly where everyone is and this is the safest place."

"What about my husband?"

"I sincerely wish I had a comforting answer for you, Kadima." Sarg gently spoke to the exhausted and frightened queen. Her children clung tightly about her legs. "To be as honest as possible, landing an Istelle in this abhorrent darkness has to be dangerous. However, if they were able to navigate through the first mountains, plains lie below." Sarg suggested with his most hopeful tone.

Kadima arched her eyebrows, confused. "What is 'plains'?"

"They are like our steppe, only lower and warmer." Queen Sjura answered her anxious friend in Tath.

"I shall continue my prayers." Kadima replied softly.

"And so shall we all." ·Sarg responded in Tath. "This is our time to wait."

The Tath tribes living along the dreary coastline of the far north, tribes used to long days of darkness, found little reason for fearfulness but much for anger. Their god tampered with the seasons and no one had prepared for the horrible, low temperature winter, a season that was supposed to arrive in three months. Even so, no one had ever experienced such a clinging darkness. Nevertheless, their provisions existed, enough if this 'false' winter quickly dissipated. Their Blue Istelles instinctively folded their fifty foot wings, and waddled ashore. The hazardous winters wreaked havoc upon those who chose to swim the icy currents.

Massive, gory, yet glorified mass suicides dotted the landscape of the Poldu Marsh, where those tattooed with the 'flying dragon' of Ashuwa dwelled. The absolute darkness, with its clingingness, convinced them that the sun died. Therefore Ashuwa's grandiose promises died as well. As the cold air froze the ponds and marshlands, the tattooed men collected about the squalid huts of the 'blue ladies' and others who preached conversion to Ashuwa's worship.

Not wishing to endure the cruel contempt and savagery of the swampers, most re-committed their lives to Ashuwa, then sank swords into their bared chests. The swampers, able to traverse the swamp even without light, burnt their hovels wherever and whenever they located them. Afterwards, as the unnatural darkness refused to leave, as its thick heaviness wrapped about their small gatherings, they reached a deadly conclusion. This time of darkness, unelevilated in spite of their efforts to cleanse the land by exterminating the bringers of Ashuwa's message, meant that this time actually belonged to the Holy One.

"An' He'es be'en to subject us ta de Juge-ment!" An older swamper excitedly exclaimed.

"But, we dun killed dem Ashuwa's peoples.....Holy One might smile at dat." Another said, nervously hopeful."

"Noper, young feller...." The swamper spat on the ground. "He come'en fer all us...Truthfully, we dun sided with de other god. You fer-gets too eazee what them monks readed us from de 'Holiness Codes'."

"Tell us! Tell us!" Came a raucous cacophony of illiterate voices, all steeped with trepidation.

"De monk readed dis. I'se quotin', mind ye...." He desperately attempted to clear his throat. "In de time of 'HIS' darkness, de Holy One tramps upon de land. Those which des-spizes Him shall He be judin' with His rightenesss."

"We ain't gots nuting ta hope fer."

"A feared not, friend....We gots but one chance not tat burn in de hell."

"Tell us, friend, what ye be'es meanin'."

"We juge us and exe-cuteses us afer Holy One done show up."

Silence ruled in the absolute darkness as the reality of their situation claimed them, one by one. No one questioned the old man's logic. No one lodged a protest against the old swamper's interpretation of the Holiness Code. No one actually quite knew how. The episode of the Holy One confronting Ashuwa at the Wall, even though now grossly exaggerated through the embellishment of re-telling, caused great anguish among the swampers. Such scenarios repeated themselves throughout the Poldu as the vengeance of the Holy One firmly established itself within the minds of the heretical Haafians. Once established, almost everyone believed the same recourse---suicide. Thusly, so they thought, their own deaths might atone for their grievous sin and the gates of the Holy One's blissful kingdom be opened to then.

Ashuwa's worshippers set forth then to renounce their allegiance to him by thrusting swords through their chests, praying the Holy One accept their penance. Whole families and villages disappeared into the bleak muddiness of death, denying their new god a people in the south.

Garht and his renegade Haafians progressed easily for two dawns before the heavy oppressive darkness obstructed their mission. Being in an unknown, unexplored territory, they fearfully set up a campsite.

"When a god creates something special, he most likely defends it in ways clearly unknown to us." Garht relayed to his brigands. "I'm not sure what this 'black stuff' is all about, except that it has stopped us, at least for the time being. Our more immediate concern is the cold. Get some fires going before we freeze."

Grumpily, as usual, the men obeyed. Self-preservation stood high on their list of abilities. Viewing each other in the faint shadow-light brought about a sense of security. They also reasoned that this heavy darkness might simply be a cloud hiding Sarg's castle from them. Therefore, their reasoning continued, like a cloud, this barrier had another side, maybe it was but a few miles thick. By traveling along the riverbank, they could pass through it. Garht believed that this plan garnered a consensus from the shivering men. He chose to follow through on it after they woke from their sleep. No unnatural darkness would keep him from his promised city, and he knew the penalty for failure.

By the second supposed dawn or day, depending upon one's frame of reference, temperatures dropped another thirty degrees, placing most of the land within freezing. Another couple of days or dawns such as this meant the end of life as one species after another succumbed to the freezing and lack of life-giving light.

At Pinduala, the battle stopped as the Light Stripers huddled about bonfires wearing both their summer and winter uniforms. Ships in the harbor, now plagued by ice floes, responded poorly if at all; few dared maneuvering without light. Requiring more heat than Haafians, the cold-blooded Kyykki, the dragons and their Demon Masters, blindly retreated into the Zuda for warmth.

Warmaker, joyfully spurring Windfire homewards towards Ashuwa's volcano with good news, crashed up against the darkness as it descended upon him from far beyond the highest clouds. Its oppressive heaviness forced Windfire down, to fly well below the clouds they originally burst through at last sunset. Warmaker totally ignored the darkness which clung to him and exhausted Windfire. His mind only focused on his punishment should he arrive late from his mission. Maintaining in his head the exact direction to the volcano, Warmaker forced his mount onward, no change in speed permitted, no deviations allowed. With such reckless abandonment, Ashuwa's premier warrior instinctively guided his mount through the thick heavy darkness. This stupid obstacle conjured by the inane Haafian god would not prevent his success. Time and time again he raised a clawed fist above his scaly pointed head to curse the Holy One, creator of this horrendous evil. The only reply he received came from the whelping of his mount, exhausted and numbed from endless flying and weakened from the greenish-red blood slowly running from his spur wounds. Warmaker indeed was the master, but the master earned only increasing animosity.

Brey, Vauk and Kinanna and the other four members of her scouting party continued their scouting without pause. Having discovered a strange partially walled up cavern located at the treeline on the northern mountains, they decided to further explore. Kinanna thought the craftsmen might have been ancient Taths, but as she knew of no Tath currently practicing such a skill, there was no way for her to prove the assumption. But, as Vauk suggested, the skillfulness of the workmanship left no doubt that wall's builders were of a highly civilized people.

"We've wound our way over three miles now, Vauk, shouldn't we be discovering something worthwhile." Kinanna spoke in halting Haafian made even more difficult to comprehend because of her nervousness.

Vauk reached out for her blue hand. "This cavern might be part of a tunnel system, possibly one reaching into Tath... In which case, we've located a secure supply route. That's the importance of continuing...." He explained to her in rough hewn Tath.

She went from her deep blue to almost a white, and hid her face from Vauk. Vauk glanced to Brey for assistance. She crossed her arms and stared him down, then almost laughed.

"What, pray tell, Queen Brey, is so laughable?" Vauk demanded, watching the two other Taths stare at him with grave looks.

"You thoroughly confused your Tath." Brey curtly admonished him. "You told her she had pretty underwear."

Then, unable to control herself at Vauk's embarrassment, she laughed again, this time almost all joined in. The echoes of their laugher bounced merrily along the cavern's rough walls. Kinanna turned round, her face returning to blue. She allowed Vauk a momentary delightfully devious glance, then resumed her official posturing as Brey's first retainer.

"I sincerely apologize for embarrassing you, Lady Kinanna." Vauk bowed as he spoke.

"You are forgiven and you will learn better Tath. I shall personally see to it." She said formally as she passed by Vauk.

This time Brey's shade turned a bit. She realized exactly what Kinanna had in mind. Vauk felt something unusual, but only recognized part of the story. After resting for the evening meal at the first juncture in the cave, some eight miles into the mountain, they decided to further explore before deciding which route to use.

"This only 'appears' to be a cavern, Brey....I'm beginning to think the entire thing was constructed."

"Simply because we haven't discovered any other passageways..."

"Yes and no." Vauk said. "Its more the floor. Usually its rough, full of those things that drip from the ceilings...... And damp, if not wet....None of these elements exists. We've had no trouble moving along because the size of the cavern has not enlarged nor shrunk, until now."

Kinanna listened intently but did not speak, but her fluttering eyebrows indicated that something important had yet to be spoken. She turned from the others and began to explore the chamber's indentations with her torch. Without warning she kicked at the wall, putting her foot clear though it. Off-balance, she tumbled before anyone reached her.

"This is the Cavern of the Five Tunnels!" She smiled through her dust covered face. "It's recorded in our ancient history, isn't it?" Kinanna asked the other Taths. None made a reply. "You have heard of the Cavern of the Five Tunnels, haven't you?" She repeated with more than a hint of frustration.

"As we listened to the stories told," One Tath guard began uneasily. "We heard the place mentioned a few times, but never in a positive way..... This place is dangerous. We should leave now, before it's too late." It took a few moments before the translating finished, and then, no one understood exactly what the guard meant.

Ignoring the guard, Kinanna dusted herself off and proceeded twelve paces from where her foot originally punched a hole in the facade. She kicked again. The unforgiving wall forced a painful scream from her. Vauk picked up her fallen torch and moved a few paces beyond her. He tapped the wall with the torch butt and smiled.

"It's hollow." He announced in Tath and Haafian while slamming his broadaxe through the powdery material. "That makes five tunnels......But Lady Kinanna must tell us why two were disguised.."

"And I shall," She said rubbing her foot. "When everyone is seated." She thoroughly enjoyed of being the center of attention. "When we had offended our god enough to cause him to deny us our homeland, two tribes immediately struck out through the pass north of this mountain. The remaining five joined to deliberately defy our god's command, beseeching him to recant his capricious action. Realizing that the Unknown One, as he was called in ancient times, could be persuaded to recant, and just as easily disappear again, or--and more to their thinking--would refuse to change anything but thoroughly enjoy bargaining with his subjects. The Taths bought as much time as possible. They became experts at delaying actions. They excelled in hairsplitting definitions."

".....In order to construct these tunnels." Vauk interrupted.

"Correct." Kinanna bluntly responded, not amused. "The Taths actually kept the bargaining alive for over a generation, then the Unknown One finally just terminated the proceedings as if they never existed."

"What then...or rather, what purpose did the tunnels serve?" Brey asked.

"They were designed to allow the Taths to return from the north."

"Then they do connect us with the tribes!" Vauk eagerly declared.

"Yes, provided the tunnels are still intact.....But that's getting ahead of the story..... The five tribes exited Paradise Valley by the same route as those who left a generation before. At that time, two tribes expected a wondrous reward for their immediate obedience to the Unknown One...... When it did not happen according to their desires, the tribes renounced allegiance to their god." She paused quietly, sipping a bit of ale to relieve the heaviness of her story.

"Those once labeled as 'non-believers'...who lived along the rivers, actually had a legitimate position?"

"Yes, Brey....But the result was war, two tribes against five. Distances kept us from the great massacres I've heard about in the your south and with the Kyykki, but the two tribes had a major success which prevented everyone from using the tunnels to return---they built the walls, some of which crumbled over time, but in each, from this juncture.... to each entrance a multitude of boobytraps exists."

Hopes rose and sank for some. The scouting party's mission was accomplished. With the knowledge currently at hand, any further movement involved too many dangers. Another larger and properly equipped expedition should clear the tunnels. Vauk sat quietly, ignoring those preparing for sleep. Those anticipating a return to daylight, especially the Taths, rested much better. In seriously contemplating Kinanna's story, Vauk recognized parallels within his people's history. He also realized, as if by divine insight, that clearing a tunnel presented few actual problems: the boobytraps could be dismantled from behind. A few well-placed rocks discharging wrongly aimed traps, and, the tunnel reaching the Taths safely opened. He needed to convince the others of this when they woke.

The incomprehensible realm far beyond the created realm, that realm whose temporary citizens feared neither time nor space, nor for their own existence, became, simultaneously, inhabited when the oppressive absolute darkness unexpectedly dropped upon the created'. In spirit form, the only matrix permitted within the uncreated domain, three spirits, later joined by a tentative fourth who was not actually numbered among the gods, deliberately withdrew from all their other responsibilities to meet the present challenger: Ashuwa.

Having entered the realm's flexible and indestructible fabric in a furious rage, Ashuwa lost precious little time in establishing the ramifications of his case. "This dung heap of the created deliberately encroached upon MY sovereign territory!" He bellowed loudly enough that the sphere of their realm expanded to twice its usual size. "I demand his immediate punishment!............ I WILL·HAVE·REVENGE!!" The realm doubled again, feeling the depth and fury of Ashuwa's indignation.

"You speak the truth you presently feel, Ashuwa." The Holy One replied without emotion. "That is why you brought the case here. However, historically speaking, are you able to ground your case in the truth?"

"How dare you raise the past! It does not exist! It does not repeat!" He screamed back, and then partially settled himself. "Therefore, it is irrelevant to the present charge. ...."

"Ooooh! You stupid ninny!" The nameless god cooed. "And you yell so strongly."

"Arrg!....If I could....."

"But you can't ....Ash Heap." The nameless one teased.

"Enough." An almost bored voice projected from the Holy One. "This name calling has no substance beyond further infuriating Ashuwa, something you're an expert at, nameless one."

"Thank you."

"Judge this capricious simpleton!" Ashuwa's words stuck to the realm's gigantic perimeter, bouncing and echoing countless time. Then he violently repeated himself. The volume increased beyond anything measurable as it ricocheted through the spirit forms of the gods.

"Can't ye be'es doin' enny better." The nameless god pushed the challenge at Ashuwa using the Haafian seafaring accent.

"Talk correctly." With his authoritative collected voice the Holy One denounced the teasing.

"Ash Heap's charge is quite unfounded.......... The territory I cleansed properly belongs to me, that includes the cesspools he claims as home. The Paradise Valley, at the onset, contained it."

"And you ran off, uncaring about your so-called people, allowing their endless prayers to seep off into nowhere....." Ashuwa rather calmly stated, causing the realm to constrict Immediately. "You totally irresponsible lout....deliberately ignoring your own people."

"I accept that condemnation fully....But what territory I was originally given has no bearing upon my personal behavior, nor does it have anything to do with my relationship to the Taths.....The issues are separate, at least to anything with half a brain."

"You ignoramus,..... you overestimate yourself!" Ashuwa taunted. "Possession is the law....You robbed me of territory which was firmly under MY control and MY jurisdiction..It has been for eons!"

"You might wish such a fantasy....The Taths were expelled from the valley not more than six centuries ago,.......... hardly any worthwhile chunk of time,.....Ash Heap!" He croaked, mimicking Ashuwa. "Some day your memory might improve!"

"Listen,.... you androgynous pea-brain!... There is no way that MY territory will return to you.... In a matter of moments I'll reclaim the entire valley for myself!.. The castle and Sarg will die!.... If you dare,.. wimp,.. try to stop me...Let's see what kind of power lurks behind your dubious exterior!"

"I refuse to fight an inferior. Fair is fair.....But then, fairness isn't found in your vocabulary. And neither is integrity, nor morality, nor credibility..... But somehow you manage to slide by on greed, incest and...."

An incredible enraged snarl erupted from Ashuwa's spirit form, so powerful as to displace the nameless god to the furthermost edge of the measureless uncreated realm. His raging continued, pounding the god without-a-name into the realm's indestructible wall. Never before had anything 'dressed down' Ashuwa before and lived. Never before had the blunt truth concerning his character been so exposed, especially at this most high level. The nameless god penetrated Ashuwa's invincible charade. Ashuwa responded in reckless fury, one flowing from his evilness. Layer after layer of his depravity came to light as he used the evils concealed there to combat the nameless one. The realm buckled and swayed with his wretchedness, his unrepentant rapacious appetite for the unholy and the unclean.

Finally, the authentic Ashuwa emerged, stripped to his basic, elemental spirit-self. The deepest-black sucking hole, whirling about itself so painfully tight as to deny gravity, light and sound their elemental existence. Ashuwa's own elemental self actually denied life. It deliberately strangled life from everything. Now, with nothing to feed upon and having used up his layers of deceit and blackest evil, Ashuwa's elemental form flopped haphazardly as it struggled for its very life. The nameless god wearily smiled as he crawled his way to the realm's interior.

"You are the brainless twerp!" He painfully chuckled at Ashuwa's wasted form. "There is no sustenance for any of us here, or did you forget?" Though severely taxed, the nameless one stood, his integrity tested.

A softer voice, one not heard from before, entered in. "Might I have the privilege to speak, Holy One."

"You may, I've had enough from these two for the rest of eternity." The Holy One spoke with a gentle vulnerable authority, the type only those who truly understand absolute power dare to use. "Dear Creation," He sighed. "Please speak."

"I thank you, Holy One.... And I also thank the unnamed god who, in his most unusual present bout of responsibility, managed to return some purity to my form.... It's exhilarating to be rejuvenated."

"So I have seen..... But what do you wish here?"

"I am no match for these two, but my heart sickens as I am forced to watch more and more of creation succumb to the degenerate filthiness of the Dark Lands. Its waste pollutes the waters, kills the fish and animals, even air is often unfit to breathe........I humbly beg permission to rectify." Her voice slowed, nervousness crept into her tones. "I am fearful of a repeat from the last peoples, though I know this time, Ashuwa is responsible."

Knowing his place, perhaps for the first time, the god without-a-name remained perfectly quiet, doing no more than listening.

"This request, Daughter Creation, have you not made it before? Did you not request that the peoples be stricken from the surface?" The Voice maintained a penetrating edge, one which forced self-examination. "Is this what you ask for now?"

"I have been foolish.... But the last peoples did self-destruct, taking most of the surface with them." She said quietly. "I hold the damned one responsible this time." She repeated herself.

"And a few of the old remain." The Holy Spoke, ignoring part of Creation's concern.

"But they are different. I do not speak about the exceptions."

"And you did a wondrous job of rejuvenating the earth, Creation."

"But only because there were extremely few people to defeat my efforts."

"That is long understood.... I recognize your vulnerability, for you alone wear a solid mantle, a surface exploited by peoples."

"And by Ashuwa!" Her accusation caused the Holy One to smile.

"Go on." He commanded gently.

"This time Ashuwa himself is personally involved in the destruction of the earth. By clogging the source of water to Paradise Valley as well as through his Dark Lands, he blatantly ignores your ruling."

"So, it's two against one?"

"Indeed."

"And rightly so." Interjected the nameless one.

"There is merit in both your cases." The Holy One said. "However, your actions will be your own." Having rendered His final word, the Holy One took leave. Their meeting ended.

As the incomprehensible realm contracted to a size that neatly encapsulated the collapsed and decimated Ashuwa, Creation and the nameless god took leave. En route to their home, Creation gently described her plan, one which she adamantly refused to allow any participation by the god without-a-name.

The original Paradise Valley river, she explained, was more than four times its present size. Moreover, that river's source also initiated at a river running through the Dark Lands to the Istellia Bay, as the Taths named it...... Ashuwa, deliberately constructed his volcano atop the river's source, diverting its flow into his cesspools, causing the Dark Lands to grow in stench-filled acridity. The lush and vibrant forest lands turned to degenerate dust bowls. As he listened, the nameless god heard the righteous agony in Creation's voice, something the 'old' god would have ignored, he sternly reminded himself. His heart and energy went out to her, but she again refused his generous offer of assistance. In spite of the numerous claims, only Creation actually owned the land. She would take sole responsibility for restoring it.

"And how do you attack the problem, Creation?"

"Simple. As it is my nature to be self-cleaning, I will increase the pressure upon Ashuwa's plug that controls the river's source. Once it blows, fresh water and... time.... will cleanse the territory and restore both rivers."

"Allowing the Taths and the Haafians to interact." He smiled.

"Peoples I do not trust...But, I warn you, don't permit these peoples to ...."

"Once was more than enough, Creation....In spite of my lousy reputation, I shall not tolerate what I did before."

"Only time will tell." She said as she descended into the earth's bowels to begin her mission.

With Creation's touchdown and the god without-a-name's return, the oppressive absolute darkness disappeared as unexpectedly as it began, leaving the peoples surprized, joyful albeit wary. However, those emerged from their shelters witnessed a vast frozen land, irregardless of where they lived. Stunned by another strange turn of events, ones surely controlled by the Holy One or the nameless one or Ashuwa, depending upon one's perspective, few peoples ventured anywhere. Fearfulness and insecurity had driven all their actions for the past six days or dawns, depending upon one's perspective of time. Everyone moved with caution.

Except Warmaker. Coated with heavy layers of ice, barely able to move, he never landed. The sudden light caused his mount, an exhausted and badly beaten Windfire, to fumble, narrowly missing the tops of gigantic pine trees. Warmaker savagely kicked its flanks. His mount gained just enough altitude to survive, mainly due to weight loss from falling ice. Warmaker painfully stretched, ripping the layers of ice from both himself and Windfire. The huge mount, thoroughly fatigued from four continuous dawns of aimless flying, truly appreciated the tremendous weight loss.

The view before Warmaker refused to register, nowhere did such a huge forest exist, especially in this territory of Ashuwa's. In all directions, as far as his reptilian eyes could discern, the pine forest flowed out into infinity. Looking up, the too bright sky refused to disclose the sun's location. In spite of the evidence, Warmaker refused to acknowledge the truth. He was lost. Windfire glided in huge circles, a bit of a respite, while its scaly master wrestled for an answer, not to ascertain their location as much as to gather another explanation for lateness. His thinking processes did not move quickly.

The sun, now able to shower the territory with her warming and healing rays, rapidly elevated the freezing temperatures. For Windfire this amounted to a death sentence. Whatever reddish-green blood remained within him due to the freezing temperatures, now slowly dripped from his flanks into the warming air. His body shook violently, his wings became spastic, uncontrollable, even as Warmaker pounded his flanks, breaking his ribs with his clawed feet. As a rock drops from a balcony, so did Windfire drop from the sky; dead from exhaustion. Screaming curses all the while, Warmaker continued beating his mount as their descent gathered speed. Within five more breaths, Windfire was impaled by a thick trunked pine tree, Warmaker had grabbed for anything his weak claws could grab. Pine branches provided no mercy for Ashuwa's first named. They broke and bent with his weight, hurtling him ever faster towards the forest floor, some three hundred feet below. The final fifty feet amounted to a free-fall. Ashuwa's last memory recorded an ugly snapping sound as his feet smashed into the needle covered ground. His heaped body, blood-covered and torn, lay motionless as the sun descended.

Taking immediate advantage of the sunlight, Feathered Goat and his party mounted their rested Istelles and flew hard for Haaf North, believing the dragons there too frozen to give battle. Each Istelle also carried a boulder, a present for the servants of Ashuwa. Within another two days, should nothing else go contrary, the Istelles would glide into Krabo.

Ashuwa's oppressive darkness took a dreadful toll on his own troops. Of the Kyykki who retreated into the swamp, over half froze to death, but in the perverse Kyykki manner, their deaths meant sustenance for the surviving. Most of the Demon Masters survived by huddling in the middle of the dragons. At the next dawn, an all-out frontal attack would be made upon Pinduala. However, over half of their force, with the dragons leading would attack the southeastern wall as a wedge. The warming sunlight and food brought a mood of confidence to their wretched camp.

At Pinduala tension ran higher the moment light reappeared; the Light Stripers expected an immediate attack in spite of the freezing temperatures.

When it was confirmed that the Kyykki retreated to the swamp, Ayhn summoned the Senior Officers of the Lancers.

"I have no doubts that on the morrow the Kyykki hordes will attack.... Apparently their asinine god forgot that his own freeze quickly....." Ayhn stopped himself, realizing that few followed his logic. "Let me backup. I don't believe that darkness only dropped on us, a trickery from the Kyykki's slimebag god. Actually the darkness fell on everything. The Kyykki are frozen in the swamp."

"You'd like a raid, Sir?"

"Indeed, but at bow range and not any closer. The dragons were not spotted."

"And the War Waggons?"

"Only as backup. They stay within sight of the walls."

"Sir, a suggestion."

"Speak."

"The Kyykki could use a little warming up....Flaming arrows may instill more fear than the regular....Also, Sir, the heaps of frozen carcasses surrounding the city are providing a ramp for the Kyykki once their attack begins....They'll slide into the city." The Officer paused as some of his colleagues snickered at such an idea. "Well, it's the truth. In some places their hides are stacked higher than the wall....That's dangerous."

"Your first suggestion is approved....But elaborate further on the second."

"I think," He then hesitated. "I think that if we placed tubs full of pitch beneath the Kyykki dead....and that if we light them as their attack begins, we might collapse the wall of carcasses as well as sabotage their attack." He paused and stepped back into line.

"Then take the engineers out to the carcass wall. Nothing better than a little conflagration to purify the air. Don't you think so Chaplain?"

"Yes," The wizened old man smiled. "Time to bring light into this damned darkness."

The amused officers rapidly put their orders into action. Almost five hundred Lancers were able to mount up. The raid went better than expected inasmuch as the Kyykki were totally unprepared. They had not posted scouts or guards. Barrage after barrage of pitch-dipped arrows connected with their half-frozen bodies. Controlled only by fear and self-preservation they fled further into the swamp. When the dragons finally roused to defend the remnants of the once-proud invasion force, the Lancers slowly galloped towards the city. Numerous burnt fingers and a couple of lame Stripers constituted the Lancer's casualties.

The lifting of the oppressive darkness brought more mocking from the hardy, independent tribes of the northern wastes of Tath. Let the foolish god have his tricks, at least this one didn't harm anyone, though the Blue Istelles wandered about confused by the extremely short winter. Some began constructing nests and then suddenly abandoned their endeavor, as if their biological clocks ran more effectively than nature's.

Almost as swiftly moving as the returning sunlight, the Elders congregated at Krabo translocated throughout Haaf, seeking evidence concerning the dawns of the oppressive darkness. Mostly they found the citizens blaming Ashuwa, the Ash Heap, for their predicament and for their loses, mainly in crops, the orchards and animals. The older citizens fared much worse than the younger, providing many funerals for the local clergy. And once the thawing began, the sewers of the larger cities no longer were as comfortable as before. The few remaining rats found themselves back in charge of their kingdom. Where tunnels existed, life kept its routine in spite of the serious limitations placed by the darkness. However, too much closeness did damage many relationships, enough to quickly empty the underground when the sunlight lit the frozen ground.

The coastal area of Haaf Bay told a vastly different story. There, due to the fiery destruction caused by the dragon's last sortie, the Haafians were without shelter. Many had begun moving inland when caught by the unmerciful darkness. The Elders discovered whole families frozen in huddles surrounding now-defunct campfires. Those remaining along the coast fared as poorly; their homes having no cellars and their towns no tunnels. Half-burnt houses provided slight refuge from the freezing temperatures.

"You can't begin to imagine the carnage. It's sickening beyond sickening." Jabbi sadly announced to the gathered Elders.

At evening, the twenty three met in the King's suite, both to share their findings as well as ascertain what might lay behind the dreadful darkness. Most still carried their winter robes or blankets.

"I assume that the swampers believed that the darkness was divine punishment from the Holy One....They committed mass suicide....The Poodle's waters will soon turn red from their thawing blood."

Oros smacked his fat hands together. "So, once again the divine fact is confirmed: evil is self-destructive." He was not happy.

"Have you no sense of compassion!" Ilty shot at the mountainous figure.

"I have a better sense of justice, Ilty...Remember the 'Blue Ladies' if you will, not to mention the Church Guards who murdered our King."

"But...."

"No room for 'buts', My Dear Lady, exceptions only create a camouflaging for the evil." Vosnob calmly acknowledged. "Not to mention the fact that none were coerced into their treachery. In every case a deliberate choice was made. Each person in that mass suicide chose wrong."

"You're beginning to sound like Sarg." Ilty responded, still a bit despondent in spite of the truth she believed.

A jarring motion swayed everything, abruptly stopping their conversations. After three swells which cracked the wall glazings, the tremors subsided.

"Ole Ash Heap just doesn't know when to quit." The Chaplain said to Baste.

"Are you that sure he's that powerful?"

"Shut up." The wizened old man shot back, smiling the whole time.

"We'll have the tremors investigated--after--we finish our reports." Vosnob said.

Baste immediately commenced his report concerning the events at Haaf North. The sooner they were finished, the sooner he'd leave to inspect his own town and visit the family. In spite of being honor-bound and duty-bound, the grandfather still only wanted to return home and go fishing with his grandsons. He began. "I imagine we'll recapture Haaf North before we have the King's funeral. Jed's troopers all but finished the tunneling to the city wall. Deep Owl and Qill also dug a tunnel parallel to the wall. The machiners are just waiting for the first half-frozen dragon to peek his ugly head over the rail."

"Does Yganak realize he's been replaced?" Oros laughed.

"You've got the erroneous version of the story, Oros." Ilty smiled sweetly as she spoke. "Actually, from what I've heard, there's talk about Yganak being the next King. Especially as Vosnob declined such an honor."

"Honor, my foot." Vosnob stomped. "The King is the one person who has no freedom whatsoever. He's watched over, nursemaided as if an invalid, denied privacy and must be open to receiving anyone at anytime." He sat back on his leathered chair and propped up his feet. "My bet is that Yganak will accept the offer only after Rux refuses it." He relaxed and placed his large hands behind his thick brown head of hair. "My bet is that some ruthless merchant needs the job." A caustic air went with his prediction.

"Actually, the last merchant King, will be one not forgotten. All ready he's become something of a folk hero." Jabbi elaborated. "Ashuwa's proclivity to evil intrigue and inventiveness have promoted him as a martyr of the Faith----at least to the serfs."

"You say that as if what serfs believe doesn't count for much!" Ilty accused Jabbi.

"Not true, Ilty." Jabbi said while eyeballing her. "But remember the serfs in the swamp."

"We need a many more females in this group. That's the whole problem."

"Alas,.......... we are without compassion."

"And we are far from our intended task, as well." Vosnob clomped his feet to the floor from the table. "Now, how go things in Pinduala..... Chaplain!"

"The Lancers mounted a surprise attack against the Kyykki early this dawn. The frozen creatures went down by the thousands... Word is...the Kyykki have too little troops left to mount another attack...Meanwhile, Ellom's using the frozen wharf area to unload his ships and load them with the wounded and injured."

"Sounds like Ayhn's been having fun."

Ignoring the spurious remark, Vosnob pressed ahead. "What news, if any, do we have from Sarg's Paradise Valley?"

"At this point, nothing. But the reinforcements safely waited out that damned darkness exploring parts of Krucik's old homestead."

"You referring to the burnt out...."

"Yes, there's quite a maze of tunnels underneath. One was stuffed with the bones of those who were sacrificed to Ashuwa. The others lead in different directions, all being mapped out."

"Another report? Or are we finished?"· Vosnob spoke hastily, he too, like Baste, wished to be elsewhere.

No one replied and those sitting on the wooden benches and the leather chairs became restless.

"We meet at the usual place following the King's funeral...In the meantime Jabbi will inform us of any irregularities in the preparations for the funeral....Let's get moving.....Listen for any information on those tremors."

Only thick dry fog remained within the meeting room chamber; twenty three Elders translocated to their respective assignments.

Simultaneously at the unexpected termination of the oppressive darkness, Paradise Valley instantly rocked with repeated convulsions, tossing the castle's unsuspecting inhabitants across floors and against walls. Far deep within the earth, close to her heart, where the primal forces of Creation herself refuse restraint, Creation sent a bolt of pure energy upwards to the source of the river incarcerated under Ashuwa's volcano. When this burst of energy collided with Ashuwa's thick molten rock plug, the reverberations in her skin rocked the face of the earth for almost a thousand miles in all directions. While everyone could not help but feel the tremors, no one with a modicum of authority claimed to understand or explain it. The times of unnatural occurrences continued. Everyone was less than comfortable.

Ashuwa's plug of molten rock, now hardened to the depth of one half mile, effectively prevented over three fourths of the water from reaching the surface for over four centuries. He allowed only enough water to keep his tunnel waterway open and enough to pretend to be the original waterfall of Paradise Valley. This latter was specifically designed to placate the god without-a-name. Ashuwa made one other provision for the water; to supply the moisture required by his living cesspools. As time passed, this filth laden water seeped into the Istelle Bay, along the way the once verdant Dark Lands became acrid, barren and desolate, a deliberate affront to Creation.

Now as her energy blasted the half mile thick plug up through the bottom of Ashuwa's volcano, Creation allowed herself the joyful privilege of righteous judgement. The plug's upward movement severely cracked the volcano's casing. Then it violently erupted into the nepes incubation areas, then into the holding tanks where the nepes lived before being dumped into the main cesspool outside the volcano. The plug violently exploded once it moved beyond the restrictive channel, bouncing enormous boulders inside the interior of the throne room. Untold millions of nepes perished either from the pure water now flooding the volcano or from the slabs of its casing smashing them.

Creation smiled quietly, proudly; this was HER time. With Ashuwa stripped beyond nakedness, to his true identity of a black empty life-sucking wind, she knew that no one would prevent her from cleansing the Dark Lands. She waited patiently now; her initial violent move began the needed healing.

Having willing divested himself of his heinous energy in attempting to destroy the god without-a-name, Ashuwa's size dwindled to where an ant might easily cart him away. Without the energy of his immense hatreds, rages, uglinesses and wrath, all particulars of himself that he used to punish the nameless god, Ashuwa finally understood the horrendous trick was actually played on him. In refusing to fight back, the unnamed god effectively drained all his energy. Now drained and devoid of power Ashuwa, still wrapped in the uncreated realm, could barely think. He balanced on the very edge of extinction, even though he remained one of the immortals.

This is worse than death, he thought to himself. I don't have enough power to even leave here....What of me still exists ..is. scattered throughout this ...convoluted realm.....I can't even leave, he repeated constantly to himself. But totally unwilling to give up on himself, Ashuwa slowly reached out his spirit to gather what fragments of himself might be floating in the realm. Once he collected enough to depart for his volcano......His plan to obtain a people would continue.

In the great room of the volcano, the room invaded by Sarg and his friends, stood the abhorrent physical form Ashuwa used. The hundred foot wide plug splintered as it passed by, crushing his grotesque form to a scaly reddish-green pasty slime. In other upper rooms, the imprisoned 'pale ladies' and their Demon Master guards met a similar fate.

From their royal suite in the marbled castle, Sarg and Sjura watched, entranced, enthralled and fearful by the disintegrating volcano. Since the tremors stopped, everyone in the castle refused to leave the windows, rightly sensing that something else had yet to happen. In the emergency, the royal suite became the obvious gathering place.

Now they witnessed another miracle. First, thousands of dragons, those Ashuwa kept for replacements as well as for the final assault on Haaf, careened from the volcano as if chased by even worse monsters. The few who few towards the castle, died of broken necks, thanks to the Istelles. The others were closely followed by exploding chunks of volcanic debris. Next, great substantial cracks appeared in the sides of the volcano through which dense blackened clouds of steam roared, then, after a few moments hissed down to nothing. Only then did the immense plates forming the volcano's sides begin to slide away. First, the plate facing the Paradise Valley slid, stopped, crumbled and then slid again, exposing the revolting interior. Suddenly it disintegrated into dozens of enormous plates that blocked the waterfall and crushed the scrawny pine forest on the upper slope. On the opposite side a plate dropped a few hundred feet, then rested. The water blasted forth, kicking the gigantic plate into the nepes cesspool, splashing out its putrid water. The remaining plates, now without support, fell in against each other, only to be lightly brushed aside by the raging column of pure water. The massive volcano disintegrated before their eyes.

Up through the clouds surged the newly released water, defiantly reclaiming its central position in the territory--a position that Creation refused to relinquish again.

From the castle, the column of water appeared as a solid beam of beautiful reflecting purity, one mile thick. The Taths, Yldans and Haafian continued to watch the column grow thicker, removing the last vestiges of the volcano. Fascinated by this natural destruction of Ashuwa's headquarters, the entire group studied the redeeming scene in reverent awed silence.

A powerful wind rudely interrupted the scene, forcing the water column's 'rain' to descend upon the acrid desolate wastes east of Paradise Valley. The god without-a-name sat high above, blowing eastward, making the most of Creation's gift. Water puddled upon the stone-hard ground in the Dark Lands, unable, at first, to penetrate. It also kicked up huge clouds of dust which later sheltered the ruined land with a coating of soft mud. Towards evening, the column slowly returned to the volcano's gigantic hollowed-out basin and disappeared. The waterfall quit flowing, consequently causing the river to drop to extremely low levels. A soft rumble escaped from the extinct volcano. The castle's inhabitants jumped.

"We better be prepared for an evacuation." Sarg said tersely. "Even though the volcano's gone, the water could still sweep this castle away..."

"Are you without faith?" One of the Tath queens asked quite innocently. "Water is the enemy of fire. Ashuwa would not collapse his kingdom's centerpiece, driving out his dragons and killing most of his creatures just to revenge himself on you."

"Maybe he would." Sarg responded thoughtfully. "We've been enemies for countless double moon cycles......I......especially with Sjura---being with our child."

"So, being a father does make a difference?"

"Yes, my dear queen," Sarg graciously smiled. "In truth, I've become more of a worrier."

Sjura seconded that remark and rose up on tip-toes to kiss her husband. "Quite frankly, I am more worried about Brey, Vauk and Kinanna. They've completely disappeared, as if the ground suddenly swallowed them..... Childbirth, on the other hand, is something quite natural....at least for some of us." She kissed her slightly embarrassed husband.

Another rumble from the extinct volcano abruptly terminated their conversation. A call from one the guards brought everyone to the windows once again. The next sight panicked most. The volcano's base had filled with water, ready to seep over the edge. Such pressure wracked whatever strength the volcanic wall yet retained. A block of white-light, emanating from the highest cloud, punched a hole through the southwestern rim. There was the slightest of pauses, as if the impounded water refused to decide which course to take, then a spacious waterfall shot out the hole, utterly destroying it. Within moments the water flowed over the cliffs. The new waterfall exceeded the old by four times. Its force buried the old pond at the base and began carving out a vast new one.

"I believe this is going to be the river my Mother's mother spoke about." Queen Sjura said to everyone in particular. She was elated with the prospect of revisiting her past.

"Now the harbor on the west end of the castle makes sense." Sarg mumbled, his mind stuffed with wonderment and adoration for the Holy One, who caused these things to be. "Now the wharves will have use."

As Sarg mumbled, the new Paradise River began as a flash flood forming at the base of the waterfall. Loaded with debris from its digging and the volcano's demise, an eighty foot wall-of-water rapidly advanced down the river's old channel, recarving its curves as it blasted everything in its path. Then, easily overcoming the old riverbed, the rushing waters grabbed the ancient shoreline, conquered it quickly and moved onward, spreading to three times its usual size.

"Sjura, this wall-of-water could erode the castle's foundation." Sarg worried even more. "Nothing can stop that....And it won't be long until it reaches us...Maybe five minutes, by your accounting."

"You exaggerate! Don't be so worried...This is the handiwork of our nameless god....Your threatening him actually did much good...."

"Can you swim?". He replied caustically.

"What is 'swim'?"

Sweat poured from Sarg's brow. "If we survive the impact, I'll teach you."

High above Sarg's solitary anxiety, deep within the mountains separating Paradise Valley from Tath, Vauk finished convincing the scouting party that to continue through the tunnel into Tath was their best plan, especially as they could all fly back. His proposal for neutralizing the boobytraps which lay ahead were tacitly accepted.

Then the tremors rolled through cavern, swaying the entire mountain, demolishing the facades covering the other tunnels--and partially collapsing the tunnel from which they entered. Dirt-laden clouds rolled through the tunnel, covering the party, making vision almost impossible and breathing difficult. Vauk fashioned temporary masks by forcing food sacks over everyone's head, Kinanna demanded a kiss first.

"I guess we don't have a choice anymore." Vauk said nonchalantly after the dust subsided. "But, He smiled. "We do know that Tath and fresh air lie on the other end of the tunnel."

"Are you sure the boobytraps haven't been set off....or, might they have bounced around altering their direction of fire?" Taert inquired in Tath. His present job was to safe-guard the 'almost' queen Brey, a responsibility he fervently accepted, much to Brey's disdain.

"I let Brey lead, then we'll know for sure." Vauk said smugly, baiting Taert. He spoke in Tath.

"I shall go first!" He claimed loudly enough to aggravate Brey.

"Enough." She interjected, unamused. "When the dust settles, we move....People at the castle are depending upon us."

"Yes, your Royal Highness."

"Not yet, Vauk. Perhaps not ever." Brey said matter-of-factly as she dusted off her tunic and checked her crossbow. "Kinanna, are there any animals...beasts.....creatures we need to...."

"No Brey." Kinanna answered too politely. "But the entrances to the tunnels are supposed to be guarded."

"Then help is closer than I thought."

After a quick meal, the party cautiously set out, Vauk leading. He tossed rocks across the path. There was no response. Heavier rocks brought no response either. With the assistance of a few others, a boulder the size of a person went careening down the corridor's flat surface. Still nothing happened.

"This bothers me." Vauk thought out loud. "The tunnel is almost perfectly shaped. The floor is flat, and supposed to be boobytrapped...yet nothing happens." Turning quickly, his cape flared out. Two iron darts rent ugly holes in it. He cursed his stupidity.

Kinanna, as could be predicted, fainted away, though no one prevented her falling to the dirty floor. Vauk examined the darts while the guards explored for their source. The darts were unfamiliar, being short and bulky with heads that were wide and rusty.

"I really don't know what I'm looking for." Taert apologized to Vauk in Tath.

"These weren't meant to be spotted." Vauk replied. "We'll just have to tease them out."

He leaned over and ripped off Kinanna's long slivered cape, placed it on a lance and wiggled it out in the tunnel.

Swoosh!

As if one, four darts passed through the cape, each from a different direction. Vauk waved the cape again. Four more darts penetrated Kinanna's cape.

"How many are there?"

"I wish I knew, Taert." Vauk said as he waved the ruined cape for a third time. Again, the results were replicated.

"Notice that the darts are aimed at hitting the waist and above."

Vauk again waved the holey cape. Four darts responded immediately.

All struck about three feet from the floor or higher, verifying Vauk's observation.

"Perhaps we have two choices. Either I can wave Kinanna's cape forever or we can crawl.....Unless anyone has another suggestion."

"May I try something?" Taert asked quietly.

"Go ahead."

"May I borrow your crossbow, My Queen."

Brey refused to acknowledge the title, but did nod her head affirmatively. Taert ripped the broad laced collar from Kinanna's cape and pierced it with a bolt. Then he cocked the crossbow as weakly as possible.

"Nice." Vauk complimented him.

"Thanks. But I really don't know what difference it will make." He replied in Tath.

"Just shoot."

The bolt slowly arced down the tunnel, the laced collar flapping. The immediate response startled everyone: thousands of darts, seemingly from nowhere zipped by the bolt. Some went high, others ricocheted off the stone floor, the majority followed after the bolt, not reacting fast enough to catch it. Taert ripped a sleeve from his tunic and repeated his experiment. The result was dramatically different; few darts flew, and these weren't very accurate.

A slight rumble went through the mountain, cracking the smooth stone floor. Darts shot everywhere. A faint hazy light appeared at the end of the tunnel, not much larger than the boulder now rolling off to the side of the tunnel. As it touched the tunnel's side another round of darts exploded against it. The floor cracked again, this time part of it dropped about ten feet. Hot smoke poured out followed by sulfur-smelling steam.

"Get Kinanna on her feet!" Vauk shouted in Tath. "Our choices have been stolen from us........Let's go before the whole tunnel gives way."

A few boobytraps erratically shot off unaimed darts. The foul smelling steam increased as Vauk led the way. He deliberately choose to crawl about piles of debris and through heaps of spent darts. This path he figured to be the safest. Complaints about the difficulty, especially from those carrying Kinanna, caused him to revert to a course following close by the steam producing crevice.

This broken path dropped them a few feet below the tunnel floor, but meandered dangerously close to the tunnel wall. The hazy light disappeared, denying a more hopeful atmosphere than this torch-lit, sulfur smelling and boobytrapped tunnel otherwise provided. Relentlessly Vauk pushed towards the tunnel's entrance, knowing full well that the scouting party depended upon him. At least there's no lava around this time, he though to himself. He perceived a change. The rumbling ceased, the tunnel had quieted a bit. Ahead, the tunnel's stoney floor lay untouched by the vibrations, but safe? Could they make a run for it?

A Tath guard brandishing a torch pushed Vauk aside and jumped up to the level floor. Nothing happen. Then he swung the torch in a wide arc, still nothing happened.

"Get down!" Vauk angrily yelled in Tath.

The guard ignored him and slowly walked on, waving his torch, crouching low. Brey ordered him to remain still, but the guard continued. He stopped at thirty feet in front of the group, motioning for Vauk to follow.

As Vauk neared the guard, the Tath pointed to the tunnel's narrowing sides. There, on the right, where the carved wall cracked, exposing a contraption he'd never seen. Unfortunately, whatever evil it contained aimed at the two men.

"Thanks." Vauk whispered angrily.

"You bis vell-kum." The guard replied in broken Haafian.

"What do you expect me to do?"

"Throw a stone one foot before me.....The machine will close off the tunnel with a poison net."

How is that you know such things?" Vauk replied in Tath.

"Grandfather's grandfather did help build it....I remember the stories.... Never believed them until now.....This is the first 'trap'......Throw a stone." He spoke, intensely impatient.

Vauk retreated to convey the story to Brey and to grab a rock. He moved forward and tossed the rock. Just before it struck the ground, the guard jumped backward, smashing Vauk to the ground. For a moment, nothing happened. Then, through the haze, the two men watched old disintegrated ropes drop across the narrowed tunnel, preventing any escape. Then, from overhead, rusty, heavy, iron-spiked nets dropped, missing the two men by a foot's length.

"That's it." The guard said happily. "Now we bis cut way out."

"After I can breathe again." Vauk coughed.

"I apologize....but we are very near the tunnel's entrance."

"Just help me up."

Before the guard obliged, Kinanna had rushed to Vauk's rescue.

"I will help." She wiped his face with a piece of her petticoat.

"That would indeed be a first."

Ignoring, though actually hearing Vauk rather well, Kinanna continued her cleaning. Her usual schemings would not land this Vauk into her net. She reconsidered her options as she assisted him to his feet.

"Now," Said the guard. "All we need is to cut through the ropes and be free....in Tath."

"Perhaps there's an easier way." Commented Brey who, with the others now stood on more solid ground. "Why not go around the contraption.. ..machiner?..Just squeeze through the crack and then head forward....I'm not sure we have the tools to slice our way out, nor the time."

"Yes, My Queen." Taert said as he squeezed through the opening. He had been in motion even before she spoke, leaving Brey wondering if this Taert might read minds. She immediately pushed the strange thought out of her head.

"There's a stairway in here." Taert called out after a couple of tense silent moments. "And lots of dust." He coughed. "Other than that, the place is pretty safe."

"Anything to get away from those stinking fumes." Kinanna responded portentously, only to be ignored by the others.

The chamber had few comforts to offer. Cut from the granite type rock, it offered barely adequate room for the scouting party. Had the rope nets not been dropped, the smallish enclosure would have prevented them from entering. Ancient heavy wooden gears, well greased and oiled, crowded the walls, along with various levers on which designs were inscribed.

"Can you read these Taert?" ·Brey asked her personal bodyguard.

He wiped a number of them clean and shook his blue head. "Aloug, read these." He commanded the guard who foolishly walked ahead of everyone else.

Aloug squinted as he attempted to decipher the symbols carved on the levers. Slowly, deliberately he roamed from one to another, never touching. Resting his head in his hands, he succeeded in intensifying the anxiety of the others. Finally he stood, jiggling a few levers.

"Don't do anything without telling us first."· Brey commanded.

"I promise not to." Then Aloug turned to the rest. "These levers control the remaining traps...At least the down pointing ones do, the others have been set off either by us or the shaking." He paused to formulate a question for Brey. "You do expect that this tunnel will be useful in the future?"

At the moment Brey's focus on their present situation far exceeded that of the future, after all, no one actually knew exactly where they were, including the scouting party. "Why do you ask, Aloug?"

"We have the power here to either eliminate the tunnel forever or renew its usefulness for the future. A few yanks on them levers will do it all."

"Why should we make that decision at all?"

"Because you are queen. Such is your personal responsibility for your people."

"We were sent to gain friends and allies against the Kyykki and their damned leader." Brey said. "In that spirit I believe that we should re-open this tunnel....Are there other opinions?"

Believing that no answer meant that everyone agreed, Brey nodded her head. Aloug yanked seven ancient levers. The reactions of the ancient machines unceremoniously dumped everyone to the floor. The walls hollowly rattled as countless darts pounded on them, great clanking noises came from dropping nets and other nameless traps they never saw. The ruckus raised another cloud of dust. This time Kinanna placed her own head in a bag.

The din soon acquiesced; the dust did not, seemingly come more to life than before, as if borne by some unfelt breeze. Perplexed, Vauk carefully stepped through the crack, back into the central tunnel. Through the clearing dust, he saw the tunnel entrance not more than fifty feet away. Outlined in the sunlight there he counted some fifteen figures, none of them bearing resemblance to the Kyykki, though he believed some carried spears or staffs. He moved towards the entrance, keeping to the shadows and the boulders. He stopped: they spoke in .Tath.

"But we cannot go in....You saw how unstable it is. The traps go off as if by...."

"Don't even think it."

"But the Istelle riders from Sjura told us of a missing scouting party."

"That's 'Queen' Sjura and nowhere is it mentioned that they ever entered a cave or tunnel. He said they simply disappeared while scouting for the ...Ky..ik..ee, or some such name, who plan to invade Paradise Valley."

"Don't you really find his story a bit too much?" Said a Tath wearing a skin hat. "This tunnel checking is good. We must repair the damage.... But to consider Taths in the tunnel, you fools?"

Vauk had heard enough: he returned to the scouting party and shared the conversation with them. At once Kinanna began to fix herself up, as an attendant of the Queen, she must look proper, especially to other Taths, she curtly explained.

"We'll meet you outside." Brey called back as the others walked toward daylight, freedom, fresh air and a successful scouting.

The freezing oppressive darkness provided Garht with plenty of time to think, something he usually shied away from. Warmaker's planning didn't add up anymore. First, neither the docks nor a ship were ready--as promised. Second, their traveling up river as shipwrecked sailors wouldn't fool anyone. The distance from the Black Water to Sarg's castle was just too great. Warmaker promised an easy entry into the castle, but how did he really know? Had the hulking demon even seen the castle? Thirdly, and the third promise broken, no merchant ship could sail up river. Hell, he thought to himself, I can walk across this stream.

The longer the horrid darkness continued, the angrier Garht became. Damn some flunky's idiotic promises--lies--that he stupidly bought into. Just like Mother always said, if it sounds too easy for the gain, it's just a big lie. He fell for the lie, now he had to regroup, a task that could be quite difficult, considering the bottom-of-the-barrel cutthroats he had hired. Well, if they wanted their pay, they'd have to change vocations. But what directions, what other means to make an undemanding living were at his disposal? Only one fit: piracy. This he contemplated as the oppressive darkness abruptly lifted. Momentarily blinded, as were the other Haafians, he lost track of his thoughts.

"Where we'es be headin' ta, bossman?"

The direct question refocused Garht's thoughts. Gathering the rough-living crew about the fire, in great vivid colors he delineated all of Warmaker's treacherous lies and warped promises that refused to acknowledge reality. As he related his embellished version of the story, Garht specifically reiterated how not one of them ever received their promised pay, yet each Haafian had remained faithful to the promises.

"As for myself, I refuse to keep a one-way promise. I'm ready to begin something new.....Who will join me?"

The rambunctious Haafians immediately signed on, not even bothering to ask what the new job might be. For them, broken promises, especially ones that were supposed to pay well, were justifiable reasons for quitting Warmaker. To a man, and as a group, all renounced dealings with Warmaker, the demonic liar.

When their euphoria quelled, Garht counseled the men on their glorious future, if they remained loyal to him, that is. While hedging the word 'pirate', Garht related how, in the future double moon cycles, this river would be a wondrous ribbon of wealth as barges from Haaf were towed up river to Sarg's castle. And then, fully loaded with wondrous magical things from the Paradise Valley, these same barges would return. Regardless of direction these most valuable commodities required protection. Protection from pirates and robbers and other unwilling to pay a fair price--protection for which Garht's men would charge their legitimate fee. What a noble occupation, how respectable, how wealthy they'd become escorting every barge both up and down the river. That tactic Garht proficiently utilized to sell his Haafian rough-necks on a vocational change.

That same evening he outlined his devious scheme. Along the river at regular intervals small forts would be built. A few men would maintain each, living by extracting a small sum for a safe journey along their measured stretch of the waterway. As leader, Garht would have the largest fort, one built where the river met the Dark Water, where vast rented wharves required his protection.

Greater and greater grandiose visions, fueled well with bitter-tasting ale, circulated among the 'new' businessmen that first normal evening, including the pair who 'volunteered' themselves as 'true pirates', just to prove that the protection one bought was the protection one required. As the moon set simultaneously with the sun's rising, the would-be 'Protectors' finally settled in.

Rising at noon the following day, Garht divided the men into two groups. The smaller headed upriver to explore and map, though they were admonished to refrain from coming close to the castle or engaging its inhabitants. The larger group retraced their travels to the river's mouth, there to reconnoiter and establish the port city and blockading of the river. When the first group finished its work, Garht commanded them to return, via raft, to Port Garht, as the primary city of protection was now named. The groups would begin their respective assignments on the morrow. This afternoon and evening Garht mandated as a time for celebration.

Two dawns later, far upriver, the first group stumbled along the river's rocky shore wondering just how any barge could navigate this thirty foot wide stream. Its depth rarely exceeded six feet and the numerous rapids constrained any barge travel to a minimum. This knowledge rapidly discouraged the 'businessmen', too eager for a quick bucket of gold. Garht's promises were seen as phony as Warmaker's. In the morning they resolved to return to Port Garht, the city of the liar. They had proved powerful enough to quit Ashuwa, then they could quit Garht.

Rumblings from upriver easily unnerved the men. They knew Ashuwa's private domain lay at the river's source, just as they also knew that the damned one had a various ways of ascertaining what his 'people' were supposed to be doing. Not wishing to push their luck, the raft's construction commenced immediately. Downstream, Garth's group also felt the rumbling, but ignored them. Just another quake coming from Ashuwa's volcano, their expert manipulator explained.

From the steep cliffs occupying the northern bank of Paradise River just about all future traffic would be visible. Garht planned for a permanent lookout there. The southern bank, an unhealthy marshy area unsuitable for his glorious city, forced Garht to relocate the port about a half mile further inland, where soft sand lay on top of the granite base. Some five hundred feet behind the river's edge, in an ancient volcanic structure, long eroded by wind, Garht imagined as his impregnable stronghold. He was unaware of the Istelles who all ready claimed the towering structure.

That evening, he sketched out another program. More men were needed to build and guard their 'protection service'. When no volunteers readied themselves to raft or swim to Haaf, Garht flew into a furious rage. They refused to see any his rationale. Their logic showed no traffic coming in, therefore no work for anyone. And with more Haafians, the less money any would have. Furthermore, Garht's concept of building a bit of an empire along the river far exceeded their capacity. After the single moon arose, three of them gathered secretly to figure a way to return to Haaf.

Sarg, holding his wife tightly as he continually prayed, watched overanxiously as the debris carried ahead of the eighty foot wave slammed into the outer curve of the castle's outer wall. The convex wall held firm, pushing the entire flood waters south of the city, maintaining the older riverbed but at four times its current size. Overhead, the Istelle riders glided silently above the water's onslaught, watching its progress and noting any relevant changes.

On the southwestern side of the city, where the rocky flatland lay, the enormous debris of massive splintered timbers, boulders and uprooted vegetation of all types came to rest. The ravaging wave, finding a more spacious environment, lost some of its earth-carving strength. Wondrously, the wharves all ready constructed there, not only held, but actually increased in size commensurate with the river's growth.

The next long miles were a deep canyon, often narrowing to fifty feet at the current level. The pounding wave swept through the canyon, widening it by slamming into the sides with the rock from a few feet upstream, then tumbled the rock to the bottom, raising the riverbed considerably.

The Istelle riders caught sight of Garht's men long before the flash flood did. The men panicked at the gigantic shadows, steering their raft directly into the rapids, where they became stranded. The Istelle riders circled closer in an effort to warn the Haafians of the impending danger. Instead, believing the Istelles another creature of vengeance sent from Ashuwa, the Haafians preferred to swim. Still hoping to aid the Haafians, the Istelles set down on both river banks, where their riders disembarked. Again, the Haafians fearfully denied the Istelles and their blue skinned riders--those types were meant to be feared. The Haafians half-waded, half-stumbled downstream, benumbed with horror, using all their energy to escape. The Istelles regained the air shortly thereafter.

Sarg's found their report as difficult to comprehend as he did the water not damaging the castle and the wharf's sudden growth.

"More traitors, I suspect." Sarg thought aloud. "Somehow Ashuwa finds ways to keep one step ahead. No sooner are we established in Paradise Valley, but we are infiltrated by the enemy."

"Sir," Commented one of the Istelle riders, speaking in Tath. "Justice is served on them. By this time tomorrow, the wave will have overtaken them..."

"That is true..... But I have little stomach for this evil nonsense. ...... It makes me sick." He replied in Tath, a sad bitterness in his voice.

"Yes, Sir."

The Istelle rider's prediction came true. Those Haafians struggling for safety downstream, found death when the flash flood's first wave of debris splattered them against the riverbed. The second party fared little better. When Garht heard the thundering rushing noise coming from upstream, most of his group ran for higher ground, more from curiosity than from any feeling of danger. Not long afterwards, cast up timbers and huge branches whistled about them, killing and maiming. Others, pinned down, drowned as the river's waters sought their ancient level.

Garht and three others sat staring at the renewed river from the safe confines of the volcanic ridge behind his proposed Port Garht. For three dawns they argued about their next venture. On the fourth, they decided to return to Haaf. Unbeknown to them, the Istelle riders watched--and waited.

Now constantly and continually, the ancient volcano once claimed by Ashuwa, bubbled over with bounteous amounts of fresh water directly from the heart of Creation. The volcano's immense crater became a hug bowl, cracked at various places to disperse its life-giving water to the whole region. After three days, Paradise River leveled off at twenty feet above its former bed. Rapids vanished under the additional water, though the strong current, until it cut meanders into the canyon and plains, moved too fast for navigation.

The beautiful, regenerative fresh water which flowed east through the Dark Lands towards Istellia Bay caused problems. The stone hardened and sun-baked lifeless valleys refused the water's blessing, forcing it to careen blindly through the desolate wasteland. The fetid contents of the 'cesspools', unmixable with the pure rushing water, formed a wedge before it, smearing its pollutants throughout the valleys of Ashuwa's territory. This further polluting would later prevent its full recovery.

To the Kyykki hordes waiting in the fringes of Zuda Marsh, Creation's renewal spelled death and mass destruction. With the land unable, unwilling to receive it, the water blasted through the acrid volcanic valleys furiously, with an innate sense of revenge. Originally a single solid cascade bursting forth from Ashuwa's favorite nepes pond, the stream split with each new valley it discovered. While its volume thus diminished, its force did not. Now, minus the resistance of the volcanic valleys, the waters reunited as they approached the upper flatlands of the Zuda, the escarpment.

The seven hundred or more surviving dragons and their Demon Master riders, along with a mere handful of Demon Lords followed the bizarre events at the volcano since the water spout first blew skyward, fearfully scattering most everything. With the greatest of concern for their own existence, the Demon Masters, Demon Lords and a number of powerful taller Kyykki who escaped from their former home, discussed and argued about their future. Being caught between Pinduala and the flooding they knew was fatal. Finding an answer continued to be their problem.

"This is what we know." Grumbled a silvered Demon Lord in such manner that the others refrained from interrupting. "Something, some power unknown to us has destroyed our homeland. Even as we speak, this 'substance' like the rivers we passed, chases us further away from home....."

"But where is Ashuwa?" A bluish Demon Lord requested. "Where are any leaders to guide us?"

"Ashuwa knows what is best for us, even if that be our death." The silvered Demon Lord returned angrily. "Listen well! Often I have been present at Ashuwa's meetings...I, like a number still living, heard him speak of a new home, a place for his people... ....We ARE his people!" He thundered. "For He, Ashuwa, did create us..... He has no reason to be here. Ashuwa made himself extremely clear....He desires for us a new homeland."

"Our great Ashuwa knew this time of evil descending upon our ancient land was coming." Added an older red-tinged Demon Lord. "Now, using His wisdom, His purpose for us, His people, we must push onward. If not, we are destroyed by our own disobedience."

Scaly pointed heads nodded in agreement: Ashuwa had no patience for disobedience, nor for failure. These consistent divine invectives of Ashuwa's were now compounded by a raging flood water which would annihilate them all.

"I might remind all of you that Ashuwa's command was to conquer Pinduala, then head southward...This command has not been rescinded, has it?"

"Your point is well taken, Green Demon Lord....It is to be considered by us all..." The silvered Demon Lord said slowly. "I offer my idea first. With the destructive water force bearing down upon us, we have little time to bicker. ...Ashuwa commanded Pinduala be destroyed. This force will do that. All ready it sweeps clear everything it touches. If it kills volcanoes and breaks down ponds, both of which are exceedingly stronger than any Haafian city, ...then allow it to destroy Pinduala. We lose nothing and the Master's command is fulfilled....As for us, I strongly suggest marching on the next Haafian city....called Daaka."

"I hear, but do we have enough Kyykki to engage and destroy this 'Daaka'?...... And, what assurance do we have that Pinduala will fall to the evil behind us?" The Green Demon Lord, a cautious beast if only from undue self-preservation, attempted to strengthen his hand in the future. "What might Almighty Ashuwa say if what you say does not come about?"

"Then we are no more destroyed than if we remain here and do absolutely nothing." The silvered Demon Lord replied, smoke oozing from his nostrils. "You offer us nothing but death. That is not good enough."

"And you have listened far to long to those renegade Haafians who died long ago....Those creatures who cared nothing for us, but only the rewards Ashuwa promised." ·Flames burst from his mouth before he finished.

"Then, mouthy slob who would destroy Ashuwa's people, prepare to die!"

"And you shall die...And we will obey the will of Ashuwa. Not some foolish scheme concocted to save yourself."

In dreadful earnest, the personal fight began. Each circled the other, backed by Demon Lords and Demon Masters who formed an impenetrable barrier about the two. Blackish smoke rose and lips curled, revealing dagger-like fangs as each Demon Lord ripped the empty air with his talons. They circled and danced past each other, each determined to wait for that one slight mistake.

The dusk came and the dance continued, all the while the waters continued their rapid devastation through the outermost volcanic valleys. The encircling Demons tightened the circle stepping in three full paw lengths; the room for dancing disappeared. The silvered Demon Lord lunged forward, claws swiping the air. His green opponent ducked and threw out a foot. The silvered Demon stumbled then tossed an overhand swipe, catching his enemy in the jaw, removing half of it from his face. As the silvered Demon jumped at his throat for the final blow, the green Demon Lord swung his clawed hand upwards against the silvered one's scaly coated abdomen, ripping through the scales, yanking out an odd assortment of slimy innards. The bite for the throat arrived, decisively ending the battle. Headless lay the Green Demon Lord, slimy greenish-red blood bubbling from his neck. His empty-eyed head crushed by the jumping of his opponent, who used one clawed hand to hold his innards in place.

Stumbling to his feet, he spoke to the rest. "In my soon-to-be death I shall be vindicated....Let the Kyykki and the dragons conquer Daaka....Let that which would destroy us, conquer Pinduala....That is my command... That is Ashuwa's will--that His people have their own land......Now go!" He shouted, sliding to his haunches. Per custom, the silvered Demon Lord knew that his commands would be followed. Therefore, alone and deserted, mortally wounded, he awaited his end with a wispy contorted smile barely visible through his blood-caked face.

Prior to the next dawn's fight, the Kyykki horde, now directed by a group of six Demon Lords, changed directions. Heading due south, with hundreds of dragons flying overhead, most gathered from the destruction of the volcano, they marched on Daaka. While the Kyykki forces were less than half of the initial force, the dragons had multiplied their force by five times.

"The dragon riders report that the evil force is catching us. We have but two dawns to clear the swamp before we are crushed." An unusual brown-hued Demon Lord told the gathering of Demons. As one of the members, his responsibility lay in ascertaining what problems existed which might deny them a new homeland.

"Then we shall march continually for the next three days. After that we rest before attacking Daaka!" An orange Demon Lord spoke with confidence.

Warmaker's attack force poised to invade Sarg's castle had successfully evaded Brey's scouting party. The combination of the oppressive darkness plus the scouting party's entrance into the cavern made such possible,. It also saved the scouting party's lives. This force of two thousand taller Kyykki sat out the oppressive darkness hidden along the ridges and ravines of the northern mountains. Their advance when daylight returned was stopped by the rumbling and subsequent destruction of their homeland's centerpiece. Unable to understand, yet too confused, disorganized to attend to the attack, they did absolutely nothing. Later, fearful of the shadows caused by the huge Istelles, they continued in hiding.

This elite force of Kyykki anxiously awaited Warmaker's return. Without his permission, attacking the castle ran paramount to disobeying Ashuwa, so they excused their inaction. Within the space of two dawns, shortly after the wall-of-water failed to subjugate the castle, an encampment order settled the taller Kyykki until some hierarchical figure enlightened them.

"What is happened?" A leader spoke to another.

"Me not know....Home is no more."

"Ashuwa says...Get new home."

"But we not go down there." He gibbered while pointing down to the gleaming marbled castle.

"Wait....We not lead-er."

"How long...wait...This be cold, then hot. Some be sickness."

"Not wait...Maybe camp be new home." His flattened frog-like face lit up, from black to charcoal.

"Ah....yes....This ...home."

"Not bad home....plenty food."

In the coming double moon cycles, two thousand of the taller Kyykki quietly transformed the wooded and rocky slopes of the mountain northeast of the castle into their new home. Living their subsistence style and used to existing without shelter, they blended into the shadowy undergrowth. To survive, the taller Kyykki learned to freeze whenever a shadow approached, be it a cloud, a waving branch or the Istelles. A handful of casualties taught them the lesson quickly. The Istelle riders reported the dead Kyykki, but they were listed as survivors from the volcano. After another moon cycle, when no more were killed, their existence was forgotten. Reinforcements were soon to arrive and Sarg and Queen Sjura had not long before becoming parents. Brey's still missing scouting party caused great concern. That was more than enough for the moment.

Chapter 9

The earth's rumblings served as a rude awakening for Feathered Goat's small flock of Istelles. They landed for rest just before the darkness hit, and had not moved since. As the Taths mounted up, the Yldan shaman quietly prayed that nothing harmful would come to his wife and children.

"Let's fly!" Feathered Goat called out in Tath. "The city is a long flight and the Istelles need something to eat."

Within minutes, the gigantic Istelles formed a loose 'V' formation and pulled hard through the crosswinds on their flight south. Now, unwilling to risk any encounter with the dragons at Haaf North prior to the King's funeral, especially because of the time element, the Istelles flew as unencumbered as possible. The old plan to dump boulders on Haaf North was ditched. By late afternoon, they paused at a swollen creek to eat. The Istelles had plenty of water, but the meager supply of fish in the creek did little to replenish their energy.

"Too bad the Haaf land doesn't produce sheep."

"Just give these half-crazy Haafians a few years and sheep will be grazing in the High Council Hall." Feathered Goat replied smiling.

"High Council Hall?"

"It's a building about one third the size of Sarg's castle. But it has no place for the Istelles to roost."

"Why would anyone construct such a stupid building? Doesn't make any sense." Questioned another Tath, one of the few with dark hair.

"Probably, you dummy, because they've never seen an Istelle before." Retorted one of his colleagues. "All they've seen thus far are stupid clumsy dragons slowly wheezing their way across the sky."

"We ought to put on a bit of a show for them Haafians."

"Hold just a minute, friends." Feathered Goat entered the rapidly expanding conversation. "We're headed to my King's funeral, not the spring circus on the steppe. ....This is a most solemn affair for the entire nation......Besides, these five will have most Haafians wetting their breeches long before we land."

The latter conception gave rise to various interesting comments, most unfit to repeat, though quite humorous. Within a short period of time they realized the most urgent need was for fish. "Haaf Bay should be reachable before sunset. That's where we'll spend the night....Is that amenable to all of you?"

"What if we the run into your Light Stripers?"

"Then we'll have ale and a great sense of directions for the following day.....Just remember one thing," Feathered Goat called back as he mounted his Istelle. "Haafians considered these beautiful creatures as sacred."

"Well, at least they got something correct." Dryly commented the dark haired Tath.

Once through the highest mountains, the flight picked up a fast tailwind, allowing the tiring Istelles to glide almost motionless. Below the ground flattened out, but it still remained devoid of vegetation. The Istelles, riding the heat currents, slowly circled higher, passing through an immense cloud bank that obscured the ground. Once through, Feathered Goat signaled 'down'. While this was not in accordance with previous instructions, Feathered Goat did spy a source of food for the Istelles. A herd of half-wind oxen grazed on shrub grasses about a half mile away. Once headed downwards, the Istelles instantly picked up the scent and dove for the unsuspecting animals.

By first moon the herd was devoured and the Istelles intoned their low voiced songs of contentment. The Taths also found roasted oxen a delightful treat, though they were unaccustomed to meat that actually required chewing, unlike their usual mutton stews.

Up and flying as the sun rose, great red-orange and clear, the five continued their southern journey. Today Feathered Goat was determined to get a bearing upon the city. It was time to catch an aerial view of the bay and possibly Haaf North, though he'd hoped that they'd be further to the east. By mid-morning Feathered Goat's hope became real. A large burnt out brownstone castle-like building lay directly before them. The Stripers tied there were frenzied by the incoming shadows. They refused to look up at the birds. They banked once, then settled in a large wheat field.

Light Striper troopers rushed to greet the Istelles, charging the birds with hands raised high over their heads.

"Keep the birds calm." The dark haired Tath shouted. "These are our new friends, we don't need them eaten."

The others laughed, but recognized the potential danger. Feathered Goat quickly dismounted as did Roosen, the dark haired Tath. Both men advanced towards the rushing Light Stripers, warning them to slow down, but to little avail. A blast from the war tuba, startled the Istelles, but, more importantly, recalled the overly-excited troopers. As they slowly obeyed, the two singular figures from the brownstone compound, burst through the line.

"Welcome, friends!" Rux laughed in Tath, startling the Istelle riders.

"Thank you." The shaman replied in Haafian. "Do you like the King's eagles?" He laughed.

"Eagles, my fat foot." Oros replied, also in Tath.

"Your feet are very fat." Roosen answered in Tath, a mischievous grin covered his blue face.

"Another wise guy, Oros, just for you." Rux commented.

"Shut up!"

"Please," Feathered Goat yelled to the troopers. "Keep your distance from the Istelles.....They are more nervous than you. ....Obviously, they are bigger than you."

Quite bewildered by a Yldan riding an Istelle, the troopers came to a standstill forming a large perimeter about the birds. From even that distance, Feathered Goat could easily believe that most of the troopers were enraptured. Even the toughened veterans stood in reverent awe of the beautiful white creatures.

"Damned if they aren't a hundred feet long."

"But those wings----over three times the size of any damned dragon."

"Just watch out for those beaks---full thirty foot chompers, with swords for teeth.......Watch when they yawn."

"And if you don't be careful where you walk, those talons will turn you into a puddle of slime."

"The King actually never saw one, did he? I mean, what he saw was part of his vision, right?"

The shaman found it strange that all comments were directed towards the Istelles, even though the troopers never saw a Tath before either. Rux and Oros proved not to be the exceptions, though they did show hospitality to the Taths, inviting them for supper. Feathered Goat never let on how the first word of Haafian they used was 'oxen roast'.

Later, Oros tried to explain that two races inhabited Haaf. The Yldans, like Feathered Goat, were fewer in number. The Taths originally believed the olive colored Haafians descended from trees, though they admitted it really didn't matter if most conducted themselves like Sarg.

Armed with a good map and verbal directions, both parties saluted each other before continuing on their respective journeys the next dawn. The Istelles would rendezvous with Raff and then reach the city the following day. This permitted the Istelles to fish for an afternoon in the bay.

To avoid casting their terrifying and indentifing shadows through the northern limits of Haaf, the Istelles deliberately flew some fifty feet above the tree tops. To provide safety from the dragons, Roosen's Istelle flew another five hundred feet above the formation, his shadow falling harmlessly upon the others. As mid-day approached, Roosen yelled as he caused his Istelle to dive in front of the formation.

"DRAGONS!" He screamed as he tore in front of the others.

Off to the right stood Haaf North, gutted and black, but with over a hundred dragons standing guard on the semi-destroyed walls and towers.

Seeing the Istelles, the dragons immediately stretched their leathery wings. They slowly rose to challenge the five Istelles who flew less than a half mile east.

"EVERYONE UP!" Yelled Feathered Goat. "TO THE·CLOUDS!"

Powerful wings pulled into the air, quickly they rose far above the dragon's ability, and then began a slow circling. An outlandish sight awaited the Istelle riders. No sooner had the dragons cleared the disintegrated east wall of Haaf North, than they suddenly plummeted to the ground. Those who launched from elsewhere did get airborne, a least for a short time and only if they avoided the east wall.

Underground, the troopers worked their machines furiously to battle the unexpected dragon attack. Jed shook his head, mystified as to why they took to the air, but he counted it as a blessing. The more the dragon carcasses littered the ground, the easier their attack on Haaf North would be.

Feathered Goat and his Taths never fought dragons before. Now they were outnumbered. They watched closely as the dragons laboriously forced their way skyward, almost as if the air wasn't their proper domain. They saw the fireballs roll towards them, watching them explode into feather-burning fragments. Fast and careful is all the advice Feathered Goat passed to the others. That is how they would attack the dragons. However, the Istelles instinctively removed control from the Taths. The dragons were their personal enemies. In one gigantic push they rolled off to the west, behind most of the dragons. Teasingly they glided motionless, baiting the clumsy winged beasts to come closer.

Most fell for the trick scrambling to ascend. Once there, they found themselves winded and in empty space. The Istelles' altitude rose dramatically rose again. At another thousand feet higher, the Istelles floated once again, baiting once again. Furious Demon Masters kicked their straining creatures ever higher: absolutely nothing would keep them from destroying the Istelles.

The painfully winded dragons strained to reach the mile high altitude where, unexpectedly, the Istelles turned and dived. Turning at high speed they flanked the dragons at a safe distance, then barrel looped about them, flying upside down. The dragons followed, but once upside down, stalled, not having enough speed to continue. In those vulnerable seconds when, disoriented, they hung in the air, the five Istelles flipped and attacked. Backwinging, talons stretched they buzzed through the congregation of dragons, snapping neck after neck after neck. Once through the congregation, the Istelles rose high into tight formation, waiting for the other dragons to follow.

Those on the ground were confounded as to the dragons' destination, for at first they saw nothing. Then they watched in awe as the dragons fell from the clouds. Finally, the Istelles dropped to bait the lumbering beasts. Action on the machines came to a standstill. The King's eagles had arrived to battle Ashuwa's creatures. However, once more dragons dropped from the sky, the troopers immediately sought safety in their bunkers.

"Keep the machines firing!" Jed commanded. "Its time to finish the dragons forever!" From his command post between the first two lines of the old defense, runners rapidly moved through the tunnels to deliver their Commander's orders.

Once again the dragons chased the Istelles higher into the atmosphere, aspiring to get close enough to deliver a fire ball. The Istelles banked and dove, then banked again, catching the dragons from below. With their long sword-toothed beaks open, the Istelles gutted the lowest flying dragons. Then, with their gigantic talons cutting through large chunks of air and dragons, the five Istelles banked and cut their way through the middle of the congregation where at close quarters, the dragons' fire would only conflagrate their own. The Istelle riders, drained of any color and almost frozen, prayed continuously and doubled any strapping knot they were able to reach.

Immediately after slashing the wings of the first rank of the congregation, the Istelles rolled out and down, single file. At this point, Roosen's Istelle, the last in line, received a fireball to its left wing. The huge white bird whelped with pain and separated from the others, heading for the shore line and water. Its wing smoked furiously.

Sensing a victory in the making, the visibly diminished congregation of dragons ignored the four Istelles to attack Roosen's. A mass formation of dragons pursued Roosen's smoldering mount. They rejoiced as they descended to levels more favorable to their meager abilities.

Only aware that massed dragons presented an undeniably beautiful target, especially when the King's eagles were chasing them, the machiners rapidly decimated the congregation. Hex-sided bolts flew as fast as the crews could load. At the ever-shortening distance, no one bothered to aim.

Roosen waved to someone on a high platform as his Istelle glided over the third defensive line. That someone seemed to wave back. But as Raff did, a single massive volley sprang from every machine under his control. The congregation of scaly beasts stopped, strangely pausing in mid-air as the massive volley slammed into their ranks. In the next breath, four Istelles attacked the survivors from the rear, wreaking death and destruction in behalf of their wounded member. Then they flew over Raff's mesmerized rear guard to aid Roosen, whose Istelle waded in Haaf Bay, a quarter mile away. Suddenly, the dragons were gone.

"It's severe enough to keep her grounded for ten days." Roosen explained to the others. "The fire ball went into the skin and the feathers on her leading edge are burnt away."

The other Istelles surrounded the wounded one, sniffing and snorting, unsure of the problem, but recognizing that something was wrong. One brought a low-finned yellow shark, but the bird refused the gift, preferring to keep her left wing under the cooling waters of the bay.

"Maybe that water will cool my leather burns. I've never been so scared in my life."

The shaking riders, color slowly returning, agreed. No one in Tath ever flew that way before, at least not anyone who survived to brag about it.

"Careful with the bay water, Yan, its salty...Might burn more than the leather did." Feathered Goat warned. "Dump your canteen water on a rag, then wrap your burns."

Yan nodded and reached for Roosen's water bottle, his being lost during the Istelles' battle. "What's them long things flying through the air?" He quizzed Feathered Goat.

"Bolts from the Light Striper machines...Something like flying swords...." The Yldan struggled to explain, then stopped.

The sound of galloping Stripers came near. The full company of Light Stripers, including Raff and a scattering of the Church Knights, clattered up the rise. Upon seeing the Istelles at three hundred feet, they instantaneously halted, without any command given, totally enraptured by the sight of the five immense Istelles. After a moment, most slid from their nervous Stripers and fell to their knees in prayer.

The Taths stared at each other, confused by the ceremony, a bit fearful of the Stripers and the small machines some troopers carried. They slowly backed under the shelter of their mounts as the company of well-wishers advanced, even though their countenances showed complete admiration for the riders.

Once again, Feathered Goat found himself in the middle, as an interpreter, a cultural expert and as the official leader of the Tath delegation to the King's funeral. Entirely surprizing the Light Stripers, he stepped out of the shadows and greeted them.

"Welcome!" He called out in Haafian. "These are Istelles, not white eagles......The fearless riders are men from the far north country called Tath...We are headed to the King's funeral."

Silence reigned as most reappraise their thinking. The Taths walked forward standing alongside of the Yldan shaman. Raff, with his personal staff also advanced.

"Running Cloud once mentioned a renegade shaman, one who wanted to fly, so he followed some birds and was never heard from again.....I suppose that's you?" He held out his hand.

Feathered Goat warmly shook his hand. "Running Cloud talks too much....I never thought I was lost forever....And I do enjoy flying..."

"I'm Raff, commander of the rear guard....Thanks for killing the dragons."

"I'm Feathered Goat....But the Istelles did the work...I just held on, barely."

"From what we saw, the whole thing came as a genuine miracle."

"You mean that last volley which dropped the entire congregation?"

"No, Feathered Goat, the appearance of the King's vision, irregardless of whatever their correct name is."

Feathered Goat translated Raff's words into Tath. The four riders became much amused. These Haafians had some strange ways of doing things, traveling overland being the most peculiar, at least from their perspective. When Feathered Goat translated this into Haafian, Raff smiled and offered each of them a Striper in return for an Istelle ride. The generous offer was readily accepted by the Taths pending one important condition: 'oxen roast' for their next meal. Laughing, though without a well defined 'why for', everyone agreed.

Before further introductions began, the Church Guards appeared, dragging a shackled Light Striper behind them. Rather unkempt, unshaven, and spitting on the guards, the man appeared a most unlikely candidate for the Light Stripers.

"Begging your pardon sir." He stood at attention.

Raff had Feathered Goat ask the Istelle riders if their mounts wanted fish. They could meet later, after this irregular matter had been completed. The Taths accepted the idea excepting for Roosen, who choose to stay with his mount and Yan who wanted to know about the machines and Stripers, the two others Taths and four Istelles went fishing in the bay. Their aerial acrobatics and dexterity brought delight and awe to the troopers watching from the shore. So much so that the Staff Masters had greatest difficulty in gathering troopers to torch the fallen dragons.

The trooper hauled before Raff was an entirely different story.

"Feathered Goat and Yan, please stay, I've been informed this trooper.... Well, let's say he really doesn't belong to us. But his story involves you."

Feathered Goat quickly translated for Yan.

Yan, knowingly, sadly shook his head. "Just like the queen, a traitor, right?" He spoke quietly. "They come in all colors, don't they?"

"What evidence do you have to implicate this trooper as a traitor?" Raff asked the corporal.

"Two specifics, sir." The corporal replied almost mechanically. "First, the other troopers with me will witness to the fact that he was going to shoot the wounded Istelle."

The four Light Stripers nodded their heads in agreement, while Feathered Goat almost laughed. The Church Guard kept the traitor on a short leash. Yan demanded a translation, but color drained from his face as he stared down the traitor.

"I will punish him myself!" Yan angrily spoke in Tath.

"But that bolt could not reach far enough to even touch an Istelle. And you are very well aware how such things merely bounce off the feathers." Feathered Goat tried to alleviate some of Yan's anger.

"That's not the issue and you know it!" Yan retorted. "It is a crime against our society to harm an Istelle....and you know that!"

Correctly recognizing that he lost the argument, Feathered Goat translated their vigorous conversation into Haafian. Twisted smiles broke out on the enlisted men's faces, but Raff and the corporal remained straight faced.

"Tell Yan I will seriously consider his offer, provided we have enough evidence to convict him for breaking our Law. Excuse me, for breaking Tath law."

Within a moment, a strong handshake from Yan indicated they had a deal. The accused's face transformed from haughty to distraught as he witnessed the transaction. He knew the swift Haafian justice, but the unknown Tath procedures proved more frightening.

"Ah, the criminal is terrified." The corporal commented dryly. "I would be too, for maybe the Istelle will have you for a snack."

"Enough, Corporal." Raff commanded. "What other evidence do you have against this trooper?"

The trooper standing behind the accused ripped off the prisoner's tunic, revealing a flying dragon tattoo carved on his upper right arm. It was the same tattoo which the renegade Church Knights, the ones who violently butchered the King, also wore.

"So," Raff said very purposefully, "You worship the Ash Heap, the so-called god who makes inferior creatures, like dragons? Answer me!"

The prisoner dropped his head and mumbled something both incomprehensible and inaudible. Yan fell back a bit, nervous.

"Sounds like an incantation." Yan shared with Feathered Goat.

"Get rid of him quickly." Without waiting for a translation into Haafian, Yan stepped forward and slapped the prisoner across his smirking face. Then he hit him again, this time everyone heard teeth break.

"Damn you blue skinned bastard, we're on the same side!" He yelled as blood trickled from his mouth.

Immediately everyone focused on Yan, who didn't understand one word of what the prisoner said. Feathered Goat quickly translated, producing an angry exchange with Yan, who spit on the ground and walked away.

"What's the problem?" Raff demanded.

"Yan and I know of a Tath queen, now dead, who sold out to Ashuwa... ..Obviously, she had accomplices.....That there are more traitors within the Tath tribes angers him."

"And how do we know Yan is not also one of the traitors?" The corporal asked, testing.

"Because I say so!" Feathered Goat blatantly denied the insinuation. "Did you not observe him killing dragons? And, while it is beyond your understanding, Yan is from the northern tribe. The central tribe's queen was the traitor."

"With new allies we also get new problems." Raff said.

"Quite true, unfortunately." Feathered Goat responded.

"First things first, tell Yan that the prisoner belongs to him. That should quell any rumors."

Even before Feathered Goat finished translating to Yan, Roosen joined the company. The prisoner begged for mercy, but none was given. Instead, the Taths lead him towards the Istelles. He fainted from fear as one of the birds gazed at him--point blank-with her huge twelve foot eyes.

Unknown to the others, one of the Church Knights received permission from his Staff Master to secure communication with the second and the first line to launch their attack against Haaf North. Once hidden by a pile of dragon carcasses, he disappeared in a cloud of dry fog. Sarg would be warned about the additional traitors.

"What are they planning to do, even though I'm not sure that I want to know?" Asked Raff.

"Four Istelles are joining the attack on Haaf North, just to insure that no dragons survive to spread the 'bad news'. The prisoner will travel by Istelle to Haaf North, where he will quickly descend to join his colleagues... any surviving demons."

Raff blanched at the thought, but the corporal readily approved. The punishment fit the crime.

"Tonight, after we've secured Haaf North, the rear guard will be taking baths." Raff instructed his Staff Master. "Any flying dragon tattoos..... Bring the troopers to me...Now, send a platoon north, to catch up with Rux and Oros. Tell them to beware of traitors within the Tath ranks. Also tell them to get this message to Sarg as fast as possible.....And I mean fast.. The message goes by runners, forget the platoon."

"Yes Sir." The young Staff Master saluted, and took off at a gallop.

"Your troopers always move so quickly?" Feathered Goat asked.

"When they're runners to begin with, yes. He'll pick up three more Stripers and two more riders before heading north....I pray he makes it on time."

"I agree, the balance isn't as good as we wished it to be."

Yganak paced the third floor above the High Council Hall relentlessly. With Jabbi, Vaal and the Captain taking a leave after conducting the interrogations of the traitorous Church Knights, he had the hairsplitting responsibility of negotiating with the Church Hierarchy concerning the King's funeral. Furthermore, even Oros along with Kofe and Nooy had somehow disappeared. Perhaps, Yganak thought, he could justify their absence, after all, they battled the Church Knights, and though none were hurt seriously, maybe they required a rest. Nadre, in spite of what transpired yesterday, demanded to work, and as Ilty needed all the assistance she could get, she got her way.

A soft knock on the door interrupted his pacing.

"What do you want?". He crankily called out.

"Well, if you don't want a visitor, I'll leave." Jelkio softly replied in partially broken Haafian.

"I'm sorry, my dear." He opened the door. "I'm not used to having day-long arguments over what colors should be part of the banner for over the King's casket.....These details are driving me crazy."

"Probably as much as being penned inside is driving me crazy." She replied in her accented voice. "I need the open spaces....I need the freedom to be without walls."

"How about a walk on the roof?....Its about as open as the guards will allow either of us." Yganak said, trying to apologize for the apparent rudeness of the Haafians. Both recognized the need for the extraordinary security measures, but that did little to alleviate Jelkio's natural claustrophobia. "I'd be honored to escort you."

"In that case we are late." She smiled politely and held out her hand.

"This is a bit like Tath." She explained to after they arrived on the roof Yganak. "It's flat and open, but you have too many buildings that get in the way." She continued on talking about her homeland and the sheep and yurts. Yganak enjoyed listening, and he cared not if it was her story or the musical lyrical quality of her voice. Today, there was something wonderful about a conversation with Jelkio. He even learned a few Tath words. Yganak received her permission for the scholars to compose a dictionary and grammar of the Tath language. This occupied the afternoon. Jelkio had no understanding of written language, let alone how someone could write down that which was only heard.

The roof of the High Council Hall had five towers rising from it; one on each corner and a spindly one, much higher than the others rose from the middle. An outside spiral staircase brought one to its summit, where there was only enough room for three persons and the wind blew constantly. Jelkio climbed it, her long skirt barely touching the steps, followed by a nervous Yganak.

"I thought I might be able to catch a glimpse of my homeland, at least the southern mountains." She spoke to Yganak.

"Southern mountains?"

"Yes." And she pointed northward. "For us they are on our southern border.. ...Someday I shall take my husband home..."

"And show him off?"

"It isn't polite to second guess a princess, Yganak,……….. especially when you are right." She smiled, then squinted her eyes.

"Jelkio, are you……."

"Look! ....In the distance!......Can you not see them?"

Yganak strained, trying to observe anything moving towards them from the north. He quietly prayed it wasn't a congregation of dragons. Unfortunately, and frustrating, he didn't see much of anything.

"You aren't seeing them, are you?" Jelkio spoke with a joy Yganak hadn't heard before. "If you did see," She teased. "Then you'd run down the staircase and call out all the clerics and nobles."

Yganak continued gazing into the northern sky, but his efforts seemed worthless. He pounded his fist on the stone railing.

"Don't be upset, my friend.". Jelkio's blue skin shone with her elatedness. "Quickly, down!...... I must find my husband!"

Yganak stumbled after the fleet-footed Tath, still desperate for an answer, still attempting to make some sense out of the empty sky. "Jelkio," He called after her. "Just what do you see that I can't see?"

"Three Istelles!" She yelled over her shoulder. "They'll be here before supper!"

Yganak's deep olive skin went white as he hurriedly clambered down the stairways after Jelkio.

Recognizing a better calendar, the pragmatic Sarg quickly embraced the Tath ten day week. Dawns became days, usually, and the terribly erratic double moon cycle could now be measured in its irregularity, but would no longer control time. Instead, as in Tath proper, four weeks became a month and four months equaled a season and three seasons became a full year. At this particular point Sarg differed with his almost-ready-to deliver wife. He decided to number the years, because the numbers did not repeat, as did the Tath animal labels.

"I, as queen, shall permit you, my dearest, to win this confounded argument. The issue is closed: years in Paradise Valley are numbered..... But not so in the northern tribal lands."

"Thank you my dear." Sarg said pleasantly then wrapped his arm about his half sleeping wife and fell asleep, exhausted from a full day of furniture making.

Since the initial wall-of-water struck, another transformation claimed Paradise Valley. The full length of the river's course surpassed the most beautiful oasis anywhere. Hardwoods all ready a hundred feet tall lined the banks and crept up the mountain slopes, fish and reptiles of unknown types splashed about the waterway and the in the nascent lakes south of the castle. Animals, both four footed and those with wings, appeared, taking their rightful place in the re-created environment. Sarg watched them descend from the rainbow lighted cloud beginning at the top of Ashuwa's water spouting volcano. New species appeared daily, many of which had never seen before.

Delegations from most of the tribes, including those of the Blue Istelles, arrived daily, but never so many as to strain the new environment's capacity. The only Istelles still unaccounted for were the rare Reds Istelles from the frozen far northeast. Word circulated however that because the skylanes over the Central Tribe's territory were now open to all, their arrival was but a matter of days.

The morning brought a puzzling question from Sarg. "Sjura, how does this kingdom fit together? First the territory belonged to your people, now it's open for anyone, with the two us as rulers."

"Quit being that way."· She responded while rummaging for one of the tent-like dresses she wasn't fond of wearing.

"I love that beautiful blue bottom of yours." Sarg snickered from the bed.

"I thought the topic concerned kingdoms." She responded tersely.

"That too." And he rolled out of bed. "We actually have two kingdoms, don't we?"

"What are you talking about?" Her head finally poked through her dress. "Two kingdoms?"

"Exactly my point. The western tribe remains under your jurisdiction as queen....and....now you also share Paradise Valley with me." Sarg spoke as he pulled his breeches up. "You'll need to travel back and forth....I don't like that, especially with a family."

"I think dark bottoms are very cute."

"Now who's off the subject?"

"Queenly prerogatives, mind you." She voice sounded stern, but the pretty gaze on her face said something much different.

"Did you realize that you had two kingdoms to manage?"

"Don't be ridiculous! Our managerial skills will successfully handle anything the unified kingdom will throw at us."

"Unified kingdom?" Sarg peered at his wife as if she were playing tricks. "When did this transpire, my love? I don't recall us ever mentioning the issue before now...... Was this something we discussed while I lay snoring?"

"Quite impossible, Sarg....You don't snore and I ought to know."

Sarg sat back on the bed, confused about having answers for a discussion which never existed. He shook his head, hoping some long lost memory might appear to ease his anxiety, but to no avail. Sjura snickered quietly as if she actually harbored the secret. Sarg cocked his head and stared directly at her, his eyes demanding full disclosure.

"You actually don't understand this, do you?" She said sympathetically. "Oh, shame on me." She blurted to no one in particular. Her countenance went from a bright blue flush to a faded light blue. Quickly she waddled over to the bed and plopped her herself, most unqueenlike, in Sarg's lap. She continued explaining after she made herself comfortable. "Do you remember when we were married?"

Sarg looked inquisitively at his pregnant wife, who smiled back in the most demure manner. "How should I forget that day?" He replied mischievously.

"I didn't say the honeymoon, you lover." She wrapped her arms about him and proceeded to kiss him.

"I certainly remember, Sjura." Sarg attempted to speak while being delightfully smothered in kisses. "But this issue is a most serious one."

"Only for you.......The kingdom matters were effectively settled the day, the very hour, the actual minute our nameless god did publicly proclaim us wedded."

Sarg flopped backwards across the bed with Sjura tumbling after him. He pulled her close and whispered. "You mean that the Western tribe as well as Paradise Valley are one gigantic kingdom." He said, quite taken aback. "You mean ...."

She continued kissing him. "Yes, yes, yes. The Queen's seat becomes the capital city for her tribe as well as its territory. ....Paradise Valley and the Northern Tribe are as one QUEENDOM." She laughingly yelled at him. "You need to use the correct words.....Your subjects definitely will despise an uneducated prince."

Sarg sighed, then with a devilish smile, attacked his wife. Her full-bodied laughter splashed through the marbled hallways of their supposedly private suite.

Later, after lunch, a more serious Sarg went out on a search party. No clues were found to even indicate Brey, Vauk and Kinanna's party had even activated their mission. In spite of the new life-giving brilliance of the world about him, Sarg dispared. He had not forgotten how their original party lost Luuft, and that when he had absolutely no control. Like an irritating specter that nightmare haunted him as he flew low and slow over the trees dotting the upper slopes of the mountain. The other two Istelle riders wondered if Sarg was watching where he headed.

An enormous shadow suddenly passed directly over him. Another Istelle just cleared the mountain's crest, but it came from the north side. Instinctively Sarg ducked and his Istelle took rapid evasive action. He stretched and flew straight up. The other two Istelles following in quick succession, only to find themselves staring at some forty Istelles heading directly for them.

Instantaneously waving and cheering broke out among both parties, as if all these people somehow knew each other. The lead bird circled, pulling alongside Sarg, wing over wing so the two riders might converse.

"Sarg, when you learn to fly by yourself?" Vauk yelled down. He however, was firmly strapped behind a strangely smiling Tath, Kinanna, no less.

"Where's Brey?"

Vauk pointed to an extremely frightened passenger on an Istelle two ranks behind. Sarg nodded, then thanked the Holy One for their safe return. When he glanced up again, Vauk pointed out the remaining persons in the search party, carefully noting that everyone survived.

"To the castle!" Sarg yelled to Vauk, then repeated his order in Tath.

After acknowledging Sarg's order, though with a fitful appearance, the Tath rider signaled the flock and, following a gusty downdraft, the forty some Istelles glided into Paradise Valley.

Intentionally ignoring the conflagration outside the stone walls of Pinduala, the surviving Kyykki horde swept past the port city, ignoring it. With dragons and Demon Masters employed as both scouts and initial shock forces, they descended upon and demolished the dry plains of northern Haaf.

Hemmed in by the incinerating carcasses, Ayhn found himself out maneuvered by the blackened horde. Captain Ellom's fleet had yet to break free of the frozen waters. With little hindrance from the defenders, the ideas Warmaker subtly placed in the Demon Masters pointed craniums brought immediate success.

"Another full day of advancing on the Haafians' northern positions will remove the threat from the raging waters." The oddly brown colored Demon Master shared with his five colleagues during a quick break.

"And we shall have the new territory, for Ashuwa's new people." The burnished red Demon ·Master added with enthusiasm.

"It can be nothing less for we are of one accord." A dust-covered Demon Master loudly proclaimed. He held forth a stout rope which ran through the blood-dripping ears of disagreeable Demon Masters. "But we are not resting, as the waters behind us do not rest....Ashuwa has sent them to motivate us."

Five ugly scaled heads nodded in agreement, then mounted up and spurred their tiring dragons into the air.

Now with tons upon tons of rough-hewn debris, from boulders to nepes to swamp vegetation, a fifty foot wall of garbage-clogged water blasted into the southern edges of the Zuda Marsh. Now, the wall spread wide. With only an occasional obstacle to impede the waters' faster movement, and without valleys forcing any route, the frothing water, propelled by its own momentum, headed directly for Pinduala.

"How long until we can see something?" Ayhn asked one of his Staff Masters.

"I'm not sure, Sir. Those damned carcasses might smolder for two or three dawns...."

"And until the pyre quiets, we're held captive in the city...I can't believe the Kyykki staged a false attack and then headed south....Just too unbelievable."

"Careful with those words Ayhn." The Chaplain chided. "We know there's supposed to be some renegade Haafians directing the horde."

"And that's unbelievable as well." He sighed.

Producing a 'long tube', Ayhn attempted to penetrate the coarse stinking clouds rising from the burning of the of Kyykki barricade surrounding the city. Even from the top of a wooden tower he had constructed above the Chaplain's quarters, vision remained considerably limited, further frustrating him.

"Might ye' bees liken to hear da good news, Commander?" Called a seaman's voice from below. "Captain Ellom saids ta tell ya as fast as possible."

"Deliver your message." Ayhn called down.

"Later dis dawn, the ice bees gone. The Captain wishes ta know iffen ya gots more wounded ta move from de port."

"Prayers can come true." Muttered the Chaplain loud enough to be heard by all on the platform.

"Quite true." Ayhn said with some restraint. "Tell Ellom to send the physicians ashore to tend the wounded. The Kyykki have bypassed the city, so its safe.... .Tell him to load the Lancers and their equipment immediately."

The seaman shook his head, puzzled. "Might I bees knowin' why, Commander? Captain Ellom will wants ta know."

"And so do you sailor. Your curiosity isn't hidden too well." The Staff Master responded, discomfitting the sailor.

"Jist bees doin' me dooty, Sir."

Ayhn interrupted the apology. "Tell the Captain I plan to sail south as soon as possible to hit the Kyykki in the flank...All those not wounded or ill can participate. ....Also, all the civilians are to be sent ashore, immediately....Do you understand?" Ayhn called down.

"Yes sir!" As he dashed to his Striper. A moment later he clattered through the emptied cobblestoned streets of Pinduala.

"I will have my opportunity yet." Ayhn smiled. His planning called for only the Lancers to leave the city, the garrison troops and the civilians would remain to clean up. The Lancers would commence landing some seventy miles south.. Realizing that the Kyykki were now poised to spearhead an attack straight through the Haafian line and then launch an attack on D'Ka, Ayhn decided to pressure their eastern flank. If nothing else, his maneuver would buy precious time for the city.

By nightfall Ellom's transportation fleet sailed against the tide. Most Lancers worked furiously preparing themselves to enter the field, especially after adjusting for a sedentary warfare. The Stripers and the half-breeds snorted into the salt-tinged air, as nervous as anyone else. Limited supplies for the war waggons frustrated Ayhn. The Lancer's movements would be restricted, especially as re-supplying from the front line barracks was an unknown factor. With guidance from his Staff Masters, Ayhn quickly modified his strategy: the Lancers' attack now shifted to hitting them on the backside, catching them at their most vulnerable. This also allowed for the re-use of some weapons.

The majority of Pinduala's citizens, too stubborn to relocate to the outer islands, found their homes and shops filthy and dank, but little stolen. Water was sufficient for the immediate future, but staples of flour, sugar and ale were another story; only enough existed for three dawns. Any surplus had been requisitioned by the Lancers.

Four frigates from the fleet immediately set sail for the outer islands, both to transfer the populace and to transport emergency provisions until the merchant ships would return. Within a few dawns, after the barricade from hell burnt into oblivion, city life expected to return to normal.

As the middle-of-the-night came and went, sentries and their torches maintained their watches. Somehow, just knowing the Kyykki moved southward relieved a lot of stress from the Light Stripers. That their self-constructed prison was soon burnt away also provided a boost to their spirits. The Chaplain called for early morning worship at the chapel. The Holy One saved them from the ravages of the Kyykki and He deserved to be thanked. Furthermore, as the Lancers now chased after the despised Kyykki hordes and their damned dragons, prayers were needed to bolster the Lancers.

A strange insistent distant rumbling which began as the torches were extinguished continued increasing in volume. With the smoldering from the Kyykki barricades denying vision, scouts fought their way through the carcass barricade to ascertain the ominous noise. At first, blinded by the sudden bright sky, the scouts perceived nothing. Then, as they gazed towards the oncoming noise, they noticed a solid black wall behind which came a long ribbon of a brown colored substance. Alarmingly, whatever it was traveled faster than dragons and it coated everything in its path. Moreover, the 'substance' headed directly for the city.

"What is it?" Yelled on of the scouts.

"I have no idea, except that it's not friendly."

"It's why the Kyykki moved out." Another scout surmized. "The damned one sent that 'stuff' to finish off the city."

"Sound the alarm!. .....Everyone to the ships!"

A squeaky metallic blast ripped through the still air, then multiplied as those at the outer wall intoned the same message: 'grave danger, to the ships'. Within moments, the just-arrived civilians were gently herded by the Light Stripers back to the wharves. Neither group knew exactly what the danger might be, except that the distant rumbling doubled its volume. Most surmized the two elements were connected, but that explained little. To those leaving the city, the noise resembled running water, except the dull enormity of the sound was unfathomable.

"Sound...'Clear the Walls'!....And run like hell. ...Save yourselves!" Commanded the corporal in charge of the scouts as he slid down the putrid smoldering heap of Kyykki.

Less than two miles distant, the enormous wave surged restlessly forward, intent on rejoining itself at the sea. Its breadth now spread to over two miles and its height reduced to eight to ten feet, but still forceful enough to scourge everything in its path.

The last scout paused at the top of the barricade to study the oncoming 'whatever'. He stood for a perilous moment, studying the oncoming force. Something about it seemed familiar to him. "Flash flood!....Flash flood coming!" He roared at the top of his lungs. Instantly, the other scouts picked up the cry. The sentries on the wall responded by yelling the message to those on the wharves, where immediate panic broke out among the gathered civilians.

"The flood will get us before the ships can sail!"

"We'll drown standing here!"

The Staff Master signaled all ships to sail, immediately. Then he commanded the Light Stripers to gather the civilians into the stoutest buildings available, the warehouses standing nearby. Immediately this procedure was underway and the last sentries were recalled. They jumped from the imperiled walls, taking cover in the substantial buildings of the city.

The wave violently smashed into the dead Kyykki barricade. The last scout slammed shut the heavy iron-barred door of the block house near the west gate. He sank to the floor, breathless and alone.

Pinduala shook and then steadied. The noise of grating and grinding, a sense of tremendous pressure, permeated the besieged city. The sounds echoed as they increased and a groaning of unparalleled dimensions rose from the wall. The Kyykki carcasses, driven by the debris laden wave, smashed against it as one huge rock, then rose up and tumbled over the fortress city's outer wall. The wall disappeared under a gigantic heaping of smoldering carcasses followed by palm trees and wave-carried boulders. Underneath surged the water, actively seeking its level irregardless of the obstacles before it.

The outer wall swayed dangerously under the impact. Then the west gate broke, snapped like a twig. The incoming water shoved the debris of Kyykki and the rest through the main street as it violently raced towards the wharves. Buildings along the main street, battered by the debris and partially undermined by the water, began crumbling, adding to the wave's destructive power. Then, as the stone buildings forced the wave into a channel, its inert strength increased along with its height. A virtual tidal wave whacked its own impersonal way into the market place.

The flash flood destroyed the lower storey of the blockhouse. The scout desperately clung to the iron weapon mounts on the wall in the upper level. He prayed to simply survive. Perhaps he just might; from the cracks in the walls, he watched the blackened debris-filled muck turn to thick brown water at which point its level slightly dropped.

Following the path of least resistance, much of the wave parted around the city, dumping thousands of stone-weight pestilence ridden garbage on the beach, but pushing most of it into the sea. Finally, under immense pressure from the wave-borne refuse, the two other gates collapsed, effectively dividing the city into four independent islands. Screaming erupted when the debris slammed into the warehouses, most of the stout buildings swayed but held, others cracked, but did not topple on the fearful citizens.

Having a greater advantage of time, the ships in the harbor had maneuvered ninety degrees: the wave caught them in the stern, bouncing them like cheap corks. A heavy merchant ship, catching the wave first, landed on a frigate trapped in the wave's gigantic trough, carving it in two with a most horrible snapping sound.

The scout looked out from his lonely perch atop the partially destroyed gate tower. Such a sight, he thought, no one would comprehend nor appreciate. Below him, the mostly debris-free water took on a light earth color while carving a bed through the main street of Pinduala. Blocked side streets, clogged boulevards and wrecked buildings formed its newly created banks. Towards the Zuda, the water kept coming, no longer a flash flood but a river. Along the outer wall, only the gate towers stood above the debris, at other places the Kyykki carcasses prevented the water from undermining the entire wall. He watched, terrified and awed as ships bounced uncontrollably in the harbor; he winced when he heard the crunching sound of them colliding.

Moments later he noticed other people standing on rooftops, each mute as they observed the destruction of their city, each filled with the same emotions as he. The sound of rushing water filled the air; water rushing through the city as well as water rushing around the city. Ashuwa's goal to incapacitate the city, to effectively remove her usefulness, had succeeded.

By afternoon, sentries re-mounted the walls and scouts headed toward the Zuda. Only a few sections of the outer wall were reclaimed. The floodwaters and the debris conquered most of the wall as no invasion ever had. The Light Stripers cleanup began by tossing the Kyykki and other garbage into the newly formed river. Its three pronged delta actually claimed and divided the city. The cleanup effort stopped when the Staff Masters realized its futility. Without controlling the rivers, clearing the walls was senseless.

Losses among the civilians numbered about one hundred, with just as many unaccounted for, while casualties among the Light Striper were slightly less. As more than ten thousand occupied the city when the wave successfully attacked, these figures quickly translated into a blessing, according to the Chaplain's perception. For many, the outer wall provided the reason for thankfulness. Most civilians blessed the strength of the warehouses.

With guidance from the Chaplain, who seemingly appeared and disappeared at will, the local administrators, both civilian and military, reluctantly agreed to abandon Pinduala. Ashuwa's effective utilization of nature effectively rendered the city uninhabitable and definitely indefensible. Recognizing their vulnerability to Kyykki attacks or dragons, as well as dreaded diseases arising from the contaminated water supply and the rotting carcasses, the city leaders decided to return all civilians to the outer islands. Martial Law was immediately imposed upon the city. The damned one defeated the city and did it in a manner that took everyone by surprize, a wretched surprize.

Feathered Goat and his two companions could not land in the capital city. Krabo's overflowing populace, upon seeing the Istelles flying in, immediately rushed to every conceivable vantage point from which to view the King's white eagles. The streets and market places were bereft of the people who had patiently awaited the King's funeral waggon to pass. All of them now crowded the towers, balconies and flat roofs.

While his two companions wrestled with the strangeness of Krabo's massive star shaped construction as well as the vast numbers of peoples contained therein, Feathered Goat circled his mount ever closer to the High Council Hall, hoping to locate someone helpful. Rux and Nadre waved to him, but he was an unknown Yldan to them. However, at the other end of the hall's flat roof stood the eminent Running Cloud with Yganak next to him.

"Will you help your friend to land?" Yganak yelled to his friend over the din of exuberant shouting by the citizens.

"I'm attempting to just that, Yganak." Running Cloud returned. "But I don't see one of your tuba players in sight."

Yganak took a look about, also discovering that no signalers made it to the roof. A perverse grin crawled across his lean olive colored face.

"Don't do anything until I know your plan." Running Cloud pointedly warned.

"I wouldn't think of endangering our friendship." The Haaf Commander smiled in return. "FIRE! .... FIRE!....EVERYONE OFF THE ROOF!......FIRE!"

Running Cloud's bronzed face paled in incredulity. "You really didn't yell 'fire', did you?" He painfully murmured, a wispy smile threaded its way across his deep red face.

"Maybe yes, maybe no." He indifferently offered while watching the Church Guards masterfully clear off the roof area. "Anyway, in a few moments your friend can land."

Seeing the roof clearing of Haafians, Feathered Goat banked away to gather his companions. Rux and Nadre caught up to Running Cloud as did Nooy and his enraptured wife, Jelkio. Kofe, buffeted by the fleeing citizens, followed far behind.

"Can we guess who yelled 'fire'?" Rux sarcastically offered as he jabbed his pointed nose into Yganak's innocent looking face.

"Running Cloud did it....I would not do anything to inspire a rioting."

"And the Church Guards are all former Kyykki as well."

"Just might be...... Stranger things are happening these dawns."

Feathered Goat's gigantic mount floated across the roof and touched down. Vaal, leading a contingent of Church Guards, found himself barely a pace away from the Istelle's ten foot eye.

"Just don't move." Feathered Goat called from atop the bird's neck. "He's quite amicable.....But," He swung himself down a rope to the roof. "He's not seen anyone in armor before."

"Anything you say, Sir!" Vaal repositioned his arms, keeping his Church Guard behind him.

They, like Vaal and the few others still left on the roof marveled at the size and graceful beauty of the Istelle. Its arrival added another measure of glory to the martyred King's history. Two soft thuds returned most everyone from their entrancement.

"The King's White Eagles have landed!" A Church Guard yelled almost prayerfully.

"Indeed," Commented Running Cloud. "His vision comes true."

Jelkio, rapidly spouting Tath to the two other riders, dragged her husband to the huge beasts. "Don't dismount! We demand a ride!"

"You demand a ride....not me dearest."

"You are so peculiar, my love.... You destroy all types of evil, but when given the opportunity to ride an Istelle, you turn it down....."

For the time being, at least, Nooy was reprieved. The tired Istelle riders had all ready dismounted. Jelkio engaged them in a rather spirited conversation to which Nooy added specific details. Then, with a few words given to the Istelles, the quartet slipped away, leaving the Istelles to the gawkers.

Shortly thereafter, the Church hierarchy, breathless and physically out-of-breath, reached the rooftop. In spite of their authority they could not persuade the people to continue with the King's funeral. Instead, they demanded the opportunity to examine for themselves, the White Eagles. It appeared that the propitious arrival of the Istelles had resurrected the King instead of allowing for his burial. A goodly number of venturesome citizens, including a scattering of Elders, had followed the churchmen to the rooftop.

Five dawns later, at mid afternoon, the Captain gamely propped up his feet on the old desk and ceremoniously lit up his favorite pipe. The bluish smoke swirled about the small room his dared to call home and then vanished out the open window. The light rain provided a respite from the exhausting regime of the past few dawns, or days, as he began to incorporate Tath into his vocabulary. The King's funeral did take place, though the proper ceremonies were accomplished a day late. The Istelles rested some miles outside the city, where the citizens could safely stare at the beautiful creatures. He knocked his pipe against the window ledge and looked out, except for the hooded renegade cleric swinging gently from the gallows below, the square was rather empty. Most appropriate, the Captain thought, the traitor deserved no audience. Then he smiled to himself. The arrival of the Istelles brought a wealth of relevant information. It also brought dubious amounts of material from the two remaining clerics imprisoned under the High Council Hall. But, whether or not their 'change of heart' might influence their sentence, was a decision he gladly allowed others to make. Right now, this peaceful time alone with his pipe was all he desired.

Jelkio found herself too busy. Running Cloud convinced members of the High Council that translating Tath into Haafian and vice versa was immediately required. As Jelkio was the only available Tath, the honor of speaking with the Church brothers belonged to her. Tath custom declared that Istelle riders could not have any other duties. Nooy sat beside her, ready to explain some of the more deadly errors that he had personally encountered in learning Tath.

Oros, with the usual tankard in hand, plopped himself in a large padded chair towards the back of the room, where Vosnob and a number of other dignitaries gathered. The Tath language and culture enticingly dangled before them. It was a new adventure--the first likable one in a long time. And with this new adventure came the Istelles, the excellent 'savior-like' creatures the Haafians were almost ready to worship, especially after exaggerated reports from the 'dragon battle' at Haaf North reached the city.

Due to the eagerness of the advance guard's efforts to reach Sarg's new city and the abilities of the unknown Elders to map out several alternate routes through the mountains, Oros and Rux had their schedule changed. They traveled as far as Krucik's destroyed brownstone castle and returned due to the King's untimely death. They had little to worry about: reinforcements were rushing north to Sarg's city without difficulty, thanks to the Istelles and their Tath riders joining with Jed's forces in reclaiming Haaf North.

The serfs, as they slowly put the pieces from the past dozen dawns together, found a sense of hope awakened within them. Had not the King's vision's proved true---and beneficial? Had not the city of Haaf North been recovered? Had not the dreadful oppressive darkness been put to flight? Had not the clergy traitors within the ranks of the Church Guard been apprehended? Had not mass suicides in the southern swamps confirmed that damned Ashuwa's allies were no more? Based upon their interpretation of recent events, the serfs regarded the Kyykki crisis as something 'ended'. The remaining bits and pieces of the Kyykki crisis had little future. Combining that with the arrival of the Tath culture, most of which was extrapolated from a few stories, a new dawn, one of endless prosperous times had commenced. Somehow, the reality of the great needless losses of their southern countrymen were forgotten as easily as the newly turned soil over the Light Striper's graves. In too many ways, the voice of the Holy One at the Wall was lost.

This not so subtle switch in the serfs' feelings gave rise to great concerns at the Elders meeting that evening. No reports from the north nor Pinduala were received because only thirteen Elders attended. This added concern to the overly optimistic view of the future. How far had this infection spread? Lengthy narratives concerning the destruction of Ashuwa's volcano headquarters and the subsequent results were presented.

"I should like to give thanks to the Holy One for this." Vosnob flatly stated. "But I believe this is only part of the story."

"You have been corrupted because you've met this 'unknown' god of the Taths."

"No, but my vision has been stretched well beyond what I thought possible." He said slowly.

"Because you've begun to believe that which is forbidden for us to believe." The Elder attacked Vosnob.

"Then why am I still here? Why am I allowed to question without being punished?" Vosnob challenged. "Answer me?"

Twelve pairs of eyes dug into the attacking Elder, some sympathetic, others not. Most found themselves alarmed at the vicious way in which Vosnob was treated.

"I cannot answer you."

"Your questions are shortsighted, my friend." Vosnob said without animosity. "Think for a moment....Ashuwa's homeland, at least a goodly part of the Dark Lands, is now being made habitable."

"It means that Ashuwa's power is gone......... He can no longer control his own land."

"That Baste," Vosnob said. "Is probably what we're supposed to believe as true..........But what if it's another devious ploy to catch us off-guard?"

"Can you explain?" Ilty asked from across the table.

"Perhaps," Vosnob offered. "But I don't claim to have all the pieces."

"We're here to listen.....Get on with it!" Oros then slammed his tankard on the table. Laughter broke out as the foaming ale drenched his light brown robe.

"Your words speak better than your actions." Baste dryly commented, his bushy eyebrows arched in mock judgement.

Vosnob broke in. "This is another way to see the loss of the Dark Lands.... ....Ask yourself, why would you allow the destruction of your home?.... I suggest that the answer is that I no longer want it, or...need it."

"You're implying that Ashuwa is going to establish his empire somewhere else."

"Why not?...The Kyykki aren't actual subjects which a god requires to survive...........And from the information we've collected, it appears that Ashuwa tried to create an empire in the southern swamp."

"And have real people to increase his strength."

"Pretty much the direction I followed, Baste."

"Then you also assume that the worst is yet to be." Ilty's brown face was tight.

"Unfortunately, I do....But may the Holy One declare me a liar.. .... Ashuwa is not dead, nor are his Kyykki defeated... And with potential new allies in the north, the Taths and their Istelles, Ashuwa finds his old homeland surrounded.......Ask yourselves, if placed in his position, what would you do?"

A subdued silence reigned. Vosnob's insight contained merit, enough to thoroughly reject the serf's optimistic opinion that all was well. And quite enough for the assembled Elders to reassess their future options and realign their strategy.

"Are we in possession of enough information to pursue your line of thinking?"

Vosnob missed the question, his mind being somewhere in the murky future.

"Vosnob?....What do you think?"

He shook is head. "What is the issue?...... I wasn't paying much attention, was I?"

"Do we actually have enough information to begin action on your 'different' conceptualization of the future?....After all, ten Elders are missing from our meeting. And the majority of those are ones on the front lines, either at Pinduala or at Sarg's new castle. ....I suggest that we wait to hear their reports before we change directions."

The Elder's remarks were accepted at face value, especially as another few dawns should not make much difference. However, if the information reported revealed evidence that Ashuwa still retained his homeland...... Obviously, action on Vosnob's ideas must wait until more evidence existed.

"Yes, perhaps I'm being a bit too hasty...Something just doesn't logically fit together, at least for me....Can we call another meeting for sundown on the morrow?"

"Only if Oros gets washed." Ilty bluntly added. "He's beginning to smell like a tavern-goer." She batted her eyelashes at the fat priest.

"Accepted." Vosnob thoughtfully agreed as thin dry fog blanketed the entire chamber.

Like an immense black blanket which refused to allow the dawn to bring another day, the Kyykki horde ploughed into the front line of the Haafian fortifications. They attacked without the usual howling, due to their exhaustion. This also allowed them to attack almost undetected. The out-numbered Light Stripers fought bravely, but vainly. The smell of food propelled the blackened horde into an unstoppable frenzy.

Before any glint of the sun broke the cloudless sky, the front lines of the lightly defended trenches were property of the Kyykki. Piles of splintered Haafian bones, still dripping with blood greeted the dawn as did bloated Kyykki, too stuffed and full to continue any form of attack. The dragons and their riders settled along the flanks, deliberately keeping the attack on a ten mile front. Then the dragons lifted off, explicitly avoiding the stoutly constructed outposts, but capturing the supply route connecting them. The buildings along this route pointed the way to D'Ka. But, if the Kyykki horde expected to conquer without detection, firing the plains was not the way to do it. With the exception of a solitary outpost, the blackened Kyykki hordes controlled fourty deep miles of the Haafian northern frontier. Now bloated from overeating, the horde stopped. On the morrow their successful push for Ashuwa's new city would begin. No Demon Master dared think otherwise. No retreat existed.

"How long can we hold out?"

"Until the end." Came the trooper's a blunt answer. "Sorry, son." Said the Chaplain. "We're the only force in the damned one's way."

"Then we'll take as many as possible with us." He aimed and slowly released the trigger. Another taller Kyykki tumbled.

The Light Stripers fought on without the advantage of the upper parapet and walkways. The tower, with its heavy weapons, could not be brought into action due to the dragons. Dense smoke engulfed most of the courtyard. This forced the troopers inside and allowed the attacking horde to boldly approach the stone fortress.

"Keep them bastards from the windows." Yelled the Senior Staff Master. "Block them up!"

He swung his broadsword in time to prevent a Kyykki from throttling a trooper, then kicked the carcass out the window.

As midday approached, the dragons fired the stone buildings. Inside, the heat became unbearable, yet to venture out meant a quick and ugly death. The upper story was abandoned. The wounded were placed in the much cooler cellars. Little by little, as the day progressed into dusk, the space occupied by the Light Stripers diminished until the living and the wounded occupied the lower stories of the central tower. The Chaplain was dead, last seen swinging a broadsword, fending off the Kyykki from the wounded. A single junior officer now commanded less than sixty able troopers.

Suddenly, the tower jarred, tumbling lances, troopers and swords across the stone floor.

"What the ...!"

"Dragon on the roof." A trooper said without much emotion.

"So its goin' cook us!" Another trooper sneered.

"I don't think so." The junior officer commented. "The tower is too small for him to breathe down the stairwell and the bastard will lose his balance if he swings over the edge."

No one spoke for several moments. Images of families and past memories floated through their exhausted minds. The oppressive heat added to their despair.

"Then we'll finish him off." A Light Striper spoke out. "No use dying from feeling sorry for myself. .....Seems this is expected of us" He said slowly as if thinking about something entirely different.

"How?" Inquired an interested trooper.

"Upstairs we gots two new machines." He said quietly. "Pointed out the slits.....Can we move them?" The trooper's voice sounded that unequivocal note of revenge, unmistakable to those who desired to even the score.

"We got four inch oak over the opening."

"The bolts will penetrate." A older trooper acknowledged quite confidently. "I've worked it before."

An excitement arising from the possibility of killing a dragon brought a hint of hope. The toll they'd extract from the damned Kyykki would aid in their total destruction. One less dragon was a good way to start. The junior officer chose six other men plus himself for the job.

As they started up the stone stairwell, the dragon began jumping about on the flat roof, frustrated. The upper stories grew steadily hotter. Water soaked cloths allowed the men to continue. On the fourth floor they stood on top of steaming rags as they slowly readjusted the massive machines. A slight breeze delivered cooler air through the tower slits. Sweating profusely, the men finally re-aimed the two machines.

In the darkness of night they impatiently waited to fire. Only one obstacle prevented them from firing. Where was the dragon sitting? Without that information their only shots would be wasted. Later, the dragon moved slowly, lumbering from side to side as if attempting to find another way to incinerate the tower's inhabitants. The junior officer measured the dragon's fairly regular pace. The dragon lumbered from corner to corner, each time pausing to lift his back feet over the oak slab covering the doorway.

He grabbed the release tethers from two troopers and sent them below. They carried a fainted trooper with them. Now he waited, coldly calculating the moment when the dragon's unprotected belly would be just above the oak slab door. A little later two regular dull thuds sounded on the stone roof. The officer gripped one tether and pulled. The bolt slammed through the oak almost before it left the cradle. The dragon's feet didn't move. All went silent--deadly silent. Green slime oozed down from the visible bolt.

He pulled again. Through the hole in the trap door and into the dragon's pierced guts shot the bolt. The men shuddered as they heard the barbs spring open ripping through the dragon's soft innards. The dragon began heaving and excessive amounts of slime ran into the tower room. The troopers evacuated, sealing the door after them.

After being refreshed by the 'somewhat' cooler air on the main floor, the troopers shared their story during a cold breakfast. This 'final' dawn soon flashed orange-yellow rays through a cloudy sky. A ruckus began immediately outside the sparsely manned walls. The determined Light Stripers, wounded included, stood, prepared for the final Kyykki onslaught. With terse grim laughter, the troopers established a kill ratio to one to ten as the requirement before anyone surrendered. However, the junior officer had to surrender first.... Then, they waited in silence.

The rambunctious noise along steadily grew louder, but no charge came. Then the noise slowly and steadily decreased, increasing the nervousness of the troopers who could not see.

"Wait until I return." The junior officer said as he bounded up the stairwell.

Within moments he returned. "They've left. Heading for D'Ka."

The stunned survivors froze, not sure if they heard correctly; almost not willing to re-think of other options. A creaky, abnormal silence existed until an old veteran breathed deeply.

"Praise be the Holy One." He said humbly. A few tears traced their way down his dirt-stained face.

Ayhn's scouts, a full three dawns ahead of the rest, had little difficulty ascertaining the direction of the rampaging Kyykki horde. A soggy brownish swath, some ten miles wide, now over fifty miles deep, cut a straight unrelenting path southwards towards D'Ka. In this stomped plain, nothing lived and little could be seen. The blackened horde annihilated trees, shrubs, small streams and huge fields of grasses. Finding the horde's path proved easy, catching up to them became the challenge.

The five-man party walked their tired Stripers beside the crushed browned earth. Eazrath, their wispy grey-haired leader, studied the Kyykki's path through a 'long tube', a now common instrument which everyone considered a divine gift. He took a swig from his canteen and then addressed the men. "I believes the front line is about thirty miles south of us....The damned Kyykki probably all ready have plowed through..."

"No way!" Countered Graych, the youngest of the five.

"Son," Eazrath said slowly. "We live by the truth, even if it hurts.....From the speed of this horde, they're well south of the fortifications."

Graych stood back, trying to understand. It was difficult. "But how?" He half mumbled.

"They never took time to rest nor eat, Son." Eazrath replied. "I expect the flood which conquered Pinduala drove them southward."

"Expect or suspect, Eazrath?" Drawled one of the Lancers.

A half empty canteen caught the large Haafian Lancer in the chest. The others laughed as he mumbled a forced apology.

"The fact is that Ayhn needs to know which direction to head... Graych, you and Thomma return to camp.....Tell Ayhn to head directly for D'Ka.........Tell him to move quickly but spare the Stripers...... .... We're going to need everyone when we catch the bastards."

Without a word, nor returning the canteen, Thomma and Graych mounted and galloped east. The quicker they caught up with the Lancers, the quicker an adjustment would be made. Both Lancers knew the stakes ran high, once the Kyykki breached the fortified line, there wasn't much to stop them until they reached D'Ka.

Eazrath mounted his Striper and headed southwards, following the path of destruction. The other two lancers moved on ahead. They possessed a terrible vision of the breached lines. In silence, except for the cool breeze from the west, the trio cantered until dusk arrived.

At next midday, two pieces of disturbing evidence came to the fore. The trio found the first set of front line trenches: filled with rotting and partially eaten Kyykki. Second, through the 'long tube' Eazrath noticed a dragon sprawled upon the keep of the outpost. As for the outpost itself, ringed by countless toad-faced carcasses, it sat quiet, too quiet.

"I fear the damned ones finished off the garrison." Eazrath informed the others. "I can't see any movements at all."

"Perhaps the Kyykki have claimed it as their own."

"That be a strain, but these dawns, anything is possible." Eazrath replied. "I mean, just afore I can retire, I get called back to active service..... Old troopers aren't supposed to be out scouting."

"Then maybe you shouldn't have friends like Vosnob, Eazrath. You're beginning to sound like an old woman."

"Then the point is all yours, my friend..... Get moving."

The Lancer's smirk quickly disappeared. Without another retort he sped along the boundary of the Kyykki trampled territory. Galloping through the burnt grassland and the rolling hills, he rapidly passed from Eazrath's observation.

"Do you think we should keep up?... Could be Kyykki hiding out there."

"I sincerely doubt that......... Such advanced tactics aren't to be found with them." Eazrath returned. "However, the youngster is bound to get lost if we don't stay on his trail. ....Let's be moving."

Stopping only a few times to use the 'long tube', the pair quickly caught up to their point man before dusk. Not more than a mile away stood the stone towered outpost, dark and quiet. From their position on the desolate hillock, the trio observed no signs of life, just the empty, hollow sound of the wind scraping the rocks of the fortification.

Eazrath kneed his Striper and the scouts slowly walked their mounts towards the darkened structure. All secured their crossbows from the saddlebags and released the cover from their quivers. At fifty paces from the outpost, Eazrath's scouting party silently circumnavigated the stench filled building. They trod upon hundreds of Kyykki, including a number of the taller type, but discovered no Light Stripers.

"I can only imagine that those unfortunate souls who didn't make it to the outpost were eaten." Eazrath dourly commented to the others.

"But they didn't die without a struggle....Just look at the piles of Kyykki....This wasn't no cheap victory for them bastards."

"To the Kyykki, price is unimportant. Only winning counts."

"What's this?" The point man suddenly called out. He dismounted to examine a small flattened path leading to the east. "They're all on foot, whoever they might be."

Eazrath rode over and studied the well defined path. He smiled. "Seems there are survivors, and they're pulling the wounded. Looks like they're making for the next outpost."

"Which may or may not exist."

"Exactly!" Declared Eazrath. "So mount up, we're going to find them before the Kyykki do.....Notice that there are no Striper prints."

Even with the double moons being at only half phase, the Light Striper's trail proved easy to follow. As they continued eastward, another raping of the land appeared in front of them, slowing their progress. The path made by the survivors cut straight across the filthy morass.

"My guess is that the Kyykki split just north of the next outpost, sensing it was easier to overrun the trenches than the stone fortifications.......... And wasting themselves on the fortifications wasn't needed.........They're headed straight to D'Ka."

"So there's twice as many as we thought?"

"I doubt that."·Said Eazrath. "By moving their line off in angles, it covered more space....My guess is that a few more miles off to the south and the two paths become one again."

"So the bastards are moving like a column instead of a fence. Rather sophisticated, I'd think."

"Extremely sophisticated, friend. The trenches were specifically designed to withstand the usual massive frontal attack. But this attack contained more than the usual ten to twelve ranks, more like hundreds..... just plowing through the land, parting like water about any obstacles."

"How poetic, Eazrath." The point man sarcastically noted.

"And yer time will come!" Then he nudged his mount forward. "Yer time will come.....Let's locate the survivors."

At late dawn, when the streaked sky fled before the brazen blue of morning, the trio finally spied the survivors. Having negotiated a brown fetid gully, the survivors had encamped on a slight knoll about a quarter mile away. Eazrath put his 'long tube' to work. The battered survivors formed a ragged but determined defensive square. The light Stripers placed the wounded on the inside, lying on travois. No officer appeared present, but two enlisted men were barking orders. Eazrath and the scouts had been spotted.

Chapter 10

Brey deliberately re-routed her journey through the celebrations at Sarg's castle. A brief 'welcome home' more than satisfied her. Having tunneled beneath the northern mountains and then returned by Istelle not only deepened her appreciation for Sarg, but also for herself. The 'motherly' lectures she received from Queen Sjura came true. She also obtained the crucial information she required in order to respond to the God-without-a-name. Therefore, the sooner she wrapped up the lingering 'queen' decision, the sooner she'd pursue her own goals. Thus, while the celebrations continued in the Great Hall and the now well-provisioned armory, she doubled back through the countless uninhabited hallways, attempting to reach the Istelles' floor alone. As much as she firmly believed in her expertise to avoid or dodge any would-be followers, something in the air reminded her that she wasn't alone after all.

She turned a sharp corner, then placed her back tight to the marble wall. The next turn led to the Istelles' roosting floor and then the enormously long staircase to the flat roof. Another set of footsteps came close, then hesitated, started and hesitated again. Brey hoped it was one of the Istelle riders checking on his prestigious mount. The steps continued closer and stopped.

"Brey, quit playing this stupid game." The familiar voice whispered down the short hallway. "It's against protocol to approach a god without a proper escort."

Brey pretended to be invisible, but Vauk was there. She didn't want company, but she also realized the truth of his words. There were witnesses when she received the offer of queenship of the Central Tribe. With an answer in hand, she knew that at least one witness would need to verify these proceedings to and for the Taths –and everyone else. A interminable moment of silence passed before she decided to reply.

"If you must, come along." She said, annoyed. "Don't get in the way."

"Thanks for the generous offer." Vauk responded smiling. He stood next to her. "Think the unnamed one will be angry with you, Brey?"

She paused, considering exactly what he meant, then tossed her head indifferently. "Just what are you inferring?"

"The unnamed god expects a positive answer. But you're intending on providing a negative one."

She turned to stare at him. Once again the conniving, persistently intimidating physician walked a step ahead of her, and they both knew it. She didn't know whether to laugh or cry, Vauk so jumbled her immediate thoughts. Vauk continually strayed into her privacy and it aggravated her. She couldn't ascertain whether his invasion was personal or professional. And, yes, the answer did matter to her, though that truth greatly annoyed her. Vauk had found great delight in the flirty Kinanna. Brey detested each and every moment of that disgusting relationship, especially when Vauk was the victim. She swallowed hard, then spoke in strained tones as she struggled to control her raging emotions. "I will make you a deal." Her voice quivered, causing Vauk to stop. "I will allow you to accompany me..... if...... and when... you are free of Kinanna." She drew in a long breath, trembling.

Vauk reached out his left hand.

"What's this for?"

"To finalize your agreement, Brey."

"Are you trying to trick me?". She cautiously replied, refusing to meet him eye-to-eye.

"Absolutely not." Came his quick reaction. "The flirt has quite a few 'gentlemen' to perform for these days...Alas, I am no longer one of her chosen few." He gave Brey a quirky smile. "Praise be the Holy One."

Brey, stunned, could not reply. Her assumptions floundered about her, leaving her directionless. Vauk's emotional assault continued unabated.

"I believe you were headed to the parapet." Vauk interrupted. "Let's get this over with. That is, provided the unnamed one is willing to meet with us there." Vauk gently took Brey by the arm. Together, in silence, they ascended the half-enclosed staircase.

Each began reorganizing priorities, anticipating something new, something unknown. Reaching the parapet, the bright mid-day sun and the soft breeze brought a wave of unbidden tranquillity to them. Not more than twenty paces away, under the shadow of an Istelle, stood the god-without-a-name arrayed in a glowing green garment.

"Greetings, my children."

"Thank you for coming, nameless one....I hoped you might heed my call, but I am humbled that you anticipated...."

"We gods have 'mysterious' ways, Brey." The god's disarming voice, his all too createdness continued to bother her.

"I thank you, My Lord." Brey said quietly as Vauk came to stand beside her.

"And you brought a witness." He chuckled.

"My Lord," Vauk interjected quickly. "I could not permit Brey to come alone. It is not proper. I am a witness."

"Most acceptable, my friend. For what may transpire requires an outside observer. In fact, the more the better." And with that the nameless god brushed the Istelle aside, revealing the entire delegation from the Central Tribe.

"My Lord!" Gasped Brey.

"All is well." Kinanna spoke, in halting Haafian, for the delegation. "We.... are....anxious to hear your words, Brey. On journey through the mountain, we.... envied......... your command of the situations as well as your..... ability to not control.........everything. Also impressive.. is...the way you work... with others to..... reaching conclusions."

"Thank you, Kinanna." Brey returned in Tath as Kinanna spoke in Haafian. "But the praise.....just doesn't rightfully fit. The scouting party was my responsibility. It's also the job I've been taught...as part of the Light Striper.....I simply did my duty."

"Well spoken, Brey." Said the nameless god simultaneously in both languages. "However, we need to dispense with a far weightier matter. Have you reached a decision concerning my offer to become the new queen of the Central Tribe?"

The delegation moved forward, anxious to hear Brey's answer. Brey took a step backwards.

"I have reached an honest conclusion in my searching for my proper role in this New Era, My Lord." Brey said, her hand gripped Vauk's.

"I thank you for your diligence in the matter. You put me to shame." The god paused, then continued. "Whatever your decision is, I hold no malice, Brey.....With the seriousness in which you did receive my offer, so with the same seriousness, shall I accept your answer."

"Thank you, My Lord." Brey felt a bit of relief, but not enough to allow circulation to return to Vauk's hand. She cleared her throat. "My Lord, delegates from the Central Tribe and Vauk." She squeezed his hand tighter. "My honest answer is that I have no desire to rule over anyone...... I would consider being queen over the Central Tribe as reaching too far....... There are many capable and faithful persons who have better qualifications and demeanor for such responsibility. A few are menfolk." In spite of the serious tone, Brey's last sentence brought a goodly amount of laughter from the nameless one.

"I apologize." The unnamed god said, then reconsidered. "Actually, that's not true....There are many thousands of well-deserving menfolk in Tath...And most of them realize that, and do the women, except that they won't publicly admit it. Brey, you merely spoke what most only dared to think...The same is true for Haafians, except that the thinking is reversed. When your officer rank is proclaimed in Krabo, there's going to be an uproar." The nameless god continued laughing, then abruptly stopped.

"I wasn't supposed to mention the future.....You aren't going to be queen, are you?"

Brey froze with fear, even though the Tath's god's voice showed nothing but understanding and compassion. Vauk's fingers, caught in Brey's tightening vise-like grip, when from white to purple. He winced.

"Please answer before you squeeze all Vauk's fingers from his hand."

Brey immediately dropped her hand away, embarrassed. Vauk stretched out his fingers, then learned over and whispered something to her. Her color returned instantly.

"My Lord," Brey began, strangely confident. "I am not the one to become the next queen of the Central Tribe."

Mixed reactions, many delicately disguised, appeared on the faces of the gathered Central Tribe delegation. Kinanna turned her back, to reappear with a handkerchief covering her face. The Taths who accompanied the scouting party stood stoically, accepting the outcome, whatever it might be.

"I find your answer not only acceptable, but also exemplary."

"My Lord?" Brey requested, more than bit confused.

The same held true for the Tath delegation, even though they remained quiet, as if anticipating another quirky response from their unnamed god, or as if some of their prearranged plans fell through.

"Kinanna," Called the unnamed one. "Stand forward, please."

Stunned by his call, though also well-pleased with the attention, Kinanna stepped into the open space between Vauk and Brey and the Central Tribe delegation. She royally curtsied before her now orange shining god.

"I dearly pray you have no such foolish idea that I might ask you to decide whether or not you should become the next queen. Such foolishness is improper." The god turned his head. "Well?" He turned and stared directly at the paling lady-in-waiting.

"Waa---waa---Why," She stammered, buying time to create a suitable excuse. "Why should I, My Lord?"

"Let's not play any more of your cute flirty games, Kinanna. Just answer the question, yes or no. Did you intend on becoming the next candidate for the queenship of the Central Tribe?"

Her countenance fell: posture went slightly, politely limp.

"Just answer me, Kinanna. There will be time for theatrics later on."

Never had so few words been so enormously difficult for her, especially as they were her trademark throughout the tribe as well as in Sarg's castle. Not that she wasn't honest, it was simply that she often received a better rewards if she 'slightly' expanded the truth. "yes." She mumbled softly as possible, all the while staring at the floor.

"Now Kinanna, speak so that everyone can hear you."

"Yes."

"Much better." The unnamed god smiled knowingly. "But telling the truth hurts you to your very heart, doesn't it?"

"yes." She murmured again.

"No matter." The nameless one replied rather indifferently. "I have a special assignment for you."

Before the god could finish Kinanna's posture straightened, she beamed for all she was worth.

"You will head a delegation of five. Your destination is the Abbey in the mountains east of the Buda Lake."

Kinanna beamed as if she were being bestowed with the queenship of all Tath. She forced herself to keep from prancing about, though she could not hide her delighted heart.

The god without-a-name finished her assignment. "Once there, the five of you are required to construct a written language for our people.... The brothers at the Abbey shall assist you in your endeavor. This work has been initiated by Jelkio, but, seeing that she is married and has other responsibilities, you are granted this special assignment."

A quizzical smile zipped by her face, one she wished had been avoidable. "The brothers are Holy Men, Kinanna." Vauk explained. "They are also scholars on various topics...But most of all, they are extremely serious men having no patience, no time for frivolity of any sort....... They don't even have padded chairs." He lied.

"I'm quite sure you'll enjoy it." Brey indelicately added.

"My dear Brey!" The unnamed god smirked. "Such a judgement! I didn't believe you could be so sarcastic. Must be the company you spend your time with." To emphasize his next point, the god stretched himself thirty feet tall. The nervous Istelles skittered to the far side of the parapet, eliminating any vestige of shade. "I accept your sincere answer Brey. Hopefully others may learn from your example...... Struggling to ascertain the correct answer isn't exactly one of your strong points, is it Kinanna?" The unnamed god spoke as he looked down upon a quivering Kinanna.

The beautiful Tath flushed and bowed her head. For once her embarrassment wasn't feigned. Somewhere deep in his heart Vauk felt a bit of pity for the sultry adventuress; an elbow from Brey returned him from reality.

"I do thank for your offer, My Lord." Brey said, shading her eyes as she gazed up at the hovering nameless god now haloed by the high afternoon sun.

Before speaking again, the nameless god decreased his stature to twenty feet, eliminating the problem. "Those of you from the Central Tribe are hereby assigned to complete the following order. By the end of this season you shall give to me the names of seven persons considered suitable by the tribe to become the next KING or Queen......Are there any questions?"

A meek, weakly disguised voice came from the middle of the group. "King?"

"Why not? Originally I chose queens, now is the time to change. May the best person possible be the one chosen to lead the tribe...... Any other questions Gymtoa?"

"No, my lord."

Taert, the Tath bodyguard whose overbearing duty mindedness almost suffocated Brey, forced his way to the front of the group. "My Lord, is anyone allowed to be a candidate?"

"Does not my original appointing of Brey as a candidate supply the answer to your question?"

"Perhaps it should, My Lord... ."

"Taert, I have definitely underestimated your potential. You are now a prince."

"A prince....like royalty?" Taert quickly lost his usual stoic composure.

"You would suggest another title?" The god without-a-name returned frivolously, a mischievous smile crossing his now ruby-toned face.

"But princes....have no real duties....They hide behind the skirts of their wives."

"I've noticed that also...Some even...Well, I'll not embarrass any in the present company."

"My Lord, I'd rather have the life of a chamberpot cleaner than that of a useless, gutless prince."

"I ought to grant you your wish." The unnamed god said. "However, that too would be a waste. ....If I might digress for a moment, I totally agree with your assessment of Tath's male nobility.....They're good looking flowerpots and full of manure."

Stirrings of nervous disagreement swept through those gathered. The truth affected a number of princes present as well as their retainers, who knew the god's words to be quite true.

"And flowerpots have uses." The nameless god continued, well aware that his terse remarks did not endear him to Tath royalty. "Princes will have uses also....... While their wives are busy attending meetings and other diverse functions required by royal protocol, their husbands shall learn the responsibilities of day-to-day administration of the tribes............ The days of freeloading and leading a meaningless existence are hereby terminated forever............I hope everyone understands." He smiled mischievously as he returned to his usual seven foot height. "Well?"

A hubbub of stifled 'yes' answers poured forth from the Taths, quite disorganized and extremely self-defensive. Vauk smiled quietly, trying to hide himself behind Brey.

"Now, that matter is settled...Kinanna, you will leave by Istelle on the dawn, as the Haafians call it. The Abbey is some six, maybe eight day's flight from here. But first you will fly to Krabo and pay proper respects to the High Council... Jelkio will insure all protocol is proper."

Kinanna immediately drew back, unaccustomed to direct orders as she was, to prepare a defense.

"My dear Kinanna," The god spoke condescendingly as if approaching an ill-behaved child. "Please remember who you are and who I am. This responsibility you carry is to benefit all our people. The new queen or king just might 'have' your delicate, but slightly inflated head--should you fail. Taert and two other guards will accompany you along with an Istelle and his rider... Yes," He paused. "I will add a priest, making your party six... So, you'll require another Istelle.... You will report here once every season until you have completed your responsibility....And you DO understand." A violet colored cloud filled with sparkling rainbows suddenly appeared as a cover for the unnamed god's relocating.

Once again a cacophony of voices raised up as many Taths found themselves struggling to implement their god's demands. A washed-out Kinanna walked over and hugged the hapless Vauk. Brey simply left the parapet.

"Perhaps I shall never see you again." She sobbed.

"Since when did that make much of a difference. You treated me as a Tath prince. That sits very poorly in my country....Perhaps your assignment will assist you in learning personal integrity."

She instantly stepped away and swung her open hand at his bronzed face. Vauk easily ducked and grabbed her wrist, forcing her to face away from him.

"I believe that's the direction you're headed. Please continue." He said disinterestedly then headed after Brey. Much later, in the armory, Vauk found Brey. She had divested her long dress in favor of her Light Striper uniform.

"You planning a trip?"

"As long as it's far away from all your filthy lies." She angrily retorted. Her defiant words tore into his heart.

"Why such a change?"

"As if you didn't know.....Still having fun with Kinanna... Setting up a schedule so you can meet with her during your traveling?" She degraded him in a most hurtful manner.

Vauk went quiet, something very near eluded him, something obvious to her but not to him. Brey's face flushed with anger and her slanted eyes narrowed to almost nothing. With hands on her hips, she walked towards him. Vauk didn't move. In fact, he was oblivious to her movement, being lost in thought.

"Jealous!" He shouted in her tightly drawn-up face. "You are jealous.... of an empty-headed flirt."

This time the open-handed blow stung his face. Brey quickly turned and began to walk away. Vauk reached out, pulling her to himself. Initially she resisted fiercely, then she wrapped her arms around his neck. Vauk slid his arms about her, leaning his head on her shoulder.

"Damn you." She cried. "You aren't supposed to know me this well."

"Too bad for you." He quietly returned, his hand playing with her long tresses.

"But why?...You know my history....I'm far worse than Kinanna."

"Will you shut up."

"Why?"

"So I can do this." Vauk turned and kissed her forehead, then the bridge of her thin nose. She lifted her face to kiss him.

"Not fair at all." She whispered.

A most pregnant Queen Sjura and Sarg inadvertently trespassed during

Vauk and Brey's encounter. It was part of their usual afternoon stroll. Sarg started to speak, but Sjura quickly and firmly placed her blue hand over his mouth. Later, when they arrived in their private hallway off the Great Hall Sarg demanded an explanation.

"You are as dense as a rock, husband."

"We've covered this territory before, my love. But what does it have to do with Vauk And Brey?"

"Have you forgotten the hours I've spent with her alone? Have you forgotten the sordid history she had to leave go?"

"I guess I did." And he said nothing further, knowing that things were going as they were supposed to go.

No Kyykki force of any magnitude was 'supposed' to have the resources to breach the 'line'. Massive evidence proved the 'line' had been breached, however. To the northeast lay nothing but the dry black ashes of the wheat and barley fields. These provided camouflage for the blackened toad-faced horde. The eastern branch of the Haaf River converted from green-blue to a thick brownish shade. Fish and water animals lined her torched banks, dead from the pollution of their habitat. But as of this dawn, no scouts had yet located the damned one's legions.

Within the fortress city of D'Ka, the Light Striper stood at full alert. All machines were readied to fire at maximum distance and aimed to utilize overlapping fields of fire. Under heavy guard, the women, children, the elderly and the infirm clogged the main northern road running into D'Ka. Also under heavy guard escort were those families heading from D'Ka to Krabo.

At the Kyykki camp council that evening, there existed a difficulty in identifying which Demon Master was which. The exhausting pace of their successful attacks left them paled, their usually robust colors fading to mere tints of what existed a few dawns ago. This, in spite of the fact that everyone enjoyed an enormous feast. Now, lying in shallow gullies and ravines, secure from the burning sunlight as well as an unfettered and relentless west wind, the immense horde rested. No guards were posted. The dragons formed a perimeter, establishing boundaries for any who might wander. It mattered not that their victory cost them over twenty percent of their forces, nor that they had broken through a ten mile wide front some seventy miles deep. The fact that they had succeeded and that D'Ka was next in line for destruction--only that counted.

"Has Ashuwa been notified of our success?" A dirty faded orange Demon Master asked the other four gathered about a bloody pile of Haafian bones.

"Indeed." Came a mumbled reply from a green Demon Master. "I commanded the red one to return to Ashuwa's headquarters via dragon. ....." He stopped speaking to pick a tendon from his fanged teeth. "He flew out....mid-day?"

"Mid-day it was." Confirmed another Demon Master.

"Then we wait until the Great Lord Ashuwa commands us to attack the city." Said the orange Demon Master.

"Impossible!" Belched the green Demon Master. "The Haafians know we have invaded. To wait is to jeopardize....."

"Ass!" Yelled the silvered Demon Master. "Remember what Warmaker advised us....Either we conquer quickly and live..."

"It's been repeated often enough....But let us fully understand that we operate without a Haafian blessing. ...They are long dead." He said in a most understated manner. "Nor can we expect reinforcements. Ashuwa's wall of water took that from us....... We are here and cannot return!"

"We have come to conquer and conquer we shall!" The silvered Demon Master exploded. "In such way we redeem ourselves before the Almighty Ashuwa.........Conquering until there are no Haafians. That is our only recourse.....Tell me, am I wrong?"

Slightly muted snarls from the older veterans greeted his simplistic appraisal. Yet, in basic bare-bones the silvered one did truthfully present their immediate future. His forceful words firmly impressed the singular truth upon them. No choices existed for the Kyykki horde and the dragons. Unable to fully comprehend the logistics nor the strategy of their isolation, the Demon Masters quickly forgot the conversation and returned to crunching Haafian bones. Morning would be time enough to renew their attacking.

Morning not only brought a steady downpour with ice-edged winds, but also a report from a dragon riding scout. The firestorms which preceded the horde alerted the Haafians. All across the southern boundary, where the fires finally died, the Haafians waited.

"Then we shall go and kill and eat them!" Yelled the silvered one.

"And if you are so damned foolish we will never fight again." Countered the orange Demon Master. "Remember, friend," He threatened. "With all our forces we DID·NOT·conquer Pinduala. Ashuwa did that alone, by use of his unlimited capability.... That is our warning from the Almighty, we are to attack when we are able to win without depending upon Him."

"You blasphemous filth!" Angrily bellowed the silvered Demon Master. "Without the Almighty, we can do nothing."

The green Demon Master shook the silvered one by his shoulders then threw him down. "Listen, you Haafian-brained moron, we need to redeem ourselves before the Almighty! We have failed once. We did not conquer Pinduala and without Warmaker's suggestion.....well, by now, no one would be alive....He is watching us, testing us and our abilities as His faithful ones....Do you understand, incompetent!"

Slowly he stood, carefully watching every move of the other Demon Masters. Having no wish to die outside of battle, he nodded his scaly pointed head.

"Then, we follow the sun until it dies.....That traveling will move us beyond the black earth." Said the green Demon Master, denying others any authority in the matter. "There will be no firestorms, nor will the dragons fly. We travel quietly and quickly."

"Then are we avoiding the attack?"

"We will turn to attack when we are assured of success…We must surprize the builders of the 'killing things'."

A few cursory commands sent the Demon Masters to moving their fragment of the unconquered horde. Westward they journeyed, strictly keeping within the confines of the shallow hollows and ravines of the broad plane. By mid-day the blackened horde began shoving their way through the tall thick grasses. Their speed progressively diminished. Late in the afternoon, the small tributaries of the western branch of the Haaf River provided food for the always-hungry Kyykki. Brown polluted water flowed out to the river, causing it to blend into the ripened wheat covered landscape.

The single moon desperately tried to enlighten the terrain far below, but the dense low-hanging clouds denied all but a handful of opportunities. The rain continued, but as a drizzle that mattered nothing to the Kyykki horde. Pushed along by their Demon Masters, the toad-faced invaders continued ever westward throughout the night. At mid-morning, they rested under the ancient willows and copses of birches lining the creek banks.

And the creeks rapidly degenerated into cesspools. All creatures desiring to live, fled southward. The herds of wildebeests, wild stripers and flocks of ducks and the song birds bolted from the expected security of their environment, terrified of the ghastly invaders who sought only to devour them. At mid-afternoon the horde swung south, to attack Krabo and redeem themselves as Ashuwa's faithful and obedient ones, to be freed from his dreadful wrath.

Ayhn quietly listened to the scout's reports. He found the Kyykki bolder and more sophisticated than expected, both items were disconcerting. He also believed that while the Kyykki horde remained an enormous destructive force, he could exploit their major weakness. No reinforcements would be forthcoming. To that end he revised the Lancer strategy once again.

The Lancers turned to head due west, directly along the path of the sun. On the second dreary dawn, they navigated the polluted east branch of the Haaf River. This proved problematic. The need for pure water in great volume justified a northward detour. Nevertheless, Ayhn continued pushing westward believing the Kyykki force had yet to descend southward to attack the cities. Scouts, continuing to follow the toad-faced horde's westward trampling, confirmed Ahyn's suspicions.

Using his Lancers to form a massive half-mile wide front, the entire regiment traversed the blackened land as an immense weapon-bristling square. On the backs of three supply waggons construction began for thirty foot lookout towers. With the grasslands re-emerging in a few more dawns, Ayhn desired no unwanted surprizes. However, if the wind blew in the right direction, he readied commands to fire the drying grasses.

Five much cooler dawns later, the Lancers posted their evening guard at the juncture where the Kyykki turned and headed south. The landscape about them, blacked with soot smeared into a vile smelling paste by the rains, and polluted by the Kyykki droppings, effectively stopped the wagons. The soft muck clogged the waggons' wheels up to the axles and the heavy morning frost, powerful enough to freeze the top layer of soil, quickly sapped the half-breeds' strength.

About a small campfire built outside Ayhn's tent, the Commander conversed with his head machiners, the Lancers whose waggons suffered the most. Many wrapped cloth about their feet and used Striper blankets as cloaks.

"I didn't plan for us to fighting at this time of year." Ayhn words flowed with a sense of self-deprecation. "Another round of cold dawns and our ill-clothed Lancers will suffer terribly."

"Not so much as you might think, Commander. We knows whets were here for. Ta rid the Kyykki from our land and render the place safe again." He drew on his pipe and shot back a streak of white smoke. "Don't worry....When ta Kyykki is spotted, there'll be plenty o' heat to go round."

In his deep laughter, several others joined him, though Ayhn remained conspicuously silent. He allowed his Lancers to suffer because he did not anticipate the oncoming seasonal change nor their venturing into the plains. His mind wandered, grappling to secure a viable answer, an immediately viable answer that might ensure the safety of those under his command.

"Commander," The old veteran continued. "We didn't come here for a vacation.....Ye does the best ye can, and let the Holy One do all else."

Ayhn nodded in tacit approval of the Lancer's age-proven wisdom, but his spirit sagged. Too much transpired too fast and he recognized that he wasn't prepared for it. His lack of experience bothered him.

"Its time for your priorities to get straightened out, Ayhn." Said a familiar voice towards the back of those gathered about the small campfire. "We aren't going to allow this freezing to effect your thinking."

Only one person in the Lancers could utter such a remark without a quick and certain reprisal: the Chaplain. Cutting his way through the officers, he stood before Ayhn. "Come now, there be no one ever who is always correct, the Holy One accepted."

Wordlessly, Ayhn dismissed the officers without additional orders. As a visit by the Chaplain was considered an honor throughout the Light Striper, Ayhn felt no embarrassment by his direct approach. Nor did his subordinates find the visit reason to disavow Ayhn's leadership qualities. A long, almost sacrosanct tradition recognized such visitations as proof of the Holy One's presence.

"Well, my friend, why is it that being here is hopeless?"

Ayhn simply stared at the frosting ground beneath his boots.

"If you find it impossible to put your concerns into words maybe those things aren't real at all....Or even....they might be a trickery of the damned Ashuwa."

Ayhn instantly rejuvenated, though a startled gaze encompassed his lean haggard face. "Ashuwa be damned!"

"We all know that to be true...The question is not about him, however.......... It's about you. Has the doubt in your mind been planted or encouraged by him?"

"How dare you!"

"Indeed I dare....Ashuwa is not faring well these days. With pure water pouring out from his Dark Lands, his own home is destroyed..........And now, his only remaining horde, so far we know, heads southward to its complete destruction......My friend, a desperate god will do anything too insure his survival.......Is he using you?"

Hot anger swelled within him, sweat dripped down his forehead. The penetrating words of the Chaplain found their target. He desperately fought even a partial chance of their truthfulness. Quietly, the Chaplain stood next to Ayhn warming his hands over the fire. Ayhn's anger soon found itself overtaken by another dreadful emotion: fear. His heart pounded, his blood raced and he felt like fainting. But on the outside, statuesque is the way he appeared to those about. The Chaplain continued standing beside the Lancers' commander.

After what seemed an incredibly long time, Ayhn spoke, his voice unsure, faltering. "I.......I have no answer for you."

"Didn't think you did." The Chaplain indifferently replied. "But we cannot afford to take unnecessary risks, can we?"

"No Chaplain, that would be quite inexcusable."

"Well put, Commander....Now, how do we get moving?"

"At this point, I'm open for suggestions."

"Then recall your officers and get moving."

Before the bleak early winter sun broke the dawn, the Lancers speedily moved to engage the toad-faced horde. Ayhn moved the column a half mile to the east, hopefully placing his force between the cities and the southward moving Kyykki. By double hitching the machiners waggons, and the supply waggons, the Lancers pulled away from the mucky path of the Kyykki and rolled across the dry grasslands. Commanded to find and then destroy the last remaining Kyykki horde brought a renewed sense of purposefulness to the Lancers as they moved southward.

A dawn later the wintry weather broke. Bright pillars of sunlight pierced the low hanging clouds, melting patches of thick frost. As evening approached and campfires warmed supper, an exhausted scouting party was escorted through the pickets by the sentries. A junior officer was dispatched to Ayhn notifying him of their return. He would receive the scouts directly. Still winded and sweating, three Lancers brought their report to Ayhn and his pipe smoking advisor.

"Where are the other two?" Ayhn asked, half-guessing the answer.

"Dead Sir!"

"Died fighting the dragon, so we might get away."

"They were brave, but no match fer a dragon with but crossbows."

"Yes, but the dragon bees missing one wing, mind you. His toad-faced vermin friends will have him for supper."

Ayhn stood listening, as did the pipe smoking senior officer. Ayhn leveled a number of specific questions at the trio. "Was the dragon also scouting?"

"No Sir!" Replied the tallest of the three. "He done spied us after we located and mapped their campment."

Ayhn smiled inwardly and then spoke quietly, motioning for his aide-de-camp to get the three something to eat and drink. "Tell me about their campment."

The trio's reporting tumbled out on top of itself, though it retained a modicum of understandability and organization. "It's about two dawns almost due south…Most of them aren't moving too fast anymore….The cold weather's got them frozen. Not all the dragons be moving too fast either, some blow hot air over the Kyykki."

"And we couldn't count their numbers 'cause they be all on top of each other…..But the campment measured almost a mile square with some sixty plus dragons. I think there are many more dragons, flying scouting missions. Each has a demon rider….Ugliest thing I ever seed…with fangs and claws and…"

"I believe I have the idea." ·Ayhn interrupted without embarrassing the Lancers. "I've seen them for myself: Evil is ugly when seen for what it is…… And those demon riders are totally undisguised depravity and sinfulness….. Please eat, I'll return for all of you later."

Taking the senior officer with him, Ayhn proceeded to the tent where the junior officers gathered. His entering surprised them, though most attempted to produce a proper 'attention'. Until they finished stumbling over themselves, Ayhn quietly waited by the tent flap. The Chaplain arrived shortly thereafter and stood behind him.

"We finished goofing around?" Ayhn enunciated each word carefully.

Every officer swiftly re-adjusted his uniform while simultaneously eliminating the smirk from his face. Now as all officers stood stoically at attention, Ayhn softened his approach. "You will not be sleeping this evening. The Kyykki campment has been located."

Coalescing emotions of elation loaded with fearfulness rushed through their frames, but was only revealed through their eyes. After studying these illuminating references, Ayhn continued speaking. "I recognize this is a most intriguing adventure for you. It is, and yet, it will be far more fearful than shooting suicidal dragons from the air." He smiled the smile of experience. "Here are your orders." Ayhn outlined the campaign in large strokes, each encompassing the officers present in various capacities. Into these capacities the officers would fit as required and, if possible, by their specializations. To keep all the 'bold strokes' flowing uniformly, Ayhn enlisted his senior pipe smoking officer to produce a logistical timetable. Once established, the Lancers' attack strategy would move forward on a regulated basis. As the force would soon be dividing into two distinct forces, one three times the size of the other, correct timing was imperative.

The small force, comprized of one third the Lancers, galloped from the campment while the hazy single moon still lit their path southward. Ten war waggons stuffed with provisions and double teamed comprized the remainder of the force. At daybreak a halt was called until their nocturnal scouts reported.

At daybreak the rest of the Lancers broke camp and followed the smaller force. Dressed and armed for battle the Lancers trotted quickly across an elongated front. By nightfall, they traveled in a path wider than deep, with both supply waggons and war waggons established in the third and fourth ranks. While the high grasses eventually slowed their progress, they also negated any signs of tell-tale dust clouds. Thick frost crunched underfoot and provided essential water for the thirsty Stripers and half-breeds. Hushed conversations laid bets on the next move or the place of their initial encounter with the Kyykki. Most believed the encounter to be within two dawns, especially as the cold weather encumbered the reptilian-like Kyykki more than the Lancers.

The night remained frigid. The wind disappeared. In these vast treeless plains, not even the double-posted sentries thought to look up. With clouds hanging low enough to become targets and so dense as to prevent all but the slightest glimpse of the moon, there wasn't any reason to. Dragons did not fly under such conditions.

Tath scouts flying silently beneath the dark night clouds circled over the encamped Lancers. The heavily clad Istelle riders numbered the campfires and returned as silently as they came.

Prior to daybreak, while the troopers stirred up the smoldering campfires, Ayhn met again with his officers.

"This dawn we form two forces." Ayhn said. "Any questions?"

"Haven't you moved up the timing by one full dawn, Sir?"

"I have. Something about this colder weather informs me that our enemy isn't as far south as he might wish to be."

"Yes, Sir."

"Send a runner to the advance company with this information." Ayhn addressed his aide-de-camp. "Other concerns, gentlemen?"

A series of long gazes indicated that everyone had prepared as much as possible. They moved into battle formation. By noon, the larger force split into two equal forces. Each formation reshaped itself as an arrowhead, the double-teamed waggons forming the last two ranks. A gulf of one quarter mile of high grasses separated the two parallel moving forces.

Pausing to rest again the following morning, the smaller force camped, awaiting for their scouts to report. The Lancers had adjusted to traveling by night rather well. By noon, their scouting party signaled by mirror to the sentries. Their full tilt gallop, however, explained quite a lot long before details were verbally presented to the pipe smoking commander: the Kyykki camp was near.

"Sir, some fifteen miles due south. Hasn't moved in two dawns..."

"But they aren't frozen, Sir."

"Just extremely lethargic, Sir." Proclaimed the corporal who lead the party. "The dragons keep the clustered toad-faced bastards alive with their fires, but not warm enough to move as they used to....Hardly any sign of that energy they had back at Pinduala, Sir."

"Draw me two copies of their camp, indicate the distances from our camp to theirs carefully. Send one to Commander Ayhn immediately." He drew in a whiff of pipe smoke through his grey beard. "Then, I need a detailed map of their camp, especially note the head demons' positions and the of the dragons, include their landing spots."

The corporal reached inside his dirty tunic and unfolded a piece of paper. "This is what you'll bees needing, Sir." He smiled and saluted. Fumbling about, the other four repeated his salute.

"Excellent work, I commend all of you." He mumbled as the pipe clogged his mouth. He carefully studied the detailed map circling with a stick the few places he where didn't understand the corporal's notations. "Will you orient the map for me?"

"Certainly Sir." The corporal twisted the map and sketched an arrow. "That bees west, following after the sun."

"Thank you, corporal... You are all dismissed. Get some rest and food."

Riding an elegant half breed, Ayhn's aide-de-camp, plowed through the parallel ranks of the Lancers searching for his commander. A gaunt stare and reddened eyes suggested to almost everyone that his message reeked of ill-boding. Most Lancers double checked their weaponry shortly after he rushed by. He caught up to Ayhn during the noon break. Roughly swinging down from his mount into the tall grasses, he stumbled into his Commander.

"You might at least salute." Ayhn called out as he raised up from the ground.

"Yes Sir." The aide saluted amidst the laughter of those attending the fire. "I request an immediate conference, Sir, in private."

A quick study of his aide demonstrated to Ayhn the aide's absolute seriousness. "As you wish. I believe there's a waggon off to the right....The Chaplain will be ousted for a short while, but he ought to recover."

"He ought to hear this, Sir."

"You sure?" Ayhn stopped next to a waggon bearing the Chaplain's insignia: a cream colored flag with a gold chalice painted in the center.

"And who be wanting me now?" Declared the Chaplain testily. He put his tankard down and came out.

"I do Sir," The aide hastily replied. "I need to speak with both of you immediately, in private."

"Well then, you're welcome inside....Just make sure there's no manure on your boots....That warm stuff stinks worse than Kyykki. .....What's the burning issue?" He plopped himself on a pile of blankets.

The aide-de-camp composed himself, without much success. "Those two scouts reported killed by a dragon....."

"I remember their report quite well...The two died so the other could escape."

"No Sir." He angrily spat out. "Their bodies were found by the advance company early this dawn....Discovered their shallow gave because the Meekying Eagles were circling overhead...Didn't make much sense until a scout examined closer...."

Deep furrows cut into the Chaplain's brow. "I care much for killing,......... especially the kind that reeks of murder."

"Were they murdered?" Ayhn carefully asked. "Did you examine their corpses?"

"No Sir, I did not see their bodies. I received a confidential report from the Commander of the company."

"Dusted with pipe ashes, I might assume." Ayhn tried and failed with his light-hearted remark.

"He did witness the bodies, Sir. ....He's preparing the two for military funeral as soon as he has your personal response and ...."

"That the Chaplain must somehow be prepared to perform the ceremony."

"No Chaplain....He wants you to declare a court-martial for the remaining scouts.....The dead Lancers had bolts sticking from their backs."

"Ashuwa's hideous shadow of damnedness never ceases, does it?" Ayhn wondered out loud, then caught himself. "I believe a court-martial is the proper response. However, with the damn Kyykki just over the next series of ridges, our time...well, we have no time for such proceedings."

"Commander," The Chaplain roughly interjected. "There is time to hold another review with the scouts...We must prevent them from construing anymore problems for us........ One traitorous deed is more than adequate for their judgement!"

"Send for them, immediately!" Ayhn snapped at his aide. "There's a singular test which will instantly permit a guilty verdict and swift execution."

The aide smiled, crookedly. "The dragon tattoos." He whispered hoarsely as he ducked out the waggon's tailgate.

Ayhn looked at his Chaplain. "Unbelievable, isn't it?....I'm recalling the lead company....Have the Lancers form a strong defensive square....I'm certain that our strategy is compromized."

"Unfortunately, I also believe you are correct....It's simply a matter of time before they'll attack us."

"Pray we have enough time to prepare before their attack begins."

"You can be sure of that much, Commander." The Chaplain called out as Ayhn dropped from the tailgate to the dry grass.

A squad of runners galloped desperately southward, knowing all-to-well that their timely arrival meant the salvation of the advance company. Simultaneously, the arrogant Lancers, hands leashed together behind their necks, were tossed to the ground before Ayhn. His judgement had been negated by the righteous anger of the guards. The five, stripped to the waist, bore the flying dragon tattoos carved into their forearms.

"Stand them up!"

The guards mercilessly yanked the five from the ground by their stringy hair. The corporal who lead the scouting party spit in Ayhn's direction. A swift kick in the groin by the guard caused him to swallow his own spittle and then cough blood.

Ayhn studied each Lancer carefully, wanting something redemptive from this despicable situation than just their executions. While Ayhn had little intention of postponing their executions, perhaps he had the opportunity to gather some information which could benefit the Lancers. To that end, he posed a series of questions. All were met with a defiant silence.

"Obviously, Ayhn, they made peace with the Holy One. If not, they ought to have spoken by now......But ...I cannot decipher their minds."

"That's quite an assumption, one lacking evidence."

"Ah...Commander, minds they have…….. Have they not chosen to murder, to corrupt, to betray, to sell their souls to the damned one....?"

"Thank you Chaplain." Ayhn said unemotionally, then deliberately switched to the current topic. "Even though they betrayed their fellow Lancers and defied the Holy Edicts of the Holiness Code, I shall not treat them as they deserve. Instead, they shall die of their own accord, ... of their own free will."

Horrified, the five looked about for support, any meagre support whatsoever. Those standing next to them also looked horrified. Suicide, irregardless of rationale, meant an eternal punishment, a dying that never quite ended, never ceased in tormenting. Such was clearly written in the Holiness Code.

"Ayhn." A sincerely worried Chaplain spoke.

"Let it go, Chaplain. We shall not murder these Kyykki mongers who sold their souls to Ashuwa.............They will do it for themselves, as is only proper for those who cowardly design to condemn the Lancers to the damned Kyykki horde....But until that time, bind each, feet and hands to a waggon wheel....If, perchance, any should try to escape......." Ayhn carried his threat no further, his tone precluded anyone misunderstanding him.

By supper the Lancers' 'restructured' defensive square lay prepared and waiting for the Kyykki attack. This particular square actually consisted of three concentric circles, with the waggons arranged as strong points within each and gathered as a keep in the innermost one. Ayhn's machiners had suggested this arrangement as the most effective way for utilizing the collective firepower of their War Waggons: all waggons could concentrate on one singular spot if required. The key factor which persuaded Ayhn to use this untested system came in the recognition that repeated volleys, totally concentrated, could be focused on another target without endangering the Lancers. Such was the machiners' theory.

The first attack, arriving at sunset, burst upon the Lancers like a rude devastating surprize. The dragons, flying extremely low, thus out-of-sight, set the tall plains' grasses afire. Driven by swiftly changing soft breezes and fueled by their own heat-created winds, the fires rapidly encircled the Lancers' fortified campment. Immediately, as the acrid smell of smoke coiled through the defenses, the Stripers and half-breeds panicked. Lancers found themselves leaping out into the flames. Others suffered underneath pounding hooves and too many mounts, desiring to escape, came to their end by impaling themselves on the defensive spikes planted beyond the outer circle.

Moments later, the flames burst through the outer circle. The tuba sounded 'retreat' as troopers battled the flames with their cloaks in an organized retreat to the second circle. Greedily the unfettered inferno rushed the waggons, rapidly passing under them in search of more easily consumed fuel. Having devoured the grasses the dwindling conflagration paused to die at the center of the Lancers fortification.

Ayhn stepped from his command waggon to survey the damage. Smoke swirled from countless piles of grass and Stripers barked in fear. The wounded were all ready being carried to the Chaplain's waggon, while the Junior Officers quickly ordered their troopers back to the front line.

"Get me a casualty report and send scouting parties out as far possible." Ayhn spoke briefly with his aide-de-camp. "Find out the location of....."

"Yes, Sir." He yelled over his shoulder as he spurred his Striper into a gallop. "We all want the pipe smoker safe-and-sound."

"He's never been the latter." Ayhn half mumbled to his staff. "Watch the fires." He ordered the sentries. "We'll not be attacked until they're out....Even demons aren't that stupid."

A quick look about the plains proved Ayhn correct. While the conflagration had entered the encampment, it also raged away from it. As far as one could see, the plains burned red with fire and then became smokey black as smoldering commenced. At present, though for a relatively short time, the fire protected the Lancers.

A similar scenario presented itself to the advanced company. However, flames charged them from only one direction, the north. With every available mount hitched to the waggons, the company galloped southward in three 'V' shaped ranks.

"Help us, Holy One." The pipe smoking commander continually repeated as the distance between the two forces steadily increased. While he surmized the fire resulted from the enemy's machinations, it now mattered little. It effectively terminated Ayhn's strategy.

Ayhn's situation became more desperate. Their southward movement placed them closer to the Kyykki horde. He ordered the ten War Waggons to the perimeter and made ready. Instantly the Lancers followed suite, loosening their broadaxes and stringing their crossbows. Grim determined smiles shot across their faces.

For most of the smoke choking afternoon, the advance company continued on, the grueling pace taking its toll on the Stripers and half-breeds. They barely walked, their sweating sides steaming the air, nostrils flared wide open as they gasped for breath. The flames still followed, never gaining, yet refusing to diminish or disperse.

A dim sparking signal from the forward scouts puzzled the scout receiving the message. From his post high in the commander's waggon, he thought he read. 'Dead dragons here. Others attack white eagle. Come quick.' Instinctively, he replied. 'Repeat'. An identical message returned.

"Commander!" The scout nervously yelled down.

"What message?"

"Dead dragons ahead. A white eagle fights against others."

The Commander removed his pipe. "You had this confirmed!" He yelled back, puzzled.

"Yes Sir!"

The Commander removed the ever-present pipe from his mouth. He wiped his sweating brow. Tales of the white eagles had been told, that was one issue, a now common one.

"Sir, what are your orders!" The scout called down.

"How far?"

"About one mile, Sir."

"Sound 'advance'!"

Though the tuba sounded the familiar signal, and the force obeyed, the pace continued at the same deliberate walk. The Lancers re-checked their weapons. The machiners restrung for extra long distance shots and then loaded the deadly spreading hex-bladed bolts. The Commander sent out another platoon to reconnoiter and assist the scouts where possible.

Strange, unfamiliar ear-piercing squawking noises, ones bizarre enough to alarm even fatigued mounts, came from just beyond the stoney knoll rising directly in front of them. After a few more paces, the hideous roaring of dragons became added to the unnatural mixture.

The advance company instantly went to 'full alert' status.

Another platoon rushed out to reconnoiter, as the first one had disappeared. They paused at the rough edge of the knoll, not quite sure of the sight before them. Down below, twice the distance of a crossbow's range, the first platoon, with their backs to an immense, white eagle, fought off both Kyykki and earth bound dragons. Over half the force lay in the shadow of the creature's huge shadow. Nine dragons with claw marks encircling their bloodied necks dotted the ground like sacks of potatoes fallen from the sky. As the white eagle turned to defend itself, the platoon noticed its left wing was charred and bleeding. Its rider, a bluish creature directed the battle from the creature's back.

"Iffen the damned dragons could fire without roastin' them toad faces, everyone be dead." Called out the corporal leading the platoon. "Blow the tuba!"

The blast caught the Kyykki and the Demon Masters by surprize; in their single-mindlessness no thought had been given to anything except killing the wounded Istelle. A dragon rose in the air to attack them, but as soon as it hovered at fifty feet a once shadowy Istelle wrapped its huge talons about its scaly neck. A bone-wrenching crunch resonated from the sky. A moment later the dragon's carcass splattered on the stoney ground. The wounded Istelle cried out in support.

Refusing to take to the air, three other dragons lumbered towards the platoon with hundreds of Kyykki following. Hunger gleamed from their desperate sunken eyes as they charged. The platoon slowly backed up to the rim of the knoll, firing with each step.

"We aren't gonna hold them.....Just try ta sucker them back to the company." The corporal directed, then sent one Lancer back to the oncoming company. "Watch out fer the dragon's fire." He yelled as the platoon slowly ascended the stoney knoll.

"Damned to hell!.... Damned to hell!" Looking down from the knoll, the corporal realized his platoon was stationed almost in the middle of the Kyykki horde. As the knoll was both steep and slippery, the Kyykki had simply bypassed it. With the exception of those Kyykki drawn from attacking the wounded white eagle, the immense horde swarmed just below them, totally unaware of their presence. Their death-dealing dragons, at least for the present, remained somewhere out-of-sight. The Kyykki's fast-paced march clearly indicated they had determined the exact location of the advance company.

The platoon's crossbows began taking their toll against the Kyykki scrambling up the knoll. To the north, the blackened horde spread out, connecting with the other side. A solid front now approached the advance company. The platoon stoically recognized that they existed as an island within an ocean of frenzied toad-faced Kyykki.

"Damned to hell!" The corporal yelled again, this time above the riotous hubbub of the swarming Kyykki.

"Yep, you got that right." Allowed a Lancer as his crossbow tumbled another Kyykki back into the ranks of his voracious comrades. After regrouping themselves, they lost little time in devouring this one who dared to knock them over. The Lancer smiled. "Anything to buy us some more time." He aimed and shot again.

"That's not what I'm shouting about." The corporal said slowly as he raised his crossbow. "It's our friends over by the white eagle.....They're gone." The emptiness from his soul reached the other eight. "Make the bastards pay dearly!" His next bolt smashed through the flattened skull of one of the taller Kyykki. While reloading he looked once again at where the huge white eagle with the strange blue figure on its back once fought. The singular color of black, filthy dirty black, now encompassed the entire area like a sea of bobbing garbage. Another sickly feeling momentarily shook his body.

"They don't gets none of us alive." The corporal called out. "Everybody understandin'?"

Staid somber acknowledgments echoed back. No one ever enjoyed dying, yet dying had always been an acceptable part of being in the Light Striper. This reality now occupied center stage.

A gigantic shadow suddenly swept down from the cloudy sky and circled the tiny island of Lancers. The Kyykki, irregardless of their present disposition, fled in terror, breaking their unified front and tearing at each other to escape. The Lancers, as terrified as the Kyykki, stood their ground. Nine puny crossbows aimed at the five hundred foot circling shadow.

"Wait until that 'thing' be in range.....We got but one chance."

The shadow dropped lower in its circle. From the white eagle's immense curved talons hung another dead dragon, its slimy entrails bouncing in the wind. Suddenly the incredible creature rose, almost straight up, then dove at the Lancer's knoll.

"Don't shoot.....It bees sent from the Holy One ta protect us." Screamed an ecstatic Lancer. "The King's white eagle!"

"Listen to 'im!" The corporal yelled as he lowered his crossbow. "Our prayers," He gulped hard, emotionally. "Been heard."

At the last possible moment, the enormous white bird pulled up and loosed the dragon's slimy carcass. Barely missing the Lancers and their panicky mounts, the airborne carcass flew over them, crashing into the ranks of the attacking Kyykki. A roar of triumph rose from the Lancers as the two hundred foot dragon smashed through the oncoming ranks of the blackened horde. The powerful momentum of the flying carcass decimated the attackers, taking out an entire fifty foot swath as it bounced down the slope. The Lancers watched in awe, mesmerized by the saving power of the white eagle's gift.

A voice, from above, startled them. "Stay where you are!" The voice called in almost a carefree manner, though the only thing in view was the huge white eagle gliding by, close enough to touch them with its wing tips. The enormous white eagle banked and the Lancers spied two men, one bluish in color, the other a Haafian. "Stay where you are...Help is coming!" The Haafian pointed low in the western sky. The Lancers counted ten more colossal shadows.

"Yes, Holy One." Said the corporal, his being lit with the knowledge of divine intervention. "Yes, Holy One,....Thank You!"

The War Waggons of the advance company fired twice before the ten white eagles descended upon the Kyykki's front line. As a sickle swings at the harvest, so with talons stretched out and swinging, the white eagles cut through the Kyykki. Swaths forty feet wide and over two hundred feet deep of slashed, crushed and lacerated Kyykki littered the field before the amazed and terribly confused Lancers. When the huge creatures rose and banked, the Lancers distinguished both bluish colored men and Haafians fastened about their necks.

"Damnedest tactic I ever saw." The pipe smoking commander quipped from his lookout. His smile belied his calm tone of voice.

"I could not agree more." Added another officer. "But the battle has yet to begin."

"Shut up, O' ye of faithlessness." He smiled benightedly. "Fire until the white eagles return!"

In spite of the accuracy of the machiners, and the devastation caused by the Istelles, the lumbering Kyykki horde, ignoring their losses, closed ranks. They easily reached the first line of Lancers before the eagles returned. Hacking broadaxes bought time for the War Waggons to readjust sights. A single sharp blast from the tuba brought the Lancers inside the waggon defenses as the machines fired point-blank into the toad-faced horde from hell. The first four ranks fell as one, but the vast numbers of Kyykki attackers completely surrounded the advance company by the next breath.

Deadly vicious hand-to-hand combat ensued along the outside wall of waggons. Lancers speared and clubbed Kyykki attempting to crawl under the waggons. In return, Lancers were ripped and torn asunder by the famished Kyykki. Groups of Kyykki tackled Stripers, bringing down both mount and rider. Lancers replied in kind. Trampling the toad-faced enemy and tossing small bags of bleach at them. The surviving machiners continued with volleys of ribbon wire, shot in a desperate attempt to slow the overflowing oncoming ranks of Kyykki. However, the volume produced did not make any difference.

"I despise this being surrounded."

"You think I like it any more than you?"

"Are the white eagles coming back?"

"Don't know, Sir....I'm just the Chaplain." He fired off to the left, killing a Kyykki standing in a waggon seat. "Quit talking and fire."

The taller Kyykki, by sheer bulk and volume, forced their way to the inner circle of the Lancer's defenses, though at tremendous cost. Once there, however, the stupid creatures stood passively, not knowing what to do next, except eat. Unable to comprehend and take advantage of their strategic gain, the hideous creatures were speedily slaughtered by the Stripers. The defenders desperately fought for each minuscule piece of territory they gave up. Even so, the territory they now held consisted of the inner waggons and a few small strong points further out. All Lancers dismounted to fight from the waggons and assist the machiners.

"I really didn't want to die today, Chaplain."

"I almost believe you....But keep shooting. I'm not ready to hack them with my broadaxe yet."

From their relatively safe position on the knoll, made safe by the continually circling white eagle, the nine Lancers watched in terrified awe as forty-nine smoking dragons forcibly muscled their way into the southern sky. In two lines they slowly navigated northward, almost drifting, allowing the Kyykki to assume full responsibility for the advance company's defeat. Their first line sought to elicit fear by breathing fire across the overcast sky. Instantly, the Lancers' protecting eagle vanished above the clouds.

The two ranks passed by the isolated platoon without hesitation. Their obvious target lay another half mile north. The second line of dragons now rose above the first, spurred onward by their Demon Master riders. At that precise moment, as the dragons struggled for altitude, the white eagles re-appeared from the clouds, striking the dragons from behind. Huge toothed beaks bit through dragon necks. Eleven carcasses tumbled earthward obliterating Kyykki underneath. The Istelles then banked tightly, smashing the ill-prepared dragons on their right flank. The birds now deftly tore through both lines, slashing the bottom rank with talons and biting off the fire-spewing heads of the upper. Following a third final attack, accomplished as a sucker feint and entrapment, the dragons and their Demon Master existed no more. The Istelles dominated the skies. Their raucous victory squawking unsettled the isolated Lancers and terrified the Kyykki.

"Set the outer waggons afire." He half-mumbled, his pipe still stuffed in his mouth.

"Yes Sir!" The pipe smoking commander's aide-de-camp responded as he grabbed the tuba from the wounded signaler.

"I can still do my part!" The one armed Lancer replied. His other arm, missing below the elbow, now survived in some Kyykki's stomach. The Lancer's saturated tourniquet dripped blood on the waggon floor as he attempted to stand. Balancing a crossbow on the waggon seat, he pulled the trigger. Another Kyykki died. Then he collapsed to floor, unconscious.

Within in moments, flames from the outer waggons effectively separated the attacking Kyykki from those caught inside. As the Lancers reformed to create a defensive square, they slaughtered the unwittingly captured Kyykki.

"Be ready to fire the last circle of waggons." The Commander ordered. "We'll fight them here." He pointed to the remaining five waggons formed in a newly tightened circle; each still firing through the flames. "Damn!"

"What now, you old man!" The Chaplain shot back.

"I been saving money for a new pipe...."

"Shut up..."

Due to the ferociousness of the attacking Kyykki and the low hanging clouds, the advance company never saw the white eagles, did not even witness the defeat of the dragons. They did, however, discern the Istelles' victory cry from all other battlefield noises, though none had any idea of its meaning nor source.

With the skies free, the Istelles began plowing deep gashes in the attackers' ranks again. However, due to the flames and smoke, their efforts continued mostly unnoticed. And, in truth, the eleven Istelles barely slowed the enormous maddened horde. The smoke and flames also denied the Lancers knowledge of long range bolts whizzing above them, just as it also refused them seeing a triple wedge of mounted Lancers cutting through the northern Kyykki ranks. Less than three hundred paces separated the two forces.

At this distance, Ayhn suddenly halted his Lancers. The erratic scattering of bolts from the advance company came too close to his forces. The piles of wounded and dead Kyykki proved too great an obstacle for the exhausted mounts and Lancers. The tuba sounded 'cease firing', but no reply returned from the besieged advance company.

Ayhn's Lancers witnessed the white eagles decimate both dragons and their earth-bound enemies. The exquisite grandeur of the snow colored birds, even in their ferocious attacks reinforced the ancient concept of chivalry: the righteous warrior reborn. Then, unexpectedly, the eleven enormous birds swept up to cloud level and formed a single line perpendicular to Ayhn's tightly packed front lines. Ayhn had precious little time to hypothesize the ramifications of their actions, his efforts being occupied by the combined low fire of the War Waggons and the triple line of lances which maintained Ayhn's force three hundred paces from the advance company. Time ran against the fatigued Lancers.

"Bring up the reserves!" Ayhn commanded. "Have them maintain a double line thirty paces behind us...They will use bows and fill in holes where the front line weakens."

"Yes, Sir!" And the signaler blasted the smokey, stench-stricken air with crisp notes from the tuba.

Suddenly, when overshadowed by a low flying Istelle, Ayhn fathomed their strategy. "Stop the War Waggons! ....Let the eagles through!" He pulled his mount about as he yelled out the order and then repeated it. Nothing happened. The War Waggons refused to stop firing. "Damn it!" He yelled as his Striper ran for the line of waggons. "Stop your shooting!..... Look!" He pointed to the Istelles. "Let them through....or you'll all be court marshaled!"

Firing abruptly stopped. Instantly, one-by-one, the gigantic creatures raked the Kyykki trapped in the three hundred pace wide alley between the two forces. With wings wide enough to cover both Ayhn's three lines and the outer smoldering waggons of the advance company, the birds slowly glided by, their razor-like talons slicing up everything. After a eleven passes, only green slime and barely recognizable parts of Kyykki existed between the two Lancer forces.

"I see a miracle!" Claimed the pipe smoking Commander. His whiskered jaw dropped. His precious pipe shattered as it bounced on the wooden floor of his command post.

"But I saw it first!"

"You're supposed to, you old fool....You ARE the Chaplain, are you not?" And he pursed his lips, shooting a long curly twist of smoke into the air. "Sound the damn tuba....We're relocating to the main force!"

As the Istelles now swooped down around the retreating Lancers, protecting their flanks, the Kyykki broke through the last circle of waggons. As before, dumbfounded with finding nothing to kill or eat, they stood silent.

"Fire the Waggons!" Yelled the old commander. Ayhn, standing up in his stirrups, waved to him. "So you enjoy miracles too!" He bellowed to his Commander.

"Why not!" Ayhn replied.

Both Ayhn and his second-in-command realized that the battle was far from being won. The Kyykki horde, through dragonless, still tremendously outnumbered the Lancers.

The advance company marshaled less then twenty percent that evening, most of them wounded. The Lancers placed great hope in the Istelles, even though only eleven provided assistance. Ayhn desired greater communication with the birds and their riders and an opportunity to get a comprehensive picture of the battlefield.

When the dim sun dropped below the horizon, the Istelles disappeared. Throughout the afternoon their tactics of circling and diving into the toad-faced horde established a safety zone between the Lancers and the enemy. While this allowed a respite of sorts for the Lancers, the Kyykki still surrounded the Lancers. From his three storey platform, Ayhn had painfully viewed this black landscape, one that swayed with innumerable Kyykki for almost a half mile in every direction. The morning's ultimate battle would be one in which the Kyykki's massive charge had a solitary objective. Completely destroy the Lancers. This grim reality choked Ayhn.

Nighttime in the Lancer encampment was marked with bright fires and a reconstructing of the War Waggon defensive positions. Using watches as full shifts, Ayhn rested as many Lancers as possible. At the machiners suggestions, wheels were pulled from the first rank of waggons. Then, utilizing makeshift cranes, the War Waggons were placed on top, creating a wooden wall some twelve feet tall. The second row of War Waggons were arranged to shoot over the first wall. In fact, except for a few heavy duty crossbows, all elected to shoot into the front ranks of the Kyykki. This included those armed with the vicious 'ribbon wire', the well-respected gift from the Yldans.

A quietly rising sun, beaming down through a cloudless sky, found Ayhn sleeping on a Striper. His aide-de-camp rudely awakened him as he excitedly shouted from his galloping Striper.

"Sir, Sir! ....The white eagle rider.....wants to talk with you!" He gasped the last word as he abruptly stopped in front of Commander Ayhn.

Ayhn shook his head slowly, returning to life. "The attack's begun?"

"No Sir! Its good news Sir!"

"Speak." Ayhn stretched and groaned.

"The white eagle's rider requests to speak with you, Sir!....He is waiting just outside the wall."

Still not entirely awake, Ayhn followed his Aide-de-camp through the masses of packed Lancers who strained to see the huge bird. Once through the defensive wall, the Istelle lowered its enormous head and two men slid off. Ayhn and his aide cantered over and dismounted.

"Commander Ayhn." Said a thin Yldan. "I am Feathered Goat...This is Hzata, the Istelle's Tath rider."

The muscular blue man bowed deeply, causing the others to bow in reply. All except Feathered Goat, that is.

"Details concerning Istelles and Taths will be answered after the battle,

Commander Ayhn." ·Feathered Goat announced. "Chaplain Commander Vosnob has the Light Striper coming up behind the Kyykki....He requires almost half day before he can attack..... Baste and Yganak, combining forces, are moving in from the east."

"How long?" Ayhn Asked nervously.

"By day afterwards, at least for their advance party." Hzata replied in a heavily accented Haafian, smiling at his surprizing the Haafians. "We have other .....other.....other......"

Feathered Goat quickly recognized his friend's embarrassing dilemma and rescued him. "Surprizes waiting."

"What might they be?" Ayhn asked. He blinked and then shaded his eyes; the dawning sun's light made him squint.

"By the grace of our god-who-has-no-name, there are enough Istelles to......to keep ......safe...you.....until sun is very high." Justly proud of his grasp of Haafian, he smiled broadly.

Ayhn and his aide-de-camp bowed at Feathered Goat's prodding.

"He is a very famous and brave prince." Feathered Goat explained as he climbed up the Istelle's wing.

Recognizing the opportunity, the Demon Lords urged their Kyykki horde forward. A single Istelle couldn't stop them all. The taller Kyykki jabbed their spears in the air as they loped forward towards the solitary Istelle. Ayhn and his aide mounted up and began walking their mounts back to the waggon stockade.

"Don't shoot the Istelles!" Feathered Goat yelled.

"I promise not to!" Ayhn yelled back.

Another breath and the two visitors and their gigantic miraculous mount flew over them.

The first Kyykki attack proved shockingly successful. By attacking the Lancers' walled encampment from all sides at once, they produced far too many targets. The Lancers not able to shoot fast enough. With their strangely twisted loping gait and toad-like hopping, the Kyykki managed to cover the 'death zone' once patrolled by the Istelles in a matter of a few breathes. The twelve foot wall might as well been three feet high.

"Now I know the wisdom behind the broadaxes." A grimly smiling Lancer shared with a friend.

He slowly walked the length of the waggon, his double-bladed broadaxe hovering just above the waggon's sideboard. Long boney fingers gripped the waggon's side, then a flattened big-eyed head appeared. In less than a tenth of a breath both head and fingers fell on top another Kyykki; greenish slime covered the blade.

"Yep, two blades means we get two with one swipe." Ducking below the waggon's side, he waited a moment before aptly demonstrating his two-for-one stroke. One head was severed whole, the other cut off at the eye level. Dark green Kyykki brains made the wooden floor slippery.

"There's too many of these damned things!" He shouted as his weapon deftly connected with another Kyykki.

His words ran all too true. In a few more breathes the Kyykki overran the waggon. It returned to Lancer possession only after the machiners swept the waggon clear. This scenario repeated itself throughout the Lancer's wooden fortress. The frequency increased as their carcasses created grizzly ramps up the waggon sides.

Inside, the Kyykki who fought free of the waggons were pursued and killed by squads of mounted Lancers. Though run through by lances as they jumped from the waggons, many Kyykki succeeded in killing the Lancer they landed upon. The Lancers learned to spear and drop the lance. However, the disadvantage of losing the lance produced increasing hand-to-hand combat, where the Kyykki's long reach equaled the bite of the broadaxe.

"Didn't that Feathered Goat promise..."

"Yes Sir, he did promise 'surprize' from the air as well as assistance by midday...."

"Haven't seen any yet, have you?"

"Not really." Replied Ayhn's aid-de-camp as he surveyed the bobbing black landscape. Then he turned his head and looked skyward. He grabbed the 'long tube' and studied the western sky. "That's not a cloud, Sir."

Ayhn grabbed the 'long tube' and studied the cloud; his drawn countenance returned to a grim smile. "Sound the tubas…Two calls…… First, 'assistance arriving' and second, 'don't shout the birds'."

The aide started to relay the commands, the paused.

"Is there a problem?"

"Sir, we don't have a call for 'Don't shoot the birds'."

"Then make one up! The Istel…les are our allies."

"Istelles?"

"Whatever they're called….Just get the message out before they arrive……Move!"

Before the message was transmitted throughout the Lancer's encampment, the gigantic white cloud partially blocked the bright sunlight. The Lancers as well as the Kyykki turned to see what the near future held. Without the aid of the 'long tube' most could not discern the Istelles.

"I believe there are well over four hundred, my friend." Ayhn said as he dropped his big-fisted hand on his aide's shoulder.

"More." He quickly replied. "Another cloud comes southward."

"Dragons from the Dark Lands?" Apprehension crept into his voice.

"Only if the damned things come in pale blues and deep reds."

"Do Istelles come in colors?" Ayhn wondered out loud.

"I have no idea….Should I send orders to shoot the blue and red birds.. ……dragons…monsters?"

"No, I'll trust the shaman and that Tath rider…..Hzata?"

The tight formation of White Istelles suddenly, silently, broke asunder. In continuous successions of ranks, the gigantic birds folded their wings, diving for the outer perimeter of the Kyykki horde, a distance beyond what the machiners could reach.

"Can't blame them for that maneuver…After all, we thought they were just a cloud." The sudden lilt in Ayhn's voice caused his aide to cringe, praying and hoping no one else heard.

"What's this stupid talk?" Yelled the Chaplain.

Ayhn's faced blanched and immediately returned. "Look at the makings of a miracle!" He exclaimed.

The trio ducked as an immense shadow covered them in instant darkness. The creature then leveled-off, extended a pair of huge talons that raked, sliced and severed a full fifty foot section of attacking Kyykki. After a quarter mile of low-level flying, the Istelle pulled up for another run. Wingtip-to-wingtip a rank of fifty Istelles followed, decisively plowing the Kyykki into the plains. Four other ranks followed suite, effectively eliminating a Kyykki threat on the western side of the waggon fortress.

Then the Istelles spiraled over the Lancers, descending in pairs that ripped through the Kyykki horde perpendicular to their formation. Relentlessly, the horde fought on, intent only on destroying the Lancers. In spite of their ever increasing losses, they still clambered over the waggon walls. Without personal regard, the Kyykki continued inflicting horrid destruction upon any Lancer within their hooked fingered grasp.

From the Chaplain's perspective, one carefully produced from studying the slower flying blue and red Istelles--if that's what they be--through the 'long tube'......"These other birds are carrying something....but I can't exactly say what."

"The bolts are almost gone, Sir!" A corporal called up to Ayhn.

"Continue firing! Be more selective about your targets...... Don't shoot the birds!"

"Sir, the scouts have made initial contact with the Kyykki."

"Thank you son." Vosnob replied. "Have the Knights make ready!"

The liaison turned to obey and then turned again. "Sir, there is one problem."

"Out with it, son. We need to make haste...Ayhn can't hold out forever."

"It's the Istelles Sir. They keep pushing the Kyykki farther and farther ahead of us.....More are pushed into the Lancers' camp."

Vosnob became none too elated by the news. "Can we signal the White Istelles....That Prince Hzata, can we reach him?"

"All ready have." Running Cloud said slowly. "I told him to drive the damned ignorant toads towards us."

"I gave no such order!" The Chaplain Commander snorted.

"Yes, you did, you just don't remember." Running Cloud said slowly. "And he's gone.....flying away to obey you." He commented without the slightest hint of mercy or humility.

"Why didn't you ride with Yganak?"

Not long afterwards, the four hundred White Istelles banked south and then hammered the Kyykki horde head on, forcing them to retreat eastward. By their decisive third pass, the four hundred Istelles had the Kyykki loping off to the east--right where the Knights waited. The Lancers immediately noticed the decreased fighting along the eastern side of their encampment. They did not know why.

"Just thank the Holy One, boys!" The Chaplain advised all within hearing distance. His admonition swept through the ranks quickly, bringing a tangible answer; one that would suffice for the moment.

In reality, the fighting continued on at an unabated pace. Fatigue hampered efforts to drive the Kyykki from the wooden walls. The promised midday salvation had yet to arrive, a salvation claimed in extremely personal terms by the oppressed Lancers.

Once again the sky darkened, this time because the 'things' carried by the blue and red Istelles came tumbling to the ground. One smashed, splattered and then dusted everything inside the encampment. Lancers rushed to find breathable air, the bleach burned eyes and clogged throats. The Kyykki died howling in unspeakable agony. More than a hundred 'gift' packages of bleach fell outside the waggon walls. Acres upon acres became dusted with bleach powder. Its toxicity thoroughly eliminated the

Kyykki's incessant assaults. The pulsing, momentary breezes scattered the bleach throughout the battle field, playing havoc with the Demon Masters' regrouping efforts.

"It's just about midday, O' ye of some faithlessness!" The Chaplain immodestly proclaimed from his perch in Ayhn's observation post.

"Get down and see to the wounded....Go dust a few Kyykki!"

"Yes, SIR!"

"Ye've insulted the Chaplain....once again." Quipped Ayhn's second-in-command. He looked most peculiar with just the broken shank of the pipe extending from his mouth. "Don't ye be worried, now." He defensively declared. "The Captain will certainly find me another one."

"Is that all you're worried about?"

"Be there anything else?"

The innate requirement for self-preservation quickly commanded most Demon Masters still living. Sensing annihilation near-at-hand and knowing no mercy existed with either Ashuwa or the Haafians, five not-so-brightly-colored-anymore Demon Masters headed westward, looking for sanctuary. Anywhere that permitted isolation from everyone and anything was their only goal. After commanding the taller Kyykki legion to commit all forces against the wooden walled encampment, they trotted down a deep ravine and quietly disappeared.

The tough intermittent hand-to-hand fighting about and within the Lancers' makeshift fortress gradually subsided. Ayhn's elite force paid an extremely heavy price for their stand. Less than a third of his initial Lancers remained. Istelles landed outside the encampment bringing supplies, Yldan shamans and a few brave Haafian physicians.

"I count about six thousand Kyykki, Vosnob....About another two hundred of the taller version and only one or two Demons." Sarg called down from a circling Istelle. "The rest are dead."

"What in the Holy One's name are you doing here?" Vosnob yelled back, a bit miffed.

"Sjura isn't due for another month....er....double moon cycle. And I owe these bastards...!"

"And the rest are with you as well, I suppose?" Sarg pointed high to the left, Brey and Vauk waved down to their Chaplain Commander.

"Well,... don't cause them to detour the damned toad faces.... I intend to destroy them all."

"As you wish, Commander Vosnob." Sarg said straight-faced, as if he had something radically different in mind.

The four-deep lines of New Knights extended for over a half mile, well-hidden behind a low ridge. The uncontrolled Kyykki did not think about where they were headed. They simply ran from the pursuing Istelles. Enough pursued to insure their panic continued. Others Istelles landed to destroy selected targets, especially any who had the faintest smell of dragon.

Hopping over each other, loping around each other, escape was the only thought of this last horde. Without pause they began lurching up the mildly steep slope.

"Forward and HOLD!" Vosnob called out.

His Junior Officers passed the order down the first two lines, the other two moved up as reserves. Deliberately the first two ranks exposed themselves to the on-coming Kyykki. As the tubas sounded 'prepare to charge' the blackened horde finally looked up----and fumbled to a complete halt. In short order they degenerated into their own worst enemy. Unable to decide which direction to move they milled about, going nowhere and losing all forward momentum. The taller Kyykki prodded the horde to charge forward, and they partially succeeded.

Taking advantage of the confusion, Vosnob ordered the fourth rank to divide and squeeze the Kyykki from both flanks. Once they were in position, Vaad brought his master before the front line, in clear view of both the Kyykki and the New Knights. Wearing his Light Striper uniform, baggy trousers and pale blue tunic, he looked much out-of-place surrounded by Haafians and half-breeds covered with steel.

"Too long," Vosnob spoke like a father to his troops. "Have we compromized with this damned product of evil....NO MORE!"

An earth-jarring shout of affirmation rose from the ranks, not once, but four times. Then silence reigned--a deadly silence to which even the Kyykki responded. Vosnob motioned for his tuba signaler to join him at the front.

"Sound the charge, son." Vosnob said quietly.

Six hundred paces later, the first line of New Knights slammed into the massed Kyykki. Their line gave quickly, like quicksand trying to entrap its victim. The knights sought no quarter. Instead of pushing through the Kyykki horde, the knights split, maneuvering to the right and left, trampling, impaling and hacking every Kyykki within reach. The second line of knights charged into the spaces left by their comrades, catching many Kyykki with their backs turned. Then as the fourth rank charged the Kyykki flanks, the first rank paused, allowing the fourth rank to pass through them. The Kyykki attackers became the chased--and then the dead. Vosnob ordered the third rank to split the Kyykki forces. With lances lowered, their tight narrow wedge sliced through the Kyykki. The knights rode almost knee to knee. Few of the horde survived this onslaught.

'Regroup!' Sounded from the tuba.

The New Knights trotted to the edges of the battlefield, free and clear of the Kyykki clustered in the middle. One rank at a time charged through the Kyykki hacking away with their heavy bladed broadswords, sparing none. The horde fought viciously, clawing at the bellies of the mounts and jumping up on knights. Small groups of dismounted knights fought back-to-back as they endeavored to extricate themselves from the horde.

Three Istelles circled the fray and then landed. Their immense toothed beaks chewed and sliced Kyykki as if they were but earthworms. Sarg's Istelle waded into the middle where it's flapping wings and razor-sharp talons did as much damage as its massive beak. The other two Istelles deliberately picked out the taller Kyykki and quickly eliminated them.

Shortly thereafter, the remaining Kyykki broke, scattering in all directions. The New Knights made short work of these. By late afternoon, the massacre ended. Baste's Light Stripers arrived in time for mopping up the battlefield, a job more dangerous than most would think. A wounded Kyykki can easily kill a Haafian with one blow.

At nightfall, a clear cold night, the Haafian forces with their Istelle-riding Tath allies camped near the Lancer's fortification-become-field hospital. While the victory was celebrated until and through daybreak, of more interest were the Istelles and the blue men who rode them.

Sarg and Hzata stood near Ayhn, Vosnob and Running Cloud softly conversing of a New Era and ruminating in their minds what sorts of new problems and promises would open before them. Brey, the only woman for miles around, and one having earned a reputation almost equivalent to Sarg's, became the object for many a Junior Officer. Little did they realize the extent of their error. In very clear terms she notified them that she, being a Senior Officer, outranked each of them. The Chaplains, meanwhile, set about making plans for morning worship for the Light Stripers, the Lancers and their still-unknown Tath allies. The victory was costly. Too many Light Stripers lay dead and thousands more wounded. This reality would temper the worship service. So would the knowledge that those who worshipped another god were present.

Chapter 11

"Imbecillic dunderhead!......... You idiotic overgrown sack of buffalo manure! I've concentrated upon this issue---this issue of the greatest magnitude for eleven long months.....and you continually refuse...."

"To back up your preposterous ideas, which, I might add, are not only illogical but a presumptuous attempt at out-and-out isogesis....You have no unconditional right to convert the Holy Scriptures to suit your own prefabricated notions.....or, and this be the truth,....to diminish your struggle with mystery....."

"I refuse to acknowledge your degrading remarks. Never once, since their untimely arrival, never once, I remind you, have I claimed the rightness of my ideas to the detriment of yours."

"As if that should create any difference whatsoever. Your foolishness might deem such a separation, but it as nonsensical as a division of God himself."

The first voice deepened with righteous anger. "What you contemplate presents, however, a situation for which direction, ultimately, is unavailable.....Think you on this issue.."

"Sometimes, especially since the 'visitors' arrived, you have entrenched yourself so deeply in 'catch-words' and phrases that you've lost any semblance of objectivity......Not everything is written within the confines of the Holy Word, and I know it."

"As if I couldn't!" The first voice sneered loudly, almost egotistically, even though that impossibility was insurmountable by either voice.

"You'll awaken the 'visitors'. Keep the volume low, you muddleheaded lummox."

"Maybe they ought to awaken, after all the sun will shortly arise...... Then I can question them again."

"And with the same familiar frustrating results." The voice sighed.

"They know so little to begin with....They never depart from their story, so the repetitious details just waste our time and energy......"

"You forget, slovenly brained one, that, in spite of our acts of kindness these past eleven months, the quartet consider themselves prisoners of war....Because of that, they have little intention of providing me with the truth, its against their Holiness Code...... Or, is that too much for your addled cranium to apprehend as truthful?"

"Absolutely not!..... As is visibly evident to everyone about." Quickly replied the second voice. "But enough of this rehashing of your incipient, even dangerous ideas..... Unless I am able to firmly...to positively....... establish that these four are who 'The Wait' concerns, no actions of any sorts....."

"'Shall be initiated'...Haven't I heard that line about six million times before?. ...However, there is nothing, absolutely nothing which shall thoroughly convince you that these..."

"Haafians, as they claim for themselves...." The second voice rudely interrupted, deliberately.

"These Haafians," The first voice continued, ignoring the interruption. "Are exactly the ones mentioned in 'The Wait'. There will be no others to follow them, just as none arrived before them......not in over....." He never finished the sentence. Once again, that sense of awed wonderment engulfed him completely as he contemplated the untimely arrival of the four Haafians, especially since they were more dead than alive when he rescued them.

"Blockheaded dolt!......... You constantly strive to understand everything.... twisting and bending it to meet your required, nay essential, conditions so that we might initiate the mission. Have you so aptly forgotten that these dark-skinned slant-eyed Haafians don't even know where they are?"

"But, simpleton, they do know......... Just ask them."

"Of course they know this is Saragoton, bumblebrain, I told them, long ago.....But they could not tell me where they were, could they?"

"They did tell. Unfortunately, your severely limited capacity to comprehend their language caused you to believe them delirious. An irresponsible mistake that cost me months of work." The first voice shouted, very agitated. "Nor did they arrive alone, you intellectual failure!"

"I remember," The second voice pouted. "The thing from hell, which is as properly cared for as the others."

"And gives us extreme consternation, if you haven't forgotten."

"Us, did you not say?..... That's impossible, as is well-known, even by the Haafians. Furthermore, as His servant, for what esoteric and oblique rationale did you expect my labors to be without difficulty, let alone testing?"

For over half the bright spring morning, the first voice continued sitting in his rough wooden chair, lost and confused by all that transpired within the last year. Essential chores and other necessities of life, such as eating, went without. Finally, he roused himself, with much obvious difficulty, to answer the hanging question.

"I'm not sure anymore.....Time has made this so lonely, so desolate.... What I want to believe and what the truth is battles within me."

"And this has been exacerbated since their strangely irregular coming." The second voice added sympathetically. "Isn't that the bottom line?"

The first voice slowly, almost motionlessly nodded his angular head, but vocalized nothing. As an answer to the divisive question, a refreshing wind capriciously blew throughout the field and whistled as it collided with the impenetrable evergreen forest surrounding it. When a cloud suddenly darkened the sun's warming light, the kindly faced man stood, bowed to the Haafians and went to work.

From their comfortable lodging, though they were usually denied the freedom to leave it, Bellah and the three scouts watched their kindly but eclectic benefactor begin his daily chores. With the exception of the seventh day, his labor had a regular ebb and flow incorporated into it. First, the bright mirrors standing in endless rows received their personal inspections including minor adjustments to catch the sunlight properly. Then he tended to all the extraordinary machines littering his so-called mansion. There were machines to sew, an iron box with fire on top--but no flames--and it cooked things inside. Other machines washed the laundry, yet another equally confusing contraption manufactured the laundry--well actually, it produced the cloth by which the clothing was made. Everything was powered by electricity, whatever such a powerful force, invisible even, that might be. Their benefactor even had machines that plowed the land.

Such unbelievable contraptions caused the Lancer scouts much anxiety. Bellah and the others initially feared this 'electricity', believing it composed of dangerous magics. In time they realized without the 'electricity' their benefactor could hardly exist. He was the sole person in this vast forest.

Since their 'unremembered' arrival, this 'man' who spoke as if he were two persons, perceived himself not as their benefactor, but as their personal servant, even to the point of having one of his machines process the Haafian language so that he might converse properly with his 'prophesied guests'. In no way were the scouts to converse in In-glish, on that point the man, unified in thought for once, remained adamant. In fact, the whole idea of the Haafian scouts learning the man's language appeared to terrify him, though no one could ascertain why.

Thus, while the four scouts remained healthy and secure, they lived in a most incomprehensible environment. One step beyond the prescribed boundaries of their prison and a buzzer went off, followed by a mindless voice calling the violator by name and warning him to step back before the lazer attacked. Ill content with incarceration and ignorant of 'lazer', Ruet had the toes of his boots sheered off the second week after he began walking again. 'Lazer' wasn't something to defy.

Bellah, Ruet, Arkkron and Mec approached almost a full year in their strange albeit benevolent captivity. Anything they requested, excepting freedom to leave, was immediately understood as a command. The four toured the machine rooms many times and learned how to work a few. They also were shown and explained the nature of the electricity collected from the huge field of mirrored panels. Nonetheless, the environment remained a constant source of stress and bewilderment. The fact that they never were quite confident as to whom they were addressing only guaranteed these feelings continued.

"Tis the most gifted man--a genius--I've ever know." Ruet shared once again. "But why are we considered the ones who were prophesied?............ And prophesied by what?"

Mec, the powerful blonde-haired member of the group, responded sarcastically. "Cause de book say so."

"Wonderful, after almost a full year of incarceration, he finally learns an entire phrase in In-glish.....Good Lord, what might he learn next?....I know, how to destroy 'lazer'!"

"That-is-not-considered-an-appropriate-action, Ruet." The mindless voice intoned unemotionally.

"So what?" Yelled Arkkron, the usually silent one. "Lazer me now, you invisible bastard."

"Such-language-is-deemed-most-inappropriate, therefore-it-will be-ignored." The mindless voice intoned again.

"Can't even get that damned 'thing' angry." Arkkron growled, disappointed at the answer, though he received the identical response countless times before.

"Something without a mind can't be angry." Mec casually added. "Just like the Kyykki."

Recognizing another verbal fight in the making, Bellah quickly interjected himself into the conversation. "I'm beginning to take this more personal, you two. Listen up and listen well. We're still on a scouting expedition."

All four began laughing; Bellah's incredulous remark struck a nerve and released some tension. This laughter brought a statement, as usual, from the mindless voice. One that the quartet refused to acknowledge, knowing that such action brought the man.

Moments later, he showed up. "And what is your request at this particular time?" He inquired sincerely, in his first voice.

"Dear Sir, for almost a year..."

"Precisely eleven months and ten days." The second voice corrected Bellah.

"We have been more than patient with our incarceration."

"Not exactly." Responded the second voice. "Unauthorized attempts to leave your security zone number twenty three. And, your homestead is not, let me repeat myself, is not, in any sense of the word, an incarceration.... You must be protected from the demonic forces which brought you harm and...."

"Nothing." Bellah angrily shot back. "Your attitude offends me. We are not little children."

"But you are." Said the first voice. "You neither can explain how you came here, you do not know the way to return, and you refuse to acknowledge Saragoton."

"We've been through all of this before." Bellah replied, his eyes rolling in disbelief. "I tried to commit suicide after wrongly believing I committed cannibalism. Mec and Arkkron, half-dead from exhaustion, inadvertently stumbled into your world....In your mercy, and with your skills, you saved each and every one of us.....For that we are humbled and grateful."

"Tis I who am grateful." Answered the first voice.

Before he could continue his usual elaborated speech concerning destinies of the world and its peoples and how that rested upon the quartet's fulfilling some exotically Arkkron scripture, Bellah cut him off. "Listen friend: we've quite had enough of your words.... Word's are cheap, easy and they disappear without any evidence to prove they were ever uttered....No more,....... either you back up your 'mere words' with actions and evidence or we will....." Bellah didn't finish the sentence, allowing their 'host' to wallow.

Though no sounds were heard, the scouts perceived that the two voices pounded at each other within the man's head. He stood rather limply, his off-white robe fluffing in the breeze until his voices reached a conclusion. To kill time and add to the man's consternation, the four deliberately tossed small items through the lazer. It was a game played out before and hopefully with the same results: a quicker answer due to the fact that their magnanimous host felt obligated to replace all destroyed items. Even when they threw multiple items simultaneously, the lazer destroyed them all, while the mindless voice reminded the scouts of their responsibility to be 'good guests'. As the four began tossing Mec's furniture across the lazer, the second room to be emptied, the man waved his hands furiously.

"All right!" He cried out in the first voice. "What must I agree to this time?" His voice grated with frustration as well as exhaustion, factors Bellah counted on, factors Bellah required if he wanted to gain release for his men.

"I detest your frivolous temper tantrums. They weary me, and for no recognizable benefit to any of us."

"Most likely because they are effective."

"Unfortunately, that is true. Your unruliness undermines the quiet orderliness of Saragoton."

Bellah ignored the man's rationale, recognizing it as another subversive means to lose the original topic.

"We demand to examine the building at the far end of the field. So far, you've prevented us from drawing near it....We believe it holds answers that might prove you a consummate liar...Prove to us otherwise.. ..... and promptly." Bellah demanded.

"I will not allow it." Said the second voice, weary albeit firm. "Too dangerous to all."

"Words, asinine words, words that keep the truth away." ·Bellah exclaimed loudly.

"No, they are the truth."

"Then you have no reason to keep us from verifying your 'so-called' truth, do you?" Ruet demanded.

The man sighed deeply, truly pained by Bellah's accusations of wrongdoing. Then he retreated to his rough wooden chair, replying only after an extensive period of self-reflection.

"Perhaps... I have not treated you as I should." He spoke in his first voice. "After all, you Haafians came from a territory I know absolutely nothing about, yet I have required that you know all about Saragoton....I'm not playing fair."

"You are beginning to sound like a person who has more than just himself to deal with." Mec said sympathetically. "Spending all these hundreds of years by yourself has proved detrimental to your own healthiness."

"Thousands and thousands of years." He softly corrected Mec, then sighed again and slumped further into his chair. "Lazer off." He mumbled in In-glish. "You are free to leave." He said in Haafian. He spoke emotionally; pain wracking his facial muscles, causing his whitish skin to tremble.

Arkkron, the intentional disbeliever, tossed a chair through the lazer's territory. It simply crashed into the mossy grass surrounding his small compound; no sparks, no fire.

"I am not deceiving you, Arkkron." The man said defensively, grieved by the mistrust heaped upon him, quite unjustifiably, at least from his viewpoint.

"Please, there are other chairs here. Come and sit." Said the second voice. "I shall answer your questions as I am able."

"And shall the other voice answer as wel?" Ruet asked suspiciously.

"There is no other voice.....I am one. I do not understand your remark, Ruet....Do you hear something unknown to me?"

The four looked at each other in disbelief: the man did not recognize himself, perhaps, could not recognize himself. Being totally isolated for thousands of years, if that were the actual truth, certainly had the potential to do most anything to a person. Perhaps he simply suffered from old-age forgetfulness. Such insight, radically different from their present thinking, arrived as a gift destined to benefit the scouting party. With this, their anger and bewilderment slowly transformed into a pity as their perception of the man took on a sympathetic dimension.

The man stared as the quartet dropped to their knees in silent prayer, something he had never witnessed before. A religious man himself, a sudden wash humility and awe engulfed him. These four were true people, unlike the terrible 'creature' locked away in the building at the far end. For eleven months he vigorously sought the proper approach in dealing with the 'visitors'. One voice saw them as unworthy of the truth because of their lack of sophistication. The other voice struggled to recognize them as those fulfilling the prophecy. Now he realized that both approaches suggested gross manipulations on his part. In regards to the four Haafians. He must establish a new relationship.

Until the scattered evening lights automatically began burning, lighting up the major facilities within the compound, both sides sat staring and wondering about the 'other', neither willing to attempt the first move. In spite of new appreciations concerning the other, a dysphoric pall encompassed both sides. This nonaction continued until the double moons rose and slipped into one of their rare eclipses; the minor moon speeding past the naked face of the major.

All five stared in awe at this mystery in the heavens, one reveling in the scientific precision of the astronomical phenomena initiated by God, the Haafians humbled by the raw power of the Creator who manipulated his creation at will. In each case, the primacy of the Creator came to the fore.

"You believe in the Creator?" The man asked haltingly in a new, a third voice, one combining elements of the other two.

Bellah looked across the twenty five feet which separated the two. His bronzed face managed a difficult smile. "You know of the Creator?" He responded hesitantly.

"Yes." Came a calm answer. "He is why I am still here, waiting."

"He is why we began our fight to stamp out the damned Ashuwa."

"Ashuwa is evil?"

"That is the name by which the damned evil one is called," Ruet replied. "At least in Haaf."· He caught himself.

"I am acquainted with him...He is not allowed here, unless He chooses to become a 'nothing'.....Ah," The man relaxed, placing his hands behind his head to watch the greater moon re-appear. "What a wondrous event that would be."

"Except the damned one won't knowingly commit suicide." Mec confidently added.

"You are most correct Mec, my son."

"I am NOT your son." The Haafian defiantly shot back. "We are not even of the same race."

"But we are." The man said thoughtfully. "And my age gives me the privilege of being everybody's father.........Please, calm down, I mean no offence." He paused, gathering his breath and his will. "I believe I've been quite in error...Eleven months we've been together, yet we're still strangers... You don't even know my name."

Bellah held his hands up. "Have you enough chairs that we might share super together?" Bellah's remarks, though in earnest, were also a testing of their benefactor.

"I invite you to my home where chairs and table await." He answered a bit more easily, acknowledging that the distance between the two parties had to decrease. He stood and motioned for them to follow, and then abruptly stopped. "My name is Benjamin."

"Benja?" Mec repeated. "A rather strange name," He paused. "So, I guess it fits."

"Not Benja,............... but Benjamin." Bellah corrected.

"And I've known your name since you arrived." He pointed to each man." Bellah, the leader. Ruet, the almost lamed-for-life. Arkkron, the quietest of the party. Mec, the bold, yet also the youngest." Benjamin aptly delivered Mec's description without offending the lanky Haafian.

As wasn't unexpected, all types and configurations of 'electronic' gadgets cluttered Benjamin's home, although the home itself was as comfortable as any back in Haaf. A small cooking stove boiled away at vegetable soup as they sat about the table where Benjamin introduced them to coffee.

Presuming the coffee to taste as good as its smell, each trooper began with a large drought. Benjamin laughed out loud when the sour-faced Haafians spit the black liquid out the open window.

"It does take a bit of acclamation." Benjamin added as a gross understatement.

"It be poison, it is!"

"No, just some dried and smashed berries I gather from bushes cultivated on the mountain slopes."

"The same slopes that brought us here?"

"That's a real possibility, Bellah, except that I'm not sure how you wandered in......You're the first visitors."

"Do you mean for us to be the last as well?" Arkkron commented dryly concerning the coffee instead of their present situation.

"Are we the last and only visitors, Benjamin?" Bellah honestly requested, pushing Akron's observation further.

"I honestly haven't any idea as to whatever our future might hold,......." His tenuous pause brought all eyes upon him. "Except that the moons will return to its original state."

"You aren't making much sense." Mec allowed.

"Probably not........ I'm assuming you know my time, a time long extinguished before your's." With that declaration Benjamin proceeded to confront the four with the world prior to this age, a world of which, by the grace of the Creator, he survived in this protected place named Saragoton.

The Haafians had some vague recollections of the Holiness Code's history of the world. True, a society preceding theirs did exist and then slowly committed suicide as the people denied having responsibility for their God-given environment. Everyone knew of a world that collapsed in its own garbage. Benjamin, their benefactor, claimed to be a citizen of that age.

"Hard to believe that we killed ourselves off, but we did a superb job at it. The comet simply placed the finishing touches upon what was all ready irreversible."

"What comet?"

"The one which drew near the moon, and which by its own tremendous gravity did pull a third of the moon from itself. That same comet sent the sewage-laden oceans running over the face of the earth, setting in motion the worst plagues we'd ever witnessed................ But this time, we had exhausted our technology ....Our false god died along with the rest of humankind." Benjamin spoke quietly, almost tearfully.

Bellah sat quietly, dumbfounded, floundering for a focus. "Seas and oceans are similar? And gravity is what causes tides? And comets are.......?"

"Like shooting stars."

"Yes, I understand....I think." Bellah said, thoroughly engrossed in Benjamin's explanation of the past. "But what are 'mankind'?"

"Our vocabulary for people. We also used to call ourselves 'humans'."

"And with great wisdom, so as to create all these mechanical devices,...... you self-destructed?"

"Unfortunately, yes." Benjamin sighed and shook his long-haired head. "Now I am seeing what I never saw before---when I was young---blue skies, sunsets and sunrises, water, drinkable from the ground, animals of all sorts and land without overcrowding."

"But that's how it's supposed to be." Mec said absently.

"There's always a huge disparity between what ought to be and what actually is,……even in your time."

"And how do you mean?" Ruet cut in, putting his face between his hands and plopping his elbows on the table.

"Aren't you here because you are pursuing an evil which threatens your civilization---this Ashuwa creature?…… Evil refuses to go away, in both our civilizations we are forced to fight it."

"But you lost." Mec added without thinking. "And that's the reason you continue to disparage yourself, isn't it, Benjamin.....Do you blame yourself?"

"As no one else is left, I am the only one qualified to carry the responsibility."

Bellah pulled up to the table. "You specifically said, 'no one else left'. That means, at one time, there were more human survivors."

"We were commanded not to leave this protected province," Benjamin returned to his running commentary. "Under penalty." His words stopped, stuck in his throat.

"Explain the penalty."

Benjamin fumbled and finished his coffee, then served soup before he felt composed enough to acknowledge Ruet's request. He continued as before while the troopers ate the soup and the dark bread. "I've never had to explain this before, to anyone." His face rippled with intense agony: the four put their spoons down.

"You never needed to, that's all, Benjamin." Bellah offered gently, emphatically.

"That's correct, but it refuses to make the story any easier."

"But that truth will free you." Arkkron interrupted.

"You know our scriptures?" Benjamin responded quizzically.

"If we both recognize the Creator, then is it not appropriate for His wisdom to continue, irregardless of our actions. After all, He is eternal."

A clunking of five emptied coffee mugs signified a unanimous consent.

The old white skinned man began. "The penalty was that once you left this protected province, returning was not possible. However, the choice to remain or leave belonged to the individual.......... Once any humans left, their memory of this place was to disappear as well."

"You remained alone?"

"No, accidents and illnesses claimed most others....But we were so polluted we could not reproduce anymore.....at least not here.....Perhaps if more had waited there would have been children." A discoloration slowly engulfed his face; Benjamin began weeping openly. "What was specifically designed for us.....a divine gift.". He sobbed. "We completely destroyed......."

A uncommonly subdued conversation arose while Benjamin continued his mourning. In restrained tones, Bellah offered his insightful explanation that Haafians and Yldans must be the descendants of those who 'walked away' from the protected area.

Arkkron and Ruet joined Mec as he stared at their sobbing benefactor. All three minds hurtled towards Bellah's own conclusion: Benjamin was, indeed, their ancient ancestor. They shook their heads at this bizarre notion, largely in disbelief. Not only did Benjamin look different with his white-tinged skin and roundish eyes, but his stature was almost a foot less than their's. Furthermore, it was incomprehensible, if not outright heresy to think 'the ancestors' were but disobedient survivors.

Ruet turned back towards Bellah. "Nice idea, but I refuse to believe it."

"And the truth will set you free." Benjamin coughed through his tears. "I believe Bellah is correct....A number of times those who chose to leave attempted to return.....Children were with them, many children." He sobbed again. "While I could see them and while I attempted to talk with them, none ever saw me. I watch them pound on some invisible wall.

Pound and pound and pound and pound.....I walked to the wall and tried to comfort them, but none could see nor hear me....Some perished at the invisible barrier.....Most left cursing and ranting about an uncaring, ruthless god.......My heart broke many times; the hearts of those still with me broke as we witnessed the devastation, the absolute ruin of our people......Some who tried to return had bluish skin,....they actually glowed in the evenings."

"There aren't any blue colored people." Mec said confidently, asserting his position.

"Careful, Mec," Bellah warned. "We don't even know the size of the world.....We didn't even know about this 'protected province'.....In fact, if we lived by what we knew, then we'd all be long dead.....You forget who patched us together."

Mec counted his toes, too ashamed to reiterate his former line of thinking, knowing it came up wanting, desperately wanting. The conversation abruptly ended as each one dropped off into a thoughtful quietness, a reflective time for each a to re-adjust his attitudes. Here, in this tranquil afternoon and evening, the present smashed into the unknown, but living past. The shock waves from its implications affected everyone, even Arkkron, whose mental flexibility didn't stretch very far. The 'what ifs' of each hypothetical scenario endeavoring to explain the time gap between now and the defection of those who once lived with Benjamin punctuated each of their thoughts.

Shortly before they were assigned by Ayhn to this scouting expedition, brash rumors concerning the world's geography circulated throughout Haaf. The north was not hot, and other enormous lands existed beyond the Dark Lands. Now Haafian cultural and historical assumptions were put to the test. Even their theological notions didn't escape scrutinization. The immense power and wisdom of the Holy One, who entered history, in all ages, thoroughly overwhelmed them.

The bright orange-grey streaks of the impending dawn rudely wakened

Bellah from his conjured scenarios. Benjamin was behind him, in the kitchen, fooling about with his peculiar machines which incomprehensibly produced a hearty breakfast. They had all slept at the table.

"This is more like it." Benjamin cheerfully proposed. He noticeably changed since the previous evening. "Friends should not be separated."

"Friends?"

"Why not?.... Are we not all here together?.... Do we not have a common purpose?"

Bellah felt an urge to suppress Benjamin's assumptions, instead he simply nodded his head waiting for Benjamin to finish.

"Understand me clearly, Bellah...There are no such things as accidents. The world would be meaningless if such were true. ......Pardon my digressing.....The fact that you and the others were able to walk through the barrier I spoke of last evening clearly indicates that God has moved onward in his plan."

"You know God's plan?" Mec asked tentatively, quite unsure of what he heard.

"I know that the only reason I was able to save you is that you penetrated the barrier which kept the others from returning.... It never happened before.....There's been a major change....I fought with myself about it."

"But we weren't returning, Benjamin, we were lost....The best excuse I can give for our predicament is that we followed a huge bird,......... one we believed our King had seen in a vision."

"Yes, you've mentioned that innumerable times before. I've seen them from a distance, but they do not come near this protected piece of land....I don't know why." He stopped to pour coffee for everyone. "You are here for a reason beyond simply being 'lost'...You are here to tell me its time for me to leave...My captivity is over........My faithfulness is finally rewarded." He danced a bit with the coffee pot, being animated as never before. "We will be leaving shortly." He grandly announced.

Mec heard only one word, 'leaving'. But that specific word was more than enough to satisfy him. "I'll take another helping......Please." He added as an afterthought.

"You are more than welcome to whatever you wish." Benjamin responded pleasantly.

Bellah reacted more conservatively. "How do you know this to be true? Simply because we got in doesn't directly imply that you are capable of leaving, or even that you are supposed to leave. And then, are we really supposed to leave? Would not our report send scouts looking for you and this land of strange electric devices?"

"Yes, but I will preempt any such invasion." He smiled in a most wisely, albeit peculiar manner. "I am taking 'myself' to your people...And all this 'electrical' stuff will be destroyed before we leave........It isn't needed anymore." He nervously assured himself. "If you four can survive without electricity, I'll learn how to do it also."

"You are deliberately demolishing all these miraculous machines?" Arkkron queried, quite disbelieving. He had been entranced by them since Benjamin toured them through his warehouses and taught them how to operate a few.

"What good are all the devices, if they keep me in captivity? I've had more than enough of being alone......It's time I begin to enjoy life again." He smiled broadly, as if thousands of stone weight dropped from his shoulders. "There's a number of things we must accomplish before we leave....The 'secret building'....Well, let me show you its horrid content. Then we can decide what needs to be done."

Arkkron quickly finished his coffee.

Bellah's incessant desire to explore the secretive structure now would be fulfilled, though Benjamin's statement gave him pause. As they approached the building, wheezing and coughing noises arose, signifying that their presence was known and unwanted.

"The creature, monster, whatever it is, I discovered two weeks, fourteen dawns in your terminology, after you were healing....It had crashed through the pine trees, as if it could fly, yet there are no signs of any wings--or electronic gadgets--to allow for that possibility......At the time, I had no idea of how intensely malevolent it is." He paused, opening the metal door. "Now the creature makes more of itself than it can deliver, nonetheless, he's a horrible sight to gaze upon."

Even Ashuwa would hardly recognize his first-named champion, Warmaker. His bloody-red coloration now paled, his fanged teeth broken and missing, his fearsome clawed hands now severely truncated, and his height diminished to that of the Haafians; his legs having been foreshortened in his rough landing. He could not stand straight nor walk.

"I removed some of his remaining teeth." Benjamin spoke as the Haafians stared. "I could not bring myself to trust the creature....That's why he can't walk so well. Both the upper and lower leg bones snapped and slid, arrested only by the next joint....Stupid thing refused to let me reset the bones....He could have been as good as new....Just like Ruet."

"You gave this stinky, filthy creature the same care as us?" An angered Ruet questioned loudly.

"I did....After all, I had no idea if you might be evil as well, did I?"

Bellah smiled patiently.

The vile creature banged about its stout metal cage without obvious direction or thought. Perhaps, its missing eye threw its balance off, or the impact of hitting the pine trees and then the ground damaged its brain. Not that the creature wasn't dangerous: it would harm anything it possible could. But as for intelligence, or purposefulness, these qualities did not exist. The creature existed as a freak animal for some showman, not unlike the two-headed chickens.

"This thing is in pain, isn't it?"

"Always has been, Mec....I can't find anything to relieve the pain either."

"Provided the creature would allow you ......" Mec returned.

"Quite true....Now, what shall we do with this creature?....He isn't traveling with us."

"The best thing to do is to relieve him of his pain." Bellah said. "We'd never let a Striper suffer like this."

"Any disagreements?"

Hearing nothing, Benjamin ushered the four from the building, then went back inside and pulled a switch. Sparks flew in all directions, the creature half-screamed once and became silent. Sparks continued to fly, setting the structure on fire. Benjamin rejoined the quartet a few moments later.

"The creature is dead." He said a bit sadly. "I wanted to relieve it of its pain long ago, but I wasn't sure if it was another arrival from your world."

"It's probably part of our world, the part that belongs to the damned one.....Such detestable ugliness." Mec said. "You are positive it's dead?"

"After the flames die away, go search for yourself." Benjamin answered. "Now I must gather up my library and destroy the electronic gadgets..... Arkkron, please saddle the horses."

"With all these miracle things, you are just taking the library?" Bellah sounded incredulous.

"No, just part of the library. Over the centuries I've lived here I've been able to ferret out which books are harmful, stupid or wrong.....No use allowing another civilization to suffer because of them." He walked towards the library, continuing the conversation. "I've all ready packed away enough books for four dozen horses, the rest we'll burn."

"You believe books have some..." Bellah fumbled for the correct words. "Awful power, awesome power, don't you?"

"What power does your Holiness Code have?"

"I understand completely, Benjamin." Bellah smiled.

The quintet ate a hurried meal while the buildings burnt to the ground. Some devices powering the lazers first extinguished the field of light-gathering mirrors, then blasted each other out of existence. While five dozen horses were prepared for their journey, the rest of the herd, once fenced in by electronics, went free.

After the meal, Bellah slowly walked the grounds he called home for some thirty centuries, talking to himself, assuring he allowed nothing behind that could prove harmful to others. Now, in the year 9514 A.D., as he peculiarly reckoned time, he sat in his favorite chair for the last time, resting comfortably. "As crazy as it seems, I'm going to take my chair along." And he tied it to one of the empty pack horses. "Time to ride, my friends!"

The Holy One, Blessed be His Name, could have almost sighed and rolled his eyes upward, except he had only a spiritual, nonmaterial form at the present moment. Once again, Creation, the most sporadic and unintentional of the 'Lesser', after an absence of only a month, returned to her labors with excessive energy. Not content with allowing the new river, the one whose source bubbled from the former stronghold of Ashuwa, to disinfect the former Dark Lands, she brought in water-laden clouds and frightening windstorms.

The sterile and putrid wastelands transformed rapidly as the torrential rains, whipped by the winds, washed away the thousand or more years of noxious sulfur deposits. Ashuwa's toxic filth washed to the sea while the moistureless water table regenerated. For over ten months this process kept the Haafians from rebuilding New Pinduala. They were not assured that the location for the new port was safe because of its proximity to 'Cesspool River'.

As the physical corruption from Ashuwa's kingdom decreased, hardy grasses moved northward and the scrub pines from the north migrated southward, both traveling as quickly to transform the land.. Creation actually pushed the rejuvenating miracle by 'slightly' altering the temperatures during the year. Never before had temperatures been so moderate and the rains so evenly spaced. Never before had chronic polluted wastelands been replenished so quickly, though the deliberateness of the actions were well-hidden from mortals.

Creation's greatest success came when she managed to transplant the magnetic poles some twenty two degrees during the peak of the annual bird migration. While sea-faring people spent two weeks in absolute confusion, millions of puzzled birds deposited thousands of seeds and tons of fertilizer while flying over strange new expanses, the former Dark Lands. Even before sailors discovered the poles were re-aligned, a smattering of trees, flowers and grasses sprouted in the most illogical of places: cracks in volcanic walls, on bare hilltops, and about brackish water pools. Without natural predators these grew swiftly. This growth brought the return of the birds and rodents; immediately followed the predators.

The Holy One, knowing full-well the eccentricities of his dearest Creation, permitted, with slight reservation, her strenuous efforts to bless the land with wellness and wholeness. That she labored so fiercely in cleansing the land, became an unintended, unintentional blessing for the Yldans, Haafians and the Taths. This dynamic went altogether unnoticed by Creation. Her sole purpose was the re-establishment what the damned one destroyed. Any additional benefits were purely circumstantial.

As the year following the destruction of Ashuwa's Dark Lands ended, Creation witnessed the reclamation of the land by countless creatures migrating from both north and south. Due to the isolation of her new river, Creation realized that no fresh water fish inhabited it. Overnight the industrious lady populated the river, its feeders and ponds with reptiles, salamanders, fish, eels, turtles, porpoises, and all manner of insects. And, though the vast interior of Ashuwa's ex-domain would naturally remain a desert, it too became inhabited, including a tentative settlement by adventuresome Haafians.

While the rains dominated the eastern part of the Dark Lands, numerous, regularly spaced confined earthquakes rocked the eastern side.

They shook the ground for almost a month. Once the dust finally settled and the covering clouds disappeared, the escarpment which once separated Sarg's territory from the rest of the Dark Lands, had seven wide ravines carved into it. The landmark waterfall continued its spectacular showering from the base of the now defunct volcano, a last remnant of the recent past.

 Having accomplished all she believed needed to be, Creation, quirky as ever, suddenly terminated her endeavors and rested. She found herself smugly satisfied that damnable Ashuwa, when he returned, wouldn't recognize his former territory nor have regained enough strength to devastate its lifeblood again. In all this environmental renewal, Creation never lost track of the fact that she numbered with the 'Lessers'. She didn't have the capacity to confront Ashuwa directly.

 That realm beyond all other realms and removed from time as well, where the actions of the gods could not influence the Holy One's creation, being nominally deserted and abnormally silent at the present from disuse, dwindled to the size of a molecule. Yet stretched so thinly as to cover over a million square miles. Within this isolated realm, where time and space were in permanent abeyance, a severely devastated, yet tenuously existing Ashuwa, once-mighty sovereign of the Kyykki and the Dark Lands, had recomposed himself. At least enough to initiate some rudimentary contemplation. His present state of existence escaped him; the painful memory of his battle with the god without-a-name did not. Once again, the truth gnawed at him.

 His present shape was identical to the molecule's, though bits and pieces of himself coalesced throughout the molecule. Ashuwa had been rendered asunder by the seemingly inconsequential god without-a-name. That truthful realization bombasted his initial thinking, adding measureless agony to his unbalanced and disembodied self. This truth of his defeat, the truth concerning his actual state of being, combined to acknowledge the termination of who he once was. With his meager strength, Ashuwa deliberately blocked this truth, exhausting himself into another extended sleep. Six months transpired before he had enough strength to collect himself to this point. Now, unwilling to face the truth, Ashuwa swept himself into the sleep, his energy spent.

When his minuscule energy, pulled together as he slept, reached its maximum, Ashuwa woke once again. This time he concentrated not on his dissolute history, but on regaining some semblance of his former self. Little by little his mind stretched out over the miles, gently gathering the bits and pieces, the molecules of himself. Each slight addition brought him strength, yet the energy expended gathering himself together produced an exhaustion which cost Ashuwa months. He had no energy to become enraged and infuriated by these frustrating endeavors, something he now truthfully realized the 'idiot' nameless god deliberately planned all along.

"D a m n d a m n d a m n d a m n d a m n d a m n d a m n........ damndamndamndamn..." The once overtly haughty god yelled at himself. The echoes from inside the realm repeated that slurry of words for weeks, their steely pinging noise interfering with his concentration. Five more particles of his spiritual self were all that remained to be gathered. Five more exhausting excursions into the ever-enlarging realm and Ashuwa, Almighty destroyer and desecrator, would wreak havoc upon the inhabitants of the world as never before, after, of course, he severely punished the one responsible for his present condition. Personal revenge consumed him.

With a vicious grab, one encompassing the entire realm, Ashuwa frantically retrieved the final particles of his once-fragmented spiritual self. The relentless god became whole. As the usual exhaustion from such vigorous action overtook him, Ashuwa soundly slept again, this time with a malevolent smirk crossing his pale wispy face.

He contentedly dreamt of his glorious imperial past, with his millions of subjects, the Kyykki, the Haafians, the dragons, the Demon Masters and Demon Lords and his first-named, Warmaker. He remembered the joy of being worshipped and the perverse satisfaction from delivering justice entirely according to his whims.

Upon returning, he would pick up where his massive Kyykki forces had stopped. He anticipated personally conquering D'Ka and Krabo. His allies in the Fluz Marsh were anxiously awaiting his signal to rise up and attack. Sarg's insolent island of resistance could wait, if need be. Even the Haafians required the ultimate heroic 'last stand' for their surviving chronicler, if any, to put it into writing. Ashuwa savored awakening, drooling in his sleep of vengeance such as Creation never dreamed. That day, when his countless multitudes of worshippers provided him with the strength required for effecting suitable punishment upon his enemies, is all Ashuwa wanted. The initial blow he'd strike, one that definitely would weaken the god without-a-name, would be to totally annihilate his base of power: 'his' Tath worshippers. Afterwards, he'd toy with the incapacitated god for countless ages. And, when he finally became bored with the miscreant god, the merciful Ashuwa would generously offer him the path to 'nothingness'.

From his absolute vantage point, the Holy One casually observed Ashuwa's theatrics. No personality changes or repentance was expected: Ashuwa unmistakably remained himself. The Holy One, however, knew exactly what transpired in the kingdoms of the mortals. In truthful terms, what Ashuwa fervently considered as his glorious future, existed only within the confines of his own capricious and twisted mind. Furthermore, considering that Ashuwa's strength ran proportional to the strength of the allegiance of his followers--who were nonexistent--any infant's foot could squash him. However, the great Ashuwa never considered requesting information from anyone, of listening to an outside opinion. Such was a sign of true weakness. His departure from the realm beyond all realms occurred sixteen months after the altercation with the god without-a-name.

The vast heavens appeared to have grown he thought to himself as he attempted to decipher time on the planet below. He continued along, totally unaware of his own size. Once through the atmosphere he turned, heading directly towards his formidable volcano, his impregnable fortress, there to catch up on some details before winning the war against the Haafians.

"Damn!......DAMN!.....DAMNDAMNDAMN!" He roared out loud. Supposedly the continent should have quaked, supposedly the seas should have risen up to inundate the coastlands, but even the lightest of clouds refused to acknowledge another pestilent insect. "I have been cheated of my rightful inheritance!" He bellowed across the water filled rim of his former volcano. The bubbling water, free and pure, paid no mind.

A swift and sudden change of attitude encompassed the damnable god of Evil. Had another trap been prepared for him? Fearfully, he randomly explored 'his' deconstructed volcano, becoming more enraged each time he discovered a mutilated particle of his former physical manifestation. A chipped tooth there, a scale thirty feet away, all beneath thousands of feet of water soaked mud and rock. These things caused him to finally realize his predetermined plans were ridiculous, if not inconsequential. Deep inside the volcano, he came across the only undamaged piece of himself, a nail from his left pinkie.

"Now we shall see who will survive!" He screamed defiantly.

Still, nothing in all creation took notice.

Approaching the nail, he reached out to grasp it, to begin reestablishing his old self. When the nail proved too heavy, too difficult, too massive for him to move, another startling revelation rudely smacked him: his size. He wasn't as big as the nail. The truth of his unambiguous situation set in. Incessant wailing and weeping went on for months as did cursing, in his more lucid moments. With all his might, Ashuwa determined to stop the river. More than once he found himself tumbling in her cleansing torrent, a phenomena which further embittered him. Worst of all, nothing paid him any heed, nothing noticed his existence. In this uncontrolled demented state he wailed until his energy gave out. Exhausted beyond exhaustion, the once and former great god, could not do anything else than allow his sallow wispy self to linger in the old volcano. Never had he been so reduced, so ridiculed before, he angrily screamed to himself as he passed into a semi-consciousness. In his contrived beatific dreams he once again commanded the nations and all feared him, the Great, the Invincible..... the Almighty..... Ashuwa.

Most unfortunately and once again, the quintet's comfortable campfire, also surrounded once again by seemingly endless towering pine trees flickering with dark shadows in night air, looked exactly as every other campfire they slept about for the last three weeks, as Benjamin counted time, that is. The four scouts' patience wore extremely thin, especially as they had no real idea of their destination or direction. Only during the evening did Benjamin allow their blindfolds to be removed. And then, Benjamin suggested only because the moons were too low to provide assistance in determining their location.

During the long days, the scouts rode the small horses where their feet barely cleared the ground. Benjamin gently led the party towards freedom. That translated 'home' to the quartet. That this arrangement, irregardless of its inconvenience, must continue uninterrupted, Benjamin regarded as a matter of trust and survival to everyone. This he painfully explained every evening because he refused to place neither temptation nor jeopardy in their lives by allowing the Lancers to ascertain the location of his old settlement. While everything had been destroyed, any number of persons might derive something from the ashes.

Benjamin's commitment to his God forbid such. Only those items useful to the cultures Benjamin had yet to meet were acceptable for transferring. Thus, in watertight saddlebags, some three thousand books slowly made their way towards the Haafian's homeland.

"I'm going to set up a university." Benjamin once again explained to the quartet.

They recognized 'university' as some type of specialized school, maybe one that dealt with electricity, or maybe it had much to do with the books and In-glish. Benjamin struggled to explain the parameters of the university most every night, to no avail. Their questions revealed they never quite understood. Perhaps, he thought, the students would be other than Lancer scouts. The gracious Creator divided many gifts among His peoples, but higher learning belonged to those who thought in less concrete terms.

"Do I have to hear about it another time?" Mec, visibly distressed by Benjamin's statement, did not welcome the recurring topic.

"No," Benjamin paused. "I will tell you about my vision last evening. Does that spark your interest?"

"Vision?" Ruet sounded suspicious. "You talking about like what we explained to you about the White Eagle?"

"Exactly."

"Just where do these visions of yours arise, then?"

"You are persistently suspicious."

"Makes for being a good scout." Ruet replied straightforwardly.

"Indeed." Benjamin smiled a bit. "The vision?"

Bellah turned towards Benjamin and placed his coffee mug on the needle-covered ground. "Tell it to us." Bellah said quietly.

Benjamin, like any good storyteller, sat back, making himself comfortable. He thoroughly enjoyed his old wooden chair. "Visions are most precious gifts. They permit the Holy things to be understood by mere mortals." He began slowly, watching the faces of the four in the dancing firelight. Seeing he had gained their attention, he quickly continued. "My vision affirmed that my exile is over. Your world would welcome my appearance and grant me a place in society."

"Running the university."

"Exactly, Mec." He paused to smile. Having lost track of the countless centuries and having witnessed the loss of all others who were part of his race, this freedom was his miracle. "I won't argue with myself anymore.... Actually, I don't need to... Anyway, in the vision, we stare down upon the brand new city-still under construction--where huge ships await and flags of the military and sovereign nations fly. Massive shadows cover us, shadows from your white eagles, along with blue and reddish ones." He sipped from his tankard.

"Perhaps, this be true, Benjamin. But what does it mean?"

"That I have regained a proper place in society." He said without thinking. "I apologize, that was most egotistical."

The Haafians, at least these four, saw nothing wrong in calling attention to oneself, especially if one were announcing the truth. Benjamin's apology was unnecessary. The politely clanking tankards revealed their impatience with his humility.

"No, actually, it means a great deal. It's part of the beginning of the New Era...... Think about it for a moment!" He exclaimed, grinning from ear to ear, his mind traversing concepts totally foreign to the four. "I am the last of the ancients! I don't even know how old I am."

"Probably a couple a million years." Ruet let out laconically, producing laughter, including Benjamin's.

"That estimate is probably true, give or take a few thousand either way." He allowed. "I'm also the last of my race..." He sighed, realizing the other side of his life.

"Then you should be dead."

"Or a liar?" Benjamin shot back. "I'm neither, as even you can ascertain.....The wear and tear of time, from such we were protected, as long as we abided by God's decree...The exceptions being those who died through illness or accident."

Mec leaned back. "I'm beginning to hear another repetitious episode."

Benjamin looked across the campfire. "You are not, Mec. I need to finish the vision."

Mec stood and bowed, formally, preposterously. "We await, O' most benevolent of the Ancients, breathlessly, for your next words."

Arkkron tossed his tankard at Mec, splashing coffee down the front of his tunic.

"A little poetic justice never hurt anyone." Bellah mused.

"Gentlemen! I request a return to my vision." An urgency sounded in his voice, one that the four understood well enough to adjust their behavior. "Tomorrow, you do not require blindfolds...... And three days from now we shall see signs of civilization...... ......your civilization."

Instantly the quartet sat up, straight.

Once again, with their undivided attention focused directly upon him, Benjamin continued. "Three things will happen once we reach the city-under-construction, a city which is also a port. First, Bellah will find his wife and children waiting, the same for Ruet...... Second, the four of you will spend the rest of your careers assisting me at the university........Third, I am to meet a great leader of your people, a peculiar man--peculiar in the right way, of course,.............. who has been re-born."

The scouts watched as tears freely ran down Bellah's bronzed cheekbones and darkened his tunic. He had repeatedly driven such hopeful desires from his mind. Initially, shortly after the Lancers became hopelessly lost, and again, prior to his attempted suicide, then during their recovery in Benjamin's ununderstandable world. Now, through a vision provided by this outsider,.

"Your family, Bellah, how many children?" Benjamin unobtrusively queried.

"Three, two daughters and a son, the oldest."

"I would be honored if the three would become my students."

Bellah nodded, tears still running down his face, though it's doubtful that he actually heard Benjamin's offer. One beautiful shock was quite enough for the evening.

"I can't contradict your vision," Ruet began slowly. "But I seriously doubt if our commander, Ayhn, will consent. We are Light Stripers, the regiment of the Lancers. Soon we'll be back with our regiment."

"Soon you will be welcomed as heroes. You'll be able to ask for most anything you want..... Including a full year of back pay!" Benjamin laughed. And your children will also come to the University."

"I never thought of that."

"Then, would you like to assist me? It's a choice you'll have to make for yourself."

"I'm not sure I can comprehend what that means."

"Some trusted friends to help in educating the Haafians and others in the ways only the four of you have witnessed...I hate being labeled a liar." He smiled tersely. "Quite frankly, I'm not sure what the effort will entail either."

"Count me in, whatever it is." Arkkron said. "I've had enough scouting adventures to last three lifetimes........I'm going to write them down and get rich."

"If you learn to read and write, that is." Mec snidely remarked. "Just don't you come beggin' to me later on."

"Gentlemen! Friends!" Benjamin shouted. "Who is this famous Haafian, one re-born?"

A rather tumultuous discussion began, one which grew pyramidally as the evening hours, as Benjamin counted time, swept by. Names and personages which meant nothing to Benjamin flew heavy and thick. Heroes of the past came and went, Kings hardly counted at all, though generals and chaplains did. Moreover, the clerics counted for a few names. But the only name Benjamin heard repeated was 'Vosnob'. The concept of someone being 're-born' never entered their conversation, being too foreign.

"Tell me," Benjamin interrupted. "Who is this 'Vosnob' person you continually refer to?"

Even as the double moons set in the still-black sky, the quartet bombarded Benjamin with the legends, lies and truths concerning the hero of the Battle and now, once again, the present leader called upon to defeat the damned Kyykki. Benjamin thoroughly enjoyed listening to their 'wondrous stories'. While listening his mind distilled as a vivid living portrait of who this 'Vosnob' actually is. His mind suddenly, unaccountably clicked. Vosnob was the Haafian in his vision. Vosnob, the great, the humble, the one known by everyone and respected by almost everybody, the warrior, the peacemaker, the practical and the wise. This had to be the one to whom he would answer. Benjamin actually felt humbled by the man all ready.

A thunderstorm, replete with dancing lightning, woke the sleeping quintet. Nervous horses pawed the ground and yanked at their tethers, ready to stampede into the forest should another bolt strike nearby. Benjamin's gentle words slowly calmed them as did the Lancers' walking amongst them.

"Should stop about noontime." Benjamin said.

"You're probably correct." Arkkron replied in In-glish, surprising Benjamin and the others.

"Excellent, my usually quiet friend." Benjamin answered in Inglish. "I'll need to teach you the alphabet, the letters."

"Would you two speak in normal Haaf, like everyone else!" Mec groused.

"Why?" Benjamin tossed the issue back to Mec. "And before you argue anymore, I've decided that In-glish will be taught."

"You're supposed to speak so that others understand you."

"Arkkron and I understand each other perfectly well.". The Ancient One easily countered.

"Forget I even mentioned the subject."

"Never!" Arkkron smiled deviously.

"Can we just get these saddlebags harnessed!" Bellah called from the far end of the herd. "These books aren't worth much of anything if the ink runs and the pages soak up water."

Each person now clutched the tethers of a dozen or so horses as in single file, they followed after the meandering Benjamin. By mid- afternoon, the sky brightened and a warm breeze swept through the forest, keeping the humidity to a minimum.

"We're beyond your forest, aren't we Benjamin?" Bellah called ahead.

"How should I know?" He yelled over his shoulder, pretending innocence.

"Because you walked this land long before the trees grew. In fact, you just may have planted the first trees." Bellah accused.

"Now why should I expend such energy?" He laughed.

The immense forest had thinned out, enough to allow the breeze to blow and small flowers to grown on the needle-covered floor. Even now their pathway widened to where the horses easily walked in trios between the trees. Benjamin's vision, now backed with evidence, added validity and hope to the final dawns, as the Haafians count time, of their strangest of journeys.

By evening, the huge pine trees lay well behind them. Their blankets lay on grasses instead of needles. Sounds and songs from familiar animals and birds filled the air, bringing a sense of peace to the four and much uneasiness to Benjamin. He refused to be consoled by Ruet's descriptions of the creatures until Ruet either captured one or pointed one out. Thus, the ancient one quickly learned of crickets, frogs, night flying birds and bats. The latter of which thoroughly fascinated him, though in a most unpleasant manner.

"The Creator must have been fooling about when He decided to place wings on rats........ How utterly peculiar." He commented.

"We believe the damned one made the bats....Because they like caves and come out only at night and their bites are full of poison." Mec offered the standard Haafian response.

"But mostly cause they're black.....just like the damned one." Ruet added. "I know they eats mainly bugs, especially mosquitoes and such, but I still keep my distance."

"Then I shall abide by your advise, my friends." Said Benjamin. "But one day I shall study these bats to learn the truth."

Bellah had ridden in silence most of the day. His thoughts were nowhere near the current topic, but on his family. He figured they waited over a year and a half for him. He also realized that, by now, the scouting party would be reported as 'missing in action'.......The 'action' they accomplished when they attacked the campsite of the traitorous Haafians and finished off the dragons. His wife and children might consider him dead. She'd be free to marry again, he thought. Cold sweat poured from his heavy brow. What if...."

"Have some coffee, Bellah." Benjamin offered. "And quit worrying about your family."

Bellah's eyes widened in amazement: Benjamin knew his thoughts. "She didn't remarry?" Bellah blurted out, exposing his deepest fear. His confession amazed the others because they had yet to consider the effects of their absence.

"Of course not. Love continues on through the hard times... Besides, you aren't dead and she doesn't believe in divorce." Benjamin deadpanned.

Bellah looked at the ancient one suspiciously. "Just what else do you know, old man?"

"Am I right or am I wrong?"

Bellah smiled to himself. "Maybe I'll need to stay with you. You are definitely more dangerous than you appear."

"I thank you for the compliment, though I believe I learned much of it from the four of you." He smiled understandingly at Bellah while pouring coffee. Deep inside he felt an ancient well-disguised hurt, a sadness that yearned for that special 'someone' he lost uncounted centuries ago. Strange, he thought he had permanently buried such feelings until he entered Bellah's personal conflict.

"See you at sunrise." He said sadly as he slowly walked to his blanket, counting the real emptiness of his years of solitude and waiting. And then how the abrupt appearance of the Haafian Lancers reminded him of the future and just how far he had drifted from being a real person. He mentally punished himself for becoming a double-voiced, double-thinking person. He fervently prayed for that embarrassing episode in his life to disappear forever. Then he realized another truth, ageing was once again a part of his life. He didn't even want to consider that his life had an ending even as it was just beginning. Sleep completely evaded him.

That morning, Mec watched as the Ancient One sewed together a new tunic. He used a small foot-powered machine. "I just couldn't leave and not bring a gift for the Vosnob, could I?" Benjamin straightforwardly explained himself and the existence of the machine.

"You told us you left all the 'electricity' behind." Mec's voice rankled, calling attention to the issue.

"My foot is not made of electricity, is it?"

"You're a peculiar man, Benjamin." Mec smiled deviously. "No tellin' what you be made of."

Bellah, with Arkkron following after, called across the flower filled meadow. "What's all the noise about?"

"Benjamin brought a sewing machine with him."

"We used to call people like you 'tattle-tales'." Benjamin grumped as he continued working on his tunic.

"So, what's the problem?" Bellah demanded. "We have all sorts of machines about us."

"This one is not from our world." Mec defended himself.

Bellah watched as Benjamin's machine literally flew through the cotton-like material. What tailors spent a full day's labor on, Benjamin's machine easily accomplished within a few moments.

"Don't worry Bellah," Benjamin explained without looking up. "There's but one machine..... A special present for your Vosnob. ....I had to see if it would work once we left the protection of the forest."

"And make yourself a fancy outfit to meet the Haafians." Bellah laughed. "Actually, leaving every machine behind was an impossibility for you....Like Lancers without weapons...."

"Or scouts without a mission." Added Arkkron.

"Well put, my friends." He paused, turned the blue material and spoke again. "Quite frankly, it's been thousands and thousands of years since I've dressed up for anything.....Don't you think this appropriate?" He held up the finished garment.

With the exceptions of the three-quarter length flowing sleeves and the blue color, the tunic was identical to the worn-out uniforms of the Lancers. As usual, Benjamin's pants remained the same, something he called 'jeans'. They fit as well as the baggy trousers of the Lancers, but were held up, not by a drawstring, but a device called a 'zipper'. Though he brought three horse loads of these with him, the Lancers kept their own style.

"Will you get me the saddlebags off my pack horse?" Benjamin asked no one in particular. He had returned to the sewing machine to hem the bottom of his tunic.

Arkkron retrieved four packages for Benjamin. "What should I do with them?"

"Pass them out. I don't want you Lancers entering civilization looking like a company of beggars. You are heroes, so its time to dress like them." Benjamin turned and looked up from his sewing.

Their new uniforms exactly matched their worn-out ones, with one major exception: the trousers, jeans as Benjamin called them, had zippers. Benjamin even constructed new boots, knee high ones having a flap extending over the knee cap, yet still flexible enough to roll down. With the primary difference being that they now rode horses instead of Stripers.

"Don't stand there..... Get the uniforms on." He ordered the four. "Today we'll probably see evidence of your civilization. They'll probably spot us."

"We'll soon have an escort?" Mec asked, welcoming an opportunity to be with others.

"No, I don't think so. We're still far beyond where the Striper patrols roam....."

"We don't roam....we explore, we scout."

"Whatever, Mec.......No offence intended."

"So who's going to find us?"

"The White Eagles with their riders should be flying about. Scouting from the air isn't only quicker, but safer and more accurate."

"Is that remark necessary?"

"Time continues to change us and how we accomplish things. I predict that more scouting will be done from flying than from Striperback in the very near future."

"But what crazy person would sit atop a bird?"

"Maybe some all ready do, Ruet. After all, I did explain to you that other peoples were incorporated into my vision."

"But who ever heard of blue people?"

"What did you think about a most peculiar white person?" Benjamin mischievously shot back to Ruet. "Did you ever hear of him before?"

"It's high time we get moving....... Saddle up!"

"Going to dodge the issue, aren't you?" Benjamin said to Ruet while he packed away the sewing machine. "When you're working at the university, you won't be able to do that anymore."

"I'll wait." Ruet mumbled tersely, then mounted up.

The expansive meadow, cut by shallow meandering streams, allowed the horses to herd for the first time since leaving Benjamin's protected territory. Their neighing and playfulness indicated an appreciation for their new environment. The sunlit meadow also made work easier for the five, no branches to duck, no stray animals to find, no water to be carried and no fodder to collect. The meadow provided more than adequately for the horses' needs.

They traveled in an eastward direction, though one so far to the north that Haafian geography didn't acknowledge its existence. The firm level ground covered with knee high grasses and flowers made for relatively undemanding travel. By mid-afternoon they noticed a huge body of water far to the northeast. The meadow, so far as they could see, ran directly to it. Their path however, was interspersed with numerous large copses of trees and dotted with dense patches of shrubbery. Their path kept them headed for the new-found lake, sea---no one was really sure what it was.

As half-expected but not prepared for, the White Eagles appeared from out of nowhere. Their huge shadows overtook them while Ruet cooked supper. After a few encircling flights by the Lancer's campsite, one of the three birds landed a few hundred paces away. The four Haafians resembled carved marble statues, completely overwhelmed by the bird's size and graceful beauty. Benjamin, on the other hand, immediately strode forth to greet the two men who were dismounting from the giant bird's neck.

"Which of you are the Vosnob?" Benjamin yelled across the fifty paces which separated one bluish skinned man and a Haafian from himself.

The two stopped their advance, apprehensive of this 'too' knowledgeable white skinned old man.

"Do not be afraid!" Benjamin called out. "I am Benjamin. Those statues over there next to the fire are Bellah, Ruet, Arkkron and Mec, famous, though long lost scouts of the Lancers of the Light Striper .... Please,...join us for supper." Benjamin laughed merrily as he continued towards the two riders. "O' what a wonderful time to live!" He exclaimed, further alarming the riders.

Almost as if to protect their benefactor, the quartet shook off their trance and ran to Benjamin's defense. The immense bird paid little attention to the rather unusual proceedings. It studied the meadow as if it were inhabited by vicious demons, its huge eyes narrowed to menacing slits as it gazed through the hazy slowly-dieing sunlight.

"Don't mind the Ancient One." Bellah called to the riders, and then caught himself. "You...you are....blue." He stammered when he actually recognized the Tath.

The lanky one-armed Haafian, wearing a senior officer's uniform of the Light Striper began laughing, then turned and spoke to the Tath in a foreign language. The Tath's eyes went wide with amazement, then he too laughed. In an ununderstandable language, the Tath returned a few lines which were translated into Haafian by the officer.

"My friend, trainer and rider of the Istelle, Ormutt," The officer explained. "Thinks that his color is exactly correct for a Tath..........and he's elated that you can recognize the color 'blue'.......... At first, he wasn't too sure of your abilities, especially as you appeared as statues."

The officer suddenly saluted. Four troopers jumped to attention.

"Sorry, Sir, Sorry." Bellah attempted to excuse their way through this lapse in military protocol. "It's been over a year and a half since we've been this scouting mission, Sir."

"So I've heard rumored, Bellah." He quickly inspected the four and ordered a 'parade rest'. "My name is Jed, second-in-command to Yganak, temporary governor of New Pinduala... My assistant is from Tath. He's a citizen of the vast steppe north of the Dark Lands.... The Istelle is his mount." He paused. "The late King's white eagle."

"Yes, Sir." Bellah barked in true non-commissioned officer form. It presented him with a familiar security he found most welcome.

"I sincerely apologize for my remark, Sir. It was totally out-of-bounds."

"Yes, it certainly was..... However, I see no reason to make an issue out of something which will never transpire again. We do clearly understand each other, Bellah?" He spoke with a transparent smile.

"Yes, Sir." Bellah smiled back.

Jed then turned to Benjamin, answering his initial question. "I did not mean to ignore you, Sir. But I thought it best to establish some of the newest dimensions of our world. Unfortunately, I am not Vosnob, the one you are seeking. However, he awaits you at New Pinduala." Jed went to his knees, followed by Ormutt.

"What is this obeisance nonsense?" Benjamin demanded as he pulled both men to their feet.

"Are you not the Ancient One?" Jed asked, perplexed by the old man's demeanor. "Are you not the 'predicted one'?"

"I am old, quite old, in fact....too old for this nonsense." He mumbled, disgusted with any and all perfunctory rituals. "And I know absolutely nothing about your predictions."

"Ancient One, I humbly confess that the prediction is not Haafian....... Rather, it belongs to the oral traditions of the Tath tribes. The prediction specifically relates that when Istelles are allowed to fly over all the territory, that is the signal for one called 'the Ancient One' to appear. That 'Ancient One' is the herald of a New Era."

The Lancers didn't miss a single word, but being 'at ease' could not say anything. Nonetheless, they readily understood that they were part of a story far greater than they ever imagined.

"Are you familiar with such a prediction?" Jed asked a clearly amused Benjamin.

"Yes, such a prophecy is made known to me in a vision....from the Creator........These four have also heard it, though from a vastly different perspective...." Benjamin pointed to the Lancers, who for the first time, appeared out-of-their-element to him. "And it is true, the Istelles now have the entire forest to fly over.....These four know of such a protected place, one whose existence.....Well, it is destroyed." Benjamin said off-handedly, then abruptly altered the course of the conversation. "....Can we go and sit?.... Is it not time for supper?"

Jed, speaking in Tath, consulted with Ormutt. Then Ormutt signaled the two Istelles circling above. Almost instantly, one headed east, its massive wings furiously beating the air. The other Istelle gracefully landed nearby, its Tath rider dismounted and joined up with Jed.

"Now we can eat." Jed finally answered. "The two Istelles will provide for our safety until the morrow."

Jed, Benjamin and the two Taths walked towards the campsite, leaving the four Lancers still standing 'at ease'. They glanced at each other, frustrated, unable to even remind the infatuated Jed of his forgetfulness. Mec loudly cleared his throat. Benjamin suddenly halted. Jed tripped over him.

"Are my assistants invited to supper?" He questioned Jed with the tone of ancient wisdom, a tone which the embarrassed Jed unhesitatingly obeyed.

"Scouts, dismissed!" He ordered as civilly as possible under the present circumstances.

"It just might be best for us to work as Benjamin's assistants." Mec quietly mumbled. "He's famous all ready.....and he certainly knows how to treat us."

While supper was definitely enhanced by fresh vegetables and fruits brought by the Taths, the evening's conversations went the opposite direction. Jed's meager translating abilities and his pre-occupation with the prophecy, especially because the Taths also wanted answers on the topic, frustrated Benjamin. More issues became muddied than clarified. Benjamin, being deliberately stubborn though kind, denied Jed much information, preferring to defer until the morrow when "The Vosnob' would be present.

Tiring of the going-nowhere conversation, the Lancers and the Tath riders, through sign language, found themselves bargaining Istelle rides for horse rides. As sojourners, close intimate colleagues with the revered Ancient One, the Tath Istelle riders held the Lancers in much esteem, just as the Haafians found themselves awed by such persons who could actually fly. This mutual admiration kept the two parties communicating until almost dawn.

In the early greyish-orange streaked cloudless dawn, a welcoming party of twenty Istelles, blue, red and white, silently landed in the nearby meadow. Their mysterious, unearthly descent clearly indicated to Bellah that the Ancient One possessed a reputation far beyond anything he might conceive. The thunder of galloping Stripers, rising from the east, added more weight to his conclusion. No one ever received such a welcoming before.

By mid-morning over a five hundred officials and their retinues, both military and civilian, had formed up in proper descending order under banner-fluttering tents pitched in the meadow. All impatiently awaited the arrival of the revered and anticipated Ancient One. A military band, the best that could be rushed forward under such short notice, sweated under the direct sunlight.

Vosnob with Blue Turtle and Yganak trailing behind him, strode over to the United Tribes of Tath delegation headed by the Queen of the Northern Tribe, Kullia. As the Central Tribe defaulted in accomplishing its God-given mission to present a new ruler to their nameless god, they sent a small delegation. The reinstated River Tribe was more than present, recognizing that with their monopoly on the central rivers, they had much to gain. Somewhere in the mix of peoples, roamed Kloshic and Oros, each attempting to defend himself through sarcasm, while sampling all the different brews the Taths had to offer. Their unofficial celebration had prematurely begun, if one was not inclined towards official protocol, that is.

Benjamin found none of this royal elitist commotion to his liking. Being surrounded by hundreds of strangers, all who held him in highest esteem simply because of his age and some prediction, didn't qualify him as someone special. He maintained this position in spite of the efforts of

Bellah and Jed. To Benjamin, this undue nonsense came close to deifying him. That singular danger he wanted no part of.

"Like it or not, you're the oldest person alive."

"Since when did simply being 'aged' mean you were important, Bellah?"

"Since your 'the Vosnob' was reborn by the Holy One." He shot back, his tone a bit icy.

"Maybe I'll have to demote you before you even become my assistant. .... And the more you haggle here with me, the more your family will have to wait to see you."

"You're telling me they aren't with the crowd." Bellah sounded worried, if not a bit betrayed.

"Only the 'so-called' important people are standing in the meadow, baking under the sun." He said. "Rather peculiar tradition you have."

"Peculiar tradition?" Bellah bounced back, hoping he'd dodge the stressful family issue, at least for the time being.

"Putting all the leaders together in a most exposed place--a place where they are all suffering in the sunlight...... What if some enemy suddenly showed up......"

"That's hardly peculiar, Bellah.....That's what we call stupid."

"Precisely! And that's why we're here in the shade drinking coffee .... Not out there sweating." He laughed.

A pompously decorated delegation consisting of Tath and Haafian leaders slowly began walking towards Benjamin's campsite. The tubas played a slow march accompanied by the musings of various drums and cymbals. Even Vosnob removed his hat. With the exception of the scrappy Chaplain from the now defunct Pinduala, everyone had bedecked themselves as if they were on a sacred pilgrimage.

"Apparently, these people have totally overrated me." Benjamin complained.

"Zap a tree with a lazer." Mec caustically poised. "Then they'll really be under your full control."

"Stop that instantly!" Bellah ordered. "That's the last thing these strangers need to know. Best to stick with the university. Understand?"

"Yes Sir!"

"Damn, I don't even have enough coffee for everyone." Benjamin confessed. "Jed, you get another bag from the saddlebags…. Thank you."

"You aren't serious?" Jed quickly responded.

"I surely am. Guests are soon arriving, we shall be prepared."

Jed willingly obeyed the white-haired man, though part of him struggled with how unnatural this encounter was going to be. Who would ever imagined that the Ancient One prepared coffee? It was like the King making tea for his servants. The apparent incongruity bothered Jed, but obviously not Benjamin, who was rummaging about the campsite for more coffee mugs.

At thirty paces from the campsite, the entourage and its leaders stopped and waited silently. Some nervousness shot through the group, for none knew what to expect, but all anticipated something pleasantly 'different'. As some quietly spoke prior to leaving the brightly decorated tents, perhaps it was a gross miscarriage of etiquette to presume the Ancient One should come to them. A few wondered, out loud, if the Ancient One might be quite offended. Now, they waited to find out.

"Did you put the coffee on?" Benjamin asked Jed. "I'll probably require another pot. See if you can find one."

"I don't know how to do it." The embarrassed second-in-command apologized loud enough for the whole entourage to hear.

"No, my mistake, Jed….I assumed you people knew about coffee. But, that's not true…And not fair to you….Let me show you how to make a great pot of coffee."

The entire entourage watched, incredulously, as the Ancient One spent a few moments detailing the steps to making coffee with Jed. Benjamin treated him as an equal and Jed accepted such treatment without protest. After one lengthy evening, Jed knew better, Benjamin despised any phoniness.

This lesson wasn't wasted on the leaders who quickly doffed much of their superfluous decorations. Vosnob commanded the band to play some dance tunes instead of marches, which momentarily confused the musicians. Those observing from a distance found themselves totally bewildered. Did the 'Ancient One' command such 'common' tunes? Was he executing judgement for their lack of proper etiquette? Was it simply music played to kill time until the Ancient One decided he would meet with the representatives from the Tath and Haafian nations?

"Are those good people still standing in the sun?"

"Yes, Benjamin, they are." Arkkron replied, a bit embarrassed by the whole scene.

"Well then, Arkkron, go down and invite them for coffee....And tell them to bring a couple of those tents....The shade's beginning to move...... And, ...we need more coffee cups."

Awkwardly, hesitantly, the usually quiet Arkkron shuffled off towards the awaiting leaders, all sweating in the sunshine. As he neared, the whole entourage straightened up, presenting their best. Arkkron abruptly stopped a few paces before the group. He stared out at the crowd of officials and dignitaries, all sweltering in the sun. He almost laughed, thinking of Benjamin's remarks.

He suddenly jammed his hands into his tunic pockets and began to address those gathered. "Welcome to the campsite of Benjamin, whom you revere as the prophesied 'Ancient One'. My name is Arkkron, one of the Lancer Scouts....... Never could have anyone expected such an illustrious welcoming of such grand magnitude, including Benjamin, the 'Ancient One'... He is humbled by your coming to meet with him."

All eyes, whether oval, roundish or slanted, riveted upon him. Their intense gaze bothered him. They did not comprehend the nature of

Benjamin. That much showed in their confused faces. Arkkron thought he should have asked for them to crawl to the 'Ancient One'. That idiocy would be fully understood and obeyed. He smiled to himself. His new boss was all ready turning the world around.

"Benjamin does have enough coffee for everyone, but not enough coffee mugs........er, tankards for all of you. Please bring some. Also, as the sun continues to move, our campsite is no longer shaded. Might a few of be so kind as to erect a few tents about the campfire....And, seeing we have but logs to sit on, except for Benjamin's ancient chair, you may wish to bring a few with you."

"You aren't serious!" A noticeably offended voice from the crowd of dignitaries shouted.

"It's a bit confusing, I assure you...But Benjamin asked me to bring the message to you...."

"He wants us to pitch tents and bring coffee? mugs?" Another voice said, puzzled.

"Don't worry." Arkkron explained with a hint of one-upmanship. "He'll help you pitch them if you haven't learned yet."

"I like this Benjamin all ready." Said Vosnob as he moved to the front. "And who are you, Lancer?"

"I'm a Lancer Scout, found, like the others, by Benjamin and brought back to health. I serve under Ayhn."

"So the rumor is true."

"Sir?"

"Did you or did you not destroy the headquarters of some Haafian traitors engaged by Ashuwa?.... Their campsite was in the swamp lands west of Pinduala."

"And we got a few dragons as well, Sir." Arkkron smiled even though he didn't exactly know who confronted him. He assumed it might be Vosnob, but the officer appeared far too youthful.

"So I've been told." Vosnob held out his hand and gripped Akron's. He pumped it vigorously. "Welcome home hero!" Vosnob shouted as he gave Arkkron a bear hug. "You saved many thousands of lives by eliminating those traitors. Thank you, son."

Arkkron struggled a bit with the personal attention, a bit mystified by it all. "Pardon me, Sir......But just who are you?"

"The name is Vosnob."

"Sir!" Arkkron quickly backed two paces and saluted.

"Just take me to Benjamin, Arkkron." Then Vosnob turned. "Do as Arkkron says and do it quickly....This 'coffee' is made especially for us, let not the 'Ancient One' wait....Kullia," Vosnob spoke in Tath. "Will you be so kind as to be my escort?"

As the unusual trio approached Benjamin, he met them with open arms, hugging both Vosnob and Kullia. "It's a wonderful day, isn't it?" He exclaimed, motioning for Mec to bring coffee. "You are 'the Vosnob'?"

"Yes."

"And you are of the Taths. I sincerely apologize, I just started learning your language last evening...." He spoke brokenly, but well enough for Kullia to understand.

"Thank you, My Lord." She responded in Haafian. "You do honor me."

She kept her eyes to the ground out of reverence, though, in truth, she wanted nothing more than to see the bringer of the New Era.

"Ah, my dear." He switched to Tath. "It does go both ways. I've not talked with a beautiful woman for centuries." He offered her his ancient wooden chair. "There is much to do...." He sighed. "But, today, we become friends first.... Can we agree to that?"

Chapter 12

Had Sarg possessed any redeeming qualities during the period of Queen Sjura's labor, they were well hidden. Perhaps, his anxiousness lay in the fact that he was irrevocably denied entrance to their bedroom. Or, through the strenuous efforts of Brey and Kadima, it lay in his disappearance. The nervously pacing father-to-be found himself strapped to the back of a Istelle, the only place where his excited jibberish wouldn't bother the entire castle staff and visitors. Sarg's present emotional state incapacitated most, if not all, of his abilities. Vauk was on hand to assist with any problems arising from that most natural process of giving birth.

Later, when presented with healthy twins, one boy, one girl, Kadima had to catch the fainting ruler of the castle. Much later, almost another day, passed before those surrounding the queen deemed Sarg proper to visit his wife. By then the sedatives Vauk mixed with his food measurably slowed him to his usual self. Sarg ranked among the proudest of proud fathers.

The timing couldn't have been better planned, for with the joyous news now traveling throughout both countries via Istelles, emissaries, ambassadors and others who dared to ride Istelles, began arriving. A new Kingdom, a combination of two cultures and with twin heirs, the latter being a most unique feature in itself, created quite a stir throughout the New World, as some called the new geography.

This great attention directed towards the new kingdom, still formally nameless, finally brought about Sarg's return to reality, at least in public. Back in the royal suite however, Sarg continued his role as a doting giddy-headed father, enjoying it thoroughly. Queen Sjura demanded that the heavy tapestries from the yurts be fastened to the walls of their suite. Perhaps this might insure some privacy, the least it could provide was relief from the echoing of Sarg's voice.

The following year, when a new, more accurate calendar, was instituted in Paradise, Feathered Goat reckoned that the date of the twin's birth was the day Benjamin, the prophesied Ancient One, left his sanctuary for a new life. For now, however, Sarg and Sjura, participated in the joyous duties of parenting. Unfortunately, as royalty with a bit more notoriety than most, the couple spent endless hours receiving well-wishers from both countries.

"Perhaps, My Love, the 'endless valley' wasn't so bad after all." Sarg said wearily as he crawled into bed and cuddled up to his tired wife.

"And you wouldn't be sleeping with me....Think about that for a moment." Sjura gently chided as she readjusted the nursing twins.

"I can't think anymore this day."

"Then you better get some rest."

"That is not really possible. The moment I get to sleep, you'll put the twins in their cribs."

"And you'll have to wake up...." She smiled teasingly. "And I'll be all by myself...."

Sarg missed her invitation by a half sentence. He'd fallen into a restless sleep. The mysterious, bothersome dream came before him once again. A man he'd never met, a dignified man of whom only a silhouette appeared, proceeded to give him directions. These concerned only his children, who, pending advise from both the Yldan shamans and Tath priests, had yet to receive their formal royal names. The matter of proper protocol in such matters as this 'unique' situation had never been approached before. The strong, yet gentle voiced stranger in Sarg's dream requested that he be given the privilege of supplying the proper names for the twins. This additional burden on Sarg caused him to shake in his sleep.

"Wake up." Sjura nudged her husband. "You're having 'that' dream again,.......... aren't you?"

Sarg rolled over and open his eyes. He lay resting in Sjura's blue arms, looking at the dark ceiling. "Yes, its the same dream....I can't figure it out."

"Don't even get started..." She cautioned him, speaking in Tath. "We both know you have little tolerance for mysteries....And I want to get some sleep."

"Do you think the Nameless One might know what this is all about?"

"You are planning on asking him?" Sjura teased him.

"Anything wrong with asking a god for assistance?"

"Listen, lover, Axendr and Geena all ready know their names... This 'others' can wait until the proper time arrives..."

"You really think so?"

"I believe I've answered you with that rationale for the past week, haven't I?"

"Indeed......But,..."

"......Do you still like mine?" Sjura cooed as she snuggled up next to Sarg and drifted off to a sound sleep.

Red Istelles from Benjamin's tentative encampment on the southern shores of Istellia Bay, arrived shortly before noon. Having found himself too enmeshed and overly encumbered by his status as the Ancient One of the Tath prophecies, Benjamin, along with his staff of four, flew away four days previous.

Benjamin actually enjoyed the quiet nights. They allowed him time to think. Such time had been driven from him in his new role. But being a prophet wasn't a role he had prepared himself for; his efforts went in another direction, establishing a university. He now realized that would have to wait. The immediate problem, dealing with the zealous Taths who jumped on his every word as if he was god, plagued him worse than any of the Haafian scouts' antics ever did. Somehow he needed to discover a way, a devise, by which he could rejoin the ranks of mortals without humiliating the overwrought Taths. Thus he eagerly accepted the offer to fly to visit Sarg and Sjura.

Vosnob quickly became a good friend. They shared a commonness unknown to others. Each of them had been reborn, renewed, revitalized--the correct, the precise word alluded both of them--for a yet to be fully divulged divine purpose. This also frightened both men, as it rightly should. Moreover, as Vosnob stood for the renewing of Haaf, the Taths quickly claimed Benjamin, the last of his 'white skinned' race, as their herald into the New Era. And, in spite of their notoriety-- neither of the two sought it--they found unnecessarily embarrassing, the two maintained the lowest profile possible. However, if, they agreed, this public acclaim would allow for the required peaceful transitions to occur within and between the two countries, then they had little choice but to maintain their present status.

Not willing to waste precious time, Benjamin enlisted Captain Ellom to begin surveying the northern seacoast with the aid of the Taths and their Istelles. He also left a copy of his computer generated blueprints for the engineers of Pinduala to study. These plans consisted of the university town Benjamin named Geneva, along with the required infrastructure to produce the town. This included airstrips for the Istelles, a port for Haafian and Tath commercial fleets, adequate grazing for sheep and cattle, and plumbing such had never before been seen. His plans for stream generated electric power he kept for the future. In his revised plans for the university, Benjamin recognized that the students would best learn by doing. As teacher, he would be their guide and mentor.

Vosnob, once Benjamin appraised him of the scope of the university and his intentions for it, first sat back, scarcely able to comprehend what Benjamin shared, finding it bordering on the impossible. A place specifically designed for specialized learning he found difficult to grasp, especially when he realized that education was the entire thrust of the university. Then Mec's observations as to what the university might offer doubled Vosnob with laughter. Benjamin managed to contain himself, just barely. Selling something far and beyond one's own experience wasn't easy.

For once Benjamin felt fortunate about the Tath prophesies, he needed all the assistance possible.

Finally, after much reflection, Vosnob pledged his full support, even if he didn't yet understand Benjamin's details. For his part, Vosnob shared with Benjamin both the immediate and far past history of Haaf, indicating that as Ashuwa appeared to be beaten, at least for the time being, then this was surely the best time for the two peoples to unite. Then Vosnob laughed, realizing that the peoples had all ready begun to unite. Nooy, the Yldan, Sarg and Feathered Goat, all had wedded Taths. Strange, he thought out loud, why haven't the Tath men taken any Haafian brides.

"You're thinking more of your own loneliness....?"

"Only as much as you are thinking of your's, Benjamin..."

"Indeed ...indeed." He sighed. "Once I had a wife....."

"Do you still miss her?"

"Inasmuch as she'll always be a part of me....yes, I do, my friend." Benjamin replied emotionally. "......Strange...the public embarrasses us with their adoration......yet the very thing we would add to our lives, they take for granted."

"I'm not sure I follow you." Vosnob replied hesitantly, as if he shouldn't even consider such a topic, at least for himself.

"Come now,......Are you not lonely?......Do you not miss that 'special someone' in your life?"

"As long as its not you." He laughed nervously.

"Trying to alter the topic doesn't erase the truth....And you Haafians have a real complex about the truth."

"You remind me too much of Yganak and Running Cloud. They get too close with the truth." Then Vosnob nodded his head in agreement.

"Perhaps there is more for us in the future.......No one in their imagination could have guessed that the New Era....."

"I know.....yes, my friend, I know." Vosnob said quietly, looking at his new face in the pool beside him, still a bit unsure as to what his divine revitalization meant.

This conversation transpired shortly before Benjamin mounted up and flew off to meet the famous Sarg, 'the gifted' and Queen Sjura. Now as he met the royal couple in their chambers, that empty feeling stirred within him once again. He longed for that closeness, that special relationship which the royal couple enjoyed.

Bellah had convinced a Tath Istelle rider to bring along his entire family. He stood two steps behind Benjamin, holding his wife's hand. Her color had returned to somewhat normal. She smiled broadly now and always, her prayers answered beyond every expectation. Her husband was now an officer and retired into the service of the Ancient One, with his strange white skin. Mec, Ruet and Arkkron stood along the white marble-like wall, amazed by its soft glowing, and being further occupied by baby-sitting Bellah's children.

The later was not necessarily a job for junior officers, especially ones itching to spend a year's back pay. However, once they realized the Tath women watched in admiration, their attitude towards child care appreciatively improved. However, time for enhancing their relationships with the Taths would wait. This moment belonged to Benjamin, the Ancient One.

So it did. News of this extraordinary man traveled fast. Sjura stumbled over the incredible news. If true, then Tath would be united as a country. A new, albeit frightening, future lay open before the Taths. After consulting with the Tath priests, she and Sarg immediately requested an audience with the Ancient One. In doing so they prepared to travel to the eastern end of Tath, but a gentle intervention by the god without-a-name prevented their arduous trip. He'd make sure the Ancient One arrived in Paradise as soon as possible. And so it happened.

A wave of shock engulfed Sarg's face. Sjura pulled him closer. "Are you sick?" She whispered.

"He's the man in my dream. He's the one with names for our children."

Nothing more was said. Benjamin had advanced within two paces. Queen Sjura bowed deeply, followed by Sarg and their entourage.

"This really isn't necessary, is it?" Benjamin said quietly to Sarg in Tath, his faced pained. "I utterly deplore these stiff ceremonies."

"You are the Ancient One, isn't some respect..."

"I have more respect than is proper." He quietly replied.

Those gathered continued with their bow, not wishing to rise until the monarch signaled.

"Then tell us to act differently." Sarg shot back hastily.

"Everyone, listen!" Benjamin spoke in firm Haafian. "Stand up before your backsides get cold."

Everyone's eyebrows went up in alarm, yet everyone did obey. After all, the Ancient One was the anticipated prophet of the Taths. About the room's perimeter and in small groups the people stood as if statues. Kadima's two children proved the exception, rushing across the polished floor to greet this wise important person, as their mother had explained Benjamin to them. He smiled as they slid across the glossy floor, then dropped to one knee, capturing the two in his wide-spread arms. Just as quickly, he stood and twirled them about. He laughed as much as they did.

For the more 'formal' types within the gathering, a flurry of disgusting looks darted across the chamber. But for those seeking a true example, the authentic prophet, Benjamin's actions answered their questions. The atmosphere relaxed, people smiled and conversed quietly. Bellah's children suddenly broke free from Arkkron and sailed across the floor, confronting Benjamin.

He looked down at them. "I have hugs for you also. It is only fair that I share with others, isn't it?" He smiled at the silent embarrassed children. Then he placed the other two back on the floor.

The five children, strangers to one another, stood less than a foot space apart, studying each other. Their silence was soon replaced by giggles.

"Do you want to see the castle?" The Taths asked almost simultaneously. Their eyes shone with anticipation. Finally they had visitors of their own age. The adults did not comprehend a word, but the conversation was not for them anyhow. Bellah's children spun about before their parents could protest and were gone.

"Don't worry Bellah, the children will be all right." Benjamin called over.

"If you say so." His words conveyed a disappointment which was betrayed by the shine in his eyes.

"Do you mock me?" Benjamin said firmly, then laughed. "This is the way of the New Era, my friends." Benjamin now spoke to everyone first in Tath, then in Haafian. "Such trust and openness are essential for our futures.....The children, bless them."

A round of applause and cheers followed, even from those steeped in traditional formality. This New Era, they realized, would have new approaches to most everything. Perhaps relinquishing the bowing and scraping which could go on for meaningless afternoons wasn't so bad after all.

Merott, a bulky Tath prince from the Central Tribe, chaffed at the changes. Enjoying a life of irresponsibility, of having a proud title which demanded nothing substantial in return, this was his tradition. His god without-a-name had intentionally stricken such privileges almost a year ago. That's when his anger began to burn, that's when his self-righteousness gained a stranglehold on his person. He kept quiet and to himself, he required assistance to return things to the past and he needed a plan. Long before the white-skinned devil, as Merott considered Benjamin, had the time to greet the Central Tribe's delegation, he dismissed himself from the celebration.

Later that evening, well past the time when even the musicians had packed up, Benjamin met with Sjura, Sarg and the late arriving Vosnob, in the sitting room of the Royal Suite. Benjamin had sent his over vigilant shadow, Bellah, off to spend time with his wife and family. Other retainers had been dismissed as well, allowing for that rare royal commodity named 'privacy'. At Queen Sjura's personal request, Kullia, queen of the northern tribes, also joined the group.

Gathered in comfortable padded wooden chairs about the fireplace Benjamin began the conversation. "I'm not quite sure I've ever seen such a commotion....I find it a bit frightening..." He spoke the first sentence in Tath, the second in Haafian.

Sarg peered around, everyone appeared to accept his remark, except for Kullia, who simply waited for Sjura to translate for her. Vosnob gently shook his head, unnerving as it was for him, the Tath women had proven records for competence. He smiled weakly, making his confession. "Benjamin, we've spoken of this before.... However, I'm still torn between what should be and the tradition I've always known.....I feel like an old prejudiced....." He spoke in Tath.

"And I, most honorable Vosnob, do feel exactly the same way..... You menfolk can be capable, I have seen that for myself,.....the old ways die hard, don't they, my friend." Queen Kullia reached over and held his hand, a movement which caught Vosnob off-guard. He found it embarrassingly delightful.

Benjamin laughed. "The touch of a woman you should never refuse." He smiled.

"But he'll probably fight it as much as my Sarg did." Sjura added as she smiled up at her husband.

"That' will be enough my dear....I'm sure we have other matters to consider this night."

"And what do you consider to be more important than personal relationships...." She quipped back, teasing and yet driving home her point quite well.

"Two points for the queen." Benjamin called out, delighted with the conversation. Then he sat back and tucked his long arms under his chin.

The others waited, a bit pensively. Benjamin spoke again. "Sjura has touched on the very subject I'm concerned about....personal relationships. If these don't exist in sizeable numbers between our two peoples, then all else we might endeavor will fail....I know this must come first.....But that might just be my personal perception." He paused, then looked over to Kullia. "What might you think?" He spoke in Tath.

Kullia thought that, somehow, her earlier touching was inappropriate. She dwelt, at present, in ways to apologize for her misbehavior. Benjamin's question caught her off-guard. After coughing a bit, and with a stern gaze from Sjura, she turned to the topic she last remembered. "Honored One, I humbly beg your forgiveness." She said pensively.

"My Tath isn't up to standards." Vosnob said flatly. "It is I who should apologize."

"No,.....I should not have touched you....Such is not proper."

Benjamin held back his laughter, recognizing Kullia's painful confession.

Vosnob answered without showing his true feelings. "Consider yourself forgiven, dear Kullia....You have done nothing wrong....For myself,...it's just been countless years since a woman has touched me.....I need to prepare myself for this New Era as much as you do."

That confession totally confused Kullia. Benjamin, to her, brought the New Era. He, the prophesied one, brought the Tath tribes together and made for this New Era. He alone, even though a male, was considered THE Leader for all of Tath. She stared at him in muted disbelief, a profound disbelief, a stare totally inappropriate for The Prophet.

Benjamin, thanks to a subtle nod from Sarg, broke into the conversation. "Kullia, you put more responsibility upon me than I shall claim .... Like it or not, I am just another person.....Yes, I am chosen for a special responsibility,...... ...... but that no more elevates me above anyone else than your queenship elevates you or........ Vosnob's rejuvenation elevates him...... or anyone else in this room......We all have issues to deal with.....Thank you for sharing your's." He reached out and took her hands, gently squeezed them and then let them go.

"Thank you." She murmured. "Now I realize that the reputation which preceded you is the truth." She said the words, but she realized it would be many days before mere words were integrated into her life. At the juncture, it was enough for her to let go of her infatuation, lest she unjustly impose upon Benjamin.

"And, is this not an excellent example of how we must learn to know each other?" Benjamin smiled. "And is this not what we must promote and establish between our two peoples?"

"It is, except...." Sjura began. "We have assumed that everyone wants what we want....Should we force this 'togetherness' upon our subjects or allow them to choose?"

"Good question." Sarg mumbled. This conversation took him far from the concrete world where he lived. As far as he was concerned, those who wanted to 'get together' simply needed permission to do so. There was more than enough room for any dissenters. "However, I am aware that many are not as open as we have been."

"You are a fine one to talk!" Sjura blurted out, somewhat amazed at her husband's sudden memory lapse. "You, who dared not touch me until the Holy One enlightened you!" She smiled broadly and laughed, igniting another discussion concerning Sarg's hidden history.

"Might I share my idea with all of you?" Benjamin asked knowing full well that the question was rhetorical, but he also wanted to refocus the discussion. He continued without much pause. "Paradise Valley, if that is the name for this place, sets forth an example for us, a divine example at that .....Taths, Yldans and Haafians all have their respective towns..........That shows an appreciation for our differences.....However, at the very center lies this castle, a unique symbol of the differences, the differences combined for the benefit of others...Such example is shown by the marriages."

"What are you reaching for?"

"Only this, Kullia." Benjamin smiled openly. "Let the example continue.....But let us set up other examples like it...."

"For instance, your new university city on the southern bank of Istellia Bay?" Vosnob arched his eyebrows.

"Yes,............But I also envision part of the Haafian fleet, accompanied by Istelles, circumnavigating the entire continent........There isn't even an accurate map for it anymore..."

"Let's think more in terms of four fleets, two headed north and two headed south on each coast.....Should get the job done much sooner." Sarg spoke well. The concreteness of an expedition he clearly understood.

"Accepted!" Benjamin grinned. "It is possible?"

That question launched the group into a conversation lasting until dawn broke. Their 'tentative final' result produced a merged fleet with all three peoples represented and one that should be ready to sail in four months. Delegating the responsibilities was the next issue, after everyone got some sleep, that is. Benjamin escorted Queen Kullia to her suite, feeding more than a few early morning risers enough gossip for a week.

"I refuse to take over." Yganak slapped the table with his open hand. "You ask too much." And he slapped the table again.

In the conference room, newly redecorated since the King's assassination, the Council of Three, augmented by the Church Hierarchy, continued their failing arguments. Yganak flatly refused to consider the nomination to be the next King.

"Give me sound theological reasons as to why Haafians cannot consider having a Queen?" Yganak hurled his question into the Church hierarchy, causing them as much anguish as they placed upon him with their insane idea. "And don't throw me the 'because' rationales......They are a pure waste of my time."

"Then," The head of the Church delegation asked, "What evidence do you require to convince you that you are the 'one' who ought to be nominated?" The thin man, dressed in the off-brown robes of a common monk asked. He, like the other clergy, had not yet encountered such obstinacy. Never had they dealt with a person so realistic.

"Quote to me from the Holiness Code......I'll not accept any arguments from tradition....traditions come and go....Nor will arguments from historical consistency help your cause...The Holy One, Blessed be His Name, has shown us the error of that line of thinking......Quote to me from the unchangeable Word..." Then Yganak sat back and drank from his tankard.

A few moments later, after the clerics finished their quiet conferencing, the old cleric turned towards Yganak; his face stressed. "Which specific questions do you require scriptural answers for?" His energy had dissipated but he remained determined. He pushed on. If someone with the wisdom and knowledge as Yganak might become King, many prayers would be answered, especially those of the Haafian royalty, many of whom now labeled themselves as serfs in order to have a livelihood.

"Just two." He replied. "One, where does it state that 'I' should be the next King?" The word 'I' carried much weight. "Two, where it is specifically mentioned that there cannot be a Queen?"

"You aren't serious?" Jabbi brought his booted feet to the floor, almost laughing.

"I'm as serious as ever." Yganak shot back. "If the Taths have Queens to rule over their tribes, what prevents us from doing the same?... Why should one-half of the population be denied the chance to serve their country?"

"I assume then," Etan lightly challenged, "That if the Holiness Code permits women to be considered---that you all ready have someone 'special' in mind?"

"Indeed."

Etan laughed until he saw the Captain puffing nervously on his pipe. The anxious clerics returned to their huddle, determined to answer Yganak. The so-called Council of Three, designated administrators for the late King, waited patiently. The day's end was coming soon; their conference had begun at daybreak. Midnight was their deadline in reaching a decision, so spoke the High Council. Furthermore, the Tath delegation awaited their decision. Only then, with royalty of equal ranks available, could international agreements actually be initiated. The problem lurking large lay in the fact that the two peoples had all ready begun their own negotiations in terms of trade, sharing information, knowledge and travel. Within another month, whatever the official government thought correct for dealings with Tath, would not matter.

Yganak was more than aware of these pressing international dynamics. He'd been deliberately blocking any progress since this official delegation began to pester him almost three weeks ago, as the Haafians had begun to record time. To his mind, which he believed to be set squarely upon the Holiness Code, the King's role was to promote the welfare of the people, not stand in their way. In the events at Paradise Valley as well as the commerce developing in the Istellia Bay, Yganak saw the handiwork of the Holy One. He was also quite impressed about the role of women in Tath, and felt deflated when he realized the wastefulness of the present Haafian policies. Thus he calculated to use the time to his advantage. He was on the verge of securing the needful answers. He took another long drink from his tankard.

"You're playing this right to the line." Etan commented as the clerics worked furiously on the answers.

"No." Yganak placed his tankard on the polished wooden table. "I'm more inclined to believe that I'm pushing for the truth. We have too much at stake to make any mistakes....The Holy One is with us, He's made changes....We err if we refuse to incorporate all the resent events into these deliberations."

With comments such as these, the clerics pushed on, believing the potential to promote a sincere believer to the throne was within their grasp. They ached for a King serve their purposes. This now included the sending of priests to Tath to convert the heathens there. Ever since Tath made itself known, the Church made her intentions known. She had no intention of putting up with some nameless god.

The Council of Three, as did most of Haaf, knew well of these future intentions. There was no unanimous opinion on the subject except within the Church. Yet, even there, caution was called for as well as restraint. Issues acknowledging the roles of the faith versus its separation from Haafian culture had yet to be explored. This included the issue of the position of women--the very issue Yganak demanded an answer for.

"We have arrived at some conclusions." A monk who might easily be Oros' double stated flatly.

Chairs slid about the wooden table in preparation for the Church's conclusions. One way or another, the stalemate would soon be over.

The head cleric began. "There is nothing in the Holiness Code that announces, 'Yganak shall be the next King.'" The cleric smiled at the obvious.

"So, I have no scriptural authorization to become King...Nor do you have the prerogative to deliberately usher me to the throne."

"That is true." Replied the rotund priest.

"And you,.....then....... have lost your leverage to push me in that direction." Yganak's forceful remark tweaked a weak smile from the clerics, a smile which allowed their unhidden design to crumble of itself. "And the answer for the second question?"

"The Holiness Code is silent on the issue of women becoming queens."

"You can do better than that." The so-called candidate's eyebrows knitted. He wasn't amused. "Do the scriptures prohibit women from having positions of leadership?"

"The Holiness Code is silent on that point as well."

"Then justify considering only a man for the top position of leadership for Haaf?" He clomped his big boney feet on the table, further angering the clerics.

"See here." Demanded the head cleric. "You push us too far. There is wisdom in the traditions which have carried us this far......You cannot demands we abandon them."

"Sounds more like you have abandoned the Code." Jabbi suggested.

"I agree." Added Yganak. "This tradition, with the exception of our last King, saw a parade of countless lackey's doing little to benefit Haaf's people..........Now, once the prominence of a legitimate King has been established, you want to enforce an unsubstantiated policy."

"No, no,........ not at all." The old priest backed off Yganak's strongly worded opinion. "It's just that one good King should follow another."

"But that has nothing to do with the bottom line for our society, namely.. .obedience to the Holiness Code.......Now answer my second question."

The fat priest pulled out a battered scroll, unrolling it as he spoke. "This is my personal copy." He explained. Then his eyes found the lines he wanted. "Allow me to read for you." He paused for his breath then read. "From the Holiness Code, from the Creation of people......."Then, in His wisdom, after all other creations had been accomplished and after blessing them so that they might be beneficial for what was yet to be accomplished, the Creator took matter from ground and molded it and blew His breath into it. Thus He did create people, man and woman, after His image...... And both were placed into His creation to rule over it in wisdom and obedience to the Creator's will." The rotund cleric paused again. "At the beginning, the Creator did not specify either man or woman as being more......anything...."

"Exactly my point!" Yganak exclaimed. "And it seems the Taths know this better than we do."

A number of eyes immediately studied the stone floor. Although Yganak clearly understood their provisions for evangelizing Tath, his knowledge of such thoroughly embarrassed them. Until one knew what actually was supposed to be, one certainly could not export the faith to another country.

"But," Countered another priest. "The Taths refuse to allow men into places or positions of authority......I see little difference."

"And you have not heard the last reports from Sarg." Etan replied.

"So what."

"Sarg reports that the Tath god, who continually refuses to yield his name, did command the Central Tribe to consider ALL persons as candidates for heading the tribes.....including men."

Jabbi entered the rapidly expanding fray, hoping to deflect the building differences into a more productive direction: finding a new leader for Haaf. "Bottom line then, if,...if.... I hear you correctly," He nodded off towards the Churchmen. "Is that there are no God-given barriers preventing a woman from taking the throne of Haaf.......... ....There is nothing in the Holiness Code specifically preventing Haafian women from assuming positions of governmental leadership." And then he laughed. "Just like Brey now commanding a full regiment of Light Stripers and other women now in training." Jabbi looked round about at their stressed out countenances. "The precedent is all ready firmly established... ....And the Holy One has yet to inform us that such is an error. ....Am I not correct?"

For an emotional eternity, silence reigned about the table. The clerics fumbled with their robes and papers, appearing to be uninvolved, detached. The Council of Three threw twisted smiles at each other, trying to avoid Yganak's gaze. They puzzled as to what he planned next. The door was open to him.

"Knowing you for a long time, Yganak, I still believe that you would make a wonderful King."

"I sincerely thank you for your complement, my friend....And I apologize for pushing the issues.....I simply want Haaf to be doing the right thing.......for the right reason.........You do understand?"

"I understand...." The old cleric announced in understated tones. "We all need to heed our baseline...."

"Then, you obviously have something.....or.....someone in mind." Etan looked Yganak squarely in the eyes.

"This is true?" Exclaimed, more than asked, the fat priest.

"Yes." And he said no more, deliberately.

"Go on." Commanded Jabbi and the old priest together.

"The tavern keeper's wife......Her name is Ilty.....I suggest we talk with her about being Queen of Haaf." And he finished off the last drop of tea in his tankard.

High above the bright waters of Buda Lake, Taert found, finally, refuge from the overly-curious onlookers at the monastery. For weeks he found himself confined between towering walls that connected immense trees together. He could hardly see the sky at times. This whole mountain territory entrapped his soul. There was no room to spread out his mind, his spirit. Today, being that Kinanna shared in another translating conference, he and the other Taths went fishing. Flying and diving down over the cool waters refreshed his spirit and renewed his faith. A smile, which began as a crooked line between his lips, now included his entire face. His charge, Kinanna, might find life at the monastery less than miserable, but not Taert. Even the Istelles preferred the open spaces of the plains and the skies.

Later that day, they landed outside a fishing village on the eastern shore of Buda Lake. Here the forests had long ago given way to pasture land, not too unlike the steppes of Tath. As expected, the Istelles immediately drew a large crowd. Once again Taert and his fellow Taths were immersed in explaining the immense birds to the locals who worshipped them. Taert listened to their exaggerated tales without smiling. He recognized some stories had their origin in the final battles on the northern plains of Haaf.

Those he left as embellished as he heard them. Others, such as the Istelles breathing fire, he instantly corrected, much to the dismay of the villagers.

As he and the other Taths spoke to the people, a lavishly decorated waggon bumped down the cobblestone street. It stopped not far from where the Istelles were resting. Upon its stopping, more than a few villagers disappeared, causing Taert to speculate.

The driver opened the waggon's door. Two extravagantly dressed Haafians appeared. Those still gathered separated before the couple, bowing all the while. Taert stood firm, waiting for the couple to approach. The gentleman violently waved a thick walking stick with which he attempted to intimidate Taert.

Unexpectedly, Taert grabbed the stick and broke it over his knee. The man pulled back, fearful, yet defiant.

"What do you mean by landing on my property without my permission?" He angrily demanded of Taert and his friends. The pot-bellied man doffed his tall hat, waving it furiously, further proclaiming the indignity he suffered from the Istelles' unwarranted invasion.

Taert looked about, the talkative villagers appeared fearful, even more so because of Taert's defensive action. The arrogant Haafian began the fight, Taert would defend himself. His friends stood to his sides, while the driver and two coachmen stood behind the dignitaries.

"Are you going to answer me or not?" He shouted as if Taert were deaf.

"Only if you answer me first." Taert calmly stood his ground. This sounded too much like the fights over pasture boundaries back home.

"You are not in charge here!.....I am."

"And just who do you think you are?"

Snickers arose from those gathered and the man's wife whispered in her husband's ear. His composure quickly changed.

"I am Baron of Leddu, magistrate of this village and its owner as well..... These fields and all that is on them belong's to me." He seemed quite pleased with his display. His self-serving pomposity caused Taert to gag.

Unsure of the meaning of 'Baron', Taert spoke quietly with his friends. They began laughing.

"What is so funny!......How dare you laugh at me!"

"Does not royalty, even in Haaf, have rankings?" Taert asked as innocently as possible as he turned to the Baron.

"Indeed....That's is why these 'serfs' bow to me." He sneered.

"So we thought as well......Then, good Baron of Leddu, bow to us."

The deep brown face went vivid white. "I bow to no foreigners!" He took another deep breath. "And I bow to no commoners!"

"I accept the foreigner part.....But we are all Princes........ Have you forgotten your manners?" Taert baited the Baron.

"Prove you are who you claim." The baron's over-dressed wife squeaked out, angrily flashing her eyebrows.

"Perhaps you ought to go first, my lady....After all, you began this trouble.....Not the villagers nor the three of us."

"You," The Baron started, his strained faced breached. "Began the problem when you landed on MY land."

Taert's friend looked puzzled and spoke. "Are you then the Holy One of the Haafians?"

Laughter rang from the crowd this time, their timidity tossed to the wind. Those who had run off, quietly returned. This free entertainment was too good to miss. Not often was the Baron confronted, let alone bested.

"I am not the Holy One.....I am a baron."

"Then you still need to bow to us.....Let's get this stupidity over so we can get to the real issue."

"And what might that be?" The Baron cautiously asked, fully aware that everyone was watching him closely. If he lost to these strangers, then his authority over the serfs would be in jeopardy as well.

"How much you owe us for breathing our air." Taert said quietly. The crowd's laughter completely drowned out the Baron's response.

"If you who can only walk on land can charge for it, then we who both walk and fly can charge for the use of the air."

"I never heard of such a thing." The Baron's wife rasped in her squelchy voice. "Take them prisoner!" She shouted to the coachmen.

"Stay your place." Taert warned.

"Are you slimy blueskinned bastards threatening me?" The Baron edged Taert on, exploiting the opportunity to win.

"I'll accept blueskinned, for that is how god chose to make me.. ...... But you shall not be forgiven of slandering my parents..." Taert, for the first time, raised his accented voice.

The villagers quieted instantly, awaiting the Baron's orders to be carried out. Taert had gone too far. "I am not a bastard......I expect you to apologize promptly." Taert continued. He stared at the Baron, eye-to-eye at four paces.

"I apologize to no one....." The Baron gritted out between clenched teeth. "....you blueskinned bastard."

Taert stepped forward and tumbled the Baron with a swift backhanded slap. He looked up, amazed and uncomprehending what happened. After shaking his head and wiping his bleeding lip on his jacket, he cursed and then yelled. "Arrest these three!......Their insolence shall not go unpunished!..."

"Do not come any closer." Taert warned the shaking coachmen once again.

Not really wishing to arrest the Taths, the coachmen obeyed. The villagers gasped, a mixture of awe and horror. While they sided with the Taths, they now knew their hanging would soon arrive. The Haafians' looks of pity and sorrowfulness collided with the Taths' calm determination.

"You have one breath----as you say---to apologize." Taert spoke to the slowly rising Baron.

The Haafian kept his arm out to protect himself from another slap. "You dare not threaten me.....It's against law!" The Baron shouted.

"Insulting my parents is also against the law!................I strongly suggest you apologize." Taert's friends signaled the Istelles with hand motions even as he spoke.

"What if....if..... I refuse?" He gloated through his swelling lip, pain reflected in his uneven gaze. "What will you do?" He came across like a thoroughly frightened bully. "What will you do?" He repeated with more than a hint of vindictiveness.

"Just this." Taert moved his hand to the right.

His Istelle, followed by the other two, moved forward, resting some ten paces behind the pretentious Baron and his wife. He motioned once again and the Baron's elaborately decorated waggon burst into thousands of pieces as the Istelle stepped on it. The six hitched Stripers took off at a gallop. The driver and coachmen ran after them, leaving the Baron and his wife standing alone, the gigantic Istelles hovering over them.

"You still have the opportunity to apologize for slandering my parents.....I suggest you push the issue no further."

The cringing Baron glanced upwards. The curious Istelle brought his head low. The Baron screamed and sprawled himself on the ground, next to his quivering wife. He blabbered about having mercy, that the bird should not eat him....He never mentioned his wife.

"Stand up, you coward." Taert's friend demanded. "Or I'll tell him to eat you."

In a twinkling, the Baron of Leddu and his wife stood on their trembling feet.

"I want my apology."

Recognizing he had no backup and realizing his true self had been exposed to the villagers, the Baron began, choking on every single syllable. "I.. did.. not.. mean.. to.. insult.. those.. who.. brought.. you.. into.. this.. world.." The last word was almost too faint to hear.

"I shall accept your apology,...Baron of Leddu,...but on this condition.... if you ever insult my parents again, you shall meet them face-to-face.....It is a seven day flight from here.... And you will dangle from the Istelle's talons until we arrive......... ....Do I make myself understood?"

The Baron slowly nodded his head, a handkerchief covered his bloodied lip. Inside he raged wildly at his defeat, at his loss of his power over the villagers, at his embarrassment before them and these damn blueskinned bastards. Outside, difficult at it was, he kept a much cooler head and mouth. The Baron loved his life. "I ...... understand.......I....do......." He slowly muttered, desperately attempting to sound sincere.

"Then you need not bow to us....I grant you permission to leave." Taert said.

The villagers remained quiet, stunned from what they witnessed, until well after the Baron and his wife walked through town and up the rise to his mansion. Then, thunderous applause broke out, counterpointed with shouts and joyous laughter. The villagers surrounded the trio and carried them to the nearest tavern. An impromptu celebration began.

The three unexpectedly found themselves seated at a table which had been placed on a raised stage-like platform. Definitely unsure of what the proper Haafian thing to do at this point, Taert called to a young lady who had stood in the front of the crowd ever since the Istelles landed.

"My Lady, might I have a word with you."

Due to the commotion, and Taert not knowing her name, the young lady did not respond. Taert reached out and touched her shoulder. She jumped, startled.

"My Lady," Taert spoke in his best Haafian. "We need some assistance."

Even above the hubbub of the joyous villagers, she heard him, but her face looked puzzled.

Over the din, Taert tried to explain. "Please, we do not know your ways...your traditions ......Will you help us?" His face quickly lined itself with marks of desperation when she did not acknowledge him. "Will you help us?........We do not wish to gain any more enemies."

With a big step up to the platform, the lady stood by their table. "Good

Sirs from Tath," She smiled brightly. "You've made more friends here today in Leddu than I can hardly count......You are to be congratulated for putting the cowardly bully in his place...... When all the other nobles left to join the New Knights, his heart didn't work right....He was forever fainting away." Her utter disgust clung to each and every word.

The crowd quieted while she spoke, then applauded her defining speech. Never a better time than now to keep the Baron in his rightful place--his mansion--and out of everywhere else. Such was the opinion of the balding tavern keeper, who dropped another round of ale before the trio.

"He's a pain, backed up by the foul thugs he hires." The young lady added as she accepted a chair offered by Taert.

"Will they be coming here?"

"Don't be so nervous....Even his brainless bodyguard knows that to touch any of you....Well,... they'll probably share the same fate as the Baron's waggon."

"This is a very poor beginning for us." Taert said to his friends and the young lady. The worry which shone from his eyes was magnified by his knitted brows. He turned directly to the young lady. "We began this morning, flying from the monastery, to get some fresh air and see open spaces again..... We did not come to stir up trouble for....."

"You've stirred up nothing that didn't all ready exist." She paused, flushed a bit. "I'm... sorry..." She spoke with downcast eyes. "We haven't been properly introduced.....But you have met my father." She smiled prettily.

The three Taths stood and bowed as they introduced themselves. The villagers applauded each one. The young lady, with her protective father, the tavern keeper, standing directly behind her introduced herself. Leye was her formal name. She curtsied very low, a borderline teasing. Her father, large hand on her shoulder, pulled her up quickly. He presented her with a knowing scowl then left to wait on other customers. Leye returned to her seat at the Tath's table.

"Shall we continue?" Leye demanded more than asked.

In Haaf, a strong-willed woman usually sent men in the opposite direction. Taert and his friends moved their chairs closer, feeling at home, comfortable, with the situation. This, in turn, caused Leye some anxiousness; perhaps Father's scowl wasn't so protective after all.

"That man....is your husband?"

Leye turned white, then blushed, caught off-guard by Taert's question turned compliment. She always thought she looked older.

"Forgive me...Lee....I have said something wrong..."

"The name is Leye." She said smiling. "That man was my father." She explained in such a way that her words politely told Taert of his mistake. "This tavern is his establishment."

"This is different, this tavern, is all new to us....We have homes--yurts--that move with us as we travel the steppes."

Leye stared at Taert with a mixture of disbelief and wonder, rumors concerning the Taths had been circulating for months. Now she had the opportunity to ascertain their truthfulness. She started asking when Taert's friend interrupted, tapping him on the shoulder.

"Remember to stay on the topic..... ...This is not a social gathering." He spoke in Tath.

Taert wasn't planning on ruining a good beginning between the Taths and the Haafians. Much the opposite had been his intention, ever since the scouting expedition with Brey and Vauk. He saw a future which allowed him--indeed, demanded of him--to make the best of his abilities. This New Era opened a wondrous future for the princes of Tath. Thus, whatever it took, that breech of broken etiquette and protocol between himself and the Baron of Leddu, had to be repaired as quickly as possible.

"Le-ye," Taert came about to look her in the face. "Without wanting to, we have created a disturbance between your Baron and the three of us....We must correct this as quickly as possible."

"The Baron of lead," She supplied the cynicism on her own. "Has few friends. He treats us like we are dirt. He treated you, wondrous famous princes from another country, as if you were nothing...I believe 'lead' has received proper recompense....."

"But that is not an issue for us, Lady Le-ye......How it is proper to make amends with the Baron?"

She blushed at the sound of royalty mixed with her name. She also found it more than a bit difficult to stay on the topic. In her fantasy, Leye wanted nothing less than to fly away with Taert on his Istelle. She'd come back a princess and set her people free from the Baron. She always wanted to be famous. A hand on her shoulder brought her back to reality.

"Leye, please answer the prince's question afore he thinks you've gone deaf." The stern but gentle voice was that of the tavern keeper. Father stood behind his daughter. "In spite of your intentions, don't count on the Baron taking a liking to any of you....In front of all of us villagers, you showed him to be incompetent. ....The only thing he responds to is power, something you..." He laughed boldly. "You have more than he does......That bird of yours ruined his toy.... He'll have you arrested for such, I'm afraid."

"Then,...its time we are leaving." Taert strongly suggested to the others. He pulled a pouch from tunic and took out a handful of glittering stones: diamonds. "Perhaps a few of these will buy him a new waggon.....Will you see to it?" Taert questioned the wildly staring tavern keeper.

"Yes....yes....I know who to contact for you." Diamonds were rare, extremely rare; the tavern keeper struggled to keep his composure. He grabbed for the stones before anyone else noticed. Taert, the tavern keeper instantly realized, had no idea of the value of diamonds in Haaf. The bag which Taert so casually flung about would easily buy the entire town three times over. "Keep the stones well-hidden, they are more valuable than you can understand." He whispered.

Taert caught on quickly. "Thank you." He fastened the pouch to his tunic. "Is there a safe way to change these into your money?"

"Yes....And we will handle the details for you." He handed Taert all but one small diamond. "This one will buy him a waggon such as has never been seen." He laughed again. "You kindly add insult upon the Baron's injury....With such a new waggon, you'll be forever in his mind.....He has too much greediness to deny himself such an expensive toy......" He got quieter and leaned over, close to Taert's shoulder. "You Tath's certainly have brought about a New Era.....Thank the Holy One."

"And this is for your hospitality." Without looking at the tavern keeper, Taert shoved a few more diamonds into his hands and stood up. "Hopefully we will return tomorrow....If Kinanna permits, that is."

"And just who is this Kin....." Leye never finished her sentence.

The Baron's guards surrounded Taert's table the moment the trio stood to leave. Their swords were drawn. They came for revenge, not justice. Taert ignored them, but sent signs to his companions: they were ready.

The tavern keeper stood by the trio. "There will be no fighting in my establishment!" He thundered at the handful of guards.

"Then your guests will come quietly?"

"My guests are free to stay as long as they so desire...This is my property....You are trespassing..."

As he spoke, women and children hastily exited the tavern. The men however, formed a circle behind the guards. These villagers recognized their opportunity to carve more power away from the contemptible Baron. They prepared themselves for a fight.

"Don't even think about it!" The head guard yelled at the men as he turned around.

"There's not much to think about.....Unless you want to leave...And we're not about to let that happen...."

The threat caused the guard to laugh, a boisterous disdainful laugh. "You worms neither have the authority nor the desire to stop us from taking these three to the Baron.....Unless, that is, you wish to accompany them." He sneered.

His men sneered. The villagers stood their ground; their circle tightened. The guards became noticeably jittery. No one moved; heavy nervous, anxious breathing filled the stilled atmosphere. Time passed without notice.

"Gentlemen," Taert spoke directly to the Baron's guards. "Would you rather work for a Baron or a Prince?"

The people, including the guards, looked at each other, puzzled at Taert's suggestion and confused as to what the answer for the Prince as employer might actually entail.

"We are the Baron's guard." The head guard spoke firmly when he finally answered. His slanted eyes narrowed to slits as he stared intently at Taert, not trusting him.

"What about being the Prince's guard?" Taert questioned the rest of the Baron's guard.

Their leader started speaking, but was interrupted by talking among his patrol. Obvious to everyone gathered, these men were not as solidly in the Baron's employment as their leader. Taert seized the moment by holding up a small diamond, one barely large enough to cast a rainbow on the table. All eyes instantly focused upon it. Eyes of greed, eyes of awe, eyes of wonderment, eyes more than willing to gain new employment.

"I pay one of these," Taert said as he held up the diamond for everyone to see. "Every month to my guards........But not just anyone can be counted among my guards....I have extremely high standards."

The guards rudely and eagerly butted in front of their leader, straining to get a better look at the diamond. Taert allowed them to study it, from a distance, then placed it back in his tunic.

"What needs we to do before we can work for you, Prince?" The raggedly guard bowed his head. Not necessarily to the Prince, but in deference to the wages the Prince paid.

"I only require three guards at this time."

A vast empty gaze shot across the guard's face, then that gaze filled with greed. Without thinking twice, he turned and plunged his sword through his former leader's chest. A deadly ruckus began as the troopers assailed each other, striving to be one of the last three. With another motion, Taert signed his companions 'time to leave'. Taert, at the last moment, turned his head, calling to the tavern keeper, "Get these people out before they get hurt....And keep Leye safe.......Very safe."

The young lady smiled up at Taert even as her father hauled her off the platform. A few more bodies piled up as the villagers ran for the door. Taert and his friends jumped through the nearby window. Shards of glass bloodied them and pricked their skin, but not enough to prevent their escape.

Moments later they were secure--airborne--flying into the darkening sky on their way to the monastery and a reporting to Kinanna. Buda Lake, dark green and tranquil, occasionally flashed reflections of the double moons. Even so, Taert couldn't relax. He'd found much more than transient respite from the monastery; he'd found a young lady he knew he'd return for: Leye's brown oval face and her flashing slanted eyes were permanently etched upon his mind.

The hour of midnight, after the lights from the double moons no longer caused shadows on the ground, the Baron of Leddu and his whimpering wife rose from their bed. Quietly they descended from the fourth floor into the basement, deliberately avoiding servants who slept soundly in their small rooms. At the basement entrance they anxiously waited. Not long afterwards, a soft knock sounded and a bloodied guard entered, carrying their dead leader.

Earlier, the guard brought the dismal news of their meeting with Taert. The enraged Baron instantly recognized the brilliant slyness of Taert's diversion. He was intrigued by Taert's divide and conquer technique and by how that diversionary tactic allowed the villagers and Taert to escape unharmed. The deaths of his guards meant little. After learning about the diamonds, the Baron realized he had to move carefully. He could not satiate his greed if Taert returned. This meant dealing politely with the tavern keeper and his daughter as well. This utterly nauseated him. He did not enjoy pretending to be nice to get what he wanted. This problem he shared with his wife. Her whimpering derived from pandering to 'inferiors'. They severely offended her royal sensibilities.

Once in the basement, the Baron unlocked a small wooden door built into the outer wall of the basement. He lit a torch and the three descended another flight of stairs. The rats scurried away, incensed by this invasion of their domain. And the smoldering torch sizzled at it burnt through the heavy cobwebs hanging from the low damp ceiling. After trudging through a winding tunnel, one wet and dripping with an oozing slime, the Baron stopped to unlock another door. This solitary wooden door, refused to move at first; its rusty hinges being unused for almost a year. Angrily, the Baron kicked at the door. It gave way, slowly swinging inward upon a sparsely decorated dry chamber. The vile stench of evil floated towards the three as they entered. Silently, the Baron lit torches spaced evenly about the circular room as the guard ungraciously dumped the leader's corpse on the floor.

In continued silence, the Baron's wife reverently dusted off the blackened altar. The charred debris from the previous sacrifices dropped to the floor, from whence it was swept down the drain hole. Prior to the Baron lighting the black candle mounted just under an engraving of the flying dragon, the three stripped naked. Only then, when fully exposed to each other and their god Ashuwa, were they properly prepared to call upon his name as they offered him the burnt body of one of his devoted followers.

With the corpse now spread-eagle upon the altar, the Baron's wife deftly decapitated it and handed the dripping head to her husband. She then cut off each extremity and piled them on the corpse's chest. Finally, as the sticky blood coated the altar's sides and ran down upon the stone floor, the Baron's wife retrieved the head and balanced it on top the corpse's limbs. The guard lit another candle and placed in a large hole carved in the altar just beneath the sickening sacrifice.

Still in complete silence, the three stood back from the hideous altar forming a circle, their bloody hands connecting. Their obscene dance, designed to beckon the great Ashuwa, began in earnest: four steps to the right, clutch the crotch to the left, four steps to the left, clutch the to right, two steps back, and two steps back in. The dance pattern repeated itself endlessly, finishing only after each experienced an orgasm, only after each was fully covered with the blood from the head guard, only after they neared a state of exhaustion produced by their repetitive repulsive dance.

Through a pinpoint hole in the ghastly chamber's ceiling, they dimly recognized that the dawn had broken. Simultaneously, they dropped to their knees, touched their foreheads to the sticky, wretched smelling floor and began chanting their prayer for Ashuwa's visitation and revenge. Though thoroughly sore, hungry and now shivering in the dampness of the chamber, until darkness fell again, they had no other choice than to supplicate Ashuwa. Without his divine assistance, the Baron's tyrannical reign would come to an abrupt ending. So they pleaded, chanting the same words repeatedly, until they no longer comprehended their own mouthings. "Almighty Ashuwa, guardian of your faithful, come to us, destroy those who hate You. Bring us Your divine blessings."

Ashuwa paid no attention to his devotees. He refused to acknowledge the trios supplication: he had a few followers left. Yet here existed his chance to regain strength, to rise from his water infested volcano to prominence once again. Here too was the opportunity to reclaim a territory for himself, had he the gumption to follow the prayers to their source. But Ashuwa contentedly did nothing; he enjoyed his self-imposed captivity in the volcano, wallowing in self-pity as he enviously watched the Kingdoms of the New Era commence before him, each occupying a portion of his former domain.

As evening finally settled in, Ashuwa sensed something more than ordinary mindless praying. The smell of burnt Haafian flesh accompanied the prayers. This wondrous smell, this odor of power, this essence of true sacrifice, immediately circumscribed his habitual inaction. He smiled to himself, recognizing true devotion, true devotees to be exact. They had life, life he required in order to grow in strength and in power. Distant but powerful memories of revenge floated back into his thoughts, supplying him motivation.

Indignation flooded through his meagerly being: a character insignificant enough for birds to ignore, and so transparent as to be almost invisible. He became utterly enraged, for the Holy One, in placing the 'truth penalty' upon him caused the gates of Hell to slam shut. The souls of the damned had their own kingdom. He no longer could steal souls by lying about being the ruler of Hell. The Righteous Judge, the Holy One, actually ruled Heaven and Hell. Ashuwa screamed and ranted. His divine punishment declared him more impotent than ever before. Still, the whiff of burnt flesh, Haafian flesh, demanded that he must respond.

The black candle sputtered as it desperately attempted to grasp at whatever wax drippings still remained. It doggedly fought for its own life. An ungodly stench, from slowly roasting Haafian flesh, clogged the worshippers' locked chamber. The depraved participants, now slightly less than semiconscious, sprawled across the bloodied floor. They had received nothing for their faithful efforts. Ashuwa sent them nothing.

Later, Ashuwa, clothed in his meager spirit, arrived to find his devotees totally fatigued, unable to recognize him. As much as this grieved him, he felt the hurtful truth, his size precluded everyone from seeing him. In all his wondrous power and grandeur, most spiders surpassed him in size and certainly in power. Thus, he did not resist the opportunity which lay directly in front of him. Three Haafians who willingly gave their souls to him. He began with the smallest, the baron's whimpering wife. Slowly he stretched himself about her mouth and nose, suffocating her. She never moved, never realized her life was terminated until Ashuwa reached forth and grabbed her departing soul. She, in a terrible panic, one in which the reality of her death and her non-existent future simultaneously came together, screamed but once. Then Ashuwa happily dined on her damned soul.

Gaining considerably in size and power, Ashuwa continued dining, murdering the guard and the Baron in the same manner. While a meal of three damned souls hardly gave him any semblance of his former self, at least he wasn't the hopeless indifferent moron he used to be. Self-righteous pride burgeoned within him. He sensed a few other followers in the village. Their souls would be relinquished to him before morning.

Wanting to be remembered for his visitation, Ashuwa blew raggedy fire into the tunnel and into the mansion. The mansion slowly began to light up the dark dawn. Furiously it burnt to the ground, the heat being too intense for the servants to do little more than to save themselves. The villagers watched in astonished awe, from a safe distance, both unable and not willing to assist the Baron. Murmurs of the Holy One's righteous judgement flowed through most the crowd. The local priest, disinclined to bless any tragedy, slipped away to prayer before the villagers set upon him for an interpretation. The tavern keeper and his daughter, Leye, felt restless, rather uneasy, as they watched the conflagration. Were the three Taths involved? For now, and until Taert returned, if ever, these thoughts remained locked away in their minds.

Even before the Baron's servants woke to the raging flames and smoke, Ashuwa had all ready visited--and dined--on his few local followers. With a total of six souls inside him, he had enough strength to detect other followers in Haaf. Though used to more than a hundred thousand souls inside him, the sense of returning to omnipotence motivated him: Ashuwa had countless scores to settle.

Planning his conquering of the nameless god, of Sarg and Vosnob and of the damnable Holy One, occupied his time as he scoured Haaf for further dining. A jubilant Ashuwa darted about the Haafian countryside, leaving a series of random deaths in his wake. As he correctly projected, no one had any hint of his return and of his rapid recovery of strength. But, his appearance was still that of a phantom, small and too wispy to be taken seriously. Ashuwa required more souls, tens of thousands more souls before he'd be capable of wreaking revenge upon certain assorted imbeciles.

After an extended respite above the village, floating about, listening to the local gossip, Ashuwa realized more food lay north of Haaf. Intently he listened to the stories of the three Taths who came to visit, then, after an altercation with the Baron, quickly departed. At that juncture Ashuwa realized the Baron called him not to worship him, but to use him to avenge his personal humiliation. Had he been able to, the damned one would have shot fire from his mouth, such was the extent of his anger at being duped. However the Baron's soul more than made up for his lack of respect for his god.

The tasty power provoking thought lingered in Ashuwa's brain: the Taths. Surely the stupid clown-faced god didn't eliminate all of his worshippers in the Central Tribe? Or did he? Perhaps he had become more thorough? Or, did brainless one continue suffering from the vile weakness of compassion, of allowing room for failure, and thus--he could have puked--forgiveness?

Days later Ashuwa roamed through the yurts of the Central Tribe. The most significant, as well as the most aggravating thing he discovered was the inordinate amount of discussion over who should become their next ruler. Even those he recognized as 'his' were involved, raising his anger once again. These people had no business finding another ruler. They still had the Almighty Ashuwa. To Ashuwa, this deliberate treason provided another rationale for dining on their souls. Two reasons for eating their souls suited him much better than one.

In future years the day was incorrectly labeled as 'the day hearts stopped'. Throughout the small clusters of yurts which dotted the high steppes of central Tath, men and women, most hard at work, simply fell over, dead. The best which was conjectured was that, for some inexplicable reason or reasons, their hearts just refused to move anymore. The horrid disfigurements of the stricken Taths firmly imbedded itself in the tribe's memory. For a reason attributed to their nameless god, not one potential candidate for ruler died that day.

That day Ashuwa feasted extremely well, having added some two hundred souls to the insatiable pit he called 'belly'. He enjoyed himself for the first time since his battle with the nameless god. Stretching out, he rested without a care, floating on the dark thunderheads high above the broad steppe. A wicked smile encased his face as he dreamed of his future revenge.

Without warning, the god-without-a-name silently appeared behind Ashuwa. Before he realized anything, Ashuwa found himself in that realm beyond time, beyond creation, that very realm where he met defeat from one who refused to fight him. With all the strength he mustered, the nameless one encapsulated the realm within an impervious invisible sphere. Then he threw the sphere far beyond all boundaries, bordering the frightening life-stifling territory of 'nowhere'.

Ashuwa's frantic ragings echoed incessantly, bouncing off the sphere's impenetrable walls. Nevertheless, he continued raging, recognizing his own 'lostness', a 'lostness' due to his own irresponsibility. Once again, the painful truth tore into his soul.

A rainbow encased god without-a-name returned to the meeting of the Central Tribe. A broad smile engulfed his entire face. His followers believed it showed his happiness. A decision concerning the next monarch was ready. The nameless one had another reason.

Benjamin deliberately called upon Queen Kullia during the next few days. Together they went for long flights on her Istelle and picnicked in out-of-the-way places. Throughout the castle flew hundreds of rumors, each moving faster than the previous one. The Queen and Benjamin returned from lunch on their fifth day to a meeting containing more gossip than substance.

Queen Kullia's initial remark canceled every possible rumor. It also precluded others being constructed. "Our oral traditions, those given by the god-without-a-name," Kullia spoke in Tath. "Do predict the coming of a prophet........However, these same traditions we rightly honor and respect add one significant dimension, presently missing, to the Prophets' identity.....That is, he must be like every other honorable man."

Every Tath within earshot went white, then paled to a reddish as they soberly considered exactly what the Queen of the Northern Tribes communicated. On the other hand, the Haafians, including Vosnob, Sarg, Vauk and Brey were but mystified by this other part of the Tath culture. The blank look covering Benjamin's lean face indicated he too required more information. Obviously, something of great significance just transpired, something which his stomach told him he was intimately involved. Yet he was baffled. However, Sjura smiled approvingly at Kullia and nodded.

Queen Kullia changed languages as she discreetly smiled at Benjamin. "An honorable man in· Tath is a married man." She explained before crossing the polished marble floor to stand next to Benjamin.

Benjamin sat down quickly as the mystery rapidly unraveled in front of him. The others stared at Kullia, not quite believing her statement and wrestling with its immediate implications: Benjamin? Benjamin as husband-to-be?

As if anticipating the thoughts of those gathered, Queen Kullia extended her hands to Benjamin. He accepted her blue hands. "Will you have me for your wife?" She quietly asked Benjamin.

Benjamin sat up, straight, gathering her hands to his lips, he kissed them. Tears fell upon her hands--his tears. Benjamin stood and embraced her and softly cried. "I could never refuse you anything." He quietly whispered to her.

Thunderous applause greeted Benjamin's supposedly whispered words. The two spun about, a bit embarrassed, more than a bit relieved. Benjamin's emptiness suddenly died as his prayer came true. Someone special did love him, someone very special to him wanted him as a husband. Kullia beamed as never before, until Benjamin arrived, her high expectations for a husband went unanswered. Indeed, she had passed the traditional age for marriage because of her demanding standards. Her prayers had an answer she long awaited.

Merott, however, was anything but elated by Queen Kullia's proposal. Another outsider gained a place of respectability and power in Tath society. How long before there are no more 'real' Taths left? He cursed to himself. These New Era unions were abhorrent to him. But, he had no plan, nor allies--at present--to pursue his goal of a 'pure' Tath society. He stomped off, unnoticed in the regal excitement, returning to the dwelling place of 'real' Taths: the yurt village.

Since Ilty accepted the offer to become Queen, the politics of Haaf almost collapsed. First, the nobility openly revolted, pledging themselves to an unidentified 'male' candidate. Second, the Church hierarchy suddenly disappeared, refusing to take a stand on the divisive issue, leaving the populace without guidance. On the other side, the serfs became elated, One of their own had ascended to the highest possible level. Yet, to a certain lesser degree, their ranks were far from unified. The very idea of a 'woman' running the country fragmented any support Ilty might receive. Even those serfs recently profiting from the demise of the traditional merchants' monopoly failed to realize that Ilty's opportunity ran parallel to theirs. The military, with the exception of the Church Knights under Vaal's command, remained neutral.

Vaal sent his Knights after the 'politically invisible' church hierarchy. Under his consistent pressure, they owned up to their irresponsibility and issued a bulletin to all clergy in Haaf. The bulletin contained a summary of the meeting held when Yganak was being pressured into Kingship. Having the Church's seal, the local clergy had no other recourse than to read the document to their parishes. When this high pronouncement promptly received formal backing from the Council of Elders, the country quickly settled down.

"Perhaps there isn't any other choice than for things to settle a bit." Vosnob spoke, attempting to focus the hubbub at the table.

"Care to explain yourself?" Oros shot back from across the room. Rainbow colors bounced off his new white robe, making him appear larger than he ever wished to be.

The colors emanated from the slowly revolving light in the middle of the room where it hung high over the table. Since the Holy One's visitation, the one responsible for Vosnob's transformation, this divine light always greeted the Elders. The supernatural light reminded the Council of the Elders of the Holy One's omnipresence.

"Only if these wonderful people will settle a bit........We're acting more like the rest of the country every moment."

"If that's a value judgement...."

"It is, Running Cloud." Vosnob said firmly.

"Then I find myself terribly insulted." The Chaplain from New Pinduala muttered.

"And you expect Vosnob to take that remark seriously?" Baste shouted loudly. Then he smashed his heavy hands together. "Please......... My grandson expects me to go fishing shortly...I have no intention of disappointing him." Baste's firmness brought order to the Elders, even though they believed they required another half-day to catch up on all the gossip. Chairs scraped the marbled floor as the twenty three Elders focused.

"Thank you." Vosnob began. "There are quite a few serious items for discussion this afternoon. I'd like to get as many done as possible."

"Sounds like you have something more personal to offer us." Oros suggested, his interest piqued by Vosnob's tone of voice.

Vosnob refused comment and plunged into the first topic. "We need to ascertain whether or not Ilty--as Queen--is still permitted to remain an Elder."

"Actually, you have the issue backwards." Jabbi commented, a bit confused that Vosnob should be so awkward about this issue. "Is it permitted for an Elder to also be counted as the highest official in Haaf?"

Ilty winced. "....Whatever....Personally, I see no problem....We have many different occupations shared here.....All equal in the eyes of the Holy One....Some others have changed occupations since being selected as an Elder....That, all of a sudden there might be a complication, I find difficult to believe."

"I do heartily concur." Kloshic pronounced as a final judgement. He flapped his thin boney arms, intimating some bizarre bird. Most laughed.

"What's your point?" Vosnob demanded.

"That you don't have an issue to begin with, and you know it. Had the Holy One wished to Ilty not to become our Queen, then this issue would never have existed.......I am firmly convinced that as we have witnessed the blessings from the Taths, that our stupidity and our downfall lay in ignoring the gifts the Holy One bestows upon women."

"I fully agree." Came the voice of the Elder living at the mill, the one who exposed the chicanery of some so-called respectable persons. "Let us move along....The will of the Holy One is being done, at least when Ilty takes her proper place as Queen of our nation."

A round of applause greeted his statement.

"I am not trying to cause problems." Vosnob declared. "Things are changing quite rapidly, some will be for the better, others not....As Elders we must guide our nation as best as possible."

Oros stood up, tankard in his pudgy hand. "We understand, my friend....." A smirk covered his face.

"Will you get serious!"

"For myself, never." He took a long swallow from his tankard. "But for the Faith, for our country and its future....yes."

Vosnob slowly shook his head, smiling all the while. Yes, he knew Oros and the other Elder affirmed the truth. He knew it before he broached the issue, but, as Head Elder, no other choice existed. He reached for his tankard and after drinking placed a summary of recent activities before the Council.

"Two Elders have relocated, permanently, to Paradise Valley. Another one is part of our delegation to the Taths. The city of....Geneva, with Benjamin......Kloshic, will you kindly do the honors of residing there.....I believe you'll find it most enjoyable."

"You bees sendin' me back ta school, are ya?" The old man smiled appreciatively, knowing full well that Benjamin brought a wealth of information and books----whatever they were.

"Why not?...You can hardly speak Haafian. Maybe you'll do better learning In-glish." He laughed along with Kloshic. Then jumped to another topic. "We are still in need of another Elder. Several names have been forwarded to me.....This is one time when I wish I might relinquish such authority..." He stopped speaking and looked about the oval table. There sat respected colleagues and friends, many he had known since the Battle. "This is not easy..."

"And it wasn't easy when you put forward Jabbi's name either, Vosnob." Baste said empathetically. He too began to realize Vosnob had something else on his mind, something as of yet, unshared.

"The name receiving the most support, I place before you as the next Elder." Again he paused.

"Go on!"

"The name is Blue Turtle."

A 'supposed' thoughtful silence followed, an understated climax to Vosnob's stressful statement. Soon smiles emerged, then laughter, forcing Vosnob to acknowledge he had been taken. The Council ran a step ahead of him.

"Vosnob, as this name has been circulating for over six months, and, recognizing Blue Turtle's name rated at the top when first presented.....you aren't telling us anything new." The Chaplain from New Pinduala spoke. "Those in favor of the nomination, take a drink."

A clanking of tankards up and down the table quickly affirmed Blue Turtle as the newest of the Elders. His mentor would be Running Cloud, next to Kloshic, the oldest Elder.

"Now," Oros spoke most seriously. "Vosnob, lets get to the bottom of things.....Since this meeting began, you've been--let me put it politely--not quite here...Tell us what is happening." He thumped his tankard on the wooden table.

After shifting nervously for a moment, Vosnob replied. "I will answer, Oros, but in my own fashion.....This last war brought immense changes to our nation. Our geography is incorrect, the serfs are more free than ever before, our New Knights make the nobility finally responsible for more than themselves and we've discovered another wonderful people, the Taths. We've also paid an extremely heavy price for being defensive...That is, we never pushed too far to the north nor did we sail about our coastline. Instead, we conveniently built our fortifications and trenches. Ashuwa's hordes plowed through them and his dragons flew over them.......Ashuwa easily infiltrated the southern swamp as well as some merchants, clergy and Church Guards....Without the divine intervention of the Holy One, the battle fought at the Wall might have easily been our defeat..... The menace commonly known as the 'blue ladies' proves we were too easily satisfied with ourselves."

"Your words are most troubling, Vosnob." The Queen-to-be said quietly.

"And might they be, Ilty......Does not the burden for our country's welfare fall upon your office?"

"I think you're deliberately trying to scare me away from it."

"Never, dear friend, never." Vosnob responded quietly. "I bring up the immediate past so we might put our actions into a more proper perspective."

"Continue."

"From the Dark Lands, we now have a new nation, Paradise Valley. A perplexing mixture of two different cultures and, like it or not, the proven existence of another god. A most ordinary one who refuses to allow his name be known. My best scout, ex-Scout officially, now that things have changed." He paused to collect himself. "Well, Sarg serves as the Prince of the territory, a land carved from the Dark Lands.....Ashuwa has become homeless."

Vosnob continued. "We have wondrous new allies in the Taths, a people who were also plagued by Ashuwa. ....Benjamin, a wiseman and prophet with strange white skin builds a university. He is the survivor from the time before our time....We have a great deal to learn from him.....The past need not be repeated."

"Do you really think he is who he claims?" Jabbi asked.

"Yes, I do." Vosnob responded with a smile. "No one could convince me otherwise. The scouting party from the Light Striper Lancers considers him a friend and a prophet as well. Bellah and the others would give their lives for him....As would the Taths, who have been waiting for him for hundreds of years..........You realize," Vosnob drawled. "We even tell time differently these days." He laughed and took another swallow from his tankard.

"I'd love to go fishing?" Baste smiled at Vosnob, gently prodding him to move along--quickly.

"Indeed, get to the point." Oros called across the table. "After all, I'm still supposed to finish the Quest.....You certainly would not want my schedule...."

"Your schedule is also my schedule, my fat friend." Vosnob's straight face belied the lightness of his words. "I'm going with you......And so is Rux... and Nadre...and Treh...and Wygga...and Taert.....and Qill plus Nooy and Jelkio....... And Captain Ellom has made room for all, including an Istelle perch....."

Stares and grins broke out as Vosnob finally exposed his major issue. Even Oros felt a strange relief, but as to why, he didn't know.

"Consider this carefully: Ashuwa is homeless...... His damnable power can yet be released against us.....Our quest is to pursue him, to gain allies in our battle against him. To gain allies before he convinces them to fight against us."

For another long moment nobody said anything. Vosnob had set a new path, one for which he was perfectly suited, both historically and by his divine rejuvenation. A homeless Ashuwa was indeed a most desperate creature. One who would never remove the idea of revenge from his vocabulary.

Finally an Elder spoke out. "So, are you going to pack up and sail about the coastline?"

"Actually, that's being done as we speak....No, we're headed directly east....into the unknown, at least... at present."

"But there's nothing out there!" Sounded an alarmed voice from the far side of the table.

"I'm going to find out if that's correct or not....Personally, I inclined to believe there's much more beyond the seas and oceans than we dare to think." Vosnob did not relate how he studied the ancient maps of the world with Benjamin. Now was not the time.

"So, if you are away....." The-ever-mindful-of-the-details Jabbi spoke up. "Who will lead the Council of Elders?"

"Provided he's not overly busy fishing, Baste will." Dry fog filled Vosnob's chair before his words filled the room.

A new life for a new mission.

THE END OF THE SAGA OF THE LIGHT STRIPER, VOLUME TWO

End note: Taert did return for Leye.

Printed in the USA
CPSIA information can be obtained
at www.ICGtesting.com
JSHW010303251023
50624JS00016B/206